EMPIRE

OF THE

DAMNED

EMPIRE
OF THE
DAMNED

JAY KRISTOFF

ILLUSTRATIONS BY
BON ORTHWICK

ST. MARTIN'S PRESS
NEW YORK

First published in the United States by St. Martin's Press,
an imprint of St. Martin's Publishing Group

EMPIRE OF THE DAMNED. Copyright © 2024 by Neverafter PTY LTD.
All rights reserved. Printed in the United States of America. For information,
address St. Martin's Publishing Group, 120 Broadway, New York, NY 10271.

www.stmartins.com

Interior illustrations by Bon Orthwick

Sevenstar logo design by James Orr

Maps by Virginia Allyn

Library of Congress Cataloging-in-Publication Data

Names: Kristoff, Jay, author. | Orthwick, Bon, illustrator.
Title: Empire of the damned / Jay Kristoff ; illustrated by Bon Orthwick.
Description: First edition. | New York : St. Martin's Press, 2024. |
  Series: Empire of the vampire ; 2
Identifiers: LCCN 2023045834 | ISBN 9781250245335 (hardcover) |
  ISBN 9781250245342 (ebook)
Subjects: LCSH: Vampires—Fiction. | LCGFT: Fantasy fiction. | Novels.
Classification: LCC PR9619.4.K74 E44 2024 | DDC 823/.92—dc23/eng/20231004
LC record available at https://lccn.loc.gov/2023045834

Our books may be purchased in bulk for promotional, educational, or business use.
Please contact your local bookseller or the Macmillan Corporate and Premium
Sales Department at 1-800-221-7945, extension 5442, or by email at
MacmillanSpecialMarkets@macmillan.com.

First Edition: 2024

10 9 8 7 6 5 4 3 2 1

I'd take a leap of faith,
But I'd lose my nerve.
In the end, I'll get the hell
that I deserve.

—TOM SEARLE

Whitesea

Bay of Tears

BLOOD DYVOK

Vellene

Avinbourg

TALHOST

Charinfel

Blind Bay

Charbourg

San Michon

Kingsgrave Bay

Avelene

Báih Side

Redwatch

Triurbaile

San Guillaume

OSSWAY

The Red Straits

Dún Cuinn

Dún Maergenn

Tolfirth

Dhahaeth

Gulf of Wolves

Sul Ilham

Sul Adair

Tuuve

Lashaame

Qadir

SUDHAEM

Asheve

Alethe

Eversea

BLOOD CHASTAIN

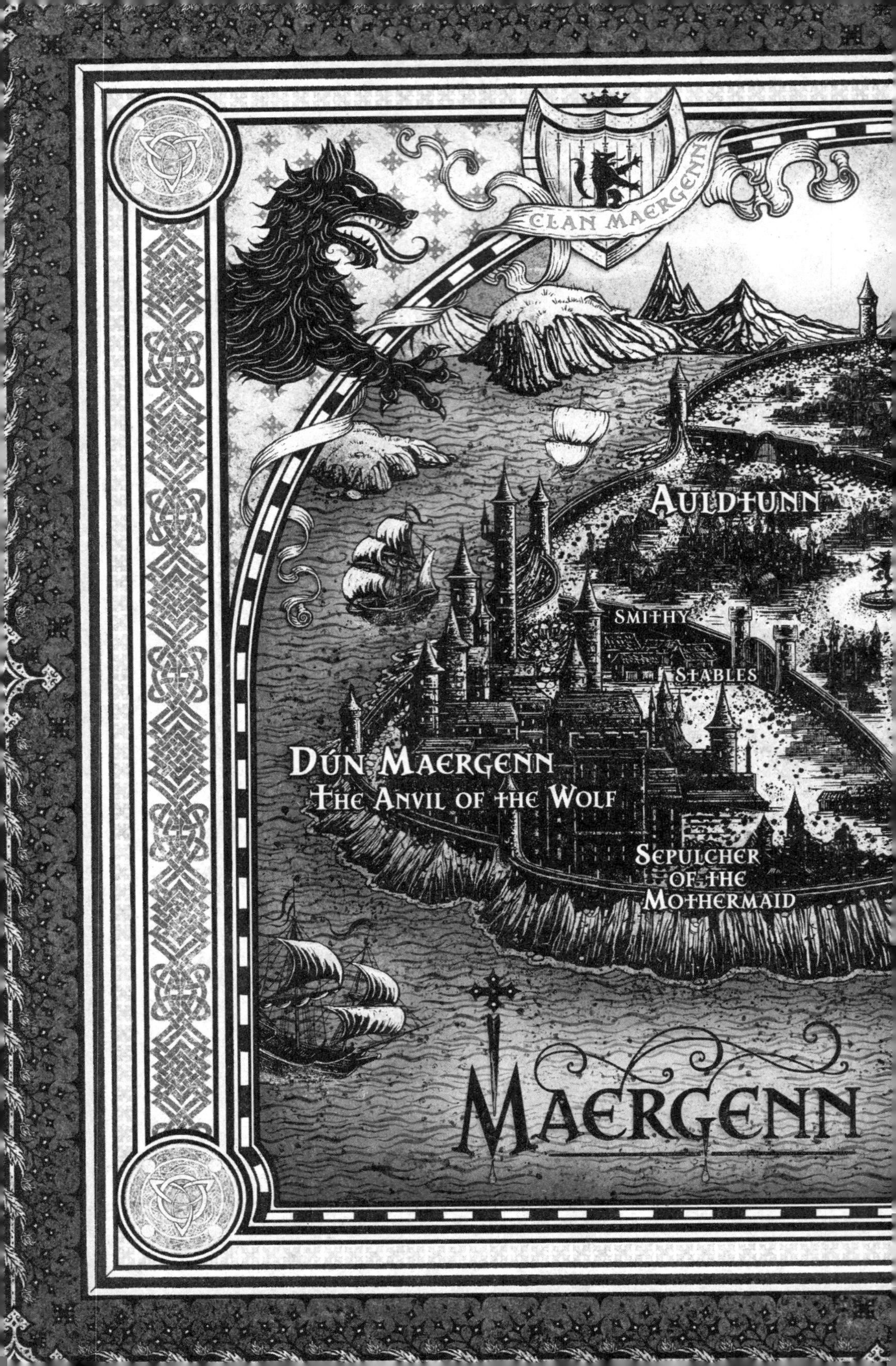

CLAN MAERGENN

AULDHUNN

SMITHY

STABLES

DÚN MAERGENN
THE ANVIL OF THE WOLF

SEPULCHER
OF THE
MOTHERMAID

MAERGENN

DRAMATIS PERSONAE

LONG WINTERS HAVE come and gone since last we visited, dear reader, and the years have not been kindest. Memory is a fickle beast, and life, too full for the recollection of every name and deed. And so, your historian offers reminder of these, our players:

Gabriel de León—The Last Silversaint, the Black Lion of Lorson, and the alleged hero of this history. Born nine years before the fall of daysdeath, when the sun was blotted from the sky across the Empire of Elidaen, Gabriel's childhood was short and cruel. He is a paleblood—born of a mortal mother and vampire father, inheritor of his sire's power and thirst both. Gabriel was recruited into the Silver Order of San Michon at fifteen, becoming a champion of that holy brotherhood before falling into disgrace.

Over a decade after his excommunication, he was a broken man, dependent on the drug sanctus to stave off his ever-rising bloodlust. But on a journey toward vengeance, our fallen paragon was introduced to a girl who would change his life forever.

Dior Lachance—Daughter of a streetwalker, orphaned at eleven, Dior began dressing as a boy to avoid trouble in the alleys and gutters of her youth. Her life of petty thievery was interrupted by the discovery that her blood could heal any wound, and cure any sickness. Accused of witchcraft, she was sentenced to death by the Holy Inquisition, but was rescued by Chloe Sauvage, a sister of the Silver Order, and friend of Gabriel.

The good sister revealed that the power in Dior's blood was no witchery, but a blessing from heaven. Dior is the descendant of a woman named Esan; the daughter of God's own mortal son, the Redeemer. And now, it falls to Dior to bring about the end of daysdeath, and fulfill her destiny as the Holy Grail of San Michon.

Celene Castia—Gabriel's sister, murdered at age fifteen when their village was destroyed by the Dead. Gabriel had thought Celene long buried, but she returned years later as a vampire, calling herself *Liathe,* and hunting Dior. Initially, the siblings were at odds, but Celene eventually saved Gabriel's life, and helped him rescue Dior from betrayal and death.

Celene is far more fearsome than other vampires of her age. She was born of the Voss bloodline, but she wields the bloodgifts of the Esani—the same mysterious line to which Gabriel's father belonged. She keeps both her face and motives hidden.

She and her brother are . . . not on the best of terms.

Astrid Rennier—A sister of the Silver Order, and beloved of Gabriel. Astrid was the bastard daughter of Emperor Alexandre III, shuffled off to a monastery when her existence became inconvenient to Alexandre's new wife. Forming a friendship with Gabriel that blossomed into love, she was excommunicated with him when her pregnancy was discovered.

Astrid gave birth to a daughter, and married Gabriel. The pair retired to the southernmost reaches of the empire, there to live as a famille in quiet happiness.

But happiness was not to last.

Patience de León—Daughter of Gabriel and Astrid. Her father had her name tattooed in silver across his fingers when she was born—a reminder to the former silversaint about what was truly important. She was Gabriel's pride and joy, the brightest light in his life.

She was murdered with her mama at the hands of the Forever King, Fabién Voss.

Know no shame, gentle reader. I also cried.

Ashdrinker—Gabriel's enchanted sword, who speaks directly to the mind of her wielder. Though the Ashdrinker experiences brief moments of lucidity, she is often confused about where and even *when* she is—she has never been the same since her blade was broken on the skin of the Forever King.

Exactly how Gabriel came to possess her is the topic of much speculation among the minstrels and soothsingers of the empire.

Aaron de Coste—Former silversaint of San Michon, Aaron was the son of a baronne and a vampire of the Blood Ilon: kith who can manipulate the emotions of others. He was apprenticed with Gabriel, and the pair shared a hateful rivalry that eventually became true friendship. He left the Silver Order when his love for the smith Baptiste Sa-Ismael was exposed, and deemed a blasphemy by their brethren.

Baptiste Sa-Ismael—A former blackthumb of the Silver Order, and the man who forged Gabriel's first sword, Lionclaw. After the discovery of their relationship, Baptiste left the Order with Aaron. The pair settled to the south, restoring the château named Aveléne.

Years later, they were visited by their old friend, who had by then taken Dior Lachance under his wing. Baptiste and Aaron offered Gabriel and Dior sanctuary, and helped defend the young Grail against the predations of Danton Voss.

Abbot Greyhand—Gabriel's former master, a son of the Blood Chastain: kith who can speak to and take the form of animals. Greyhand tried to instill a sense of duty in the young Gabriel, warning him never to succumb to the thirst in his blood.

Years later, he was appointed Abbot of the Silver Order, and was instrumental in Chloe Sauvage's quest to find the Holy Grail.

Chloe Sauvage—Sister of the Ordo Argent, childhood friend to both Astrid and Gabriel. Chloe helped Gabriel foil Fabién Voss's invasion of the Nordlund; a feat which saw Gabriel knighted by the Empress at sixteen years old.

Years later, Chloe came across her old friend once more, recruiting him to help defend Dior Lachance. Chloe intended to bring Dior to the San Michon monastery, where daysdeath could be undone through an ancient ritual she'd unearthed in the library. But when Gabriel learned that ritual involved Dior's sacrifice, he was outraged, killing Greyhand, Chloe, and half a dozen other silversaints in the innocent girl's defense.

Saoirse á Dúnnsair—A member of the Company of the Grail—those heroes recruited by Chloe Sauvage to protect Dior. Saoirse was a warrior of the Ossian Highlands, wielder of an enchanted axe named Kindness, and companion to the mountain lioness, Phoebe.

She and Phoebe were slain in battle by Danton Voss at San Guillaume.

Père Rafa—Another of the Company of the Grail, scholar of the Brotherhood of San Guillaume, and friend to Chloe Sauvage. Rafa accompanied Chloe on her journey to find Dior, often butting heads with Gabriel over matters of faith.

He was also killed by Danton during the San Guillaume massacre.

Bellamy Bouchette—A soothsinger of the Opus Grande, and a member of the Company of the Grail. He journeyed with Gabriel, Dior, and the others through the wastes of southern Nordlund, never shy of sharing a story or song.

And oui, Danton murdered him too.

Forgemaster Argyle—Chief smith of the Silver Order. The old black-thumb fought alongside Gabriel, Aaron, and Baptiste at the Battle of the Twins, where the Forever King's invasion was defeated. He was present for the ritual to murder Dior, but fled Gabriel's attack on the San Michon Cathedral.

Talon—A seraph of the Silver Order. Talon was a cruel man, never Gabriel's closest confidant. He succumbed to the *sangirè*—the red thirst—a hereditary affliction that eventually drives all palebloods mad with bloodlust. He was killed by Gabriel and Greyhand.

Fabién Voss—The Forever King, Priori of the Blood Voss, and perhaps the oldest kith in existence. Fabién was the first Priori to weaponize the wretched—a mindless breed of vampire that became abundant after daysdeath—mustering them into an army known as the Endless Legion. Despite being delayed by Gabriel's efforts, Fabién eventually conquered Nordlund and swept east, taking over much of the Elidaeni continent.

His broodchildren, the seven Princes of Forever, were instrumental in his invasion. He took exception to the murder of his youngest daughter, Laure, at Gabriel's hands, and years later, exacted bloody revenge against the silver-saint and his famille.

Danton Voss—The Beast of Vellene, Fabién's youngest son. Danton was sent by his father to capture Dior Lachance, though why the Forever King wants the Grail of San Michon *alive* remains a mystery. He slew most of the Company of the Grail at San Guillaume, and pursued Dior and Gabriel all the way to Aveléne.

He was killed by Dior, wielding the enchanted blade Ashdrinker, which had been anointed with her holy blood.

Laure Voss—The Wraith in Red, and Fabién's youngest daughter. Laure scouted the Nordlund to prepare for her father's invasion, bringing her into conflict with Gabriel, Aaron, and Greyhand. She tore off Greyhand's arm, scarred Aaron's face for life, and was set on fire by Gabriel. In retaliation, she traveled to Lorson, burning the town of Gabriel's birth to the ground and murdering all therein, including his baby sister, Celene.

She was slain by Gabriel at the Battle of the Twins.

Valya d'Naél—A sister of the Holy Inquisition, who along with her twin, Talya, pursued Dior for the crime of witchery across the empire. The pair captured Dior and Gabriel in the city of Redwatch, torturing them both brutally. Dior broke loose, murdering Valya's sister, Talya, and rescuing Gabe from torment.

Isabella Augustin—Wife to Alexandre III, and Empress of all Elidaen. She was a patron of the Ordo Argent, restoring the Order to greatness after centuries in decline. She knighted Gabriel after the Battle of the Twins, and used him as her right hand during subsequent years, overseeing his rise to fame and glory.

Maximille de Augustin—A warrior king who began the unification of five warring countries into the great Elidaeni Empire, more than six centuries ago. Maximille was killed before his dream came to fruition, but his dynasty rules the empire to this day. The Church of the One Faith named Maximille the Seventh Holy Martyr as reward for his earthly efforts.

Michon—The First Martyr, a simple huntress who became a disciple of the Redeemer, and carried on his holy war after his execution upon the wheel. Unbeknownst to most, Michon was also the Redeemer's lover, and together, they had a daughter named Esan—a name meaning *Faith* in the tongue of Old Talhost.

Esan—Daughter of Michon and the Redeemer. Four centuries ago, Esan's descendants raised rebellion against the Augustin dynasty; an uprising that became known as the Aavsenct Heresy. Their rebellion was put down by crusaders of the One Faith, and most of their number slaughtered.

Dior Lachance is the last scion of their line.

And now, mes amis, we begin.

From holy cup comes holy light;
The faithful hand sets world aright.
And in the Seven Martyrs' sight,
Mere man shall end this endless night.

—AUTHOR UNKNOWN

SUNSET

THE DEAD BOY opened his eyes.

All was still and silent, he among it, and most of all. A statue he was, his only movement in the yawning of his pupils, the soft parting of his bloodless lips. There was no quickening of breath as waking claimed him, no deeping drumbeat beneath his porcelain skin. He lay there in darkness, angelic and bare, staring at the timeworn velvet canopy above and wondering what had woken him.

It was not nightfall, to be sure. The daystar was yet kissing the horizon, the dark not yet quite sunk to its knees. The mortals who shared his grand four-poster bed were peaceful as corpses; motionless save for the featherlight shift of the beau's arm across his belly, the smooth rhythm of the maid's breath against his chest. There was no hunger in a bed so laden, nor chill amid beauties so ripe. So what then, had dragged him from slumber?

He'd not dreamed during the day—those of the Blood never did. But still, he realized sleep had brought him no comfort, frail daylight no rest, and emerging now fully from the death-deep murk of sleep, all at once he understood.

What had woken Jean-François was the pain.

He remembered now; hand drifting up toward his neck as the images danced like corpseflies in his head. Iron-hard fingers, sinking into the ashes of his throat. Wine-stained fangs, bared in a snarl. Storm-grey eyes, brimming with hatred as Jean-François was slammed into the wall, red smoke boiling from his skin.

"I told you I'd make you fucking scream, leech."

He'd been only a few moments from his ending, he knew it. Had Meline not intervened with her silversteel dagger . . .

Imagine it.

After all you've seen and done.

Imagine dying *right there in that filthy cell.*

Lying there in the darkness, Jean-François caressed the place Gabriel de León had hurt him. Picturing those grey pitiless eyes veiled in red smoke, the dead boy felt his jaw clench. And for a moment—just the space of a single, mortal breath—the Marquis experienced a sensation he'd imagined consigned to the dust of decades.

"There is no one more afraid of dying than things who live forever."

His movement had disturbed the girl beside him, and she sighed before sinking back toward sleep. A pretty flower she was, Sūdhaemi born, with soft dark curls and deep olive skin. She was on the scrawny side—but weren't they all these nights—a handful of years older than Jean-François when he'd received the Gift. But her skin was warm, and her touch oh-so-clever, and whenever she looked at him, her deep green eyes swelled with a hunger at wondrous odds with her ingenue's façade.

She'd served in his stable almost four months now. Wanton and willing. For a moment, Jean-François wished he could remember her name.

His eyes roamed the promise of her bare body; the lush line of the artery running the inside of her thigh, the delicious tracery of veins at her wrists and up, up to the sharp blade of her jaw. He watched her pulse thrum gently below it, hypnotic, soft with sleep. The thirst stirred inside him—his hated lover, his beloved enemy—and Jean-François pictured Gabriel de León again, the silversaint's face hovering just inches from his.

Fingers sinking deeper.

Lips close enough to kiss.

"Scream for me, leech."

The historian levered himself onto his elbow, golden curls tumbling about his cheeks. Behind him, the young beau sighed objection, hand questing over cold sheets. He was a Nordish beauty, that one, raven of hair and creamy of skin, near twenty years old, Jean-François supposed. The Viscontessa Nicolette had presented him a few weeks past—a bribe from his blood-niece in exchange for a kind word in the Empress's ear, and though he hated Nicolette like poison, Jean-François had accepted. The beau was lean as a thoroughbred, the flesh at his wrist and throat and nethers faintly scored by needle-sharp teeth.

His name definitely starts with a D . . .

Jean-François traced marble fingertips over the maid's skin, gentle as the first breath of spring. Chocolat eyes narrowed in fascination as her flesh reacted—that telltale trail of prickling hair as one razored fingernail grazed the bite marks at her throat. The monster leaned in, tongue flickering swift, over, around the tightening swell of her nipple, and the maid's breath quickened, shivering, waking fully now. The warmth of the blood he'd drunk before they'd all tumbled into sleep had faded—his lips must have been cool as melting ice. Yet she moaned as he suckled deeper, biting hard but not *quite* hard enough. And parting her thighs, she dared to run a hand through his golden hair.

"Master . . ." she breathed.

The beau was awake now; roused by the maid's sighs. He scattered kisses across the Marquis's bare shoulders, and slow as melting candle wax, his hand quested over the coldblood's hips, across the pale muscle of his belly, down toward Jean-François's nethers. The vampire allowed the Nordling to touch him, stroke him, willing his blood southward and hearing the beau groan as he grew iron-hard and heavy in his hand.

"Master," he sighed.

The maid was pressing gentle kisses along his throat, ever closer to the wounds de León had left. Jean-François seized a fistful of her curls, and she gasped as he dragged her back. Her pulse was a war drum now, and he kissed her, hard, allowing his fangs to slice her lip and spill a few drops of ruby-bright fire across their dancing tongues.

The thirst *surged* then, and for a moment, it was all he could do to bring it to heel. But the Marquis was a creature who enjoyed the hunt as much as the kill, and so he broke their bloody kiss and guided the maid toward the rock-hard beau behind him.

She understood at once, lips parting as the Nordling knelt up to meet her. He groaned as she took him into her mouth, pulse thumping harder beneath smooth, warm skin. The Marquis watched the pair sway for a time, the play of shadow and light on their flesh. The scent on the air told Jean-François that the maid was wet and warm as summer rain, and the merest brush of his fingers along her quim made her shiver all the way to her curling toes, pushing back against his hand, needing, pleading.

"Not yet, love," he whispered, eliciting a moan of protest. "Not yet."

Jean-François rose, languid, kneeling on the bed behind the breathless beau. Brushing long black locks from the Nordling's neck, the Marquis felt the mortal tremble; a predator at his back now, sharp claws skimming over his skin. The Marquis's hands roamed down delicious swells and valleys of muscle, finally encircling the heat of that throbbing cock. And gazing down over the plane of his prey's heaving belly to the maid, he growled a low, hard command.

"Finish him."

The maid moaned, eyes locked on his; a priestess, lost in worship. The beau was shaking, taking hold of the maid's tresses as the monster's fangs grazed his skin. Jean-François could still feel the silversaint's fingers around his throat.

"Scream for me," he whispered.

The beau did just that, one hand tangled in the Marquis's hair. The maid plunged him into her throat, deep and deepest, and as Jean-François felt it— that pulsing, rushing heat flooding up through the beau's nethers and into her waiting mouth—he bit down, past that brief, intoxicating resistance of skin, unleashing the rush of bliss-thick life within.

There was nothing then. No trembling body in his arms. No cry of ardor echoing on the walls. There was only the blood, aflame with every mote of the beau's passion; an elixir of life and lust entwined and lifting him ever upward into boundless skies.

Alive.

Jean-François drank just as greedily as the maid, wanting only more, only this, only *everything*. In nights before the daystar failed, he'd have taken just that. Yet sheep were too rare now, their lives too dear to waste, and so, he sliced his thumb with one sharp fingernail, pressed it to the beau's lips. The mortal gasped, latching on, suckling, one hand still entwined in the maid's curls, drinking deep as he pumped his hips, a perfect communion, consuming and consumed, all the world around them bathed in—

"Master?"

The call sounded at the bedchamber door, followed by brisk knocking. Jean-François recognized the perfume under the heavenly scent of blood.

"Meline," he sighed, mouth dripping red. "Enter."

The door to his boudoir opened, admitting echoes of steel and stone, faint whispers of servants in halls above. The château was waking now; a dozen faint notes of bloodscent hanging in the air as his majordomo swept into the room.

Meline was clad in a whalebone corset, a stunning gown of black velvet damask, only slightly worn with age. A lace choker was cinched about her throat, long red hair bound into thin braids, a half-dozen strung artfully across her eyes in the seeming of thin chains. She looked a madame of middle thirty, though in truth she was closer to fifty; the relentless charge of time slowed by the blood she supped weekly from his veins. She stood framed in the doorway, tall and stately, casting an ice-cold glance over his half-savored feast.

The beau was on his back, drained pale but still hard as steel. At the sight of Meline, the maid's mood fell, and she drew the sheets up over her naked-ness, gaze downturned.

"What is it, Meline?"

His majordomo curtseyed. "The Empress wishes to see you, Master."

The historian slipped a robe over his shoulders. Its fabric was pale and fine, but beginning to fray at the hems—no new silk in a land where nothing grew. He brushed fingertips across a chymical globe, bringing light to the palatial bedchamber around him. The walls were lined with oaken shelves, brimming with the histories that so fascinated him. His desk was scattered with charcoal sticks, artful studies of animals, architecture, naked bodies. Jean-François sprinkled some ground potatoloaf into a glass terrarium, smil-ing as five black mice emerged from the little wooden château. His familiars fell to their meal, Claudia snapping at Davide as she always did, Marcel squeaking for peace.

He glanced to his majordomo.

"We have a sitting scheduled on prièdi, do we not?"

"Apologies, Master. But Her Grace commands your presence now."

The historian blinked, his attentions sharpened. Meline was still curtsey-ing; perfectly motionless, perfectly trained. But he caught the discord in her tone, the tension in her shoulders. Padding toward her, silk whispering, he touched her cheek.

"Speak, my dove."

"A herald has arrived from Dame Kestrel, Master."

". . . The Iron Maiden has accepted Her Grace's invitation," the Marquis realized.

Meline nodded. "As has Lord Kariim, Master. Envoy arrived late this morning, bearing news of the Spider's intent to attend our Empress's Convocation."

"The Priori of the Blood Voss *and* Ilon?" he breathed, bewildered. "Coming here?"

Jean-François turned toward the bed, his voice iron-hard.

"Out."

The maid sat up quick, taut with fear. Pulling on a nightdress, she urged the beau to his feet, draping his arm about her shoulder. She avoided Meline's cold stare—always a clever little thing, this one—helping her stablemate toward the door. But as they passed, the Nordling met Jean-François's eyes, gaze still burning with the madness of the Kiss.

"I *love* you," he whispered.

Jean-François pressed one claw to the beau's sticky lips, and aimed a pointed stare at the maid. No further warning was needed, and the pair vanished swift out the door.

Meline watched their exit, bristling.

"You do not like them," Jean-François murmured.

The woman lowered her gaze. "Forgive me, Master. They are . . . unworthy of you."

"Oh, my darling." Jean-François caressed the thrall's cheek, lifting her chin so she might look at him again. "My dear Meline, envy does not become you. They are but wine before the feast. You know it is only you that I trust? You that I adore?"

The woman dared to cup his hand to her cheek, scattering his knuckles with kisses.

"Oui," she whispered.

"You are the blood in my veins, Meline. And if I have one fear, my dove, my darling, it is the thought of an eternity without you by my side. You know this, do you not?"

"Oui," she breathed, near weeping.

Jean-François smiled, trailing his finger down her cheek. He watched her pulse run quicker, her bosom heaving as his hand reached the choker at her throat. Then he hooked one sharp claw beneath her chin, almost hard enough to break the skin.

"Now dress me," he commanded.

Meline shivered, whispering.

"As it please you."

II

IT WAS ONCE said by the soothsinger Dannael á Riagán, if a man sought proof that beauty could be born of atrocity, he need look no farther than Sul Adair.

Built in the frozen heart of the Muath Mountains in east Sūdhaem, the cityfort was a testament to both the ingenuity and cruelty of mortal men. It was said that Eskander IV, the last Shan of Sūdhaem, spent the lives of ten thousand chattels to build it. The dark ironstone that gave the château its name—Black Tower in the local tongue—was quarried almost a thousand miles distant, and the route by which it was transported has forevermore been known as Ne'seit Dha Saath—the Road of Nameless Graves.

Sul Adair sat nestled in the Hawkspire Pass, safeguarding the goldglass mines at Lashaame and Raa, the grand cityport of Asheve. Those treasures were faded now, but Sul Adair remained, uncorrupted by the hand of fate or the teeth of time. And it was atop these frozen peaks that the Empress Margot Chastain had raised her throne.

Jean-François strode the halls, footfalls echoing on high-flung ceilings. Meline had dressed him in his finest—a frockcoat of white velvet, a mantle of pale hawk's feathers. The twin moons and wolves of the Blood Chastain were stitched at his breast, and the long hair his Empress so adored flowed about his shoulders like molten gold. Meline walked three steps behind as was proper for a thrall, the dark damask of her gown whispering.

Servants glided the shadowed halls, falling to their knees at the sight of him. Animal familiars—cats and rats and ravens—watched his approach, slinking away as he drew near. He saw other kith; mediae and fledglings of Margot's Court of the Blood, bowing or curtseying as he passed. But the Marquis breezed by most with barely a glance, gaze fixed on the walls around him, the gables soaring overhead like the boughs of heaven.

The château's interiors were decorated with the most breathtaking frescoes in all creation. The grandmaster Javion Sa-Judhail had toiled thirty years in the painting of them. It was said when the grandmaster received word of the birth of his first son, he did not even look up from his toil. When the Sūdhaemi warlord Khusru the Fox launched his ill-fated campaign to wrest the city back from Augustin control, Javion continued to paint even as the armies of the Emperor and would-be Shan clashed upon the battlements. And when his beloved wife, Dalia, hurled herself from Sul Adair's highest tower in protest at his neglect, the grandmaster did not even take the time to attend her funeral rites.

Jean-François admired the mortal's passion. But more, what he'd created with it.

A beauty that would endure, long after its creator had fed the worms.

The château was built in five magnificent tiers, and Javion had painted the walls of each level as a step on the ascension to heaven. The first level was dedicated to the natural realm, and God's favored children, humanity. The second was adorned with parables of the saints, the third, a tribute to the Seven Holy Martyrs. Above them flew the angels of the heavenly host— Eloise, Mahné, Raphael, even dear old Gabriel—spreading dove-white wings along the towering walls of Sul Adair's fourth tier.

Jean-François climbed ever higher, Meline breathing soft behind him as finally, they ascended the château's highest level. Here, a grand hallway stretched before them, blood-red carpet swathing dark flagstones. Beautiful chandeliers adorned the rafters, like great spiderwebs of glittering gold-glass, hung thick with the shadow of roosting bats. And upon the walls, where Javion Sa-Judhail had painted his decades-long homage to God Almighty, the sovereign of heaven himself, there was now only featureless black stone.

The grandmaster's lifework had been sanded completely bare, and replaced with dozens of paintings in golden frames. Different portraits of the same subject, over and over again. Striding past steel-clad thrallswords, Jean-François reached the tall doors to his dame's inner sanctum. And there he stopped, studying the portrait above the entrance.

She who had obliterated heaven, and supplanted its rule on earth.

"Enter," came the command.

Thrallswords pushed open the mighty doors, unveiling the grand chamber beyond. Meline stepped forward, speaking in a loud, clear voice.

"The Marquis Jean-François of the Blood Chastain, Historian of Her Grace, Margot Chastain, First and Last of Her Name, Undying Empress of Wolves and Men."

A road of deep red carpet stretched into the dark, flanked by tree-tall pillars. The Marquis felt a chill in the room, banishing the bloodwarm passions of his bed. Entering alone, he followed the carpet, hands clasped like a penitent, accompanied by the bright song of a lone castrato somewhere in the shadows. With every step, that chill pressed harder on his skin, along with the swell of a dark, impossible power.

A low, warning growl rang out ahead. The Marquis stopped immediately and dropped into a bow, deep enough that his beautiful golden curls brushed the floor.

"My Empress. You commanded my presence."

"I did," came the reply, rich and earth-deep.

"Your word is my gospel, Your Grace."

"Look upon me, then, Marquis. And pray."

Jean-François lifted his gaze. The carpet was a river of blood, flowing down from a magnificent throne. Four wolves, black and fierce, lounged on a dais about it. To one side, a page in Chastain livery knelt with palms upturned, holding a leather-bound tome almost as big as he. And behind the throne, twenty feet high, loomed another portrait of the Priori of the Blood Chastain, the eldest of the line of the Shepherd, dread sovereign of all her kin.

The Empress Margot.

It was not the best he'd painted—Jean-François had painted *all* the portraits in this keep—but it *was* Her Grace's favorite. Margot was depicted sitting upon a golden crescent, clad in a beautiful onyx gown. Twin wolves flanked her feet, twin moons kissed her sky. She was a maid in form, but a goddess in stature, pale as the sun-bleached bones of her foes. The portrait had been replicated countless times, sent to duchies of the Blood across Sūdhaem; a reminder of she to whom they had sworn fealty eternal. The Empress was an infamous recluse—this was the only version that most of her subjects would ever know.

And beneath his portrait, sat the Empress herself.

At least, the version *Jean-François* knew.

She was not the towering figure he had painted on the canvas. In reality, Margot was slight in stature—even short, a fool might remark. She was not a buxom youth, nor a perfect blond beauty. No maid had Margot been when she Became, but a woman of middle age. And now, carved of white marble and black majesty though she was, still she bore the marks of a mortal life hard lived, years unkind, preserved in the forever tale of her flesh.

But that was the beauty of it for an artiste like the Marquis. And his path to Margot's favor. Because there was no mirror, nor glass, nor pool of moonlit water that would cast a vampire's reflection back to them. And the years since the Empress had seen her own face in anything save the portraits Jean-François flattered her with were nigh uncountable.

Margot was so old, she couldn't even remember what she looked like.

The Empress of Wolves and Men fixed Jean-François with eyes as black as heaven. Her shadow stretched out before her, caressing his own, and though not a breath of wind moved in the chamber, the Marquis felt his curls stir in a chill breeze. Her clawed hand stroked the closest wolf—a vicious old dame named Malice—and the Empress spoke with a voice that seemed to come from the air all around him.

"Thou art well, Marquis?"

"Perfectly, Your Grace. Merci."

The Empress's lips curled gently. Another wolf—a sleek beauty named Valor—growled as she spoke again.

"Come ye closer, child."

Jean-François ascended the dais and knelt at his Empress's feet. Even sitting above him, Margot was almost smaller than he, and yet, her presence dwarfed his completely. The shadows lengthened, and she raised her hand so swift it seemed not to move, but *blink* from her lap to his cheek.

Jean-François's belly thrilled as Margot lifted his chin so he might look upon her. It had been fifty years, and he still remembered her murderous passion the night she'd killed him. The dark joy in her eyes as he'd risen from the bloody floor of his studio, aghast with horror and wonder that she'd not destroyed him, but *gifted* him a life undreamed of.

"Thou art injured still."

Scream for me . . .

"A trifle, Your Grace."

"Six nights and this trifle lingers?"

"Yet slowly heals. I assure you, Mother, it is unworthy of your attentions."

The Empress smiled. "Who am I, my son?"

"You are rightful sovereign of this empire," he replied, voice rich with pride. "Conqueror and sage and soothseer. Ancien of the kith, and Priori of the Blood Chastain."

"Think thee, then, I am unable to judge what is and is not worthy of my attentions?"

The Empress's tone was gentle, fingertips brushing his wounded throat.

Vampires could not choose which of their victims were granted the Gift, and most ended up rotting for days before they turned, arising as that vile breed known as *foulbloods*. Jean-François was the last highblooded vampire Margot had ever created, and he knew many in the Empress's court whispered that she indulged her youngest. But as Margot pressed harder, as he felt just a *hint* of the monstrous strength inside her, a chill trickled down his spine.

"I apologize, Your Grace. It is not for me to say what should not concern you."

"Say'st thou, this *should* concern me?"

"I . . . say nothing, Your Grace."

A thumb strong enough to crush marble ran gently over his larynx. The chill deepened, shadows bending, *screaming*.

"Of what use be a historian who doth not speak?"

". . . Mother, I—"

A soft chuckle rang in the chamber, sharp fangs glittering as the dark fell still.

"I sport with thee, love." Margot cupped his cheek, black eyes gleaming. "Thou art so boyish, ofttimes. So *young*. I would warn thee to 'ware such weakness, if it did not make me adore thee all the more. And adore thee I do, my beauty, with all a mother's heart."

Her smile fell from her lips like dead leaves.

"But thou dost reek of the sheep ye rut with, Jean-François. Back now."

The third wolf, an elderly dame named Prudence, watched as the Marquis retreated, head low. Jean-François kept his face a mask to hide the storm within—ardor, shame, fear, devotion. His mother always set him off-balance, always left him feeling such a . . .

The Empress glanced to the boy beside her. The page had remained motionless all this time, that brass-trimmed tome upon his palms. Though the boy had a thrall's strength, his arms still must have burned with the agony of holding it—that was the point, Jean-François supposed. He knew the Empress did not approve of the way he spent his nights. Gifting him this display of casual cruelty was her reminder of what he was. What *they* were.

The wolf frets not for the ills of the worm.

"I have perused thy chronicle," she said.

"Does it please Her Grace?"

"Thy artistry is wond'rous as ever. Yet I found the tale somewhat . . . incomplete."

"It is a work in progress, Your Grace."

Jean-François felt a chill breeze, and his Empress simply disappeared—one moment, she sat upon her throne, and the next, that throne sat empty. Brushing his hair back from his face, he saw her now standing at one of the tall windows looking to the north.

"They run blind, who run quick," Margot murmured. "Impatience was the end of the Forever King, and no intent have I to follow pretty Fabién into hell." Margot turned pitch-black eyes to her child. "But matters grow . . . pressed, my love."

"You speak of the Iron Maiden. And the Spider."

Margot's lips twisted into what a fool might call a smile.

"They are actually coming *here*," Jean-François breathed, walking to her side.

"Aye. And word have we 'pon the winds that the Draigann approaches o'er the oceans, our invitation clutched in his beggar's hand. They shall arrive before the feast of Damesday."

"The Priorem of *three* bloodlines. Voss. Ilon. Dyvok. All here within the week." Jean-François looked out on the mountains in wonder. Small figures in black steel roamed the battlements below, firepots blazing like stars upon impregnable walls. "And you intend to grant them Courtesy?"

"'Twould hardly be polite to refuse. Given 'twas I who proposed this Convocation."

"Such a gathering has not occurred once in *hundreds* of years. We have waged shadow war with the other Priorem since time immemorial. How can we trust them?"

The Empress actually chuckled at that. "We cannot, sweet Marquis. But their desire for self-preservation? *This* can we trust. These wars hath bled this land dry, my child. And every petty fiefdom carved by upstart bloodlords, every mouthful gnawed by rampaging packs of mongrel foulbloods, the closer we all stumble toward catastrophe. Kestrel knows this. Kariim knows this. E'en the Draigann knows this."

Margot shook her head, lip curling.

"But e'en drawn here willingly, they shall ne'er bend the knee. We require advantage to achieve that end. And e'en now, it lies screaming in the hole where ye left it."

Jean-François clenched his jaw. "He is dangerous, Mother."

"Of course he be. How think ye, he hath survived a world this cold otherwise?" Margot's fingers caressed the hurt beneath his cravat, gentle as whispers. "Yet they are the key, my son. This riddle, this weapon, this Grail—they alone hath the keeping of its fate."

"De León *loathes* our kind, Mother. He has told us *nothing* wh—"

"Why suppose ye, I set thee this task?"

He frowned, befuddled. "I am your historian. There is no one in your c—"

"Because thou art *young*, Jean-François. Young enough to recall what it is to be a man. There be potency in that. Comfort and comradeship a clever wolf might turn to advantage." Margot waved to the history in the thrallboy's hand. "Pon those pages is the tale of a man whose cup overflows with rage. And grief. But above all, *pride*. Protest he may, but doubt it not—Gabriel de León hath *desire* for the world to know his story. Such is the profound depth of his vanity. And the key to his undoing."

Margot's black gaze flickered to Jean-François's throat.

"And he feels a kinship with thee, sweet Marquis. The murder of his famille. His bond with Dior Lachance. Think ye, so intimate his confessions would have been to me?"

"Intimate?" Jean-François's jaw clenched. "He tried to *murder* m—"

"Thou hast taken thy sport," she snapped. "Time hath come to swallow wounded pride, little one, and gift the kindness that the wise proffer after cruelty."

The Marquis shivered, chill crawling his spine as she caressed his cheek.

"'Tis only thee to whom I would vouchsafe this task, Jean-François. Not in thy siblings, nor cousins, nor in any other within our court do I place such faith. Of all the horrors I have wrought, dost thou not see it is only thee I trust? *Thee* I adore?"

Margot tilted her head, searching Jean-François's eyes.

"Oui," he whispered.

Behind him on the dais, the fourth of the Empress's wolves—a hulking brute named Fealty—licked his dripping jowls. Margot moved without moving at all, in one blinking touching his cheek, the next holding out her hand. And upon her upturned palm lay a glass phial filled with blood-red dust, and a heavy iron key.

"Bring me what I need, child. Bring me an empire."

Jean-François bowed, murmuring.

"As it please you."

III

THE KILLER STOOD watch at a thin window, still waiting for the end to arrive.

The room was not as he'd left it when they'd dragged him down to hell. The flagstones had been scrubbed near-clean, an old lambswool rug draped over the bloodstains. The hearth was bereft of flame, but not heat—they'd lit a fire a few hours past, banishing the chill. Two antique armchairs stood in the room's heart, a small round table between. Two golden goblets sat upon it; empty, yet full of promise.

All had been put in order again, like pieces on a game board just waiting for the players to arrive. But though they'd taken efforts to make it more comfortable this time, the Last Silversaint knew this room for what it was.

Still. Better than the prison he'd just left.

Six nights he'd spent, starving at the bottom of an empty well in the tower's belly. His tongue a riverbed of cracking clay. His throat a desert plain. Agony had been his only company; agony and blood-flecked screams and smoke-soft dreams of *her*.

He'd been delirious when they finally hauled him up, gifting him a lungful of sanctus so sweet he'd actually wept at the taste. A cadre of thrallswords had escorted him to a bathhouse in the château's heart, where two pretty mortals—a green-eyed Sūdhaemi maid and a dark-haired Nordish beau—had sunk him up to his chest in wondrously warm water. They'd bathed him slow, combing the blood and filth from his hair as his lashes fluttered on his scarred cheeks. By the time they were done, Gabriel had almost felt half-human again. And so when he'd felt the beau gifting soft kisses along his shoulder, the maid running slow fingertips up the inside of his thigh, he found himself sighing instead of itching for a sword.

"What are you doing?" he'd croaked, throat still cracked from screaming.

"Our master bid us see to your needs, Chevalier," the maid replied. "All of them."

"What are your names?"

The lass blinked in confusion. "My . . ."

"Your name, mademoiselle," Gabriel had insisted.

". . . Jasminne."

"Dario," the beau had murmured, teeth tickling Gabriel's ear.

He'd pushed them away gently, hands and lips both.

"Merci, mes chers. But I'm not that kind of hungry. Nor that kind of bastard."

They'd dressed him in his old leathers, now washed; boots polished, tunic spotless. And after three bowls of rabbit ragout, and half a bottle of a wine so rare it might have paid for a château in Nordlund, Gabriel had been escorted under guard back up the tower stairs, there to await the pleasure of the Marquis Jean-François Chastain once again.

He did not wait long.

As Gabriel stared out the window to the mountains beyond, he felt a tickling, as if a hand was brushing his hair back from his neck. Turning, he saw the coldblood standing twenty feet away, chairs and table and empty goblets between.

"I trust you are feeling refreshed, Chevalier?" Jean-François asked.

The Marquis was dressed in pale finery, golden curls flowing about marble cheeks. His ruby lips were quirked, fresh blood staining the whites of his eyes. Though he'd not seen the historian once in the last six nights, Gabriel knew this monster had been behind every moment of his torture. Punishment for his assault the last time they'd spoken.

"How's the throat?" he asked.

"Better."

"I can remedy that."

The coldblood's smile became something darker; something that hunted true smiles for sport. For a moment, the air ran thick and dark as heartsblood.

"I thought we might try again, de León," Jean-François declared. "I thought we might talk as gentry, the red ledger between us marked even, and all our hurts forgot." The Marquis gestured to the armchair. "Will you sit?"

"What happens if I don't?"

"Bloodshed, I'd wager." Jean-François reached into his frockcoat, unfolding a small blade from a gleaming pearl handle. "And not the pleasant kind."

Gabriel glanced at the knife. "A little small, isn't it?"

"'Tis not the size of the blade, Chevalier, but one's skill in wielding it."

"A song sung by every short man I ever met."

The Marquis chuckled and snapped his fingers, the cell door opening. Jean-François's faithful thrall Meline waited on the other side, her black, wasp-waisted bodice tumbling into a waterfall of heavy skirts. Drifting into the room, she placed a golden platter on the table.

Gabriel saw a chymical globe, a bowl of steaming water, draped with a strip of muslin. A lump of actual soap rested on a dish beside a small horse-hair brush.

His eyes drifted back to the monster's little blade.

"You're jesting."

"This flesh was never old enough to cultivate more than a shadow of one, but I am told beards can be rather . . . irritating." Jean-François winced. "And in all honesty, Chevalier, yours looks less a beard and more a blasphemy."

"I *do* have a reputation to maintain in that regard."

"Consider my service apology. Comfort bestowed after comfort denied. Unless of course . . . you do not trust me with a knife at your throat?"

The monster smiled, the air crackling with sadistic amusement. Gabriel knew the game being played here, the cruel purpose behind it. To suffer six nights of agony, then be dragged back to this thing's feet to acknowledge he was still within his power. To bare his throat to this leech and pray it didn't slice him open.

To *surrender.*

Tossing his hair off his shoulders, Gabriel eased himself into that ornate leather chair. The monster smiled down at him, relishing his subjugation. And closing his eyes, Gabriel tilted his head back. Trusting the scorpion not to sting.

The space of three long breaths passed before the muslin was draped over his face, warm with sweetwater. Gabriel breathed steam, skin prickling as he heard the coldblood's footfalls to his left. Fighting down instincts he'd honed through years of slaughter and war, the primal urges of fight and flight in his head, willing his heart to cease thundering.

Patience, a voice inside whispered.

Patience . . .

"My Empress read your story, Chevalier." The monster's voice was soft, behind him now. "Your apprenticeship in San Michon. Your journey with Dior Lachance, and your battle with the Ordo Argent for the Grail's life. A saga worthy of the ages. Her Grace was pleased."

"Well, that's a weight off my mind," Gabriel murmured.

"And mine, I assure you."

"Frightened of disappointing Mama, coldblood?"

"Terrified, actually."

The muslin was removed from his face, and Gabriel felt Jean-François whisking the soap to a lather across his jawline. The scent wasn't entirely unpleasant; fools' honey and woodash, the faintest notes of bluebark.

"She did, however," the Marquis mused, "offer critique of the tome's length."

Jean-François was on Gabriel's right now, the silversaint's jaw tensing as he felt the first touch of razor to flesh. Fingers pressed light to Gabriel's chin, the monster skimmed the blade down his cheek in one long, smooth stroke.

"She was eager at the prospect of a continuance."

The razor was sharp as glass, whispering as it kissed his skin again. The Marquis's touch was stone-hard but gentle, warm from feeding. Gabriel held himself steady, but the beast inside him was on edge to be so vulnerable—invisible hackles rippling down his spine as the Marquis deftly curled his blade across the bow of Gabriel's upper lip.

"Though we have had our disagreements, de León, I am not a vindictive soul. But Her Grace has made her desire plain. So while I have no wish to gift you further torment, I shall be forced to, should you defy her. And neither of us truly wishes that."

Gabriel felt the razor again, curling down toward his neck now. A blood-warm touch at his throat, the light brush of the monster's crotch against his hand.

"Do you sleep with women, coldblood? Or men?"

The blade paused.

"Why do you ask, Silversaint?"

A shrug. "Indulge me."

Gabriel felt a rock-hard thumb at his lip then, ever so gently wiping the soap flecks free. "Male, female . . . such matters are trifles to immortals. Sinking swift in the ocean of eternity. Beauty may be found across any boundary."

"So when you're bedding your beauties, do you warm them up first? Or do you just bend them over and have at it?"

The razor fell still again. "Are you—"

"To put it plainer." Gabriel finally opened his eyes, looking up at the Marquis. "If you're going to try to fuck me, vampire, at least have the decency to buy me a drink first."

Jean-François's jaw clenched, razor hovering over Gabriel's jugular.

The silversaint only smiled.

Gabriel knew he *was* in danger here. But tortured and weary, in the end he was still no fool. Truth was, if these monsters wished him dead, he'd be just that, and though they'd dragged him to the frayed edge of sanity, they hadn't let him fall. He knew what they wanted. The tale of how San Michon's Grail was broken. To know if there was some way they might still turn her to advantage. And so, while trusting a scorpion not to sting might've seemed a fool's wager, Gabriel had known he'd nothing to fear sitting in that chair.

Baring his throat to this bastard was no surrender.

It was a *conquest*.

And closing his eyes again, he tilted his head, alllll the way back.

"The Monét if you have it, chérie."

". . . See to it, Meline," Jean-François commanded.

Gabriel heard the door creaking shut, the key twisting—the thrall considered him dangerous enough to lock it behind her now. The sanctus they'd given him to smoke had been barely a thimbleful, but his senses were still sharp, and as the Marquis pressed razor to flesh again, Gabriel counted Meline's steps down from the tower.

He knew now that the heavy iron door below led out into the château's western wing. Every step from those stairs to the dining hall had been tallied in his head during his march back up here. Every thrallsword marked. The tall windows a man might leap from, servants' doors a man might slip from, all stowed in the ironclad vaults of his memory.

The Marquis continued shaving him in silence, his smug air of triumph evaporated. The razor skimmed his throat one final time, murder just a whim away. But finally, the monster wiped his blade clean and folded it back inside his coat.

After a moment, Jean-François pressed his hands to Gabriel's face, cool and wet. The silversaint smelled sharp alcohol, and beneath, just the faintest note of . . .

Flowers.

Gabriel opened his eyes again. Jean-François was gazing down at him, golden curls swaying as he smoothed the grooming water over his cheeks.

"Apologies, de León," the monster murmured. "I am afraid silverbell is one of the only pleasant fragrances we can still fashion these nights. I am aware it was your wife's favorite bloom. Your daughter's also. And if the scent gives rise to memories unpleasant, I ask forgiveness. As I said, I've no wish to see you suffer."

Gabriel lost focus, looking back on distant days. That little lighthouse by the sea. The warmth in Patience's smile and Astrid's arms. The song of waves and gulls and distant shore, and three knocks falling like hammers upon the door.

"Come in," Jean-François murmured.

Meline slipped back into the room with a green glass bottle, filled with a delicious red. Gabriel inhaled the wine's perfume, watching the artery pulse beneath Meline's choker, eyes drifting over the milk-white curves of her bosom as she leaned forward and filled one of the goblets. His blood ran quicker, and he avoided her eyes as she handed him the glass.

"Do you desire anything else, Master?"

Gabriel hadn't even seen the monster move, but Jean-François was now seated on the chair opposite. A leather-bound tome rested in the cold-blood's lap.

"Not for the moment, my dove. Leave us."

"Your will be done." The woman glanced at Gabriel. "I shall not stray far."

Gabriel winked and raised his glass, and Meline retired. The silversaint tipped back his head, emptying the goblet in one draught. Leathers creaking, he poured another. And with cup filled to trembling brim, he leaned back, grey eyes on the monster opposite.

"What the Forever King did to your famille . . ." Jean-François shook his head, eyes to the narrow window. "I confess the tale struck me to my heart, Silversaint."

"You have no heart, coldblood. We both of us know that."

"I am no stranger to cruelty. But there *is* a threshold over which only the truly monstrous dare tread. And Fabién Voss *was* that, by any measure. But in ending him, you have authored a calamity. This empire teeters on knife's edge, de León. If the Courts of the Blood are not united, there can be but one ending to this tale."

"And you think the Grail will help you?" Gabriel scoffed. "I told you before, coldblood. The cup is broken. The Grail is *gone*."

"It matters not what I believe, Gabriel. Neither of us wants to see you thrown back down that hole. But that is *exactly* where my Empress will leave you, if you do not give her what she wants."

". . . And if I do?"

"Immortality. Perhaps the only sort any of us truly know."

The coldblood produced a wooden case, carved with wolves and moons. He drew out a long quill, black as the heart in Gabriel's chest, placing a small bottle upon his armrest. Dipping quill to ink, he looked up with dark and expectant eyes.

"Begin," the vampire said.

The Last Silversaint sighed.

"As it please you."

BOOK ONE

SAINTS AND SINNERS

For three centuries had that noble brother-hood endured. Though condemned by birth and damned by God, they rose above their cursed natures to light a silver flame, burning twixt humanity and the horrors that hunted us. A hope for the hopeless. A light in the night.

What cruel fate to know that at the last, 'twas not the dark that dealt them their deadliest blow. But the hand of one of their own.

—ALFONSE DE MONTFORT
A CHRONICLE OF THE SILVER ORDER

NOTHING BUT DARKNESS

"WHERE SHALL WE start?" Gabriel asked.

"The place you left off seems wisest," Jean-François replied.

"If it's wisdom you're looking for, coldblood, you're talking to the wrong man."

"Alas, then, that you are the only man in the room."

Gabriel scoffed, leaned back in his chair. "Story of my fucking life."

"To continue it, then." The historian plucked an imaginary speck of fluff from his frockcoat sleeve, lips pursed. "You had journeyed halfway across the empire, on a quest for vengeance after the murder of your wife and daughter. Intent upon destroying the Forever King, Fabién Voss, instead you had ended up as guardian of the girl, Dior Lachance, last scion of the holy Redeemer's line. Your brethren among the Ordo Argent had tried to murder you, and your old friend Chloe Sauvage had attempted to sacrifice Mlle Lachance in an ancient ritual intended to end daysdeath. But, with the aid of your sister, now revealed as one of the kith and calling herself *Liathe*"—here the vampire's lip curled in contempt—"you ascended San Michon's heights, butchered your former comrades like holy piggies in a row, and rescued the Grail from certain death. Happy endings for all."

Jean-François waved his quill, eyebrow raised.

"Unless you were a member of the Silver Order, of course."

The Last Silversaint said nothing, staring at the chymical globe between them, and back across far-flung years. A skull-pale moth had crawled from some nook within the cell, and was now flitting about the light. He watched the insect beating in vain against the glass, remembering the flutter of a thousand tiny wings as he'd plummeted from the monastery's heights after his so-called brothers cut his throat. The taste of ancien blood on his tongue, hauling him back from the brink of death. A pale figure in a crimson great-coat, dragging aside her porcelain mask to reveal the face of the monster, the horror, the sister beneath.

"Why didn't you tell me, Celene?"

"Because everything I have suffered, everything I am, is because of you."

The Last Silversaint took another slow swallow of wine.

"Because I hate you, brother."

"De León?"

"Do you ever wonder where this ends, Chastain?" Gabriel finally asked. "When the last mortal throat is opened? The final drop of us drained dry? When your Empress's folly about the Grail is laid bare, and your kind fall on themselves like dogs over the last bone? Will you go down fighting, do you think? Or will you die on your knees?"

"There is all manner of bliss to be found on one's knees." The historian smiled, brushing his quill across his lips. "But I assure you, I have no intention of dying."

"Neither did she, vampire."

The silversaint sighed, his gaze still lost in the light.

"Neither did she."

Gabriel de León leaned back in his chair, the globe flaring brief in the storm-grey of his eyes. The air was chill, still, save for the warm whisper of his breath and the soft hymn of his pulse and the velvet kiss of bat wings on the night sky outside.

The historian held his quill poised over the page.

All the world held its breath.

And finally, the Last Silversaint began to speak.

"I can still remember it like it was yesterday, you know. I can see it so clear, it's almost frightening. The pair of us, standing before that altar. The cathedral empty and silent. The smoke rising to the ceiling and the miserable daysdeath dawn spilling through the windows and the statue of the Redeemer looking down on the carnage I'd wrought. But the thing I remember most is the blood. Cooling on the floor. Thumping in my veins. Spattered all over the face of the girl beside me.

"Dior was still swathed in the ritual robes they'd meant to murder her in. A price they thought worth paying to save the world. She stood there in the ringing quiet, blue eyes wide and bruised and fixed on me. Her sinner. Her savior. And dragging her tumble of ash-white hair from her face, she whispered, 'What do we do now?'

"'I suppose you should come meet my sister,' I sighed.

"'. . . Sister?'

"'Long story.'

"Dior watched mute as I knelt beside Chloe's body. My old friend's mouse-brown curls were soaked with gore, empty green eyes staring up in sightless accusation at the man who'd condemned this world to darkness. I pressed her lids shut with bloody fingertips, then trudged up the aisle, doing the same with every silversaint I'd murdered. Big de Séverin, little Fincher, old Abbot Greyhand. Friends. Brothers. A mentor. I placed their swords upon their chests, closed their eyes forever. But I didn't pray for any of them. And peeling aside Greyhand's bloodied greatcoat, I found . . .

"'Ashdrinker!' Dior cried.

"I drew my old broken sword from her battered scabbard. Her dark starsteel glittered, glyphs etched down her curved blade, six inches snapped from her tip when I'd tried and failed to kill the Forever King. Despite the blood on my hands, the beautiful dame on the hilt smiled at me as always, her arms spread along the crossbar as if to embrace me. Her shout echoed in my head, silver and glittering with joy.

"*Gabriel!*

"'Good to see you, Ash,' I whispered.

"*D-D-D-Dior, i-i-is she—*

"'She's here,' I cooed. 'She's well.'

"*Give me to her, give me t-t-to—*

"I handed the blade over, and Dior took her with a smile. I couldn't hear the words Ash spoke into Dior's mind, but I heard the girl's reply.

"'I'm aright, Ash,' she murmured. 'Nothing to forgive.'

"Dior hung her head, tucking one pale lock behind her ear. Then she smiled, bright as the long-lost sun, and as she would a sister, Dior hugged the broken sword to her chest.

"'Merci, Ash.'

"Dior gave the blade back to me, and her weight was a perfect comfort in my bloody hand. I squeezed her leather-bound haft tight, grateful beyond words to have her back at my side. One surety in a world slipped into chaos and madness.

"*We cannot linger here, Gabriel,* she whispered. *Though it m-may have the look of it, no sanctuary there be 'p-p-pon this hallowed ground for we, for we.*

"'I do *so* enjoy your habit of telling me shit I already know, Ash.'

"*Fortunate. Because as ever, ye n-n-n-need me to.*

"Sheathing the blade with a small smile, I took Dior's hand, and together, we trudged up the aisle and into the struggling dawn. The air outside was freezing, thick snows tumbling among the monastery's great pillars, the grand gothic buildings looming atop them. San Michon was impregnable; a bastion that had stood even as most of the realm fell to darkness. But though Ashdrinker was as mad as a bucket of wet cats, she'd spoken truth—there was no respite here for us. Dior's destiny wasn't to be found at the end of Chloe's knife, but I was certain the girl *did* have one, and we couldn't simply hide here among the bloodstains. If nothing else, other silversaints would eventually return from their Hunts to discover their abbot murdered by my hand on holy ground.

"Not a conversation that would go well, I wagered.

"But wintersdeep had come to Nordlund now, the rivers frozen solid; no hindrance to the vampires I knew were still hunting us. The Forever King had set his youngest son upon Dior's tail, and though Danton was dead, Voss wasn't fool enough to risk his entire stake on one throw of the dice. Stepping off hallowed soil, we were stepping into the wolf's maw.

"Damned if we left. And damned if we stayed.

"I heard a winch rattling, and looking across the cloister, I saw a dozen sisters of the Silver Priory at the sky platform. Three Brothers of the Hearth stood beside them, led by the hulking form of old Forgemaster Argyle. They were wrapped in furs, carrying hastily gathered possessions, and wearing the hunted expression of folk fleeing for their lives.

"Fleeing *me,* I realized.

"Argyle raised a silversteel mallet at the sight of us. The old blackthumb had been present in the Cathedral for the ritual; content like all the rest of them to doom an innocent to save the world. But he'd fled as I set about rescuing Dior. I recalled the old man as he'd been in happier days, hard at work in his beloved forge, crafting the weapons that'd saved my life on the Hunt more than once. But he spat on the stone as he stepped between me and the holy sisters now, the burn scars on his pale face etched in livid red.

"'Nae closer,' he warned.

"'Argyle—'

"'*Back,* Gabriel de León! Stay those bloody hands, I warn ye!'

"I could have stopped them, I supposed. If they lived, they'd tell the tale of what happened here to any who'd listen. And what was a few more murders after what I'd done? But I only watched in silence. I knew what these people saw when they looked at me. Not a hero who'd saved an innocent child, but a traitor who'd desecrated their monastery, killed their friends, condemned their world. One of the sisters made the sign of the wheel, Forgemaster Argyle's grey beard bristling as he growled.

"'I pray ye live to rue this sacrilege, villain. May God *damn* ye for it.'

"The platform descended, down through the wailing snows. I felt bitter winds burning my eyes, the girl beside me squeezing my bloody hand.

"'You're not a villain, Gabe.'

"I squeezed back, smiling at her sidelong.

"'I'm a villain when I need to be.'

"Arm wrapped about her, we trekked to the Priory, our shoulders hunched against the howling gale. The grand old building was hollow now, our footfalls ringing on cold stone as we climbed the stairs. Dior showed me to the room where she'd slept, and kicking open the door, we found her clothes neatly folded on her cot, her boots sat beside it.

"'Thank the Mothermaid. I'm freezing my tits off in this *idiotic* robe.' She raised a warning finger. 'And no cracks about needing to have them to lose them.'

"I raised my hands in surrender. 'I didn't say a word.'

"'Keep it that way.'

"'Sweet Redeemer, you make one jest about the size of a dame's baps and spend the rest of your life apologizing for it.'

"'I think there's a lesson in that for all of us.'

"I scoffed, and as she tore off her bloodied robes and cast them to the floor, I turned my back, keeping watch on the corridor outside. Dior wasted no time, dragging on the stout britches I'd given her, the shirt and waistcoat, the fine frockcoat—pale with golden curlicue, lined with good fox fur. And brushing her hair back from the dark beauty spot on her cheek, she did a small pirouette, sweeping her arms out at her sides.

"'Better?'

"I glanced over my shoulder, making a face. 'Passable.'

"'Bastard,' she scoffed. 'You're no oil painting yourself, you know.'

"'I am, actually. There's a good one of me hanging in the Imperial Gallery at Augustin. Moulin painted it.' I scratched my chin. 'I mean, at least it *used* to hang there. Before I got excommunicated. They've probably hung it in the privies now.'

"'Appropriate.'

"'Fuck yourself.'

"'Such a *scorching* wit, Chevalier.'

"'Wit is wasted on the witless, mademoiselle. Now, we've places to be, and precisely *none* of them are here. So get your boots on your feet before mine find your arse.'

"She scoffed, patting her backside. 'You'd have to catch it to kick it, old man.'

"Dior Lachance was a girl who'd survived on the streets since she was eleven, and those years had left her with a gutter-sharp pragmatism, a bawdy wit, a courage that'd put most warriors I knew to shame. So even though she'd almost been murdered by someone she'd thought of as a friend, I'd supposed some gruff jesting between us would make her feel on familiar ground. And she played the game at first, ever giving as good as she got. But as she tried to tie her cravat, I saw that her fingers were fumbling.

"'You're cold,' I lied, stepping in to spare her. 'Let me.'

"She lifted her chin, allowing me to gather up the cloth at her throat. As I tied the knot, I could see Dior was avoiding my eyes. 'I s'pose it's lucky Sister Chloe left my gear laid out,' she murmured. 'Considering she never meant for me to come back here.'

"'Luck. Or the devil loves his own.'

"'Glad *someone's* looking out for me. God surely won't be after all this.'

"'God.' Scoffing, I scruffed her ashen hair. 'You don't need God. You've got me.'

"Her eyes finally met mine, her voice a whisper.

"'. . . Do you mean it?'

"Meeting the girl's stare, I could see her hurt, swimming now to surface. She was hard and sharp as steel, was Dior Lachance, but I realized that for all her front, she was still only sixteen years old. Thrown face-first into a world she couldn't possibly have imagined. Everyone she'd ever cared about had either left her or been taken away. Her trust wasn't easy to earn, and to have given it to Chloe only to be rewarded with a knife at her throat . . . well, I could see that betrayal had wounded her deeper than I first supposed.

"'I mean it,' I told her, searching her eyes. 'By the Blood, I *vow* it. I know not where this road will lead us, girl. But I'll walk it with you, to whatever fate awaits. And if God Himself should tear us asunder, if all the Endless Legion stood in my path, I would find my way back from the shores of the abyss to fight at your side. I'll not leave you, Dior.'

"Reaching down, I squeezed her hands tight as I dared.

"'I will *never* leave you.'

"She fought it a moment longer, dragging her hair down over her eyes, pulling on that armor of bravado she'd learned to wear as a child . . . a child, Seven Martyrs, what the hell did I think she was now? But much as she fought it, it broke loose, the dried blood on her skin cracking as her face crumpled. Tears came then, spilling down her cheeks as she hung her head and snarled.

"'Fucking *coward* . . .'

"'Sweet Mothermaid, girl, the *last* thing you are is a coward.'

"I reached out to her, awkward, and as my hand touched her shoulder, she sobbed aloud, throwing her arms around me. I hung still a moment, paralyzed. But finally I gathered her up, holding her as she wept. Her whole body shook with sobs, and I rocked her back and forth as I'd done with my own daughter, what seemed a lifetime ago. The memory was jagged as a broken blade, and the thought of ma famille brought a lump to my throat.

"'Hush now,' I murmured. 'All will be well, I promise.'

"She sniffed hard, crushing her face into my chest as if to smother her question. 'Did . . . did w-we do the right thing, Gabe?'

"'. . . What do you mean?'

"'The *ritual*,' she hissed. 'Daysdeath. We c-could have ended it! All of it!'

"My chest ached at that, my bloody deeds in that cathedral weighing heavy. I'd cut my old brethren to pieces to save Dior, and though I couldn't pity folk who'd been willing to murder a child, I was still aware that the rite I'd disrupted might have actually *worked*. From the moment I'd made that choice, every orphaned child, every murdered mother, every moment of suffering beneath that daysdeath sky . . . all of it was now in part *my* fault.

"But not hers.

"'Hear me now.' I pulled her back to look her over. 'You put a stopper in that bottle of bullshit, you understand me? The choice was mine alone, and if there's a price to be levied for it, then *I'll* pay the forfeit.' I scoffed, trying to sound more certain than I felt. 'The writings in this monastery are mostly pig-spunk and bullshit anyway. Celene told me if I let the Order kill you, all would be undone.'

"'. . . Celene?'

"'My baby sister. The one you know as Liathe.'

"Dior's tear-stung eyes grew wide. 'That bloodwitch in the mask? She's been trying to get her claws in me since we left Dhahaeth.'

"'She also helped us fight Danton and his brood. She's no friend to the Forever King.'

"'So the enemy of my enemy . . .'

"'Is usually just another enemy.' I looked to the window then, the dim light beyond. 'But she saved my life. She helped me save yours. We should hear what she has to say at least. It's not safe for us to stay here, Dior. You must decide which path we take next.'

"She blinked at that. 'Me? Why me?'

"'Because this is *your* life. *Your* fate. You're the Holy Grail of San Michon. I'll stand beside you, ever and always. But your road is your own. *You* should have the choosing of it.'

"She sniffed and swallowed hard. 'What if I choose the wrong one?'

"'Then we'll get lost together.'

"She looked up into my eyes, and I saw that old spark kindling in hers.

"'The road is black ahead,' I told her. 'And it's hard to keep walking when you can't see the ground beneath your feet. But that's what courage *is*. The will to keep walking in the darkness. To believe the end is just beyond your outstretched hand, rather than a million miles away. And while some might falter, some might fail, some might curl up like babes rather than walk on through that lonely night, you are not that girl.'

"I squeezed her hand and searched her eyes.

"'You are *not* that girl.'

"She squared her shoulders in her fine frockcoat, stood a little taller, dragging those pale locks from her face. And though she was still small, tired, God, so *very* young, in those shining eyes, I caught a glimpse of the woman Dior Lachance might grow up to be.

"And just for a moment, the dark seemed not so dark anymore.

"'Come on, then,' she said. 'Best not keep famille waiting.'"

II

HOWS AND WHYS

"WE DESCENDED TO the valley below, and there was only one thought in my head. Not relief to have learned my sister wasn't dead, nor horror to discover she was Dead instead. Not suspicion at the strange gifts she'd displayed, nor curiosity about how she'd spent the last seventeen years. As Dior and I rode the sky platform slowly down, my questions, my wonders, all were whispers, drowned out by a single fear.

"'Celene made me drink her blood.'

"Dior glanced up from chewing her nails, spitting a ragged sliver over the side. 'I'm new to all this admittedly, but don't vampires usually do it the other way around?'

"'Greyhand cut my throat. Celene's blood stopped me dying.'

"'Doesn't sound too bad, then?'

"'It's exactly one-third of the way toward fucking disastrous.'

"The girl shook her head, looking blank.

"'There's power in vampire blood, Dior. Strength. A cure for mortal hurts. It even slows old age. But there's darker magiks too. Drinking from them gives them *power* over you, and that power only deepens the more you drink. Sup from the same vampire on three separate nights, and you'll be enthralled. Naught but a slave to its will.'

"'That's why silversaints smoke blood,' she murmured. 'Rather than swallow it.'

"I nodded, looking at the frozen river below. 'Greyhand told me a tale once. About a vampire named Liame Voss. He was a fledgling Ironheart, birthed in Madeisa maybe fifty years back. A silversaint named Marco was sent to the city when folk started to go missing.

"'Marco was a wily hunter, and he did what any wily hunter would. He

— 37 —

investigated Liame's tomb, spoke to the man's famille and fiancée; a pretty lass named Estelle. Marco almost got his quarry too, catching the vampire striking a streetwalker near the docks. He took Liame's arm off with his blade, near blinded him with a silverbomb. But the leech leapt into the bay, swimming into the murk where Marco couldn't follow.

"'Strange thing was, Liame had been claiming a new victim almost every night. But after Marco near killed him, the murders stopped cold. Our good frère lay low, certain Liame would strike again, but he never did. Not one more victim. Marco supposed the vampire had fled for safer hunting grounds. It wasn't 'til years later he learned the truth.'

"Dior spoke, her voice hushed. 'And that was?'

"'Well, this was back when the sun still shone bright in the sky. And to safeguard him while he was helpless during the day, Liame had thralled his fiancée. Estelle watched over him as he slept. Lured in victims that he might feed off them. Even disposed of the bodies sometimes.' I shook my head, face grim. 'A thrall will kill for her master, Dior. Die for her master. Commit *any* atrocity for the one she's bound to. But Estelle genuinely loved Liame. All the ardor of her mortal life, compounded by the serfdom of the Blood. And so completely *terrified* was the mademoiselle after her beloved Liame was almost killed by Frère Marco, that she fashioned a way to protect him forever.

"'It was nine years before it all came to light. In the end, Estelle was struck by a runaway carriage. Crushed beneath the horses' hooves. And as she lay dying, she told her priest the truth—not to confess, mind you, but to beg he continue her blessed work.

"'The priest escorted the militia to her home, broke through her cellar wall. And there, they found Liame. A starving bag of bones, still comatose as they dragged him up into the sun. Estelle had buried her fiancé while he slept, you see. Bricked him up, where nobody could hurt him. She'd been feeding him through a drain, stoppering her ears with wax, so she'd not be able to hear his commands to release him. Wanting nothing more in all the world, but to keep her beloved master safe.'

"Dior shivered and made the sign of the wheel. 'Forever.'"

Jean-François suddenly scoffed, the historian leaning back in his armchair. "What *utter* nonsense, de León."

Gabriel glanced up at the Marquis, sipping his wine. "As you like it."

"I assume this fiction was supposed to frighten the poor girl?"

"Life is stranger than fiction, vampire. But the tale was *supposed* to teach

Dior that blood serfdom is no trifling affair. And in some folk, it gives rise to a devotion that borders madness." Gabriel nodded toward the shadow under the door; Meline lurking ever outside. "You should be wary of that. *Master*."

Jean-François pursed ruby lips, gifting the silversaint a withering glance.

"But even if you avoid insanity," Gabriel continued, "after three drops over three nights, you're still naught but a slave. I'd drunk once from Celene already, and I knew her blood would be at work in me now, softening my heart. No matter what she'd become in the nights since I'd last seen her, my baby sister and I had been thick as thieves when we were young. Her blood in my veins would only make that love ring deeper. And truth was, I couldn't trust her. Not as far as I could spit the blood she'd forced down my throat.

"We continued our descent, chains creaking as the wind rocked the platform. The Mère Valley was dressed in its winter gowns, the frozen river gleaming like dark steel. The peaks of the Godsend loomed on the northwest horizon, the Nightstone Mountains to the southwest, shrouded in storms. The land was cloaked in snow, ash-grey and thick.

"Dior had rolled herself some traproot cigarelles in black tinderpaper— Benedict, one of the old brothers who worked the monastery Breadbasket, had been a hopeless addict, and the girl had commandeered his stash. She lit one on her stolen flintbox now, pale smoke drifting from her lips as she murmured. 'So what happened to her?'

"'Celene?'

"'Oui.'

"I dragged back my windblown hair and stared out at the lands of our birth. 'Aaron and I fought one of Fabién's daughters when we were initiates. Her name was Laure. The Wraith in Red. I set her ablaze during the battle, and she set fire to the village where I was born as revenge. Killed everyone. My mama. Stepfather. Baby sister. Everyone.'

"'Great Redeemer.' Dior squeezed my hand. 'I'm sorry, Gabe.'

"'Celene was barely fifteen years old.' I sighed. 'She died because of me.'

"The platform touched down with a heavy *thump*, and I looked about the freezing valley, seeing no sign of my sister. Trudging to the stables, I noted horses missing, probably taken by Argyle and the others. Celene hadn't seen fit to stop them, but perhaps she—

"'God be praisssed.'

"I spun toward the soft hiss behind me, hand on Ashdrinker's hilt. Beneath my furs, I felt a warmth forgotten, now rekindled; the fire of faith renewed, running through the silver tattoos on my body, my aegis burning in the presence of the Dead. A figure stood behind us, tall and graceful and swathed in crimson, like a bloodstain in the snow.

"She was just as I remembered, but my heart still quickened at the sight. Locks of midnight-blue running to her waist, long red frockcoat, silken shirt parted from her pale chest. She wore that same mask; white porcelain with a bloody handprint over her mouth, red-rimmed lashes. Her irises were pale as her skin, and what should have been the whites of her eyes were black instead. Her stare was a dead thing's, utterly drained of light and life.

"'You live,' Celene whispered.

"We stood there in the chill, so much weight and so many words between us, the air felt harder to breathe. Half my life had passed since I'd thought my baby sister murdered, but to see her again after all those years, my heart felt ripped anew from my chest. And though I'd a thousand questions to ask, I couldn't think of a single thing to say.

"'Dior Lachance,' I managed, 'this was Celene Castia.'

"Dior nodded, mumbling around her cigarelle. 'Thought you preferred Liathe?'

"'Liathe is our title. Not our name.' Celene sank to one knee, like a chevalier before a queen. 'But call usss as you wish, child. We are ssssimply over-joyed you are safe.'

"Dior blinked, uncertain. Celene's voice was that same strange whisper, lisping and sibilant—like the point of a knife being dragged along a sheet of cracking ice.

"'You sssaved her, brother,' she said, turning to me. 'We had our doubtssss.'

"I stared hard as she rose to her feet, echoes of the blood she'd fed me lingering on my tongue. Even hours later, it burned with a potency I'd never tasted. The blood of an ancien vampire, somehow welling inside the veins of a fledgling only seventeen years in her grave.

"'Your title,' I said. 'What does it mean?'

"'Liathe. Old Talhostic for *crusader*. Or *knight*.'

"'Knight?' I scoffed. 'Of what?'

"'The Faith. The Faith*ful*.'

"'Why did you follow me?' Dior demanded. 'What do you want?'

"'You must come with usss, child. You are in danger. And with you, all the soulsss of this realm. 'Tis the Forever King who stalksss you now, but it is only a matter of time before the other Priorem seek to bend you to their wills. You *cannot* fall into their handsss.'

"'The hell is a Priorem?' the girl growled.

"'The most powerful of the kith,' I replied. 'The heads of the four great bloodlines.'

"'Five,' Celene said, gaze shifting to me. 'There are *five* bloodlines, Gabriel.'

"I stared at my sister, remembering our clash at San Guillaume, the battle on the Mère we'd had with Danton. She'd fought like a demon at both, stronger and faster than a fledgling had any right to be. But moreover, she'd wielded a blade made of her own blood. Boiled the blood of other kith by touching them, just as I could. I knew almost nothing of the vampire who'd fathered me, but like all palebloods, I'd been granted a measure of his power—speed, strength, and a hint of blood sorcery named *sanguimancy*. And it seemed Celene somehow shared that same dark gift.

"My sister dug a thumbnail into her palm, dark red welling forth. The scent hit me like a fist, and I could feel my tattoos burning hotter on my skin. As Dior's eyes widened, the blood flowed up from Celene's hand like a viper, shaped by her will into a familiar crest; the same unearthed by my beloved Astrid in the library above, half a lifetime ago.

"Twin skulls, facing each other on a towered shield.

"'Esani,' I whispered.

"'That's Old Talhostic too,' Dior said. '*Faithless*. And my ancestor, the daughter of the Redeemer and Michon, her name was Esan. *Faith*.'

"'What the hell does all this mean, Celene?' I demanded. 'You told me the Wraith in Red killed you when she burned Lorson.'

"'She did. Dear mama Laure.' A long sigh slipped from behind my sister's bloody mask. 'You robbed me of my vengeance when you ssslew her, brother.'

"'If Laure made you, you're born of the Blood Voss. How is it you can work sanguimancy? That's the bloodgift of the Esani.'

"'Sssso much you do not know. Years spent in your little tower, learning to kill faekin and coldbloods and duskdancersss. And you know *nothing* of what you are.'

"'Teach me, then,' I spat. 'Instead of being bitchly about it.'

"Her head tilted, bitter wind blowing her coat about her like smoke.

"'The Esana are not just a bloodline, brother. We are a *belief*. I ssstudied at the feet of one of the Faith's greatest acolytesss. An ancien named Wulfric.' The sluice of red before her shivered, formed itself into a long, dripping blade. 'It is from *him* that our giftsss flow.'

"'So why did this Wulfric send you after me?' Dior exhaled smoke, eyes fixed on that rippling sword. 'What is it you want?'

"'The sssame thing Gabriel's misguided brethren wanted. The Redeemer's blood will end daysdeath, child. You will bring the sssun back to the heavens. And an *end* to this empire of the damned.'

"The air hung heavy with anticipation. The promise of revelation. The butchery I'd committed up in that cathedral was *my* choice, and I'd have done it all again to save Dior's life. But I'd have been a coward to turn my face from the price the world might now pay for it. I'd stopped the Silver Order from ending daysdeath, and all the suffering that came with it. So now, I'd have to end daysdeath myself.

"And it seemed my sister might know the way to do it.

"I could feel the weight of the word Dior spoke next. It seemed as if all the world had fallen still, even the wind shushing itself so it might hear her frightened whisper.

"'*How?*'

"'We . . .' Celene hung her head. 'I . . . do not know yet.'

"The wind began its wailing again, the world its turning, the stillness shattered by my bark of incredulous heartbroken laughter. 'You *WHAT?*'

"Celene looked up at me, hissing soft behind her mask.

"'Are you *jesting?*' I spat. 'You dog our arses halfway across the empire, almost murder me *twice* trying to snatch Dior away, and you don't even know—'

"'I said I do not know *YET*!' Celene's roar rang on black stone. 'Master Wulfric was *murdered* before he could teach me! But there are *other* Esana, Gabriel! Creaturesss who walked the earth when this empire was not even a dream! The greatest warrior of the Faithful abides but a few weeksss' journey from here! We will seek the lair of Master Jènoah, and within his hallsss, we will learn the truth of all Dior must do to bring back the sun!'

"'A few weeks? In the depths of wintersdeep? Where the hell is this place?'

"'Somewhere in the Nightstone Mountainsss. A citadel known as Cairnhaem.'

"'. . . *Somewhere?* You've never been? Have you even met this prick?'

"'It mattersss not!' she snapped. 'In your gentle keeping, the Grail almost lost her life, and the world its sssalvation! You have no understanding of what is at stake here, Gabriel! Thisss is the path the child must walk, and she need not walk it with you!'

"Celene stamped her boot, vicious, and for a moment, she seemed not a blood-drenched monster, but my sister again—a child, a fury, a hellion with a temper I'd both feared and adored. And pale eyes narrowed, she raised one shaking hand to Dior.

"'Now come with usss.'

"I glanced to the girl beside me, and back to this thing that had been my kin.

"'You're out of your fucking mind,' I said, drawing Ashdrinker.

"*Ohhh,* my blade whispered. *Pretty coat redredred outside and in, pretty fl—*

"'Thisss is no game, brother,' Celene spat. 'You cannot protect her from what is coming. You have not the first *inkling* about the answersss she needs. The child comesss—'

"'The *child* has a bloody name,' Dior snapped. 'And perhaps we should all take a breath here. I mean, those of us who breathe at least . . .'

"'I warn you, Gabriel,' Celene hissed, the air between us now crackling with dark current. 'This life is mine because of you. All I am, all I do, is because of *you.* We are taking Dior to Master Jènoah. Stand not in our way.'

"'When it comes to this girl, I'm in the *world's* way.'

"Celene raised her bloody blade.

"Her voice sliced through the chill between us.

"'Then we will make you move.'"

III

BAD BLOOD

"CELENE FLEW AT me; a red blur across grey snow. I pushed Dior aside before she struck, that bloody sword scything at my throat. My aegis was burning, but I'd no time to unveil it—barely time enough to parry with Ash. I felt the terrible strength behind Celene's blow, twisting and kicking her in the spine as she overextended. Momentum sent her into the granite pillar behind me, splintering the stone.

"Dior cried, 'STOP!' as Celene turned, her sword painting a crimson ribbon on the air. And crashing blade to blade, heartsblood to starsteel, my sister and I began to dance.

"Celene had been a terror as a child, like I said. Our dear mama used to tear her hair out at my sister's unladylike pursuits, and chide *me* for encouraging them. My hellion always claimed she'd no desire to wed, speaking constantly of a life of adventure instead, and she and I would play at swordfighting around my stepfather's forge when our chores were done. But strange as it might sound, Celene and I never fought each other. Instead, we'd stand back-to-back, sticks in hand, facing down endless legions of imaginary foes.

"*Ever outnumbered*, we'd say. *Never outmatched. Always, Lions.*

"And there, in San Michon's shadow, it seemed at first we were children again—that at any moment, Mama might yell at us to set aside our sticks and come in for supper. But as I fended off her next assault, blade to blade to blade, I realized Celene played no games here; that my heartwarm memories were just the echoes of her blood in my veins.

"*This is not your s–s–sister, Gabriel*, came Ash's whisper.

"Red droplets flew as our swords kissed.

"A hiss of pain as her blade sliced my cheek.

"'GABE!' Dior shouted.

"*DAMN YE, FIGHT!*

"Dior charged across the snow toward Celene and me, shouting for us to 'HOLD!' I cried warning for her to back off, but that girl had more balls than fucking brains sometimes, I swear it. And with my eyes off my sister, Celene lashed out with a kick that damn near broke my ribs, sending me flying back like a cannon shot. Right smack into Dior.

"We collided with a grunt, the *crack* of my forehead into her face. Dior's breath exploded from her lips along with her cigarelle as we crashed into the snow together, tumbling now to rest. I rolled up into a crouch, blade held tight, glancing at the girl I'd struck; only dazed and winded, to my relief. But my pulse thrashed quicker and my mouth ran dry as I saw it spilling from her nose in a slick of bright, brilliant red.

"*Blood.*"

Gabriel breathed deep, thumb tracing the teardrop scars down his cheek.

"Now. It's been said by some that I was the greatest swordsman who ever lived, coldblood. The songs they used to sing about me claimed I could cut the night in two. And though drunken prattle around the pisshouses of Augustin and Beaufort is nothing to measure your manhood by, it's true I was never a slouch with a blade. I'd trained at the feet of masters since I was a boy. I was born of Nordish blood; the blood of Lions. And looking at that girl bleeding in the snow beside me, I felt that lion in me awaken.

"'You *fucking hurt her,*' I spat.

"I sprang at Celene, falling upon her like an avalanche, aegis burning beneath my skin. It was clear now that my sister wanted me dead, Dior in her cold clutches. And glancing to that winded girl, rolling over in the snow and dragging her knuckles across her bleeding nose, I remembered what I'd promised, what I'd already sacrificed to see her safe.

"The fate of the entire world.

"*FIGHT!*

"Celene lunged, the tip of her blade shearing toward my chest. Skipping back, boots crunching, I dragged her off-kilter. Dancing in close, I begged another strike, and she obliged, reeling and unbalanced, hissing in fury. But I turned the blow downward, driving her swordpoint into the snow. And slipping behind her with all the grace those pisshouse minstrels sang of, I brought Ashdrinker down across her back.

"Celene's coat split apart, a gout of blood hit the snow as Ash whistled through skin and bone. My sister shivered in the howling wind. And before my wondering eyes, her whole body splashed into a sluice of gore at my feet.

"I heard a sound, soft—a crunch of snow at my back, turning as a red blade erupted through my chest. The blow cleaved just shy of my heart, blood bubbling into my mouth as Ashdrinker tumbled from my hand. Celene stood *behind* me now, dead eyes narrowed, the figure I'd struck low just a puddle on the frost—some trick of the eye, I realized, some spell of the blood.

"'F-fuck my . . .'

"Dior screamed, Celene *twisted,* cleaving my ribs as she wrenched her blade free. I fell, coughing blood, rolling onto my back as the thing that had been my sister raised her sword high. I was but a breath from death, I knew it. But desperate, gasping, I felt that fire yet burning beneath my skin. And dragging off my left glove, I held up my hand.

"The sevenstar on my palm flared, and Celene hissed, one hand to her eyes. In the wars of my youth, that ink had burned silver-blue, lighting the battlefield with the fire of my faith. But now it burned red as the hate-struck heart of hell. There was no devotion to the Almighty left in my heart after what he'd done to me, to ma famille. But as my old friend Aaron had told me, it mattered not what I held faith in, so long as I held faith in something.

"And I held faith in *Dior.*

"Celene staggered back, half-blind. Wheezing, I tore my greatcoat and tunic open, baring the burning lion on my torso. Pink froth at my lips, spitting blood, I snatched up Ashdrinker and rose from the steaming snow.

"'N-not today, sister.'

"But Celene only raised her hand.

"I felt her touch, like a fist about my chest, iron bands *squeezing* my whole body. I gasped, unable to move, to even *breathe.* My sister's eyes narrowed as by some unholy measure of her dark arte, she seized hold of the very blood in my veins.

"*Her* blood.

"Celene curled her fingers into claws, and I gasped in agony as the blood she'd gifted me began to boil. Her hand shook and red steam rose from my skin, a scream ripped up from my throat as she hissed behind her mask. 'Not today, broth—'

"Pale fingers twisted through her hair, yanking her head back. And from behind, a silversteel dagger was pressed to her throat.

"'Not *ever*, vampire,' Dior spat.

"My sister fell still, holding me just the same. 'Child—'

"'*Stop* calling me that. Let him go.'

"Celene glanced to me, her grip still steel in my veins. For a moment, I wondered why she was so afeared—she was born of an elder Ironheart, after all. But looking closer, I saw Dior's dagger didn't only gleam silver, but *red*—her blood not just smudged on her nose and lips now, but smeared on her blade. Celene and I had both seen that blood burn a Prince of Forever to ashes. And all of us knew what it could do to her too.

"'We mean you no harm, chérie. You mussst—'

"'I must nothing, *chérie*. Now let. Him. Go.'

"Celene's dead gaze fell on me, fury melting to fear. '. . . He will kill usss.'

"'Maybe. But I don't think so.' Dior met my eyes, speaking as much to my sister as me. 'He's too smart for that. If I *am* the key to ending this, and you know where the lock is, seems perhaps we all need each other. You're not *taking* me anywhere. But . . .' She sniffed hard, breathed deep. 'We can come with you. We'll seek out this Master Jènoah together.'

"The girl spat red into the snow, raised one brow in question.

"'Unless someone's got a better suggestion?'

"Her gaze was fixed on me, pale blue eyes glinting with question. I could see distrust in her. Trepidation. Anger that Celene had hurt me. But still, there was curiosity too. About the Esani. About her truth. About how she might actually fix this awful, broken world. Though I'd little faith in my sister, Celene seemed to know *something* of what Dior must do to end all this. Which was more than I could say for myself.

"And so, straining against Celene's grip, my own better judgment, I gave a small nod.

"'But if you don't let him go *right now*,' Dior whispered, tightening her grip in my sister's hair, 'your brother won't have to kill you, Celene, I swear to fucking God.'

"Like I say, Dior had grown up in the gutters of Lashaame. Only the Almighty knew what she'd done to survive them. Hard times and hard stone breeds hard people, children hardest of all. This girl had killed inquisitors. Soldiers. Sweet Mothermaid, she'd killed the Beast of Vellene himself. When she swore to God, I believed it. And Celene did too.

"The grip on my veins eased, and I collapsed into the snow. Wisps of red steam seeped from my skin, and I pressed one hand to my punctured chest. The wound slurped and bubbled with every breath, the taste of salt and copper on my tongue.

"'Gabe!'

"Celene straightened her silken scarf as Dior skidded into the snow beside me, eyes on the blood pulsing between my fingers. The girl hauled off her glove, lifted the dagger to her scarred palm, ready to cut. The blood of the Redeemer was miraculous—I'd seen it heal wounds that would've put any ordinary man in his grave. But I was no ordinary man.

"'Don't hurt y-yourself,' I whispered, still glowering at my sister.

"'But you're bleeding!'

"'Not for long. Palebloods don't d-die easy.'

"Glancing down, I saw my wound already beginning to close; sobering testimony to the power in the blood Celene had fed me. While I could boil another's blood by touching them, she'd done so with a gesture—it seemed every drop of herself was hers to command. Her display of sanguimancy had been awe-inspiring, terrifying—without Dior here, my sister might well have bested me, and I wondered what else she was capable of. Because kneeling there in the chill of San Michon's shadow that morn, staring at my Dead sister and down the black road we'd now apparently all be walking together, I had one certainty, sure and true.

"'You sure you're aright?' Dior asked. 'You don't need me to . . .'

"'Save your blood, chérie,' I sighed.

"Celene nodded, whispering.

"'Where we are headed, you ssshall need it.'"

IV

LOST TOGETHER

" 'SON OF A rat-fiddling ... goat-sucking ... pig-fucking *whore!*'

"Dior's shout echoed on the ice, teeth bared in a frustrated snarl.

"'You realize you're only insulting my mama when you call me that?' I called. 'It's not actually an insult to *me* at all?'

"'Eat shit, you cack-gargling twatgoblin.'

"'See, that's the spirit,' I smiled. 'Now pick it up.'

"Dior spat into the snow. 'I'm no *good* at this, Gabriel!'

"'You're shite. But how do you suppose one *gets* good?'

"We were stood on the frozen surface of the Mère River, mist hanging thick in the morning gloom. Frost billowed from Dior's lips as she cursed again, dragging the sweaty tumble of hair from her eyes. But stubborn as a wagonload of drunken mules, she sighed, reached down to the ice, and picked up her training sword.

"'Were *you* this terrible when you started out?'

"'Doesn't matter.' I took a swig of vodka, tucked my flask inside my great-coat. 'Measure yourself not by where others are, but where you used to be.'

"I raised my sword, eyes on hers.

"'Once more with feeling.'

"We'd been trekking downriver nine days, San Michon lost in the deepening snows behind us. We'd set out the morning Celene and I clashed, accompanied by three tundra ponies 'borrowed' from the monastery stables. They were a sturdy trio, that hardy Talhost breed known as sosyas, and they'd been raised to be unafraid of the Dead—good news, considering the strange new company we were keeping. But my sister was off scouting now, and the beasts stood easy in the shelter of twisted trees on the riverbank, watching as Dior and I began trying to dash each other's brains out again.

"We used wooden swords, filched from the Armory along with a stash of silvershot, chymicals, sanctus, and a princely sum of monastery vodka to boot. I hadn't been able to find the saber Dior had taken from Danton's corpse, so I'd armed her with my old silversteel dagger and a new longblade from Argyle's armory. She couldn't swing a sword to save her life yet, but I could recall the sight of the Beast of Vellene as he burst into flames from the mere touch of her blood. And I knew this girl was a weapon leeches would learn to fear.

"'Northwind,' I commanded.

"Dior lifted her training blade and took up the offensive stance I'd demonstrated. Her breath was coming quick, cheeks flushed with exertion.

"'Blood Voss,' I demanded. 'What are they?'

"'The *Ironhearts*. Brood of Fabién.'

"'Their creed?'

"'*All Shall Kneel.*'

"She came at me quick as silvershot, running the pattern I'd shown her; belly, chest, throat, repeat. I parried each blow, our swords cracking against each other as we danced.

"'Very good,' I said, backing away across the ice. 'What are their gifts?'

"'They shrug off hurts that'd end other coldbloods. Silver. Fire. And the older ones can read people's mi—'

"I dodged a clumsy thrust, poked her ribs as she stumbled past.

"'You're giving your game away with your eyes. Don't look where you're set to hit. *Feel* your way. Now, what's the proper term for older vampires?'

"She turned on me, breath hissing. 'Ancien.'

"'Good. Southwind stance.' Dior shifted to the defensive at my command, turning a blow that I threw at her face. 'Blood Ilon next. Name and creed.'

"'The *Whispers*,' Dior said, backing off. '*Sharper Than Blades.*'

"'Their gifts?'

"Dior winced as I struck, barely fending off my assault, panting for breath. 'They play with emotion. Twist you madder or happier, tumble your passions all around. Make you act in ways you wouldn't, say things you shouldn't, feel things that aren't real.'

"'The *Push*,' I nodded. 'Not quite as flashy as breaking swords on your skin or punching down walls. But when you can't trust your own heart, you can't trust anything.'

"We fell into another flurry, Dior gasping as she parried my next few strikes. Her hair was damp with sweat, her breath coming hard and chill.

"'Excellent,' I nodded. 'Now, Blood Dyvok. Name their creed.'

"'*Deeds Not Words.*'

"'Who are they? What can they do?'

"'The Untamed. Their ancien are so strong they can crush steel in their fists, smash down castle walls with their bare hands. Even the young ones are—'

"I feinted low, then tapped her shoulder. 'What do we call newborn vampires?'

"'Fledglings,' she wheezed.

"I struck at her chest and head. 'And the gifts of ancien Dyvok?'

"'They command people. Bend a person's will with the power of their voice.'

"'Like the Ilon?'

"'No.' She shook her head, chest now heaving like a bellows. 'The Ilon are subtler. They whisper, and people agree. Dyvok roar, and people *obey*.'

"'They call it the *Whip*. Subtle as a sledgehammer. But just as effective.'

"I renewed my attack, quicker than before; chest, belly, throat, belly. Dior turned each blow aside, and I caught myself smiling when she read my feint. But as she danced away, she slipped on a treacherous stretch of ice, and I smacked her wrist hard enough to leave a bruise. Dropping her sword, she bent double and spun on the spot.

"'*Goddamn it!*'

"'Fighting is dancing. Always mind your footing, Lachance.'

"'That *fucking* hurt, Gabriel!'

"'If this blade were steel, you'd have no fucking hand. You think that'd tickle?'

"'I tried to move!'

"'Trying isn't doing.'

"'Right, but there's no need to be a prick about it!'

"'*You're* the one who asked me to teach you this,' I growled. 'A blade and half a clue are twice as dangerous as no blade or clue at all. So if you insist on swinging one, there's every reason under heaven to be a prick about teaching you to do it proper. This world won't give you what you want just because you asked nicely, girl. Not respect. Not love. Not peace. You get what you earn. You eat what you kill.'

"I took another burning swig of vodka, pointed to her fallen blade.

"'So kill, damn you.'

"She scowled. She swore. She spat a few more colorful insults about my mama, and the fact that I forgave them all should give you some indication of how fond I was growing of this girl. Because for all her griping, Dior never relented. She earned a few more bruises, I drilled her until she was drenched with sweat. But she never stopped working until I told her enough. And seeing the steel in her eyes, I understood why.

"The entire Company of the Grail had given their lives to protect this girl—old Père Rafa, Bellamy Bouchette, Saoirse á Dúnnsair and her lioness, Phoebe. Aaron de Coste and Baptiste Sa-Ismael had been willing to risk the whole city of Aveléne to protect her. I'd drenched San Michon Cathedral red defending her.

"*She wants to be able to defend herself.*

"'Aright,' I grunted. 'Breakfast will be ready.'

"Dior lowered her blade, wheezing. Too exhausted to even backchat me, she staggered toward our cookfire on the banks, crashing face-first onto her furs. I followed, stowing our blades on our spare pony—a silver roan I'd named Nugget. My own pony, a big dun I called Bear, stood beside him, snuffling in his feed bag.

"'Thought of what to call her yet?' I asked, stirring the cookpot.

"Dior's voice was muffled by her furs. 'Mnnff?'

"I nodded to a shaggy chestnut mare, sheltering in the shadow of a fungus-riddled oak. 'She needs a better name than Pony.'

"'Gabriel, the last horse I named hurled herself off a cliff a few days later.'

"'And your theory is that happened because you gave her a name?'

"'I'm just saying I ended up sleeping *inside* her,' the girl said, still look-ing queasy about it. 'So you'll pardon me if I'm not in a hurry to name another.'

"I glanced at Dior's beast, lips pursed. 'What about Blanket?'

"'Oh, God, *STOP IT!*' she wailed, burying her face and kicking her heels.

"I chuckled, ladling out bowlfuls of rabbit-and-mushroom soup. I was no cookmaster, but the fare was hot and rich, and better than most we'd enjoyed on this road. Settling beneath a frozen elm with a steaming bowl in my lap, I leafed through one of the tomes I'd 'borrowed' from the San Michon library while I ate.

"'What are you reading for?'

"I blinked, glancing up from the illuminated pages. Dior was sitting cross-legged, slurping her soup and watching me across the flames.

"'I don't think I've ever been asked that question,' I realized. '*What* I'm reading, certainly. Never what I'm reading *for*. You don't like books?'

"She shrugged, shoveling in another mouthful. 'Never saw much use for them.'

"'Not much . . .' I sputtered, outraged on behalf of every scribe, librarian, and bookshop owner in the imperium. 'They've a *thousand* fucking uses, girl!'

"'Name one. *Aside* from reading,' she added as I opened my mouth to quip.

"'Aright.' I started counting off on my fingers. 'You can . . . light them on fire. Throw them at people. Light them on fire, *then* throw them at people, particularly if those people are the sort of bucktoothed shitwits who don't like books.' Dior rolled her eyes as I pulled the tome up in front of my face. 'They can serve as a brilliant disguise.' I balanced the book on my head. 'Fashionable headwear.' I slipped it under my backside. 'Portable furniture.' I tore off a page corner and pushed it into my mouth, chewing loudly. 'Good source of roughage.'

"'Fine, fine,' she sighed. 'They've their uses.'

"'Damn right they do. The right book is worth a hundred blades.'

"'All I'm saying is a book won't cut your next purse or steal your next supper.'

"'But they might teach you a better way to do both.' My voice turned serious, then, all jest vanishing. 'A life without books is a life not lived, Dior. There's a magik like no other to be found in them. To open a book is to open a door—to another place, another time, another mind. And usually, mademoiselle, it's a mind far sharper than your own.'

"Dior spoke around another ambitious mouthful, tapping her temple with her spoon. 'Sharp as three swords, me.'

"'Wooden ones, maybe.'

"She scoffed at that, kicking a toeful of snow in my general direction as I returned to my reading. Still smiling, we finished our breakfast in companionable silence, Dior cleaning the gear and packing it in our saddlebags while I saw to the horses.

"'Put your ghostbreath on,' I reminded her. 'You'll have sweated it off training.'

"'Do I have to? It's disgusting.'

"'So are corpses. Which is exactly what you'll be if you don't put it on.'

"Dior groaned, but reached for the chymical concoction I'd brewed. It was a small bottle marked with a wailing spirit, pale liquid inside. It didn't smell a bouquet, sure and true, but the hunters of San Michon used ghostbreath to mask their scent from the Dead, and as long as I'd traveled with her, the Dead had seemed drawn to Dior like flies to honey.

"'That will not work,' came a whisper.

"Dior startled, but I kept myself steady, brow raised as I glanced behind us. My sister had returned from scouting, it seemed, watching us now from a copse of dead trees. Long dark hair framed her porcelain mask, that bloody handprint over her mouth.

"'We can sssmell her miles away if the wind is right,' Celene said.

"'You're a highblood,' I replied. 'And a sanguimancer. Who knows whether simple wretched will be able to smell her as well as you.'

"'They will. They *do*.'

"'We'll see.'

"Celene shook her head, Dior watching her through the falling snow.

"'. . . What do I smell like?' the girl finally asked.

"My sister fixed Dior with her dead stare, cold wind whispering between them.

"'Heaven,' she replied.

"Dior lowered her eyes, throwing a nervous glance at me. It had been the girl's idea for us to travel this road together, and she'd spoken truth pointing out we'd no better prospects than to seek this mysterious Master Jènoah. But it seemed none of us were too comfortable with the arrangement.

"My sister had been journeying with us nine days, though truly, she kept our company only half that time; the rest spent scouting for the nameless danger she *insisted* was coming. Celene moved like a knife, swift and cold, keeping her distance even when we walked together. She told us she'd no wish to spook the horses, but honestly, I think she was as uncomfortable in my company as I in hers. My sister was a vampire. I was a man who'd spent his life *killing* vampires. And we were all still coming to grips with those truths.

"But beyond the strangeness of her presence, the inexplicable power she wielded despite her age, another unease had been gnawing me for days now.

"*I'd never seen her feed.*

"Depending on her age, a vampire can go days, perhaps a week without blood before her thirst becomes unbearable. But I'd not seen Celene drink a drop—not once in all the time we'd traveled together. And while I supposed my baby sister might've been hunting in her long treks away from our side, I was acutely aware of how little I truly knew of her.

"'How much farther?' Dior asked.

"Celene glanced down the curve of the Mère; the grey ice, the black trees encrusted with frozen blooms of shadespine and beggarbelly fungus. To the southwest, the shadow of the grim and frozen Nightstone peaks could be seen rising above the deadwood.

"'Perhaps a fortnight, moving ssswift.'

"'It's getting bloody cold out here,' Dior said, blowing into her hands.

"'It'll be worse in the mountains,' I warned. 'The winds up there can freeze the very blood in your veins. We *might* consider sheltering somewhere warm awhile. Aveléne's not far from here.'

"'No,' my sister snapped. 'Aveléne takes us from our path. Every day the sssun fails to shine, more lives are squandered. More soulsss lost. We are heading to the Nightstone.'

"A scowl darkened my brow. 'We owe Aaron de Coste and Baptiste Sa-Ismael a debt, Celene. Without their help, Dior would be in Danton's clutches right now.'

"'All the more reason not to darken their door,' Celene replied. 'The Beast of Vellene is dead, but Danton was not Fabién's only child. If the Forever King had not already set more dogsss on Dior's tail, he *will* be unleashing them now. You cannot protect her from her destiny, Gabriel. She mussst be prepared. She mussst face what—'

"'I am fucking *sick*,' Dior sighed, 'of you two talking about me like I'm not here.'

"'You mussst face what you are,' Celene said, not skipping a beat. 'What you mussst do to end the death of days. Those secretsss lie in Master Jènoah's lair, not some river hovel. Have faith in yourself, chérie. In the path you have chosen. Aveléne is a fool'sss errand.'

"I scoffed. 'And visiting someone who refers to his home as a *lair* sounds a perfectly fucking sensible course of action.'

"'This *is* a dangerous road,' Celene nodded, still watching Dior. 'We do not deny it. And there *are* other eldersss of the Faith we might seek. But they are far-flung, or deep in the territory of our enemies. We cannot promise the journey to Master Jènoah will be without peril, Dior. But we *can* promise he will show you truth at the end of it.'

"Dior looked between us, clearly torn. We were taking an awful risk trusting Celene, and a warm hearth and hot meal in Aveléne was a tempting prospect. But this girl carried the fate of the world on her shoulders now, and despite my reassurances, I knew some part of her still felt the weight of that red dawn in San Michon. Questioning if I'd been right to save her. Guilty that she lived while so many others suffered beneath our blackened sun.

"'Celene's right, Gabe,' she finally sighed. 'I *have* to learn how to end all this.'

"I pursed my lips, nodded slow.

"'Lost together, then.'

"Our strange trio set off, Dior and I plodding along on horseback while Celene skulked in the distance. We left the river, cutting into a long stretch of deadwood crusted with glittering fungal snarls. Riding into danger as we were, I determined to do everything I could to prepare Dior, and as we traveled, I shared wisdom from a lifetime fighting the dark—mostly talk about coldbloods, though I dispelled some mistruths about faekin and duskdancers just to break the monotony. Our shoulders were hunched, the gale howling through the trees, our tricorns filling slowly with snow. Dior was puffing on those cigarelles like they were paying her for the privilege, and I was drinking steadily, a constant scowl at my brow. I knew Celene was right—despite my fears, I couldn't keep this girl sheltered forever. And it *was* a relief to think that there might yet be a way to end daysdeath.

"But what price was I actually prepared to pay for it?

"I looked about for my sister, but again, she'd disappeared among the snows. Taking another swig, I pondered the question of where she'd been all these years. I wondered about this Jènoah we were headed for, how Celene had fallen in with the Faithless after she died. And in quietest moments, I wondered if she knew something of my *own* father; the vampire who'd seeded our mother, and started our famille down this road to hell.

"'Gabe.'

"Dior's voice dragged me from my musings. She was sat tall atop Pony now, cigarelle dangling from her lips as she pointed south.

"'Gabe, look!'

"Peering through the tangled woods, I spied a dark figure in the distance, stumbling in our direction. He was a tall Ossian fellow, his skin ghost-pale, square jaw dusted with blood and stubble. Sandy-blond hair was brushed into a whip of short spikes and shaved in an undercut, and he wore a dark greatcoat, its hem rippling behind him as he hobbled onward. He was clearly wounded; right arm hanging limp and a crimson trail spattered on the snow in his wake. Pausing to draw one of five wheellock pistols strapped across his chest, he fired behind him with his good hand. And squinting through the falling snow, I spied his targets.

"A pack, loping on all fours through the icy scrub, dashing swift among the trees.

"Dead-eyed, half-rotten, all hunger.

"'Vampires,' Dior whispered."

V
OLD TIMES

"THEY WORE THE clothes they were murdered in.

"Peasants' smocks and gentry coats. Soldiers' kit and dirty rags. They were a filthy band, wretched all, but at least two dozen in number; tricky odds in the open even for—

"'A silversaint,' Dior whispered, finally spotting the sevenstar at his breast.

"'Shit,' I breathed.

"'Do you know him?'

"I made no reply, watching the man limping through the wood.

"'Gabe, we have to help him,' Dior declared, hand to her blade's hilt.

"I was struck by those words, looking now to the girl beside me. The Silver Order had tried to murder this child not a fortnight back, and yet here she was, ready to defend one of their number with a sword she barely knew how to swing. For all the wounds she'd been dealt in her life, underneath her scars, she still had a golden soul, did Dior Lachance. Eyes that saw the hurts of the world, and a heart that wanted to fix them.

"She reminded me so much of my own daughter, it made my chest ache.

"'*We* don't have to anything,' I pointed out. 'I help. *You* applaud.'

"'Gabe . . .'

"Slipping down off Bear, I looked around for Celene, but could still see no sign of her through the frozen trees. I tipped a dose of sanctus into my pipe, tamping down the sticky powder before lighting it with my flintbox. Boiling red smoke filled my lungs, the familiar bliss of the bloodhymn flooding all the way to my fingertips, fangs stirring in my gums.

"I glanced to Dior. 'Wait here.'

"'Gabe, they're only wretched.'

"'There's no *only* about it,' I warned. 'They're still vampires, and they'll still gut you like a lamb at a butcher's ball. You're nowhere near ready yet, Dior. Wait *here*.'

"The girl muttered beneath her breath as I stalked away, shouting to get the fleeing silversaint's attention. He squinted through the dead trees and tumbling snows, raising one hand as he bellowed reply. I lifted a glass phial from my bandolier, lobbed it into the wretched closing behind him. The silverbomb exploded, a deafening burst of fire and silver caustic that scattered the mob, set fire to a few low branches. None of the monsters dropped, mind you, but the blast gave the 'saint the breathing room he needed.

"I studied him as he hobbled toward me, blood dripping from his broken arm, spattering on his boots. He'd changed in the years since I'd last seen him—late twenties now, more muscular, though he moved quick as ever. He'd added more ink to his aegis too; burning silvered roses now threading along the sides of his skull, glowing thorns and blooms scrolling down his cheek. His wounded hand was gloveless, the letters *W I L L* etched in silver below his knuckles. Emerald eyes were edged with kohl, but the whites showed no trace of red; looked like he'd been caught in the open with no sanctus in his veins. And glancing to his waist, I saw no scabbard or sword.

"Disarmed. Literally and figuratively.

"'Sloppy work, youngblood,' I whispered. 'You were taught better than that.'

"The wretched gave chase, deathly silent and deadly swift. Drawing closer, the limping 'saint finally recognized me, kohled eyes going wide. A shout rang out behind me, and glancing over my shoulder, I saw Dior drawing her longblade from her belt. Quick and sure, she flung the sword overhand, silversteel glittering as it arced through the snows.

"'Catch, monsieur!'

"The 'saint snatched the blade from the air with his good hand, turning on his heel with a flourish to face our foes. The wretched came on swift behind him, claws gouging the frozen ground. Tossing sandy hair from his eyes, my new comrade tore open his tunic to reveal the roaring bear of the Dyvok inked in glowing silver across his chest. And back-to-back, swords raised, we stood our ground as the vampires washed over us in a flood.

"I'd been killing these monsters since I was sixteen years old. Born and bloody bred for it. And though the horror of fighting wretched had faded with time, part of me always wondered who the things I slew had been before they died. A big man charging at me with callused hands outstretched—a

mason, perhaps—beheaded with one sharp blow. A rotten lad in minstrels' motley, not enough left in him to make a sound as I hacked his legs out from under him. A young woman with a troth ring on her bloated finger; perhaps a husband somewhere to mourn her, children somewhere to miss her, but no one here to pray as I cut her down, Ashdrinker singing in my head all the while.

"There was an old woman who r–r–ran a fine inn;
"She throttled her guests and made drapes of their skin.
"She flayed off their flesh and she ate it like beef,
"Made soup of their gizzards and broth of their teeth.
"She ground up their bones and she p–pickled their eyes,
"The rest of their leavings, she baked into pies.
"There was an old woman who r–r–ran a fine inn;
"Run quick as the devil if she asks you in.

"The 'saint beside me moved slower, weary and bloodied, but even with a broken arm and no sanctus in him, his strength was crushing. His blows cleaved heads from necks and limbs from torsos; all the unholy might of his bloodline unveiled. And at the end of the slaughter, snows drenched with gore and smoldering bodies, we stood side by side as we'd done in years long past, gasping for breath as we met each other's eyes. Ashdrinker was smoking in my hand, her voice bright and silver in my head.

"*Oh, p–p–prettyone! W–w–w–w–we rememememember you . . .*

"'Bonjour, Lachlan,' I said, raising my broken blade between us.

"He scowled, his voice a soft Ossian brogue. 'Been a long time, Gabriel.'

"'You look good,' I said, eyeing him bonce to bloody boots. 'All things considered.'

"'Course I do.' He lifted his chin, jaw clenched. 'I'm *me*.'

"His eyes sparkled. My lip curled. Lachlan was the first to break, but I followed close behind, both of us bursting into laughter and falling into a hug so fierce it might have killed an ordinary man. Even wounded, one-handed, he picked me up like I was made of feathers, his roar ringing through the deadwood.

"'GABRIEL DE *LEÓN*!'

"'Careful, pup, you'll break my fucking ribs!' I groaned.

"'Damn yer ribs! Bring me those cherry lips, ye beautiful old *bastard*!'

"'I'm thirty-three, you little prick!'

"He kissed my cheeks loudly, one apiece, then planted another square on my mouth. Laughing, I fended him off, and after another breathtaking hug, he put me down with clear reluctance, squeezing my shoulder tight enough to make the bones creak.

"'Good God Almighty be praised. I never thought to see ye again, Master.'

"'Master,' I scoffed. 'You're not an initiate anymore, youngblood.'

"'Old habits die hard, apparently. Just like old heroes.' He dragged tattooed knuckles across his bloody grin, looking me over with shining eyes. 'God's truth, I thought ye dead, Gabe. What in the *Mothermaid's* name are ye doing up here?'

"'Gabe?' came a soft voice behind.

"Dior stood close at my back now, her pale blue eyes drifting from the butchery on the snow around us to her sword, still dripping in Lachlan's fearsome grip. Wiping my hand clean on my greatcoat, I gave the girl's a swift squeeze.

"'Frère Lachlan á Craeg,' I declared, 'this is M. Dior Lachance.'"

High in the black tower of Sul Adair, Jean-François noisily cleared his throat. Gabriel glanced up from his goblet of wine, annoyed at the interruption. The historian was working on one of his artful illustrations—a beautiful piece depicting the silversaint, his sister, and the Grail together. But his eyebrow was raised in question.

"What is it, vampire?" Gabriel sighed.

"I am wondering why you continued Lachance's pretense of being a boy."

The Last Silversaint stared a long moment, then slowly shrugged.

"Because she wanted me to, I suppose. Dressing as a lad was a ruse that had kept Dior out of harm's way for much of her life. Like she'd told me, the gutter doesn't fuck boys the same way it fucks girls. I knew it wasn't a ploy that'd serve forever either—thin as she was, she was growing older, and I could see it was getting harder for her to hide the truth. But as long as she wanted to wear the ruse, I'd ride along with it. After all she'd seen, all she'd been through, I wanted her to feel . . ."—Gabriel shrugged again—". . . safe."

"Mmm," Jean-François murmured, lip quirked. "That's all rather—"

"Indulgent? Soft? Matronly?"

"Moving," Jean-François said, brushing back a long golden curl. "You're rather a gentle touch when you wish to be, de León. It surprises me, is all."

"*Fuck* off, vampire."

The historian smiled as the silversaint returned to his tale.

"'Pleasure to meet you, Frère.' Dior nodded to Lachlan, her voice cool and measured as she met my eyes. 'You two are old comrades, by the sound?'

"'So it might be said,' I replied, scruffing Lachlan's ridiculous hair. 'This young pup has the dubious honor of being the Black Lion of Lorson's first and only apprentice.'

"'And this old dog taught me all his tricks,' Lachlan laughed, knocking my hand away.

"'Not all of them, youngblood.' I raised a warning finger. 'I saved a few in case you ever got too big for your boots.'

"Lachlan flashed Dior a smile that could make a nun reconsider her celibacy. 'Godmorrow, M. Lachance. Any friend of Master Gabriel's . . .' He looked over the blade Dior had thrown him, dark and gore-struck in his hand. 'But a friend worthy to wield silversteel? There's few in the empire can claim that honor, lad.'

"'I'll take it back now, if it please you,' Dior said. 'I earned that blade.'

"I saw a sliver of trepidation in the girl's eyes now, question rising in Lachlan's. In truth, I couldn't fault either of them—the Silver Order *had* tried to murder Dior, after all, and for Lachlan's part, it must've been seven kinds of strange to find a boy carrying a brand-new silversteel sword and wearing gear clearly taken from San Michon.

"'Ye're come from the monastery?' He looked to me, lips twisting. 'I'd have wagered on bloodshed between Gabriel de León and the man who chucked him out of the Ordo Argent. But from the look of ye, Abbot Greyhand gave ye welcome?'

"I was overjoyed at this unexpected meeting, my mind momentarily afire with memory. But Lachlan's question brought me down hard, and one glance at the sevenstar on his greatcoat weighed my rising heart with sorrow. I pictured the cathedral of San Michon then, the bloody massacre I'd committed before that silent altar. In my mind's eye, I could see my fingers closing around Greyhand's throat, my old mentor's blood boiling as I hissed the last words he'd ever hear on this earth.

"*Who the* fuck *told you I was a hero?*

"'Hell with me,' I replied. 'What are you doing out here with a busted arm, no blade, and a pack of wretched chewing at your clumsy arse?'

"'I've a sensational arse. And envy doesn't become ye.'

"'Good thing you remembered to pack your wit when you left your sword behind.'

"With a wince, Lachlan sank to his haunches in the bloody snow, there to gather himself. He'd taken worse beatings in his life, sure and true, but I could see he'd still been dealt a serve. Without thinking, I reached for my pipe and sanctus.

"'I've been in Ossway at Greyhand's command.' Lachlan glanced southwest, his handsome face gone grim. 'Helping refugees over the border, like.'

"'Strange work for a silversaint.'

"'It's bloody business, brother. Whole country's gone to shite in the last few months. Worse than it was back in the day.' He winced, pawing at his bleeding arm as his voice grew dark as pitch. 'The Blackheart has taken Dún Maergenn.'

"'Seven fucking Martyrs.' I glanced to Dior, all awonder. 'We came across some refugees on the road a few months back. They told us the Dyvok had razed Dún Cuinn to the ground. But now they've got the capital too?'

"'Aye. Bastards tore the place six new arseholes, way I hear it.'

"I packed my pipe with a goodly dose, handed it over. My old 'prentice nodded thanks, breathing deep as I cupped the bowl and struck my flintbox.

"'Well, that still doesn't explain what you're doing here without a sword, Lachie.'

"The young 'saint held his breath a long moment. Letting the sacrament wash over and through him, his eyes flooding crimson as he finally exhaled.

"'I got word from the abbot on the winds about six weeks back,' he told me. 'Recalling all silversaints to the monastery. Every brother, no matter their task, was to return to San Michon with all haste. I was following the Mère north when I saw the smoke yesterday.'

"'Smoke?'

"'Aye.' He dragged in another lungful, breathing red. 'From Aveléne.'

"Dior tensed then, stepping forward as my heart skipped two beats.

"'Why was there smoke coming from Aveléne?' she demanded.

"Lachlan shrugged, spitting blood on the frost. 'Because it was afire, lad.'

"'Sweet Mothermaid,' I breathed. 'What the hell's happened?'

"'Never got near enough to see much.' Lachlan finished the pipe, shivering as the sanctus did its work on his wounds. 'Two highbloods hit me out of the dark. Cut my sosya clean in half. Lost my sword and most of my gear.' Here he patted the five wheellocks on his chest. 'I gave them a few new holes to ponder, but there were more wretched than I'd shots to spare. I had to leg it afore I could end them proper. But from what I saw, Aveléne was in the worst way. The keep on the hill had been smashed like glass.'

"My blood ran chill as Dior met my eyes.

"'Aaron,' she whispered. 'Baptiste . . .'

"My stomach was a knot of oily ice, my breath too cold to catch. Trudging up a small rise, I lifted my spyglass southward. The snow was tumbling thick, and I could see no sign of Château Aveléne through the veil of rotten trees. But now that Lachlan had mentioned it, high and faint on the wind, I swore I smelled . . .

"'Smoke.'

"Dior walked to my side and dragged the windswept hair from her face, an unspoken question in her stare. But I met it square, shaking my head.

"'We can't.'

"'But Aaron. And Baptiste . . .'

"'I know.'

"'You were all set to visit them this morning! I'd be *dead* if not for them!'

"'I *know*. But it's too dangerous now.' I clenched my jaw, heart aching. Every word I spoke next weighed a fucking ton. 'It's better to be a bastard than a fool.'

"'Gabe, we can't just leave th—'

"'We can't risk it!' I snapped, lowering my voice to a whisper so that Lachlan might not hear. 'We can't risk *you*. Not after all we've risked aready. This is war, Dior, and Aaron and Baptiste are soldiers. Believe me, they'd understand.'

"She pursed her lips, glancing downriver. 'Well, I'm no soldier. And I *don't*.'

"Boots crunching in the frost, Dior stormed up to Lachlan and snatched back her bloody sword. Stomping over to the sosyas, she slung herself up into Pony's saddle.

"'Where the fuck do you think you're going?' I sighed.

"'Your papa's house,' she spat. 'To rump your mama while he watches.'

"'My mother's dead. As was the man who rumped her on the regular.' I walked across the snow and grabbed Pony's reins. 'And you're not going anywhere, Dior.'

"She pursed her lips, aflame with anger. 'You said this road was mine to choose.'

"'That was before you chose to jam your head up your arse.'

"'Oh, *very* droll. You want to help me or mock me?'

"'Fancied I'd mock you, actually,' I snapped. 'Because not that I'm an expert on vampires—oh, wait, I fucking *am*—but you've not the first clue about the unholy shitstorm you're charging toward. The strength Lachie is describing? To cut a horse in half? To crush castles like chalk? That's the strength of the *Dyvok*, Dior. The Untamed. Strong as demons all, blooded by two decades of all-out butchery in the Ossian campaigns. If they're still at Avelène, they're a war we can't hope to win. And if they've already departed, you've *no* wish to see what's left in their wake.'

"'Gabe speaks truth, lad,' Lachlan said, dragging back his blood-crusted hair. 'Trust me, there's few under heaven who know the cruelty of the Untamed better than I.'

"I glanced to my old pupil as he spoke. I could still remember the day I'd found him; barely more than a bairn, fangs bared in a snarl, fighting for his life on the walls of Báih Sìde.

"God, to think where he'd started.

"What a man he'd become . . .

"Dior spoke beside me then, her voice soft, yet sharp as knives.

"'I know it's dangerous, Gabe. I *know* it takes us from our road. But we can't just ride on without at least learning what happened to Aaron and Baptiste. They *love* you. You love *them*. Your friends are the hill you die on, remember?'

"I looked up into her face, breathing deep.

"'It's not *my* dying that has me afeared, Dior.'

"'I know.' She smiled, eyes shining as she squeezed my hand. 'But we have to stay true to the ones we care about. We have to *try*. Or what the hell is all this for?'

"Glancing southward, I felt torn all the way to my bones. I could've forced Dior to leave—hogtied her to a saddle and dragged her away. But she'd never forgive me that. I could've gone to the château alone, but there was no way in hell I could leave Dior here with Lachlan after my comrades had tried to kill her in San Michon.

"I sighed, heavy with sorrow. The years my old 'prentice and I had spent apart were but moments now, the years we'd fought side by side so near I could touch them. We'd not always seen eye to eye, Lachie and I, but God, meeting him again . . . I realized how much I'd missed him. He crouched in the frost, silver roses scrolling down his cheek, hard green eyes locked on mine. I'd taught him all I knew; my pupil, my friend, my brother through oceans of blood, and if we were headed south, I could surely use his blade at my side. But in the end, he was the loyal son of the Ordo Argent I'd raised him to be. And that made him a threat now.

"To Dior *and* me.

"'You need a horse for the ride back north?' I asked.

"'Ye mean to go on?' Lachlan raised one brow. 'I know ye were close to them, brother, but the Silver Order named Aaron de Coste and Baptiste Sa-Ismael traitors.'

"'They named *me* a traitor too, Lachie.'

"'Maybe. But I *know* ye, Gabe.'

"'Do you? Really?'

"*Who the* fuck *told you I was a hero?*

"I shook my head, helping my old friend to his feet. 'It seems a cruel fate, to be reunited after so many years, and parted so swift. But . . . I fear this is adieu.'

"'Yer out of yer skull.' Lachlan rolled his shoulder, wincing in pain. 'There's only one reason the Untamed would've struck a fortress like Aveléne, and we both know it. But if yer set to start a scrap with the Blackheart's brood, there's no way I'll let ye do it alone.'

"'I thought the abbot had recalled you to San Michon?'

"'All respect to Greyhand. I love the grumpy old bugger. But he can wait a sunset or two.' Lachlan clenched his now-healed hand, squeezed my arm fondly. 'I've not seen ye in ten years, brother. This'll be just as it was in yesterdays. The Black Lion of Lorson could ever count upon the blade of Lachlan á Craeg. Although . . .' He looked toward Dior, gifting her a cheeky smile. 'I might have to borrow one.'

"Dior stared at the young 'saint, uncertain and mute. After all that had happened at the monastery, keeping company with a member of the Silver Order posed untold danger. Moreover, though she was still nowhere to be seen, Celene was sure to make an appearance sooner or later, and God only knew what my old 'prentice would make of *that*.

"But to pass up Lachlan's help when we walked so surely into peril . . .

"'Why are you wearing all those pistols?' Dior asked, glancing to the brace of wheellocks across his chest. 'Are you that shite a shot?'

"Lachlan chuckled, refusing to rise to her bait. 'It's like my old master used to say. Even the best marksman has the occasional bad day.'

"I smiled, nodding to the girl. 'Lachie's a safe pair of hands, Dior.'

"The girl sighed then, tossing her silversteel. 'Just give it back when you're done.'

"Lachlan caught the sword with a flourish, tipped an imaginary hat. 'I'll return it in one piece, lad, I vow it. Assuming *any* of us are in one piece by journey's end.'

"I climbed onto Bear's back, turned my pony south toward Aveléne. If what I suspected was true, this was now the fool's errand Celene had promised. But as I'd always said—as Dior had reminded me—my friends were the hill I died on. And though this took us from our path, to abandon them without even looking . . .

"I glanced at Dior from the corner of my eye. The girl was right. And the girl was wrong. And I knew not what else to do, save trust the only faith I had left.

"'I swear, sometimes you are enough to give my arsehole a headache,' I muttered.

"She pulled her tricorn down against the wind, smirking. 'That's a good one.'

"'Been working on it since I met you.'

"'Well, they say the brain *does* slow down as a man gets older.'

"'Could you try a little harder to be a bitch about this?'

"'Oui.' She shrugged. 'Right now, I'm not trying at all. This is just raw talent.'

"I hung my head, rubbing my stubble to hide my smile. Behind us, Lachlan had climbed aboard Nugget, kohl-rimmed eyes narrowed on the deadwood ahead. God only knew how bloody the road before us would be, but in truth, my heart *was* lighter to have friends on it with me. For a moment, it almost seemed like old times.

"What a fool I was, to forget how dark those nights had actually been."

VI

RUINATION

"I SMELLED THE truth long before we saw it.

"The first hints were gentle, like snowflakes on a chill breeze. Wood ash and charcoal; a cold hearth on a wintersdeep morn. But as Dior, Lachlan, and I rode down the Mère, I began to catch other notes on the wind. The sharp tang of scorched metal, scratching at the back of my throat. Charred hair, entwined in the rancid tang of burned shit and leather. And beneath it all, like a knife between my ribs, came a sickening perfume, boiled black and crusted upon still-cooling stone. My whole body *thrilled* with it, the monster in me both repelled and inflamed, teeth grown razor-sharp against my tongue.

"*Great Redeemer . . .*

"I'd sworn to my Astrid the day I buried her that I'd never drink from another, and it had been more than a year since that Worst Day. But my vow had been broken for me by my sister now, and as my thirst *seethed* at that awful scent on the breeze, I could only take a long swig of liquor to drown it, teeth gritted so hard they creaked.

"*It's never felt like this before . . .*

"'What's that smell?' Dior whispered.

"'Blood,' I replied, swallowing hard.

"Lachlan nodded, glancing at me. 'Blood and fire.'

"I pushed thoughts of my thirst aside, set my mind to the danger we courted coming here. The monsters that had hit Aveléne might be long gone, they might be but a heartbeat distant, and I knew it would've taken an army of the Dead to crush a fort so well-defended. Every step closer had me deeper afeared—not for myself, but for the fate of Aaron and Baptiste, the people they safeguarded, but most, for this girl beside me. Dior Lachance was many things: lady of liars, queen of thieves, would-be savior of the empire. But watching her from the corner of my eye, running my thumb over the name of my daughter inked across my fingers, I was beginning to realize how much this girl truly meant.

"Not to this empire. But to *me*.

"'Where the *hell* is Celene?' I whispered.

"I'd not seen my sister since before we found Lachlan. Though she could disappear for hours at a stretch, she'd surely return soon, and I was still pondering how to explain her presence in a fashion my old 'prentice might understand. Lachie had more reason to hate coldbloods than most, but I dare not mention the Grail to him after all that had happened at the monastery. Ashdrinker was a comforting weight in my hand at least, the beautiful dame on the hilt ever smiling, her voice a stuttering silver song in my head.

"I c-c-can't remember, Gabriel . . .

"'Remember what?' I murmured, eyes on the snow-clad tree line.

"The night the p-prettyone led ye to the B-Butcher. C-C-C-Crimson Glade. There was a woman, was a woman, wasawoman. A . . . q-q-queen?

"'No queens in Ossway,' I replied. 'She was a duchess. Niamh Nineswords.'

"Ahhhh, Niiiineswords. Hair of g-g-gold, voice of thunder, m-m-mother of many?

"'That's her.' I sighed, glancing southwest. 'I hope she and her daughters escaped Dún Maergenn before the Blackheart crushed it.'

"'Ashdrinker still talks to ye, eh?'

"I glanced to Lachlan, scratching his stubble as he stared at the blade in my hand. 'She sings a lot these nights. But oui.'

"'She still call me Pretty One?'

"I scoffed. 'She never called you Pretty One.'

"Redhand elderson p-p-p-prettyone . . .

"'Good to see ye again, Mlle Ash,' Lachlan called, doffing a tricorn that wasn't there.

"P-p-p-prettyone . . .

"'Aright, that's enough,' I grumbled. 'Mind on the job now, eh, Ash?'

"There once was a locksmith named Jobb;

"Who had an astonishing kn—

"'What happened to her?' Lachlan gestured to Ash's jagged edge. 'Her tip's broke.'

"I met my old 'prentice's eyes. Mind swimming with visions of a lighthouse by the sea. I fancied I heard little feet then, crunching in the snows behind us as bright laughter rippled on the wind. Warm arms about my waist. Warmer lips pressed soft to my cheek.

"'Mind on the job now, eh, Lachie?'

"'Seven Martyrs . . .'

"It was Dior who whispered, sitting up straighter and raising one shaking hand. She'd said barely a word on our trek south, sensibly subdued by Lachlan's presence. But I looked to where she pointed now, and saw as she did—a gust of wind parting the snows ahead and revealing our goal, rising like a shadow before us.

"'Château Aveléne,' I murmured.

"Even distant, it dominated the Mère's gloomy shoreline; a solid mont of Nordlund basalt, black as my bride's hair. Its base was encircled by thick walls, and a spiraling road wound up its slopes, dotted with hundreds of little houses. Crowning the peak was a castle of that same dark stone, keeping stoic watch over the valley below. A light in a sea of darkness, tended by men I loved more dear than any on earth.

"At least, so it had been a few weeks ago.

"And now . . .

"'It's ruined,' Dior whispered.

"The watch fires on the walls were extinguished, the battlements all unmanned. Smoke rose from the houses; broken black fingers winding up into iron skies. Through the snow, I could see the hilltop keep had been shattered just as Lachlan had said, its walls sundered, towers toppled like trees.

"I wondered if anyone had been alive to hear them fall.

"'Aaron . . .' I whispered.

"But the more I studied this picture, the less of it made sense. Aaron and Baptiste were apprenticed at San Michon, and their home had been designed to stand against the Dead. Yet though the keep was destroyed, the battlements around the mont were hale and whole—as if there'd been no siege here at all.

"I could still hear the crowd gathered on those ramparts the day I set out to save Dior, their eyes alight with hope: 'The Lion rides! THE BLACK LION RIDES!' But now the only sound was a soul-sick wind, and the croaks of glutted crows.

"'Hello?' Dior cried, sitting up in her saddle. 'HELL—'

"'*Will* you kindly shut your flapping trap, Lachance,' I hissed, grabbing her arm.

"'If anyone is alive—'

"'If anyone is alive down there, Lachie and I will go find them. Ideally without alerting every coldblood from Vellene to Asheve our cocks are on the block.'

"'I'm coming too,' Dior declared.

"'It's not safe. We've no idea what's still in there.'

"'You're telling me waiting here alone with my arse in the wind is safer than sticking like a fly on shite to the most famous vampire slayer who ever lived?'

"I glanced to Lachlan, the young 'saint's lips twisting in a wry smile. 'Seems yer new apprentice is as sharp as yer old one, brother.'

"'Oui,' I admitted. 'Good point, well made.'

"Dior tipped her tricorn. 'Merci, messieurs.'

"The girl lifted a black cigarelle to her mouth and lit it. I leaned over and flicked it right off her lips, sparks spraying into the biting wind.

"'Oi! The fuck was *that* for?'

"'Comparing me to shit, you little shit.'

"'. . . Good point, well made.'

"Lachlan drew one of the five wheellocks from the bandolier across his chest, sharp green eyes scanning the snows ahead. Looking downriver to the remains of Aveléne, I was torn which way to tread. We were upwind at least, so the Dead wouldn't smell us coming. Rushing in blind here was madness, but it was a couple of hours to nightfall, and if we *were* heading into trouble, we should do it with dim daylight on our side.

"'Why burn the houses?' Dior murmured. 'I thought vampires hated fire.'

"'They loathe it,' I replied, loading my pipe.

"'Coldbloods can't enter a home uninvited, lad,' Lachlan told her. 'So when they take a city, they have their thrallswords set fire to the roofs. Gives the people inside a choice, aye? Leave shelter and risk slaughter. Or stay inside and burn.'

"Dior blinked. 'Thrallswords?'

"'It's what we called them in the Order,' I replied. 'Mortal soldiers of the kith. Grim as it might sound, there are some folk who fight *for* the Dead rather than against them.'

"Dior looked aghast. 'Godssakes, why?'

"'Some join willingly. Out of lust for power, or darkness of heart. Others are just fools who think they'll live forever if given the bite. But most are simple captives, offered the choice between becoming a slave or a meal.'

"She shook her head, bewildered. 'I'd *die* before I served these bastards.'

"'Most would say the same.' I sighed. 'But truth is, nobody really knows what they're made of 'til they get offered that choice. Get on your knees and swallow, or get in the cage and be fucked with the rest of them. It took a while, but the coldbloods have got *very* good at what they do. Fear is their blade. Despair their cloak. And there's no shortage of folk who'd feed their kin to the wolves if it'd spare themselves the teeth.'

"Dior gritted her teeth, hissing frost. 'I'd rather *die*.'

"'But that's the thing of it, lad.' Lachlan met Dior's eyes, a shadow darkening that emerald green. 'The bastards don't kill ye. They keep ye *alive*.'

"Dior made the sign of the wheel, lips pinched thin as she looked back to the ruins of Aveléne. Meeting Lachlan's stare, I breathed a red sigh, binding my collar up over my face and tossing him a couple of spare silverbombs.

"'Aright, we head down together. Dior, don't leave my sight, and be ready to bolt if I tell you. You see anything moving, shout. Or scream. Whichever takes your fancy.'

"'Depends how big it is, I s'pose.'

"Lachlan chuckled, and with him beside me, Dior behind, we rode on, Aveléne looming larger with every step. Our sosyas' hooves crunched in the frost, my hand on my blade and my heart in my throat as we approached what was left of the sanctuary my friends had built. The snow was a grey veil, a bitter gale snapping right in our faces, and my blood ran chill as I finally spied movement through the flurries ahead.

"'Hold,' I whispered, raising my hand.

"'Mother and bloody Maid,' Lachlan breathed. 'I *knew* it.'

"Dior shook her head, squinting. 'What *is* that?'

"I raised my spyglass, belly sinking as all my awful fears were realized.

"'Meatwagon,' I sighed.

"It was sat on the ice near the château pier, drawn by a team of four skittish horses. A heavy wooden wagon, iron bars rising up from its tray to form a large, rusted cage. Within was pressed a multitude of figures, and my heart twisted as I realized all of them were children, grubby and bloodied, jammed together like dry rations. Dim beneath the howling wind, I could hear weeping, cursing, barked commands. More figures were at work around the wagon, forcing little ones inside at swordpoint—a dozen soldiers in dark armor, hulking thugs all. But beyond, shuffling about the ice or staring hungry at the terrified captives, were at least two dozen wretched, dead-eyed and soulless.

"I drew breath to warn Dior to back off slow, but true to form, the Almighty took the chance to slip his cock into my earhole. At that moment, the wind shifted, west to northerly, howling now at our backs. I saw one of the wretched tense—a rotten old man in rags, head swiveling immediately toward Dior. More of the Dead turned to us, lips peeling back from jagged teeth, low hisses rolling down their line.

"'Shite,' Lachlan hissed.

"It was just as Celene had said; the ghostbreath apparently did nothing to hide the girl's scent. As a shout rang among the soldiers, I rolled the dice in my head. We could flee if we chose, barrel back up the ice on horseback, faster than they could chase. But if an army had struck Aveléne, this *seemed* to be its leavings—a few thrallswords and wretched left behind to clear out the dregs of a city already lost. I wanted to know what had befallen Aaron and Baptiste. But more, *most,* the sight of those poor children in that cage was giving birth to fury. Dark memories of darker days; days of blood and glory, of holy war and grim atrocity and mournful pipes singing over a crimson glade.

"A thrall let loose a long peal on a raised horn, the note hanging on the frozen air as I glanced to Lachlan beside me.

"'Fancy a dance, brother?'

"My old 'prentice smiled, hand to his hilt. 'Yer back. My blade.'

"The horn's echo was ringing down the riverbanks now, and I heard footsteps crunching on the frost in answer. And looking through the veil of mist and snow, I saw them; three highbloods emerging from the château gates side by side, my skin running chill at the sight.

"'Seven fucking Martyrs . . .'

"The first was a lad, seventeen or so when he was killed. Ossway-born, his skin was marble, long rust-brown hair framing flat, flint eyes. He was big and brutish, dressed in furs, tattered cloak, heavy boots, a hauberk of dark mail. A bloody handprint was smeared on his face, and the greatsword he carried was bigger than I was.

"The second coldblood was a mountain of bearded muscle, six and a half feet tall, near as wide. Despite the cold, he wore naught but a kilt and heavy boots, hands big as feasting-plates clutching a warhammer that could crush a castle wall to rubble. His head was shaved and strangely bereft of ears—only two nubs of flesh remaining on either side of his skull.

"From the fresh holes in their armor, the hateful stares they threw his way, I guessed these two were the pair who'd slain Lachlan's horse. But fearsome as they were, I spared each only a glance, my eyes drawn instead to the monster walking between them.

"She was *tall*. Broad. A daughter of Ossian warriors. Her skin was pale as frost, eyes green as the grass of days long dead. Her long copper-brown hair was bound in slayer's braids, and she wore leathers and furs, decorated with jewelry of human bone.

"A massive warmaul was held in both fists, solid iron, its head the size of a child's coffin, wrought like a roaring bear. Her belt was hung with a half-dozen iron manacles, clinking as she strode toward us. Her kilt might once have been woven with colors of her birthclan, but was now black, stitched with bears and broken shields: the sigil of the Blood Dyvok. She trudged from the ruined château with heavy tread, flanked by the bruteboy and the earless mountain, and at the sight of her, my fury gave way to a cold and perfect rage.

"'I thought we killed you, bitch,' I whispered.

"'. . . You *know* them?' Dior asked.

"'Never met those two.' I nodded to the pair at her sides. 'But the woman is Kiara Dyvok. The Wolfmother. She ran stock raids for the farms at Triúr-baile.'

"Dior blinked in question as I unbuttoned my greatcoat.

"'Slaughterfarms,' Lachlan explained, stripping himself shirtless. 'The Untamed built them when they launched their first invasion of Ossway, fifteen years back. They kept their captives there. Men. Women. Children.'

"'Why woul—'

"'For *food*, Dior.' I saw her eyes widen as she took my meaning. 'People kept like cattle to sate the thirsts of the Dyvok armies. The Silver Order liberated Triúrbaile when I was nineteen years old. The leeches were feeding the bodies of the dead to their captives to keep them alive. Hundreds of cages. Thousands of people. I can still smell the fucking stench when I close my eyes.'

"I glowered downriver at Kiara, fangs growing long in my gums.

"'And that hellbitch helped fill them.'

"Dior looked sickened to her stomach, swallowing hard. Again, I glanced around for Celene, but I could see no sign through the windswept snows. Slipping down off Bear, I stowed my gear, tightening my bandolier about my bare chest as I glanced to the girl.

"'Back off. Three or four hundred feet downriver. Things go bad, keep running.'

"'Gabe, I don't need you t—'

"'I *know* you've a mind to prove yourself. But Kiara Dyvok is a monster with a century of slaughter under her belt. You don't even have a sword. Pick your battles, Dior.'

"I turned Pony about over the girl's protest, smacked the sosya's rump. Pony bolted, Dior yelping and hanging on for dear life as Lachlan and I turned toward the enemy. The dozen thrallswords had formed up alongside Kiara, but after sensing Dior, the wretched had just come charging upriver toward us. The wind was freezing on my naked skin, yet my aegis burned brighter as the Dead drew closer. That long-forgotten warmth brought a surprising comfort, blood-red light smoldering through the lion on my chest, my daughter's name on my hands, mingling with the silver flame of Lachlan's dauntless faith.

"At the sight of that glow, Kiara held up her hand, roared at the charging wretched to halt. Yet only about half the monsters obeyed, the rest not breaking stride as they dashed toward us. I raised Ashdrinker in grim salute, my aegis now burning with bloody heat as Lachlan started firing, shot after shot from his brace of trusty wheellocks. And as the Dead plowed into us, eyes narrowed against our blinding glow, my blade and I danced like in days of glory. Limbs were hacked from rotten torsos and heads tumbled from gushing necks as Ash hummed an old song in my head, the tune bittersweet—a nursery rhyme I'd sing to Patience back when she was a little girl, woken by terrors in the dark.

"Sleep now, my lovely, s-sleep now, my dear,
"Dark dreams will fade now your papa is near.
"Fear not the m-monsters, fear not the night,
"Papa is here now and all shall be right.
"Close your eyes, darling, and know this b-be true,
"Morning will come, and your papa loves you.

"At the end of the slaughter, corpses were scattered across the ice at our feet, smoldering and sundered. Lachlan was spattered head to foot in red, Dior's sword dripping in his fist, bodies cleaved like meat on the butcher's block all around him. Ashdrinker was smoking in my grip, her blade dusted grey, dipped red. The light of forgefire blazed on my skin, bloody eyes now falling on the Wolfmother.

"*We know her know h-her.*

"'That we do.'

"*We hate her* hate *h-her.*

"'That we do.'

"Kiara stood fifty feet downriver in the château's shadow, the bones she wore clinking in the wind. A dozen wretched were held poised before her, trembling with animal desire for the kill, the two highbloods beside her glowering at the lion burning upon my chest. A child in the wagon cried out to me as a thrallsword slammed the cage door, the horses whinnying in fear of the Dead around them. Lachlan reloaded his pistols. But I stared only at Kiara, mind filled with images of the day we liberated Triúrbaile.

"Dead bodies hung and butchered, the remains of the lucky used to keep the less-so alive. Stick-thin fingers reaching toward me through rusting bars. Charnel pits full of bones.

"'The Black Lion,' she snarled. 'And his traitor cub.'

"The Wolfmother's voice was a thick west-Ossian growl, the wretched hissing in reply. The brute beside her slid that terrible greatsword off his shoulder, the earless one hefted his warhammer, but I paid them little mind, just staring as Kiara reached to a small golden vial about her throat and took a long swallow.

"I tipped my tricorn. 'Been a while since Crimson Glade. How do, Kiara?'

"Baring red teeth, she raised her double-handed maul in marble fists.

"'I heard ye were dead, de León.'

"'Heaven was full. And the devil was afraid to open the door.'

"'Then the devil is a coward.'

"'Speaking of.' I looked her over, eyes narrowed. 'Rumor had it you got ended the night I took Tolyev's head. Looks like you saved your own skin instead.'

"The Wolfmother glowered as Lachlan fixed his eyes on the brutes beside her.

"'What are yer names, coldbloods?' he called.

"'Kane Dyvok.' The younger vampire lifted a golden vial around his neck, similar to the one Kiara wore, taking a swig. 'Though most folk call me the Headsmun.'

"'Well, ye murdered my Cinder, Headsmun. I've had that horse since I was a bairn. So I think I'll just call ye Cunt.' Lachlan flicked a sluice of dark blood off his blade, glancing to the largest of the trio. 'What about ye, big boy? What name do they call ye by?'

"The bearded one quaffed from his own vial, snarled with blood-red fangs.

"'Rykard Dyvok.'

"'Nae, that won't do a'tall . . .' Lachie pursed his lips, thoughtful. 'What about Dick fer short? Childish, I know, but ye've the look, what with the bald head and nae ears, like.'

"Lachlan looked back and forth between the vampires, smiling.

"'Dick and Cunt. Nice symmetry, aye?'

"Rykard and Kane glowered as I raised Ashdrinker, my eyes still locked on Kiara.

"'We have bones to pick, you and I.'

"'Aye,' Kiara replied, hefting her maul. 'That we do.'

"'You've *ten thousand* deaths to answer for, bitch.'

"'And ye've only *one*, bastard. But we'll repay the both of ye fer it now, I vow it.'

"Kiara looked to the wretched and thrallswords about her, weighing the odds against the hate in her heart. The sun was yet up, and as I'd guessed, whatever force had struck Aveléne, this seemed to be the dregs of it. But still, she had the numbers. And lips peeling back from her fangs, the Wolfmother spat as if she'd a mouthful of venom.

"'*Kill!*'

"Her wretched surged into motion, like wild dogs off their chains, Kiara running behind the mob with her cousins and thrallswords beside her. Lachlan hurled his silverbombs to break up the pack, but as the explosions cracked and boomed, the drays chained to the meatwagon startled, bucking and stomping. Beasts of earth and sky *loathe* the Dead, coldblood, and the animals were already terrified. As Lachie's bombs burst, as the echoes rang, the poor drays reared up in a panic and broke into a run, dragging the wagon of screaming children behind them out onto the ice.

"Kane was swinging left to outflank us, and thinking him the smallest of the trio, Lachie and I both dashed to meet him, fixing to end him quick. But fearless, fearsome, the vampire swung that massive two-hander in a whistling arc, his body sailing forward with it, driving him right toward us in the first few spinning, thundering steps of a Dyvok Tempest."

Jean-François lifted a brow in question. "Tempest, de León?"

The silversaint nodded. "The Untamed wield weapons far larger than mortals can carry—for intimidation, as well as effect. That sword of Kane's weighed a good three hundred pounds at least. God only knows about Kiara's maul or Rykard's warhammer. Thing is, even if you're strong enough to swing a weapon that weighs as much as you, its *weight* is still going to drag you with it when you swing it. That's just the way mass and force work. So, the best Dyvok warriors fight in an ancient coldblood style called the Anyja. The Tempest. They use the weight of their weapons to fling themselves around as they strike. Moving with the momentum, spinning and shifting direction, cutting anything in their path to bloody pieces. It makes the Dyvok near-unstoppable on the battlefield. And absolutely fucking terrifying.

"Kane scythed toward us, boots skidding on the ice as his blade tore the air. But frightening as it was, Lachlan and I had spent long years fighting his kin in the Ossway, and while the Untamed are strong as devils, their flesh is butter compared to an Ironheart's. Dropping to our knees, we let momentum keep us skidding along the ice beneath Kane's blow, the pair of us rising up now beneath it. Lachlan's blade sheared through the vampire's belly, long spools of desiccated guts spraying through the air, and as the angels on my arms carved blurs of light on the gloom, Ash sheared his arm off above the elbow.

"'KANE!' Kiara bellowed. 'WARE YE!'

"Bruteboy roared, slung off-balance by his blade now, and I turned about to end him. But the wretched plowed into us then, blinded and thrashing, all in a tumbling mob. I felt one crash onto my back, teeth ripping my skin as we fell. I bellowed, punching the monster in the mouth, twisting to my feet as Lachlan hewed another pair into quarters. Big Rykard was flying toward me now, Kiara beside him, swinging that terrible maul of hers like it weighed a feather. Her steel moved so swift the air fairly *boomed* behind it, and I was forced into a desperate parry—*never* a good idea when the weapon being swung at you weighs more than a man. Even turned aside, the force of her blow sent me sailing down the river and smashing onto my back, black stars bursting in my eyes. I heard someone scream, thumping footsteps, and panicked horses, spitting blood as Ash sang in my head.

"*G-G-Gabriel, are ye well?*

"'Didn't n-need those r-ribs anyw—'

"A wretched loomed over me, lunging with a voiceless hiss. I managed to roll aside, taking off its legs with a swipe from Ashdrinker's blade. But Rykard was thundering toward me again, flanked by Kiara, her eyes alight with hatred. And looking past the Wolfmother through the driving snows, I felt my heart drop like a stone in my chest."

"Allow me to guess," Jean-François murmured. "Lachance had returned?"

"Like a case of the scratch," Gabriel nodded. "That bleeding heart of hers had started gushing at the sight of those little ones in that wagon, and she was chasing them out onto the ice now, compassion bidding adieu to common sense. She couldn't ride worth a damn either, almost spilling from her saddle, crying out as she made a desperate leap into the driver's chair. But she managed to snatch up the reins, dragging the panicked beasts to a slow and slipping halt in the middle of the river. Dior was out of the chair in a blinking, crawling over the cage's roof to its door. But with a curse, she found it locked, the wailing captives sealed inside.

"Kane had scooped up his fallen greatsword, he and Lachlan now carving their way across the ice in a brutal, spectacular brawl. My old 'prentice was born of the Dyvok line, and of deeper pedigree than most. But he was still only a paleblood, and Kane's strength was *terrifying*—even one-handed, the Headsmun was somehow giving as good as he was getting. Kiara was stalking toward me, maul dripping with my blood, Rykard beside her. But with sinking heart, I saw her thrallswords had now turned on Dior. And stubborn fool that she was, the girl turned to face them, drawing her silversteel dagger in one pale fist.

"'No, Dior, go!' I roared.

"She glanced at me, back over her shoulder to the helpless children in that cage. Outmatched as she was, I could see she was determined to defend them. The thrallswords were closing, the Wolfmother and Rykard between me and her rescue.

"'Damn you, girl, *run!*'

"I cut down another wretched, reeling back as Kiara's maul ripped the air. Half-blinded by my aegis, the Wolfmother's next blow sailed wide, the weight of her weapon sending her skidding past me. Rykard bellowed as he swung his massive warhammer, the river beneath us crackling as I slipped aside the blow. Kicking the bastard's knee with my silvered heels, I struck at Kiara's back, a smoking gash carved through her flesh as she roared and dropped her maul onto the ice. I could boil their veins dry if I managed to get my hands about their necks, but though the sun was in the sky, the pair were undaunted, and one solid strike from their fists would smash my bones like glass.

"Behind my foes, Dior raised her knife, lashing out at the thrallswords with a ragged cry. Her strike missed by a mile, but the soldiers backed off, circling and wary. Kiara lunged at me bare-handed, my belly rolling as she seized a fistful of my hair and ripped it out at the root. Snarling, I reached for her throat, catching only that golden vial about her neck. The chain snapped, vial sent flying as a blow from Rykard's warhammer hit me like a runaway carriage. I felt my ribs splinter, blood and spit exploding from my lips as I flew, weightless, senseless, tumbling through the air as all the world ran to grey. I must have landed another fifty feet upriver, too stunned to even feel the impact as I crashed onto the ice.

"Rolling onto my belly, I coughed red and struggled to rise, to *breathe*. I could hear Dior shouting over the ringing in my ears, groping about on the ice for my sword.

"'I'm s-starting to suspect the Almighty m-might be *genuinely* annoyed with me . . .'

"*Ye committed m-m-mass murder on sanctified ground n-not two weeks ago.*

"'They were b-bastards, Ash.'

"*So are ye, Gabriel.*

"'. . . Touché.'

"Kiara and Rykard were charging toward me, Lachlan still brawling with Kane—I had to get up, had to *move*, blood in my eyes, head tolling like funeral bells as my fingers closed around Ash's hilt. Spitting red, I leaned on her and tried to rise, failing, slipping back to one knee, too hurt to even meet my death on my own two fucking feet.

"But I heard footfalls on the frozen river then; soft boots on new snow. Kiara and Rykard slowed their charge, boots skidding on the frost, eyes narrowed to papercuts. Drooling blood, I looked up to find a slender figure standing now beside me, clad all in red. The light spilling off my skin glinted on the porcelain of her mask, threw a long shadow onto the ice between us and the Untamed. Dropping into a low, courtly bow, Celene hissed.

"'Greetingsss, Dyvok.'

"And with those words, she dragged her mask aside.

"I'd seen it before, but my stomach still turned as the horror of my sister's face was laid bare. From the cheekbones up, Celene was a comely maid, fine-boned and beautiful, so akin to our mama it made my heart ache to see. But the skin on the bottom half of her face had been ripped away; ropes of muscle and pale bone exposed, fangs gleaming in her lower jaw, the once-temple of her flesh now a ragged, broken ruin.

"Rykard stared at my sister in the falling snow, fangs bared.

"'Who are ye, cousin?'

"'No cousin of yoursss,' she replied.

"My sister crossed one hand over another, dragging sharp fingernails along her palms. Blood flowed like twin serpents, one sluice forming itself into a curved sword, the other a whip-long flail as the scent . . . God, it struck me like a spear to my aching belly.

"'I am Celene Castia. Sssword of the Faithful. Liathe of dread Wulfric.'

"Dead eyes gleaming, Celene raised her blade toward the Untamed.

"'And I am deliverance. For you and all our accurssed kind.'"

VII
BY THIS BLOOD

"RUBY SPOOLS HUNG from my lips, broken ribs grinding beneath my skin. Celene swept her greatcoat aside with a flourish, brushing a fleck of snow from the brocade as she stared down her foes. Kiara and Rykard shared a silent glance, uncertain; the pair knew not where Celene stood, save now she was between hunter and prey.

"'I've bloodclaim on that one, cousin,' Kiara snarled. 'Stand ye aside.'

"But Celene shook her head, replied simply.

"'No.'

"The Wolfmother narrowed her eyes, looking again to the vampire beside her, the meatwagon still out on the ice. I saw Dior standing pale and alone, dagger in hand—Celene had murdered every one of the Dyvok thrallswords around her, the ice washed crimson. Kiara's eyes drifted back to the bloody blade in my sister's hand, fangs bared as she spat.

"'Then *die*.'

"And with a roar, she and Rykard launched themselves across the ice.

"My baby sister moved like winter wind, brutal and chill, cutting to the bone. She stepped aside Kiara's booming strike, a blur of red, larger cracks spilling out beneath us all as that maul struck the river's frozen crust. Swift, silent, Celene lashed out with her blade, striking the ironwood haft of Rykard's hammer and slicing it clean in half. Thrown off-balance, the big coldblood was gifted a spine-deep strike as he stumbled past, marble flesh parting like smoke. Quick as silver, Celene seized hold of the Wolfmother's wrist. And just as mine had in the shadow of San Michon, Kiara's blood began to boil.

"My skin tingled at the sight of it unleashed, the scent thick upon the wind; the same dreadful power my unholy father had given me.

"*Sanguimancy.*

"The blood bubbled into Kiara's eyes first, whites flooding crimson. The Wolfmother roared as her marble skin blackened, spreading outward from my sister's grip like cracks in a dry riverbed. But Kiara was no whelp to be so easily mastered, and bloody fangs gritted, she struck Celene backhanded, sending her flying like a bag of chaff.

"I rose in the chaos, hand pressed to broken ribs. Head still ringing, I charged the Wolfmother, Ashdrinker singing silver in my mind. Kiara turned, hissing hatred, stepping aside my strikes; belly, chest, throat. We were both of us wounded now, desperate, Lachie still brawling with Kane, Dior stepping forward with dagger raised as I roared.

"'No, stay back!'

"I twisted away as Kiara's maul whistled past my chin—God, the strength in her was enough to level a bloody mountain. If it were nighttime, I'm certain she'd have leveled me too. But dim daylight still held rule of the sky, and my aegis burned bright, and wounded as I was, fighting to defend that girl before the walls of Aveléne, my mind rang again with the truth its lord had spoken to me, not so long ago.

"*It matters not what you hold faith in. But you must hold faith in* something.

"Kiara's maul crashed against my blade, the force sending me skidding back across the ice and then again to my knees. I rose, gasping, but as the Wolfmother spat blood and readied to charge, we all of us were shivered by a dreadful cry behind us.

"I turned to see Rykard on his knees before Celene. My sister's foe was bloodied, one arm a smoking stump at the elbow, the other cleaved off at the wrist. Her strength was *terrifying*—the fact a fledgling Voss stood so tall against a veteran warrior of the Dyvok made no sense at all. But Celene seized Rykard's shoulders, the exposed muscle flexing obscenely along her jaw as she opened her mouth wide, wider. And I watched in horror as my sister sank her teeth into her enemy's throat."

Gabriel shook his head, running one finger gentle across his lips.

"They call it the Kiss. The rapture a vampire's victim feels as those fangs pierce skin, as that blood rushes hot and thick. No drug can hold a candle to it. No sin of the flesh can compare. Once tasted, some folk will do *anything* to experience it again; sacrifice their freedom, their very lives just to shiver through that bloody bliss one more time. And I saw it take Rykard too; his lashes fluttering, a shuddering lover's moan slipping his lips as Celene drank deeper. But then horror broke through the heaven of it, the big coldblood's eyes widening, flooding with fear as they met mine, as we both realized the awful truth.

"Celene wasn't stopping.

"Rykard gasped, struggling, but Celene dug into the vampire's throat like some starving tick, drinking, *swallowing*. The big coldblood bucked once, feeble, as what was left inside him clawed the bounds of its immortal shell. And with one final, earsplitting scream, his body trembled toe to crown, and burst to dust in my sister's cold arms.

"Celene stood, dragging knuckles across her bloody mouth. And though it might have been a trick of the dying light or the hurts I'd suffered, I *swear* the wound at her face had lessened some. Muscle thickening on bone. Translucent skin stitching onto dead flesh. The shade of her irises had deepened; from the ghost-white of death, to a faintest hint of the brown they'd been in life. They rolled back in her head, lashes fluttering, euphoric.

"'By thisss blood,' she breathed, 'shall we have life eternal.'

"I'd hunted vampires half my life, Historian, but I'd no fucking clue what I'd just seen. And more to the point, apparently nor had the Wolfmother. Kiara was mediae, a vampire with a century or more under her belt; not as wily as an ancien with hundreds of years to her name, but no fledgling either. And despite the murder of her kinsman, her vendetta against me, I saw the Wolfmother was at a loss now. Kane was still brawling with Lachlan out on the river's heart—he'd be no help to her at all. Fury burned in Kiara's eyes as she glanced to the captives, to Celene, boiling over into hatred as her gaze fell back on me. But you don't live forever by being a fool, and I could see her jaw clenching as the tally in her head now came up wanting.

"'Another night, Lion,' she spat.

"The Wolfmother lifted her maul high over her head. All the world seemed to spin in slow motion, my heart falling still as that hammer fell.

"I turned and roared warning to Dior.

"Kiara slammed her maul into the ice.

"And the surface of the Mère exploded."

VIII

TALON AND TOOTH

"THE FROZEN RIVER split asunder, foot-thick ice shattering as if it were glass. Jagged cracks arced toward us like lightning, powdered snow blasted high into the howling air. And with a deafening *boom*, the Mère collapsed beneath us.

"I heard Celene shout warning as I rolled to my feet, diving across the crumbling ice. Roaring at Lachlan to run, my sister to follow, *FOLLOW!* I sprinted, the ground pitching and rolling as we scrambled, stumbled, leaping again as the collapse spread.

"*Run rabbit run-r-r-rabbitrunrunnn . . .*

"The sound was deafening, impossible. I heard screaming horses, a faint whisper beneath the thunder, more snow thrown skyward as the tectonic shift rolled on. But the bloodhymn sang in my ears, and I was paleblood born, after all; a burning shadow leaping toward the shoreline, aegis ablaze, finally crashing to rest on the frozen banks.

"Spitting blood, I dragged myself upright, broken ribs grinding as I gasped for breath.

"'Dior . . .'

"Looking about, I saw the devastation was terrifying, the Wolfmother's strength beyond *anything* I'd expected. There was no sign of her nor the Headsmun nor my old 'prentice either, but the Mère was smashed bank to bloody bank, fissures stretching near a thousand feet down her length. The air was tumbling snow and raw chill, echoing with the cracking of tortured ice. And stomach twisting, I heard a scream amid the chaos.

"'GAAAABE!'

"I squinted through the howling snows, and with sinking heart, I saw Dior was still out on the river. The meatwagon had fallen partway into the water as the ice split, the drays pulling it in their panic. The children inside were screaming, reaching out through the bars as the wagon began to sink. And refusing to let them die, Dior was crouched atop it.

"'*GABRIEL!*'

"'Fuck my face . . .'

"'You mussst save her.'

"I turned to Celene, her toes poised at the very edge of the smashed ice, red hands slipping her mask back over her blood-slicked face. She'd overtaken me as we fled the collapse, great, long leaps bringing her safely to the banks. I'd still no idea what I'd just borne witness to, but no vampire can cross running water, and to head back out there . . .

"'You *must*—'

"But I was already gone, sheathing Ashdrinker and coughing blood as I dashed back out onto the broken river, slick as glass and rolling under my boots. The wagon was jammed between two slabs of ice, listing ever farther as the floes broke apart. The horses were in the water already, screaming and dragging at its weight.

"Stumbling toward them, I saw Dior raising the dagger I'd given her, cutting the beasts free from their harnesses so they'd not haul their cargo to its doom. The wagon shook as the ice splintered again, children inside still wailing, and I bellowed, 'GET OUT OF THERE, GIRL!' But ignoring me completely, Dior sheathed her blade and withdrew her trusty wallet of thieves' picks from her boot. And mad as a drunken Ossian, she crawled back over the cage and started sweet-talking the padlock.

"I leapt from one frozen chunk to another, wind screeching, snow blinding, almost falling half a dozen times into the freezing depths. Casting desperate eyes around for Lachlan, I could still see no trace of him. But with one final leap, I crashed against the bars of the cage. Dior grabbed my hand to steady me, blue eyes bright and wild.

"'I told you to get the *hell* out of here!'

"'You're honestly lecturing me *now*?' she shouted. 'I'm trying to pick this fu—'

"With a snarl, I seized the cage door and tore it off its rusted hinges, hurling it into the river behind me. Dior blinked in utter astonishment.

"'. . . Right, that works too.'

"The wagon shuddered, dropping two feet, the current churning as I reached in for the first child I saw. 'Run! All of you *go*!'

"Every breath jagged, bleeding, I dragged the children forth, two and three at a time, tossing them onto the ice. Some were little more than toddlers, most barely teenagers, all absolutely terrified. The slab buckled beneath us, splitting, tilting, freezing water rushing up over the wagon's wheels as it continued to sink. The young ones still inside wailed in horror, clawing each other in their panic to get free as Dior roared from the doorway.

"'Gabe, are you—'

"'I'm fine, go, GO!'

"The girl leapt down, snatching up a tiny blond lass and throwing the child over her shoulder as she cried, '*Follow me!*' The other children obeyed, olders grabbing youngers as they fled, cracks spreading wider, deeper. Freezing water flooding up to my thighs, I waded into the cage and dragged out the remainder, fingers and lips already turning blue. The last child I grabbed was Ossian-born by the look—an older girl with reddish-brown hair, who'd stubbornly refused to leave 'til the last captive was freed.

"'Go!' I roared at her.

"'Are y—'

"'GO!' I bellowed, throwing her out the door.

"I bent double, broken ribs stabbing my lungs as the water swirled up over my waist. The chill was shocking, bone-deep and numbing, and for a moment, it was all I could do just to breathe. Grabbing the bars, I hurled myself out, red drool spraying from my lips as I hit the splintering ice and the wagon disappeared into the depths behind me.

"I was up and stumbling, leaping slab to crumbling slab. My every breath was a war, the river's surface seething like a herd of thundering horses. Blood in my mouth, knowing one mistake would send me down into that freezing current, I staggered on. The shoreline was in sight, twenty or thirty feet to go now, but leaping long and landing heavy, I felt my luck finally fail, the ice splitting beneath me.

"'Shit, not ag—'

"Down into that hellforged cold I fell, cursing as I reached out for something, *anything* to grab onto. Water closed over my head, dark and freezing, and I felt my lungs empty at the shock. But I'd still breath enough to scream, bloody bubbles spilling from between my fangs as something razor sharp and crushing closed around my wrist.

"I was dragged back up from the water, roaring in agony as the teeth—oui, fucking *teeth*—sank farther into my flesh. Something had me in its *mouth*, a beast, a monster, my forearm splintering like kindling in its jaws. Its shape was a rust-red blur through the snow and pain, all gleaming golden eyes and pearl-white fangs, and I bellowed, slamming my fist into its skull as it hauled me out of the river. I punched it again and it let me loose, but Dior was at my side now, screaming my name. Lachlan was beside her, cursing aloud, his leathers drenched in freezing water and his bare chest splashed with blood, helping the girl drag me back to the shoreline, where the ice stretched all the way to the river's bed.

"Safe at last.

"'Seven bloody Martyrs,' the young 'saint wheezed, collapsing onto his backside.

"'Gabe, are you aright?' Dior cried.

"I rolled onto my back, coughing, freezing, gasping. 'F-fucking marvelous . . .'

"The girl squeezed my shoulder, whispering a prayer of thanks. Blinking hard, gazing about, I spied a huddle of frightened little ones on the riverbank, gazing at Dior with wonder and me with awe. Spitting blood off my tongue, I looked to a gasping Lachlan.

"'Kiara?' I croaked. 'Kane?'

"The 'saint answered with a shake of his head, a shrug toward the broken river and its roiling floes. Hauling myself off the ice, my right forearm torn to the bone, I drew Ashdrinker with my left. And squinting through the swirling snow, Lachlan rising up beside me, I turned at last toward my mysterious savior.

"A cat.

"Well, a fucking *lion*, if I'm being honest.

"The beast sat on its haunches at the shoreline, licking my blood from its snout with a flat pink tongue. Its fur was russet red, eyes speckled gold. An old scar cut down its right cheek, and another was sliced fresher into its shoulder and chest. It was *huge*—one of the big mountain breeds that had haunted the Highlands before all the predators perished for lack of prey. The children backed away in clear terror, that Ossian lass ushering the youngest of them behind her to shield them. But the little blond girl Dior had saved pointed one finger, absolutely delighted.

"'Kitcaaaaaat!'

"'My God,' Dior whispered, rising to her feet. 'Gabriel . . .'

"The lioness held us in her golden stare, tail switching side to side, and

I felt my breath leave my lungs as I finally recognized her. I couldn't quite believe what I was seeing, wondered if I'd gone mad. But there she was, big as life and twice as bloody.

"A ghost.

"An *impossibility*.

"I heard a whisper then; a razor on the wind. A figure flew from between the dead trees, a whip of long black hair streaming behind her, bloody sword raised.

"'No, Celene, *don't!*'

"My sister struck the snow without a sound, swinging her blade toward the she-lion's back. But the beast moved, swift as silver, red as rust, twisting aside from the blow with a furious snarl. Ears pressed back to her skull, the lioness bared fangs long as knives, spitting a bellowing *ROAR* at my sister. Lachlan was a sudden blur, hissing, '*Coldblood!*' as he drew his silversteel, wide eyes locked on Celene as I dragged in a breath to—

"'*STOP* IT!'

"Dior's shout brought sudden quiet to the riverbank, the lioness and vampire and silversaint all frozen still. The children we'd rescued looked on in silent fear, and I placed a hand on Lachlan's shoulder, shaking my head in warning as Dior stepped forward. The girl shot a hard glance to Celene, the young 'saint beside me, hands raised to placate the beast. Her voice was soft with wonder as she spoke a name I'd never thought to hear again.

"'*Phoebe?*'

"It was her, sure as I breathed—the lioness who'd traveled with Saoirse á Dúnnsair and the Company of the Grail. Phoebe had fought beside us at the Battle of Winfael, seen us safe through the Forest of Sorrows, been our guide in dark nights and darker places. But Danton Voss had murdered the big cat and her mistress both at San Guillaume. He'd split Phoebe's chest clean open with Saoirse's own axe, then smashed the lioness to pulp on the monastery's flagstones.

"I'd seen it with my own fucking eyes.

"'You were *dead*.'

"Phoebe's fangs gleamed as she licked her bloody jowls. She growled warning at Celene, but my sister didn't advance, standing with blade poised and dead eyes narrowed. Lachlan was a statue of knotted muscle and burning ink beside me, my gentle hand on his shoulder all there was to hold him still.

"The dusk was silent as tombs, pregnant with menace.

"Phoebe looked toward the sinking sun, closed those glittering eyes.

"And then . . . she began to move.

"Not prowling nor stretching nor slinking, no. I mean her *body* began to move. To ripple. To *bend*. She bowed her head, the children behind me gasping as her limbs elongated, hips widening, twisting, *shifting*, as a long, low growl rolled through her whole length. I'd never witnessed the like of it, but from my years in San Michon, I knew full well what I was seeing. Understood at *last* what Phoebe actually was.

"Lachlan cursed in wonder as the change continued, while I could only stand gobsmacked. Phoebe's fur receded, and on the pale and freckled skin beneath, I saw inkwork, same as Saoirse had worn; *Naéth*, the warrior tattoos of the Ossway Highlanders. Blood-red spirals trailed up her right arm, beneath her breasts, wending over her hips and down her left leg to her ankle. She arched her back, growling, feline, the scar cutting through brow and cheek twisting her lips into a lopsided snarl. And where once a lioness had sat, a beautiful woman with fierce emerald eyes now crouched on the riverbank, naked as her saintsday save for the collar of leather everknots about her throat.

"But no, on second glance . . . *not* a beautiful woman. Not *quite*. Her fingertips were black, cruel, curled like talons. Her ears were pointed like a cat's, protruding from her mane of thick auburn curls. And strangest of all, looking to the snow beneath her, I saw the shadow Phoebe threw in the glow of my aegis was still that of a lioness.

"She stared at me, dragging knuckles across her bloody nose, the scent of her thrilling me from aching head to trembling toes and everywhere in between.

"'Fine hook, Silverboy.'

"'Night save usss,' Celene hissed.

"Phoebe glowered over her shoulder. 'Wave that pigsticker at me again, ye'll need more than prayers to save ye. I'll take yer hand off at yer *neck*, leech.'

"'Phoebe . . . ?'

"The woman turned at Dior's whisper, lips curled in a sudden, joyful smile.

"'Hullo, Flower.'

"The girl shook her head, utterly bewildered. 'But . . . you were *dead*.'

"'Near to it.' Phoebe tossed a long braid off her shoulder, her chin raised, jaw set. 'But *near* counts nae wi' my kind. I was wounded deep and bitter.

Carved to the very bone. But I've been trackin' ye both since I was well enough to limp again, love.'

"'Sweet Mothermaid, Gabriel,' Lachlan whispered. 'You *know* this thing?'

"I could only shrug, voice soft with awe. 'I thought I did.'

"'How . . .' Dior shook her head. '*What* are you?'

"Phoebe looked to the ruins of Aveléne, the children we'd saved, emerald eyes narrowed. She was mid-twenties by my guess, tall, fine, completely unabashed by her state of undress. Most of the little ones looked mystified, horrified, but the Ossian lass I'd rescued shepherded a few more youngers behind her skirts, hissing soft.

"'Duskdancer.'

"Dior's eyebrows climbed toward her hairline.

"'I'm a wealdling, Flower.' Phoebe nodded, glancing to the Ossway lass. 'What folk of the Lowlands might name a duskdancer, aye. I am blessed by the strength of Father Earth and the grace of Mothermoons. And in the short breath between day and night, I can dance between this woman's seeming and the shape ye knew. The wealdskin. The Beast.'

"'Why didn't you . . .' Dior briefly flailed, looking at Phoebe as if her world had been entirely upended. 'You traveled with us for *months*. And all along . . .'

"'Forgive me,' the woman replied, green eyes gone soft. 'I'd nae wish to deceive ye, love. But cousin Saoirse knew my mind enough to speak fer the both of us, and there's a toll to be paid for the dancin' I do. Heavier in these blighted nights than ever.' She nodded to the fallen sun, the dying daysdeath light. 'So now I dance only as oft as I must.'

"'We thought Danton *killed* you.'

"'Only silver can kill me. Silver, magik, and the cold teeth of age. The Bastard of Vellene wounded me deep. But in the Mothermoons' light, all a wealdling's hurts mend in time.'

"'Then . . .' Dior blinked, suddenly brightening. 'Is Saoirse—'

"'Nae.' Phoebe scowled. 'A warrior o' the Moonsthrone she was, brave and fair. Daughter o' the Auld-Sìth, a seer and a dreamwalker. But nae wealdling.' The woman clenched her jaw. 'My cousin is dead.'

"The words hung heavy, and Dior looked crestfallen. Though they'd known each other only a few months, the girl had been fond of Saoirse—hell, *more* than fond, if the kiss I'd caught them in was anything to go by . . .

"'Condolences for your kinswoman,' I murmured. 'Saoirse was a brave—'

"'I've nae need of condolence, Silversaint,' Phoebe spat. 'I need five *seconds* alone wi' Danton Voss. I swear by Fiáin, I will eat his godless heart. I will breathe his *bloody ashes*.'

"'Danton's dead.' I nodded to the lass beside me. 'Dior killed him.'

"The children murmured, yet more wonder in their eyes as they gazed at Dior. Lachlan looked incredulous at my claim, but Phoebe only lifted her chin, lip curling. The duskdancer wasn't as broad as her cousin, nor as brawny—Saoirse had been an axe, heavy and sharp, but Phoebe was a sword, sleek and swift. I could see a dangerous shadow prowling behind her eyes as she rose to her feet. And I knew then that while her cousin had been a warrior, Phoebe was a *predator*.

"The duskdancer stalked toward Dior, black talons curled. The girl shrank back to my side, and my hand went to Ashdrinker's hilt, Celene bristling with threat, Lachlan's grip tightening on his blade so hard that the very metal groaned. But Phoebe came to a halt a few feet away, lowered herself to one knee on the ice. Curtains of flaming hair tumbled about her scarred and freckled cheeks as she bowed her head.

"'Then were I not bound to ye aready by augur of my kin, I would still be bound to ye now.' The woman lifted her eyes to the bewildered girl. 'Dior Lachance, by the heart of Fiáin and in sight of Father and Mothers, my fate is fixed to yours. If by my blood or boon or breath might ye be kept safe, I do here vow to give them all in yer service.'

"Phoebe drew her claws down her breast, opening scarlet ribbons in ghost-pale skin, and God in heaven, the *scent* of it struck me like a sword-blow, dizzying and feral, blazing a flaming trail from my brain all the way down to my aching nethers. Swallowing hard, cursing it, I pulled my thirst into check, my jaw clenched tight as Phoebe spoke.

"*Dead shall rise, and stars shall fall;*
"'*Weald shall rot to ruin of all.*
"'*Lions roar and angels weep;*
"'*Sinners' hands our secrets keep.*
"''*Til Godling's heart brights hea'en's eye,*
· "'*From reddest blood comes bluest sky.*'

"Holding out her hand, Phoebe let crimson droplets fall to the snow.
"'I am yer talon and tooth, Flower. By my heartsblood spilled, I vow it.'

"Dior looked to me, mystified. I could only shake my head, just as baffled. The little ones gazed on in wonder, Celene folding her arms and glowering, Lachlan bristling beside me. The air was thick with the stink of death, danger, and distrust.

"And across the frozen breadth of Nordlund, dusk gave way to night."

IX

MUCH A MONSTER

"THE SUN HAD tumbled to sleep, skies as dark as the shadow on my shoulders. My leathers were sodden and my feet freezing, blood dripping from the ragged bite wounds in my arm. Phoebe was wrangling the children we'd rescued, Celene was off skulking, Lachlan scouting downriver to ensure the Dyvok didn't creep back and fuck us in the dark. And Dior was walking beside me, torches in our hands and hearts in our throats as we wandered the ruins of the city my brothers had built.

"The stench of blood was so thick, it made my stomach growl.

"A tale of horror and sorrow awaited us inside Avelène's walls, but we'd soon discovered a mystery also. The gatehouse soldiers had been dispatched with such force it chilled the blood; necks twisted, faces pulped. But the portcullis and gates were intact, open as if to invite the world inside. There had been no siege here, no bloody defense of these mighty battlements. As I looked across the ruins, my mind was a storm of *hows* and *whys*.

"And my God, I was so *thirsty* . . .

"'Poor souls,' a soft voice murmured. 'Almighty God, gather them in yer arms.'

"I glanced up from the wreckage of the gate guards, looking at the lass beside me.

"'I fear he doesn't take requests lately, mademoiselle.'

"The lass signed the wheel, making no reply. She was a little older than Dior, slender and small—the last captive I'd rescued from that sinking meat-wagon. After the calamity on the riverbank had died down, she'd introduced herself in a soft Ossian brogue as Isla á Cuinn, a resident of Avelène, notable among those we'd saved only in that she was the eldest. Her pale skin was smattered with freckles, long reddish hair tied in plaits, twin beauty spots on her cheek. I could dimly recall her at the welcome feast Aaron threw for us a few weeks back, serving drinks after the Godthanks. But beyond that, I knew her not at all.

"Scowling, I surveyed the destruction. 'What the hell happened here?'

"'They came in the night, Chevalier,' Isla replied softly. 'Merciless and swift.'

"'But they didn't break through these gates. Did they come over the walls? In force enough to take the city, but without a bloodstain on the battlements?'

"'I did not see.' The lass shivered, arms wrapped about herself in the rising chill. 'I was asleep in the château. Woken by the sound of thunder. And screaming. Great rocks were being flung at the keep from the city streets below, falling in the courtyard like hail.' Isla shook her head, awestruck. 'It was the Dead, Chevalier. They were *throwing* those boulders. Tossing chunks of houses about as if they were pebbles.'

"'So they were already inside the outer fortifications by the time the attack sounded?' I clenched my jaw, eyes narrowed. 'That makes no fucking *sense.*'

"The lass only shook her head, mute and trembling. We walked onward, fat crows jeering as we passed, rats skittering through the shadows. Ascending the cobbled road to the château on the hilltop, we saw signs of furious battle everywhere. The fire throwers Baptiste had built on the battlements had left long scorch marks on the rock, flagstones littered with coal and ash. The smell of burned wood alcohol and blood stabbed my aching belly. Unlike the outer walls, these inner gates were gone—not broken, mind you, but torn free and tossed back down the hill with a force that reduced the houses they'd struck to rubble.

"I knelt beside a dead soldier, his skull smashed open, brains crusted on the ice. Prying a leather flask from his frozen fingers, I unscrewed the lid, sniffing once.

"'Holy water?' Dior asked softly.

"I shook my head. 'Vodka.'

"'He died with liquor in his hand?'

"'That's the way I'd want to go.'

"Dior rolled her eyes, scoffing softly. I sighed, studying the corpse on the cobbles before me. Barely a whisker on his chin, the poor bastard.

"'A soldier will take comfort in prayer, Dior. In thoughts of famille, the love of his brothers, the light of his God. But there's nothing like a dram of courage to hold you steady when the screaming starts.'

"I took a long gulp from the flask before tossing it aside, standing to study the carnage. Within the château walls, the destruction was terrifying. The keep was demolished, solid basalt smashed like cheap pottery. The chapel where Astrid and I were wed had been gutted by fire, its roof collapsed. I could imagine its bells tolling during the attack, desperate citizens fleeing to the only sanctuary they had left—that of holy ground.

"'The soldiers told us to shelter in there,' Isla explained. 'Women and children. But the smoke flushed us all out eventually. We youngest were the last wagon loaded.'

"'How many more?' Dior asked softly.

"'I know not,' Isla murmured, fragile as glass. 'But many.'

"'We mussst away, brother.'

"The Ossian lass startled at the soft hiss, and I glanced upward, jaw clenched. Celene was crouched like a crow on the broken battlements above, long hair and coat blowing in the bitter wind. Her hands were now lily white, but her shirt was spattered red—the leavings of that unholy feast I'd witnessed on the river. She nodded southward; the way we supposed Kiara and her cousin had fled.

"'Dark has fallen. If the Dyvok return in force, they will crusssh us.'

"'Lachlan is awatch,' I told her. 'He'll sing if he sees them.'

"'Ah, the wisest of plansss. Set the man who would gladly see half of us dead standing guard over all our lives.' My sister shook her head, dead eyes glinting like broken glass. 'Why is he here, Gabriel? What were you *thinking* letting him c—'

"'I fought alongside Lachlan á Craeg through two years of hell, Celene. Right now, I trust him more than I trust *you*. Now unknot your fucking pantaloons, I'm not fixing to build a house up here. But we've a moment to figure out what happened to our friends.'

"Celene hissed disapproval, and Isla signed the wheel, glancing between us with wide eyes. My sister had helped save the children of Aveléne from the Dead who'd captured them—that was plain. Yet plainer still was the fact she was Dead herself. This poor lass had no idea what kind of shite she'd waded into, only that she wanted to be out of it.

"'What happened to Baptiste?' Dior asked.

"'I did not see,' Isla replied, wringing her hands. 'But he'd have tried to stand beside Capitaine de Coste, I'm sure. Their love burned brighter than silver, and no evil could part them. But whether he fell in battle or was taken by the Dead . . . I know not.'

"'And Aaron?' I murmured.

"'I saw the capitaine.' Isla shivered as she pointed. 'There, atop the walls. Glowing like silver flame in the night. He was battling one of the high-bloods. Both fighting like demons. But then . . . h-he was hit. A r-rock the size of a *wagon*.'

"'Oh, God,' Dior whispered.

"I gritted my teeth, not wanting to believe as I studied the highwalk where my brother had fought. It was smashed by some colossal impact; dozens of tons, horrifying to see. A massive chunk of masonry sat across the courtyard, a huge runnel torn through the flagstones in its wake, stained dark with blood.

"I walked like a man to the gallows, images of Aaron shining in my mind's eye. I recalled our youth—our hatred forged by hellfire into a friendship I cherished above all others. I saw him standing beside me the day Astrid and I were wed here, trading the rings Baptiste had forged with his own two hands. I remembered them both sharing my tears the day Patience was born. Embracing me as I set off after Dior, aching that they couldn't ride at my side one more time into darkness.

"My gorge rose at the sight of an awful smear, a blood-drenched boot crushed under the masonry. And wedged in the splintered rock . . .

"'Gabe?' Dior whispered.

"I knelt to retrieve the object, but found it stuck fast. I felt my fury rising, fangs grown long and sharp as I tried to drag it loose. My muscles stretched taut, Dior touched my shoulder, but I only cursed and leaned back into it, gasping as I finally wrenched it free.

"I stood there in the night, the falling snow, a scream building inside my chest. The thing in my hand was heavier than a lifetime unloved. Its crossbar was bent, but I could see the raven's wings, the grinning skull, the long flowing robes of silver.

"'Mahné. Angel of Death.'

"Dior whispered, 'Is that . . . ?'

"'Aaron's sword.'

"'Oh, God . . . Oh, Gabe . . .'

"I hung my head, the shattered hilt tumbling from my hand, fighting that scream inside me. I closed my eyes against the sight, I wouldn't believe it, *couldn't* believe it, telling myself over and over it might not be him, it might be another man, another soldier who somehow took up Aaron's beloved blade, who somehow . . .

"*Somehow* . . .

"'Gabriel.'

"I looked up at that hateful whisper, into hateful eyes.

"'We *mussst* away from here,' Celene hissed. 'Cairnhaem awaits.'

"'But . . . what about the children?' Dior asked.

"A whisper, cold as ice. 'What about them?'

"'We're just supposed to *leave* them?'

"'We are.' Celene took in the wreckage of Aveléne with a wave of her thin hand. 'This is only a *taste*, Dior. The entire world will look thus if we do not find Master Jènoah. Every moment you tarry from your path, you wassste time, you wassste hope—'

"'You waste breath,' I snapped. 'Repeating what you've already said.'

"'We have no breath to wassste, brother. Thanks to you.'

"My heart sank at her jab, but I refused to bite back. Dior chewed her lip, watching me as I gazed about the sanctuary my brothers had built. Listening to the lonely calls of twice-glutted crows among the ruins. The echoes of another dream destroyed.

"'Whatever we do,' I finally sighed, 'we can't stay here.'

"We trudged back down the hill to the children below. They were twoscore in number, boys and girls, most near Dior's age but a handful far younger. They'd scavenged what food and clothing they could from the ruins, wearied and heartsick from their ordeal. But a few of the older ones stood taller as they saw Dior, looking at her with numb gratitude and quiet awe. Phoebe had scrounged clothes in the burned houses—britches, a stout jerkin, a winter cloak, all stained with soot. But a pair of boots had apparently eluded her. She gifted a warm smile to Dior, a cold glance to me. But Celene, she fairly glowered at.

"This was going to be trouble . . .

"Speaking of, I heard crunching footsteps behind, turning to find Lachlan stalking through the gates, shoulders kissed with new snow. Our eyes met, and I could see anger, distrust, barely held in check. He was disciplined enough not to voice the questions I could see roiling behind his fangs. But I knew a difficult conversation loomed on our horizon.

"'No sign of Kiara or her kinsman,' he reported. 'But dark is deeping, and the Dead run quick. We should off afore they're up us. Where is the question.'

"'We keep to the path,' Celene said. 'West to the Nightstonesss.'

"Phoebe waved to the frightened children. 'With *them* in tow? Fine plan, leech.'

"'No one asked your opinion, flessshwitch.'

"'No one asked me to save your brother's hide, neither. And call m—'

"'Enough,' I snapped. 'First things last, we need to get the hell away from here. If the Untamed return, we're fucked harder than a bishop at a cardinal's convocation. We head back north, away from their tracks. *All* of us,' I added, glowering at my sister. 'Get some miles under our feet and sleep in our pockets.' I clapped my hands. 'Let's move, soldiers.'

"At my barking, the young ones formed up, making ready to leave the only home most had known. The air was heavy with sorrow and chill, and Dior gave my hand a squeeze, lips pressed thin. I squeezed back, throwing off the cloak of my own grief, turning thought to simple survival. And sighing, I looked to Phoebe, patting Bear's saddle.

"'Mesdames before messieurs.'

"The woman raised one eyebrow. 'Shove yer chivalry up yer arse, man.'

"'My chivalry fell on its own sword a long time ago. But if I've the right of it, you're stuck in that shape at least until dusk amorrow. So unless you've a burning desire to walk for the rest of the night through freezing snow in bare feet . . .'

"Phoebe looked me up and down, hands on hips. I rolled my eyes.

"'Don't make me beg, mademoiselle.'

"'I like it when yer kind beg.'

"'. . . My *kind?*'

"Tossing her hair, Phoebe turned and lifted a young girl onto Pony's saddle. Hefting two older lads up behind the lass, she gave Dior's fingers a squeeze as she handed over the sosya's reins. The girl stiffened slightly at the duskdancer's familiar touch, but Phoebe seemed unconcerned, taking up watch at Dior's shoulder like a guardian at the gates.

"I helped a gangly young lad into Bear's saddle instead, lifting another child behind him before stooping to pick up a third. She was the blond lass Dior had carried from the river, I realized, maybe six or seven years old. Her dress was grubby and spotted with blood, a handwoven moppet doll clutched in one dirty hand. And about her neck, I saw a prize that had once adorned a Wolfmother's throat.

"A golden vial on a broken chain.

"'What's your name, chérie?' I asked softly, crouching before her.

"She looked to her feet, frightened, replying with a tiny voice, 'Mila, monsieur.'

"'And where did you get that, Mlle Mila?' I asked, pointing to the vial.

"'Found it.' She risked a glance. 'After kitcat lady bit you and you said a badword.'

"'I said a *very* bad word,' I nodded, solemn.

"She risked a shy smile, clutching the moppet to her chest. 'You *did*!'

"'May I see it?'

"She looked up at me; blood-flecked skin and dirty-blond hair and big brown eyes that had already seen far too much of this world. And though she'd just lost everything, that little girl slipped the chain off her neck, and placed it in my open hand.

"'Keep it.'

"'. . . Truly?'

"Mila nodded. 'You said a badword. But you're a goodman.'

"I slipped the vial into my bandolier and kissed her forehead, lifting her up behind the others. Looking about, I caught Dior smiling at me, waving her off with a scoff and a scowl. Lachlan raised a young boy onto his shoulders, another youngster riding him pig-a-back. And eyes narrowed against the bitter winds, collar dragged high and tricorn low, I led our little company out of Aveléne's gates, and into the frozen night beyond.

"The children walked mostly in silence, a few murmuring prayers, others sobbing softly. Lachlan was apoint, casting wary glances to the trees about us, behind for the Dyvok who might be stalking us. Celene strode far out on our flank as always, stealing glances at Phoebe all the while. Monster though she was, my sister was clearly unsettled to have another monster riding with us, and God's truth, I shared her concerns. The brethren of San Michon had raised me and Lachie on stories of duskdancer savagery, taught us they were accursed by God and twisted by heretical magiks. A foe to be both fought and feared.

"Phoebe walked beside Dior like a second shadow. Barefoot, she left no tracks in the snow, and seemed completely unbothered by its chill. But strange as she was, her talons were draped around the girl's shoulder, protective. She'd helped us on our journey through Ossway, saved my arse out on that ice today. And she was no friend to the Dead.

"Apart from the sharpness of her tongue, she didn't *seem* much a monster.

"After a few hours' ride upriver, Lachlan spied the ruins of a fisherhovel in a shallow dell, walls and roof crawling with shadespine and moldweave. Following a brief search, he emerged with a small nod, and I ushered our young charges inside.

"The little ones were exhausted, collapsing onto the hovel's floor. Most were settling into shock now, too numb for tears. My heart was bleeding for Aaron and Baptiste, but there was enough misery in this company already. And so, while Lachlan went out to keep watch, Celene to scout for the Untamed, I set my boots by the fire and cooked a passable supper with stores I'd scrounged from a taverne in Aveléne; fucking potatoes, sadly, but enough for all. I set the pot boiling, chopped the fare, pausing to take a hit of sanctus from my pipe, or a swig from a bottle I'd filched with the spuds. For all my troubles, the thirst shouldn't have been one of them—not with all the liquor I had and the sacrament I was smoking. But still, I could smell it in that damned room. Taste it at the back of my throat.

"Blood.

"*Blood.*

"Isla was slumped in a corner, twin beauty spots etched under haunted eyes. Dior sat near the hearth, Phoebe slinking down beside her, smooth and swift. Again, the girl tensed as the duskdancer laid a head on her shoulder, but Phoebe simply sighed in contentment, as certain of her welcome and as heedless of personal space as any feline I'd ever met. I was certain if Dior scratched her back, the woman would start purring.

"As I served supper, I asked about the attack; who saw what, and when.

"'They came as smoke, Chevalier,' one of the older boys assured me, stroking the fuzz on his chin. 'Creepin' through the gates like mist.'

"'Bollocks,' another lad scoffed. 'This is no time for your tall tales, Abril Durán.'

"'Shut up, Sergio, I seen 'em! Smoke they was!'

"'I saw no smoke,' a thin girl whispered. 'But I saw the one who led them. A devil in black. Soaked in red. God, when she *looked* at me . . .'

"Chinfuzz glanced behind him. 'Were these the same devils as took Dún Cuinn, Isla?'

"Isla glanced up from the flames, drawn and haggard. 'I don't know, Abril.'

"I looked at the girl anew, remembering those refugees Dior and I had met on the road months back. 'You were at the fall of Dún Cuinn, Mlle Isla?'

"The maid's face was pale as she nodded, murmuring in her Ossian brogue.

"'Aye. Six months gone now. They came in the night back then too. Thunder with n-nae clouds. Boulders falling like r-rain.' She shook her head, making the sign of the wheel. 'You know, Capitaine Aaron used to tell us you only appreciate the sunshine after you've felt the pouring rain. B-but sometimes it feels like it's been raining all my life.'

"The lass hid her face in her hands, fighting back tears. Trying to head off an unwanted flood, I filled a bowl from the cookpot and offered it to her.

"'You should eat something, Mlle Isla.'

"She glanced up, frail and trembling. 'What's the point?'

"'Of potatoes?' I risked a smile. 'I've wondered the same mys—'

"'Of eating!' she snapped, slapping the bowl from my hand. 'It's all gone to *hell*, can't ye see that? Ye think some half-cooked slop will make any of this better?'

"The older children around the room hung their heads, a few of the little ones began crying. But Dior looked up from oiling her dagger, pale blue eyes shining.

"'You fight harder on a full stomach, Isla. Keep heart now.' Dior glanced about, her voice rising. 'Keep heart, *all* of you. I know the road looks dark ahead, but th—'

"'Dark?' Isla cried. 'Dark isn't the half of it! I had someone who *loved* me! Even in all this, I found my Ever After, and now . . .' She glared at Dior, rising to her feet as her tears began falling. '*God*, I wish ye'd never unlocked that cage. Why couldn't ye leave me be t—'

"'Don't,' I warned, temper flashing. 'Feeling heartsick is one thing, mademoiselle. But wishing yourself dead is insult to every man and woman who *died* defending that keep.'

"'Hell with them!' She glared at me, pawing her cheeks. 'Hell with *all* of ye!'

"The lass stormed from the hovel, sad whispers and sobbing children in her wake. I stared at the fallen bowl, the meal spattered all over the floor.

"'And I thought *I* hated potatoes . . .'

"'Mother and Maid,' Dior scoffed, shaking her head as she looked at me. 'You are a heartless prick sometimes, Gabriel de León.'

"'I've heart aplenty. More's the pity.' I stooped to lift a crying child; grubby red hair and bloodstained dress. 'But woe-is-me theatrics at a time like this helps no one, Dior.'

"Dior slipped her dagger back into the sheath at her wrist, staring after Isla. 'She's only a girl, Gabe.'

"'There's nae *only* to it.'

"Dior and I glanced toward Phoebe as she spoke. The duskdancer was nursing little Mila in her arms, dirty face and tear-filled eyes.

"'Hate to admit it, but yer silversaint's right, Flower.'

"'Damn right I'm right,' I muttered.

"'Don't let it go to yer head, man. Every dog has his day.'

"'Dogs eat cats last time I checked, mademoiselle.'

"'Mothermoons,' she scoffed. 'I wouldn't let ye eat me if ye paid me for it.'

"'Fortunate, then, that I wasn't offering to.'

"Phoebe shifted the little girl in her arms, fixing Dior with her emerald stare.

"'There's a time and place for tears, Flower. An' there's a solace to be found in sadness. It's easier fallin' downhill than climbin' up. It hurts to punch on with broken hands. But it's when darkness falls around us that we find the fire within. An' I see it in ye, sure and true.' Phoebe searched Dior's eyes, speaking fierce. 'Yer the fire that will burn away this dark, Flower. And *yer* a girl. So stick that *only* shite where the sun don't shine.'

"I glanced upward. 'The sun doesn't shine anywhere anymore, Kitcat.'

"'Then stick it anywhere ye like, smartarse.'

"'Quiet as tombsss out there,' came a whisper, and Celene stepped through the door. The children immediately fell into frightened stillness as my sister brushed snow from her shoulders, out of her midnight-blue hair. 'And jussst as dark.'

"'No troubles?' I asked softly. 'No pursuit?'

"'Nothing movesss save wind and snow. But we cannot linger here.'

"'We need to rest. Including you.'

"'You know nothing of what we need, brother.'

"'I know coldbloods need to sleep like the rest of us. Take an hour or two.'

"Celene blinked around the sea of frightened faces. 'In *here*?'

"'Where else? I'll watch with Lachlan.' I shrugged, grateful for any excuse to escape that room. 'No way I can sleep with a fresh pipe in me anyway.'

"My sister gazed about the hovel, meeting those unsettled stares, her eyes finally returning to mine. 'Perhapsss an hour, then.'

"I nodded, rocking the child in my arms. Celene sank down in the corner, as far from the fireplace as could be. But still, those closest shuffled farther away. Despite what I'd seen on the river that day—the memory of her fangs locked on Rykard's throat—the sight still struck a sad chord in me. Even here in our refuge, my sister was forced to keep herself apart, and the air was thick with fear. Hers of the flames. The children of her.

"'Where will we go now?' someone asked softly.

"'Beaufort, mebbe?'

"'South? That's where they *came* from, Sami.'

"'I'll not go near the Forest of Sorrows,' Chinfuzz vowed. 'Not for all the silver in Elidaen. The faequeen Ainerión has woken, she and her flowerknights—'

"'What about the others?' an older girl demanded, her voice trembling. 'All the p-people they took? Our friends? Our f-famille?'

"Hush fell then, broken only by frightened sobbing.

"'We could take them to Redwatch.' Dior looked to me, hopeful. 'That's not far.'

"'After the shit you pulled there last time?' I scoffed. 'They'd hang us both.'

"'God, you kill one inquisitor and spend the rest of your life apologizing for it.'

"'I think there's a lesson in that for all of us.'

"'We are *not* going to Redwatch,' Celene hissed, interrupting our chuckles. 'We have no time for petty compassion, Dior. We mussst continue west. We *mussst* find Master Jènoah.'

"'Ye'd do well not to tell us what we *must*, leech,' Phoebe growled, nursing that little girl in her talons. 'Last I looked, ye were as far from our friend as a snake can slither.'

"'You know nothing,' my sister replied.

"'I know when we fought at San Guillaume, ye tried to kill me *and* yer brother.' Phoebe glanced at me, eyes flashing. 'What I *don't* know is why he hasn't put ye in yer grave fer it.'

"'Because he is not a fool, fleshwitch.'

"'I like how ye did that. Implying I *am* without actually havin' the courage to say it.'

"Celene stared bloody daggers at the duskdancer's throat, and I interceded before trouble started. 'Do you have another suggestion, Mlle Phoebe? Or are you just stirring shite for the sake of it? Where do *you* propose we go?'

"'I give nae a single whisker off my sweet cunny where *that* goes.' Phoebe glared at Celene, then looked to Dior. 'But *we* should head to the Highlands, Flower.'

"Celene scoffed. 'Madnessss.'

"'Every leech we've met on this road has tried to *end* Dior. What's mad is following a leech's advice about which road to take now.' Phoebe glowered at me. 'Last I heard, your kind *hunted* the Dead, not clung to them like a babe to tit.'

"'You don't know me, mademoiselle.'

"'I know silversaints have hunted nightthings for generations. Our greatest queen perished at the hands of one of yer kind. But now yer happy to follow a corpse about?'

"'I've never hunted a duskdancer in my life. Never even *seen* one 'til I met you. And the Ordo Argent aren't *my* kind.' I met the woman's stare. 'You. Don't. Know me.'

"The pair of us glared at each other, neither blinking, neither flinching. Logs crackled in the fire, and Dior spoke into the uncomfortable silence.

"'What's in the Highlands?'

"Phoebe broke our staring contest, meeting the girl's eyes. 'Sanctuary. As much as can be found in this Time of Blighted Blood anyway. Yer coming was augured among the All Mothers of my kin, and long have the folk of the Moonsthrone awaited yer birth. Ye'll find sisterhood there, Flower. Sanctity. Magiks, old and true.'

"'Dior.'

"The girl looked to my sister as she hissed.

"'Your truth liesss with Jènoah,' Celene said. 'The fate of every soul under heaven dependsss upon you reaching the Nightstones.'

"Dior scruffed her fingers through her hair, glancing to the frightened faces around her. 'What about the souls in this room?'

"'Don't fret on it for now,' I told her. 'There's no call to be made tonight that won't keep 'til the morrow. And you'll see clearer come morning light.'

"The little girl in my arms was calmed at last, and as I tucked her in on a blanket near the fire, I gazed about the commonroom. The children were pale and frightened, bloodied and weeping and numb. I'd seen this story before; a hundred towns, a thousand lives, all destroyed by coldblood hungers. But it's just as I learned when I was a boy, vampire: When your whole world is going to hell, sometimes all you need is someone who sounds like he knows the way.

"'Sleep now, all of you,' I told them, hand at rest on my sword. 'No Dead shall trouble your dreams. All songs cease, little ones. All cities fall. But so too must end darkness. And I will watch over all of you until the breaking of the dawn.'

"The children hushed, the last of the sobbing ceased. And grabbing up my bottle, matching Dior's small smile with my own, I headed out to the cold night alone."

X

THE HATE OF YOU

"I CLIMBED THE rise above our hovel, breathing deep of the blessedly fresh air. All around was cold and lightless, the heavens above, a silent void. But as dark as the world had become, I had a full dose of sanctus in me, and the night itself was alive.

"The howling song of wintersdeep wind. The scurryings of nightthings about their business, uncaring of any man's sorrows. The promise of peaceful dreams. When I was a boy, the night had been a time for fear, the place where monsters dwelled. But for all its horror, all its mystery, the night can be radiant sometimes, vampire. The night can be—"

"Beautiful," Jean-François murmured.

The Last Silversaint looked up from the chymical globe, gaze falling on the historian's latest illustration—a picture of Gabriel at watch in the dark. As the vampire lifted those chocolat-brown eyes, deep enough to drown in, Gabriel slowly nodded.

"Sometimes," he agreed. "Sometimes it can be beautiful."

Jean-François's lips curled as the silversaint swallowed another mouthful of wine.

"But all the beauty was lost on me back then. Alone with a moment to breathe, my eyes burned at the memory of Baptiste's final embrace, of Aaron's last good-bye. I pulled the cork from my bottle, wanting only to be numb. One more loss. One more thing *taken*.

"And as I stared into the dark, I realized it was staring back.

"My heart twisted at the sight of a ghost-pale figure, standing among the trees. She was clothed in naught but the wind, a beauty spot painted beside her bloodless lips, her eyes deep as dreaming. Her hair was the night itself, velvet and black, and as her shadow reached toward me, across the wall of death, I saw the want in her gaze, a perfume of silverbell and blood hanging in the air, just as it had the night *he* knocked on our door.

"*'My Lion,'* she whispered.

"Much as I wished it, I knew this wasn't my bride—just a thirsting madman's dream. But though I knew her for a phantasm, the sight of my Astrid still filled my eyes with tears, and my heart with longing for a home I could never return to.

"The home Fabién Voss had *taken* from me.

"*'I miss you . . .'*

"She was behind me now, a dark angel enfolding me in her arms. The nights of passion we'd shared ablaze in my mind, memories of her blood, hot and burning down my throat, filling me with awful, wondrous want. I took off my gloves, fangs stirring in my gums as I pressed my lips to her wrist, bitter cold winds blowing her long black hair about us.

"'We *miss you . . .'*

"And in the gloom I saw her then, my heart sinking, tears rising. A familiar shape, willow slender, so young, God, far *too* young. She wore cloth as black as ravens' feathers, her skin pale as death. Her mama's hair and her papa's eyes, staring at me from the dark.

"*'Patience,'* I breathed.

"*'Papa . . .'*

"She stretched out her hand, my beautiful baby, beckoning me to join her in the shadow. I trembled with the ache of it, knowing how easily I could be with them again; peace just a knife twist away. But I had business unfinished. A vengeance I'd only *begun* to taste. And another girl who needed me now, almost as much as I needed her.

"'Wait for me a little longer, loves,' I begged.

"'Gabriel?'

"I sniffed hard, pawing at my eyes.

"'Up here, Lachlan.'

"I heard silver-heeled boots in the snow, banishing all fancies of ma famille as Lachlan á Craeg stalked up the frozen hillside toward me. Tipping his imaginary tricorn in greeting, my old 'prentice tucked his gloveless hand into his armpit for warmth, breathing a plume of frost. Dior's sword was still sheathed at his waist, and I felt a flicker of threat despite the history between us, gleaming on that sevenstar at his breast.

"'Aright?'

"'Nae sign of the Dyvok,' he replied softly. 'If that's what yer asking.'

"'Merci, brother,' I nodded. 'For keeping an eye out.'

"Lachlan shrugged. 'Yer back. My blade.'

"'You should get some sleep.'

"He stepped up to me then, the anger he'd long kept checked glinting in sharp green eyes. 'I think it best ye and I have a word first. 'Saint to 'saint, like.'

"'I'm not in the Order anymore, Lachie.'

"'I know. I was there when they tossed ye, remember?' He searched my eyes, gaze burning. 'And excommunicated or no, I still respect ye, Gabriel. Ye *know* I do. But I'd like to think I'd earned the same in the years we shared. Enough for the truth at least.'

"'. . . Truth about what?'

"'About that girl yer riding with. And who the hell she is.'

"'Well, she's a he, for starters.'

"'Don't lie to me, I beg ye. Ye didn't train a fool, Gabe. She's bleeding.'

"'After that brawl with the Dyvok, of course he's—'

"'Nae,' Lachlan interrupted. 'She's *bleeding*.'

"'. . . Shit.'

"I rubbed my brow, breathed a weary sigh. I'd drunk near a whole bottle of vodka and fled the hovel to avoid the scent of it, but still . . .

"'I hoped you wouldn't notice.'

"'How could I *not*?' Lachlan demanded. 'I've never smelled the like. Is it true what ye told that duskdancer on the river today? That slip of a girl slew the Beast of Vellene?'

"I said nothing, avoiding Lachlan's kohl-rimmed stare. But still he pressed.

"'Last I heard, ye were retired in Sūdhaem with yer mistress. Why trek all the way to San Michon with that lass now? And what did Greyhand say to ye when ye arrived?'

"I wanted to speak the truth, to confess all I'd done, God help me, I did. Lachlan was a brother-in-arms. A friend. But I remembered my *other* brothers in arms, my *other* friends, men I'd also fought and bled beside for years. Chaining me to the wheel at San Michon. Bearing witness as Greyhand slit my throat, ear to fucking ear.

"'The abbot said nothing of consequence,' I murmured.

"Lachlan pursed his lips, scowling. 'D'ye remember Chloe Sauvage?'

"My head was light; liquor and sacrament dancing arm in arm. But I still felt that sword in my hand, cleaving through Chloe's chest. I could still see the disbelief on my old friend's face as she grasped the blade, blood spilling from her lips with her whisper.

"'*All the work of his hand is in accord with his plan . . .*'

"'Fuck *his plan.*'

"'I remember,' I said. 'What about her?'

"'She left the monastery near two years back. Rumor had it she convinced Greyhand to let her look for a treasure. A *weapon* to be wielded against the endless night.'

"'Chloe ever spent too much time in that library, Lachie.'

"'I thought the same. Yet six weeks back, I get a message, recalling all 'saints to San Michon. And then I find ye a thousand miles north of where yer supposed to be. The Black Lion. The greatest hero the Silver Order *ever* produced, in league with duskdancers and *coldbloods*? With a lass in lad's cloth hid under his wing and the ashes of Danton bloody Voss fresh on her boots? This makes nae sense!'

"'You want a world that makes sense, Lachie, best start digging.' I took another pull from my vodka, polishing off the bottle. 'Two feet wide and six feet deep should do it.'

"'Who *is* she?'

"'None of your concern.'

"Lachlan's hands curled into fists. 'But she *is* the concern of that bloody skinthief down there? That fuckin' *leech*? Sweet Mothermaid, Gabe, have ye lost yer—'

"'In case you missed it, that skinthief saved my life today, Lachie. And that *fucking leech* is my baby sister.'

"He blinked then, that awful truth sinking into his skin. 'Yer—'

"'Sister, oui. And merci for inquiring after the rest of ma famille, by the by.' I tossed the bottle aside, squaring up to him now. 'You've a dozen questions about Dior, but not a single *breath* to ask about Astrid? You knew her almost as long as you knew me.'

"Lachlan clenched his jaw, breathing deep. 'Yer mistress is nae concern—'

"'She wasn't my fucking *mistress*, Lachie, she was my *wife*.'

"He shook his head, the old wound between us tearing open. 'She was yer *ruin*, Gabe. She's the reason ye *left* us. I said it then, and I'll say it now; that jezebel was—'

"My punch took him on the jaw, swift and hard enough to split his lips against his fangs. He struck me back, unthinking, the terrible strength of his Dyvok heritage sending me sailing into a nearby oak with a spray of blood and spit. I crashed against the trunk hard enough to make the whole tree groan, a blanket of snow crashing down atop me, wet and freezing. Lachlan was horrified, one hand raised, stepping forward to help me up.

"'Seven Martyrs, brother, I'm s—'

"With a roar, I crashed into him, mashing my knuckles against his teeth. His head snapped back on his neck as we tumbled into the snow. He was stronger than me, my old 'prentice, but I'd taught him all his tricks, the pair of us punching, kicking, flailing—

"'You boysss should play more gently.'

"I froze at the voice, Lachlan's hand at my throat, my bloody fist poised over his face. Glancing over my shoulder, I saw a pair of dead eyes among the wasted trees.

"'Somebody will ssstart crying,' Celene whispered.

"Lachlan shoved me off, snaking upright with a dark curse. His hand went to his blade, silver ink across his knuckles burning bright, his glare locked on my sister's.

"'I should send ye straight to hell, coldblood.'

"'I have been there, Sssilversaint.' Her head tilted, a long lock of ink-black hair spilling over her mask. 'Would you like to know how it tastessss?'

"'Enough, the pair of you,' I said, rising to my feet.

"'I don't take orders from ye anymore, Gabriel,' Lachlan growled.

"'What if he shouted? You monastery boysss do ssso love a good *strong* man to—'

"'Shut up, Celene,' I snapped.

"Lachlan stared at me, his eyes hard and cold. I couldn't fault him for his rage, his disbelief. He'd been at my side through the battles of Tuuve, Qadir, our blades drenched with the ashes of dozens, *hundreds* of slain vampires. And now . . .

"'How d'ye plan to explain all this when we get back to Greyhand?' he demanded.

"I shook my head. 'We're not going back to San Michon, Lachie.'

"'The monastery's but ten days north. Ye've three dozen orphans 'neath yer skirts, Gabe. Wintersdeep will see them all in their graves afore ye find someplace better.'

"'A pity, that would b—'

"'Shut *up*, Celene,' I growled.

"Lachie glanced back and forth between us, a look of dark incredulity on his face. I watched in silence, wishing more than anything that I could tell him the truth.

"*Who the* fuck *told you I was a hero?*

"'Well, I can see ye two have much to whisper about,' he finally spat. 'I suppose I should take my leave.'

"'Get some rest, Lachie,' I warned. 'No poking sleeping duskdancers, oui?'

"He met my eyes then, shaking his head. Matching Celene's gaze, he spat blood on the snow. And without another word, Lachlan turned and stomped off into the gloom.

"Knee-high boots crunched in the frost behind me, cold whispering on the back of my neck. My sister was announcing her approach rather than simply appearing from the darkness as she was so fond of, but still I felt threat tickling my spine as I turned to face her.

"'We must be rid of him, Gabriel.'

"'When you say *we*, do you mean you and I, or you and you?'

"'He is a member of the Ssssilver Order. He is a danger to Dior.'

"I studied Celene in the darkness, the snatching wind and falling snow. She still had the appearance of the girl I'd known in my youth; while I'd aged in our years apart, she'd remained exactly the same. And yet, I knew full well she was something else entire.

"*Leech.*

"*Coldblood.*

"*Granddaughter of the Forever King himself.*

"'You should be sleeping,' I said. 'I'm out here freezing my arse off so you can rest.'

"'We all know why you are out here. The blood of Voss flows in these veinsss.'

"My eyes narrowed as I caught her meaning. 'Stay out of my head, Celene.'

"'Then guard your thoughtsss with greater care. We can *feel* the thirssst in you. Perhaps now you understand why we cannot linger here. Those lordling's clothesss cannot hide the truth of the woman Dior is become.'

"'I know,' I sighed, belly clenching at the memory. 'Lachlan smelled her. And so do I.'

"Celene's gaze slipped to the pipe in my bandolier, back up to my blood-red eyes. 'But the sanctusss does not sate you at the scent, as once it did.'

"'That's none of your concern.'

"She inhaled, and I could feel her thoughts in mine, slipping like gentle fingertips into my skull until I snarled and slammed the door. 'I told you, stay out of my head.'

"'You have been . . . *drinking*.' Her head tilted. 'From Dior?'

"'*What?*' I spat, sickened and outraged. 'Fuck no, of course not!'

"'Who, then? How long?' Cold eyes roamed my body, down to the troth ring on my left hand. 'A *wife*? Tell me you were not foolisssh enough to drink from her?'

"'You are on *thin* fucking ice, Celene. God help you when it breaks.'

"She stared a moment longer, the gulf between us wide and deep as graves. My hands were balled fists, Lachlan's blood still smudged across my knuckles, and for one terrible, endless moment, I had the near *irresistible* urge to lick it off my skin. But my pulse slowed, my want eased, and finally, Celene raised her hands in surrender.

"'We did not come here to quarrel, brother.'

"I breathed deep, pushing anger and thirst down to the silvered soles of my boots.

"'Oui,' I nodded. 'We should talk. Sister.'

"'We must be rid of this silversaint,' Celene began. 'Those accursed children, and that *ssskinwitch* too. Dior heeds your counsel, Gabriel, and we have wasted time en—'

"'Stop,' I snapped.

"Celene blinked. Standing in the falling snow as if she were carved of stone. I realized I could hear no heartbeat in her breast. Feel no warmth in her veins.

"'*We*,' I said, gesturing back and forth between us, 'should *talk*.'

"She sighed. 'And what would you have ussss talk about?'

"'Oh, shit, I don't know, the price of a footjob in San Maximille? What do you fucking think? How about you start with what I saw on the river today? You drank that Dyvok to *ashes*! Or maybe you explain where you've been the last seventeen years? What are the Esani? How do you wield their bloodgifts if you're born of the Voss? Maybe explain how you're caught up in *any* of this shit?'

"'And if I do not?'

"'Then how about I finish what you began when you tried to *murder* me at San Guillaume?'

"'Suppose you are that foolish. How will you find Jènoah?'

"'Who the hell says I need to? The Highlanders apparently speak legends of daysdeath too, and Phoebe can tak—'

"'Fleshwitches and skinthieves,' Celene spat. 'Dior is the descendant of heaven's sssovereign. It is through *his* servantsss this world shall find sssalvation. Not some sty of inbred heathens, rutting in filth and howling at the Mothermoonsss. And no member of the Silver Order can set foot in the Moonsthrone Mountains and live, excommunicated or no.'

"Celene shook her head, looking me up and down.

"'If you go to the Highlands, you will *die*.'

"She spoke true, I knew it. But more, it struck me—to hear my sister speak of heaven and salvation, when all knew that vampires were children of the damned. Even now, I could feel my aegis burning beneath my skin in her unholy presence. But Celene spoke like . . .

"*Like a believer*, I realized.

"'Dior listensss to you, Gabriel. And though you've turned your back on the Almighty, he has not turned his back on you. Master Jènoah will teach Dior what she must do to sssave this empire, and all the souls within. Including my own. *If* you give a damn about it.'

"Sighing, I dragged one hand back through my hair.

"'Of course I do,' I said softly. 'You were my baby sister, Celene. And one night, I might muster courage to beg forgiveness at my part in what happened to you. But if you'll not tell me of what you are and became . . . after what I saw today . . . how in God's name can I trust you at all?'

"'I owe you no explanation, brother. We have sssaved your life twice now by our counting. But if still you need proof of my fidelity, consider thisss.'

"Celene stepped forward, and my hand slipped instinctively toward Ashdrinker's hilt at the rage burning in those dead eyes.

"'All I have sssuffered, all I have ssseen, is due to *you*. I look upon you and feel the blood in my veins *boil* for the hate of you. But you are bound to the Grail, and she to you. That much is plain for any with eyes to see. So I sssswallow my hatred. I drink the poison of your name. I endure your presence, as the Redeemer endured his tortures upon the wheel. Because the fate of every sssoul under heaven hangs in the balance of this.'

"Celene smoothed her hair from her mask again, calm returning.

"'So if you trust not in my word, trust in my hate. And understand how important this all must be, for me to sssuffer another *sssecond* of your company.'

"My heart bled to hear her speak so. I knew it truth, I knew it just. But she'd been my little sister once. Celene stared a moment longer, just a shadow of what she'd been. Then without another word, she turned to leave.

"'You were an aunt.'

"She froze. I let those words hang in the dark, watching her reaction. Celene remained motionless, only her coat and hair rippling in the howling wind. But as she glanced over her shoulder, I caught a small flash across the pale arc of her eyes.

"'Were,' she repeated.

"I nodded, running my thumb over the name inked across my knuckles. I searched the night around us for those ghost-pale figures again, but of course they weren't there; they'd *never* been there. Words weighing upon my shoulders like broken wings.

"'Your niece was murdered a year ago. Along with her mama. And *I* was the one who invited death to our door. So if you've naught but hate for me in your heart, sister, believe me, I sympathize. Your fire is a candleflame compared to the hate I keep for myself.'

"I took a step across the snow, and Celene turned to face me as I spoke.

"'So that girl down there is my world, now. I give no fucks for the souls under heaven. I ask nothing of its sovereign, save the chance to spit in his face before he sends me below. I *shit* on your Redeemer, sister. Upon his wheel. Upon the cartwright who carved it and the woodsman who felled it and the son of a whore who planted its seed. And you feel free to hate me if it makes you feel better. I'll keep Dior on this road for as long as she wishes to walk it. I've a mind to see where it leads myself now. But if you're drawing her into danger, if you or this Jènoah harm but one hair on her head, whatever you've suffered these last seventeen years will be nothing—*nothing*—compared to the hell I'll gift you afterward.'

"I stared at Celene in the falling snow.

"My sister. And my sister no more.

"'I am glad we underssstand each other. Brother.'

"And spinning on her heel, she stalked into the dark."

XI

FRAIL AS BUTTERFLY WINGS

" 'I F I C O M E up there, am I getting punched in the face?' someone called.

" 'Depends on the face,' I replied, hand to my sword. 'And who's attached to it.'

" 'Savior of the Empire,' came the reply. 'Slayer of a Forever Prince. And some would say a dazzling wit and beauty besides.'

" 'Doesn't sound like anyone I know.'

"It was past night's deeping, and my watch had been quiet. The cold was blade sharp, but my vodka kept me warm, cheeks flushed, feet and tongue numbed. I'd heard Dior coming, of course; boots crunching up the snow-clad slope. I'd smelled her too, but the bottle I'd demolished thankfully kept most of my thirst at bay, and the rest of it so repulsed me that I shoved it back, slammed the door inside my mind, cursing it and myself besides.

"Dior drifted now out of the dark, wrapped in the coat I'd gifted her, eyes shining above the scarf about her face.

" 'What are you doing out of bed?' I growled.

" 'Thought you'd want a rest.'

" 'Sleep when you're dead.'

" 'Thought you'd want some company, then. Grumpy prick.' Lighting one of her black cigarelles, she leaned against a rot-riddled ash beside me. 'Seen anything?'

" 'Savior of the Empire. Slayer of a Forever Prince.' I frowned at her. 'Those smokes are a good way to ruin your dazzling beauty, by the way. And as for your so-called wit . . .'

"Dior flipped me the Fathers. 'Bastard.'

" 'You realize I take that as a compliment, no?'

"The girl gave a weak chuckle, and I, a weak smile in kind. And settling into thoughtful silence, she sighed a lungful of pale grey smoke. I could tell she was searching for words; some magikal combination of consonants and vowels that would set this aright. She might as well have been searching for rain in a cloudless sky.

"'I'm sorry, Gabe,' she finally sighed. 'About Aaron and Baptiste. I know you loved them. I know you'd give anything to . . .'

"She hung her head, and again my heart sank at the thought of my brothers' fates. But it wasn't her shoulders that deserved the weight of them. 'It's not your fault, Dior.'

"'Of course it is. Please don't pretend you're an idiot, Gabriel.'

"'I never pretend I'm an idiot. Those days I sound like I know what I'm on about? *That's* when I'm pretending.'

"The girl refused to smile, jaw clenched. 'Savior of the Empire, my arse . . .'

"'Oh, ye of little faith.'

"'*You're* one to talk.'

"'Touché. But I'm not totally bereft since I met you.'

"'Not sure why.' She scowled, breathing smoke like some dragon from a child's tale. 'You say I'm supposed to save this place, but it's worse than ever. And each night, mor—'

"'Have you noticed the way they look at you yet?'

"She blinked. 'Who?'

"'The little ones you saved from that cage.' I nodded to the hovel below. 'Those children just lost everything, Dior. But when they look at you, the one who risked all to save them, I see a spark in their eyes. It's a tiny thing. Frail as butterfly wings. But it's the foundation of *everything* to come. It's the gift you're going to give back to this empire.'

"'What gift?'

"I shrugged. 'Hope.'

"She squinted at me long and hard. 'How much have you had to drink?'

"'A skinful,' I grinned. 'Still not enough to lie to you, though.'

"Turning to the howling black, the girl dragged on her cigarelle. I could see the tension in her frame, the weight of the dark around her, the road before her, the blood inside her.

"'Where the hell are we going to go, Gabe? We can't just abandon these children.'

"'Way I see it, we have two options.'

"'All ears, you may consider me.'

"I breathed deep, looking into the wailing night. To the north, I felt the shadows of the Godsend, and south, the ravaged wastelands of Ossway. Eastward, the bitterbleak tundras of Nordlund awaited. But northwest, I could feel it. A tiny flame in this dark.

"'First option,' I sighed. 'We all seek sanctuary in the Barony of León.'

"Dior raised an eyebrow, whistling smoke. 'Still can't believe your grandfather's a baron. Some folk just get born with Angel Fortuna's lips on their cocks, don't they?'

"'Anytime you want to trade boots, Lachance, you just sing.'

"'He's still alive?'

"'Far as I know.' I scowled, shoulders hunched against the chill. 'I've never spoken to the old prick. He cast my mama out when she fell pregnant with me. But our young charges will be safe in the House of Lions. She's a cityfort on the coast. Good limestone walls. Garrison of a thousand men. Harder to get inside than an Ossian princess's chastity belt.'

"'I need to meet an Ossian princess,' Dior smirked. 'Always up for a challenge, me.'

"'Not many left these nights, by the sound of things.'

"She nodded then, smile fading. 'And our second option?'

"'Lachlan takes the children, and we continue on to the Nightstone with Celene.'

"'You think he's in the mood to do you favors? After the chat you had?' Dior's gaze turned sour. 'That was a very handsome face you just tried to kick in, you know.'

"I scowled, pawing at the blood in my stubble. 'He's had worse.'

"'I think you hurt his feelings.'

"'Lachlan's feelings aren't exactly top of my list of priorities right now, Dior. His blade at your fucking throat is.'

"'I'm not sure he'd do that. I mean . . . he doesn't seem the type.'

"'And Chloe did?'

"Her face fell at that, looking to her feet as she breathed grey.

"'I know you want to see the best in folk,' I said gently. 'But there's none more fearsome in their faith than sinners redeemed. Lachlan á Craeg was a boy raised in hell, Dior. It was my hand that saved his life, but the Silver Order gave that life *purpose*. And though I love him like a brother, once he learns what I did at San Michon . . .'

"'You mean what you did for *me*.'

"'And would do again.' I squeezed her hand. 'A thousand times over.'

"Dior dragged on her cigarelle, breathed grey into the awful, rising chill.

"'Phoebe is pressing me hard about heading to the Highlands. Her folk are gathering soon for some big festival called Wintermoot. The leaders . . . Riggan someone? Old She?' Dior shook her head, sighing grey. 'Anyway, she says I need to meet them.'

"'Rígan-Mor. Auld-Sìth. War-Maker and Peace-Bringer. Every Highland clan has a pair of them. All power up there is shared, see.'

"'They don't have kings or emperors?'

"'Once.' I shrugged. 'A warrior named Ailidh the Bold was the last. Stormbringer, they called her. She was a duskdancer who united the Highlanders about a century back. Led an army into southern Ossway. Conquered near half the country.'

"'Why only half?'

"I winced, rubbing my stubble. 'A silversaint assassinated her at the Emperor's command. That's one of the problems with queens and kings, Dior. The greatest suit of armor is only as strong as the buckle holding it in place. The Highlanders have been at each other's throats ever since. There's three bloodlines up there. Dozens of clans. Phoebe's kind are known as leófuil. *Cat-kin*. Then there's velfuil—*wolf-kin*—and úrfuil. *Bear-kin*. And they all get along about as well as you'd expect a pack of hungry carnivores would.'

"'Bloodlines?' Dior raised one brow. 'All the stories I've heard about 'dancers said you have to get bitten by one to become one.'

"'Horseshit.' I pulled up my sleeve, revealing the still-bleeding bite marks in my forearm. 'Duskdancer claws and teeth can end a vampire quick as silver. This'll leave a scar that'll last the rest of my days. But their curse is passed parent to child.'

"'Phoebe called this *the Time of Blighted Blood*. You know what that means?'

"'No clue. But blight and bullshit aside, the trek from here to the Highlands is seven shades of savage. And duskdancers *loathe* silversaints. I'll follow you to the end, Dior. You know that. But if you've any desire to avoid my brutal fucking murder, maybe we should give the mountains full of bloodthirsty heathens who hate my guts a miss.'

"'We're at least bringing Phoebe with us?'

"I raised one brow, noting her shift in tone. 'Made an impression, has she?'

"Dior shrugged, all innocence. 'Smarter to have her on our side than in our way.'

"'She's too old for you.'

"The girl blushed, pawing her hair down over her eyes. 'No harm in looking. What did she mean anyway? When she said there's a toll to pay for the dancing she does?'

"'Her claws. Her ears. Her shadow. The more a 'dancer takes the shape of her beast, the more the beast leaves its mark on her. Eventually, they lose themselves to it utterly. Trapped forever in the skin of animals.'

"'How d'you know all this if duskdancers are so rare you've never actually *met* one?'

"'Remember when I told you to give reading a try? The soldier arms herself in the smithy, Mlle Lachance. The empress, in the library.'

"Dior rolled her eyes. 'The right book is worth a hundred blades.'

"'Well said, my young 'prentice.'

"I glanced at her sidelong. Stubborn. Impulsive. Too softhearted for her own damn good.

"'Speaking of advice you don't listen to . . . I couldn't help notice you risking your narrow arse out on that ice today when I told you not to.'

"'You've got very good eyes for a man your age.'

"'I'm serious, Dior. I know you're keen to prove yourself, but you're t—'

"'Gabe, I'm not afraid of these bastards.' She turned to meet my gaze, fire in her own. 'And I'm not some wide-eyed babe with her thumb in her gob and shite in her pants. Seventeen years in this hole, I've learned how to take care of myself.'

"'. . . I thought you were sixteen?'

"'It was my saintsday five weeks ago.'

"'Why the hell didn't you tell me?'

"'I was inside a horse at the time.'

"'Oh. Well.' I shrugged. 'Happy saintsday, Mlle Lachance.'

"She scoffed, smiling at me through her mop of hair. 'Merci, Chevalier.'

"I patted my pockets, coming up empty. 'I don't have a gift. What the hell do you get the Savior of the Realm anyway . . .'

"My voice softened, then faded entirely. Standing taller, I peered into the gloom, my whole body tensed. Dior drew breath to question, but I held up a hand, and wisely, she held her tongue. Sobering swift, I drew Ashdrinker into the dark.

"*I was dreaming about . . . f-f-flowers. Roses of red and bells of silver. Do you remememember why they c-call violets* violets, *Gabriel? Weren't they b-b-b-blue?*

"'Wake up, Ash,' I whispered. 'We've company.'

"*. . . Invited?*

"'The other kind.'

"*Ohhh, delightlightlightful.*

"Though she knew not what troubled me, Dior was still all business, stubbing out her smoke and drawing her silversteel dagger from her sleeve. I nodded out into the wood, finger to lips, and crouching low, the pair of us stole through the black.

"Dior was quiet as an empty coffin—a knack she'd learned as a pickpocket in Lashaame. I was no slouch on the sneak myself, and I was too well-practiced to be stumbling after a single bottle of vodka. And so we moved, wraiths wending through the dark, off toward the sound I'd heard. It was muted under the howling wind, but still, unmistakable.

"Slow, shuffling footsteps.

"We slipped through dead and twisted trees, fungal blooms glittering like ice sculptures about us. I could hear it clear now, and Dior could too, the girl's grip shifting on her blade. And skirting west, past rotten oak and elm and ash, the corpses of kings that had ruled this little wood in brighter days, we finally found the source of the steps.

"'Wretched,' I breathed.

"Just one this time. Standing in a small clearing, shrouded in falling snow. I knew not if it was a straggler from the Dyvok attack, or just a rogue, wandering the wood alone. But either way, it was more trouble we didn't need.

"It'd been young when it was murdered, mid-twenties maybe. Lank hair was plastered to its skin, marbled with a web of dark veins. It was naked as its first saintsday, right arm hacked off at the elbow—probably a soldier in life. There were hundreds of those among the foulblood ranks; young men wounded on the battlefield, drained to death by the coldbloods they fought, and if they were unlucky, rising thereafter into hell on earth.

"We were upwind, side by side, safe as castles. Dior shot me a hopeful look, pointing to herself and making a stabbing motion. But I was hardly going to let the Grail of San Michon get into it with a coldblood after only two weeks of sword practice. I gave no shits if it was armless, toothless, and chained to an iron post with a target painted on its arse.

"I shook my head. *No.*

"Dior held up a single finger, disbelieving. *There's only one!*

"I glowered harder, putting my three years as a commander of the legions of Emperor Alexandre III—not to mention my decade as a father—to work in my scowl.

"*No, young lady.*

"Dior scowled right back. *You're not my papa, old man.*

"I could see the sharpness in her eyes, honed on gutter's edge and alley stones. It was true what she'd told me—she'd been looking after herself half a lifetime before I stumbled along. And I wondered, what the hell was I training her for, if not this?

"I breathed deep, sighed long. And finally, I tossed Ashdrinker through the air. With a fierce grin, Dior snatched the blade in her hand, gazing at the figure on the crossguard with admiring eyes. Testing the weight, her eyelids fluttered as she listened to the silver song in her head. I knew she was in safe hands; Ash and Dior had put an end to Danton Voss together, after all, and a bond ran between them now, deep as oceans.

"The coldblood was still sniffing the air, its back to us, filthy hair whipping in the wind. Skirting the clearing's edge, I checked my wheellock, cracked my neck. And with a glance to ensure my young 'prentice was ready, I stepped out to distract her foe. What happened next played out over maybe three or four seconds.

"But in truth, it'd change the rest of our lives.

"'Oi, twatgoblin!'

"The wretched whirled as I shouted, quick as winter chill. Dior was already dashing at the coldblood's flank, Ashdrinker raised high. But as a gust of wind whipped the hair back from the monster's hollow cheeks, my belly froze into a knot of oily ice.

"Its face was that of a thing long dead. Pallid, rotten, wasted. But down its brow, across its sunken eyes, I saw a thumbprint, smeared in fresh blood. And as it glanced to Dior, charging toward it through the night, its lips split in a ragged grin.

"'*There thou art.*'

"Ashdrinker fell like the hand of God. The wretched didn't even try to defend itself, Dead flesh parting like water under the girl's blow—a swift northwind strike from the arsenal I'd shown her. As it toppled in two pieces, smoking and scorched, Dior skidded to a halt in the bloody snow, gawping at the sword in her hands in near-disbelief. And glancing up at me, she grinned in triumph, squeaking loud as she dared.

"'Sweet bloody Mothermaid, *did you SEE THAT?*'

"The girl danced on the spot, twirling Ash in her hand as she leaned down to crow at the sundered corpse. 'Eat every *inch* of my shapely arse, you ugly f—'

"'Seven Martyrs,' I hissed.

"Dior paused her victory celebrations, glancing up at me. 'Eh?'

"My heart sank down into my boots, guts crawling up into my throat. I knew we'd be setting foot into the wolves' den as soon as we left the bounds of San Michon, yet a foolish part of me had hoped the wolves might not track us so swift. But looking to the deadwoods about us, then back to Dior's wondering eyes, I drew one shaking breath, and spoke with the fury and fear of a man who had the fate of the entire world cupped in his shaking hands.

"'Fuck . . .'

"I glowered about the darkness.

"'My . . .'

"I stared down at the corpse.

"'*Face!*'"

XII

NOTHING LASTS FOREVER

" 'WE NEED TO move,' I snarled.

"'Move, what d—'

"Dior yelped as I began dragging her down the slope, away from the foulblood she'd butchered. 'We need to move *now*.'

"'Gabe, I killed it, why are you bleating like a sheep on the rag?'

"But I paid her no mind, kicking in the door to the fisherhovel with a bang.

"'Ware! Up now, all of you!'

"Celene snaked upright, Lachlan springing to his feet, hand to his borrowed blade. The children were a mixed bag; some crying out in alarm, others pawing at the sleep in their eyes. But I saw that Isla had returned after her little outburst, and the Ossian lass took one look at my face and started dragging the younger ones to their feet. Confused but apparently still a pragmatist, Phoebe was already snatching up armfuls of possessions.

"'Gabe?' Lachlan called. 'Aright?'

"'No,' I snapped, hefting tackle and knapsack. 'Move your arses, soldiers!'

"'Gabe, what the *hell* has got into you?' Dior demanded from the doorway.

"'They saw us. They saw *you*.'

"'They? Who the fucking hell is *they*?'

"'What newsss, Gabriel?' Celene demanded.

"But I paid my sister no mind, grabbing our gear and hustling our young charges back out into the screaming wind. Our sosyas were asleep, Pony snorting in disgust as I threw her saddle atop her back and turned to Dior with hand outstretched.

"'Get up here. Now.'

"The girl complied, frustration rising as she climbed atop her mare and snapped. 'It was *one* wretched, Gabriel! And I killed it! One shambling bag of mindless—'

"'*Not* mindless,' I spat. 'Dead that far rotted can't think for themselves, let alone *speak*. Something else was in its head, Dior.'

"She paused at that, swallowed hard. 'Speaking for it.'

"'Vosssss,' Celene hissed, searching the dark around us.

"I nodded. 'Ironhearts can bend the minds of the wretched. Direct them with a thought on the battlefield. But their ancien aren't limited to commanding the lesser Dead. They can *ride* them, Dior. Mind in mind. As simple as you ride that damned mare.'

"Phoebe scowled. 'Why would they—'

"'Scouts,' I replied. 'Voss don't step blind into danger when they can send others to spot it for them. There's none more terrified of dying than those who live forever.'

"'Aye,' Lachlan murmured, kohled eyes on Dior. '*Especially* if one of us has got the ashes of Fabién's bonny boy on their boots aready.'

"Dior met my eyes, fear finally overcoming anger. 'Is it . . . *him?*'

"'I've no fucking intention of finding out. But we need to move. They're close.'

"Phoebe frowned. 'Close? If these Voss can ride rottens across the empire—'

"'Not the empire, flessshwitch,' Celene said. 'Even the ssstrongest Ironheart can only ride a puppet forty, perhapsss fifty miles.'

"'Forty miles,' Isla breathed, glancing over her shoulder. 'Oh, *God . . .*'

"Lachlan stepped to my side, our quarrel forgot, murmuring so the children wouldn't hear. 'We could head back to Aveléne? Defend there? The walls are intact at least.'

"'There's still the Dyvok to fear. And there's no *we* here, Lachie.'

"My old 'prentice met my eyes, his own narrowing to knifecuts. 'Ye don't mean—'

"'That's exactly what I mean. You're taking these children with you to San Michon.'

"'Yer out of your mind, Gabe. I'll not aband—'

"'Whatever's on our tails will be coming hard, brother. We've not horses enough for the little ones, and they sure as hell can't make the trek alone. Leave us to it.'

"'There could be a fuckin' army comin' for all ye know. Ye'll need my—'

"'Dead armies travel on foot, Lachie. If anything catches us, it'll be highbloods on thralled horses.' I mustered a smile for my old friend's benefit. 'This isn't my first grand ball, brother. I taught you all the steps. Trust me, what's the worst that could happen?'

"'They ignore ye completely and just ride after us?'

"'. . . Aright, what's the second worst that could happen?'

"'They butcher ye like a Firstmas hog and ride us down anyway?'

"I scratched my chin. 'That's probably worse than the first thing.'

"'This is no bloody *jest*, Gabe!'

"I took his arm, leading him out of earshot, gesturing at our little band. '*Look* at them, Lachie. They won't last a heartbeat against a pack of hungry Ironhearts. But you can run for safety while I lead the Dead away. The Voss are after *us*, not a passel of children.'

"'Aye?' His gaze flickered to Dior, back to me. 'And why might *that* be?'

"'Fuckssakes, why doesn't *matter*! What matters is they've a better chance breaking for San Michon with you. God's truth, I wish it otherwise. You know damn well there's no one under heaven I'd rather have with me in a scrap.' Here I glanced to Celene, to Phoebe, lowering my voice further. 'But you're the only one here I trust to lead these children to safety.'

"Lachlan clenched his jaw, gazing around the riverbank at the now-terrified children. I searched his eyes then, offered my hand; the same hand that had dragged him up from the abyss I'd found him in, all those years ago.

"'Have faith in me now, Lachlan. As you did back then.'

"My old 'prentice breathed a heavy sigh. He glanced once more to Dior, sharp green eyes burning with question, suspicion, uncertainty. But reluctantly, he nodded.

"'Aright. For ye, brother.'

"And as I sighed with relief, he finally shook my hand."

"Bravo, Silversaint."

Gabriel glanced up as the historian spoke, his brow darkening. The scratching of Jean-François's pen had momentarily ceased, the vampire offering a polite smatter of applause.

"For what, exactly?"

The historian raised his hands, as if to placate a guest for insult not yet given.

"Understand I've no desire to offend . . ."

"Oh, heaven forbid."

". . . But even you must admit that you are hardly the subtlest of protagonists, de León. Yet every now and then, you wield a deftness of touch even the Ilon might envy."

"The fuck are you on about?"

Jean-François lowered his voice, doing a passable impression of Gabriel's. *There's no one under heaven I'd rather have with me in a scrap. But you're the only one here I trust to lead these children to safety.* The vampire scoffed, ruby lips curled. "A performance worthy of the Théâtre D'Or in Augustin. It was not that you trusted your old apprentice to protect those children from peril. You simply didn't trust *him* around Dior. And in order to untangle your silver cub's eager little paws from your pretty hair, you lied right to his face. A man you called *brother*. A man who still thought of you as a hero, despite it all."

The Last Silversaint crossed his legs, fingertips drumming on his boot.

"Better to be a bastard than a fool."

Jean-François smiled. "You are not a bastard, de León. You are a *cunt*."

"Well. You are what you eat, vampire."

"Charming."

"My wife certainly thought so."

The vampire chuckled and dipped his quill, turning to a fresh page.

"Led by the older children," Gabriel continued, "the little ones began trudging upriver—silent and sad, but clearly grateful to be gone. Chinfuzz shook my hand as he departed, Isla nodded to me and mumbled apology, others gifted Dior sad smiles or solemn bows. Little Mila hugged my leg tight, lifting her doll's hand to wave at Phoebe.

"'Bye, Kitcat.'

"'Au revoir, Mlle Mila,' I said, kissing her brow. 'Look after Lachlan for me, eh?'

"The aforementioned lifted the girl up onto Nugget's back, storm clouds above his head. I knew sending him away was wisdom, but still, this parting was a wound, worsened by the knowledge of what awaited him at San Michon.

"'Au revoir, Lachie,' I said, embracing him tight. 'Walk safe in the light.'

"'And ye.' He patted my back, clearing his throat as he broke our embrace. 'Gabe, what I said before . . . about Astrid. She's a fine woman. It was wrong—'

"'No harm, brother. Water beneath the bridge for friends like you and I.'

"He smiled weakly, looking north. 'Any message for Greyhand or the others?'

"My stomach dropped at that, the wind blowing a different kind of cold.

"'Lachie, when you get back to the monastery . . .'

"He raised a brow as my voice faded. 'Aye?'

"I looked to Dior. To my blade. Again, I felt that urge to confess all I'd done, to wash some of that blood from my hands. But I knew sure and true what would come of it.

"'Raise a glass for me with the brothers, eh?'

"He smiled, slapped my shoulder fondly. 'Aye. There's still plenty of us who speak of ye fondly, despite all that happened. The Black Lion will always bleed silver.'

"Turning to Dior, my 'prentice drew the longblade from his belt.

"'Told ye I'd return it in one piece, lass. My thanks for its keeping.'

"The girl looked from the gleaming silversteel to the frightened children around us, back to the silversaint's eyes. 'You hold on to it, Frère. Keep them safe with it.'

"Lachlan's gaze was clouded as he looked the young girl over, toe to crown. But with a smile that might make angels swoon, he finally sheathed her blade.

"'I vow it.'

"The group departed, threading back upriver, into the rising dark. I was heavy with guilt, raising my hand to Lachlan in farewell. I'd no knowing what peril they'd meet on their frozen road, but as I'd said—those children had a better chance with him than with us. The feeble dawn was approaching and with it, the monsters who pursued Dior. Princes of Forever or a Forever King, I knew not. But I owed them vengeance, either way.

"I could see them now in my mind's eye, gathered like vultures outside my home the night their dread father came knocking. Kestrel. Morgane. Alba. Aléne. Ettiene. Danton. Devils all, cloaked in menace and malice, come to witness the Forever King's vengeance for the murder of their youngest sister, Laure.

"They'd stood and watched while he did it. They'd *laughed* as my angels died. And I'd sworn I'd see every one of them dead for it. But I focused on the ink across my fingers, scribed by the woman I loved in honor of the beauty we'd created. And her name was the prayer I whispered to drown out the roar for revenge in my head.

"'*Patience* . . .'

"I climbed aboard Bear, Phoebe slipping up onto Pony behind Dior, Celene's eyes fixed on me. Lacing my collar about my face, I spoke.

"'Let's be off. Sunset waits for no saint, and the Dead run quick.'

"'What direction is the question?' Phoebe said.

"Dior breathed deep, gaze roaming from Celene, to Phoebe, to me. I could see the choices before her, all the paths she might take. Southward to the war-torn wastes of Ossway, and the protection Phoebe promised in the Highlands. Northwest to León, a fortress that offered safety, but none of the answers she needed. Or west toward Master Jènoah and whatever truth and peril that trusting my sister would bring.

"To risk her life. Or risk the world.

"For a girl like Dior Lachance, a choice like that was no choice at all.

"She pulled her scarf up over her face, looked me in the eye, and spoke the word that would doom us all.

"'West.'"

The Last Silversaint fell silent, eyes on the goblet in his tattooed fingers. He studied the ink below his knuckles, the name of the daughter long gone. Jean-François was sketching in his book—finishing his portrait of Gabriel while his prisoner collected his thoughts. But eventually, the vampire frowned in the creeping silence.

"De León?"

"It's a hell of a thing," the silversaint murmured. "Being a father. You want to shield your children from the worst of the world, even though you know that'll leave them unprepared for what they'll find. But the sooner you let them see the horror of it all . . ."

"Oui?"

The silversaint stared into the bottom of his goblet, his voice soft.

"Do you remember your father, coldblood?"

". . . I beg your pardon?"

"Your father. You didn't spring from your mama's purse full-formed by magik."

Jean-François glanced up, annoyance darkening his eyes. That he felt annoyance—that he felt *anything* where his father was concerned—irked the vampire all the more. A half dozen rebukes rose swift to his tongue before he remembered his mother's counsel.

He feels a kinship with thee, sweet Marquis.

One a clever wolf might turn to advantage . . .

"I remember him," the historian replied. "Though not with much fondness."

"You *do* strike me as something of a mama's boy, vampire."

"If ever you have the fortune to meet my dark mother, de León, you will be left with absolutely no misapprehensions as to why."

Gabriel smiled, crossing one long leg over the other. "Who was Papa, then? Some fat baron or sodden lord? You've the look of one from monied stock."

"Look closer, then," Jean-François replied, setting aside his quill. "My papa was a farmer from the squalid outskirts of San Maximille. Not a brass royale to his name."

"Bullshit. You've never done an honest day's work in your life."

"I admit that I proved somewhat impervious to the rustic charm of the provinces at an early age." The Marquis smiled. "Papa was . . . enthusiastic with his remonstrations."

"He beat you?"

"Some would say *beat*. Some *tortured*. It is a complicated thing, is it not? The struggle between fathers and sons?"

"Try fathers and daughters," Gabriel scoffed.

"From what you have told me of your life, de León, I would rather not."

The smile died swift in the silversaint's eyes, faded slower from his lips. Sitting straighter, he downed the last of his wine, scowling as if it tasted bitter. The room seemed suddenly chill, that ghost-white moth flitting about the chymical globe again, and Gabriel snatched it up in his hand, swift as a knife in the dark.

The Marquis cursed himself. He knew he must tread softer here.

"Apologies, Gabriel. That was a poor jest."

The silversaint opened the cage of his fingers, and the moth fluttered free again.

"Truth is the sharpest knife," he replied.

The moth returned to its futile courses, beating frail wings in vain upon the globe's false starlight. Jean-François looked toward the cell door. "Meline?"

The lock clunked, the door swung aside, and there his majordomo stood, ever-dutiful. Clad in her long black gown, red curls cascading over pale shoulders, Meline dropped into a deep curtsey, her emerald eyes downturned.

"Your desire, Master?"

"More wine for our guest, dove."

"Your will be done." She risked a glance upward, ruby lips parted. "And for you?"

The vampire's mouth quirked in a dark smile. "Later, my darling."

Meline curtseyed again, swept from the room. The vampire and his pris-oner were left alone once more, air hanging chill, darkened by the shadow of an empty lighthouse and the murmurings of still-remembered ghosts.

"I ran away."

The Last Silversaint looked up from his goblet. "What?"

"From Papa. I ran away." Jean-François studied his long fingernails, scratching at an imaginary speck. "I was young. Foolish. I thought to find ap-prenticeship with an artiste of repute. And so I set out for the fabled streets of Augustin, there to seek my fortune."

"Did you find it?"

"She found me, Gabriel."

A knock rang on the cell door.

"Come, love," Jean-François called.

His majordomo slipped back into the room with a fresh bottle. Jean-François watched Gabriel watching Meline as she leaned forward to fill his goblet. The silversaint's storm-grey eyes roamed the treasures swelling abun-dant above her corset, the curve of her collarbone and the artery thudding at her throat. Jean-François could tell his prisoner was inflamed at the sight; shifting in his chair now, pulse thumping ever harder. The vampire's eyes drifted from the straining buttons at the silversaint's crotch to those strong, callused hands, the memory of them around his neck slipping unbidden into his mind.

"Scream for me."

"Will there be anything else, Master?" his majordomo asked.

"Not yet, love," he smiled. "Not yet."

Meline curtseyed, departing in silence. Gabriel downed his glass, met the Marquis's eyes over the goblet's edge, heartbeat thick in the air with whispers of what might be.

"Why did you run?"

The vampire blinked. "I beg pardon?"

"Why did you run away from your father, Chastain?"

"I think not, de León," Jean-François smiled, patting the tome in his lap.

"My Empress already knows my story, after all. Call it the will of the Almighty, or the vagaries of cruel chance; the fate of this empire undying rested not upon the shoulders of a humble farmer's son, but a baronne's bastard from the spires of San Michon, and a whore's daughter from the gutters of Lashaame."

"And a dreamer from the Highland snows." Gabriel drummed his fingers on his leathers, leaned back in his chair. "A princess never meant for a throne. A conspiracy of holy fools. And a king who wanted an empire that lasted forever."

Gabriel smiled.

"Except *nothing* lasts forever."

"Your tattered company made it safe to the Nightstone, then? Duskdancer and vampire, fallen chevalier and Holy Grail?"

"Oh, we made it to our destination. But safe? Even without the Voss dogging our heels, we were entering the world of the Esani now, vampire. The lies at the heart of it all. The Aavsenct Heresy. The Red Crusades. The Wars of the Blood."

The Last Silversaint shook his head.

"None of us would ever be safe again."

BOOK TWO

SHADOW

OF THE SON

A broken line of sorcerers and cannibals, damned even among the damned. Spit their name from thy tongue as thou wouldst the blood of pigs, and guard thine own blood lest they wrest it from thy veins:

Esani. The Faithless.

—Lûzil the Tongueless
Nightfall in Elidaen, a bestiary

I

CAIRNHAEM

" 'OH, LOOK!' I roared. 'Another impassable chasm, how lovely!'

"We stood on the crest of a frozen rise, looking into the ink-dark drop below. Chill wind snapped and bit at our skin, howling up the treacherous mountain pass behind. From her seat on the saddle behind me, Celene snarled into the howling gale.

"'Cease your wretched whining, brother!'

"'I'm not whining, I'm bellyaching—there's a difference!' I dragged my coat tighter about myself and scowled. 'You want to hear me whine, just wait 'til my vodka runs out!'

"'We await the day with bated breath!'

"'The Voss must be right on our arses by now. Where the *hell* is this place?'

"'We seek a creature old as centuriesss! A being whose name is a *whisper* among a cabal who call the shadowsss home! And you complain he is difficult to find?'

"'Damn right I do, I'm freezing my jollies off!'

"'Would that your tongue shared their fate!'

"Dior wailed, head bowed against the blinding snow. 'I can't feel my bloody feet!'

"I shook my head, teeth chattering as we turned about. 'I can't feel my *anything*!'

"Such had been our lot for a fortnight. After parting with Lachlan, we'd set off at a gallop, stabbing westward, desperate to stay ahead of the Ironhearts at our backs. The cold was blistering, but our beasts were Talhosti stock, and more, over three nights, Celene had fed both her blood. I was wary of thralling our beasts to my sister, but God's truth, we needed the pace, and bolstered by her strength, Bear and Pony carried us across the cold tundra of Nordlund, through the frozen Scarmoors, and into the Nightstone Mountains.

"The path up those grim peaks was rough from the outset—miles of snow-capped rubble and jagged, deathly chill. Ever since daysdeath, the snows of Elidaen had fallen grey, not white as in winters of my youth. The noon skies were dark as dusk, and the whole mountain range seemed shrouded in freezing ash, reeking of brimstone.

"I tried to keep the mood light, griping with Dior as we climbed ever higher, horses forging shoulder-deep through the frozen grey. But the dread of not knowing what awaited us, coupled with the threat of the highbloods behind us, had me wound *tight*. We'd eluded the Voss thus far, but I knew it wouldn't be long before they ran us to ground. As we fled higher into clawing winds and deepening snow, our supplies were dwindling, along with our spirits. We were running out of time."

"And liquor?" Jean-François smiled.

"Oui." Gabriel sighed, topping up his goblet. "Fucking nightmare."

"'Why is this bastard hiding all the way up here anyway?' Dior shouted.

"Celene answered behind me, her long dark hair whipping about my face. 'The Faithful have ever been creatures of the ssshadows, chérie. But have no fear. Our Master Wulfric told usss the markersss by which Master Jènoah might be found.'

"'I thought he was a damn vampire?'

"'By Master Wulfric's accountsss, Jènoah was *the* vampire. Second only to Mother Maryn among the warriorsss of the Esana.' Celene shook her head, looking up the broken black slopes. 'It is said he was a blood-drenched horror in his youth. A peerlesssss swordsman and terror of the night, undefeated in a thousand battles. His name was whispered in terror by his foes, and in awe by the Faithful.'

"'Well, then, doesn't he need blood to survive?' Dior demanded. 'We haven't seen a living thing in days! What the hell does he eat all the way up here?'

"'What indeed?' I growled.

"Celene met my stare as I glanced over my shoulder. I could still recall the sight of her drinking Rykard to dust on the Mère. The ecstasy on her face as the awful wound Laure had left her with diminished. The words she spoke as the lust faded from her eyes.

"'*By this blood, shall we have life eternal.*'

"It was a line from the Book of Laments. The covenant the Redeemer made with his followers—that through his sacrifice, their souls would be saved. I still knew not exactly what I'd witnessed that day, but I recalled my youth in San Michon; stolen moments in the library with Astrid and Chloe. My beloved had been the first to discover the name of the Esani bloodline, hidden in the pages of a bestiary long forgot. But that tome had described my forebears by another word, far grimmer.

"*Cannibals.*

"'All will be made clear, chérie,' Celene promised. 'We know you have questionsss. But in Master Jènoah's hallsss shall we have sanctuary, and you, the answers you sssseek.'

"Dior shivered, glancing about. 'I just hope he's not g-going to be too upset when we come knocking. He seems to have g-gone to an *awful* lot of trouble to avoid guests.'

"My sister's eyes twinkled. 'Your visssitation will be as an angel from heaven. If only you understood what your coming truly meansss.'

"I nodded, drumming Ash's hilt. 'Just so long as *we* understand each other, sister.'

"'Perfectly,' she replied. 'Brother.'

"The air crackled between us all; tension and distrust and dark foreboding. If this journey proved a fool's wager, I'd soon be filling a fool's grave. But Dior blinked then, sitting taller, a smile banishing the cloud over her head as she cried out in joy.

"'Phoebe's back!'

"I squinted through the blinding snows, and oui, here came the dusk-dancer, returning once more from her scouting. Phoebe wore the shape of her beast as she'd done for a week now, rust-red and cutting the grey like a sword. By some measure of her dark magiks, the lioness seemed little affected by the elements; despite her weight, she came bounding across the *top* of the snows rather than sinking into them, leaving no tracks in her wake. Dior shouted, waving and grinning at the sight of her.

"The pair had ridden together on the first leg of our journey, which I fear hadn't done much to relieve Dior of her unrequited crush. But the duskdancer moved faster, saw keener in her wealdshape. And though she'd seemed none pleased about it, once we reached the Nightstone, Phoebe had stripped herself bare by the fire, and with the vow 'See ye when I'm lookin' at ye,' ran off naked into the gloom. I'd heard footsteps receding, a shift in tempo, as if where two feet had once fallen, now fell four. And thereafter, we saw only the she-lion; a blood-red shadow on ash-grey snows.

"I found that odd, truth told—for the rest of our journey, Phoebe never once changed back to exchange a word or human moment. Her manner was akin to a big cat's while in her wealdshape; one minute warm and playful, the next completely aloof, and looking into her golden eyes around the fire each night, I found it hard to believe there was a woman inside there at all. After the sun rose, she'd be gone for hours, sometimes a day, but ever she returned at dusk, sleeping by the side of the girl she'd sworn to die defending.

"Dior jumped off Pony's back as Phoebe pranced toward us now, the girl laughing as the duskdancer pounced and brought her down into the snow.

"'What newsss, fleshwitch?' Celene asked.

"Phoebe looked up from sporting with Dior, huffing the frost from her snout. Her eyes narrowed, tail switching side to side as she stared at my sister like an especially annoying mouse. But finally, she shook herself nose to tail and peered off to the south.

"'She's found something,' I realized.

"The duskdancer growled and met my eyes. And licking the frost from her jowls, she bounded across the snow again, light as feathers, turning and waiting for us to follow.

"Follow we did, on through the blinding grey. The winds pushed us back, as if the skies themselves counseled against our coming here, and for the thousandth time, I wondered if I were a fool. A part of me wanted the answers Celene had promised Dior too; my father was of the Esani line, after all. But always in my head came the maxim I'd learned as a boy, the words that had steered me true through nights of war and blood and fire.

"*Dead tongues heeded are Dead tongues tasted.*

"We struggled on after Phoebe, the morning sun disappearing behind the wall of a gathering storm. The Voss were doubtless close to our heels now, and there were still the Dyvok to fret on. But here we were, blundering about like—

"'There!' Celene cried. 'Look!'

"I squinted into the gloom, one hand shielding my eyes from the wind's claws.

"'Seven Martyrs,' Dior whispered. 'Are those . . . giants?'

"'Oui,' I breathed in wonder. 'But not the sort who'll grind your bones for bread.'

"They rose up from the snow before us as we climbed out of our saddles, silhouetted against the rumbling heavens. Buried to the thighs, still they towered far above our heads. God knew how long ago they'd been carved, hewn by impossible hands from the very bones of the Nightstone itself. Ageless and beautiful, caked in frost; statues of cold dark granite.

"The first was an elderly man, his beard long and his hair flowing free. He wore a robe, carved with such skill it seemed almost to ripple in the shrieking winds. His right hand was pressed to his heart and his left was outstretched, palm upturned and empty.

"'The Father,' Celene whispered, head bowed in reverence.

"The second was a young man, alike in features to his elder, but crueler of expression. His beard was trim, his eyes fierce and fearless. He wore archaic armor, held a sword and a helm, encircled with a crown. It was strange to see him such—most oft, he was depicted upon the wheel in the moment of his death. But this statue showed him not as he'd died, but as he'd *lived*. A warrior. A leader. A would-be conqueror.

"'The Son,' Dior breathed, frost at her lips.

"Almighty and Redeemer. Father and child. The God who made this world, and the savior who'd founded his church upon it. The statues were beautiful, awful, and I wondered what manner of thing had carved them. Dior was staring up at the younger, questions in her eyes. She was of his line, after all. Bearer of his holy blood. But she was also a gutter-rat, a thief and trickster, as far from a warrior king as one could be and still be breathing.

"And yet . . .

"Phoebe's snarl snatched my attention, dragging my eyes away. The lioness stood atop a ridge at our backs now, staring down the frozen pass behind, hackles rippling. Reaching into my greatcoat, I raised my spyglass. And there, in the grey distance . . .

"'Well, well,' I breathed. 'God pisses in our porridge at last.'

"'Gabe?' Dior called. 'What is it?'

"I turned toward her, that child who slew the Beast of Vellene with her own two hands, standing in the shadow of her ancestor. I tossed my spyglass, and she snatched it from the air, lifting the glass to her eye. And a cold curse slipped her lips as she saw what Fabién had sent in his baby boy's wake.

"'Seven bloody Martyrs . . .'

"They were maids, a pair of them, sat atop dark horses on the ridge far below. Willow tall, sharp chins and sharper cheeks. Their hair was long and straight as swords, cut in severe fringes above their lashes, and though the stormwinds howled about them, not a single strand of it moved in that rising gale. They wore jodhpurs, knee-length boots, and both carried riding crops in hand. Elegant coats were cut in a feminine style, and each wore a slash of crimson paint on her lips; like knifewounds in those beautiful, terrible faces.

"They raised their hands in unison toward us, though where one pointed with right hand, the other pointed with left. It was as if each was a reflection of the other, not only in movement, but seeming. For the first had black hair, ebony skin—a daughter of the Sūdhaemi plains. The second's hair was ash blond, her skin marble—a child of the Elidaeni mountains. Their cloth they wore for contrast, light on dark, dark on light. But the eyes of both were bottomless pools, flooded utterly black by the uncounted centuries they'd walked this earth with deathless feet.

"'God help usss,' Celene whispered behind me.

"White-hot rage coursed my veins as I shook my head. 'He's not listening, sister.'

"Alba and Aléne Voss. The Terrors. The Forever King's eldest children. Creatures so ancient, none could say how old they truly were. Some rumor held it they'd been Voss's first victims; virgin priestesses plucked but a few nights after Fabién himself Became. Others whispered they were hunters of the dark; sorceresses sent to kill him, instead bested and corrupted by his blood. Whatever the truth yesterday, they were creatures of impossible power today, almost equal of the dread father who'd set them on Dior's trail. And now . . .

"'They found me,' she whispered.

"The Terrors spurred their horses, coats flowing behind them as they sped like arrows across the snows toward us. With a curse, I watched Dior bound forward onto Pony's back, my heart pounding like a war drum.

"'We are close!' Celene called. 'We will be sssafe once we reach Cairn-haem! No child of Voss dares ssset foot upon Esana's sacred ground!'

"'Ride!' I bellowed.

"And so we did. As if all hell came behind us, thunder rumbling as storm clouds seethed above. I rode hard, paleblood eyes watering in the chill, Dior and Pony galloping beside me. Phoebe dashed out in front, sleek and bloody red, Celene clinging to my back, whispering under her breath in a cadence I finally recognized as a prayer; the old Benediction for Battle that Greyhand had taught me back in San Michon.

"'*The Lord is my ssshield, unbreakable.*'

"On through the bitter-bleak day.

"'*He is the fire that burnsss away all darkness.*'

"On through the deepening snows.

"'*He is the tempest rising that shall lift me unto paradise.*'

"On through the wind, the chill, the fear, we rode. Our beasts were terrified, and I could feel it also—a weight hung in the very air now. It seemed as if the storm above were alive, yet a stillness gripped my heart, a *wrongness* as we galloped onward, *onward*, thunder cracking above and the black wind screaming ahead like the voices of the damned.

"*Go back*, it cried. *Back while ye may.*

"*The living are not welcome here.*

"'Gabe?' Dior called.

"'I feel it too,' I told her.

"I reached out toward her, brushing the tips of her fingers.

"'I've got you,' I promised.

"Dior smiled, thin and frail. 'I've got *you*.'

"Lightning struck the sky, a blade of blinding white slicing the gloom to ribbons. And in that brief flash of brilliance, my sister raised one bloodless hand and called.

"'There!'

"Breathless, we pulled up our bone-weary horses. A cliff edge waited before us, begging a drop into a howling dark. A tower rose up from that gulf; a sheer granite spire, joined to the cliff's edge by a thin stone bridge. Below the span's arch hung iron gibbets, suspended on long chains over the wailing chasm below. Statuary lined the railings; saints and angels so lifelike, I fancied they'd not been carved, but *cursed*—bewitched by some fae trickery, turned from warm flesh into cold stone. And across that bridge . . .

"'Cairnhaem!' Celene cried, leaping down into the snow.

"In truth, it looked less a lair, and more a cathedral. Gothic towers stabbing the sky, windows of stained glass so beautiful they almost hurt the heart to see. Cairnhaem's design struck me hard—coldbloods were monsters spat straight from the belly of hell, and yet, this place wore the façade of holy ground. Its scale was awe-inspiring; it seemed not a church built for men, but gods, and I boggled at the genius, the will, the fucking *time* it must have taken to carve all this out of nothing . . .

"'How did this get here?' Dior breathed. 'How can this *be*?'

"'One can accomplish great things, chérie,' Celene replied. 'When one has faith.'

"'Great things,' I muttered. 'Or terrible ones.'

"I cast a wary glance over my shoulder, and though I could see no trace of the Terrors, I could *feel* them, coming on through the snarling snows. Yet riding across that bridge toward the safety Celene promised, my sense of unwelcome, that weight of dread, only intensified. My hand was on Ashdrinker's hilt the whole time, half-expecting the stone saints to spring to life, to tear us to pieces and cast us from the bridge into the gulf below.

"Breathless, frozen, we reached the span's end. Vast stairs led up to a pair of enormous doors, wrought bronze, corroded green with countless years. Above them, two massive disks were set in the stone, rimed with frost, ornate and beautiful—*clocks,* I realized. Yet as I climbed off Bear, I saw they tracked no hours nor minutes, but the movement of moons and stars, and the slow passage of *centuries.*

"The doors were slightly ajar. As if we were expected. An inscription was visible through the frost above them; a snatch of scripture from the Book of Vows.

"*Enter and be welcome, those who seek forgiveness in the light of the Lord.*

"Dior dismounted, trembling with cold and fear. 'D-do we knock, or . . . ?'

"'Follow,' Celene commanded. 'Sssay nothing, do *nothing* unless we bid you. Heaven only knows how long it has been sssince the master of this house had guests.' Celene glowered at me, eyes flashing. 'And God help anyone who draws steel in these hallsss.'

"'God help anyone who forces me to,' I replied, arm around Dior.

"'I mean it, brother. We dance now on razor's edge. The creature beyond these doors has seen the rise and fall of empiresss. He hasss tasted heaven in the Red Crusssade, and drunk ashess in the Warsss of the Blood. Ancien. Esana. Lieutenant to dread Maryn herself.' Dead eyes fell on Dior, shining with fervor. 'But he will teach you your truth, chérie. And this world shall find sssalvation from night eternal. We *know* it.'

"Phoebe growled, golden eyes fixed behind us.

"'I concur,' I said, glancing back down the bridge. 'Get the fuck on with it, Celene.'

"With a final, burning glare, my sister turned and squeezed through the doors. Phoebe followed, shoulders bunched, stalking like to prey. And hand in hand with Dior, my heart thumping, mouth dry, I stepped beyond the threshold and into Jènoah's church.

"Snow was piled high in the gap between the doors, spilling across the cold stone floor. A grand entry hall awaited, vast and circular and freezing, and the feeble light of my lantern spilled only a few dozen feet into the black. We saw a great hearth of dark stone, big enough to fit a carriage inside, flanked by blood-red drapery. Twin staircases arched about it like a pair of open arms, leading to the floor above. Hundreds of candelabra, pillars thick as trees, and on every wall, strangest of all, we saw . . . pages.

"'Seven Martyrs,' I whispered, lifting my lantern high.

"Illuminated pages, torn from the Testaments—thousands upon thousands of them. Different languages, different scripts, different parchments, but at heart, all the same. The entire room, every *inch* of stonework was plastered with the holy words of God.

"'Master Jènoah!' Celene was on bended knee, head bowed as she called. 'I am Celene, Liathe of Wulfric! We are come with dark tidingsss and joyousss revelation!'

"My sister's voice echoed on cold stone, into the hidden reaches overhead.

"'Master Wulfric is gone to his final rest! But we have not been idle sssince he fell!' My sister called louder into the dark. 'We have *found her*, Master! The one promised in the starsss! The Scion of Heaven! We have brought her to you, that ssshe might learn the truth of herself! To part the veil! To end this darkness, and save our damned soulsss!'

"No answer save the winds, the roll of hollow thunder.

"Celene lifted her head. 'Master?'

"Dior squeezed my hand, and despite Celene's warning not to, I found myself drawing Ashdrinker from her sheath. Lightning cracked the sky; a brief illumination spilling through stained glass. And as it faded, so too did hope.

"'Oh, God . . .' Dior whispered.

"*Death d–d–danced here . . .*

"I gripped Ashdrinker tighter as I stepped forward, lighting a nearby candelabrum with my flintbox. The light grew, adding to the illumination from our lanterns, and my belly sank toward the flagstones as it became clear where we stood.

"Not a sanctuary.

"A *cemetery.*

"Burn scars scorched the floors, the walls, charring the Testaments pages back to bare stone beneath. Old bloodstains were splashed across the walls. The dust of decades covered all, but worse, I now saw evening gowns and frockcoats, even a suit of ancient armor scattered across the foyer; all empty save for handfuls of cold, grey powder.

"Celene lifted her hands, brushing it from her palms.

"Not dust.

"'Ashesss.'

"'What happened here?' Dior asked.

"My sister hung her head. Her fingers curled closed, her whole body trembling. She slammed a clenched fist into the floor, shattering the marble flagstone into a hundred pieces, and my heart ran chill as I truly understood the depth of our failure. Dior gazed about, crestfallen, and looking into her eyes, I saw the truth now dawning. After so much risked, after so much promised . . .

"'He's fucking dead, isn't he?'"

11

THE FIRE BURNS

" 'HELLO?'

"'*Hello? Hello?*'

"Dior called again, hands to her mouth. 'Oi!'

"'*Oi! Oi!*' came the reply, off in the dark.

"We stood in the quiet of Cairnhaem, naught to break that dreadful still but the thunder outside and our own echoes within. Celene had stalked off alone, obviously in no mood for company. Phoebe and I were still well aware of the Ironhearts who pursued us, and with a nod to me, the lioness had slunk back out into the storm, silent as smoke. And so, Dior and I roamed the château together, looking for answers in that quiet dark.

"Ashdrinker gleamed in the light of Dior's candelabrum as we searched those vast halls, but in my aegis, no light burned at all. We found an armory— ancient suits of plate and beautiful weapons arrayed in racks, all spackled with rust. A set of graven doors revealed a huge room with a checkered floor, and statues carved in the likeness of great chess pieces. Every surface was covered in dust and ashes. Every wall plastered with the word of God.

"Yet of the truths we sought in coming here, we'd found no word at all.

"We stood on the mezzanine of a grand library now, looking out on a sea of beautiful shelves and tomes, untouched for uncounted years.

"'Hello?' Dior called again.

"'*Hello?*' came the echo in the gloom. '*Hello?*'

"The girl stood on tiptoe, drew breath to shout again. 'Is anyb—'

"'Lower your voice, for fuckssakes,' I growled, grabbing her arm.

"Dior blinked. 'How will they hear me if I lower my voice?'

"'Sweet Mothermaid, girl, look around us.' I gestured to the dusty books, the empty halls. 'There's no one been in here for fucking years.'

— 155 —

"'Well, if there's no one to hear me, why would I lower my voice?'

"'If there's no one to hear you, why would you shout?'

"She shrugged. '. . . Because it's fun?'

"'Fun?' I scowled.

"'She smirked and shouted again. 'ECHO!'

"'*ECHO! ECHO!*'

"'Seven Martyrs.' I pinched my nose, sighing. 'The master of this place was supposed to *protect* you, Dior. He was *supposed* to teach you the meaning of all this, and he's good for bugger-all except gritting the garden path. The Terrors are likely only waiting for nightfall to strike us. Do you have any idea what's coming for you? Do you understand how deeply, spine-shatteringly *FUCKED* WE ARE?'

"'*FUCKED WE ARE? FUCKED WE ARE?*'

"The girl flinched as I shouted, the smile fading on her lips. Crouching on the stone and dragging her hair over her eyes, I still saw a little of the spark in them die.

"*Let her enj-j-joy herself, Gabriel,* came a whisper in my mind.

"I looked to the silvered dame in my hands, gleaming in the lanternlight.

"*She wears the smile to cover the b-b-bleed inside. That is her strength. Steal not what j-j-joy she finds, but rejoice she finds it at all. She thinks the world of ye. Would ye be the one who m-m-makes her burn brighter, or casts shadow 'pon her flame herflame?*

"I hung my head, ashamed at that. I was frustrated, aching with thirst, marveling at the mistake I'd made in bringing Dior here at all. But as always, my blade spoke true. And though this girl might think the world of me, she meant the same to me too.

"'Apologies!'

"'*Apologies! Apologies!*'

"Dior glanced up, scowling as I stood on tiptoe and shouted again.

"'Sometimes I'm something of a cunt!'

"'*Cunt! Cunt!*'

"The girl narrowed her eyes, lips twisting a little as she yelled. 'Prick!'

"'*Prick! Prick!*'

"I smiled. 'Wanktruffle!'

"'*Truffle! Truffle!*'

"Dior grinned, climbing to her feet and bellowing, 'Cockwombler!'

"'*Wombler! Wombler!*'

"'Fuckweasel!' I countered.

"'*Weasel! Weasel!*'

"'Twatgoblin!'

"'*Goblin! Goblin!*'

"'Oi,' I glowered, poking her chest. 'That one's mine.'

"'I know.' She grinned, fire burning once more in her eyes. 'I learned from the best.'

"'Come on,' I chuckled, tossing my head. 'Even if the master of the bloody house is dead, there must be *some* clue about all this Esani business in here. I'm buggered if I walked all the way to the Nightstones for nothing.'

"Dior lifted her light again, and we set out through Jènoah's lair, searching for some hint, some crumb, some scrap of wisdom. We found servants' quarters. A music room. Cold chambers and armoires shrouded in dust. The walls of Cairnhaem rumbled as thunder rolled, a gathering storm blotting out the daysdeath skies. But if that ancient keep held any answers about bringing the sun back to the heavens, they were well hidden indeed.

"'Why do they call them the Terrors?'

"I glanced to Dior as she spoke, her face underscored by dancing candlelight. Her voice was steady, her eyes ahead, not nearly as afraid as she should be.

"'You sure you want to know?' I asked.

"She nodded, just once. I took out my hipflask, downed a burning swallow.

"'The first city the Forever King conquered after he crossed the Bay of Tears was named Lucía. When Fabién's legion broke through the gates, he unleashed his children to have their sport, as was his way. The soldiery were slaughtered, the Baron killed—there seemed nowhere to run. And so, folk fled to the sanctuary of Lucía's grand cathedral. It was a magnificent place. Designed by the master Albrecht. Six centuries it had stood in the city's heart, and three thousand of Lucía's citizens squeezed into its hallowed halls. Desperate. Weeping. Praying. And that's where Alba and Aléne found them.

"'As butchery unfolded in the city around them, the Terrors made the folk in the cathedral a proposition. The twins could set fire to the roof, they called, and burn all those within to death. But they'd no desire to destroy an edifice of such beauty. And so, they promised half of the people within would be spared. If the other half were given up for slaughter.'

"Dior stopped walking, turned to meet my eyes. 'What happened?'

"I shrugged. 'Folk turned on each other, of course. Like rats in a sinking ship. For fear of death, of those teeth, the poor turned on the wealthy, the strong on the weak, the normal on the strange. Murder and mayhem erupted in the cathedral's heart, innocent blood washing the floor of God's house. Defiling it. *Profaning* it. Sacred ground no more.

"'And with nothing now to hold them at bay, Alba and Aléne Voss kicked in the cathedral doors and murdered everyone inside. Man, woman, and child.'

"I shook my head and sighed.

"'Terror is what they are, Dior. Terror is what they *do*.'

"She nodded slow, and though the fire still burned in her eyes, I hoped the tale instilled some sense of the darkness that was coming for her. We walked onward through long-abandoned galleries, furniture and tapestries all paled with time. A dining room was set with a dusty feast, the desiccated bodies of dozens of servants sat about it—all poisoned, by the look. Climbing higher, we found a palatial boudoir, wind howling through the chill peaks outside. I gazed at the grand four-poster bed, dreaming of just one night's decent sleep as Dior pushed through a set of grand double doors behind us.

"'Oh my *GOD*!' she cried.

"'What? What is it?'

"I shouldered past her, ready for bloodshed. Figures waited beyond; dozens silhouetted in the dark. I raised Ashdrinker with fangs bared, but my foes remained motionless. And squinting harder, I saw they were wrought not of flesh, but wood and iron.

"'More statues,' I realized, pulse still thundering.

"'Not statues,' Dior corrected, stepping in beside me. '*Clothesmen*.'

"'You almost gave me a fucking heart seizure, girl.'

"Dior mumbled a reply, incoherent, eyes wide as she peered around us. I saw now that we stood in the velvet and satin rows of a vast and kingly wardrobe; shirts and jackets and dresses and greatcoats of finest cut and richest cloth.

"'Great *fucking* Redeemer,' she whispered. 'Tell me I'm dreaming.'

"I shook my head, motioned back out to the hall. 'Come on. Let's keep moving.'

"The girl looked dumbfounded. '*Surely* you jest, Chevalier.'

"'Do I look like I'm jesting? It's only a few hours to sunset, we need to find—'

"'Gabriel de León.' Dior folded her arms, looked me over. 'You are currently wearing a greatcoat older than I am, wrapped in what appears to be the remains of a dead dog.'

"'It's a wolfskin. And who gives a fuck what I'm wearing?'

"'Me. *I* give a fuck. You may have been born the grandson of a baron, but take it from someone who wore rags and slept in gutters all her life.' Dior planted her candelabrum on the floor like a flag on a conquered shore. 'There are *always* fucks to give for fashion.'

"And turning, she dove in among the racks with joyful abandon.

"Dior soon emerged with armloads of fabric, tossing them to me before plunging back into the breach. I sighed, dragging off what I had to admit were leathers that had seen *far* better days. Candlelight gleamed across the silver ink on my skin as I shouldered my way into a black velvet shirt, a fine greatcoat of blood-red velvet with midnight-black trim. It was a handsome cut, ankle-length and lined with good fur—fashionable or no, it'd keep me a lot warmer than my old gear had. There were no mirrors in a coldblood's château to inspect the results, of course, but Dior soon emerged from the racks and put hands to hips, proudly declaring, 'You look *fucking* fabulous.'

"'Shut up.'

"'*You* shut up.'

"'Touché.'

"The girl had abandoned the clothes I'd given her—tattered and travel-worn after long miles and bloody months. She was now resplendent in an embroidered golden waistcoat, and a frockcoat and tricorn of lush, blue-grey damask. Performing a pirouette, she dropped into a curtsey and looked to me for opinions.

"'Not bad,' I conceded. 'Waistcoat's a bit showy.'

"'This is the nicest waistcoat I've ever worn in my life.'

"'Does that say more about your life or the waistcoat?'

"'Silence!' She raised a hand, imperious. 'Ruin this for me, ye shall not.'

"'Want to bet?'

"I grinned, and she laughed, and the warmth between us served to banish Cairnhaem's chill better than any greatcoat under heaven. We were hundreds of miles from nowhere, in the castle of a monster long dead. The answers we'd sought had been denied us, and the Terrors were only a sunset away. My thirst was growing, drowned only by a constant diet of sanctus and liquor, and my stores of both were running low. Hope seemed a distant star, lost in the darkness that had covered the skies since I was a boy. But looking into

Dior's eyes as she smiled, it wasn't so hard to remember how warm the sun had been.

"I fished inside the lining of her old coat, retrieved the phial of my blood that I'd given her. By the small tricks of sanguimancy I'd mastered over the years, I could still *feel* that blood, and I'd used it to track Dior in the past. The girl sighed, but made no objection as I broke the stitching of her new hemline, and slipped the blood inside.

"'Just in case,' I told her.

"Dior rolled her eyes, gave a long-suffering sigh. 'Oui, Papa.'

"We both stopped as she spoke that word. Meeting the other's eyes. The weight of it was lead, too heavy to carry, and I brushed it aside as I nodded to the hallway, gruff.

"'Come on. Your answers won't find themselves.'

"The girl nodded, squaring her shoulders and tossing me an overstuffed saddlebag. Peering inside, I saw emerald silk, pale fox fur, raising an eyebrow in question.

"'Something for Phoebe,' Dior explained.

"'Mlle á Dúnnsair doesn't strike me as the type, Dior.'

"'Because you lack *vision*, Chevalier,' the girl grinned.

"Her smile faded to a thoughtful pout, eyes drifting back to the fabrics around us.

"'We should get something for Celene too, I s'pose.'

"I looked at the ceiling above our heads, scowling.

"'Hell with Celene.'

"On we walked, through the dark and chill hallways of that silent crypt, no grand revelations or ancient wisdoms to be unearthed in any of them. But in the end, we climbed to the reaches of Cairnhaem's topmost level, and found a scrap of hope at least.

"Another set of mighty bronze doors loomed before us, embossed with twinned skulls on a towered shield. Beneath that sigil were wrought two words in Old Elidaeni, carved on a scroll in an ornate script. Recalling what I could of that now-dead tongue, I realized with cold dread that somehow I already *knew* these words; that some part of me had always known them. A voice in my head whispered of years long passed, of creatures long dead, of a legacy long forgot.

"'Do you remember the creed of Blood Voss?'

"Dior blinked at my strange question, answering by rote. '*All Shall Kneel.*'

"I smiled soft. 'And the Dyvok, my young 'prentice?'

"'*Deeds Not Words.*' She looked over the design on the door, blue eyes widening. 'Is that what *this* is? The sigil of Blood Esani?'

"I nodded, my fingers tracing the shapes of those graven skulls. 'I first saw it years ago, in the pages of a book Astrid discovered in San Michon. But I never noticed before.'

"'. . . Noticed what?'

"'Look close. What do you see?'

"Dior stepped nearer, brow furrowing. But her eyes were sharp and her mind sharper, and in the end, she spotted it, same as I. Clear as crystal water once unveiled, never to be unseen; a shape, wrought in the negative space between the skulls.

"'A cup,' she whispered. 'A chalice.'

"'No chalice,' I said, meeting her eyes. 'The Grail.'

"'Seven Martyrs.' She breathed deep, lips parted in wonder. 'What are the words?'

"I ran my fingers over the letters, their weight now thrumming in my veins.

"'*Judgment Comes.*'

"We pushed through the doorway, dead skulls seeming to stare at us as we passed, the image of the Holy Grail burning between them. And beyond the threshold awaited the strangest room we'd yet discovered in that silent tomb. It was huge. Freezing. The last thing a sane man might have expected to find in the lair of one of the damned.

"'A chapel . . .' I breathed.

"But no chapel I'd seen like of. A great circular room, echoing with the song of the rising storm. In its heart rested a round granite altar, ringed with stone pews. Above it hung a statue of the Redeemer, strung upon his wheel, and before it, like a penitent, knelt my sister, hands splayed upon cold stone.

"Unlike the rest of Cairnhaem, the walls of the chapel were not decorated with scripture, but a great bas-relief circling the entire room. Gazing about us, I saw hundreds of figures, clad in archaic armor and carrying standards of the One Faith. They were embroiled in some vast battle, fighting and killing and dying.

"'Gabriel,' Dior whispered. 'Their teeth . . .'

"Looking closer, I felt a chill run through me. For while they'd seemed as men and women at a glance, I saw now the canines of those warriors were long and sharp as knives.

"*Not teeth*, I realized. *Fangs.*

"Before the altar, I saw a stain on the ground, etched in black. A burn, I realized. A burn in the shape of a man. It was spread-eagled, mirroring the pose of the Redeemer above, nothing but ashes. My sister was knelt before those remains, head bowed as if in prayer, curtains of midnight-blue hair tumbling forward to hide her face.

"Upon the altar rested an open book; or the statue of one at least, wrought of the same dark stone. Stepping closer, Dior beside me, I saw the left page was etched with a familiar verse; that snatch of prophecy Chloe had taught me, back when all this began.

"From holy cup comes holy light;
"The faithful hand sets world aright.
"And in the Seven Martyrs' sight,
"Mere man shall end this endless night.

"The right page was similar to the left; another stanza once carved upon the stone. It had been smashed by some terrible blow, its pieces scattered in the dust long ago. And yet . . . on the very edge of that broken page, letters were still faintly legible among the cracks.

"'*This black* . . .' I squinted, trying to make out the words. 'Does that say *well?*'

"'*Veil*,' Dior whispered.

"She ran her fingers over the letters, trembling as she spoke.

"'This blackened veil shall be undone.'

"The girl looked up into my eyes, her own gone bright and wide.

"'The right book is worth a hundred blades.'

"This was it, then. The clue we'd come here seeking. It seemed there was another half to the prophecy, perhaps the answer to the riddle of all Dior must do. But the one who knew the whole of it lay in ashes on the floor, and the verse itself was shattered; our answers just beyond our reach. Dior sank to her knees, trying to piece together the tiny fragments, to make some sense of all this. I gazed around the bas-relief, those warring kith, armies of vampires slaying each other. I looked up to the statue of the Redeemer, so similar to the one in San Michon; all I'd done, all I'd risked coming here now ringing in my head.

"'What the *hell* is this, Celene?' I demanded.

"My sister was still knelt before those ashes, her voice hissing, hateful.

"'A sssin too monstrous to forgive.'

"Dior looked up from the broken pieces of the page, jaw clenched. 'Look here, I know it's what you do? But the cryptic deadgirl shite is wearing awfully thin, Celene.'

"My sister murmured, bowing her head deeper before the statue of the Almighty's son, making the sign of the wheel. And as she stood and turned toward us, I saw with astonishment that she was *weeping*—bloody tears streaming down her porcelain mask, staining her pale cheeks red as murder.

"'He killed them, Dior.'

"Celene's whisper trembled with impossible rage as she gestured to the floor. And there, beside the ashes where she'd knelt, I saw words daubed in old, black blood.

"This wait, too long.
"This weight, too heavy.
"Father, forgive me.

"'Master Jènoah,' Celene hissed. 'He took the lives of his servants and liathe, and then, he took his own. Committing the greatest sin, consigning himself to the fires of hell, and a thousand shriven souls along with him.'

"Dior shook her head. 'I don't understand . . .'

"'He could not bear it. The years. The burden.'

"Celene lifted her chin, resolute. She began pacing then, wringing her hands as she spoke her tumbling thoughts aloud, voice fraying at the edges.

"'But fear not, chérie. Jènoah was not the only Esana remaining, as I said. Mother Maryn herself residesss beneath Dún Maergenn, but a month's march from here. The journey will doubtlessss be perilous, but we c—'

"'I mean I don't understand *any* of it!' Dior roared, rising to her feet and gesturing to the carvings around us. 'What the hell *is* all this? What does it *mean?*'

"Celene stopped her pacing, lifting her eyes to Dior.

"'We do not have all the answersss, chérie.'

"'At this point, I'll settle for one!'

"'I am only liathe. I was not ssshown the path to your destiny, I do not—'

"'Oh, enough *bullshit*!' the girl shouted, her temper finally breaking loose. 'You've dragged us to the arse end of nowhere, and all we have to show for it are dust and ashes! The Voss will be on us like maggots on a corpse as soon as the sun goes down! Hell with my destiny, this is my *life*! Gabe's life! Phoebe's life!' Dior stepped forward, pale blue eyes burning now in fury. 'I don't give a shit about the pieces that are missing, I want the pieces you have! Right fucking now! Or we are done, Celene, you hear me?'

"My sister glowered at that, pale eyes hard as stone. Dior met that Dead stare, jaw clenched, gutter-hard and alley-born. I was surprised at her outburst, her frustration and fury. She was but seventeen years old, this girl, a few months of war under her belt, a few hundred miles, facing down a monster with the power of centuries at her fingertips.

"But in the end, for all that strength, it was Celene who lowered her gaze.

"My sister stared down at her empty hands.

"Hung her head and sighed.

"'We will tell you what we know.'"

III

FAITHFUL

THE LAST SILVERSAINT leaned back in his chair, crossing one long leg over the other as he brushed a lock of black hair from his eyes. Jean-François could feel the man watching as he drew smooth lines across a blank page; a portrait of grim Cairnhaem, its mighty towers wreathed in snow and mystery.

"Are you ready for this, vampire?"

"Ready for what, de León?" the Marquis asked, not looking up.

"Hard truths."

The vampire scoffed. "I was not aware there was any other kind?"

"I knew a man once. Père Douglas á Maergenn." The Last Silversaint lifted the bottle of Monét, topped up his goblet as he spoke. "He was a brother of the Order of Our Lady of Miracles. Accompanied the Nineswords' armies in the Ossian campaigns. Young fellow, about my age—I was barely more than a boy back then. And while I fancied myself a true believer, Père Douglas put my devotion to shame. He didn't even fight with a sword, the mad cunt; the only thing he carried into battle against the Dead and their minions was the silver wheel around his neck, and I tell you, that thing shone brighter than the aegis of most silversaints I've known. He was a beacon. A *flame* of faith. I asked him once how he managed it. How he could run at a wall of thrallswords barehanded without fear.

"'Why fear death?' he told me. 'When beyond lies the kingdom of God?'

"Douglas fought with us for a year. Never picked up a weapon, not once. He charged the seawall at Báih Sìde, helped break the line at Saethtunn, made it through the assault on Dún Craeg without a damn scratch. All the way to Triúrbaile.

"And then he saw those slaughterfarms. Those cages. What the Dyvok had done to their captives. What God had *allowed* them to do. I found him behind one of the grindhouses—the abattoirs where the coldbloods took the bodies of the dead and turned them into food for the living."

Gabriel downed his goblet in one draught, swallowed with a wince.

"There was a . . . a pit. Hundred foot square, I don't know how deep. *Filled* with bones. Men. Women. Children. Thousands. *Tens* of thousands. Scraped clean of every scrap of meat, and then boiled for broth. Just . . . fucking . . ."

The Last Silversaint hung his head.

It took a long slice of silence before he found voice again to speak.

"Père Douglas was knelt in the middle of it. Black robes on that sea of white. I watched him reach up to that wheel that had shone like silver flame and tear it from his neck. Drop it into those bones. I called his name as he walked away. He met my eyes, and the look in his . . . sweet Mothermaid, I'll never forget it. Not rage. Not sorrow. *Heartbreak.*

"We found him next day. Out in the deadwoods. He'd taken some soldier's sword. The only weapon he'd ever picked up. Put out his own eyes, and then fell on it."

"I take it there is a point to this tale of woe?" Jean-François asked. "Other than to showcase the savagery of the Untamed? Kith are not all alike, de León. We are n—"

"Point is," Gabriel interrupted, "it's a difficult thing, to have your faith shattered."

"And you think you will shatter mine?" The Marquis chuckled, bloodless and cold. "To paraphrase your young Mlle Lachance in regard to her . . ."—Jean-François waved at his chest—". . . feminine accoutrements, one must have a thing to lose a thing, Gabriel."

The Last Silversaint poured himself another glass with steady hands.

Drawing a deep breath as if before the plunge.

"Have it your way, coldblood.

"So. Dior and I stood in Jènoah's chapel, the storm raging outside, the shadow of the Terrors growing longer all the while. Lightning arced across stained glass, painting all in blood-red and shades of long-lost blue. I could see hesitation in my sister's eyes now. Fear. But Dior met that cold stare with her own, sitting among the chapel pews and folding her arms, expectant.

"'All thisss was told me by my Master Wulfric,' Celene began. 'Earned after a decade of service, and but a ssscrap of the knowledge I might have attained had he lived. By sharing these truths, I break a covenant. A sssacred trust from master to lia—'

"'Get on with it, Celene,' Dior spat.

"My sister breathed deep. Thunder rolled above.

"'The first kith to walk this earth numbered not four, but five.' Celene stared down at her open palms, voice soft as velvet. 'The first dwelled in the peaksss of northern Elidaen, building a dark dynasty by the name of Vosssss. One called the wildsss home, communing with beastsss of earth and sky and begetting the line Chastain. Another claimed the frozen wastes of Talhost, carving the blood-soaked name of Dyvok among the terrified populace. The fourth dwelled in the cityports of Sūdhaem, there weaving the endlessss webs of the Blood Ilon. But the last of the Priorem would claim no dominion, wandering the earth and falling into darknessss with her firstborn broodchild, and love of her life.

"'Her name was Illia. And his, Tanith.'

"Celene dug her claws into her skin, and the blood flowed, heady, thick, weaving from her upturned palms into a pair of figures; male and female.

"'Illia had been a deeply wicked woman in life. Some rumors even held it she was an acolyte of the Fallen, her nights devoted to bloody sin and bloodier idolatry. After they Became, she and Tanith lived as betrothed, wandering the realm and glutting themselvesss upon the blood of the living. Their devotion to each other was the sssingle spark of humanity in a life of ever-deepening brutality and decadence.'

"The figures in Celene's hands wove together, locked in a lovers' embrace.

"'But after centuries of darknessss, Illia came to sssee unlife as an abomination, and herself, a prisoner, locked in purgatory unending. Rather than depravity, she sought *meaning* in eternity.' She nodded to the statue above the altar, the son of God upon his wheel. 'And she found it among the teachings of the One Faith, now spreading across the realm in the wake of the Redeemer's martyrdom. Illia reasoned eternal life might not be a curse, but a *gift*, to be spent in search for the salvation of her damned soul.'

"The female figure slipped from her lover's arms and sank to her knees on Celene's palm, praying.

"'She consulted prophets, priests, the pages of the Testaments, ssseeking a salve for the emptiness in her heart. And finally, deciding that her thirst was a testing from God, she declared she would no longer sssate it on the blood of innocents. Her broodchildren pleaded that she feed; even her beloved Tanith came to her, begging that she sssee reason. And haunted by visionsss, tormented by the memory of her countless past misdeeds and driven to blind frenzy by her rising thirst, Illia murdered her beloved, drinking him to ashesss.'

"The figure rose and struck at her lover like a viper, latching onto his throat. And as Dior and I watched, the male form was drawn into the female, until nothing remained.

"Celene met my eyes with hers, cold and lifeless.

"'The Priori was ssstricken with grief. But soon after the murder, Illia realized if she listened, she could hear Tanith's voice in her head. And even though kith do not dream, her beloved would visit Illia in her sssleep, whispering she had not destroyed, but *sssaved* him.

"'Illia reasoned she now carried Tanith's soul within her body, and that by consuming him, she had ssspared him the fires of damnation that await all kith after death. Naming her deed *communion*, Illia believed God had ssshown her the purpose of her existence, just as she'd prayed for, and she declared it the duty of all her line to redeem those other poor sssouls fallen to the vampiric curse—consuming their bodies, and carrying their spiritsss safe within until the Day of Judgment promised in the Testaments.

"'Some of her brood came to see as Illia did, devoted to the sssalvation of their eternal souls. Those who refused? Illia sssimply ssslew and consumed.

"'For the next two centuries, while war raged across five kingdoms, and seven martyrs died to bring the One Faith to the corners of the mortal world, the Illiae hunted and slew countless vampiresss of the other lines, in what became known as the Red Crusade.'

"Blood sluiced back into Celene's palms as she gestured around us. My eyes roamed the bas-reliefs; vampires fighting and killing and dying. I saw figures in the battles now, latched onto each other's throats like leeches, and I recalled Celene digging into Rykard's neck on the Mère likesame. The ecstasy in her eyes as she drank him to dust.

"Insanity.

"Insanity and bloody depravity.

"Dior took out a cigarelle from her case and lit it. Breathing deep and exhaling grey, she fixed my sister with eyes like blue diamonds.

"'So what do I have to do with any of this?'

"'*Everything*,' Celene replied.

"She gestured again to the carvings, the warring coldbloods, the teeth and ashes.

"'Illia's crusade met with frightening successss. A vampire's heartsblood thickens in consuming another's, and those who drank the soulsss of other kith were blessed with the bloodgifts of their victimsss. Vampires of the other lines were drawn to the teachingsss of the Priori, and Illia proclaimed them her liathe. Her knightsss. Her *crusadersss*. The Illiae became less a bloodline, and more a . . . religion.'

"'A cult,' I muttered. 'A *madness*.'

"'As you like it,' Celene replied.

"'Gabe, is all this true?' Dior whispered.

"I sighed, looking to the walls around us. 'She speaks of the time before empire. The centuries following the Redeemer's death, eight hundred years gone. The library in San Michon made no mention of any of this, but it made scarce mention of the Esani either.'

"'This is truth, chérie,' Celene promised. 'Gifted to me not by the pages of sssome dusty tome scratched by mortal men. But ssspoken by those who *lived* it.'

"'*Survived* it, you mean,' I growled. 'Something happened. To this Illia *and* her bastard cult. Else I'd have heard a whisper of all this before now.'

"'My ancestor,' Dior realized, looking toward that crest on the doors. 'Esan.'

"Celene nodded. 'You have wisdom, chérie.'

"'Tell me,' Dior demanded. 'Tell me the rest of it.'

"My sister sighed, bowing her head.

"'The Wars of the Faith were won. The warlord Maximille de Augustin had forged five feuding kingdoms into a single empire, united under a single religion, and his descendantsss ruled with iron fistsss from atop their Five-fold Throne. But in the depthsss of Talhost, rebellion was brewing against the Augustin dynasty.'

"I scowled, remembering Père Rafa's lessons in Winfael. 'The Aavsenct Heresy.'

"Celene nodded. 'Mortal descendants of the Redeemer's daughter, Esan, hidden long centuries and by now, a dynasty unto themselvesss. Their ancestor was the prince of heaven himself, and they believed it their *right* to rule the kingdomsss of the earth. Faced with this threat, the mortal church and the

Augustins declared Esan's descendants heretics. All around the realm, armies of faithful soldiersss were raised to purge their blight. And Illia became convinced that *here,* at last, lay her chance at redemption.

"'Renaming her brood the Esana—the Faithful—Illia and her liathe threw their weight behind the Redeemer's line, seeking to protect them, and finally redeem *themselves.*

"'But in the shadowsss, opposition to Illia's brood had been building for centuriesss. There is no love lost between the Courtsss of the Blood, yet in the wake of the Red Crusades, even the most paranoid of elders came to sssee the Faithful as a threat. An alliance was forged—a cadre of ancien and mediae, mustered from among the four other lines. Calling themselves the Knights of the Blood, they descended on Talhost to purge Illia's brood from this earth. They were led by a fearsome capitaine, legendary among the kith even then. Cold of hand and iron of heart.'

"Celene pointed to the reliefs again, and among those warring figures, I saw a youth, beautiful, terrible, carrying a blade in one hand and a raven on the other. Fierce eyes. Fangs bared. Only an artist's rendition, but skillful enough for me to recognize him.

"'Fabién . . .' I hissed.

"'The Forever King,' Celene nodded. 'Fearful of the Esana's growing power. Hateful of the love and light of God. Dragging a rabble of blind and envious *foolsss* into the ruin of all our kind. And thisss conflict, mortal against mortal, vampire against vampire, would be known in the pages of kith history as the Warsss of the Blood.'

"'Wars that Illia must have lost,' I said. 'Because those same histories call her brood the Esan*i,* not Esan*a.* Faith*less,* not Faith*ful.*'

"'Is that why Voss wants me?' Dior gazed about, bewildered. 'Some holdover from a heresy that ended *centuries* ago?'

"'We know not why the Forever King huntsss you. And Master Jènoah took any wisdom he held about it to his grave.' Celene looked to those ashes, the fragments of that verse crushed upon the floor, and she sighed. 'There are no answersss to ending daysdeath here. Nothing of truth remains in these hallsss.'

"Kneeling before Dior, Celene squeezed her hand.

"'But have faith, chérie. These trials are sent by God to test us, and we will *not* fail him. There is one other of the Esana within our reach. The eldest of usss. Priori of the Faithful. Mother of Monstersss and broodchild of Illia herself. If any on this earth know the truth of what you must do to bring back the sssun, it is she. We must find her, Dior. We have no choice now. We *must* ssseek Mistress Maryn in Dún Maergenn.'

"I scowled, bristling at the sight of Celene's hand on Dior's. 'Dún Maergenn is fallen, Celene. The Blackheart and his brood took it months back. And why the hell would we tru—'

"My sister tensed, snaking to her feet just as my own ears pricked up. I heard it too now; clawed and padded feet thumping swift on the floors. I turned to see Phoebe barrel through the chapel doors at full sprint, talons scratching on slick stone as she brought herself to a halt at Dior's feet. The lioness was damp with snow, flanks steaming from what had obviously been a flat sprint for God knew how many miles.

"Dior crushed out her smoke, knelt at the duskdancer's side. 'Phoebe?'

"Sunset was still a few hours away—the duskdancer would be trapped in her wealdshape until then, unable to talk. Instead, the lioness unsheathed her claws and raked furrows into the stone floor; two long scores, meeting at a point. The letter *V*.

"'The Voss,' Dior whispered, looking to me. 'They've found us.'

"'Only a matter of time.' I breathed deep, stood taller, trying to buoy her spirits. 'But know no fear. We've good defensive position here. Ancient blades and coldblood magiks and 'dancer claws. And old as Alba and Aléne are, at least there's only two of them.'

"Phoebe met my eyes then, glittering gold. And as the lioness growled, so deep and low I could feel it in my gut, my heart sank down to join it.

"'. . . How many?' I sighed.

"In reply, Phoebe tore at the floor with her talons once more, dozens of knuckle-deep scores ripped into ancient stone. Over and over and over again.

"Thunder rocked the walls.

"Dior met my eyes.

"'*Too* many.'"

IV

WHAT MATTERS MOST

"HOW DO YOU do that?" the vampire asked.

The Last Silversaint was staring at the chymical globe, that pale moth battering ceaselessly upon the glass. The thirst was a constant presence, spreading black wings about his shoulders and running burning hands down his throat, chest, belly. The wind was howling about the keep outside, and Gabriel could feel the chill, real and remembered, echoing in the abandoned chambers of Cairnhaem, the hollow halls of his heart. But he glanced up as the vampire spoke, annoyed.

"How do I do what?"

Jean-François waved his quill. "That thing you do with your eyebrows."

"The fuck are you talking about?"

"You're doing it again," the historian said. "It's not quite a frown . . . more like a frown had a drunken ménage à trois with a glower and a pout. It's very good, you must have practiced it at length in the mirror."

"Benefits of having a reflection, you soulless prick."

The historian chuckled as the silversaint met his eyes.

"So that's it?" Gabriel demanded. "I tell you the secret history of your species, and you dribble nonsense about eyebrows? Does it not concern you th—"

"You presume much, Silversaint." Jean-François had returned to sketching, his ruby lips pursed. "I suppose you cannot be blamed. You were raised by a passel of ignorant halfbreeds, after all. Folly your bread, and deceit your wine. But the Esani were not the only kith to fight in the Wars of the Blood. And while mortals may have expunged all mention of the Faithless from the annals of antiquity, the Knights of the Blood remember."

Gabriel's eyes narrowed, a slow smile spreading across his lips.

"Margot told you. Interesting."

"Not particularly." The Marquis yawned. "I *am* her favorite, after all."

"She had other favorites in her time, way I hear it. Your Empress of Wolves and Men. Those Knights of the Blood shared more than a battlefield, if rumor is true." Gabriel leaned forward, trying to catch Jean-François's eye. "Did she grieve Fabién when he died, I wonder? I heard they hated each other in the end, but you never forget your first true love."

"Please," the Marquis sighed. "You embarrass yourself, de León. We are not here to discuss the exploits of my dame's youth, nor the lovers she has outlived. Your mortal mind cannot contain the smallest drop of the ocean that is she." The quill's golden nib sank into the pot of ink, and Jean-François met the silversaint's eyes. "So. Voss's hounds had run you to ground. Four of you to defend a castle against an army. You lived, that much is obvious." Chocolat eyes roamed Gabriel, boots to brow. "The question is how?"

"No." The Last Silversaint steepled tattooed fingers at his chin, dragging his thoughts back to the night it all began to fall apart. "The question is what I paid for it."

Gabriel shook his head and breathed deep.

"Cairnhaem's best point of defense was its bridge—a narrow passage where whatever numbers the Terrors had would count for less. If Jènoah had built himself a damn *drawbridge* over that chasm instead, his home might've been impregnable. But I supposed an ancien so powerful in a lair so remote had little fear of unwelcome guests."

"Age breeding arrogance," Jean-François murmured.

Gabriel glanced at the fortress around them. "Wonder who *that* reminds me of."

"Ah, sarcasm. The whelp's excuse for wit."

The Last Silversaint smiled thinly, toying with the stem of his goblet.

"Still, even without a drawbridge, Celene, Phoebe, and I might hold a pass that narrow. So, while the sun sank ever closer to the horizon, and Dior snatched some much-needed sleep, my sister and I tore down the statues lining the bridge, piled furniture from the château around them, creating five choke points. I draped the barricades with tapestries from the halls, sheets from the boudoirs, and—glad Dior wasn't around to see it—every stitch of clothing from Jènoah's wardrobes. The gibbets dangling below the bridge were rusted and useless, but we used every spear and sword from the armory, jammed in among the furniture and statues; a bristling thicket of blades pointed at our foes. Alba and Aléne would smash through them like glass, but they might slow down thrallswords or wretched. And for the final touch, we doused the lot in liquor we found in the château's cellar.

"It was Talhosti vodka for the most part. That shit will strip the varnish off floorboards if you let it sit too long, so I knew it'd burn hot, and if there's one thing all vampires fear, it's fire. The bottles were blue—a touch of cobalt in the glass, I supposed—but as I finished dousing the fourth barricade, I saw Celene upending a bottle of dusty green onto our last line of defense.

"'The *fuck* are you doing?' I cried.

"'Preparing our—'

"'Are you *insane*?' I snatched the bottle away, looking over the lamb and wolf on the label. 'This is Château Montfort! One bottle is worth an emperor's ransom these nights!'

"'Do we know any captive emperorsss? It is liquor, Gabriel. What matter—'

"'This isn't liquor, it's *gold*.' I looked the bottle over, relieved to find it mostly full. 'There's not enough alcohol in red wine to burn anyway. You're just wasting it.'

"'And guzzling it like a hog at trough is perfectly acceptable usssage?'

"'Now there's a thought.' I lifted the bottle in toast and took a long swallow. 'Santé, sister. Your blood's worth smoking.'

"We stood at the top of the stairs when we were done, those great bronze doors looming at our backs. Celene had raided Jènoah's wardrobe before we consigned the rest to the barricades, and her new greatcoat was the rich red of heartsblood, velvet brocade brushing the cobbles at our feet. I surveyed our makeshift defenses, drinking slow from the Montfort, savoring the rich, heavenly taste of the first wine I'd drunk in *years*. The bridge to Cairnhaem stretched out before us; a narrow gauntlet, reeking of spirits and gleaming with spears. We'd surely make our foes bleed for every inch. But God only knew the strength coming at us, save that two among them were Princes of Forever.

"'It isss not much,' Celene sighed. 'But Fortuna willing, it will be enough.'

"'We'll need more than an angel's blessing to see us through this storm, sister.'

"Celene brushed her hair from her mask, her embroidered sleeve slipping back from her wrist. 'What other strength would you ask for, brother?'

"The air grew still between us, my eyes narrowed. I could see thin blue veins beneath the marble of her skin, remember the taste of her blood crashing upon my tongue as she forced me to drink at San Michon. That blood had given me a strength I'd never known, and God knew I'd *need* strength if Dior was to live through this. But two more drops over two more nights, I'd be Celene's thrall, and I'd as much desire to deepen the bond between my sister and I as I had to cut my own fucking throat.

"But a deeper fear in me was whispering, never quite silenced now. A tiny ember burning in my chest, bursting slow to vicious flame these last few months. I'd confided it to none, but smelling Lachlan's blood, Dior's blood, Phoebe's blood . . . I had to admit the thirst in me *was* worsening. Growing more difficult to drown, no matter how much I smoked or drank. A word was echoing in my memory; a dread taught to every acolyte in San Michon. The name of the madness that eventually consumed every paleblood alive.

"'Sangirè,' Celene whispered. 'The red thirst.'

"'I warned you to stay out of my head,' I growled.

"'We would love nothing more.' Celene plucked her cuff down over her wrist. 'But your thoughtsss bleed, Gabriel. The same way your beloved Astrid bled every night onto your fool'sss tongue. We can *feel* the price you now pay for it.'

"Anger flared at the mention of my bride's name, bitter and broken-bottle sharp.

"'Spare me the preaching, Celene. And mind your own fucking business.'

"'This *is* our businessss. The Grail is our only hope of sssalvation. We must do all we can to protect her. From her enemies without. *And* within.'

"My eyes narrowed at that. 'What do you mean, *within?*'

"'God Almighty,' she sighed, rounding on me. 'Do you not sssee? You are a *danger* to Dior, Gabriel. We all know it. Stumbling drunkenness aside, it is only a matter of time before the bloody madnessss budding in you comes to bloom. We know you care for the girl. We know why. But when this night's butchery is done, you would do well to leave her. To the only one who can truly protect her.'

"I squared up to Celene then. Hissing through clenched teeth.

"Hear me now. If the legions of heaven stood between me and that girl, I would slay every angel in the Host to get back to her side. She and I have walked through hell together. I will *never* leave her, you hear me? And I would *never* hurt her.'

"'Not tonight. Perhaps not tomorrow. But we sssee your thirst growing every day. How long until it consumesss you utterly? And the ones you claim to care for?' Celene tilted her head, hissing behind that hateful mask. 'Did they not warn you? Your preciousss Silver Order? What would happen if you indulged your desires night after night? Or were you sssimply too drunk with lust of the flesh to give a damn about your immortal soul?'

"'You dare lecture *me* about souls? When you're part of a cult that *consumes* them?'

"'You have no *idea* what we are part of. Communion is a holy task, given unto—'

"'*Holy?*' I crowed, incredulous. 'I saw the look in your eyes when you drank Rykard Dyvok to ashes, and there was nothing *holy* about it! This is about hunger, Celene. And *power*. And deeds so dark a monster like Fabién fucking Voss convinced a legion of hate-filled leeches to work together to wipe it from the earth!'

"'You. Know. *Nothing!* Nothing of what I have seen! *Nothing* of—'

"'I know after tonight, you and I are done! Damn your fables, *damn* your masters! You promised answers and delivered ashes, and I'll not play the fool for you twice over! We win through the hell that's coming for us tonight, I'm taking Dior to the Highlands tomorrow!'

"'There are no *answersss* for you in the Highlands! Only *death*! Dior must go to Dún Maergenn! Mother Maryn awaits her there in eventide, and we c—'

"'The hell is eventide?' I held up a hand as she began to answer. 'On second thought, spare me. I won't be able to hear you over the deafening roar of the fucks I don't give.'

"'You cannot do thisss, brother.'

"'You can't stop me, sister. Dior listens to *my* counsel, not yours, remember?'

"Celene's eyes narrowed as the winds of our homeland clawed the gulf between us. I stood a head taller, glowering down at her, just as unyielding as she. We were both our mama's children in that moment, stubborn, prideful, the blood of lions roaring in our veins. I recalled Celene as she'd been—my hellion, my baby sister. But she was only a shadow of herself now. And though in part the fault of that was mine, I knew I'd been an idiot to trust her. Perhaps it had been guilt that drove me to the spires of Cairnhaem. Perhaps it was her blood lingering in my veins, or the desperate hope my actions at San Michon hadn't doomed the world. But I saw this all now for the folly it had been.

"'You're right, Celene. I don't know what you've seen, nor done. But I've spent my whole life hunting monsters, and I know one when I see one. And I see one in *you*.'

"And spinning on my silvered heel, I strode into the keep.

"I cursed as I slammed the mighty doors behind me—I knew damn well it was foolish to push my sister, that I'd need her strength tonight if any of us were to make it out alive. But the thirst in me was roiling, *pounding* like a fucking hammer on my skull as I pictured that faint blue scrawl upon her wrist. That fear was growing, that *word*, echoing now in my head as I took another long gulp of wine to drown it. I remembered the Red Rites I'd seen in San Michon as a boy. Those silversaints who gave up their lives before they succumbed to the madness in our blood. '*Better to die a man than live a monster,*' they used to tell us. And though I'd leveled the charge at Celene, I could feel that same monster now in me."

"Why did you do it?" Jean-François asked.

". . . Do what?" Gabriel replied.

"You *had* been cautioned by the Order. You *knew* the insanity that all palebloods succumb to, and that indulging your thirst would only hasten its onset." The historian's dark eyes fixed upon the silversaint's wine-stained lips. "So why drink from your wife night after night, de León? Your famille's blood runs hot, oui. But are you such a slave to passion?"

Gabriel drank down the last of his goblet, staring now at the monster opposite. All the light in the room seemed to coalesce in the dark pools of its eyes, shining like stars. His skin prickled as he thought back on those long, slow nights of blood and fire and sin. Smooth curves beneath his roaming hands. Thumping pulse beneath his flickering tongue.

He sat forward, elbows to knees. Beckoning Jean-François with one finger. The vampire stared a long and breathless moment, silence thick in the air, finally leaning close. Gabriel smoothed back a golden curl from the monster's ear as he whispered.

"Because she always said *please.*"

The vampire turned his head, meeting the silversaint's eyes.

"I shall remember that."

"So," Gabriel continued, leaning back. "We had perhaps four hours to dusk.

I knew I should rest, but a tempest was ringing in my skull as I stood in Jènoah's foyer. Dior had drawn back the faded draperies from that massive hearth, lit a tiny fire in its vast hollow. Bear and Pony were tethered and slumbering near the stairs close by, safe out of the weather. Dior herself lay on a chaise longue near the flames, Phoebe curled up beside her, both sleeping. And content the duskdancer would keep the girl safe, I trudged up the arc of the eastern stair with my wine in hand, searching for some measure of salvation.

"It's a strange thing, that silence before the storm. I've stood on the eve of a hundred battles, coldblood. I've seen every way a person deals with that fear. Some drink and carouse, desperate to wring one last drop out of life before they dance with death. Some seek solace in another's arms, a moment of living in those warm, soft places where nothing else matters. Nearly everyone prays. People say the test of a man's mettle is on the battlefield, but that's not the truth. You want to know a man, look into his eyes the night *before*. Before the shouting and screams drown out the voice inside his head. Before he gets drunk enough to think himself brave. When it's just him, and the things he's done, and the things he might never do.

"That's when you'll see us as we truly are.

"I let my feet lead me, and rather than taking me to the chapel, I found myself in Jènoah's chess room. It was a vast space, lit by dim daysdeath light. Stained glass. Checkered floor. Like all other statuary in Cairnhaem, the pieces had been carved by a master's hand; the bright were opalite, the dark, black opal, the tallest among them near my height. A game had apparently been underway when Jènoah decided to end himself; now never to be finished. Wandering among the figures, pondering the battle to come, I found my lips twisting as I noted the light side was running the Rousseau gambit."

"Rousseau?" Jean-François asked.

Gabriel blinked. "You don't know chess?"

"Not yet." The vampire smiled. "I was planning to master it in a century or so."

"It's a famed technique. Feign weakness to draw your opponent out of position in his haste to finish you. Then you strike. High risk. High reward. Looking around, I could see the bright player had been using it to claw back control of a losing game.

"I circled the dark emperor, watching rainbow veins glitter in his stone. The storm outside put me in mind of the tempests we used to get on the coast back home, a lighthouse burning now in my smoke-and-wine-addled mind. Pushing my knuckles into my eyes, I fancied I heard small footsteps behind me, running feet and laughter, turning to glimpse a child, a little girl, long black hair and bloodless skin, flitting among the pieces. I heard her calling for me—*Papa! Papa!*—my wife's song in the kitchen rising over the howl of the wind, and those three awful knocks that brought it all to an end.

"*Thump, thump, thump.*

"'There you are,' came a voice.

"I looked up to find Dior standing at the entrance, and at the sight of her, my heart grew warm again, those ghosts at my back falling blessedly silent. But looking closer, blinking hard, my smile faded like their voices on the storm.

"She was still dressed in Jènoah's stolen frockcoat, but she wore a long shirt of chainmail underneath now. She'd given her silversteel longblade to Lachlan when we parted, but she'd replaced it with a sword from the armory. The blade was too big for her, hanging at her belt in an ornate scabbard that dragged along the floor as she marched into the room. She carried a helm under one arm, plate gauntlets encasing her hands, heavy greaves on her shins. Some sleep had done her a world of good, but she still looked pale. Pale and frightened and very, very young.

"'What are you all dollied up for?'

"'What do you think?' she said, clanking to a halt in front of me.

"'I think your other waistcoat suited you better. What happened to all those fucks you gave for fashion?'

"'Fashion can wait, Gabriel. The Terrors are coming.'

"'Oui,' I nodded. 'But a chain shirt won't help much against monsters who can punch through platemail. Armor is heavy. Noisy. Slow. Even when it's made to fit you. And that lot fits you about as well as a nun's skirts would fit me.'

"'What the hell else am I supposed to fight in, then?'

"'Who says you're fighting at all?'

"'Me. *I* say.'

"I breathed a weary sigh, tired in my bones.

"'Dior, you can barely hold that sword, let alone swing it. You're not sporting with the puppies anymore, you're running with the wolves. Cutting down a lone wretched is one thing, but fighting toe-to-toe with ancien is another battle entire. When hell starts raining down on that bridge tonight, you're going to be nowhere near it. And if hell makes it through the door, you don't stand your ground. You *run*. Agreed?'

"She breathed deep, scowling. 'You know, I hate it when you do that.'

"'Do what?'

"'Tell me what I'm doing and then put a question mark at the end as if you're asking.'

"'Perhaps I should leave the question mark off in future, and see if you actually do what you're fucking told.'

"'Fat fucking chance.'

"'Thought fucking not.'

"The girl clenched her armored fists, glancing at the stone pieces around us.

"'Celene told me about the argument you had.'

"Hackles rippled down my spine, the memory of my sister's words on the bridge hanging in the air. I could almost hear that viper's hiss at my back.

"*You are a* danger *to Dior . . .*

"'It's unwise to be talking to her alone, Dior. Celene's a fanatic. A madwoman.'

"'This Mother Maryn she talked about is supposed to be the broodchild of Illia herself. The oldest Esani still on earth. The answers we need are bound to be in Dún Maergenn, but Celene said you want to take me to the Highlands instead?'

"I took a long pull from my wine. 'That's right.'

"Dior glowered. 'Did you ever think to ask what *I* wanted?'

"'Dior, it's not what you *want* that matters now. It's what you *need*. Nobody doubts your spirit, but you've no inkling of the monstrous fucking evil breathing but an *inch* from your neck. And the fact you want to *risk* that neck in battle tonight only proves it.'

"I sighed, shaking my head as I gazed to the stained glass above.

"'And how *could* you know? You've never seen it. You're a child, for fuckssakes.'

"'Oh, merci,' she spat. 'Papa.'

"We stood in silence, scowling and stubborn, and it occurred to me how ill-suited I was for all this. Patience had only been eleven years old when she was taken from me. Dior had raised herself from the time she was my daughter's age, and God only knew the things she'd done and had done to her in kind. She loathed being told what to do, and yet she desperately *needed* to be. But who the fuck was I to tell her anything at all? She was right; I wasn't her father. Sometimes I barely managed to be her friend.

"Dior had turned away from me, scowling, wandering among the chess pieces to search for calm. I took a gulp of wine, waved at the board with my bottle.

"'You want to play?'

"She glanced over her shoulder, ice-blue eyes dark with anger. 'I don't know how.'

"'You want to play for money, then?'

"She chuckled despite herself, hanging her head to hide her smile in the tumble of her hair. I laughed aloud to see that smile, and at the sound, Dior laughed too, her eyes sparkling. The tension between us melted a little, like dew on a springtime morn.

"'You're drunk,' she said, only half-scolding.

"'I'm merry.' I motioned to the other side of the board. 'Over there. I'll school you.'

"'I'd rather you school me in northwind stance again, truth told.'

"'This game is older than empire. There's lessons in it well worth learning.'

"Dior pouted, skeptical, but relented nonetheless, clanking over to stand behind the bright army. She withdrew a black cigarelle from her case as I waved toward her new suit.

"'You'll just wear yourself out walking around in all that metal.'

"She scowled and lit her smoke, ignoring me. Shaking my head, I pulled the last swallow from my Montfort, patting the dark piece in front of me on the shoulder. He stood tall as I, clad in platemail, a longsword in his hands, and a crowned helm upon his head.

"'This is the Emperor,' I declared. 'The most important piece on the board. He can attack any direction he pleases, but he can't move far. So he tends to stand here at the back of the line, commanding the rest of these pieces to do his will.'

"'Sounds like a boy I knew from Lashaame.' The girl breathed smoke into the air, scowling. 'One of the Narrowman's crew. We used to call him *Blister*.'

"'Blister?' I lifted one brow. 'Why?'

"'He only ever showed up after the hard work was done.'

"'There *are* privileges to wearing the crown.'

"Dior scoffed. 'I wouldn't know.'

"'Perhaps these little bastards will be more familiar to one of your colorful upbringing, then.' I nudged a smaller piece with my boot; a row of them, waist-height, fashioned like infantry in archaic armor. 'The Peon. They're the front line of your army. Cheap. Expendable. They open the board up for the rest of your pieces to really play. This here is Château. This one is Chevalier. And this is Pontifex. Church and state. They move in different ways, but their task is the same; go out onto the battlefield and inflict carnage in their Emperor's name. They're your specialist pieces. You protect them if you can. But in the end, you can lose them all and still win the game.'

"I demonstrated the method of moving each piece, lifting them easily with the dark strength in my veins. It occurred to me this was a set that only coldbloods were truly meant to play with; that Dior would struggle to move them by herself. But still, she watched on now, blue eyes shining as she dragged on her smoke, her natural curiosity blossoming.

"'What about that one?' she asked, breathing grey.

"'This is the Empress.' I patted the piece she nodded to. 'The power behind your throne. She moves as far as she pleases, in any direction she likes. She's your executioner. Your red right hand. Swift. Versatile. Deadly.'

"Dior smiled. 'I *like* her.'

"'Don't get too attached. In the end, she's just as expendable as the rest.'

"The girl frowned. 'Why? She sounds the strongest piece on the board.'

"'She's not.' I tapped the dark Emperor's shoulder again. '*He* is. The object of the game is to capture your opponent's Emperor. In the end, nothing else matters.'

"'That's foolish. He can't do half of what these other pieces do.'

"'He does what *none* of them can do. He wins you the game.'

"'That's not fair.'

"'Fair is for dead men and losers, Dior.'

"'But it makes no sense.' She scowled, breathing grey from her nostrils. 'How can the coward who doesn't fight be the difference between winning and losing?'

"'The Emperor does fight. If he's *forced* to. And when he does, like any good leader, he can swing battle's tide. But you don't risk your most valuable piece on the front line. Not when all these other pieces are willing to fight for him. Not when losing *him* means losing the *game*. That's not just foolish. That's suicide.'

"Dior folded her arms and stared across the board. 'I'm beginning to see why you wanted to teach me this game.'

"'Oui?'

"'Your metaphor is showing, Chevalier de León.'

"'Why, Emperor Lachance, whatever do you mean?'

"'I'm not a piece on a board. And my life isn't a game.'

"'You're right. It's not. And yet, you continue to treat it like one.'

"She dragged on her cigarelle, breathing fire. 'Another lecture. Just what I needed.'

"'You *do* need it,' I scowled. 'You're a seventeen-year-old girl.'

"'And is it the fact I'm seventeen or that I'm a girl that brings out the bitch in you?'

"'Don't give me that shit, I've never treated you less for what's between y—'

"'I don't need you to fight my wars for me!' she snapped. 'You were younger than I am when you won the Battle of the Twins! When you ended Laure Voss! And *I* killed a Prince of Forever too, in case you missed it! And saved your sorry arse in the process!'

"'Dior, listen to me! You are the most important person in this empire! The Scion of San Michon, the end to daysdeath, the hope of the realm! Without you, *all* is lost!' I lowered my voice, knowing I was stepping onto thin ice. 'I know you still feel guilty about Chloe's ritual. I *know* a part of you wonders if perhaps all this might've ended if she'd but ended *you*. And so you put yourself arisk, time and time again. Ignoring me on the Mère. Ignoring me at Aveléne. Ignoring me now.'

"'Enough people have died on my account already!' she shouted. 'Aaron! Baptiste! Rafa! Saoirse! Bel! I'm not just going to sit by while you give your life for me too, Gabriel!'

"'I know you won't, and that's my point! He! Doesn't! Matter!' With unholy strength, I hurled the Chevalier across the room, Dior flinching as it shattered against the wall. 'These? Don't! *Matter!*' One by one, I lifted the beautiful pieces, dark and bright, Peon and Château and Empress, smashing and hurling them aside—'None, *none*, NONE of them!'—until only two pieces remained. And chest heaving, I lifted the dark Emperor over my head, and with a roar, brought it down at the bright Emperor's feet with all my strength.

"The flagstones shattered like glass, a hollow *BOOM* echoed among the gables. The dark Emperor broke into a dozen pieces, dust and fragments spilling across the smashed tiles. The room was deathly silent as I turned to Dior, chest heaving, fangs bared.

"And in that quiet, again I heard the sound of little feet and laughter.

"My wife's lonely song on the ocean winds.

"'Victory,' I hissed. 'Over the darkness. Over *him*. That's what matters, Dior.'

"She held my stare a moment, then looked to the floor. The once-beautiful pieces were scattered, fallen on their sides, splintered and broken. The girl shook her head, pale-blue gaze drifting over the bright Emperor, standing alone on the ruined and broken field.

"'Gabriel, if this is victory . . . what the hell does defeat look like?'

"'Goddamn you, girl . . .'

"Taking one last drag on her cigarelle, she dropped it onto the tile, crushing it under her boot. 'You're drinking too much. I'm really worried about you.'

"And turning on her heel, she clanked out the door."

V

THE BASTARD AND THE FOOL

"THE SUN HAD slunk to sleep beyond the mountains. Jènoah's church was caught in the storm's quiet eye. And in the brief and starless lull between one tempest and the next, the Dead had come to Cairnhaem.

"'That delightful expression of yoursss,' Celene murmured. 'Remind me?'

"I dragged my hand through my hair and sighed. 'Fuck my face.'

"We stood behind the first of our five barricades across the château bridge. I'd stowed my greatcoat and shirt in my saddlebags, my old wolfskin wrapped about me like a cloak, Ashdrinker glittering in my hands. Lightning pulsed in the distance, illuminating the frozen slopes above. The things watching us. I'd wondered why the Terrors had taken so long to run us down after tracking us to Avelène. But in the weeks we'd wasted searching for Jènoah's tomb, it seemed Alba and Aléne had gathered all hell to their sides.

"'Tell me what you see,' I demanded.

"Beside me, Dior peered through my spyglass, breath steaming in the deeping chill. A shadow hung between us now; anger and misgiving, resentment and fear. Despite it, the girl had still marched out to see what was coming for her; dressed in her stolen armor, a cowl of padded mail and iron helm dragged down over her hair. All that damn metal must have weighed most of what she did, but she wore it still, stubborn as a toddler at bedtime.

"'A host of thrallswords,' she replied. 'And a *lot* of wretched.'

"She spoke true. The vanguard of the Voss force were foulbloods one and all, perhaps a hundred deep. They stared across the frozen expanse between us—beggars and lords, soldiers and peasants, parents and children. Their brains rotted to ruin, their bodies mere shells for the thirst that drove them, each still strong and swift as a dozen mortals.

"Soldiers stood behind them, geared for battle, a band of a hundred at least. They were veterans by the look, the white raven of the Voss set upon their shields or tabards. Their helms were fashioned like skulls, their pauldrons, skeletal hands. Swordsmen stood in front, riflemen at the rear, wheellocks at their shoulders and death in their eyes.

"'And what don't you see?' I asked.

"Dior wiped snow from the spyglass, squinting into the dark again. 'The Terrors.'

"'You understand now?' I pointed to the mongrel Dead. 'Peons. Cheap and expendable. They get thrown first to test us.' I nodded to the thralls. 'The specialist pieces come next. They grind us down. Sap our strength. But you don't see the Emperors upon the field, do you? When they have a choice, even *immortals* don't risk themselves on the line. So you need to get the hell back behind ours. Because we're in a swamp of shit here, girl, and you've not got the boots for it.'

"'They want me *alive*, Gabriel,' Dior insisted. 'Those riflemen won't dare shoot with me standing here beside you. And the wretched won't charge mindless in case—'

"'In case what?' I demanded.

"She squared her shoulders, defiant. 'In case they hurt me.'

"'That's right!' I snapped, all my fears made plain. 'In case they *hurt* you!'

"I could hear it again now, rising above the howling wind and the thunder of my own heart. Little footsteps and laughter, flitting among the barricades at my back. The echo of my bride's voice, soaring in the dark behind my eyes along with Ashdrinker's broken song.

"Sleep now, my lovely, sleep now, my dear,
"Dark dreams will fade now your papa is near . . .

"'Get back inside, Dior.'

"'Perhaps you should take a breath, brother?' Celene whispered. '*You are angry.*'

"I snarled at the bloody shadow at my back. 'You think it wise to risk her like this?'

"Celene stood tall in the howling wind, dark hair whipping about her ghastly mask. Her lifeless gaze slipped to me, then Dior, gleaming with fox's cunning.

"'We agree with the Grail. She can hide in the shadowsss no longer.'

"'Finally!' Dior crowed. '*Merci*, mademoiselle!'

"'You treacherous fucking sow.' My sister narrowed her death-pale eyes as I glowered at her. 'You'd risk Dior's life just to score a point off me?'

"'You flatter yourself,' Celene sighed. 'We have alwaysss said Dior must embrace what she is. What she was *born* to be. She showsss valor standing against this foe, and she should be lauded for it. For all your hubris and fury, this is not about you.' She shook her head, eyes burning behind her dreadful mask. 'But they were alwaysss the Black Lion's favorite sins, no? You are damned by Pride, Gabriel. *You are ruled by Wrath.*'

"Fury darkened my heart further, my teeth grinding. My frustration was rising, my temper, my fear, the echoes of that accursed song in my head.

"Fear not the m-monsters, fear not the night,
"Papa is here now and all shall be right.

"I slammed Ashdrinker back into her sheath, turning on Dior with a growl. 'Aright, enough horseshit. Get back inside. Now.'

"'Gabriel, I'm an *edge* here,' she insisted. 'I killed Danton. I can fight!'

"'One lucky strike, and you think you're ready for a war? What was the first lesson I taught you?' I grabbed her by the belt, metal singing as I ripped the blade from her scabbard. And with fangs bared, I hurled Dior's sword over the railing, down into the chasm below. 'A blade and half a clue are twice as dangerous as no blade or clue at all!'

"'Calm yourself, brother,' Celene whispered. '*Your anger deepens . . .*'

"'Damn right it does! And if you knew what these fucking monsters were capable of, there is no way in *hell* you'd be pitting a *child* against—'

"'I'm not a *child!*'

"Dior's cry cut me off, but it was the look on her face that held me still. So much pity. So much grief. So much love in her gaze it near broke my raging heart to pieces.

"'But that's what this is about, isn't it?' she said.

"Her voice fell then. Just a whisper.

"'God, what it's *always* been about . . .'

"Tears shone in Dior's eyes as she reached for my hand, squeezing it tight.

"'I know you're just scared for me,' she said. 'That you can't stand the thought of *losing* someone else. I know you're thinking about Patience and Ast—'

"I slapped her then. Swift. Right across the face. Her head snapped sideways, and her mouth dropped open as thunder rolled, echoing my daughter's name. The sound Dior made was strangled, something between a gasp and a sob. And as she staggered back, hand to cheek, she looked at me as if she couldn't quite believe what I'd done.

"None could fault her for it."

Gabriel shook his head.

"I couldn't believe it myself."

The Last Silversaint met his jailor's eyes, glittering in the dark of their cell. Silence hung heavy between them, yawning like the abyss beneath the Cairnhaem bridge, until—

"Well played, I say." Jean-François shrugged, returning to his tome. "Lachance was being a fool. Almighty only knew what would happen if she fell into the Forever King's clutches. You were the master; she, the pupil. You did well to remind her of her place."

"No," Gabriel replied, staring down at his open palm. "It's the lowest kind of man who raises a hand to his child and calls it love."

"She was not your child."

"Famille is not always blood."

"And love is not always simple. But you *did* love her. You knew what it might cost. Yet you decided to risk bruising the girl's heart, rather than see it torn from her chest. You are not a bad man, Gabriel de León. Sometimes you simply do bad things."

The Last Silversaint drank deep from his goblet, wiped his eyes.

"Coming from you, vampire? That means absolutely nothing."

The historian pursed his lips as Gabriel slipped back into the darkness.

"That slap's echo was like a wheellock shot. Dior licked the corner of her mouth, and my heart sank, belly *twisting* at the sight of her blood. I felt the Dead host stirring behind me; a ripple rolling among the wretched as that red scent kissed the air. And as the thirst rose inside me, hateful and bleak and furious, God help me, I raised my hand for another.

"'Get inside.'

"'You *prick*,' Dior hissed. 'You f-fucking *bastard*.'

"'Better to be a bastard than a fool,' I growled. 'Because God Almighty knows you're being fool enough for the both of us, Lachance. Get the fuck inside. *Now*.'

"Her lower lip trembled. Her eyes welled with tears. I could see such *awful* hurt in them, it might have cleaved me to my heart, if that heart weren't already overflowing with rage. But she didn't let them fall. Instead, she snarled with a fury to match my own. And with one last burning glance to Celene, she turned and ran, off through the thickets of spears, back across the bridge and squeezing through the crack in Cairnhaem's massive doors.

"My pulse was hammering, mind a tempest, half-disbelieving what I'd done. I fumbled for my pipe with shaking hands, eyes blurred with the sting. Loading a full day's dose, I lit it swift, dragging down the bowlful in one burning breath. Celene watched me sidelong, pale eyes gleaming as the storm's eye closed, winds howling between us.

"'You are crying,' she whispered.

"'*DE LEÓN!*' came the cry.

"I sniffed hard, spat into the brink beside me, turned my eyes to the foe. Etched in black on the slopes above, I saw two silhouettes now; maids both, once fair and fine, twisted to horrors by the dread hands of time. Their twinned voices rang as much in my mind as upon the winds, a duet of bloody centuries and bleak majesty.

"'*Good eve to thee, Lion! Thou art in finer form than when last we laid eyes 'pon thee! Our dread father bids us give thee greetings, his assurance that he still awaits thee in the east, and condolence 'pon the feast he made of thy daughter and bride!*'

"Celene glanced to me, grim understanding in her eyes. My teeth ached as I clenched my jaw, hand closing around Ashdrinker's hilt, leather creaking as I *squeezed*.

"'*Shall we parlay?*' the Terrors called. '*Shall we offer concord? Or shall we presume poor brother Danton hath aready played that song to deaf and foolish ears? We shall allow thee safe passage if ye beg it, de León! Gift us the girl, and we shall gift thee thy life!*'

"I felt a hammerblow on my thoughts then; clawed fingers trying to push through my eyes and into the secrets beyond. But the aegis was burning now on my skin, and colossal though the force of those ancient minds were, I forced them out, off, *away*. Touching my flintbox to the barricade before us, I saw Celene flinch as the tapestries burst into hungry flames. And drawing Ashdrinker in one clenched fist, I roared over the rising wind.

"'Get on with it, you fucking maggots! We'll see how many dogs it takes to slay a lion!'

"*Where are w-w-we, Gabriel?* Ash whispered, bewildered.

"I watched the wretched begin to move now, loping down the hill in dark waves, silent and breathless and oh so hungry.

"'We're in trouble, Ash.'

"Oh dear ohd-deardeardear. Where are Astrid and P-P-Patience?

"I looked up to those twins on the hill, silhouetted in the dark just as they'd been the night their father came knocking. Inhaling smoke and exhaling hatred.

"'They're at home, Ash.'

"Oh good g-g-gooooood.

"Celene lifted her arms, dragged her fingernails along her skin. Her claws sliced through porcelain white, brilliant red sluicing her fingertips. The scent stabbed my lungs, pitter-pattered on the flagstones as she glanced at me.

"'Good luck, brother.'

"'Go to hell, sister.'

"'I have been there, Gabriel. They found my company just as disagreeable as you.'

"Her blood rippled, coalescing by dark arte and darker will into her long-blade and whip-length flail. I shouldered off my blanket, Celene hissing as my aegis was unveiled, burning brighter than the barricade we stood behind. Hefting a torch in my free hand, I touched it to the flames, watched the hempcloth begin to burn. Through the rising blaze, I saw the wretched coming, dozens upon dozens, silent as tombs and hungry as wolves.

"Gaze b-black teeth bright sniksnaksnikSNAK!

"I closed my eyes as that horde came on, hair tumbling about my cheeks as I hung my head. I took the span of three breaths, listening to those rushing feet, and in every one, I had to resist the temptation to pray. We were all that stood between Dior and the Forever King now. The only light in her night. But the Almighty had put her down here, after all, with me of all fucking people. I just hoped he knew what the *hell* he was doing . . .

"'You remember when we were young?' I murmured. 'Playing around the forge?'

"Celene nodded. 'Ever outnumbered. Never outmatched. Always, Lionsss.'

"'Just like old times, eh?'

"And then they hit us.

"Shapes out of the dark, hollow eyes and blacktooth grins, skimming viper-swift round the burning barricades and into our bottleneck. I was waiting, my sister beside me, blades hissing as they cut Dead flesh to ribbons. Ashdrinker was singing again; not a nursery rhyme now, but an aria, soaring silver bright inside my head. And I danced to her song, veins flooded with bloodhymn, air burning with the light of the flames on my skin. The wretched reeled as they charged us, hateful, blinded, stumbling. We cut them down, grey snow at our feet slicked red, giving slow ground to the sheer weight of their numbers. I took the hands off a grasping horror, thrust my torch into the tangled nest of another's hair. Celene's bloodblade was a whisper as it killed; a knife through butter on a summer's day, cobbles splattered with the bubbling leavings.

"But as I warned Dior, this was only a probe to test us. And with quickening heart, I realized where the Terrors' opening move would *truly* come from.

"More wretched had swarmed from the dark, using their accursed strength to avoid our barricades entirely. They were coming now, scuttling like spiders along the sides of the bridge, or leaping from gibbet to rusting gibbet, and seething over the railings at our rear.

"'They're flanking us!' I roared. 'Fall back!'

"I cleaved a grinning boything's head from its shoulders, stabbed my torch into the face of leering fiend. Claws ripped my back as I dashed toward the second barricade; a tumble of broken statues and furniture, bristling with a thicket of rusting spears. I heard a series of cracks, sharp, metallic, and the air about me whistled as I vaulted the barricade. The first of the wheellock volley struck the wood by my hand, another shot blasted a line of fire right through my shoulder, another my hip, and I barely held on to my sword. As I hit the flagstones, bleeding, gasping, I heard a voice bellow for a reload, the crunch of boots through snow that told me the swordsmen were advancing on the bridge.

"The Terrors were moving their next pieces into the game.

"Celene vaulted the barricade beside me, and I lit it with my torch, just as the first wretched came tumbling over after her. It was an elderly man, thin and grey, his charge harried by the two spears broken off in his chest and belly. There was enough in him to scream in bewildered pain as fire caught on the barricade and his skin, more shapes barreling over him, a clawing, flaming tumble. Celene shied back, terrified of the blaze, foes in front and at flank. And again, side by side, my sister and I danced."

The Last Silversaint leaned forward, fingers steepled at his chin. The historian was writing swift, caught up in the rush of the battle now as if he too lived it. But the silence stretched on, like a strand of sticky crimson between sundered throat and pouting lip.

"...De León?"

"Some say war is hell, coldblood," Gabriel said. "Others name it heaven. There's thousands of songs and sagas that try to capture the essence of it. That chaos. That mad, blood-drunk ... *thresher*. The minstrels sing of heroism and cowardice. Historians write of the twist of strategy, the boon of technology, the touch of destiny. Grim fate and pure will and dumb fucking luck. They all have a hand to play. But you want to know the card that trumps them all, vampire? The simple, undeniable fulcrum most battles tip upon?"

"Tell me, Silversaint."

Gabriel sighed.

"It's *math*. No songs sung for it. No shrines built in its name. But it's how kings claim thrones and usurpers carve empires." The silversaint shrugged. "Simple math. A man can only swing a sword so many times before he tires. A rifleman can only fire so many volleys before his pouch runs dry. And two people can only hold a stretch of stone one hundred feet long and twenty feet wide for so many minutes before midnight starts to chime, no matter who those two might be. Peerless swordsaint. Deathless bloodmage. Paint the cobbles red as you like, scatter the stone with ash and bone, move like a song and bleed like a martyr and slay like all the winds of winter. If every enemy you kill costs you sixteen inches of ground, your foes need send only seventy-five bodies into the breach before you've nowhere left to run. And the Terrors had brought *hundreds*."

Gabriel dragged his hand down his scarred face, and sighed.

"Math is a bastard.

"We cut them to shreds, Celene and I. My arms weighed like lead and my breath burned like fire, flesh torn by claws and cleaved by blades, split by fists and rent by shot, and still I fought, drooling red, long black curtains of gore-soaked hair about my face. Celene hovered beside me, at the edge of my aegis's forge-red light, porcelain flesh torn, greatcoat in tatters, just as spent as I. And when we'd given all we had, when we'd no strength left but to stand, pressed back to our final barricade with the bronze doors of Cairnhaem looming behind us, then, finally, those dark emperors took the field.

"Alba and Aléne drifted through the dying flames, black and white, hand in hand. They were surrounded by a fresh company of swordsmen—slaved brutes all, clad in Voss livery and armed to their crooked teeth. The storm howled, whipping the Terrors' long coats through the rising smoke, but their hair moved not at all—as if it were wrought of iron like their flesh, like their hearts, as they stepped with squelching boots over the carnage we'd made of their men and monsters, sparing none of them a glance.

"They stopped twenty feet away, behind their wall of thralled meat and swords. Neither of them had yet suffered a scratch, but my muscles were burning, breath ragged, Ash's haft slippery with gore in my trembling fists.

"'We might be in shite here, Hellion . . .'

"Alba and Aléne's eyes flickered to the clocks above the door—the motion of stars, and track of centuries. They blinked in unison, and I saw each had bloody eyes painted upon their lids, giving the uncanny impression they could still see, even with those eyes closed. I reached out and lit our final barricade, hoping to see them step back from the flames. But the Terrors didn't flinch. Leech flesh burns like tinder, and even ancient coldbloods fear fire. But in a contemptuous display, Alba and Aléne removed their riding gloves, one finger at a time, stepping forward to hold their hands in the flames between us, as if to *warm them.*

"They stared at me as they did so, eyes black and unblinking, completely unafeared. After a moment, they withdrew, standing with fingers entwined among their minions once more, and though the flesh of any other leech would've been charred to fucking cinders, I saw the marble of Alba's skin had been merely singed; from bone white to pale grey.

"I nodded, swallowing hard.

"'Oui. We're in shite.'

"'*Kneel,*' they said.

"The command rang in my head, in my heart, and exhausted as I was, bleeding and breathless, I almost succumbed. I could feel their minds, *smashing* against my own, trying to breach my walls. But I pictured my wife and daughter, filled my thoughts with the warmth of their love, and my heart with the fury of their fates.

"'Ladies f-first.' I wheezed, patting my coin pouch. 'I'll m-make it worth your while.'

"'*How puerile thy song, de León.*' Their heads shook simultaneously. '*A boychild's innuendo masking a boychild's fear. Know thee no other tune?*'

"'Why do you ssseek the Grail?'

"The Terrors blinked, gaze shifting from me to Celene. My sister lurked beside me, mask underscored by the firelight, her long, bloody blade unveiled in her hands. And at the sight of her dark magiks, the Terrors hissed, voices thick with hatred.

"'*Esani . . .*'

"'What does Fabién want with Dior?' Celene demanded.

"Alba and Aléne narrowed those ink-black eyes, bristling with rage. Indignity. And oui, perhaps a touch of fear now. '*Who art thou to question us, thieving whelp? We are daughters of the Blood Iron. The Blood Royal. We are thy elders and thy betters.*'

"'I am no *whelp,*' Celene spat. 'I am the last begotten child of Laure, your sister, the Wraith in Red. The blood of the Forever King flows in these veins.'

"The Terrors paused at that, exchanging a brief and black glance.

"'*Bring the girl to us, then, petite nièce. Break the silvered dog beside thee, lay the Grail here at our feet, and the Forever King shall grant thee reward undreamed of.*'

"'But he already has, mes chères tantes.'

"Alba and Aléne tilted their heads. '*Indeed?*'

"'Oh, oui.' Celene nodded, hands rising to her face. 'He brought you here to me.'

"Thunder rolled as my sister dragged her mask away, exposing the awful ruin of her face. Skinless jaw and lipless fangs and beneath her scarf, the skin of her throat ripped free like a troublesome glove—torn away by Laure Voss the day she murdered her.

"'Tonight, we drink your heartsblood, mesdames,' Celene vowed. 'Tonight, I take *all* that was yoursss, and reclaim a little more of what was mine.'

"The thrallswords drew their steel in answer, firelight gleaming on skeletal helms. Across the bridge, the riflemen raised their wheellocks, aiming at our bloodied chests.

"But the Terrors were yet still as stone.

"'*Our dread father yet awaits thee in the east, Lion,*' they told me. '*One last chance we offer, to seek for thy beloved bride and babe, the vengeance due.*'

"I hissed, bleeding, gasping, lifting Ashdrinker in shaking hands.

"'You tell Papa I'll see him soon.'

"And looking over their shoulders, I bellowed into the thunder.

"'*Now,* Phoebe!'

"A shape blurred from the shadows across the bridge, striking from behind the wheellock line. The lioness moved among the riflemen quick as lies, ripping bellies and throats to tatters. She'd struck so fast, four were dead before the screaming began. The remainder tried to recover, but it's hard to bring a longarm to bear at close range, harder still to reload when those golden eyes fall on you and that roar shakes your bones and she charges across the blood-soaked snow, quick as the shot you missed her with.

"But *she* didn't miss.

"Phoebe never missed.

"With the guns silenced, Celene and I retreated up the steps, tore the mighty doors wide between us and fled inside. Enraged, the Terrors sent their thralls flooding after us, spilling into the vast hollow of Cairnhaem's foyer. My aegis burned in the gloom, long shadows stretching out from the feet of those mighty pillars, falling across the great hearth, its blood-red drapes rippling in the wind. Celene and I took one staircase apiece, me backing up the east and she the west, both of us hacking at the thralls that came behind, furious, fearless, soaking the Testaments pages on the walls red. And slow, inexorable, the Terrors stalked after their footsoldiers, content to spend every one, grinding at us until we fell.

"We fought like the Fallen, Celene's bloodblade and flail whispering as she sliced the air, Ashdrinker's aria reaching a silver-bright crescendo in my head. But math is a bastard like I said, coldblood. And all knew in the end, we both of us would falter.

"Celene and I were back-to-back now, atop the mezzanine, thralls still pressing, Terrors still coming, death but a few breaths away. And at last, as those ancient feet touched the balcony, as those red lips curled in triumphant smiles, I roared at the top of my lungs.

"'GO, DIOR!'

"Lightning split the sky as she charged, draperies flung apart as she barreled out from the massive hollow of the hearth's belly, knuckles white on Pony's reins. A sword sliced my shoulders as I flung myself over the balcony rail, striking the foyer floor and swinging up onto Bear's back. Celene was lither, landing on the saddle directly behind me, arms flung about my waist. And Dior in front, my sister and me behind, the three of us charged back out the open door, toward the empty bridge and the slopes now cleared beyond."

"Feign weakness," Jean-François murmured. "Draw your foes out of position in their haste to finish you. Then, strike."

Gabriel smiled. "Rousseau."

The vampire gave an appreciative nod. "Perhaps I should learn chess, after all."

"We galloped down the stairs, the Terrors roaring behind us as thunder answered overhead. Dior caught my eye as we leapt the first barricade, my belly rolling as I saw the bruise on her cheek, the split at her lip, and God, my heart near broke at the sight. I couldn't believe I'd hit her, that wasn't like me, that wasn't . . . *me*. But there'd be time enough to beg forgiveness once we were safe and far from here.

"I only ever wanted the best for that girl.

"I only ever wanted to keep her safe.

"We rode on, through the corpses and smoke and cinder rain, steeds swift as silver. Dior charged ahead, gold-trimmed coat streaming behind her. I came next, Celene holding my waist, wheeling around the barricades and through the rising smoke.

"I didn't see the blow until it struck.

"It came like a thunderbolt, scything so fast the air *boomed* behind it. A warmaul, as long as I was tall, its head the size of a child's coffin and wrought like a roaring bear. It hit Dior's horse with the force of a cannon shot, not so much tearing Pony's head from her shoulders as reducing it to a blast of fine, red mist.

"Dior screamed as she was flung from the saddle.

"I reached toward her and roared her name.

"And Kiara the Wolfmother lifted her hammer for another blow."

VI

BURNING BRIDGES

"I DRAGGED ON my reins, desperate. Dior sailed through the air, wailing. And Kiara's blow came down like God's own fucking thunder.

"Bear was dead before he knew what hit him, the impact an earthquake. Kiara's strength was terrifying, her maul driving what was left of my brave sosya into the stone so hard it shattered. I flew through the air, arms pinwheeling as I crashed into a still-burning barricade, feeling my ribs break, face split. Dior had been flung from her saddle as Pony died, crashing into the stone and now lying sprawled on the blood-soaked flagstones. As Kiara's maul turned Bear into paste, the impact shook the whole bridge, gibbets swaying on their chains and crashing like rusty wind chimes below.

"Celene leapt from the saddle behind me, bloodblade gleaming, eyes narrowed as she cut through the dark like a knife. But though Kiara had been surprised by my sister's arrival that day at Aveléne, she was ready tonight, stepping aside from the arc of Celene's blow and following through with a thunderous strike of her own.

"Her maul hit Celene square in her chest, and my heart dropped as my sister's body simply blew apart, nothing left but a red spray across the sky. But I caught a flash of crimson *behind* the Wolfmother then, realized Celene had used the same ploy she'd used on me at San Michon—that trick of the eye, that spell of the blood. As her doppelgänger evaporated, Celene struck from behind, cutting into Kiara's back, once, twice, cleaving Dead flesh and bone. The Wolfmother staggered, but kept her feet, turning with a bloody roar.

"Celene was one of the finest blades I'd ever seen. Kiara was a tower, a tempest. I've no knowing who might've proved the victor had they faced each other on even ground. But my sister was already bloodied from our battle against the Voss, and Kiara was fresh, swift, and deathly strong. They hewed at each other, bloodblade and warmaul, flail and fist. Yet in the end, the dice they played with were loaded. Celene wrapped her flail about Kiara's wrist, looking to disarm her and end the brawl. But the Wolfmother proved the stronger, dragging my sister off-balance, slayerbraids whipping through the air behind her like serpents as she brought her maul around in a double-handed strike. The blow hit Celene in the middle of her spine, and I heard every rib in her chest shatter. My sister flew, head flung back—just *flew* like a fucking kickball through the dark, up and over the snow-clad slopes behind us, her blade and flail reduced to a spray of red behind her.

"Kiara turned to me, her grin dripping with horse gore.

"'Hullo again, Lion.'

"I'd lost Ashdrinker in my fall, barehanded and gasping as I dragged myself off the bloody stone. With a cry, I flung myself past Kiara's strike, feeling that iron bear's head scythe just shy of my spine. The blow struck so hard that the cobbles split, cracks arcing out across the bridge's surface toward the mooring stones.

"I caught sight of more figures back where the bridge met the cliff. Kane—that brute who'd brawled Lachie at Aveléne, astride a black tundra pony. He was flanked by two snowhounds, and another figure I'd never seen; a mortal lad, handsome and knife-sharp. The Headsmun's arm was still partway missing—a wasted limb of raw bone and fresh flesh growing from the stump that Ashdrinker had left him with. But he still carried that massive greatsword, the kind of weapon only the Blood Dyvok could wield with any skill. I'd no idea where the hell Phoebe was; God knows I could have used her with these odds. But Kane made no move toward me at least.

"The Wolfmother, it seemed, had claimed me for herself.

"I was exhausted, bleeding, unarmed—it was only the light of my aegis that saved me, I swear it. Stabbing bright into the Wolfmother's eyes, sending her terrifying blows wide, each one shaking the bridge in its bones with a sound like thunder.

"'Ye owe the Dyvok blood, Lion.'

"*WHOOOSH.*

"'And blood now I claim.'

"*BOOOOM.*

"If I could get my hands on her, I could boil her veins dry with my father's gift. But I was bleeding, broken, gasping. Rolling aside from an overhand strike, I rose to my feet and reached toward her throat, but Kiara clipped me on the backhand; a touch still hard enough to shatter every bone in my arm, to send me flying like a toy into the railing, breath bursting from my lungs. I saw stars, black and blinding, trying in vain to roll to my feet. This wasn't the place I ended, I knew it—I had business with the Forever King, I'd not fall to some Untamed *lackey*. But the Wolfmother loomed above me, maul raised high, and looking up, I saw Mahné, Angel of Death, reach out his hand.

"'When ye meet great Tolyev in hell,' Kiara hissed, 'tell him it was me who sent ye.'

"The scuff of boots.

"The whisper of a chain shirt.

"The glint of fresh blood on starsteel.

"Dior rose up behind the Wolfmother, Ashdrinker in hand, smeared in the girl's own blood. Teeth bared in fury, she plunged the blade toward Kiara's back. And for a moment, my fool's heart thought it would end just as it had when she killed Danton on the Mère.

"But now, unlike then, she wore metal armor—heavy, noisy, slow.

"Now, unlike then, Kane cried warning as she struck.

"And now, unlike then, Dior got caught red-handed.

"Kiara turned, raising her maul and catching the girl's blow across its haft. Ashdrinker bit the iron, sparks flying as she scraped her way down the hilt. But for all her fury, and despite her courage, Dior had only four weeks' training under her belt. Her foe had the strength of a goddess, and the experience of blood-soaked decades.

"'Oh, *shit* . . .' the girl breathed.

"Kiara smashed Ashdrinker aside, the blade glittering like the star it had been forged from, sailing over the railing and into the void below. I croaked warning as the Wolfmother seized Dior's throat, lifting her in a grip that could grind iron to dust. The girl's eyes grew wide, feet kicking, fingers clawing, my heart frozen in terror as I awaited that awful *snap* . . .

"'*HOLD!*'

"Kiara blinked, turned toward Cairnhaem. Ears ringing, chest bubbling, I saw two figures drifting through the ember rain behind us. A cadre of bloodied thrallswords marched behind them as they threaded the wreckage and dead horses, wreathed in smoke.

"'Hold?' Kiara glowered. 'By what right do ye command *me*? All west of the Mère and north of the Ūmdir is province of the Blood Dyvok. Ye trespass in the dominion of my dark Laerd.' The Wolfmother drew herself up to her full impressive height. 'I'll have yer names, cousins. And mistake nae demand for request.'

"Chill wind struck the bridge, smoke parting, unveiling the Terrors in all their pallid glory. The white and black of their brocade was spattered now with red. Their dark eyes burned with fire, and oui, perhaps a touch of dread at the sight of the girl in that monstrous grip. They regarded Kiara a long moment, heads tilted at precisely the same angle.

"'*We are daughters of the king of this kingdom eternal. Iron of heart and royal of Blood. Have ye but one drop of merit in thy veins, knowest our names, dost thou.*'

"Kiara seemed to shrink a little as recognition sank in. 'Lady Alba. Lady Aléne.'

"The Terrors inclined their heads.

"'I am—'

"'*Kiara Dyvok.*' Ink-black eyes skimmed her cohort, lingering on the iron manacles dangling from her belt. '*We know thee, Wolfmother.*'

"'Then ye know I am daughter to the Priori of my line, dread and unconquered sovereign of all Ossway.' Kiara motioned toward me with her gore-slick maul, Dior still struggling in her grip. 'The debt between this—'

"'*Thy debts concern us not. The girl is ours alone.*'

"'Girl? I—'

"'*Ours,*' the Terrors repeated. '*And preach not of sovereignty to the Voss, whelp. Thy paupered line hath not the knowing of the word, let alone its keeping.*'

"'. . . Whelp?' Kiara spat. 'I am thirdborn of Nikita the Blackheart! Broodson of Tolyev the Butcher himself! I have walked this earth a hundred and—'

"'*Heartbeats. Blinkings. Give her over. Then get thee and thy rabble gone.*'

"The Wolfmother fell mute, glowering. Her pride was bleeding to be spoken to so, but I thought for certain she'd yet obey. Glancing to the Headsmun and houndboy behind her, she cast Dior to the floor, the girl squealing as she hit the flagstones with a *crunch*. Kiara snapped her fingers, held out one hand. The Headsmun glowered, yet reached to his throat, and there I saw a golden vial—the same kind I'd snapped from Kiara's throat at Avaléne. With a scowl, the Headsmun tossed the vial to the Wolfmother, who snatched it from the air in one heavy paw. Taking a draught, she swallowed deep, shivering all the way to her toes. And when she spoke next . . . well, in truth my jaw near hit the damn floor.

"'These lands are dominion of the Blood Dyvok. All prey within is *ours.*'

"The Terrors glanced at each other, incredulous. But as the—"

"*Ahem.*"

Gabriel stumbled to a halt as Jean-François cleared his throat in dramatic fashion.

"Really?" he scowled. "You're interrupting now?"

"Why did Kiara's defiance surprise you, de León?" the historian asked.

"*Now?* To tell you what you already fucking know? This is one of the classic contests! Ironheart versus Untamed? That's like wine versus whiskey, or blonde versus brunette, you can't just—"

The historian began tapping his quill on the page, eyebrow raised.

Tap Tap Tap Tap Tap Tap Tap.

Gabriel hung his head, dragging one hand down his face, brow to chin.

"Look," he sighed. "Coldbloods hate each other like poison. Throw two lions into a cage together, one ends up shitting out the other's bones. There's only three chains holding your so-called society together, and without at least two, the whole shitshow would've gone up in flames centuries ago."

Gabriel held up his hand, counting on his fingers.

"Servage. Famille. Soumission."

"Explain," Jean-François demanded.

Gabriel rolled his eyes. "*Servage* is blood slavery. Leeches forcing other leeches to drink from their wrists. Once. Twice. Even three times. *Famille* is self-explanatory—so long as they don't fuck with each other's food, leeches of the same brood tend to tolerate each other's presence. Last, and most important, is *soumission*. The longer a vampire has lived, the more powerful it becomes. So if you're a fresh-faced cub who wants to be a lion one night, you'd best pay the lions around you respect. Or, like I say. Shit and bones."

The Last Silversaint sipped his wine, shaking his head.

"It was no real surprise Kiara had been dismissed by the Terrors—even with a hundred years under her belt, she'd have seemed an infant to creatures as ancient as Alba and Aléne. But hearing a mediae giving lip to a pair of monsters who predated empire . . . well, let's just say you're more likely to hear me turn down another bottle of this fine Monét."

Gabriel threw a meaningful glance at the almost-empty wine on the table.

"That was a hint, Chastain."

"And one possessed of your usual featherlight subtlety," the historian murmured, still writing in his tome. "But please, continue."

Gabriel swirled his goblet and took a mouthful. "So. Despite *all* common sense, Kiara stood tall. Dior was crumpled on the stone at her feet. I lay in a puddle of my own blood, my left arm shattered, face broken, trying to breathe through punctured lungs. Kane Dyvok and that houndboy lurked at the edge of the bridge, their dogs watching with blood-red eyes. The Voss thralls stood with weapons raised and jaws clenched. And the eldest daughters of the Forever King stared at the Wolfmother, as if truly noticing her for the first time.

"*'Taken leave of thy senses, hast thou?'* they demanded. '*Queens we were, when thy wretched forebears were but beggars in the mire. Ancient we were, when thy ancestors didst slither from betwixt their mothers' thighs. And were we not thy elders, still we would be thy* betters. *We are Ironheart. Our line ruled the dark when yours still cowered in their tombs for fear of moonslight, Dyvok. And when our dread father sits 'pon the fivethrone of this empire, thou shalt cower again.'*

"Kiara scowled. 'All Shall Kneel?'

"The Terrors smiled. '*All. Shall. Kneel.'*

"'Know ye, what we Dyvok say to that?'

"The Wolfmother lifted her warmaul above her head. Her eyes flooded red with the blood she'd drunk, burning with murderous fury as she flung herself into the air; the first deadly step into the fury of a Dyvok Tempest.

"'DEEDS NOT WORDS!'

"Thing is, the Terrors didn't even bother to step aside. The strength of the Untamed is terrifying, but the Voss aren't named *Ironhearts* for nothing. And as the Wolfmother sailed through the air, bellowing in rage and bringing her maul down with all the unholy strength in her veins, the Terrors reached up to ward off her blow.

"Not with their hands, mind you.

"With their smallest *fingers.*

"Truth told, I wasn't surprised. Ashdrinker had broken on Fabién's skin, after all, and she was enchanted starsteel. An ordinary weapon would shatter upon the skin of an ancient Voss like glass. So, I think it was something of a shock for *everyone* when Kiara's blow struck home—not at the Ironhearts themselves, mind you, but at her true target:

"The flagstones at their feet.

"That maul struck the Cairnhaem bridge like the hand of God. I felt the impact in my *bones.* And impossible as it seemed, the rock that had spanned the gulf between those spires for heaven knew how many millennia . . . well . . . it just fucking *disintegrated.*

"The impact rippled outward, stone dust blinding, granite split asunder.

The Terrors had time enough to blink before they were falling, down with the rubble and horse bodies and screaming thralls, not a hair on their heads out of place as they plummeted into the chasm below. Cracks spread and rock groaned, the whole structure rolled like the ocean in a storm. And my stomach turned a dreadful flip as I saw the railing Dior was slumped against crumble, and with a bloody croak, the wounded girl tumbled backward into the gulf.

"'NO!'

"With a roar, I threw myself across the span, knowing it was already too late. But skidding on my belly across the bloodied rock, I almost sobbed with relief as I saw Dior dangling from one of the rusted gibbets below, metal flaking away in her grip.

"'GAAABE!'

"'Hold on, I'm coming! I'm—'

"A vise grip seized my neck, bones grinding as Kiara ripped me off the deck. Her grin was sticky sharp, eyes alight with vengeance, the snap of my spine just a *squeeze* away—

"A shadow flew from the dark, swift as lightning. I heard Kane roar warning, caught a glimpse of rust-red as Phoebe struck, talons sinking into the Wolfmother's shoulders. The lioness was torn, bloody—I supposed the Untamed had mistaken her for an ordinary beast, kicked the living shite out of her, and left her for dead. But only silver can kill a duskdancer, coldblood. Silver or magik or the cruel teeth of time. And despite her hurts, Phoebe fought on, true to her heartsblooded vow to Dior.

"*If by my blood or boon or breath might ye be kept safe . . .*

"Kiara roared and dropped me, and with a cry, I hit the railing and flipped over into the gulf. As I grabbed the ledge, desperate, the impact snapped the rusted bracket holding Dior's gibbet in place. I heard the girl shriek as the metal broke, and with a gasp, a curse, I seized the falling chain in my right hand, clinging to the bridge with my shattered left. I roared in agony, helpless, Dior hanging from the cage, me holding its chain, only a few links of corroded iron between her and the gulf below.

"'Dior!'

"'Gaaaabe!'

"'C-climb!'

"'I c-can't . . . !'

"'I c-can't hold it, damn you. Climb!'

"Broken and bloodied, teeth slicked red, the girl hauled herself upward.

The cage snapped away from the chain, and she lunged, catching the icy links with a curse, the impact sending a wave of white fire up my broken arm. I closed my eyes, pain lancing through my body as she crawled ever higher. Phoebe yet danced with Kiara above, but I could hear Kane had joined the fray, despite his mangled arm. The duskdancer now fought two on one, and I knew we'd only moments before Phoebe fell.

"'*Climb!*'

"Bridge shaking.

"Cracks spreading.

"Fingers slipping.

"'Dior . . . f-for Godssakes, *CLIMB!*'

"I felt my grip failing as she seized hold of my bloody fingers. I felt my heart sink in my chest. I looked down into her eyes as the chain fell away into the brink below; a brief second, desperate love filling my chest despite the hurt between us, whispering the same lie my wife had whispered to my daughter the night he knocked on our door.

"'All will be well, love . . .'

"My grip on the bridge gave out. Our fall began. Down into dark. Down into sleep. But from the black above, a figure reached out, and I roared in agony as she seized my broken hand in hers. Jerked to a halt, I looked up, saw my sister dangling upside down, legs wrapped in the railing, eyes narrowed against my burning light, her skin smoking and spitting at the touch of the silver on mine.

"'CLIMB, CHÉRIE!'

"Dior scuttled up my body like a bleeding, gasping spider. Planting a kiss on my bloodied cheek, she lunged, seizing Celene's free hand. My sister pulled the girl upward scrabbling, scrambling, safe from the fall. But not the doom above.

"Phoebe yet fought the Untamed, fleet as the wind. The Headsmun had caught the worst of her fury, on his knees clutching his bloodied face with his one good hand. But at last, Angel Fortuna turned her back on us, just as she always did. As the duskdancer lunged at the fallen coldblood, Kiara seized a fistful of russet-red with one bloodied fist. And with a strength beyond any mediae I'd seen, she swung the duskdancer by her own tail, smashing her back and forth with force enough to shatter the flagstones.

"'Filthy!'

"CRUNCH.

"'Fucking!'

"CRUNCH.

"'*Whore!*'

"With a final roar, Kiara flung Phoebe off the shattered bridge, the lioness's body spinning limp and broken, out through the black. Dior screamed Phoebe's name, thunder rocking the skies above. Breath burning, arm screaming, I looked up into Celene's eyes. My sister dangled yet upside down, one hand holding the minced remains of mine, my blood oozing through her fingers. We were all that remained now; the last two pieces on the board, enemies closing in around our Emperor above. Just like when we were children, fighting back-to-back around our papa's forge. Ever outnumbered. Never outmatched.

"I grinned with bloody teeth. 'Just like old times . . .'

"'No.'

"Celene met my eyes, gleaming with hatred.

"'*Nothing* like old timessss.'

"And she let me go.

"I saw her scissor upward, arm flung out as she summoned her bloodblade again. I felt thunder split the sky as she flew back over that railing toward Kiara's back. I heard Dior scream at the top of her lungs. And then, the descent was all that remained.

"Rushing wind in my ears.

"Breaking heart in my chest.

"And down, down into the dark, I fell."

VII

BELLY OF THE BEAST

THE LAST SILVERSAINT tilted his head back, drinking deep. The historian watched from the armchair opposite, one blond eyebrow arched. Gabriel finished his wine, sighing as he reached for the Monét and, despite all hopes to the contrary, found it finished.

"No song so sad as an empty bottle," he murmured.

"She let you fall," Jean-François mused. "Your sister."

"Well, for the sake of historical accuracy, it's probably safer to say she dropped me."

"That was rather mean-spirited of her."

Gabriel nodded, rueful. "Celene was a *behemothic* cunt."

Jean-François chuckled. "Still. It seems a fool's gambit to toss you aside before the battle was won. Dread sanguimancer she might've been, but she was wounded. Spent. Your Hellion had little chance against two highblooded Dyvok alone."

"Phoebe had already cut them to ribbons. Wounded and unarmed, I'd not have been much help in the fight anyway, and Celene knew if I somehow made it off that bridge alive, I'd make good on my promise and take the Grail to the Highlands. If she ended me face-to-face, Dior would never trust her again. But if I simply slipped from her grip in the heat of battle . . ." Gabriel shrugged. "My sister played the cards she'd been dealt."

"And what cards did the Wolfmother play in response?"

"Well, that's the problem, coldblood." The silversaint stroked his smooth chin. "I've no fucking idea. I was rather preoccupied, gravity being what it is."

"You survived the fall, that much is obvious."

Gabriel nodded. "Palebloods don't die easy. But the roads I found myself on afterward led me places I'd not imagined. It'd be months before I heard word of Dior again."

"So." The historian sighed, looking to the thin window. "We come to it at last."

". . . Come to what, Chastain?"

"My dove?" the Marquis called.

The cell door opened swiftly, hinges creaking. Meline awaited on the other side, head bowed and dutiful, adoration in her eyes. "Master?"

"Bring the good chevalier another bottle, my love. We must keep our guest amused in our absence." Jean-François glanced to the silversaint. "Unless I could tempt you with something stronger? Meline could entertain you, if you wish?"

Gabriel glanced to the woman, and for a moment, Jean-François saw she met his gaze. The Marquis knew his majordomo hated the silversaint—she'd never forgive his attack on her beloved master, after all. But the vampire also knew the look of desire, and he saw Meline's skin prickling as her gaze drifted over the silversaint's mouth, the arc of his lips. In the end, no drug could hold a candle to the Kiss. No sin of mortal flesh could compare. And as much as she despised him, Gabriel could give her *that*. Clawing and cursing, bare and begging and biting, the promise of it thudding along her jawline, rising in her quickened breath . . .

Jean-François smiled as Gabriel tore his eyes from Meline's throat.

"Wine is fine."

"I could have my boy bring refreshment if you've desire of a different flavor." The Marquis frowned, befuddled. "What was his name, dove?"

"Dario, Master," Meline replied.

"Ah, oui. *Dario*." The vampire sighed the name, his smile, razorblades. "He has not served me long, but he is *exquisite*, de León. I can easily arrange a sampling? Or if you like, he and Meline could *both*—"

"Wine," Gabriel growled, "is *fine*."

Jean-François chuckled. "See to it, love."

With a last glance to the silversaint, Meline curtseyed and left the room, locking the door behind her. Jean-François took a kerchief from his frockcoat, Gabriel frowning as he watched the vampire cleaning the golden nib of his quill. Stowing it in a wooden case, the historian closed the leather-bound chronicle in his lap, and with another, longer sigh, he rose from his armchair, smoothing the lines of his coat with one slender hand.

"Where are you going?" the silversaint asked. "The night is young."

"And I shall return before its end, mon ami," the vampire smiled.

"I thought your Empress wanted the whole of my tale?"

Jean-François adjusted his cravat about his wounded throat. "I think we may consign pretense to the flames, Gabriel. My Empress wishes the story of the Grail. And indeed, Dior Lachance's tale is in large part your own. But for now at least, the threads of her tapestry seem to have slipped your clever fingers, and it falls to another to weave for a while."

"What the hell are you talking about?" Gabriel scowled. "What *other*?"

"You are not the only prisoner in this château, Silversaint."

"Of that, I've no doubt. But the cup is broken, Chastain. The Grail is *gone*. And there's none alive who know her tale better than I."

"No," the vampire agreed. "None alive."

The Last Silversaint's eyes narrowed. The armrests of his chair creaked dangerously as he squeezed. "You can't mean . . ."

"Can I not?"

"No," Gabriel snarled, incredulous. "Margot's not *that* fucking stupid."

Jean-François raised a hand as the silversaint rose from his chair. "I would advise against any outbursts of temper, Gabriel. I am certain you would rather wait here in the company of good wine and willing flesh than walk with me back to hell. Because hell is *exactly* where I am headed." The vampire met the silversaint's eyes, the air crackling between them. "You may draw cold comfort from that at least."

"You can't believe a word she says," Gabriel spat. "That bitch is made of lies."

"Whereas I am certain every note you have sung to me thus far is God's own truth." Jean-François smiled, almost affectionate. "Every coin has two faces, mon ami. Every tale, two tellings. We shall return to yours presently, no fear. But until then . . ."

The door swung open silently, Meline stepping back into the room. She carried a fresh bottle of Monét and a gold bell, wrought with howling wolves. Her skin prickled as she placed both on the table, glancing at Gabriel through the long, sooty haze of her lashes.

"Do you wish me to . . . remain, Master?"

Jean-François raised a lazy eyebrow in Gabriel's direction. The silversaint was silently seething, his hands in white-knuckle fists. And for the first time since they'd met, the vampire fancied he caught a sliver of true fear in those storm-grey eyes.

"I think our guest would prefer solitude for now, love." The historian glanced at the bell on the tray. "Ring if you've an itch, de León. Someone will be along to scratch it."

"You've no idea the devil you waltz with, Chastain."

"Perhaps not." The vampire inclined his head. "But I do *love* to dance."

The historian strode from the room, velvet frockcoat whispering about his heels. He could feel the silversaint's gaze burning a hole in the back of his head as Meline shut the door behind them, locked it firmly. The six thrall-swords outside the cell bowed low, their eyes downturned as the Marquis reached into his pocket, lifting a small black mouse on the palm of his hand. Gazing into the creature's dark eyes, he murmured.

"Keep an eye on our guest, Armand."

Placing his familiar on the flagstones, the vampire followed the stairs down to the château, Meline walking swift behind. With every step, the smile he'd proffered for the silversaint's benefit faded, the grim amusement he'd felt at de León's fear grew more distant. The watchful familiars and deathless courtiers he passed were but shades, a darker shadow now swelling in his mind. He knew he was in no true danger, that his mother would risk no harm to her favorite child. But the thought of this . . . *abomination*, the litany of its crimes, the notion he must somehow win its trust . . .

Ironbound doors were unlocked at his command, and he descended into the château's bowels, past the limit of all light and hope. If Sul Adair's upper reaches were a hymn to heaven and earth, the dungeons beneath were an ode to the abyss; silent and dark and utterly forgot. Thrallswords marched at his side, Meline his ever-dutiful second, boots ringing crisp on black stone as they wound down hidden paths, farther and farther from the light. And at the last, in the deepest, darkest pit within Sul Adair's belly, the Marquis Chastain and his company stopped outside a pair of heavy stone doors.

They were banded in silver, sealed with a lock and chain of the same. Jean-François withdrew the key his dame had entrusted to him, handed it to his majordomo. Wincing with discomfort, Meline loosed the silver padlock, Jean-François stepping back as the thralls unwound the chains. And at a nod, straining, the men dragged the heavy doors wide.

A cell waited beyond, black as pitch and smelling faintly of blood and char. Its walls were cut from raw rock, rough-hewn and hasty, ringing with the song of rushing water. Fifty feet wide, fifty feet deep, it ended at a jagged drop into a rushing tumble of dark water, still flowing despite the ever-winter gripping the world far above.

An underground river.

Three thrallswords stepped into the cell, cautious, placing an ornate leather armchair at the water's edge, a mahogany table beside it. A chymical globe, two crystal goblets, and a bottle of green glass were set atop it. Their work done, the men retreated with torches held high, never once turning their backs on the river, the dark shore beyond.

Meline wrung her hands, pleading. "Master, I . . ."

Jean-François kissed his fingertips, pressed them to the woman's lips.

"See to de León. I will call if I have need."

Her eyes shone with fear as she bowed her head. Jean-François glanced to the man looming beside him—six and a half feet of thralled muscle, flaming torch in hand. His dark hair was slicked back from a widow's peak, beard trimmed so sharp it might cut the lips.

"If I *should* have occasion to shout, Capitaine Delphine, *do* come quickly."

The capitaine placed his right hand on the Chastain livery at his breast. "Marquis."

Jean-François stepped into the cell, his leather-bound history pressed between his palms. The doors thumped closed behind him, all the world muted through the stone, under the river's babbling rush. He listened to the chains being fixed in place, the padlock snapping shut, faint breath and crackling torches and the thudding of Meline's fearful pulse. He looked about the cell; featureless, cold, and save for the chymical globe at the river's edge, utterly lightless. As deep and dark a prison as his Empress could fashion.

And then, he looked to the thing who called that prison home.

She was tall, slender, pale as frost. Lurking on the cusp of the light at the river's far shore. Powerless to cross. Her head was bowed, long midnight-blue hair draped about porcelain cheeks. She wore leathers and torn silks and a beautiful, ornate coat, fit for the Emperor himself. The fabric was crimson, trimmed with golden filigree, stained with old blood and new ashes and the ruins of hateful ambition. The lower half of her face, her jaw, her dreadful, murderous *teeth* were locked behind a muzzle, set with silvered bars. And she watched him, silent, rage burning like an angel's blade, stare black as a devil's soul.

"I am Marquis Jean-François of the Blood Chastain, Historian of Her Grace Margot Chastain, First and Last of Her Name, Undying Empress of Wolves and Men."

The monster said nothing.

"You are Celene Castia, Last of the Liathe."

Still, the monster named Celene made not a sound. Her eyes burned like candlelight in the dark; the air felt sticky-black and lush. It seemed for a moment that the Marquis stood not at the edge of a river, but the abyss itself, and that only the cold press of those *teeth* to his throat might save him. But he turned aside, set his history upon the table, scratching at the wound beneath his cravat. And smoothing his frockcoat, Jean-François took a seat in the leather armchair, looking back across the water.

"Will you say nothing, mademoiselle?"

The Liathe remained mute, shaking like a newborn foal, eyes fixed on his throat.

"I can wait all night," the historian said. "And as many nights thereafter as required. How many have you languished down here already? Seven? Eight? The pain must be unspeakable. But it can all end, mademoiselle, if you will speak to me instead."

The monster stayed mute. Wracked and shivering.

"Alas, then." The Marquis sighed. "You do not mind if I sit and read awhile? Your brother was quite forthcoming, and there is much to review."

Jean-François crossed his legs and opened the tome in his lap. Sucking soft upon his bottom lip, he let his eyes roam the pages, bold dark script flowing like the waters between them, drawing him back to the battle at Cairnhaem, the—

"Gabriel."

Jean-François felt a small thrill in his belly. Turning another page with a steady hand.

"Hmm?" he murmured, glancing up. "I beg pardon, Mlle Castia?"

The thing glowered on the light's edge, her stare black and hard as stone. Through the silvered cage locked across her mouth, Jean-François fancied he caught a flash of fangs.

"My brother is . . . *speaking* to you?"

The historian patted the tome in his lap. "At some length."

The monster hissed then, a single word, dripping such venom it might have burned a hole in the stone at her feet.

"*Coward.*"

The Marquis smoothed a lock of curling blond from his cheek. "Some would call it wisdom, to bend rather than break. For break we all must, cousin, you and I know better than most. The thirst *always* wins. But my pale Empress wishes to hear your story, mademoiselle. Rather than leave you here to rot in the dark, in her infinite generosity, Margot has offered you opportunity to speak. Of your past. Of your exploits."

"Of the Grail."

"Oui." The historian smiled, chocolat eyes shining. "And of the Grail."

The monster hung her head, her voice soft as velvet.

". . . What has Gabriel told you?"

"As much as he can, for now. I am dearly hoping you might bridge some of his gaps. We last spoke of the battle at Cairnhaem, he and I. The Terrors. The Wolfmother." The vampire drummed his fingertips upon the page. "Your betrayal."

"*My* betrayal?"

"So he named it."

"And you believe him?" The monster shook her head, voice trembling with cold rage. "My brother is a drunkard. A braggart. But above all, a *liar.*"

"Well," Jean-François smiled, thin. "All men have their frailties. But I have every confidence you shall set his record straight."

"No, sinner," she hissed, low and dangerous. "I am disciple of dread Wulfric. A liathe of the Esana, sworn to a covenant old when this empire was but a babe, squalling in its fivefold crib. I am bearer of a hundred shriven souls and a *thousand* stolen years. Granddaughter of a Forever King. And servant of the King of Heaven itself."

The monster shook her head.

"No coward, I. Nor traitor, neither."

"A shame." The Marquis trailed one sharp claw along his lip, and gave a grudging nod. "Yet, one cannot deny the courage you display with refusal, considering the torments you suffer. I commend your integrity, Mlle Castia. In fact . . .." The historian turned to the table, lifting the bottle atop it. "I shall drink to it."

And with a smile, he cracked the black wax seal with one long fingernail. The perfume struck him; heady, thick, iron-bright. Jean-François heard the monster across the water hiss through grinding teeth as he poured, filling one goblet, then the other. The blood was still warmed by the body heat of the thrall who'd carried it, flooding into the crystal; a dark meniscus so smooth it might have cast a reflection if only the Marquis had one to throw. And inhaling deep of that brilliant bouquet, the historian raised his glass to the thing across the river.

Though Jean-François had neither seen nor heard her move, the abomination stood much closer now. Feet poised at the very water's edge. Her eyes were locked on the blood, claws biting bone-deep into her palms. Yet the veins beneath her skin were so parched, her hunger so profound, the wounds bled not a drop.

"Santé," the historian smiled.

Jean-François sipped the blood, shivering as that liquid fire kissed his tongue, rich as goldglass, deep as oceans. He closed his eyes, let it slide down his throat, uncoiling from his belly and out to every finger's tip. When he opened his eyes again, the monster was still staring, *shaking*, poised on the very brink of that rushing flow and fighting with every mote of her wretched soul not to fling herself into the water in a vain attempt to cross.

To drink.

Oh, God, to *drown* . . .

He lifted the second goblet, filled to its brim. Rising slow to his feet, he held out the cup to the thing across the river.

"Will you still not speak, mademoiselle?"

The Last Liathe hissed, hate and misery and famine bubbling in her throat. Jean-François lifted the glass he offered, studying the play of light in the crimson.

"As you like it."

And with a sigh, he tossed the goblet into the water.

The glass struck the edge as it fell, splintering, droplets of blood gleaming like dark rubies on the stone. The monster dropped to her knees, lunging with a scream toward the water, hand outstretched and twisting, clawing. But the river might well have been a wall of flame, and as the goblet vanished into the flood, the Liathe hung her head, a shuddering, heartsick moan slipping over her teeth.

"Oh, *God* . . ."

"My mistress has time, mademoiselle," the historian lied. "Time in abundance. I shall return amorrow, perhaps the night thereafter, and meanwhile, you may weigh your agony against your integrity. Scream as loud as the former demands and the latter permits. We have buried you too deep for even your Almighty to hear."

The historian picked up his tome. And leaving the open bottle to weave its perfume in the dark, he strode back toward the doors.

"Wait . . ."

He stopped. Ruby lips curling.

"Great Redeemer, *w-wait* . . ."

Jean-François turned. The monster was yet on her knees by the water's edge, head hung low, fingernails clawing the stone. For all the stolen power in her veins, for all the horrors she had wrought, Celene Castia seemed for a moment to only be that which she'd *been*. A maid from the Nordlund provinces. A sister. A daughter.

A girl.

"Give us the b-bottle," she begged. "And we will give you what you w-want."

Jean-François lifted his chin, glowering. "Be this some ruse . . ."

"No ruse. God help us." Something between a growl and a sob bubbled in her throat, and the historian realized the monster would be weeping, save that she'd not blood enough left inside her for tears. "Give us the b-bottle, sinner. And we will speak."

Jean-François walked slow back to the table, heel-toe, heel-toe, and by the time he reached the water's edge, Celene was shuddering so badly, it seemed she might simply fall apart. The historian had once gone four nights without sating his thirst, and he could only imagine the agony she now burned with. But still, to see her—this horror, this *legend*—so abased, filled him with something close to contempt.

This *is the thing I feared?*

He tossed the bottle across the water, fifty feet, glass glinting in the light. In her haste to snatch it, she almost dropped it, blood sluicing from its open throat and splashing upon her hands. Desperate, the monster pressed the bottle's lip against her silver muzzle and upended it, spilling the bounty into her waiting mouth. She drank without pause, starving, utterly wretched, reaching the bottom and moaning as the dregs dripped onto her tongue. And though her mouth was caged behind bars of purest silver, still she licked the blood from them, from her hands, tongue and fingers sizzling on the metal, wisps of black smoke rising into the air.

Jean-François took his seat, glancing to his own goblet on the table beside him.

From his coat, the historian produced a wooden case carved with two wolves, two moons. He drew a long quill from within, black as the stare of the thing that watched him, placing a small bottle upon the armrest of his chair. Dipping quill to ink, Jean-François looked up with dark and expectant eyes.

Celene drew a deep breath, inhaling the scent of blood and silver.

"Begin," the vampire said.

BOOK THREE

THE
UNTAMED

Crimson Glade. Ah, just to speak its name lights a fire in the hearth of my old heart. Silvered saints and deathless fiends, blessed warriors and mindless corpses, so much blood they say thirteen years later, the snow is still stained red. And among it all, ink burning so bright it seemed all the fires of heaven blazed upon his skin, he stood triumphant, the barrowking's blade naked and drenched in his hand.

I was there, my friend. And to this day, I dream of it. I have danced the places in-between, supped nectar from twixt the thighs of the faemaids of Baanr Aóbd, trod the everroad at the End of All Things, and I tell you now, no horror nor wonder have I known so deep as the day Gabriel de León won the war in Ossway.

The day dread Tolyev died.

—DANNAEL Á RIAGÁN, SOOTHSINGER
THE LAST SONG, A MEMOIR, 674 AE

LITTLE MOUNTAIN

"WHERE SHALL WE start?" Celene asked, dragging one sharp fingernail along the stone. "Shall we speak of my childhood in Lorson? Of those sunbright years before daysdeath found us, and my brother and I learned to loathe each other? Shall we pretend any of it matters?"

"To discern the pattern in the threads, one must study the tapestry entire." Jean-François offered the most charming smile of his arsenal. "And as I told your brother, in my not inconsiderable experience, histories are best begun at their beginning."

"For creatures such as you and he. But there is an ocean between you and I, sinner."

"You wield that word as if you intend insult," the historian mused. "Yet in your brief handful of years, you have been the architect of more atrocity than most ancien I know of. There is a saying about glass houses and thrown stones."

"*There be no room for sin in a heart filled with the fire of God.*"

Jean-François frowned at the unfamiliar quote. ". . . The Book of Vows?"

"No."

The historian tapped his quill against his lip. "You are still of the delusion, I take it, that the cause of the Faithless was righteous? How to rationalize that, given the enormity of your failure? If you *were* chosen of God, as the insane ramblings of your Priori claimed, how is it that Illia and every one of her followers now rots in a well-deserved hell?"

"Not every one," Celene replied.

"True. *You* rot in my Empress's cellar instead."

"I am where God wishes me to be."

The Marquis chuckled. "I was under the impression, mademoiselle, that we all are."

"You introduce yourself as *Historian*. Yet you call us *Faithless*. That name is a lie. If you were worthy of the title you lay claim to, you would know that."

"I know that history is written by the victors. And the Esani were *far* from that."

"This war is not over yet."

"Forgive me." Jean-François smiled, motioning to the bare rock around them. "The world must look very different on your knees."

"It does. That is why we pray there, little one."

Jean-François's temper prickled at that. "*Little* one? You are younger than I, girl."

"Girl?"

The prisoner tilted her head.

"*Come here and call us that.*"

The historian stared at the vampire across the water. She still lingered at the very edge of the shore, as if she desired to be as close to him as possible. Her gaze was locked on his, midnight-blue hair framing the silvered cage on her jaw, her eyes as dark as his dame's, flooded to their edges, black and bottomless. If he stared too long, he felt he might drown in them, sinking into the cool dark of oblivion just as he'd done the night his mother murdered him, on her knees before him, ruby lips grazing his skin and teeth sinking deep, pain entwined with awful pleasure as the heat was dragged up from his—

No.

Stop.

"Stop," he hissed.

Jean-François blinked. He realized he stood where once he'd sat. His boots were poised at the river's edge now, dark current tumbling just beyond his toes. No kith could cross running water save at bridges or by flying high above it, but had he taken one more step, he might have tumbled in; swept along in that flood as the flesh washed off his bones.

And the terrible thing was, he'd *wanted* to. Because she'd *willed* him to.

The historian looked back up into those bottomless eyes, a jolt of perfect fear arcing all the way down his spine. His teeth grew long and sharp in his gums.

"Impressive," Celene whispered.

"Do *not* do that again," he snapped. "Or I swear by the Night I will leave you here to languish until your screams can be heard all the way to Augustin."

Celene upturned her palms in supplication, her eyes hard as black pearls. "*Forgive us.*"

The historian returned to his chair, opened his tome and took the space of three breaths to find his composure. The contempt he had felt mere moments ago was replaced with fury and dread now, with some small understanding of this thing lurking on the far shore. There was a reason his Empress did not wish to conduct this interrogation herself. A *reason* why Celene Castia had been buried in the darkest pit his dame could conjure. She might have the appearance of a maid from a Nordlund backwater. She might have but a handful of years to her name. And had he tumbled into those black waters, still she would have been imprisoned here, helpless on that dark shoreline; but that would have been small comfort to his corpse. Looking again into those jet-black eyes, Jean-François at last understood. Trapped and cornered though it might be . . .

This thing is dangerous.

"What did my brother tell you of our childhood?" she asked.

The historian licked at dry lips, sipping from the goblet of blood beside him.

"You grew up in the Nordish provinces," he replied. "The youngest daughter of Raphael Castia and Auriél de León. He, a blacksmith, a cur, fond of his whores and liquor and beating his children. She, the noble daughter of a baron, a lioness, who did her best to raise her children in the light of the One Faith."

A chuckle rang behind that silver muzzle. "Is that what Gabriel told you?"

Jean-François blinked. "You sing a different tune?"

"My mother was no lioness, sinner. Auriél de León was a prideful, cosseted *brat*. My father did what few men would have, in marrying a woman heavy with a monster's child. And she repaid him with nothing but scorn. It was in Gabriel that Mama placed the fullness of her faith, her time, her love. For the rest of us? She left scraps and named it a feast."

The monster shook her head, dragging nails across the stone.

"My father was no cur either," she said. "He had a good heart, Raphael Castia. Even as a child, I could see what it was doing to him; to be unwelcome in the bed he'd built with his own two hands. He was a big man, strong as an ox, yet ever he walked like he carried a weight upon his back. He drank too much. He strayed too far. No saint, my papa, but still, he tried. And he never laid a hand on my mother, or my sister, or me."

"But he beat Gabriel like—"

"Like a disobedient stepchild?" Celene nodded, eyes glittering in the dark. "Because he *was* one, Chastain. My mother filled my brother's head with such rot, he could not help himself. Feeding the fire of his pride until it burned bright enough to blind him."

The historian pursed his lips. "Your brother spoke quite a different tale."

"Of course he did. No matter how oft he makes mention of them, Gabriel's greatest love has never been liquor, nor licentiousness. It is *lying*."

Jean-François frowned, glancing toward the tower high above.

"Let us speak plainly, little Marquis," Celene said, entwining fingers in her lap. "Your Empress would kill us if she dared. She cares not where I came from, nor what we became. Margot Chastain desires Celene Castia's story only in so far as it is also *another's*. La demoiselle du Graal. The Red Hand of God. We were there the day the name *San Dior* was first sung to the heavens, and we heard what heaven sang in reply. So while histories are best begun at their beginning, and while my sweet brother enjoys little more than talking about himself, let us assume you are here at purpose other than the assuagement of my ego, and allow us to impart the tale your mistress actually wishes to hear."

Celene leaned back, legs stretched out before her, palms flat to the stone.

"We assure you; you will learn all you need know of *us* in the telling of it."

The historian inclined his head, lifted his quill.

"As it please you, Mlle Castia."

"So." The monster lowered her chin, watching the historian through the dark haze of her lashes. "Where did my beloved Gabriel leave you?"

"The bridge at Cairnhaem," Jean-François replied. "You had sought an ancien of the Esani among the peaks of the Nightstone, but found him dead by his own hand, and in turn, been found by pursuers of two different Courts of the Blood. In an astonishing display of strength for a vampire her age, the Wolfmother had done away with the Terrors, but only you and Gabriel remained to defend Dior against the Dyvok. And you betrayed him."

"Betrayed." The monster sighed. "Dear brother. Dear liar."

"You deny you let him fall?"

"We say only that a traitor has no right to bleat when he feels the knife in his own back. And that my brother let me fall *long* before we deigned to return the favor."

"You thought it wise to fight alone?"

"I had been alone most of my life, sinner. Why would that night be any different? The hell I had seen, the places I had been . . . I knew what Celene Castia was made of."

"And that was?"

The monster gazed into the rushing waters, those black eyes suddenly far away.

"My mother and I were in a fight once. Years after the sun failed, this was. A rough-and-tumble scrap of a girl I was back then. All skinned knees and scuffed knuckles. A fool might have called me a tomboy, if he held no regard for his teeth.

"My eleventh saintsday was coming, and I'd asked for a belt knife like Papa and the other men of Lorson carried. Mama told me I was getting a new dress. We fought about it for weeks, but she'd not give an inch, insisting I must set aside childish fancy and learn what it was to be a woman. '*Grow up*,' she'd tell me. '*Godssakes, Celene, grow* up.'"

The monster looked down at her body, frozen forever at childhood's edge.

"In tears, I sought Papa. I found him in his forge as ever, bent over the refuge of his anvil, and I asked how he could stand it. To live like that. To live with *her*. He thumbed the sweat from his brow and smiled. 'What is the name of our famille, daughter?'

"'Castia,' I replied.

"'In old Nordish, it means castle. And are castles made of steel?'

"'No, Papa.'

"'Are they made, then, of ice?'

"'Castles are stone, Papa.'

"'Good. And what are castles for?'

"'Princesses live in them.' I scowled. 'They go to stupid dances and dine with stupid princes and wear *stupid* dresses.'

"He laughed, and he put down his hammer and lifted me in his big, broad arms. He was a giant, my papa. A rock. Strong as the roots of the earth.

"'Castles *endure*, love. They weather storm and fire and flood. Steel rusts. Ice melts. But stone stands. And that is what *we* do. We stand the weight, that others might be spared the burden. We endure the unendurable.' He smoothed back the hair from my face, Nordish fire burning in his eyes. 'Castles are made of stone, Little Mountain. And so are you.'"

Celene stared silent into that water, perfectly motionless.

"And so," she finally sighed. "When faced with opportunity at Cairnhaem to rid ourselves of my fool brother and blame it on battle's tide, we took our chance. His arm was shattered. His sword gone. That accursed light on his skin made it just as difficult for us to see as our foes, and even if he lived, the thirst in Gabriel was growing every day. It was only a matter of time before he fell to it. All things weighed, we were better off without him."

Jean-François raised his quill, frowning. "Forgive me, Mlle Castia, but I am a touch confused. When you say *we*, do you mean you and Dior, or—"

"I mean *us*, sinner."

The Last Liathe took in her body with a wave of one slender hand. "*All* of us."

The historian met her gaze, lightless and deep as hell. He remembered Gabriel's tale of the battle at Aveléne; of Rykard Dyvok being drunk to ashes. He recalled the atrocities attributed to the Esani during the Red Crusade. And looking into the black of this monster's eyes, he wondered just how many monsters were looking back at him.

"The bridge was smashed in half," Celene continued. "The remainder barely clinging to the cliff behind us. Dior scrambled toward the safety of a burning barricade, Gabriel plunging into the abyss below as we hurled ourselves back over the railing and into the fray. And laying eyes upon the Wolfmother and Headsmun, drenched in animal gore, we flicked our wrist and willed our bloodblade back into being."

"Sanguimancy," the historian murmured.

The monster glanced up at that, a sly glint in her eyes.

"The gift of the Faithful. Mastery of the Blood itself. Are you curious about its workings, sinner?" She nodded to the bottle beside her. "We'd give demonstration, if you'd be kind enough to fetch us another draught."

The Marquis ignored those dark eyes fixed on his neck. "The blade *was* made of your blood, then. Wearied as you were, there must not have been much left inside you."

"No," the monster replied. "But while the Wolfmother's strength was fearsome, the fleshwitch had already wounded her deep, and while we were wounded too, the fire of God burned yet in our heart. So, we'd thought to quench our thirst presently."

"You and your brother *do* share some kinship, then," the historian mused.

"Meaning what?"

"Arrogance seems to run in your *famille*."

"It should have worked," Celene snapped, impetuous, voice cutting the dark. "Kiara's blood was thinner than ours. The power of ancien flows in these veins. I had delivered dozens of kith just like her during my studies with Master Wulfric, and others *far* deeper in the Blood since." Celene shook her head, quietly furious. "She *should* have fallen.

"But as deep as we stood, Kiara was somehow stronger—far, *far* stronger than she should've been. Our first blow opened her belly to breast, but her riposte almost smashed us off the bridge. The advantage in speed was ours, but God, the strength in her was *unholy*. The first blow we turned aside shattered our arm, so we were forced to dodge rather than parry, slipping aside as Kiara threw herself into the booming, sweeping arcs of the Tempest. Each near miss from her maul cut the air so swift that thunder rolled in its wake. Her comrade Kane was on his feet now too, yet another blade to dance away from, and the Wolfmother did not even seem to feel the blows we carved in her flesh.

"We could not go on like this much longer.

"And then, we caught movement from the corner of our eye; Dior rising to her feet. The girl was gasping, covered in stone dust, blood, ash. But ever dauntless, she drew the silversteel dagger from her sleeve and made ready to step into the fray. I was forced to admire her courage, even as we cursed her foolishness. A thin line is drawn between both, after all, and we wondered if this child would live long enough to learn the difference.

"'No!' we cried, holding up our hand. 'Back, *chérie*, *back*!'

"The blink of an eye is enough to alter the course of history. A moment's distraction can mean the difference between life and death. We are creatures who walk between the rain, awake in the forevers between seconds. And as we felt Kiara's grip close around our outstretched arm, we knew in that second what an awful mistake we'd made."

Celene Castia shook her head, her voice grown soft and distant.

"There is a kind of dog in Ossway called a cùildamh. A staghound. They are rare these nights. Expensive to keep, firstly, and there are no stags left to hunt, after all. But the most valuable ones were the females with no toes. Do you know why, Historian?"

Jean-François nodded. "Cùildamh were famed for their ferocity. Breeders would have young females bite into a deer carcass, then haul them skyward and begin snipping their toes off. The more toes a female lost before she released her quarry, the more ferocious her offspring would prove, and the worthier she was judged to breed."

Celene nodded. "A good Ossian staghound will die before she releases her prey. And while we never saw Kiara Dyvok without her boots, we'd not be surprised if you removed them and discovered she had no toes. She slung us around like a bag of rocks, slamming us back and forth into the cracking flagstones, never once releasing her awful grip. Our arm broke in a half dozen places, our blade pierced her chest, her throat, but still, she didn't let us go. It was our left arm she had us by, and we fought hard as we might, but dazed, skull cracked and wracked with pain, we gasped as her fingers finally closed around our sword hand too. Our mask had shattered as she whipped us into the rock, but no matter how we struggled, cursed, her strength was terrible. *Impossible.* Kiara met our eyes, blood drooling from her teeth as she growled.

"'This is fer cousin Rykard, pretty one.'

"And rearing back like a serpent, she slammed her forehead into our face.

"The blow was so terrible, it tore our arms clean from their sockets, pulped our skull, sent us sailing back through the air like a blast from a cannon. We crashed into something hard and sharp, smelled something burning, heard someone screaming, so stunned we barely recognized our name. And it was then we realized the hardness and sharpness we'd crashed into was the last of our flaming barricades, that the voice we heard screaming was Dior's, and the thing we smelled burning was us.

"It was *us.*"

Celene looked down at her hand, flawless and pale.

"Have you ever been set aflame, Historian?" she asked softly.

Jean-François didn't look up from his tome, his quill flowing smooth over the page. "A few misadventures with candles in the boudoir notwithstanding, no."

"It's . . . *awful,*" the monster replied, her voice suddenly tiny and frail. "It's as if the Almighty Himself were reaching down from heaven to show you how . . . *small* . . . our kind actually are. *All I have given you,* he seems to say, *all I have made you—strong as a hundred men, swift as a thousand spears, timeless and deathless and fearless—all of it can be undone by the simplest of my gifts. The first I gave to my* true *children. The gift that kept them warm in the dark at the dawn of time, and safe from evil like* you.

"*Never forget,* the fire tells you. *Never forget who He loves most.*

"We barely had sense enough, strength enough, but as those awful flames tore up over our coat, our hair, our flesh, we summoned the very last of our power. And we felt our body tremble, and our pieces fly apart; a thousand tiny droplets bursting into flight, a thousand tiny wings spiraling up into storming skies. The fire chased us like it had a will to end us, leaping from moth to moth, more of us consumed, ashes drifting earthward like snow. But a few tiny pieces of us escaped, twisting into the night, a blur of consciousness above the burning bridge, the triumphant Wolfmother, the cemetery that was Cairnhaem.

"We'd brought Dior to that place hoping she'd find the ancien wisdom of the Faithful, the shelter of Jènoah's protection. Instead, she'd found only death. Her hopes dashed and her protectors stripped away one by one until she was almost utterly alone."

The Last Liathe reclined on the cold stone, as if a queen on a velvet divan. Slipping her hands beneath her head, one knee crooked, she stared at the dark rock overhead. Again, Jean-François was struck with the brief notion she was but a maid; an innocent, sprawled among the blooms in some flowering field and talking of childish things to childish friends. But he understood something closer to truth now.

"Forgive me, Mlle Castia," he said. "But if you parted ways with the Grail at Cairnhaem, then I fail to see what light you can shed on her story. Perhaps I would be better served returning to the Black Lion's company."

"We are certain you would simply *loathe* that, sinner."

The historian sighed. "It seems you and your brother share a fondness for sarcasm as well as arrogance. But when my Empress learns how little use you actually are, you may find yourself wishing you'd put that scalpel tongue of yours to better use."

"And if you stop interrupting us, little Marquis, we shall do exactly that."

"How? Kiara Dyvok beat you to a bloody pulp, tore your arms off, and then set you on fire. You barely escaped with your existence. I have no use for hearsay or secondhand babble, and after the thrashing you took, you cannot possibly know what came next."

"Can we not?"

"You said Dior was alone."

"We said she was *almost* alone. She was many things, Dior Lachance. Ofttimes a courageous girl. Others a headstrong and terribly foolish girl. She could be a resourceful or cunning or ruthless girl. A hateful girl. A vengeful girl. But above all, sinner, Dior Lachance was always a *fortunate* girl. And while this seemed her darkest hour, while it seemed she had been left completely bereft, the Almighty had not abandoned her."

For the first time since Jean-François had met her, the Last Liathe laughed; hollow, cold, and utterly unnerving.

"Even if she did not know it at the time, that girl had one last trick up her sleeve."

JAWS OF THE BEAR

"A LONE FIGURE stood upon a broken bridge. Empty heart and empty hands.

"She was shrouded in smoke. Smudged in dried blood and caked with ashes. Wild embers spiraled upward toward the lightning's pulse above. Her knights had fallen all around her, and bloodied and torn though they were, Kiara and Kane Dyvok still stood. Dior edged backward, closer to the flaming barricade, blue eyes wide, ashen hair thick with gore and soot. She looked to the vampires before her, the fate awaiting her, and then, over the railing beside her. That dark drop, whispering.

"*Escape.*

"*Sleep.*

"*Peace.*

"'I am not that girl,' she sighed.

"Kane Dyvok had been a cruel and brutish-looking young man before he died, and death had done nothing to soften his edges. Already sharp and thuggish, his face had been rent to the bone by the kiss of Phoebe á Dúnnsair's claws during the battle. It twisted now, furious, bloody, and the Headsmun lifted his greatsword, large enough to cleave a full-grown bull spineward. Raising it above his head, he readied to treat Dior likesame.

"'Hold, cousin,' the Wolfmother said.

"Kane hesitated, glancing over his shoulder.

"'Hold?' he growled, his Ossway brogue thick and dark. 'I'll split her throatways and lick her leavings off my hands. I've earned a feast from this night's foolishness, by God.'

"'Aye,' Kiara replied, looking Dior over like wolf to lamb. 'But nae this feast.'

"'Who is this mouse to us?' Kane demanded. 'We came for vengeance. We came for the Lion.'

"'Aye. But the Voss came for *her*.' Kiara met Dior's eyes, stone hard. 'Why?'

"The girl remained silent, fists clenched in her mismatched armor.

"'*ANSWER*,' the Wolfmother demanded.

"The Whip, they call it, those children of Dyvok. The strength in their veins made manifest in their words. 'Tis no subtle arte, like the Push wielded by the Ilon. There is no poetry to it, no glamour. It is a hammerblow, a battering ram at the gates of will, sending most folk to their knees. And while Kane was but a pup, incapable of wielding it, Kiara was mediae, her voice reverberating with a century's power, echoing on the stone at Dior's feet.

"'I don't know why the Voss want me,' the Grail spat.

"Kiara peered over the railing into the gulf where the Princes of Forever had fallen. She was no elder, the Wolfmother, but no fool either. Thirdborn of Nikita, cunning enough to have risen to ascendency in her Priori's favor after the slaughter at Crimson Glade, and cruel enough to have remained there ever since.

"She stepped forward, quick as winter wind despite her size. Dior lifted her silversteel to her skin, but before she could anoint the blade, the Wolfmother had her, one gloved hand around her wrist, the other, her throat. Dior hissed, Kiara lifting her off the ground effortlessly, dangling her over the yawning drop. Dior struggled, curses choked between her teeth, but her strength was a child's fist against a mountainside.

"'Sleep now, little Mouse,' Kiara said.

"The vampire *squeezed*, just enough to cut off the blood flow while sparing the bone. Dior's face purpled as consciousness faded. She'd fury enough to hawk up a mouthful of saliva, yet not enough breath to spit it, her defiance simply spattering on the Wolfmother's vambrace. But as she struggled— one last burst of rage—that bloody spittle *trembled*, shivering, snaking a few more inches up the leather on Kiara's forearm before finally freezing still. And limp as a boned fish, the Holy Grail of San Michon slipped into darkness.

"Kiara was already reaching to the iron manacles at her belt, locking a pair about Dior's wrists, another her ankles. 'If the Ironhearts have desire of her,' she explained, 'the Count will desire her too. Simple butchery be not the only way to his esteem, cousin. If ye knew that, perhaps ye'd stand higher in his favor.'

"'Stand in his favor,' the Headsmun scoffed softly. 'Ye mean kneel in his boudoir.'

"Slinging the girl onto her shoulders, Kiara tossed back the golden vial Kane had loaned her, meeting the younger Dyvok's flint eyes.

"'I dinnae quite hear ye over the wind then, cousin. It *sounded* like insult to my maker, yer own blood uncle, and Priori of yer line. But surely not. Mind repeating it?'

"Kane made no reply, fixing the vial back around his neck with a sullen scowl, and the Wolfmother turned to the mortal boy waiting at the bridge moorings. He was a pretty one, Nordish-born, cheekbones sharp as knives, and long hair, thick and black as ink. He gazed at Kiara with unmasked adulation, flanked by his two big snowhounds.

"'Storm is worsening,' she called. 'Can ye lead us back to the others in this?'

"'If you will it,' he replied, 'I'd lead you through the fires of hell and back.'

"'No poetry tonight, boy. I didn't ask if ye would, I asked if ye *could*.'

"The lad knelt in the snow beside his hounds. They were a fine pair; a shaggy dark-grey male and a lighter female, both of that swift Nordish breed known as lancers.

"'Matteo and Elaina led us here, Mistress. They can lead us back.'

"'Be about it, then, Poet. And swift. Time tarries not, e'en for the timeless.'

"The boy bobbed his head and led his hounds back up the hill. The Headsmun climbed aboard his thralled sosya, impatient to be gone. But the Wolfmother turned back toward Cairnhaem, studying its sword-sharp spires with narrowed eyes. Lifting her mighty warmaul off the stone, she ran her fingertips over that roaring bear's head, staring down into the gulf where my brother had fallen. Her eyes were still crimson from the blood she'd drunk, lips peeled back from her grin as she spat into the drop.

"'Sleep well in hell, Lion.'

"And with the fate of every soul under heaven unknowingly slung over her shoulder, Kiara Dyvok turned and trudged toward her frightened horse."

"How do you know?"

The Last Liathe shifted her gaze from the rough-hewn ceiling to the historian across the river. Jean-François was sat in his leather armchair, still writing in his tome by the dim chymical light. But his question hung in the air with the echoes of rushing black water.

"Know what, sinner?"

"What Lachance was doing," the Marquis said. "What she was thinking."

"The Grail's mind was ever a locked door to the Dead," Celene replied. "We did *not* know her thoughts. Nor have we claimed to. We have only told you what we observed."

"But how? You were clearly not present through this ordeal, Mlle Castia. And yet you tell the tale as one who saw it. Heard it. Lived it."

The light of the chymical globe sparkled in jet-black eyes. And though her lips were mercifully hidden behind her silver muzzle, Jean-François was sure Celene smiled.

"Patience, coldblood."

The Last Liathe shifted her gaze back to the ceiling and continued.

"It would take the Untamed three nights to reach their goal, but Dior woke near dawn on the first. Lifting her head in the dark, she found herself bound, gagged, and blindfolded, curled against something warm and shaggy as a muted storm raged all around her. She tried to speak, thrashing briefly before a pair of hands held her still. A gentle voice bid her, 'Hold now, mademoiselle. You'll hurt the dogs.'

"Her blindfold was loosed, and she discovered she was in a small hunter's cover; little more than a few strips of oiled canvas providing shelter from the storm. The space would've been cramped with her alone, but she was squeezed in beside that knife-sharp mortal boy and both his dogs. Uncomfortable as it was, the space was warm at least.

"'Are you thirsty?' he asked. 'Mistress said you could drink if you wished it.'

"Dior was still muffled and manacled, and could do little but nod. The boy untied the leather gag from her mouth, lifted a waterskin to her lips. When she'd drunk her fill, Dior caught her breath, tossing hair from her eyes. Her voice was soft, cautious, not all the way frightened. 'Merci, monsieur.'

"The boy nodded, sipping what smelled like sharp, reeking liquor from a hipflask.

"'Where am I?' Dior asked.

"'Warm.' The boy gestured to the shelter around them. 'Safe.'

"She scoffed, bitter and hard. 'Where are the vampires?'

"The boy nodded out into the storm. 'Sleeping.'

"Dior peered around the shelter again, taking closer note of her surrounds. She'd been stripped of her mismatched armor, clad now in her golden waistcoat and heavy frockcoat, the dark grey damask spattered with blood and ash. They'd left her boots on at least, and her lockpicks were still nestled snugly inside, but her hands were shackled behind her. She strained against her bonds, and one of the dogs licked her face with a big pink tongue. Dior winced at the reek of blood on its breath.

"'Elaina likes you,' the boy smiled.

"Wiping her sticky cheek against her lapel, Dior looked the lad over more careful. 'I *know* you,' she murmured. 'I mean to say . . . I've seen you before.'

"The boy's smile was darkly handsome, and he obviously knew it. 'We span a jig together. After you waltzed with Capitaine Baptiste. You're a terrible dancer.'

"Her skin prickled with goosebumps. 'You're from Aveléne . . .'

"'Oui.' The boy winced as he sipped from his flask again. 'I was the kennelboy there. My name is Joaquin. Joaquin Marenn.'

"'We freed some of your people!' Dior gasped, trying to sit up straighter. 'A pack of children from a wagon on the river! A girl named Mila and another named Isla and—'

"'You saw Isla á Cuinn?' The boy's eyes widened, and he pointed to his cheek. 'Two beauty spots here and—'

"'Oui!' Dior cried. 'Just a fortnight back!'

"Looking closer, Dior saw the boy's hipflask was embossed with the letters *J&I*.

"'You're the beloved Isla spoke of!' she breathed. '*You're her Ever After!*'

"The boy smiled then, dark eyes sparkling. 'She . . . she called me that?'

"'She did! I know where she's headed, I can take you to her!' Dior tried to roll over, proffering her bound wrists. 'Get me out of these damned things, I can—'

"'No,' the boy replied simply.

"'. . . No?'

"His smile was gone, his face drawn cold. 'My mistress forbade it.'

"'Your *mistress*?' Dior blinked. 'You mean that godless leech?'

"A change came over him then, storm-swift, red and sudden fury in his eyes.

"'Don't speak of her that way,' he snapped, raising a finger in warning. 'She bid me keep you safe and so I shall, but I'll not hear one crossed word about her, I *vow* it.'

"Dior's eyes narrowed, her jaw clenched, for as he'd lifted his finger, Joaquin had revealed a strange scar atop his left hand. It was fresh, scabbed dark against his skin. An odd mark, geometrical, cut into his flesh and rubbed with ash to preserve the design. Gabriel's voice almost seemed to ring in the air then; the words he'd spoken at Aveléne.

"*Some join willingly. Out of lust for power, or darkness of heart. Others are just fools who think they'll live forever if given the bite. But most are simple captives, offered the choice between becoming a slave or a meal.*

"'That's no scar,' she whispered, staring at his hand. 'It's a brand.'

"The boy met her eyes, Dior's skin prickling with horror.

"'You're a thrall.'

"'Scorched, they call us.' He smiled, running a thumb across the mark. 'They who are chosen to serve. A gift, you see. To show their love for us.'

"'That's not love, Joaquin,' Dior hissed. 'They destroyed your home, killed your friends, murdered Aaron! That fucking bitch is—'

"The girl got no further, Joaquin pushing her face down into the floor. Gone was his gentle manner, and as Dior howled protest, Joaquin dragged the leather thong back into her mouth with a terrible strength. Dior's breath was hissing as he climbed off her back.

"Rolling over, she glowered at him, teeth clenched on her bit. But Joaquin's eyes were on the shelter's flap as he reached out to scratch the male hound's chin, absent-minded.

"'You'll see,' he said. 'She'll be awake soon. You'll see how *wonderful* she is.'

"Dior lay still and quiet, heartbeat thumping quick. Joaquin said no more, and over the next few hours, she snatched some fitful sleep, moaning as she dreamed. Eventually, she was woken as the boy slipped from the shelter, pulling herself up onto her elbows to peer out after him. Night was new-fallen outside now, and under the sound of the roaring wintersdeep winds, a crunching noise could be heard, as of a spade in fresh snow.

"The thrall was digging his masters from their beds.

"Dior was soon dragged out of the cover by a pair of hands, one pale and whole, the other skeletal, wrapped in ropes of new-grown flesh. Hauled up by the lapels, she found herself face-to-face with the one called Kane, his stare as hard and cold as the earth he'd slept in. His features were still scarred by Phoebe's claws; four rents torn brow to bloodless chin. He looked her over, hunger prowling back and forth behind those cruel, flint eyes. Dior shivered, trying to pull away as he drew her closer, cold lips brushing her neck.

"'Ye smell good enough to eat . . .'

"She could say nothing behind her gag, but her eyes still begged him.

"*I dare you.*

"'Enough,' came a growl. 'Leave her be.'

"Kane turned to Kiara, saddling the horses with a doting Joaquin. 'She smells like—'

"'I smell her as well as ye. But the Voss think her a prize, and we've a long ride ahead. If ye've a thirst, ye can sate it on that lackwit Shae at the end of it.'

"'Shae's aright,' Kane mumbled.

"'He's thick as pigshite,' Kiara scoffed. 'Ye wasted good blood thralling that fool.'

"'I scorched him for his swordarm, not his wits. He slew a dozen men at Aveléne.'

"'And no few women besides,' the Wolfmother scowled. 'You'd best put a leash on that dog, cousin. We didn't drag our arses hundreds of miles from Ossway for rape and slaughter. We came to Nordlund for *food,* and a corpse feeds naebody but the worms. I've half a mind to throw that bastard in the wagons to replace the stock he ruined.'

"Dior still hung in Kane's grip, his arm as unmoving as an iron bar as he replied.

"'There'll be yet more ruined by this delay. Nightstone took us *weeks* from our road. If we don't get back home with the cattle soon, they'll be frozen solid.'

"Kiara scoffed, her smile like razorblades. 'I just killed the Black Lion of Lorson, cousin. The commander of the Crimson Glade. Slayer of great Tolyev himself, laid low by mine own hand. That's worth a few dead cows, and nae bloody mistake.'

"'We saw him fall,' the Headsmun pointed out. '*Not* die. I wager the Contessa would be none too pleased to learn our arrival was delayed for a *maybe,* cousin. Nor that ye lost yer vial scrapping with the Lion on the Mère, and had to beg me mine to replace it.'

"The Wolfmother stopped working, turned to regard the younger vampire. Boots crunching in the snow, she strode up to the Headsmun, tall enough to meet him eye to eye.

"''Twould be a shame,' she nodded, 'if someone were to tell her that.'

"The pair stared at each other, the Grail dangling between them like a shank of meat between two snarling bears. The vampires were still as statues, eyes locked, bristling with monstrous threat. But after a breathless age, the younger kith averted his stare.

"'Aye,' he murmured. 'A shame.'

"The Wolfmother smiled a mouthful of knives, the Headsmun turning away. Dior could say nothing, teeth clenched tight on her bit, hands in fists. She was slung onto Kiara's pony, wretched and cramping as the vampires rode into the howling night. The weather was cold enough to freeze her blood, eyes closed tight as they trekked down the mountain, farther and farther from the site of Gabriel's fall.

"But if she mourned my brother, Dior did it quietly.

"It was near dawn, three nights after Gabriel had plunged off the bridge at Cairnhaem, when the smell of woodsmoke kissed the air. The male lancer, Matteo, barked, and a shout rang in answer in the dark. Dior lifted her head, peering through her mop of frozen hair as figures emerged in the gloom; men in mail, longblades at their waists, bearded and burly. Behind them, she saw the silhouette of a hunter's hut, encrusted with shadespine. The men sank to their knees when they laid eyes on the Wolfmother and Headsmun, a tall, blue-eyed devil at their head. He'd ruddy red hair and a thick beard, dried gore beneath his fingernails, and the roaring bear of the Blood Dyvok stitched on his battle-stained tabard.

"'Master Kane,' he said, dipping his head. 'My Lady Kiara.'

"'Shae,' the Headsmun replied. 'What news?'

"'We tracked those bairns down, just as you commanded, Master.' The man kept his eyes lowered, though he stole one ice-blue glance at Dior. 'Caught them on the westroad. Lars and Quinn have already taken them south to meet Lady Soraya.'

"'Splendid.' Kiara replied before Kane could answer, climbing from her saddle. 'Talley, see to the horses. Jean, get the boy and this one fed.' Lifting a spade from her saddle, she tossed it into the snow beside the redheaded man. 'Ye may have the honor of digging our beds, Shae. We set out at first dark. But Lord Kane needs his beauty sleep first.'

"'Aye, Lady,' the red-haired man replied, not daring to look up.

"The Headsmun rubbed at the scars on his face as Kiara trudged toward the hut. Her boots scuffed as she came to a thoughtful halt. 'Oh, and Shae?'

"'M'lady?'

"'Nae unpleasantness is to befall this girl while Lord Kane and I slumber. Ye don't touch her, ye don't speak to her, ye don't even look at her, ye ken?'

"'Perfectly, m'lady.'

"'Splendid. Dig quick. The Headsmun's nae pretty as once he was.'

"Three of the men chuckled at the jest, but the redhead simply scowled.

Young Joaquin lifted Dior from the saddle easy as he'd heft a goosedown pillow, and she was hauled inside the hut—a thatchwood hovel with walls of daub, now overrun with fungus. It stank inside; sweat, rot, and feet. But it was warm at least, a fire burning in a little hearth. Dior was propped in a corner, still bound and gagged, trembling hands bunched in white-knuckled fists. Her captors had given no clue where they were headed, or what her fate would be at road's end. But surely, it must be a dark one.

"Joaquin stood near the fire, his hounds stretched out beside the flames. The other men came inside as they finished their duties, five in total. As they tugged off their gloves to warm themselves, Dior stared at the brands atop their left hands, carved by knifework and ash. There were two different symbols among them—one shared by Joaquin and the cook, Jean, and an older man inexplicably called Dogshank, and a second mark borne by Talley, the cockeyed one who'd tended the horses. As he ducked inside and scruffed the snow from his greasy red hair, Dior saw the one named Shae also shared that second brand.

"Two different marks. Two different masters.

"'Who's the slip, Freshmeat?' Talley asked, glancing Dior's way.

"'Some girl we found in the Nightstone.' Joaquin spoke softly, eyes downturned. He was younger, and obviously new among this ragged band—lowest in their pecking order. 'She was with the one that the mistress hunted. The Black Lion. They came to Aveléne together a month or so back. Capitaine Aaron knew them, I think.'

"Talley sniffed. 'Wot's she dressed like a boy for?'

"'We could undress her.' Shae grinned with dirty teeth. 'Find out?'

"'Mistress said she's not to be touched,' Jean growled, looking up from the fire.

"'Aye, keep it in your britches, Shae,' Dogshank spat. 'Lest Mistress tear it off.'

"The redhead gave a bark of cruel laughter, sharing a dark glance with Talley. But he said no more. Eventually, Joaquin brought over a bowlful of thin soup, removing Dior's gag long enough to let her eat. He offered a sip of those foul-smelling spirits from his flask, but she grimaced and refused. Joaquin was gentle in feeding her, but careful too, retying her gag tight and checking her manacles before returning to his grubby comrades.

"Outside in the raging storm, deep beneath frozen earth, Kiara and Kane

Dyvok slept the day away. Legs curled beneath her, Dior began inching her fingers toward the lockpicks in her boot, eyes closed as if she slept, blue lips moving swift all the while.

"She was frightened enough to pray now, you see.

"They were wary, the five thralls—one ever sat watch, waking a comrade after a few hours to take turn on guard by the flames. But all the while, the Grail was at it; drawing the leather wallet from her boot and setting to work with her picks. She'd surely sweet-talked a thousand locks in her time, but none that her life truly depended on. Sweat filmed her brow now, her fingers trembled, but near dusk, the manacles gave way, and her hands were free.

"Dior opened her eyes a sliver. The one named Dogshank was awatch, but he was nodding by the dying fire. All was silent now, save for the storm roaring outside the hovel and the snores rumbling within. She brought her hands out from behind her back, setting to work on her ankle irons. And after twenty tortured minutes, her legs were also loose.

"Stretching and wincing, she dragged that wretched gag out of her mouth. Slipping off her boots, she rose soundless as shadows, creeping on stocking-clad feet. As she lifted a backpack and waterskin, the floorboards creaked beneath her, and she froze still as stone. But the only one who stirred was Elaina, the snowhound opening her eyes and wagging a hopeful tail. Dior pressed finger to lips, and the lancer raised one ear. And swift as winter wind, the Holy Grail of San Michon slipped out the door.

"Dragging on her boots, she climbed onto the Wolfmother's sosya. The pony startled from sleep, nickering in annoyance, but with hands wrapped tight in the gelding's mane, the girl gave a swift kick, and he was running, hooves thundering on fresh snow.

"A cry of alarm rang out, but she was already gone, galloping through the rising dusk. She'd not have had any clue where she was headed, of course; only that she must *away*, charging downwind where the Untamed might not smell her and praying like a saint.

"She was city born and bred, this girl—no true rider—clinging with nails and teeth and sheer bloody will to the sosya's back. But she was gutter-sharp too; a child of broken locks and filched purses and lies too many to count. Galloping into a stretch of corpsewood, she kicked her horse harder, *harder*. And steeling herself, she leapt from the gelding's back, into the arms of an old, twisted oak. The breath left her lungs as she and the tree collided, spit and frost and flecks of blood. But old man oak caught her true, and she clung like grim death as her stolen sosya charged onward through the trees, tracks carved clear in his wake.

"Gritting her teeth, she leapt into the twisted crown of another tree nearby. Then, she jumped again, again, threading across the wood until she was a goodly length from the gelding's tracks. And slipping down into the snow, the Grail began running, stumbling, wheezing, stopping only to catch her breath and listen for pursuit.

"It came soon enough—the drumbeat of approaching hooves. Whispering prayers to God, Mothermaid, and all seven Martyrs, she cut away from the gelding's path, weaving into the tangle of dead trees. Her eyes were wide, heart thundering, waterskin thumping her flank as she ran. But she smiled as she heard hooves rush up at her back and fade again, following the horse, not her. Grinning like a thief, she ran through the mist and twist, whispering soft.

"'Bonsoir, maggots.'

"She was free."

III

DOGS AND LEASHES

"SHE MADE IT eleven miles before they caught her—a laudable effort to be sure. She was exhausted by then, bramble-scratched and breathless. It was Elaina who found her first; the snowhound barking in the night, but Matteo followed, shooting out of the trees like an arrow. Dior shrieked as the big lancer walloped into her, bearing her down into the frost. She cursed, flailing, wincing as her fist found the poor fellow's snout. Elaina was on her then, dragging her back down as she tried to rise. The hound tore her coat, not her skin—well trained by the kennelboy of Aveléne, sure and true. But her brother was less gentle, biting into her boot as she roared.

"'No, Matteo!' came a distant shout. 'Soft!'

"Dior tried to tear herself free, rolling and kicking. Footsteps came then, running quicker than ever a man could, and awful, strong hands were suddenly lifting her by the collar. She glimpsed greasy red hair and ice-blue eyes as the one called Shae slammed her into the trunk of a weeping willow, hard enough to make her gasp.

"'Clever little—'

"Rank breath sprayed as her knee met his nethers, doubling Shae up with an agonized curse. She kneed him in the head as he buckled, turned to run as more hands grabbed her, hounds barking, Joaquin pleading, 'Hold, hold, I don't want to hurt—'

"Her elbow met his jaw, his lips split against his teeth—not the graceful dance my brother had schooled her in, but gutterfighting from the alleys of Lashaame. Punching and kicking, spitting and biting, blood on her knuckles and in her mouth. But not hers.

"*Not hers.*

"Something hit her, hard, heavy; a bootheel to the back of her skull. She grunted as she rolled off Joaquin, dogs barking as a weight pressed hard on her chest.

"'Fucking *sow*,' Shae hissed, the curse wet and thick with blood. He punched her in the face, bleak night crashing into blinding day, thunder in her pulse and suns in her eyes.

"The blurry form of Joaquin rose at Shae's back. 'Mistress said she wasn't to be—'

"'Harmed?' the big man snapped. 'She broke my nose, I'll fuckin' *gut* this piglet.'

"The thrallsword pressed a long, cruel knife up under Dior's chin. 'You hear me, you little rat quim? I'm going to carve you a new hole then ponder which to fuck.'

"A gob of bloody spittle struck him in the face, Dior hissing through red teeth.

"'Eat shit, you limp-dicked *coward*.'

"Shae pawed the spit off his lips, furious. 'Now, *that's* gone and done it . . .'

"He raised the blade, Dior writhing to free herself, overpowered yet defiant to the last. But it was the kennelboy who saved her, Joaquin planting a kick square between Shae's shoulderblades and knocking him into the frost, spit at his lips as he roared.

"'*Mistress said she wasn't to be harmed!*'

"'*Your* mistress, not mine,' the man hissed, rolling to his feet.

"'Lord Kane obeys m'lady, and so do you!'

"'Who the fuck do you think you are?' Shae demanded, pawing at his broken nose. 'Barely two weeks scorched, and lecturing *me*? Kiara wouldn't have wasted a drop on you, save she needed your fucking dogs for her damned hunt. That fool bitch insults and shames my master with every breath, but I'll be *damned* if I take likesame from you!'

"Shae lunged, Joaquin tried to grab the arm that held the knife, Matteo crashing into the man's legs. Dior crawled back in the snow, blood spilling down her lips as the scorched and hounds fell into a tumble. A yelp rang in the night, and Matteo went flying, tumbling through the frost. The wet sound of metal sinking into flesh cut the air, a gasp, a whimper. And tossing the blood-soaked hair from his face, Shae rose up from the steaming snow.

"Joaquin lay on his back, red breath bubbling at his lips. Dior scrambled away from Shae, fingers clawing through the snow for a branch, a rock, *anything*.

"Shae raised his knife, blue eyes cold and cruel. 'Now about that new hole—'

"A horrid sound rang in the dusk; a dozen greenstick *snap*s and the wet *pop* of bursting lungs. Shae stared stupidly at the fist that had burst from his chest, drenched red and clutching a fistful of steaming meat. The man had time enough to recognize his own still-twitching heart before the fist closed, crushing the organ to paste. And then the hand was torn back out the gaping hole in his rib cage, and Shae himself was torn apart.

"His pieces flew like fireworks at a feastday, trailing not light and flame, but gore, Dior flinching as she was splashed with a great red gout. And where her attacker had stood, now stood Kiara Dyvok, drenched head to foot with his best, boots covered in his worst.

"Wiping red sludge from her eyes, the right hand of the Priori Dyvok knelt in front of the gasping girl, her voice soft as gravel. 'Ye run swift for a little mouse.'

"'What in great Tolyev's name . . .'

"The Wolfmother glanced over her shoulder as a furious Headsmun reached the clearing, looking about the carnage. Joaquin was on his back, stabbed thrice in the chest, the snow soaked red. Elaina was at the kennelboy's side, whining and licking the blood from her master's fingers. Matteo lay on his belly, the hound bleeding from a wound in his neck.

"'What happened here?' Kane demanded. 'Ye slaughtered my man?'

"'I warned ye to put a leash on that dog, cousin.'

"'He was my property!' Kane spat, drawing himself up tall. 'Scorched by mine own hand! He served me well, a score of years, and now he's done for *what*? Bruising a peach ye insist neither one of us can have a bite of? Ye've lost yer fuckin' mind, Kiara.'

"'Mind yer tongue, cousin.' The Wolfmother stood slow, turning to face the Headsmun. 'Or ye'll lose far more.'

"The younger vampire snarled, but he kept his rebuke behind gritted fangs. With a warning glance to Dior, Kiara walked to Joaquin's side, looming over the bleeding boy. He reached up with a blood-soaked hand, unable to speak, yet begging with his eyes. His chest was gushing, the frost soaked through with red. She might feed him from her wrist, heal the wound with her blood, but the Wolfmother moved not an inch to help him.

"'Hunt's over, Poet,' Kiara murmured. 'Nae much use fer a houndboy anymore.'

"Joaquin whimpered, eyes bright and wide. The Angel of Death raised his sickles, and the boy's bladder loosed for the terror of it. He looked to his beloved mistress, perhaps for one last measure of comfort, fingers trembling as he strained simply to *touch* her before he died. But Kiara Dyvok remained unmoved as Joaquin held out his hand.

"And so, Dior Lachance took it."

Jean-François's quill ceased scratching, one blond eyebrow rising.

The Last Liathe breathed a sigh, studying her outstretched fingers.

"You will wonder why she did it, of course. Why she tore his tunic open, wiped the blood from her bleeding nose onto her palm and pressed it to Joaquin's chest. Why she chose to save his life, when in truth, she owed him nothing, and to show these monsters what she could do placed herself deeper in peril. Some would call her fool for it, no doubt. Some would call her noble. Some would call her young or softhearted, headstrong or thoughtless. But all would have some opinion to share. That is the way of things these nights, is it not? Folk who know nothing still insist on saying *something*."

"And you, Mlle Castia?" Jean-François asked. "What would you call her?"

"What I have always called her, little Marquis."

The monster's eyes twinkled in the dark.

"The Holy Grail of San Michon.

"Kiara and Kane Dyvok watched in mute amazement as Joaquin's wounds stitched closed, the touch of the Grail's holy blood hauling him back from the very edge of death. The boy's breath ceased to bubble, the pain in his eyes giving way to baffled wonder. Dior looked him over, helping him sit, one bloody hand still pressed to his chest.

"'Are you aright?' she whispered.

"'I . . .' The boy's mouth hung like a broken door, his face death pale. 'I—'

"'How did ye do that?'

"Dior looked up as Kane spoke, the Headsmun's cruel eyes gone wide.

"'*Answer me!*' the vampire demanded, grabbing her collar.

"Dior flinched back, her red, sticky hand grabbing at the Headsmun's wrist. And as her blood touched his Dead flesh, white fire bloomed, setting Kane's newly regrown hand aflame. The Headsmun roared in agony, toppling backward and flailing, kicking, finally plunging his burning fist into the snow and extinguishing the holy fire on his skin with a long sharp *hissss*. Snarling, Kane lifted his now-blackened claw from the steaming slush, eyes boiling with hate and fear fixed on Dior.

"'Ye still think this peach worth bruising, cousin?' the Wolfmother murmured.

"Kiara seized Dior by the scruff and hauled the yelping girl into the air. Dior clawed at her grip, but unlike her cousin, Kiara wore heavy hunter's gauntlets, the Grail's bloody hand doing nothing but staining the hardened leather. The Wolfmother looked Dior over, the girl choking out every colorful insult my brother had taught her as she struggled to free herself. But her cursing turned to a pained gasp as Kiara squeezed hard enough to make her spine creak.

"'Be still now, little Mouse.'

"'L-et m-me—'

"Kiara *squeezed* again, her strength enough to grind stone to dust. Dior wailed at the agony of it, forcing herself to be still, muscles corded at her clenched jaw.

"'I care nae for the hows of it,' the vampire murmured. 'Nor the whys. But if ye try to run again, I'll have my men put out yer eyes. Burn yer toes off. Carve their names in ye while ye scream. Oh, I'll leave ye livin', have nae fear. Our foes have a wanting of ye, and thus, so must we. But by time I'm done wi' ye, ye'll envy poor young Shae here.'

"The girl whimpered in that titanic grip, face red, teeth clenched.

"'At least t-tell me . . . where you're t-taking m-me.'

"The Wolfmother blinked, as if the answer were obvious. 'We take ye to the court of Nikita the Blackheart. My own dread maker, and Priori of Blood Dyvok.'

"Dior's eyes widened at that, goosebumps prickling her skin. She was in the clutches of horrors; helpless and small and obviously terrified. Yet not by chance, nor whimsy, but through Almighty God's own providence, it seemed she was also headed to the *exact* place in the empire she most needed to be. The city where the truth of all she must do awaited in eventide. The resting place of Mother Maryn herself.

"'Dún Maergenn,' she whispered."

In the shadows beneath Sul Adair, the historian dipped his quill, murmuring scripture to himself. "*All on earth below and heaven above is the work of my hand.*"

And across a black river, a monster smiled behind the cage on her teeth.

"*And all the work of my hand is in accord with my plan.*"

Jean-François met Celene's eyes, a sudden chill upon his skin.

"Does that frighten you, sinner?" she asked. "To see his will at work in the world? To witness his divine design unfold *exactly* as he intended? Because were I you—heartless, faithless, purposeless—it would *terrify* me."

The historian arched one brow, expectant.

"You are in danger of boring me, Mlle Castia. Continue."

Celene inclined her head, amusement sparkling in those black eyes.

"Dior still hung in the Wolfmother's grip. But after Kiara's revelation, her struggles had ceased. Satisfied, the vampire released her hold, let the poor girl hit the snow.

"'Let's be off, then,' the Wolfmother grunted. 'Time tarries nae for the timeless.'

"The Wolfmother trudged back across the red clearing, absentmindedly licking Shae's gore off her lips. She paused at the edge of the trees, looking back to Dior and slapping her thigh, as if calling a hound. And with all desire to flee now vanished, the bruised and beaten girl wiped her bloody face with snow, and dragged herself upright.

"'Joaquin?' the Wolfmother called. 'On yer feet, Poet.'

"Dior looked to the lad beside her. Joaquin was still sat in the frozen red, chest and hands drenched likesame. Elaina snuffled at his face, tail wagging. Poor Matteo was dead, pierced through the throat by Shae's knife, and the boy's eyes were fixed on the hound's, brimming with tears. But more than sorrowed, Joaquin simply looked . . . bewildered.

"'It's only a dog, boy,' Kiara called again. 'Come. Now.'

"'Joaquin?' Dior asked softly.

"The kennelboy looked up at her, like a lad awakened from the dream of a roaring fireplace only to find himself in the cold deep of night. But as Kane growled impatience, the boy came back to himself, sparing the Headsmun a frightened glance.

"'Coming, Mistress,' he murmured.

"Joaquin pressed his lips to Matteo's brow, and rising, he ran after the Wolfmother. Elaina snuffled about Matteo's body, but at a call from Joaquin, the hound bounded off through the snow on his heels. Dior realized only the Headsmun remained now, watching her with dark, hungry eyes, his hand burned into a black claw by her blood. And with Kiara's threat hanging in the air above the greasy spatter that had been Shae, Dior ran after her, Kane following with a soft curse.

"Red drenched the snow behind them; Shae's blood mixed with Joaquin's and the Grail's. And as a cold wind blew through those dead trees, the latter began to tremble.

"To move.

"Droplets of her holy blood, shivering as if the earth were quaking, running in thin rivulets across the frost as if to return to the veins of their mistress. But the wind blew harder, the red ran cold, those lonely drops freezing now to ice.

"And all was still once more."

IV

CIRCLE OF HELL

"TWO WEEKS PASSED, frozen and bleak, trekking southward, ever southward. The dark company skirted the edge of the northern weald, crossing the frozen Ròdaerr River and cutting around the grim cityfort of Redwatch. If Dior thought of Gabriel—the journey they'd taken together across these same frozen wastes, growing fonder with every step—she gave no hint to her captors. The bruise his hand had left on her face was faded now.

"Who could speak to the bruise on her heart?

"The Dyvok fed from their scorched—only a mouthful each night so as not to weaken them, but both vampires were clearly hungered, and their men clearly stretched. They'd found Dior's lockpicks after her recapture, nevermore leaving her unguarded, but after learning of her destination, the Grail made no further attempts to escape. Instead, she lay trussed up like a Firstmas hog behind the Wolfmother, riding ever south toward Dún Maergenn, praying through every mile of that frozen hell.

"It was on the banks of the Volta she at last found reprieve. They trotted beneath the shell of San Guillaume, Dior's eyes shining as she looked up to the monastery where the Company of the Grail had been slaughtered by the Beast of Vellene, only a few months and a hundred lifetimes ago. But passing beneath those lonely cliffs, their pace slowed, and after countless leagues and wintersdeep nights, in the cold light of the rising sun, the girl saw with horror what they'd been chasing all this while.

"A convoy. Three dozen wagons, gathered around a roaring bonfire, guarded by fifty thrallswords and twice that many foulbloods, chained in a rotten mob. The wagons were the same as we'd seen at Aveléne—rusty iron cages rising up from wooden trays. And just like at Aveléne, every cage was filled near to bursting.

"Men. Women. Children. The ragged remnants of Aaron de Coste and Baptiste Sa-Ismael's dream, now reduced to nothing but cattle.

"Over a *thousand* of them.

"Kiara spurred her pony on, Dior's head bouncing mercilessly off the beast's flank until they drew to a halt at the inner ring of carriages. Cries of 'The mistress! Mistress Kiara returns!' rang among the wasted trees, soldiers in Dyvok livery taking a knee around the flames. Dior shivered, her breath catching at the awful sights about her—frostbitten fingers curled around rusted bars, and eyes bereft of hope peering out from between them.

"'Ah, dear Wolfmother,' a low, sweet voice said. 'I thought we'd lost you.'

"Dior dragged her eyes from the poor souls around her, searching for the one who'd spoken. It was a short woman in fine dark leathers, a fawn frock-coat and tricorn, a mighty greatsword at her back. Her black hair was bound in braids, so long they near brushed the frost at her feet. She looked perhaps thirty, possessed of sharp, dark eyes and a perilous grace, two circles of what must have been blood daubed on her cheeks. Sūdhaemi born, the woman's skin was dark like all her kinfolk, yet greyed by the grim pallor of death.

"Another vampire.

"'I am certain, sweet Soraya,' Kiara said, 'your heart *bled* at the thought of my fall.'

"The smaller vampire's lips twisted in a mirthless smile. The Wolfmother nodded to an iron box atop one of the wagons, wrapped in heavy chain.

"'How fares the bairn?'

"Soraya shrugged, tossing her braids back off her shoulders. 'Still not drinking willingly. But he drinks eventually.'

"Kiara chuckled, dark as poison. 'Don't we all.'

"Soraya tipped her tricorn back, looked the bigger woman over. 'You seem of a pleasant mood. I'd have bet you'd be shitting blood at thought of our delay. Good hunting, was it?'

"'That it was, little sister. That it was.'

"The smaller vampire prickled at the diminutive, sharing a swift glance with the newly arrived Kane. 'Good enough to warrant whatever happened to your face, cousin? The bloodwitch who got Rykard take a slice from you too?'

"The Headsmun scowled as he dismounted, the claw scars across his features only deepening. But Kiara patted Dior, trussed up on her saddle, and the third vampire's gaze sharpened as she noted the girl for the first time.

Breathing deep now, Soraya pressed the tip of her bright red tongue to a sharpening canine as she looked Dior over like ripe fruit.

"'Now *what*,' she breathed, 'in great Tolyev's name, is *that*?'

"'A *prize*, little sister,' Kiara grinned. 'One the Blackheart will thank the bearers of. We return with Lion's blood on our hands, sweet Soraya. And raven's gold in our purses.'

"Soraya frowned, clearly confused. Kiara only grinned the wider.

"'Get our mouse stowed, Poet.' The Wolfmother glanced to the kennelboy, arriving now with the other scorched. 'Throw her in with the other valuables, safe and warm. Lady Soraya and I have *much* to talk about.'

"Joaquin bowed and lifted Dior effortlessly, cradling her in his arms as he trudged toward one of the sturdier wagons closest to the fire. Another thrallsword unbolted the heavy door, and the people within shrank back, wide-eyed and fearful. Joaquin's brow darkened, glancing around the other wagons circling the flames.

"'They're all full?'

"'We've snatched up some more refugees on the way 'ere,' the man said, scratching his rough beard. 'And Lars and Quinn brought another bundle down six nights back. Those brats from Aveléne that the Lion cut loose. Makin' a break for León, they was.'

"Dior paled at those words—it was clear the man spoke of little Mila and the other children who'd been left in the care of Gabriel's old apprentice. She gazed around those cages, then up at the boy who held her, plaintive and pained. Joaquin Marenn had called Aveléne home, after all; scorched out of simple expediency so Kiara might track Gabriel better through the Night-stone, and left for dead once his usefulness had run out. But if any affection for the folk he'd grown up with remained within, there was nothing of it in his eyes as he nodded to the wagon.

"'There's no room,' he pointed out.

"'Allow me,' came a growl.

"Kane stepped forward, reaching into the cage and grabbing the first mortal he saw—a young fellow not much older than Dior. The youth cried out as the vampire's hand closed about his wrist, other folk screaming as he was dragged out the door. He wailed, struggling with all he had, but his captor held him in a grip like iron. And as Dior watched, wide-eyed, Kane bared long bright fangs, and sank them deep into the poor fellow's throat.

"She'd never seen a vampire truly *feed* from a mortal before—the few sips she'd witnessed on the road here held no candle to the full horror of it all. Because it was not fear that welled in the youth's eyes as those teeth punctured his neck. It was *bliss.* He groaned as Kane drank deeper, eyes rolling back, lips curled in a euphoric smile. And were they not pinned at his sides, he'd have surely thrown his arms around the thing that was killing him.

"Because Kane *was* killing him . . .

"'Stop,' the Grail said.

"She struggled in Joaquin's implacable grip, horrified and furious.

"'Make him . . . No, stop! *STOP!*'

"The Headsmun paid her no heed. The youth in his arms stiffened, breath rattling now, smile gone blue. But still, the vampire drank, groaning, growling. With one final gasp, his victim shivered, like a lover reaching his ending, every muscle taut. And then Kane released his murderous grip, letting the body drop, *thump,* lifeless into the snow.

"The Headsmun sneered, rubied spools of stolen life stretching between his lips.

"'*Now* there's room for ye, girl.'

"And turning on his heel, he stomped after Soraya and the Wolfmother.

"Dior looked down at the dead youth, struggling not to retch. Joaquin exchanged a glance with the other thrall, but breathing deep, he lifted Dior and shoved her into the stink and crush of the other 'valuables' in the cage, locking the door behind her. His comrade picked up the fresh corpse like it were straw, and without a backward glance, the pair stomped toward the bonfire, Elaina following on her master's heels with wagging tail.

"'Joaquin?' a voice cried.

"The houndboy stopped, turning back to Dior's wagon, blinking at the figure now reaching through the bars. It was Isla, of course; the Ossian lass who'd snarled at Gabriel over potatoes, who'd told Dior she should've left her to the Dyvok.

"'Isla?' he whispered.

"'Aye, it's me!' The lass pressed her face to the bars, twin beauty marks on a cheek wet with tears. 'Oh, God, Joaquin, I thought ye were dead! I thought they *got* ye!'

"The houndboy glanced at the thrallsword beside him, the Dead around him, the chill dawn wind blowing flurries of snow between them. The way

Isla had spoken about her Ever After, these two had loved each other true before Aveléne's fall. But now, reunited, Joaquin stared at his beloved as if she were a stranger. Cold. Hard. Eyes like stone.

"'They *did* get me,' he replied.

"And without another word, he trudged off toward his fellows.

"Dior bit her lip as Isla called her beau's name. Another scorched bellowed for quiet and cracked his truncheon across her hand, the girl wailing as she pulled it back inside the bars. Cold iron pressed against Dior's cheek, her heart thumping with a dreadful cadence now; the horror of where she truly was finally laid bare. Miles into bleak wilderness, headed toward a land she'd never seen, in the captivity of monsters she'd never imagined.

"She met Isla's eyes, the girl giving her a small nod of recognition, her lips pinched tight as she nursed her wounded hand. Dior's voice was soft in the gloom.

"'Where did they catch you?'

"'A few days north of Aveléne,' the girl replied. 'We didn't get far without ye.'

"Dior sighed. 'What happened to Frère Lachlan? Did he fall?'

"Isla shook her head. 'He *left* us.'

"'Left you? He was supposed to look after you, why would he—'

"'We met other silversaints on the river,' Isla murmured. 'Heading south. Frère Lachlan spoke with a big man with a hand made of iron. I heard not what they said, but the frère grew upset. Furious, even. And with barely a word, he sent us on toward San Michon alone, and headed back south with his brethren.'

"'Shit.' Dior hung her head, breathing deep. 'I'm sorry, Isla.'

"'The fault isn't yers, Mlle Lachance. This is the will of—'

"'Mlle Lachance?'

"Dior's pale blue eyes widened and she turned toward that voice, breath catching in her lungs. And she saw him then, squeezed in tight among the prisoners but tall enough to loom above them, his disbelieving smile bright as the sun had once been.

"'*Baptiste?*'

"She whispered the big Sūdhaemi's name as he started pressing toward her, struggling through the tight-packed bodies. Dior plunged into the crush, smaller than he, slipping her way past elbows and ribs, and somewhere in the thick of it they reached each other, the blackthumb struggling to get his big arms around her.

"'Great Redeemer, Dior, it *is* you!'

"'Baptiste!' she sobbed, hugging him like a drowning girl hugs driftwood. 'Oh, thank the Martyrs and Mothermaid! We thought you were dead!'

"'I'm fine, sweet child,' he breathed, dark eyes shining with tears. 'God's truth, I never thought to see you again! The scouts we sent never returned, and then the Dyvok . . .'

"The blackthumb shook his head, drawing her back to meet his eyes. He was a handsome man, the smith of Aveléne; strong jaw and dark skin, hair cropped short, salt and pepper at his temples and in the whiskers on his chin. He wore dark leathers trimmed with pale fur and stained with blood, big, forge-callused hands squeezing hers gently.

"'How comes it you're here? Godssakes, where is Gabriel?'

"It must have hit her then, to finally hear my brother's name. For weeks, Dior had been mired in a world of enemies, not daring to show weakness, to reveal how deep she bled. But there in the blackthumb's arms, something appeared to break inside her; some dam of pain and grief, crumbling now to rubble in his embrace.

"'He f-fell,' she whispered, tears spilling down her cheeks. 'I d-don't know if . . .'

"Sorrow washed over Baptiste's face; grief and pain and despair as one more loss was added to his tally. The blackthumb wrapped the girl up and hugged her as she sobbed, her whole body shaking with anguish. Smoothing her bloodstained, ashen hair with one gentle hand, he murmured comforts, his own eyes shining with grief.

"'Hush now, chérie,' he told her, jaw clenched. 'No tears for the faithful fallen. They dwell in the kingdom of heaven, at the right hand of the Holy Father.'

"'Forgive m-me. I know you've your own grief to bear.' Dior pressed her brow to his chest as if to steady herself, and breathing deep, she looked up to meet his eyes. 'I know about Aaron, Baptiste. I'm so sorry.'

"A shadow seemed to fall over the blackthumb then, his shoulders sagging, a murmur of cold horror rippling through Isla and the others crammed into that awful cage. Baptiste's voice was thick and raw, and he frowned as he searched Dior's face.

"'How could you know about Aaron, chérie?'

"'Gabe found his sword at Aveléne. Broken in half. God, I'm *so* sorry, mon ami. I know you loved him true. He might not have died if—'

"'Chérie . . .'

"Baptiste was trembling now, anguish burning in the coals of his eyes. He glanced toward that iron box atop its wagon, wrapped in heavy chain, tears spilling down his cheeks. He tried to speak, but it seemed as if he had forgot the shape of words. Isla spoke for him then; the girl's face drawn and pale, her mouth downturned in sorrow.

"'I was mistaken when I spoke at Aveléne, Mlle Lachance. Capitaine Aaron is not dead.'

"Dior's face fell as the lass shook her head.

"'He is Dead.'"

V

DÚN MAERGENN

"DIOR'S EYES OPENED to a song of screams.

"So it had been every night for the past three weeks. Crammed in with the other captives, flogged south and west across endless, frozen miles through the Ossian wastes, past ruined dúns and decimated farmland and the old feasts of fat crows. Her journey was torture, despite the answers that might await her at the end of it. Though the 'valuables' in Dior's wagon were fed better fare than the other prisoners, they were still so tight-packed, there was no room to curl down to sleep, and the wagon floor so filthy, only a madwoman might lie on it anyway. Dior dozed upright instead, crushed in beside Baptiste and young Isla á Cuinn, grabbing what rest she could during each day's stop.

"And every dusk, the screaming woke her.

"It was like some grim cock's crow, heralding the fall of the sun. The scorched would rouse themselves to its tune, setting to work with shovels and picks to dig their masters from the cold cradles of their beds. They would rise, those Dead things, and brushing black earth from their cold hands, the vampires would make the screaming stop.

"'Oh, my poor, sweet Aaron . . .' Baptiste whispered.

"Dior held the blackthumb's hand, whispering that it would be over soon. It had been even more awful to begin with—Aaron had screamed for *hours* in those first few nights the Grail was imprisoned, beating the box they'd locked him in so hard that its iron walls buckled like parchment. It was Kane who fashioned the solution—cruel, cold Kane, looking up from the corpse he'd just made, red dripping from his chin as he asked,'Why don't we just cut it off him?'

"And the Wolfmother had dragged her teeth from the gasping dame she and Soraya had been sharing, sticky lips quirked in grim amusement.

"'Nae your worst idea, cousin.'

"Dior's eyes had welled with tears as they'd dragged Aaron from that box. The brave capitaine of Aveléne had been a giant when she last saw him, standing on the battlements of his mighty château. Beautiful blond hair blowing in the wind, scarred face twisting as he spat defiance at the Beast of Vellene, and risked his entire city for a girl he'd only just met.

"*My name is Aaron de Coste*, he'd roared to Danton, *son of House Coste and the Blood Ilon. I have been slaying your kind since I was but a boy, and I am a boy no longer.*

"No giant it was, that the Dyvok dragged from that coffin. Aaron de Coste was a pitiful figure now, lordly clothes filthied, long blond hair and beard matted with dried blood. His eyes were red, wild, his voice cracking with agony, and Dior sobbed as she looked into his screaming mouth and saw his canines grown long and sharp.

"'Oh, merciful God,' she'd breathed.

"They'd held him down, Kane and Soraya, tearing the tunic from his back, and unveiling the source of his agony—the aegis that the sisters of San Michon had inked into Aaron's flesh as a boy. Once, it had served as his shield against the horrors of the night, but now, it was only silver; a cursed, poisonous bane burning beneath his Dead skin. And taking a short, sharp knife from her boot, the Wolfmother had knelt over Aaron's writhing body, and begun relieving him of it.

"Naél, Angel of Bliss, sleeving his left forearm; Sarai, Angel of Plagues, at his bicep; a beautiful portrait of the Redeemer covering his entire back—all these the Wolfmother flayed away with her blade. She was deft as a butcher with a fresh flank of venison, Aaron's pallid flesh carved red as he roared and bucked. Baptiste had gripped the bars of their cage so tight the iron cut into his skin, his face twisted in anguish and rage as he watched.

"'Don't look,' Dior had told him. 'Don't let them torture you too.'

"The man's eyes were fixed on his lover, welling bright with pain.

"'Baptiste, don't listen,' Dior begged. 'Talk to me. Tell me something good.'

"He shook his head, whispering, 'There is no good left now in this world, chérie.'

"'Tell me how you two met.' She kissed the man's big, callused hand, now suddenly so small and frail in hers. 'Tell me how you fell in love.'

"Baptiste glanced to the girl at his side then, and a glimmer of light shone through the shadow that had fallen over him. His dry lips curled in an almost-smile.

"'Aaron and I did not fall in love, sweet child. We *plummeted*.'

"The screams had seemed to fade around them then, Baptiste's eyes shining as he left that freezing cage and wandered instead through the summer-warm halls of memory.

"'We met in the Gauntlet of San Michon,' he sighed. 'I can still see him that morn if I close my eyes. I was new-apprenticed to Forgemaster Argyle, and he to Frère Greyhand. He was practicing swordplay, and the sigil of his bloodline was fresh-inked upon his chest, so he fought shirtless. And when I saw him . . .' Baptiste smiled truly then, awestruck. 'He seemed a statue of some myth come to life. Brave Thaddeus or mighty Ramases, etched in marble by the hands of masters, then blessed with life by the lips of God Himself.

"'Our eyes met across the circle. We said our introductions, formal and cool. But when we shook hands, his touch lingered a breath too long, and in that breath, I knew I had found what I'd sought all my life. Somewhere to belong. Someone to belong *to*. No matter the danger, nor the cost. He would be mine, and I, his. Forever.'

"The big man hung his head, glancing once more to Kiara.

"'I did not know back then, what an awful word *forever* could be.'

"Dior put her arms around the blackthumb and squeezed, tears shining in her eyes as she found herself back in that cage, that cold. The butchery was near its ending, though; Kiara had almost finished her dreadful work. She'd seemed to take particular pleasure in the last of it—the intricate sigil of the Ilon bloodline inked on Aaron's chest. Taking her time, cutting deep and hard and finally hurling those beautiful serpents and roses into the fire.

"'Nae Whisper now,' she'd smiled. 'Untamed are ye, through and through.'

"'Damn you,' Aaron had managed to spit. 'Goddamn y-you and all your cursed kind.'

"'Nae my kind, my bonny boy.' She leaned close, planting a cold kiss upon his scarred cheek. 'Our kind. Ye are reborn to the line of great Tolyev, grandchild of Nikita the Blackheart, king and conqueror of this land. All the empire now trembles at the name of my dark father, boy. All Ossway kneels at his feet. And soon, so too shall ye.'

"Tears spilled down Baptiste's cheeks as his beloved was thrown back inside his coffin with the dregs of Kane's feast—another torture that Aaron's kin fashioned for him, to be locked in a box with his thirst and the cooling corpse of someone he'd sworn to protect. But at least the silver had been stripped from Aaron's skin, and awful as it had been, Dior had supposed the capitaine would now be spared that pain for the rest of his eternity."

Jean-François chuckled, the historian pausing to sip from his goblet of blood.

"Save that we kith awake each dusk in exactly the same state we died in. Only fire or silver or the darkest of magiks might gift us a hurt that lingers longer than a sunset. No mere steel would be enough to spare de Coste his torments."

"No," the Last Liathe murmured. "And his captors well knew it. So, each day, his tattooed flesh would heal. Each night, Dior's eyes opened to the dreadful song of his screams. And Kiara had her dark son dragged from his box, and flayed him all over again."

"Such savagery." The Marquis sighed. "Nikita's brood well deserved their fate."

"Do not feign outrage, Chastain," Celene replied. "You may have finer tailors, but you and your kin are cut from the same cloth exact."

"You misjudge us, Mlle Castia," Jean-François replied. "The Blood Chastain has no penchant for unnecessary cruelty, nor our Empress desire to rule a wasteland."

"But Margot still has desire to *rule*. And while your kin may not openly revel in brutality as the Untamed did, you still call yourself *Shepherds*, and God's true children *sheep*." The Liathe shook her head. "You are an abomination in his eyes, sinner. Unrepentant, unashamed, unafraid, even in the face of the hell awaiting you. And its sovereign shall make a *feast* of your rotten soul."

The historian smiled, licking his thumb and turning a new page. "'Tis a strange thing, to be called a monster by one more monstrous."

Celene Castia shrugged, looking back to the ceiling.

"I was always my mother's daughter.

"And so it was, over a month after Gabriel had fallen, Dior found herself in the duchy of the legendary Niamh Nineswords; the chill and barren wastes of Ossway. To the far north, the dark spine of the Mìchaich na Baloch—the Moonsthrone Mountains, where the twin goddesses of old Ossian folklore rested their heads each dawn. To the west, the jagged shores of the Elea Brinn—the Splintered Isles, where Daegann Ironhand was hurled to earth in the Age of Legends. And across the frozen breadth of the Òrd River, towering upon a great promontory of the Wolftooth Coast, stood the once-mighty capital of Niamh's realm, and the final resting place of the Mother Maryn—the grand cityfort of Maergenn.

"'This place used to be the jewel in Niamh's crown,' came a soft voice.

"Dior glanced to Isla beside her, saw the faraway look in the girl's green eyes. She was an odd one, Joaquin's beloved. She'd seemed traumatized after her rescue at Aveléne, but she'd proved solid as stone these past weeks in captivity. She'd seen the fall of Dún Cuinn, after all, survived more trauma than most, and a strength shone in her now the shock had worn off. Isla helped the other 'valuables' keep their spirits up, even giving up some of her rations so the children locked in with them might eat a little more. And though he ever ignored her, it seemed a fire came into Isla's eyes whenever Joaquin was near.

"'You've been here before, Isla?' Dior asked.

"The lass nodded. 'Ma brought me here as a little girl. We came on pilgrimage to see the Sepulcher of the Mothermaid. I'd never laid eyes on anything like it.'

"'This city used to be one of the mightiest fortresses in the empire,' Baptiste murmured. 'Anaen dú Malaedh, they named it. The Anvil of the Wolf. The armies of four clans united broke upon these walls. It was said not even God Himself could breach them.'

"The blackthumb made the sign of the wheel and sighed.

"'Sweet Mothermaid, look at it now . . .'

"Dior's eyes were wide as she stared out through the bars at the grand cityfort. The Ossian capital was enormous; one city built outside another, ringed by half a dozen walls. The innermost city, known as Auldtunn, was all grand buildings of fine-wrought stone, high gothic towers and wondrous architecture, a beautiful old dockside named Portunn on its southern flank. The outer city, Newtunn, was an urban sprawl, grown like fungus on the skin of the first. Both Auldtunn and Newtunn were encircled by mighty battlements, and upon the very point of the promontory rose a grand keep of dark stone—the château that shared the city's name, and the name of the clan that had built it.

"Dún Maergenn.

"'God, what happened here?' Dior whispered.

"'Same as happened at Aveléne, chérie,' Baptiste murmured beside her.

"A battle. And a terrible one, by the look. The city's outer walls were crushed to rubble, many of her buildings collapsed or burned or simply blasted apart—it seemed the very stone of Maergenn itself had been torn apart by the hands of spiteful giants.

"The smothered sun was sinking, Dior looking to the armored figures upon the ramparts above. The Newtunn gates stood forty feet high, wrought of heavy, ironbound lumber. A great wolf had once been painted on the wood, rampant against nine blades. But the beast had been painted over with blood, the sigil of Clan Maergenn defaced by a roaring bear and broken shield, a motto scrawled beneath by heavy, red hands.

"'*Deeds Not Words* . . .' she whispered.

"A shout rang above, and the gates were drawn wide. The great portcullis beyond rose up with the song of greasy iron, and with a command from Kiara, the convoy rolled inside; wagons and highbloods first, thrallswords next, foulbloods trailing last as always.

"Newtunn was a ruin; smashed dwellings and tumbled towers. Snow clung to broken eaves, filled gutted shells, wagon wheels *thud*ding and *thump*ing as the convoy was led up a shattered thoroughfare. The prisoners looked about in horror at the destruction. The highbloods were tense, watching the buildings around them with narrowed eyes as crows sang in the deepening gloom.

"Baptiste pointed, whispering, 'Sweet Mothermaid, look . . .'

"Dior's grip on the bars tightened as she saw figures emerging from Newtunn's ruins, creeping through the shadows of the sinking sun. Foulbloods. *Thousands* of them. Soldiers in dirty livery, embroidered with wolf and swords. Hollow-eyed women, ragged children flitting among the wreckage like wraiths. Dior shrank back as their stares fell on her; sharp teeth and soulless smiles. Dozens lurched forward, thin and famished, but the Wolfmother bared her fangs, and the foulbloods cowered, backing away like whipped curs.

"Kiara glanced toward the Headsmun. 'Kane, see the dogs off, will ye?'

"The younger vampire scowled but yet obeyed, opening the rearmost wagon. Folk wailed as Kane reached in and plucked a body at random from within; one of the boys Dior had rescued on the river at Aveléne, his chin fuzzed with soft whiskers, face twisted as he screamed and flailed. Holding him aloft, the Headsmun proffered the lad to the foulbloods who'd followed them from Aveléne, as if waving a treat to a mob of hungry pups.

"'Dior,' Baptiste murmured. 'Don't watch, chérie.'

"But the Grail ignored the blackthumb, jaw clenched, tears shining in her eyes as the Headsmun twirled the boy like a sack of straw, then hurled him out into the mob.

"The foulbloods fell on the poor lad, sharks to red water. The wind was howling, but not enough to drown the boy's screams. Kane dragged another figure from the wagon; an older woman, fighting with all the desperate strength of the doomed. But the Headsmun only laughed, throwing the poor soul like a rag doll, out into that ocean of claws and teeth.

"Dior's hands were curled into bloodless fists. Her lips moving, her words unheard. Beside her, Baptiste lifted his eyes to the sky, made the sign of the wheel.

"'Merci, Almighty Father,' he whispered. 'Merci.'

"Dior hissed then, incredulous. 'What the *hell* are you thanking him for?'

"Baptiste met her eyes, his own wet with tears.

"'For not making me like them, chérie.'

"The girl gritted her teeth. The foulbloods tore their feast. And without a backward glance to any of it, Kiara ordered their convoy onward.

"A horn rang in the dusk, and a second set of gates opened into the city's inner ring; tall tenements, well-appointed homes, cobbled streets. The buildings in Auldtunn were mostly intact, and trundling up the thorough-fare, Dior whispered in wonder as she saw figures—not coldbloods now, but *people*. Soldiers dressed in Dyvok livery were stood atop a butcher's wagon, distributing shanks of raw meat to a disheveled, shouting crowd.

"Looking out over Portunn and the Gulf of Wolves, circled by a third tier of walls, a mighty dún rose into the deepening night ahead. As the convoy rolled into its vast bailey, a horn blast pierced the sky, great flocks of crows taking to the wing and sailing up into the snows.

"The castle was huge—even Aveléne seemed a mud hovel beside it. But as their wagon came to a halt, Dior's eyes lingered on the broken battlements, fallen spires, sundered walls. Masons were at work with barrows and mortar, but the scars of the attack still ran deep. The air was thick with the reek of fresh death. The hymn of fat flies.

"Everywhere Dior looked flew the standard of the Dyvok—that roaring bear triumphant with its broken shield, white upon deep blue. On the north side of the bailey, great barracks loomed beside a smoking ironworks, a dis-tillery that smelled like an open privy, a stable large enough to horse an army with barely a beast left within. On the courtyard's southern side, a grand cathedral stood, reaching up into the storm-washed heavens. Its spires were tall and graceful; a gothic marvel wrought in dark stone. But it was half-destroyed now, roof collapsed, mighty walls gutted by flame.

"'Amath du Miagh'dair,' Isla murmured. 'The Sepulcher of the Mother-maid. Built upon the earth where the Testaments say she was delivered unto heaven.' The girl signed the wheel, head bowed. 'Thank ye, holy madame, for delivering us from the wilderness.'

"The bailey was in tumult now, wagons being unlocked and captives dragged out by dutiful scorched. Dior stumbled as her boots hit the cobbles, saved only by Baptiste. She'd no time to thank him; a truncheon cracked across her back, and she was shoved into a line of prisoners, bewildered and babbling. She looked about her in a daze, men and women in Dyvok colors watching from the walls, shoving at the captives, dividing them into groups.

"'Whatchado, boy?' a gruff voice demanded.

"Dior blinked, turning to the man who'd spoken. He was an ill-favored fellow, blood on his tabard and pig iron in his eyes. Dior saw a tablet of dark stone in his left hand, an intricate thrallbrand atop it—a black heart encircled by thorns.

"'Whatchado?' he asked again.

"'. . . Do?' she asked.

"He cuffed her, hard enough to make her ears ring. Baptiste caught her from falling, glowering at the little man, his fists clenched with impotent rage.

"'Yer in with the valuables, ye must 'ave a trade,' the little man said. 'So whatchado? Farrier? Farmer? Fletcher? Wot?'

"Dior shook her head. 'I don't do anything.'

"'Right.' The fellow marked his ledger, glanced to the thug beside him. 'Feast.'

"'Hold now,' Baptiste said, standing tall. 'I'm a smith, this boy is m—'

"A truncheon cracked into Baptiste's legs, and he hit the cobbles, knees blooding the stone. Dior cried out, rough hands grabbing her scruff and squeezing horribly tight.

"'Blackthumb, eh?' the little man nodded. 'Marvelous. One of ours just got hisself et by the mongrels tryin' to escape. We've call for another.' He marked his tablet, nodded to a hulking brute beside him. 'Take 'andsome 'ere to the forge, have Knacker break 'im in. Throw this little pigdick in the stocks. Don't think they'll need more tonight, but if they do—'

"'Let me go!' Dior snapped. 'Get your fucking hands off—'

"Her arm was twisted behind her back, and she gasped, her bones but a twitch from snapping. She spat a vicious curse, struggling, when a sharp voice cut through the flurry.

"'Hold, Petrik. This mouse is mine.'

"The scorched froze as still as stone, the little ledgerman turning to find the Wolfmother at his back, her skin pale as marble in the flickering torchlight. Chill wind tousled her thick slayerbraids, and she looked at the ledgerman like something she'd dislike to dirty her boots with, but would swiftly step in nonetheless.

"'My dread Lady Kiara,' he said, bowing. 'Of course.'

"'Come, Mouse,' the Wolfmother beckoned. 'Yer laerd awaits.' She glanced to the controlled chaos around her. 'Bring the tally to me when yer done, Petrik. The Bloodlords will bid for their share come the morrow, but I'll be claiming mine afore the dawn.'

"'. . . As it please, m'lady.'

"Kiara held out her hand. Dior looked to Baptiste, but on his knees, the man could only nod, affirming she obey. Isla whispered a blessing, squeezing Dior's hand, telling her not to fear. All around, she could see a struggle of life and death, as grim and cruel as any battle she'd witnessed, playing out not with swords and steel, but sticks of chalk and stone tablets. Terrified people being weighed on some awful scale, their worth not measured by deeds, nor words, nor anything so simple as human compassion, but by their usefulness to the monsters who'd captured them. Children ripped from mothers' embrace, wives torn from husbands' arms. The sight was too awful to witness, too sickening to believe.

"'Little Mouse,' Kiara growled. 'Come. Now.'

"Dior hung her head. The words Gabriel had spoken seeming to ring in the air.

"*It's a tiny thing. Frail as butterfly wings. But it's the foundation of everything to come. It's the gift you're going to give back to this empire.*

"But hope seemed so very far away now.

"And with no other choice, the girl took the vampire's hand."

VI

FEAST OF THE BLACKHEART

"*YOU CANNOT GET blood from stone*, the old saying goes. But as Dior followed the Wolfmother down a long, cold hallway, the rock beneath her feet was remarkably free of stains. It hung in the air, old but sharp—faint hints of the awful butchery that must have unfolded when this city was conquered. The towers were toppled. The ramparts crushed. But there were no stains on the floors at least.

"Truth is, you can get anything from stone if the servants scrub hard enough."

Jean-François frowned, glancing up at the shadow across the river.

"I don't think you've quite grasped the meaning of that saying, Mlle Castia."

"Fortunate, then," the shadow replied, "that we do not care what you think."

Celene lay on her back, eyes fixed on the ceiling above, lost in the mists of time. The historian scoffed, dipping his quill as she continued.

"Kane and Soraya stalked behind Dior, carrying Aaron de Coste's iron coffin between them. Such had been their haste, they'd not had time to flay the fledgling's skin tonight, and he could be heard within, whispering prayers to the God who had forsaken him. But the Wolfmother's eyes were fixed ahead, her voice a low growl as she addressed Dior.

"'Speak only when spoken to if ye value yer tongue. Climb not off yer knees if ye've want of yer legs. My father will suffer no slight in sight of his bloodlords, and his only use fer fools is to feed his guests. To disrespect here means death. D'ye hear me, Mouse?'

"Dior replied softly, jaw clenched. 'I understand.'

"'Nae.' Kiara stopped suddenly. 'Ye cannae possibly. My Laerd Nikita walked this earth before the first Augustin drew breath. He survived the Ashen Inquisition, the Sixty Years Plague, the Wars of the Wyrm. When yer beloved Gabriel destroyed great Tolyev at Crimson Glade, this bloodline near tore itself to *pieces*. And the Blackheart dragged it back together with his own two bloody hands, and carved the kingdom upon which ye stand. Ye've never been quite so close to death as now, little Mouse. So don't pretend to understand.' The Wolfmother towered over Dior, decades of murder in her eyes. 'Just *obey*.'

"They walked to a set of tall double doors, flanked by men in dark steel and Untamed colors. Despite the somber surrounds, the sound of revels rang out within; loud talk and crashing laughter and metal striking metal like a booming gong. Kiara rolled her shoulders, lifting her hand to knock, yet not letting her knuckles fall.

"'You look nervous,' Dior murmured.

"Kiara scowled, but the Grail spoke true; on the threshold of her triumphant homecoming, the Wolfmother appeared entirely ill at ease.

"'You return in glory, sister,' Soraya said. 'The blood of a Lion on your teeth. Our father shall surely smile upon you. Even *she* must be of good cheer at de León's fall.'

"The Wolfmother shook her head and muttered, 'She's *never* of good bloody cheer.'

"Kiara pounded three times, knuckles leaving deep dents in the ironwood. And pushing the doors open, the Wolfmother led Dior into a carnivalé of horrors. A vast room of dark stone, lit by chymical globes and flickering candlelight. Minstrel song washed over the Grail in waves, and she gagged at the reek, copper-bright and iron-heavy on her tongue.

"So much blood.

"The Hall of Plenty, it was called—a room far larger than the feasthall of Avelène. A vast map was painted upon one wall, depicting the Empire of Elidaen in exquisite detail; from the Splintered Isles in the west, to the Spear Coast in the east. No fire burned in the three great hearths, but the air was still warm with the press of bodies, and the stink of new murder. Dior's face ran bloodless as she looked up and saw *people* strung from the rafters; chained upside down by the dozen, hands bound and mouths gagged, naked as babes. Mortal handmaidens in rich finery stood below them; beautiful gowns, sumptuous hairstyles, and powdered skin. Each maid held a sharp knife and a tray of goblets in her hands, and their shoes were sticky red.

"Great tables framed the hall, arranged in a headless square, long and broad enough to seat thirty at a side. And those seats were *filled* with vampires.

"They wore noble trim or slayer's garb, leather and steel or silks and lace. One was clad in the robes of a holy sister, a broken wheel strung about her neck. Another was dressed in jester's motley, save his colors were all bleached grey. Soldiers, noblemen, brutes in hide and fur—they had the look of folk from all across the realm, every walk of life. But each was bereft of that life, malevolent and cold and grave pale; highbloods all. And Dior Lachance was struck mute at the awful sight of it.

"A Court of the Blood.

"A contest was underway in the Hall of Plenty's heart; a grim parody of a knightly tourney before a mortal king. The first combatant was a tall and wiry highblood, his hair long and snow-grey, his beard reaching to his belly. He'd stripped down to his britches, and his lean arms and back were carved with beautiful tattoos—maids with fishes' tails, grim monsters of the deep— and as he smiled, the two fangs in his upper jaw glinted gold. His foe was a sleek-cut woman in black leathers, her dark hair clipped back to uneven stubble, like a heretic bound for an inquisitor's pyre. She was shorter than her opponent, but her swords were as long as Dior was tall, and she wielded one in each hand, the blades *boom*ing as she flew through the air in a whirling, scything dance. Highbloods around the tables jeered as she blooded her opponent; a blow that near took his arm off and sent him skidding back across the flagstones, snarling and cursing.

"The big highblood rallied, relieving the woman of one blade with a blow so fierce it cracked some of the windows around the hall. The woman brought her other blade down, cleaved her foe's shoulder all the way to his rib cage. But with one bloody hand, the man snatched her up and slammed her into the floor with force enough to splinter the stone. The woman punched back, shattering his bearded jaw, blood spraying bright. But the tattooed brute didn't let go, pounding the woman's head back into the shattered floor, again, *again*, until she slapped her hand on the stone three times.

"'Yield!' she groaned. 'I yield!'

"A thin roar went up, a few highbloods lifting goblets, others rolling their eyes and raising only their brows. The tattooed hulk rose to his feet, drooling red, offering a hand to his vanquished foe. Her bleeding lips split in a savage grin as she took it.

"'Almost.'

"'Ye broke my damned jaw, Alix,' the fellow slurred, rubbing at his sopping beard.

"The woman stood on tiptoe, licked the blood from his lips. 'I'll kiss it better later.'

"The man chuckled as the sleek woman slapped his rump, the pair staggering to a nearby table. The woman caught the eye of a handmaid standing beside one of those ghastly chandeliers, held two fingers aloft. Dior blanched in horror as the maid curtseyed, lifted her knife, and sliced a young man's throat—as casual as if she were picking flowers for the centerpiece. Steaming blood gushed from the slice, the man not even struggling as it flooded over his chin and onto the floor. None of the folk hanging beside him made a whimper as the maidservant filled a pair of goblets to their trembling brim.

"'Sweet fucking Mothermaid,' Dior whispered, stepping forward.

"A cold grip closed around her arm, hard enough to make her bones creak.

"'Disrespect means death,' Kiara murmured.

"Trembling, sheened with fresh sweat, Dior watched as the handmaid filled the other goblets on her tray. Leaving the fellow to drip his last onto the stones, the woman took the cups to the wounded combatants, gifting each a draught, then proceeded to carry drinks around to the other guests. Dior closed her eyes at the horror of it all, lifting hands to her face and whispering a fevered prayer.

"'Come,' the Wolfmother growled.

"That iron grip closed on her arm once again, and the Grail was dragged down into that gathering of devils, Kane and Soraya on her heels. The minstrels played on—a merry tune utterly at odds with the macabre surrounds, trilling close to the edge of madness. But conversation hushed as the quartet passed by, Dior almost slipping on the bloodstained stone. It was palpable now. Thickening the air. The attentions of monsters, shifting from the casual cruelty around them to the pale, frightened waif among them.

"At the end of the Hall of Plenty was a dais, as long as the tables around the square. A magnificent window of rainbow glass loomed behind it—a triptych so large it took up the entire wall. The Mothermaid was the central figure, beatific and serene, flanked by the Father Almighty, and their son, the Redeemer, bleeding from his trials upon his wheel.

"Looking into her ancestor's eyes, Dior clenched her jaw to stop her teeth chattering.

"Two thrones waited beneath that window, wrought of ornate black iron-wood, one sitting just below the other. Servants gathered in the shadows around them, and two figures reclined upon them, still as marble statues. All conversation had ceased now, even the minstrel song had hushed, the eyes of every vampire in the room fixed on the Wolfmother's quartet as they approached those graven thrones.

"'Kneel,' the Wolfmother murmured. 'Now.'

"Pale, reeling, Dior obeyed, withering to her knees. Kane and Soraya placed Aaron's iron box on the sticky stone as Kiara bowed, one hand to her long-dead heart.

"'My Laerd and Count Nikita,' she said, addressing the higher chair. 'Firstborn son of Tolyev the Butcher, conqueror of Ossway, and Priori of the Blood Dyvok.' The Wolfmother turned to the second. 'My Contessa Lilidh, beloved broodsister to my laerd, eldest child of Tolyev, and Wife of Winter. I bid ye humble greetings, elders, and pray Night I find ye well.'

"Kane and Soraya sank to one knee, heads bowed, fists over their hearts. The figure on the first throne spoke then, his voice as deep and cold as winter sky.

"'Welcome ye back, my blood.'

"Dior looked to he who spoke, lips parting in awe. Nikita Dyvok was young in appearance, early twenties when he'd been taken, though he defied a notion like 'time' as a hawk defies gravity. He was an idol wrought of onyx and pearl; an incubus carved of firelight shadow and the dreams of heartsick maids. His long hair fell in a black tumble over one side of his face, and a circlet of iron fashioned like a wreath of thorns kissed his princely brow. He wore dark silks and an ornate greatcoat of ocean blue, and a necklace of vampire fangs graced his throat, alongside another of those golden vials that Kiara and her kin all wore. A naked greatsword, longer and broader than a man, leaned at rest on the back of his throne. Its hilt was wrought like roaring bears, its edge notched by a thousand battles.

"Dior Lachance's first kiss had been with a girl—she'd told my brother that she'd never had a passion for men. Looking at Nikita, her body was flush with heat, her pulse thumping. But as stunning as the one they called Blackheart was, she spared the First Laerd of the Dyvok only a glance, her gaze dragged to the figure at his left hand.

"She was a maiden in form, Lilidh Dyvok. A sumptuous gown of black trimmed blue hugged her hourglass form, cascading to her feet in velvet waves. Her long blood-red hair reached near to the floor, her ears and fingers dripped with gold, and her brow was circled by a crown of spiraled ram's horns. She sat with one hand at rest upon the head of a great wolf, lounging beside her throne. The beast was white of fur, broad and sleek, though a deep scar ran down the left side of its face, and one of its eyes was missing. Its other—pale blue flushed with red—was fixed upon Dior.

"Lilidh's own eyes were rimmed thick with kohl, her lips, fresh blood. The Heartless, some named her. The Winterwife. She was attired like a daring noblewoman at court, but she had the seeming of some nameless goddess in a temple long forgot; a statue carved of marble that had endured long after the men who worshipped it had gone to the grave. Until the statue moved, that is, speaking to Kiara with a haunting voice that carried the length of that bloodstained hall.

"'Sweet niece. Our hearts gladden, to see thee again. It seems an age of this earth hath come and gone since last we gazed 'pon thy beauty.' The statue lifted her alabaster hand from the wolf's head. 'Come, let us kiss thee, and share heartfelt joy at thy return.'

"'M'lady. Ye honor me.'

"Kiara bowed lower, yet threw one swift glance to her dark father. Dior tensed as a current crackled through the room; as if the hackles of a hundred wolves were now raised. Nikita remained mute, unmoved as Lilidh beckoned with painted fingers.

"'Prithee, niece. Come ye closer.'

"Kiara obeyed, stepping up the dais under the gaze of every devil in the hall. The great pale wolf growled as she drew near, but Lilidh hushed the beast with a murmur. And as the Wolfmother leaned close, the Heartless seized hold of her scruff. Dior winced as she heard cartilage popping, bone grinding, Kiara falling to her knees as Lilidh *squeezed*. It seemed an impossibility—that a slayer so mighty as the Wolfmother could be bested by one so slender, so fair. But no maiden was Lilidh Dyvok; no statue upon this throne, but a monster, ancient and strong enough to claim it for her own.

"'The hour of thy arrival is late, niece Kiara,' she said. 'Deathless are we, but the cattle in the city outside share no such blessing. And the children *ever* hunger.'

"Kiara could only gurgle reply, her throat too crushed to draw breath.

"'Two moons passed since ye were sent to refill our larder.' Lilidh twisted, dark eyes roaming the gathering. 'Our bloodlords were in danger of growing

parched. And the Draigann can only beat so many of his lovers bloody afore we all tire of the spectacle.'

"Soft laughter rang around the hall. The tattooed man raised his goblet and grinned, gold fangs glittering through his gore-soaked beard. The monstrous maiden laughed in kind.

"'Sister,' Nikita said.

"The laughter stilled; a babe smothered in its crib. Lilidh's eyes broke from the gathering, shifting to her brother's, the count's voice cool as autumn's breeze.

"'Peace.'

"Lilidh's lips curled in an ingenue's smile, though no warmth reached her eyes. And pecking Kiara on the cheek, she released her grip. The Wolfmother staggered back, the red stain of Lilidh's lips on her skin. The pale wolf licked its jowls, eyes yet fixed on Dior.

"'Thy arrival *is* much delayed, daughter.' Nikita frowned, pale fingers steepled. 'Stock in the Auldtunn pens grows scarce. How comes it thou art delayed so long?'

"'Laerd and Father, I beg pardon,' Kiara croaked. 'But winter's chill and foulblood hungers have drained yer lands of what little cattle remained. As ye warned us, beyond yer borders we were forced to roam to find more than dregs to fill yer cup.'

"'But filled it, thou hast?'

"'Filled and more.' The Wolfmother lifted her chin, eyes shining as she looked upon her lord. 'I am come from Aveléne with its dust on my heels, its bounty in my arms, and the blood of Gabriel de León upon my hands.'

"At the mention of my brother's name, the mood in the room dropped through the floor. The tattooed one named the Draigann rose to his feet, glowering. 'The Black Lion . . .'

"'Deliverer of Báih Sìde,' Lilidh smiled, mirthless. 'Liberator of Triúrbaile.'

"'And *murderer* of our noble father,' Nikita growled.

"'A foe we thought dead and well-buried.' The Draigann hurled his goblet at the wall, crimson spattering the stone. 'Say ye now that thrice-damned whorespawn lives?'

"'*Lived*,' Kiara corrected, gazing around the room with a feral smile. 'But nae longer. And *mine* are the hands that wrought his end, cousin.'

"The hall was all in a furor now, and Dior knelt in the midst of it, head hung low. She had ever been a believer in my brother, in his vow that he would never forsake her. But surely even *she* doubted he could have survived his fall into that frozen abyss. Chaos rung in the air around her, vampires rising to their feet, crying questions, raising goblets, spitting Gabriel's name as if it were holy water on their tongues.

"'*SILENCE!*'

"The command rang like a cannon blast, its echo cracking upon the stone. Lilidh gazed among the kith, her stare brooking no dissent.

"'My son.' Here, she looked to the Headsmun, black eyes gleaming. 'Spake the Wolfmother true? The silvered cur who slew great Tolyev, slain now in turn?'

"Kane glanced to Kiara, the older vampire bristling with silent threat.

"'The price was steep, Contessa,' Kane muttered. 'Cousin Rykard slain on the banks of the Mère. But the Black Lion is fallen. By my dear cousin's own hand.'

"A great roar went up in the hall, and the Wolfmother stood taller, chin raised high. As the walls echoed with bloody adulation, Kiara looked to Nikita.

"'Joyous tiding be not all I have brung ye, great father,' she smiled. 'Another gift I offer, to sweeten this triumph all the more.' With a flourish, Kiara stepped aside, gesturing to the iron box on the stone behind her. 'A bonny grandson of yer line.'

"A murmur rippled around the room at that, Nikita leaning forward on his throne.

"'A fledgling of thy making? Highblooded?'

"'Avelène's laerd.' Kiara's eyes shone with dark pride as she glanced at the monsters around her. 'Aaron de Coste. A capitaine, Father, a nobleborn warrior and son of San Michon. Toe-to-toe we battled 'pon his walls, nae quarter asked nor given. His sword I shattered, but his dagger now I gift ye, along with his keeping. May ye judge him worthy of yer blood.' Kiara's eyes fell once more on her dark maker, her voice grown thicker. 'And she who made him, who slew yer great enemy, worthy of yer blessing.'

"Reaching into her cloak, Kiara produced a short blade in a battered sheath. An angel glittered on the hilt—the same as the broken silversteel blade that Gabriel had found at Avelène. At the sight of it, Nikita's lips curled in a small perfect smile.

"'Well done, my love.' The ancien inclined his head. 'Proud of thee am I.'

"Meeting Nikita's bottomless eyes, the Wolfmother brushed her braids from her shoulders, fangs gleaming as she preened—had she a pulse in her veins, she'd surely have blushed like a springtime maid. At the same time, Kane and Soraya unlocked the heavy chains, unwound them from the iron box, and opened the lid.

"And with a hate-filled roar, Aaron de Coste flew at the Wolfmother's throat."

VII

ALLEGIANCE WRIT RED

"IT WAS A fool's gambit. De Coste was starving, outnumbered and out-matched in the belly of the beast. But as they say in Ossway, sinner, 'tis not the size of the dog in the fight that matters, but the size of the fight in the dog. And de Coste had that in abundance.

"He was dirty and disheveled, beard caked with blood, but still, *magnificent*. Alabaster muscle and golden hair, silver ink gleaming on his bare chest. He struck the Wolfmother's jaw, splintering teeth and splitting lips. As Kiara staggered, Aaron seized the silversteel dagger she held, and twisted with such force, her wrist shattered like ice. Hand on hers, de Coste drove his blade up into her chest.

"'Burn in hell, leech,' he hissed.

"Kiara's good hand closed around Aaron's throat. '*Tha's my boy.*'

"The Wolfmother lifted the fledgling off his feet, and slammed him down into the flagstones. A *boom* rang out as the court of monsters roared in approval. Dior was half off her feet when she felt a hand on her shoulder, strong as a dozen men.

"'Nae foolishness, girl,' Kane warned.

"Kiara lifted Aaron like a sack of feathers, and slammed him down like a barrow of bricks. His skull shattered, blood spilling from his nose and ears. He twisted the knife in her chest as she slammed him down again, again, the walls trembling as if the earth quaked. And already weak and starving, and wounded now enough to end any mortal man, Aaron's hand slipped off the hilt of his old blade. Kiara released her dreadful grip, braids tumbling about her red grin as she balled her fist to crush his face.

"'Daughter.'

"The Wolfmother glanced up to Nikita, frozen. But the ancien's eyes were fixed on Aaron, gleaming with fascination.

"'Stay thy hand,' he murmured. 'Too fine to spill, this wine thou hast brung us.'

"The tumult died as Nikita rose to his feet, straightened his coat, and descended the dais. Dior looked utterly helpless, wretched, seething. That awful grip tightened on her shoulder; she couldn't rise no matter how much she wished it. But we suspect still she might've tried, had Aaron himself not caught sight of her. The fledgling blinked in confusion, bewildered to see her there, but begging her hold with a shake of his head.

"Nikita loomed over Aaron now, dark gaze roaming silver ink and muscled flesh.

"'Ye fight with heart, Golden One. But thou art silversaint no more.' The ancien gestured to the tattoos on Aaron's flesh, bereft of the light of faith, the love of God. 'Thy Almighty hath turned his back upon thee. Thou art ill-used, and now discarded by heaven's callow king. Come ye, set aside mortal pride, and pledge thy blade to a sovereign worthy of it. Thou art *remade*, child. Reforged in the blood of Dyvok, the blood of mighty Nikita, who hath crushed all Ossway beneath his heel. Not even great Tolyev managed such a feat. Yet in two short years hath the Blackheart brought this nation to its knees, and sits now as king and conqueror 'pon the Nineswords' throne.'

"Nikita gestured to the ironwood chair behind him, an iron ring embossed with the sigil of his line glinting upon one marbled finger.

"'Kneel before us. Press ruby lips to our seal and pledge red allegiance to thy Priori.' Nikita smiled, black and bleak. 'If think ye thou art worthy of his blessing.'

"All eyes were on the fledgling now, Aaron's face twisting as he rolled onto his belly. He looked around the hall, saw the hopelessness of his plight, Dior begging beneath her breath that he obey. Golden hair wet with blood, face twisted with the agony of broken bones and burning silver, Aaron crawled across the rubble. Inch by inch. Drop by drop.

"He reached the Blackheart's boots, the iron bear upon that signet ring gleaming as Nikita offered his hand. The fledgling took it, looked up into ancient, smiling eyes. And with a snarl, he spat a mouthful of blood onto the Dyvok sigil.

"Dark murmurs rippled among the congregation as Aaron balled his fists, and despite his wounds, rose to stand on trembling feet.

"'I am Aaron de Coste,' he declared. 'Lord of Aveléne and son of San Michon. I have slain more of your kind than I can count, leech. And though you say my God has turned his back on me, I'll not turn my back on him.' His eyes welled with bloody tears, voice trembling with hatred. 'For I would be truly damned, if *ever* I knelt before the likes of you.'

"Nikita smiled wider now, all the way to his gleaming fangs. He lifted his palms and glanced about the gathering, as if asking that flock of devils to bear witness.

"'He kneels for none. His worth proven. His blood Untamed.'

"'Untamed!' Soraya cried, raising a goblet. 'Santé!'

"'Santé!' came the cry, echoing around that bloodstained hall. 'Dyvok!'

"Nikita moved, so swift it was difficult to see. His hand was at Aaron's throat, lifting him as if he weighed no more than smoke and dreams. Aaron tried to break that awful grip, but the ancien only raised his wrist to his teeth and bit deep. And pressing the bleeding vein to Aaron's mouth, the Laerd of the Dyvok's tongue became a Whip.

"'*DRINK.*'

"Aaron ceased his struggles at once. As if commanded by God's own voice, he clutched Nikita's wrist. And as Dior looked on in horror, Kiara with a darkening scowl, Aaron drank like a man dying of thirst. Nikita smiled, a sigh of dark pleasure slipping bloodless lips, looking the fledgling over with void-dark eyes.

"'All my power,' he whispered, 'all my hatred, all my rage be now thine, child. And two nights hence, thou shalt also be.'

"Nikita gasped, lips parted, his own fangs grown long and hard as Aaron drank. The Blackheart allowed the beautiful capitaine of Aveléne to swallow one more moaning mouthful, running a red tongue over his lips before tearing his wrist free.

"'Enough for now, Golden One.'

"And with a twist of his wrist, Nikita snapped Aaron's neck.

"The fledgling's body dropped to the stone, and Dior cried his name before a torturous squeeze to her shoulder stilled her. Nikita turned to Kiara, his smile a blade.

"'I thank thee, daughter. A worthy gift. Relish do I, the thought of playing with it.'

"Kiara bowed low, but a shadow of her scowl remained, her eyes now drifting to Aaron, sprawled upon the bloody floor. A pair of thrallswords dragged the capitaine's body from the hall, Nikita retiring to his throne, admiring his new dagger. The silversteel sizzled as the beautiful monster pressed it to his smallest finger, a wisp of smoke rising from marble skin. Whispers passed among the gathering—the court clearly intrigued at the news Nikita had a new grandchild born of hunter's stock, and that the Blackheart intended to keep him.

"But Lilidh only stifled a yawn.

"'A vulgar display.' Those black eyes fell on her niece once more, golden nails drumming on her chair. '*Weeks* o'erdue, our foulbloods starving, cousin Rykard slain, and thou wouldst appease our displeasure with dead kittens and another mouth to feed?'

"'My wagons are filled to bursting, m'lady.' Kiara bowed with hand to her long-dead heart. 'The seed our Priori planted well come to bloom. O'er a thousand head await yer pleasure in the courtyard. But one last prize have I brung ye. A treasure worth any delay, and the weight of all my crop in nights to come, I'll wager.'

"'Treasure?' Lilidh lifted one pale hand, brushing one of the long horns of her crown. 'Another whelp to ruin our floors with?'

"At last, Kiara motioned to the girl kneeling far behind her, and Lilidh's ancient gaze fell on Dior like an anvil from the sky. The one-eyed wolf had been watching the Grail intently since she entered the hall, but now, all in the room focused on her. Dior's heart was thundering, her palms gone damp and slick. She'd met elders before, stood against the youngest son of the Forever King and won. But the pride she'd felt at that feat must surely have seemed the darkest sort of vanity now, and the heated words she'd spat at Gabriel when he'd tried to tell her the danger she was in, the whining of a foolish child.

"Nikita frowned. 'What worth, this slip of a boy?'

"'No boy, brother,' Lilidh replied, looking Dior over with rising fascination. 'A maid we mark her, and finest cut at that. Chaste angels would tremble at her perfume.'

"Nikita sniffed the air, his attentions sharpened—the ancien only breathed when he needed to speak. But now he rose again from his throne, rippling like black silk, and Dior shrank back from the dreadful hunger in his eyes. How small she must have felt then. How weak. Looking around the room and seeing how little she meant, how easily these things could twist her open and snuff her out, just one more mouthful in their brimming goblets. Nikita's lips parted, and the Grail shuddered at the gleam of the fangs beyond.

"'Father,' Kiara said.

"Nikita glanced at his daughter, annoyance in pitch-black eyes.

"'Forgive me.' The Wolfmother lowered her gaze. 'But nae mere draught have I brung ye to sup and toss. This girl traveled in the company of Gabriel de León. And on the field where I felled him, Kane and I also crossed blades with two Princes of Blood Voss.'

"Lilidh looked to her broodson, and Kane nodded once more.

"'Lady Alba and Lady Aléne, Contessa.'

"Nikita shrugged. 'The Lion's feud with the Ironhearts be well known.'

"'Aye, Father,' Kiara nodded. 'Yet the Terrors sought nae the Lion's death, but the life of this bairn here. Captured. Nae killed.'

"The gathering was bristling now, tension rising as more of the monsters caught a hint of Dior's scent under the reek of blood. But Lilidh was staring at the Grail, her eyes dark and fathomless, hungrier than the wolf beside her.

"'Worm?' The Heartless snapped her fingers. 'Where art thou?'

"A lass appeared from the shadows, as if conjured by magik. Her hair was a bright strawberry blond, and she was dressed in homespun linen— common servants' attire. She scuttled forward, diving onto her belly before Lilidh's throne. Gathering her splendid gown, the Heartless used the young woman like a footstool, stepping onto her back and then to the floor. The wolf rose to its feet, stalking beside her, ladies-in-waiting flocked at her back. There were three of them, mortals, and rare beauties all. Two redheaded maids, like enough in seeming to be sisters, and an older dame at their fore; a woman with piercing blue eyes and a scar down her chin, stooping to lift the long train of Lilidh's dress.

"Lilidh moved, serpentine, seeming almost to float in the sudden still. Kane bowed and melted away, leaving Dior alone on her knees. The girl kept her eyes averted, the peril now grown so thick about her, her skin prickled at the chill. The shadow Lilidh threw on the floor was all curved horns and clawed hands; not so much a maid's as a devil's.

"'Who art thou, mortal?' the Heartless demanded.

"'Dior Lachance,' she whispered.

"The white wolf growled, ears pressed back to his skull.

"'Hush, Prince,' Lilidh murmured.

"'How comes it ye kept company with the murderer of our lord and father?' It was Nikita speaking now, eyes boring into her own. 'How knew ye Gabriel de León?'

"Dior glanced around her; an ocean of wolves, and she, the bleeding lamb.

"'A sister from San Michon saved me from the Holy Inquisition,' she replied, her voice frail and small. 'She asked Gabriel for help protecting me . . . b-but then she died. And Gabe is a man who keeps his promises.'

"She faltered then, licking at dry lips.

"'I mean . . . h-he was.'

"'And why do the daughters of our hated foe seek thee?' Lilidh's voice was the smoke of a cigarelle, drifting soft over Dior's skin. 'What doth Fabién Voss want with thee?'

"'I don't know . . .'

"The Grail shivered as Lilidh's hand brushed her jaw. The Heartless slipped one finger under her chin, lifting Dior's face so she finally met the ancien's black gaze.

"'*Speak truth*,' Lilidh commanded.

"Dior flinched as the Whip in those words cracked in the air, echoing on the walls around her. She cried out, terrified, shrill.

"'I don't *know!*'

"'She has gifts, m'lady,' Kiara said. 'One of the scorched I claimed at Aveléne was wounded in a scrap. Stabbed thrice through the chest, all but a corpse. Yet this girl, she . . .' The Wolfmother shook her head, still bewildered. 'She laid hands 'pon the wounds, and at her command, his dying heart was made well.'

"'But have a care, Mother,' the Headsmun warned, raising his still-scarred hand. 'Her blood is a venom to our kind. Burned me to *cinders* where it touched me.'

"The Heartless smoothed back Dior's ashen hair, peering deep into her eyes.

"'Sorceress, art thou? Faeborn lamb, or servant of the Pit, or concubine to gods of old? By what magiks burn thee flesh immortal, and wrest failing hearts from death's cold hand?'

"Dior's reflection gleamed on those perfect black eyes; small and pale and completely alone. But despite her terror, or perhaps *because* of it, cunning remained.

"'I don't know how I can do it,' she lied. 'I don't know what I am.' She shook her head. 'And I don't know why the Forever King hunts me.'

"'*Speak truth*,' Lilidh demanded, the command reverberating in Dior's skull.

"'I don't *know*! I swear on my father's grave!'

"Lilidh leaned back, exchanged a dark glance with her brother.

"'Worm?' The Heartless patted her thigh, as if beckoning a pet. 'Come.'

"The serving girl lying facedown before Lilidh's throne rose immediately, scuttled forth swift as rat to drainpipe and sank once more to her knees.

"'Your command, Mistress?'

"The girl's eyes were filled with ardor as she looked upon the vampire. They were mismatched—one bright green, the other deep blue. Her skin was lightly freckled, her hair like summer flame. A thrallbrand was scorched atop her hand—an ornate crown, set with twisted antlers, matching those on the maidservants now gathered at Lilidh's back.

"Dior blanched as the Heartless drew a dagger from her embroidered bodice. The weapon was ornamental, yet still deadly, its blade sharp and thin, golden hilt wrought with a roaring bear. As the monsters in that bloody court looked on, Lilidh handed the serving girl the blade and glanced to her niece Kiara.

"'Three times in the chest, ye say?'

"The Wolfmother nodded. 'Thrice if it was once, m'lady.'

"Dior's eyes widened. 'What are you—'

"'*Stab thyself,*' Lilidh commanded.

"Not a breath, not a beat, not a blink passed before the maidservant obeyed, plunging the knife into her breast. Dior screamed, reaching out to stop her as the Heartless spoke '*Again.*' The serving girl obeyed, eyes bright with pain, breath already rattling as she dragged out the blade and buried it deep. The ladies-in-waiting looked on horrified, but none moved a muscle to stop the madness. Dior lunged for the knife, but with one hand, effortless, the Contessa Dyvok held her still. And black eyes still fixed on the serving girl, she spoke.

"'*Again.*'

"'NO!'

"The girl obeyed, wrenching the knife from her bleeding heart and thrusting it back to the hilt. Her hands were soaked with blood now, her face gone white and her bodice drenched red. But still, she looked up at Lilidh with mismatched eyes brimming with love, twisting the knife free and holding it poised, as if anticipating her mistress's next command.

"The Heartless smiled. 'Our thanks, Worm.'

"The girl smiled in return, a ribbon of blood spilling from her lips. And pale, wheezing, she crumpled like a broken doll to the stone.

"'Are you *fucking insane?*' Dior cried, trying to twist herself free.

"Lilidh released her grip, turned her gaze upon the girl. 'Demonstrate.'

"Dior looked to the maidservant, lying on her back in a pool of her own blood. The lass stared yet at her mistress, lips moving perhaps in prayer, breath bubbling in her throat. She was but a few heartbeats from death—to do nothing was to consign this poor girl to her grave. But if one listened, my brother's voice could almost be heard upon the air.

"*You're not sporting with the puppies anymore, you're running with the wolves.*"

In a dark cave below the cellars of Sul Adair, Marquis Jean-François of the Blood Chastain rolled his eyes, shaking his head as he dipped his quill. Black water babbled in the space between chronicler and storyteller, Celene glancing across the dark river.

"You sigh, Historian? Does our tale bore you?"

"No. I am simply dreading another effusive barrage about the saintliness of one Dior Lachance." The vampire waved his quill in dramatic fashion, doing a passable impression of Gabriel's growl. "*Eyes that saw the hurts of the world, and a heart that wanted to fix them.*"

Celene scoffed. "Is that what my brother told you?"

Jean-François thumbed back through his tome that he might quote directly. "*She reminded me so much of my own daughter, it made my chest ache.*"

"Almighty Redeemer. That man never met an aggrandizement he wouldn't dip his wick into, I swear it." The Last Liathe levered herself onto one elbow, regarding the historian through long dark curtains of hair. "Let us tell you the truth about Dior Lachance, Chastain. For while there will be some in this tale who name her Saint, the Grail of San Michon was as far from that as heaven is wide. She was no pious angel, nor selfless martyr. She was a gutter rat. A whorechild. A girl raised on cold, hard streets with cold, hard choices. Steal or starve. Lie or die. Dior Lachance was a grifter. A thief. But above all, an *opportunist.*

"It would have been obvious from the moment she entered that city, the second she witnessed the reaping in that courtyard, how little life mattered to these monsters. And though her mind remained ever closed to us, though we knew not her thoughts, it was plain she had no intent to be just one more fool strung up from their ceilings.

"Dior snatched the blade from the serving girl's fingers, and sliced the heel of her hand. As the perfume of her blood kissed the air, every vampire in that hall bristled and sighed. Lilidh wet her lips with a long red tongue as

Dior cut the maid's bodice ties, loosed the blood-soaked chemise beneath. And as Lilidh and her beautiful brother watched, utterly enthralled, the Grail pressed a red hand to the maidservant's wounds.

"And before their Dead eyes, those wounds stitched closed.

"A murmur rolled among the assembly; the Count and Contessa matched undying stares. Dior wrapped a grubby kerchief tight about her sliced hand, then helped the maidservant sit up, still pale and drenched in red. The girl looked utterly astonished, staring down at her unpunctured chest, then up into the Grail's ice-blue eyes.

"'Sweet M-Mothermaid . . .'

"'A bloody miracle, sure and true.' Lilidh fixed Dior with a gaze so hungry and deep it spanned an age. 'And thou hast no ken how this working be thine?'

"The Grail stood, pale lips and liar's tongue. 'I've always been able to do it.'

"Lilidh nodded. Her midnight eyes narrowed in thought, and she sucked slow upon the plump swell of her lower lip, looking Dior over from head to heel. And finally, lifting one clawed hand, she dragged it across her neck, cutting deep into porcelain flesh. Dior's eyes widened as the vampire slipped an iron arm about her waist, drew her close—

"'Sister,' Nikita said.

"Lilidh looked to her brother, expectant.

"'Hold,' he told her.

"'Why?' she demanded, meeting his stare. 'A prize Nikita hath claimed aready this night. A feast of them, by our counting. A grandson to bolster the ranks of his lords, a brace of cattle for his larder, a blade for his armory. Wouldst he lay claim this prize, also? What, then, remains for Lilidh? Think from her maid's seeming, she shall be satisfied with a maid's portion? Thou art her Priori, brother, but *not* her elder.'

"The ancien matched stares, the gathering stared at them. It seemed the politics of Nikita's court were a thorny snarl—power divided between this prince who wore the crown, and his older sister who somehow vouchsafed it. But while the eyes of the courtiers were fixed upon the Count and Contessa, Dior stared only at that slice in Lilidh's throat; the blood spilling thick down the vampire's décolletage.

"*A thrall will kill for her master. Die for her master. Commit* any *atrocity for the one she's bound to.*

"'We shall not break her, brother,' Lilidh promised. 'Simply break her *in*.'

"Nikita pondered an eternal moment. But finally . . .

"'As it please thee, sister.'

"Lilidh smiled, and this time, it reached her eyes. And without more ado, she wrenched Dior tight to her body and pressed the girl's lips to her wounded throat. Dior gasped, face twisting in revulsion, crimson smudged slick and sticky across her mouth. But try as she might, she could not resist that hellborn grip, nor break that hateful embrace.

"'Drink,' Lilidh whispered.

"She might have fought. Fruitlessly, certainly, but sometimes to resist without hope of victory is the only victory to be won. Yet Dior Lachance was ever a gambler, and with so much at stake, it seemed she resolved to keep the few cards she had close to her chest. And so, beneath the hungry stares of that court of monsters, wrapped in that ancien's pale arms, the Grail of San Michon breathed deep.

"She closed her eyes.

"And oui, she drank."

VIII

THE TRICK UP HER SLEEVE

" '*BEFORE HE BURNS his bridges, a man should learn to swim.*'

"Dior knelt on the floor of her cold cell, staring up at those words on the wall. They'd been carved there God knew how many years ago, probably by the hand of one long dead.

" 'Wonder if he drowned,' she whispered.

"The dungeons of Dún Maergenn were a dank and chill pit, carved deep below the château's foundations. Dior's cell was barely five foot at the square, a moldy blanket for her bed and a bucket for her privy and only a small slot in the banded ironwood door to let the light in. She had been dragged there at Lilidh's command, cursing as the thrallswords dumped her on the stone, the ancien's blood yet smeared on her lips.

"They locked her in, the gloom punctured by a single chymical globe in the stairwell. Once their footsteps had faded, she crawled over to the bucket in the corner and thrust her fingers down her throat, heaving up her bellyful. Red and thick. Gasping and spitting. She likely knew her efforts were futile, but still, she tried all the same. And when she was done retching, she gathered her breath, dragged her hair from her eyes. Rising to her feet, she stood in the center of her cell. And there, she began to dance.

"Not a jig or a line or a waltz, no, but the steps my brother had shown her. Northwind stance. Front foot forward. Belly, chest, throat, repeat. She practiced with an invisible sword in her hand and fire in her eyes. Hewing imaginary foes, over and over, until her breath was burning and her skin sheened with sweat and she had perhaps regained a tiny fraction of the control they had taken away.

"It was only after she stopped for a breather that she felt it; a soft tremor on her skin. Dior paused, uncertain, but dismissing the sensation as fancy, she took up southwind stance and made ready to begin anew. And then she felt it again. Unmistakable this time.

"Something was inside her shirt.

"It was too big for a flea, but Dior was ever afeared of rats, and Mothermaid only knew what other tiny horrors might call this dungeon home. She cursed as she felt the tremor again, ripping her grubby grey frockcoat off her shoulders. Swatting at the sensation, shrieking as she wrestled with her waistcoat, she dragged her travelworn shirt over her head. And twisting toward the dim light, she spied it, nestled up the inside of her arm.

"A moth made of blood.

"It was pressed tight to her pale skin, no bigger than a thumbnail. It beat its tiny wings, delicate as snowflakes and pretty as rose petals and red as all life's ending.

"Dior's eyes widened, an incredulous whisper slipping her lips.

"'*Celene?*'"

"Ah," Jean-François smiled. "So, we come to explanation at last. Here I was, wondering how you knew what had befallen the Grail since you parted. But you had never parted at all." The historian lifted his goblet in toast. "Santé, Mlle Castia. Most ingenious."

The Last Liathe was still propped on her elbow, watching across the waters with hungry eyes. "Save your flattery for my brother, sinner. It means little to us."

"Little is more than Nothing." The historian smiled, toying with the knot of his cravat. "And not so far from Much. And one cannot help but note that you share Gabriel's penchant for drama, mademoiselle—saving this delightful morsel until now, rather than revealing it to me immediately. You and your brother are more alike than you realize."

"Careful, Historian. You will hurt our feelings."

Jean-François chuckled. "You had been with her since Cairnhaem?"

The Last Liathe nodded. "That small part of us, oui. But the flames had left little else, and thus, we could only listen back then. *Feel.* It had taken weeks to re-form the rest of ourselves enough to follow Dior's trail, to press our will upon that tiny fragment we had left her. But now, we reached out across the dark toward that sliver, that droplet, that tiny *mote* of us, and bid it beat bloody wings light as baby's breath upon her skin.

"*Tap.*

"'Oh, sweet Mothermaid, it's *you.*'

"*Tap.*

"Dior looked around her cell, furtive, a giddy smile twisting her lips. We could feel her pulse quicken under her skin, her flesh prickling beneath our tiny feet. Strange how so much can be learned by pressing so close. How much truth there is in the flesh. Standing on tiptoe to peer out the barred window, Dior could only see the cell opposite—she'd no clue who might overhear her speaking. And so she hunkered down in the corner, low and small as she could, whispering as if her very soul depended upon it.

"'What the *hell* happened to you? Are you well?'

"We made no reply, save to patiently flutter those tiny wings.

"*Tap.*

"*TapTap.*

"'You can't speak, right, aright.' She pawed her lips, nodding. 'But you can hear?'

"*Tap.*

"'One for oui, two for non?'

"*Tap.*

"'Good, that's good,' she breathed, her pulse now all agallop. A moment ago, she must have thought herself utterly lost and alone, but now, she was breathing quick, dragging a shaking hand through her hair. 'Is there . . . more of you? I saw you burning on the bridge, but . . .' She regarded our tiny mote, whispering. 'Is this all that's left?'

"*TapTap.*

"'Aright, good, good. Is the rest of you with Gabe?'

"*TapTap.*

"Her voice dropped then, edged with fear. 'Do you . . . do you know if he's alive?'

"*TapTap.*

"'Shit.' Biting her lip, the Grail hung her head. '*Shit.*'

"Dior sat in the dark for a long and silent moment then. Hands in fists. Eyes shut tight. We knew not what she was thinking, but we guessed well enough.

"'Aright,' she finally whispered. 'The rest of you, then. Are you close?'

"*Tap.*

"'Can you get me the *fuck* out of here?'

"The span of five deep breaths passed in that dark, but Dior took not a single one.

"*Tap.*

"*Tap Tap.*

"'Oui *and* non?' She shook her head, eyes wild. 'The *hell* does that mean?'

"We fluttered our tiny wings, Dior hissing in obvious frustration. We could not feel her mind, nor speak to her thoughts; as helpless as any other Voss to pierce her veil. But as she watched, that mote of us crawled over her skin, across and up and down her bare arm, deliberate, painstaking. It took a moment for the girl to see our game, but as we've said, this guttersnipe was no one's fool. And finally, she realized the pattern we trod formed letters. A crude method, agonizingly slow—no use for little more than a word or two. But that is what we gave her, spelled out on her skin at glacial pace by small red feet.

"'*Hurt,*' she finally whispered. 'You're still hurt.'

"*Tap.*

"'Fuck my face . . .'

"*Tap Tap.*

"She slumped lower, frustration rising in her voice along with her fear. 'These things are fucking *crazed,* Celene. They treat people like . . . like animals. Like *cattle.* And they're feeding me blood. They want to know what I am, what I can do. If they thrall me, I'll have to tell them about all of it. The Esana. Mother Maryn. You. I have to get *out* of here.'

"We turned a tiny circle on her arm, wings trembling.

"She sighed, ashen hair in her eyes as she hung her head. 'But you can't help me . . .'

"*Tap Tap Tap Tap Tap Tap.*

"Dior's body tensed as footsteps descended the stairs, harsh, familiar voices echoing on the dank walls. We crawled up her shoulder, her neck, settling in to watch from beneath the mop of her hair. She threw on her dirty shirt, her waistcoat, rising on tiptoe to peer out the barred slot just as a pair of hard emerald eyes loomed on the other side.

"'Enjoying yer lodgings, Mouse?' Kiara asked.

"The girl flinched back but made no reply, pulse thrumming beneath our tiny feet.

"'Lady Lilidh will gift ye finer accommodations soon, nae fear,' the Wolfmother said. 'Soft sheets. Pretty dresses. A nice wee cushion fer yer tender knees. Ye should be honored she's chosen ye to serve her.'

"'I don't *serve* anyone,' the girl hissed.

"'Two nights hence, ye'll sing different.' Kiara met her eyes, lips curling in a cruel smile. 'Beware when the devil takes ye under her wing, girl. It's warmer than ye think.'

"Dior scoffed. 'You're fucking—'

"*Tap Tap Tap Tap Tap Tap.*

"'Where shall we put 'im, m'lady?' a gruff voice asked.

"'Yonder,' Kiara said, nodding to the cell opposite. 'Let him suffer the scent of her.'

"Dior watched through the slot as Joaquin and Dogshank dragged a still-broken Aaron down the stairs. He wore only his leather britches, but he'd been bathed and brushed, wrists and ankles bound in chains so thin we thought he must surely break them when he woke—until we saw they gleamed silver. Soraya waited nearby, her braids trailing down her back, and her skin the smooth grey of death. Joaquin's face was a mask, and though Dior sought his eyes, ever the houndboy kept them downturned.

"The two scorched hauled Aaron into his cell, dumped him on the stone floor. Kiara's brow was dark, her voice a murmur as she looked at her broodson.

"'Ye caught his eye, my bonny boy. It seems Fortuna smiles on ye.'

"'And us, sister,' Soraya said. 'Who brought great Nikita this prize. His pens refilled. A grandson of high blood. De León slain. The Blackheart will surely reward us.'

"Kiara's heavy gloves creaked, one thumb rubbing at the top of her hand.

"'Not like he used to.'

"Soraya rolled her eyes, her full lips pursed. As the younger vampire tapped at her throat, we saw the familiar glint of the golden vial strung about her neck.

"'I've need of another draught, sister. I drank all I had when we took Aveléne.'

"Kiara seemed to come back to herself then, nodding slow. 'I'll speak to the Contessa. See what his majesty has fer us.' The Wolfmother turned to her thralls. 'There's meat needs sorting in the bailey. Go help that louse-house Petrik. We'll be along presently.'

"Joaquin met Dior's eyes, pity in his own. But then the houndboy was gone, up to the courtyard with his fellows to help sort the cattle that had once been his friends. Kiara was still staring at Aaron, eyes narrowed as she regarded the fallen capitaine in his cell. But with a final glance to Dior, the highblood turned and stalked up the stair. Soraya blew the Grail a kiss, and then she too was gone, following in her older sister's wake.

"Dior sank down onto her moldy blanket, knees under her chin. Making the sign of the wheel, she whispered a prayer for Isla and little Mila and most of all Baptiste, her palms clasped tight as she turned her eyes to heaven.

"But if he heard her, the Almighty gave her no sign.

"The dungeons of the Dyvok were quiet now, and Dior clearly exhausted after so many miles and trials. She was still in deepest peril; even our tiny eyes could see it plain. Absent-minded, she licked at the corner of her mouth, the Contessa's blood still smudged on her lips, copper-sweet. Almost immediately, Dior realized what she was doing, spitting again and scrubbing her mouth on her sleeve. But still, as her tongue had touched that stain, we had felt her skin prickling, her pulse tripping a shade quicker.

"Despair.

"Dread.

"Delight.

"'I'm fucked,' she whispered.

"A flutter on her skin then, soft as moonslight. A simple touch in the dark. And she breathed deep, nodding, because even if she had never trod quite so close to hell as this, even hellfire is easier to bear with a friend at your side. And so, the Grail curled down on that cold stone and closed her eyes, seeking the strength she would find in sleep.

"But there was no sleep for us.

"Instead, once she was slumbering, we fluttered out from the shelter of the Grail's coat, and took to the wing. Flitting up through the dark, quick and silent, intending to search every shadow in that keep, in that damned *city* if we needed to. Despite the danger Dior was in, we could not help but see the providence in this, and the will of God Himself at work here. We had been denied at Cairnhaem by Jènoah's final, terrible sin. But as I'd told my fool brother, other ancient of the Esana slumbered in eventide around the empire.

"Wise Oleander below Augustin.

"And the eldest and most powerful of us, here, deep beneath Dún Maergenn.

"Sure as iron to lodestone, as fated to fate, the Almighty had brought us *right to her.* All on earth, the work of his hand. All the work of his hand, in accord with his plan. And so, wings silent and eyes swift, we set out to find she who might help us.

"To unearth the resting place of mighty Maryn, Priori of the Faithful.

"To wake the Mother of Monsters."

IX

BENEATH THE UNDERTOW

"ALL WAS DARKNESS when she opened her eyes.

"Pitch-black. Cold and deep and complete. For a moment, Dior's heart was sent galloping with fear, and she snaked upright, clawing at the floor beneath her. But she felt the hard stone under her hands then, smelled the mold and rot and rust around her, and her hands curled into helpless fists.

"And then, screaming.

"'Aaron,' she whispered.

"Dior dragged herself to her feet, grasping the bars in the door slot. Dim light shone from the stairwell, the cries echoing on chill black stone, all the way down her spine.

"'Aaron!' She stood on tiptoe, shouting to be heard over his cries. '*AARON!*'

"The screaming stilled—a muffled gasp, a heartsick groan. And then came a tiny whisper, so wracked with misery and pain that tears filled her eyes.

"'D-Dior?'

"'It's me!' she nodded, squeezing the bars. 'I'm here, Aaron. You're not alone.'

"He had no need to breathe, the doors of life now closed to him forever. But still, we heard the brave Lord of Aveléne inhale as if to steady himself. 'Where is h-here?'

"'The dungeons under Dún Maergenn. They locked us in last night. Lilidh and—'

"'Nikita,' Aaron breathed.

"'Oui.'

"We heard him moan then, the sound of something dull and heavy thumping against the stone, over and over. His skull, we realized.

"'Oh, Aaron . . .' Dior sighed.

"'It h-hurts, Dior. Almighty God in heaven, it *b-burns*.'

"'I'm sorry,' she whispered, anguished. 'I'm sorry, what can I do?'

"'Talk to m-me,' he begged. 'Tell me how you came to b-be here.'

"'Kiara and Kane caught me in the mountains. Brought me here in the convoy from Aveléne with the others. Baptiste was in the cage with me.'

"'I-is he . . .'

"'He's alive. And he's safe. Safe as he can be in this accursed city anyway. They lost their last blacksmith, they said. They need him to work.'

"We heard Aaron whisper thanks to God, and as we crawled down Dior's arm to rest upon her hand, we found ourselves marveling that one who had suffered so much could still thank his maker for so small a blessing. So different to our faithless brother, this one. So near, yet so far away. A tiny kinship we felt then, for this fallen son of Aveléne. This martyr yet walking. He was but new to the Blood; the tattered remnants of his humanity unshed, his mortal ties yet unbroken. But sitting upon Dior's knuckles, wings fluttering in the dungeon air, we could smell the faint tang of burning flesh, hear the soft sizzle of silver chains on his skin. We remembered the sight of him drinking from that dark prince's wrist just the night before. And we knew he was as damned as we were.

"'And Gabriel?' he whispered. 'Where is h-he?'

"'I don't know.'

"Dior shook her head, glancing now toward us. And perhaps it was imagination, or a simple trick of the light, but I swear we saw a glint of suspicion in her eye. The lips she licked at still stained with Lilidh's blood.

"'I don't even know if he's alive,' she said.

"'If he is, he will c-come for you.'

"The Grail drew a deep breath, looked around her dank cell; the cold stone and hard iron and dim, flickering light. 'I'm not sure we can count on Gabe, Aaron.'

"'You can. You *sh-should*. I h-have known Gabriel de León since I was a boy, Dior. He is no saint, believe me.' The capitaine of Aveléne chuckled, drew a trembling breath. 'But h-he does not abandon those he l-loves. And he loves you, doubt it n-not.'

"'Maybe. But I'm not waiting for Gabriel. I've escaped darker holes than this, and I'll figure out a way to free us both. I c—'

"'No,' he hissed. 'No, tell me n-nothing, chérie. If you do discover a way to freedom, I pray God you get my Baptiste to safety. But breathe no word of it to m-me. For when the Blackheart binds me with his blood, he may command me to t-tell all I know of you.'

"Her pulse thumped harder, the scent of sour sweat moistening her skin. 'They're binding me too,' she said. 'They forced me to show them what my blood can do. Then Lilidh, she . . . she forced me to drink.'

"We heard a sigh then, thick with sorrow. 'God help you, child . . .'

"'Maybe we can fight it?' she hissed, defiant. 'Gabe said it was like love. I've been in love before, but I was still *me*. I wouldn't ever—'

"'It is no mortal love, chérie. That corruption in their veins. It is a dark counterfeit, bereft of truth, but no less potent for its lack. It is a *cruel* love they bestow, Dior. An envious, possessive love, dragging all sweetness and honesty beneath its undertow. I have seen it make wives kill their husbands with a smile. Parents butcher their children in defiance of all God and nature's law. It is a love hellborn.'

"'There must be *some* way to break it?'

"'If the one you are bound to is slain, that will end the spell. And even if they live, after a time spent without drinking, the bond will fade—not years mind you, but decades. But other than that . . .'

"Aaron's voice came easier now, as if he almost had a grip on his agony. Yet between each trembling breath, we could still smell the burning on his skin.

"'I gave up all I had to be with my Baptiste. All I'd worked for. My future. My place in the Silver Order. Ma famille. I turned my back on all of it, and felt not one drop of regret. Such is the love I bear him. Have *always* borne him. My beautiful man.'

"He sighed like a little boy, lost in the dark.

"'But two nights from n-now, when the blood of that devil touches my tongue for the third time, I will be *his*. And should he command it, I would cut my beloved's throat in a blinking, and try not to get any on my boots. That is the depth of it, Dior. That is the h-horror. Three nights is all it takes to forge a forever hell.'

"'You wouldn't do that.' Dior shook her head. 'I don't believe it. I've *seen* the way you two look at each other. Heard the way he speaks of you, and you of him. You *love* him.'

"'I do,' he breathed. 'But love is mortal. Blood is eternal.'

"She opened her mouth to protest, to defy. But footsteps on the stair stilled her tongue, and as I crawled swift back up her sleeve, she shrank away from the door, jaw clenched tight. Her heart was all agallop, heat rising on her body as the feet stopped outside, the lock clicked. She balled her fists, ready to fight, but when the door creaked open, a young woman waited on the other side.

"'The Contessa Dyvok commands you follow me.'

"Dior blinked, unknotting belly and hands. She would have recognized the maid, of course—despite the lack of knife wounds in her chest. Her hair was still the color of fire in summertime, her scowling, mismatched eyes fixed on Dior's.

"'The Contessa does not abide waiting,' Worm snapped. 'Come. Now.'

"The maidservant walked brisk toward the stair, Dior following with clear reluctance.

"Aaron whispered a prayer. 'Almighty g-go with you, child.'

"She was led up the dungeon's stairs, past a desk where sat a heavyset man with close-cropped hair and hawkish eyes, wreathed in traproot smoke. The jailor returned Worm's nod, and with a covetous glance at his cigarelle, Dior followed into a corridor beyond. Night was fallen outside, the mighty keep lit by chymical lights—leeches would allow few flames in their havens, after all. The dún was busy; soldiers and servants rushing, the sound of steel and heavy boots ringing in the courtyard outside, hundreds of crows calling in the black heavens above it all.

"Dior followed on the maidservant's heels into the dún proper, dark stone around her, long woven rugs beneath her feet. We were perched at the line of her jaw now, pressed flat to her thumping pulse, watching from beneath her tangle of pale hair. We were afeared at all this, and clearly so was she. But our search for Mother Maryn had so far proved fruitless, and we were still helpless; forced to bear mute witness and beat our small wings against Dior's skin every so often, simply to remind her she was not alone.

"Despite the cracks in the walls left from the Dyvok attack, the opulence of this place was breathtaking; high ceilings and stained glass and décor fit for royalty. We entered a great hall with far-flung rafters wrought with everknots, the walls lined with beautiful suits of plate armor and weaponry. Grand green tapestries embroidered with wolves hung beside portraits of proud women, their brows graced with circlets of gold. They were attired as highborn ladies, save they often wore breastplates of steel and carried swords, and men dressed in noble cloth stood at their right hands.

"'The Hall of Crowns,' Worm murmured by way of explanation.

"These were Laerd Ladies, we realized—the women who'd ruled this dún and clan in years past. Centuries after it had been brought into the fold of the One Faith, Ossway was still a matriarchal nation at heart, venerating the feminine, the lifegiver, the wellspring. The Ossian interpretation of the One Faith centered the Mothermaid, not the Almighty; a bastardized holdover from pagan days when these folk spilled the blood of enemies on altars devoted to the Mothermoons. And though this country had sworn fealty to the Augustin dynasty, in truth it had not been ruled by the emperor, but a conquering queen.

"In the nights before the Dyvok came, at any rate.

"Dior looked at her statue now, looming before the twin arches of a stair winding up from the Hall of Crowns. A young woman, fierce as lions, clad in platemail and clancloth, a longblade held in one raised fist. The statue was granite, but the sword itself was real—the actual blade she'd forged from the melted weapons of her vanquished foes.

"'Niamh á Maergenn,' Dior read on the plaque. 'The Nineswords.'

"'Do not tarry,' the maidservant snapped, glancing over her shoulder. 'There is but one lady of this realm now, and her name be not á Maergenn. And should you leave her waiting, your life shall pay the forfeit of her patience.'

"Dior looked the maid over, lips pursed. She was nineteen at a guess, and we'd have marked her Ossian by her freckled skin and fiery hair. But she spoke with an accent as mismatched as her eyes—half-Elidaeni by the sound, only a hint of Ossway in her vowels.

"'What's your name?' Dior asked.

"'The Contessa Dyvok calls me Worm.'

"'But what's your *name*?'

"The girl blinked at Dior, and replied as if she were an imbecile. '*Worm.*'

"Turning on her heel, she strode up the stair, down a long corridor lined with more armor, thrallswords at guard. They came to double doors, embossed with the wolf and swords of the Maergenn clan, a river running beneath. And as the girl called Worm pushed them open, Dior looked dizzied by a perfume near forgot.

"A bathhouse, we realized, hung thick with steam. A large copper tub sat at its heart, the water already drawn. There was little in the way of flowers in the empire anymore, but what could be done to sweeten the air clearly *had* been; garlands of fools' honey hung on the walls, and sticks of woodash smoldered in golden bowls.

"'Undress,' Worm commanded.

"Dior blinked. 'Most folk offer a drink firs—'

"'I am to make you presentable for your audience,' Worm snapped. 'If I fail, the Contessa will be displeased. And you may not be there to mend the stab wounds next time.'

"Dior swallowed hard. 'I'm sorry. If I'd have known what she was lik—'

"'I've no need of your apology, bloodwitch,' Worm glowered.

"'Well, I'm giving it all the same,' Dior replied, jaw squared. 'You were hurt on my account, and I'm sorry for it. And I'm no witch either, by the by. I'm not like them.'

"'I know sorcery when I see it,' Worm replied, looking Dior up and down. 'And deceit when I hear it. But if you'd truly make amends, do as I say and *get undressed.*'

"Worm busied herself at a cupboard, while Dior stood in the bathhouse's heart, motionless and mute. After Lilidh's declaration yestereve, the maidservant was obviously aware that Dior was a girl. But the Grail's pulse was still thumping with uncertainty, and her skin was clammy cold—after so long pretending to be something else, she was clearly frightened to be unveiled as she truly *was.*

"With Worm's back turned, we fluttered free from Dior's hair, hiding among the shadows of the rafters above. Turning away from the other girl, Dior discarded her travelworn clothes with clear reluctance, glancing over her shoulder to ensure Worm wasn't watching. Her trembling fingers traced a small bulge hidden in her hemline; Gabriel's phial was still secreted under the stitching, and to abandon her frockcoat was to abandon her last link to him. But aside from swallowing it—or solutions more unsavory—she'd nowhere else to hide it, and in truth, none of us had any idea if he was even alive. And so, dropping the coat and stripping off the last of her underthings, Dior slipped quickly into the water.

"Despite her unease, a smile curled her lips as she lowered herself into that warmth, a blissful sigh slipping her lungs. 'Seven Martyrs, I can't remember the last—'

"Her words were drowned by a bucketful of water, dumped over her head without ceremony. As Dior sputtered, Worm tipped a ladleful of viscous sludge onto her hair—soap, apparently, the tang of ash and quicklime sweetened by more fools' honey. The maidservant was ungentle, scrubbing hard enough to bring tears to Dior's eyes, but the Grail tried to hold herself still, arms folded to protect her modesty, eyes shut against the sting.

"It wasn't until Worm lifted a horsehair brush that Dior finally objected, trying to twist free of the grip that closed about her wrist. But like Joaquin, the maidservant was blessed with a thrall's terrible strength, and Dior's arm was hauled skyward, Worm scrubbing her armpits and chest with no regard for the younger girl's bashfulness.

"'What is *your* name?' Worm demanded.

"Dior yelped as the maid hauled one leg from the water and began scrubbing. Worm looked up briefly, her eyes glittering. They were peculiar to be sure—one bright blue like the skies in old paintings, the other the green of long-gone leaves. Old folklore in Lorson had it that folk afflicted suchlike were cursed with ill-fortune; that such a mark told of an ancestor who'd had truck with the fae. But we noted that the Grail was staring at them.

"'Dior,' she replied, squirming with discomfort as the scrub brush crept higher.

"'Where are you from?'

"'Sūdhaem. A city called La—'

"'I did not ask where you were born,' the faeling snapped, dropping her foot. 'I asked where you were *from*. Who are your family? Of what stock were your kin?'

"'I never met my papa.' The Grail shrugged, matter-of-fact. 'He was a wanderer, from what Mama told me. I don't even know his name. Mama was from Elidaen, originally. She was a . . . well, the polite phrase is *courtesan*. Though she never visited court in her life.'

"'Well, you are in a court now, by God,' the maid replied, grabbing her other foot. 'A Court of the *Blood*. And if you do not comport yourself with due dign—'

"The doors slammed open, and Dior startled, water sloshing over the tub's lip. Standing on the bathhouse threshold, we saw a dark angel, carved by a devil's hand, our frail wings trembling with hunger at the mere sight of him.

"'Count Nikita,' Worm whispered, dropping to her knees.

"The Priori of the Blood Dyvok loomed at the entrance, gazing about the bathhouse with the voids that passed for his eyes. He was utterly naked save for his necklace, strung with fangs and that gleaming golden vial. His every muscle was carved of alabaster, long hair spilling over his graven shoulders and chest like a black waterfall. He stood so still and silent, he might have passed as a sculpture on Jènoah's dreadful bridge, save that he was *covered*—hands, chest, face, privates—in fresh blood.

"'Night's blessings, sweetlings,' he smiled, his voice deep as graves.

"Dior averted her gaze, looking anywhere but at that dark and bloody prince. As we watched from on high, she crossed her arms to cover her nakedness again, sinking as low in the bath as she could. Her heartbeat was so loud we could hear it, that dreadful tempo only doubling as the Count Dyvok walked across the boards before the prostrate maidservant, and without ado, climbed into the tub opposite Dior.

"The bath was an opulent affair, large enough for four. But the Grail flinched as Nikita reclined, staining those waters sticky red, his toes brushing light upon her thigh. The vampire said nothing, simply staring, black presence and leaden silence thickening in the air, until Dior at last was forced to raise fearful eyes to his.

"'Mind me not,' he smiled, waving one lazy hand. 'Be about thy business.'

"Dior was up and halfway out of the bath before his voice pinned her still.

"'Hold, sweetling.'

"Save for the hammerblow of her heart, the girl froze. Slowly, she turned to the one they called Blackheart, sunk now in the water up to his chiseled chest. His face was yet spattered with blood, bright and gleaming. We wondered briefly who it belonged to.

"'Thy hair.' He pointed, fingernails long and sharp. ''Tis yet unclean.'

"'Forgive me, Laerd,' Worm began, rising with ladle in hand. 'I was about t—'

"'Nono.' The monster's black gaze drank Dior in, head to toe. 'Allow me?'

"Dior clenched her teeth to stop them chattering. 'Most generous, Laerd, but th—'

"Laughter cut her protest off, left her mute and trembling. From above, we watched Nikita shake with amusement; head thrown back, razors gleaming in his gums. There was a beauty to him, undeniable, no matter the heady peril of it. A youth in life's prime, pale and fey and shadowborn, preserved forever at the moment of a dark perfection.

"'When Nikita asks,' he said, smile dying on his lips, 'he is seldom *asking*.'

"Dior made no reply, bare and vulnerable, lowering her gaze once more. We saw horror dawn on her face as she realized he cast no reflection in the water they shared.

"'Turn about,' Nikita whispered, twirling one finger in the air.

"Dior glanced up to us; that bloody mote, helpless but to watch and seethe. She looked to Worm, who appeared near as terrified as she. But the maidservant met her eyes and nodded, almost imperceptible, lips pressed thin. And so, Dior turned her back on that beast in the tub with her, arms still wrapped tight about herself, sinking back down into the steam. Nikita stirred behind her, rising, the troughs and valleys of his rock-hard belly now pressed against her spine. She shivered as he hooked one sharp fingernail beneath her chin, tilting her head back. And lifting the ladle, he lathered water gently through her ashen hair.

"'Thou art a maid, as my sister spake it,' he murmured. 'And a winsome bud at that.' His eyes roamed her body, falling on the clothing she'd discarded. 'Why veil hind's splendor 'neath crude hart's cloth, and shackle such bounty 'neath tight-bound rags?'

"Dior remained mute, flinching as he poured more water, his claws running soft through her hair. We knew a terrible strength was hid behind Nikita's touch, but only his smile betrayed the wickedness in his soul, his hands as gentle as a lover's own.

"'My sweet sister would claim thee for her own. And I have given blessing. Nikita is Priori, but Lilidh is eldest, and to keep the peace of his court, he must keep the Heartless and her children pleased. Yet the *scent* of thee . . .'

"He lowered his head now, wolfish, inhaling deep and sighing long.

"'My Headsmun names thy blood a venom. Yet thy perfume promises bliss. Might fire be found in but a single drop of thee? I wonder, pale poison . . . should I risk a taste?'

"His lips brushed her neck as he whispered, and Dior trembled like candleflame at his touch. His fingertips danced slow along her shoulders, lower now, diamond-hard nails skimming her prickling skin. The dark pull of him swelled at her back, dragging her in, bottomless and black. His fingertips danced down the arms she'd wrapped about her breasts, and the faintest prick of his fangs pressed upon her throat as his hands closed about her wrists, prying them away ever so slow and leaving her utterly bare.

"This was surely her nightmare, rage and pity filling us to the brim as we watched it unfold. The bitter irony of it all—to have hidden what she was all these years, and be set upon the very *second* she let it be known—God, how we cursed our helplessness then. I looked down into her eyes, praying God she might endure this, might become the Mountain I had learned to be. But that was to pray for a sun already risen.

"If she'd been but a maid, she'd surely have melted; sighing submission as countless others over countless years must have done. Yet she was no mere child, Dior Lachance. She was a daughter of the Redeemer born. And far from sinking into the bleak promise of that black prince's arms, we saw her fists clench with fury at his unasked-for touch, at the notion of this leech gnawing at her throat. We knew what her holy blood would do to him, and we prayed she might beg him bite. Let him *burn*. But we all of us knew that song would end badly, no matter its sweet beginnings. And so, iron-willed, she gritted her teeth instead.

"'Get your *fucking* hands off m—'

"'Count Nikita, I beg forgiveness,' Worm blurted, wringing her hands. 'But my beloved mistress bid me bring the girl with all speed. She will be displeased if I tarry.'

"The vampire glanced toward the maidservant, needle-sharp fangs yet poised at Dior's neck. An age passed, empty and breathless, the very air itself crackling with desire and danger. But in the end, the vampire's bloodstained lips curled in a small smile.

"'Far be it from us, little one, to keep our elder waiting.'

"Nikita held Dior pinioned a moment longer, breathing her in like a fiend at his wretched pipe. And then the Laerd Dyvok released his grip and sank back slow into red water. Dior near flew out of the bath, Worm wrapping her in a linen towel with eyes downturned. Ushering the Grail from the room, the serving girl was stopped at the last by Nikita's voice.

"'Worm.'

"The maidservant paused, chest heaving. 'Aye, Laerd?'

"'Maids' cloth suits thee better than thy former attire. Ye serve thy new mistress well.' The vampire draped a steaming cloth over his face. 'But forget not who is master here.'

"'Aye, Laerd,' she breathed.

"With a swift curtsey, and Dior on her arm, the maid fled the room."

X

A DAGGER OF TRUTH

" 'PUT THESE ON. And damn your eyes, be swift about it.'

"Dior stood in the belly of a grand wardrobe, magnificent coats and gowns arrayed all about her. She was draped only in a damp towel, and we fancied the chill of that ancient monster lingered at her back. Yet she was young, this bowerbird, and ever possessed of a weakness for shining things, having grown up so sorely in lack of them, we suppose. And so, her mouth was agape as she stared at the finery on display around her, the shadow of Nikita Dyvok fading in that rainbow of bold chiffon and rich satin and gold-thread twill.

" 'Fuck my—'

"A silken chemise hit her in the face, followed by a barrage of accoutrements—hose and garters, elbow-length gloves, dainty pointed heels of embroidered velvet damask. Dior did her best to catch the pieces and maintain her towel, finally surrendering hope of the former for the sake of the latter as the volley continued. Worm finally emerged from the wardrobe's depths carrying a wondrous white gown of crêpe and lace.

" 'This will ser—' She stopped short, bristling. 'Why are you not dressing?'

"Dior looked about the scattered clothes, back into the maidservant's eyes.

" 'Violetta Tremaine,' she replied.

" 'Who in the Mothermaid's name is Violetta Tremaine?'

" 'A girl I shared a squat with after my mama died. She was the second dead body I ever saw. And the state they left her in when they were done with her is the reason I cut my hair and dressed as a boy ever since.' The Grail shrugged, her voice hard as alley cobbles. 'Damn my eyes all you like. I've no idea what I'm doing with any of this shite.'

"Worm paused at that, studying Dior, toe and crown and all between. She seemed to regard the girl in a new light after her defiance of Nikita in the bathhouse, her outrage at his unwanted touch. But setting her face in a scowl, she plucked the chemise off the younger girl's shoulder.

"'Raise your arms.'

"'My towel will come off.'

"'As shall my head, should the Contessa lose patience.'

"Dior yelped as Worm dragged her arms skyward, her towel dutifully falling to the floor. The maidservant hauled on the chemise, kneeling to tug up the silken hosiery and bind it with garters at Dior's thighs. Worm's fingers were skirting terribly close to dangerous places, and while a servant was certainly used to this sort of thing, we saw Dior was blushing to be stripped naked and manhandled so. Worm finally stood, wrangling the heavy gown over Dior's head, following with a corset of boned velvet and lace.

"'I've never worn a—'

"She gasped as Worm drew the ties, cinching the fabric tight. Wincing as her insides adjusted, Dior looked at the gentry's frockcoats about her with unmasked envy.

"'Who did all this b-belong to?' she managed.

"'Niamh á Maergenn, once Laerd Lady of this dún, and Duchess of all Ossway.'

"We looked to a painting on the wall, looming above the silks and velvets. It showed the same woman as that statue in the Hall of Crowns—the legendary Nineswords. But rather than a sculpture of a conqueror, this painting depicted the Duchess with her famille. She was seated on her ironwood throne beside a striking man with a red beard and dashing smile. He stood behind the Duchess, to her right; a partner surely, but not an equal. The couple were surrounded by children—four daughters, all fine and strong.

"'She looks so young,' Dior murmured.

"'That was painted long ago,' Worm said, binding the corset ties. 'In happier nights.'

"'What h-happened to them?'

"'Laerd Aidan died many years ago. During the Clan Wars.' The maidservant nodded to the daughters, one at a time. 'Lady Aisling was killed leading the defense of Dún Cuinn. Lady Una was commander of the Nineswords' legions, and Lady Caitlyn, a captain in her fleet. Both were murdered when the Untamed conquered this city.' Worm glanced to the last of the girls—a pretty child with deep red hair and sharp green eyes. 'Lady Yvaine is in the east. Married to an Elidaeni lord.'

"'And what h-happened to the Nineswords?'

"'Nikita Dyvok.' Worm finished with the ties, lips pursed. 'Now turn. Sit.'

"'Sweet Mothermaid, it'd not kill you to say *pl*—'

"Dior was twisted on the spot by the thrall's strength, thrust onto a stool, sputtering as the maid threw a handful of pale powder into her face and stifling décolletage. Worm raised a stick of kohl, Dior closing her eyes only just swift enough to avoid a blinding.

"'Stop squirming, curse you.'

"'I don't wear this shite, I told—'

"'Eyes shut! Lips likesame!'

"The maidservant set to work, squinting in the dim light. The Grail tried to sit obediently, lips pursed, body motionless. But obedience had never been Dior Lachance's strongest suit, and she was soon mumbling again, fingers fidgeting in her lap.

"'That tickles.'

"'Be quiet.'

"'Careful, you'll have my bloody eye out!'

"'Flinch again, and see prophecy fulfilled!'

"The Grail settled down again, sullen and pouting.

"'You know, I always suspected the business of being pretty was *utter* bollocks,' she finally hissed. 'Now I know for certain. So I suppose thanks are in order, mademoiselle.'

"'I live to serve.' Worm sighed, a half dozen hairpins pressed between her lips as she surveyed her work. 'You've honestly *never* worn a dress before?'

"Dior shook her head, eyes still closed. 'Not since I was eleven. Thank God. Best thing about dressing as a boy is avoiding the ludicrous fuckaboutery that comes with being a girl.' The Grail shrugged, lips quirked. 'Not that I've an aversion to the end result, mind you. But there's not much use for a corset when you're pinching some fool's purse, and I doubt running from the watch would be helped by seven additional layers of underth—'

"Something cinched tight about her neck, near-choking. And then . . .

"'Open your eyes.'

"A stranger was sat before Dior when she obeyed. It was only when she lifted her hand and the young lady opposite moved likesame that she seemed to realize she was staring into a looking glass. Her lips—not ashen now, but bright red with paint—parted slow, and she touched her face as if to ensure her eyes spoke true. Her flesh was powdered death pale, lashes and the beauty spot on her cheek picked out in dark, sharp relief. A choker of blood-red rubies was fixed at her throat, a pearl-white waterfall of skirts tumbling below her ornate cream corset, down to a pair of beautiful pointed heels. Worm stood behind her, fixing her hair with iron pins before lifting the pièce de résistance into place—a pale, ornate wig, styled with the gaudy flair usually reserved for the finest of nobility.

"Dior Lachance was a girl who had hidden as a boy most of her life. This was the first moment she'd been unveiled as a young woman. And while that young woman was impressive—stunning, in fact—still, her expression was clouded as she looked at her reflection, the shadow of that beast in the bathhouse rising at her back once more.

"'What is wrong?' Worm asked. 'You look passable.'

"Dior shook her head. 'I feel . . . *naked*.'

"Worm met her eyes then, a touch of pity finally softening that emerald and sapphire. 'No purses to filch nor watch to flee here, Mlle Lachance. But though it's a strange truth, all this *ludicrous fuckaboutery* can serve purpose. Silk will prove stronger than steel on the right battleground. Beauty can be a kind of weapon, and bestow a rare power. The only kind they will allow you in this place anyway. But wield it well and she will mark you.' The maidservant's voice dropped low. 'And *she* can protect you from *him*.'

"Worm stepped back, motioned to the door.

"'Now hurry. The Contessa awaits.'

"The maidservant swept from the room, and more subdued now, Dior followed, hiking up her skirts and wobbling on her uncomfortable shoes. We followed, flitting rafter to rafter on tiny red wings as Dior was led stumbling and cursing down a long stone corridor.

"The air was heavy and chill, ringing with the song of crows. A trail of bloody footprints stained the floorboards before her, leading to a pair of grand doors, flanked by two young gallants in steel breastplates and Dyvok colors. They were redheaded Ossians both; handsome of face and green of eye, their chins dusted with the scrawny beards of boys who long to be men. The stench of murder ever hung over Dún Maergenn like a pall, but we felt it stronger here, deepening with every one of Dior's wobbling steps.

"The pair nodded to Worm, watching Dior's unsteady approach with bemused expressions—obviously as unsure as she was. But with eyes on the boys, and hands full of skirt, the Grail stepped in one of those bloody

footprints, slipping, almost falling, and in a blinking, both lads near dropped their swords in their lunge to catch her.

"'Ye well, m'lady?' one young gallant asked, holding her steady.

"'Oui,' she said, finding her footing. 'Merci, messieurs.'

"'Best be careful.' The other flashed a bright smile. 'Not that catching ye wasn't a pleasure, but it's a long fall off those pretty heels.'

"Dior smiled back, lowering her eyes. It seemed a light moment, a harm-less flirt, commonplace in any taverne or court in the realm. But looking to their hands, Dior saw each lad was scorched with a brand—a black heart, circled by thorns.

"'Nikita's mark,' she whispered.

"'Aye,' the taller one replied, eyes shining. 'Praise be, our laerd and master.'

"Her smile died then, the moment with it, and the flirt seemed not so harm-less anymore. Studying them from above, it was hard for us to not wonder who these boys had been. Soldiers, obviously; sworn to the Nineswords' service before her city fell. But had they fought before they bent the knee? Or had they bowed to save their own skins? Did it trouble them to serve this evil? Or did the love they bore it now swallow their shame?

"Worm nodded thanks, glanced to Dior to ensure she was steady. Satisfied, the maid knocked once, brisk, then flung the doors wide. And Dior flinched, hand up to her face as the stench washed over us all in a red, reeking wave.

"*So* much blood.

"A parlor room awaited; polished mahogany, velvet and satin, chandeliers of gleaming goldglass. Two doors opened left and right into boudoirs so palatial they could bed dozens—obviously the chambers of the former lady and laerd of this keep. Dior's face was still ashen as Worm pulled her within, and we flitted inside behind them, up, up, nestling at last in the shadows of the rafters above, every part of us now afeared.

"Closing the doors behind them, the maidservant urged the Grail to her knees before the figure waiting in the room's heart. Cold as tombs, motion-less as mountains, as beautiful as the first snows of fresh fallen winter.

"The beast named Lilidh Dyvok.

"She reclined on an ornate chaise longue, her great white wolf beside her, its one blue eye flushed scarlet and locked on Dior. The vampire was flanked by three ladies-in-waiting, all immaculately attired; beautiful ballgowns and powdered cheeks and ornate hairpieces. Yet Lilidh Dyvok was not dressed as a noblewoman like her entourage—in fact, the Heartless was hardly dressed at all. A sleeveless black robe was draped over her shoulders; two strips of sheerest silk, barely protecting her modesty. A half-corset bound her ribs beneath, cinched her waist; black velvet and whalebone. Her bare legs were crossed, demure, but her eyes burned with dark promise as she gazed upon the Grail.

"A golden circlet sat on her brow, and her hair spilled over her shoulders to the floor in red rivers. Her skin was porcelain pale, yet now unveiled, we saw it was decorated with beautiful inkwork—fae spirals wending up her right arm and down her left leg. Not as intricate, but assuredly similar to those that adorned the skin of Phoebe á Dúnnsair.

"*Naéth,* we realized. The tattoos of the Ossian Highlanders.

"Another servant in a beautiful gown was on her knees, scrubbing the bloody footprints off the stone. We recognized the twin beauty spots on her cheek at once; young Isla, Joaquin's beloved Ever After. To have survived the fall of two cities only to be press-ganged into the maidservice of these monsters was a cruel fate. But at least she lived.

"The lass met Dior's eyes, risking a small nod.

"Dior's gaze followed the footprints into one of the boudoirs, and there she saw naked people about the room; on the floors or silken sheets, one even dangling from the chandelier. Many of them were the 'valuables' she'd been brought to Dún Maergenn with; pretty young men and women she'd known and suffered alongside. They were dead now. Every one. Throats torn open or heads torn away, bellies ripped wide and privates ripped off. Dior had surely seen cruelty before—on the streets of childhood, in her journeys with Gabriel, but she still blanched at the sight of such wanton slaughter. We remembered Nikita in the bathhouse then, drenched head to foot in blood. Understanding at last where it had come from.

"'Mistress,' Worm declared. 'The prisoner has been prepared, as commanded.'

"'We thank thee, Worm. Artful handiwork, as always.' Lilidh pressed one finger to crimson lips, thoughtful. 'Yet . . . thou art somewhat tardy in thy arrival.'

"We saw Worm tense then, heard her heartbeat quicken as she pressed brow to boards. 'Forgive me, Mistress. Count Nikita came upon us in the bathhouse. He w—'

"'Thou wouldst blame my brother for thine own ineptitudes?' Lilidh frowned. 'A Lord of Night, a king of dark heaven's splendors, to be held account for a servant's failings?'

"'No, Mistress. Of course, the fault was mine. Please . . . I beg forgiveness.'

"Lilidh smiled, indulgent, waving one pale hand. 'Of course, love.'

"Worm sighed, like a man who receives pardon just as he steps onto the gallows.

"'Kiss ye my feet,' Lilidh commanded. 'And all sin shall be forgiven.'

"One might have expected the young woman to flinch, to balk, God help her, to refuse. But without hesitation, Worm scuttled forward, low as her namesake. A look of revulsion crossed Dior's face as the thrall prostrated herself. And as Lilidh stretched out one long leg, the maid pressed her lips to the dead goddess's pale, ring-clad toes, one at a time.

"Dior appeared uncertain where to look—at the girl being humiliated for the sake of a few minutes' wait, or at the innocents slaughtered for the sake of a madman's meal. But she settled on the latter in the end; the former was in part her fault, after all.

"The Heartless followed Dior's eyeline, dark smile dimming.

"'Thou shalt excuse my brother his peccadillos,' she sighed. 'Many nights hath passed since our larder o'erflowed with such bounty. A king must have his catharsis.'

"Lilidh's eyes fell on Worm, lifting her lips from the last of her toes.

"'Have those served with the evening meal,' she ordered, waving to the leavings of her brother's feast. 'There be yet dregs in them, and the children ever hunger.'

"'I live to serve, Mistress,' the girl breathed, her voice thick with devotion.

"Worm whisked into the boudoir and lifted the first corpse she saw; a young man, missing both throat and privates. Dior stared as the maidservant slung the body over her shoulder like a sack of feathers, and lifting a lass likewise mutilated, Worm hurried from the room, Isla scrubbing furiously at the spatters in her wake.

"'Thou hast the look of muddied blood.'

"Dior flinched—she'd apparently not heard Lilidh move, but the vampire now stood only inches away. Lilidh gazed down with jet-black eyes, the ink on her skin visible through her sheer silks. Reaching out, she caressed Dior's cheek, soft as spring rain.

"'Those eyes,' Lilidh mused. 'Those lashes, those *lips*. Elidaeni stock, surely.

But thy complexion be Ossian, through and through. From whence dost thou hail?'

"Dior swallowed hard, averted her eyes. From on high, she somehow looked more exposed than the Contessa, despite the finery she wore. To us, she seemed not a beautiful maid in a dazzling gown, but a soldier without her shield. A knight without her armor.

"'I grew up in a city called Lashaame.'

"'We know it.' Lilidh nodded. 'We visited with our brothers, twelve decades past. A pit of lepers and vipers, we thought it, beggared of beauty and reeking of dung.'

"Dior smiled faintly. 'It hasn't changed much since then, I fear.'

"The caress at her cheek slipped lower, the dark goddess lifting the Grail's chin so she was forced to meet her eyes.

"'Thou shalt refer to us at all times as Mistress.'

"Dior's faint smile died beneath that monster's stare. It was bereft of anything approaching life. Warmth. Compassion. It was the gaze of a shark closing in on a drowning swimmer, mouth slipping wide to reveal endless rows of jagged teeth.

"'Mistress,' Dior murmured.

"Lilidh's lips curled. 'Thou art a beauty. Fey and fine. Pray, why did ye hide it?'

"'The streets I grew up on were cruel to girls, Mistress.'

"'There be no street under heaven that is not. But we learned long ago the solution to that dilemma is not being afraid, poppet. It is being *feared*.'

"Dior gazed into Lilidh's eyes at that, lips parting. We knew the Contessa's blood would be at work within the Grail now, softening her will, warming the halls of her heart. And though perhaps it was my own fears speaking, it seemed a moment of understanding passed between the pair; the girl on her knees and this goddess to whom she knelt. It was hard. Sharp. A *dagger* of truth. The Heartless fussed with Dior's outfit a moment; gold-dipped fingers straightening the bodice, adjusting the choker of rubies around the Grail's throat. And standing back to admire her work, the ancien finally nodded.

"'Walk with me.'

"Lilidh stalked from the room, silk flowing about her, wolf slinking at her side. From the glares the ladies-in-waiting shot her, Dior realized she was expected to follow first, and she wobbled to her feet, hurrying to catch up as the women flocked around her.

"There had been swans on the lake near Lorson when I was a child, and flitting above them now, we fancied Lilidh's ladies moved like those birds once had, regal and graceful. All three were scorched with Lilidh's mark—the same antlered crown that Worm wore—yet we noted their brands were fresh, and that all were marred further somehow; scarred hands or sliced faces or missing fingers. Wolves were embroidered on the fabric of their dresses, and all wore some shade of green. Noble colors for the nobleborn.

"These must have been the ladies-in-waiting to the Duchess á Maergenn, we realized. Now forced to serve the murderer of their mistress by the power of her blood.

"And Dior was only two drops away from that same hell.

"Lilidh led us down a corridor lined with beautiful armor, draped with clancloth of the Maergenn—two shades of green, hatched with black and blue. Reaching a set of double doors, two bowing thrallswords drew them aside. A freezing wind struck our wings, but though she wore next to nothing, Lilidh walked onto the balcony as if into a summer's day, her white wolf beside her. As Dior followed, we saw dark ocean beyond the battlements; whitecaps crashing on the Gulf of Wolves. The great snow-clad bailey below was all abustle, a multitude of folk lit by flickering torchlight, shouts rising above the song of the waves.

"It took a moment for us to comprehend what we were seeing.

"The folk Dior had traveled with from Aveléne were clustered outside the ruined Sepulcher of the Mothermaid; over a thousand, guarded by thrallswords in Dyvok livery. Upon the broken cathedral's stairs stood Soraya, doffing her tricorn to the flock of vampires before her. The tattooed one named Draigann and his paramour, Alix, the sister with the broken wheel about her neck, the grey jester, Kane, Kiara; all the members of the Untamed court were assembled. And pointing to a bedraggled group of men on the steps beside her, Soraya called aloud.

"'A half dozen head, unskilled, but strong and hale, all! What am I bid?'

"A young vampire wearing a cloak of what looked to be children's skin called above the clawing winds. 'Three nights. Fifty swords.'

"'Three and fifty to Bloodlord Rémille!' Soraya cried. 'Do I hear four?'

"The jester raised his hand, his voice like oily smoke. 'Four and fifty.'

"'Four to Bloodlord Grey! Hear us five?' Soraya looked around the gathering, dark eyes gleaming. 'Fresh from the Nordlund, this lot! Well fed, and unspoiled!'

"Dior watched on, her face running pale with horror.

"'They bid nights of service to my brother,' Lilidh murmured beside her. 'One drop of water is worth a fortune in a desert. And while crowns are often won with steel, they are always kept with coin.'

"Dior said nothing, staring down into the dark. A cart waited near the dún's doors, corpses within, naked and mutilated. As the Grail watched, Worm threw two more bodies onto the pile. People were being hauled from wooden pens over by the stables—elderly folk, all—pushed into a wagon by more scorched. We recalled that foulblood horde within the walls of Newtunn then, understanding the depths of the depravity at work here.

"The frail and elderly would be fed to the wretched outside, the young and strong auctioned off to purchase the loyalty of Nikita's court; a brutality and callousness from the darkest of nightmares. Gabriel had warned Dior of the evil of these things, but to witness it firsthand was another trial entire. Her eyes fell on a gaggle of children, ragged and tearstained, not one older than ten. Among them stood a small girl with dirty-blond hair, a handwoven moppet doll clutched in one hand.

"'Mila . . .' Dior whispered.

"'This troubles thee to see?'

"Lilidh's voice dragged us back to that balcony, to Dior's own jeopardy. The girl licked at ash-dry lips, swallowing hard.

"'Oui. Mistress.'

"'Why? Be this so different to a farmer and his sheep?'

"'Of *course* it's different,' Dior hissed, bewildered. 'They're *people*.'

"'People they are. But animals also. And though it may seem cruel to thee, so too the spring cull to the lamb'—Lilidh gestured to the beast beside her—'or the wolf's teeth to the doe. In the wild, there be no rabbit nor deer who dies peaceful in his sleep, poppet. Young or old, in the end, they perish in *anguish*. Torn apart by predators, all of them. Such hath it been since time's dawning, for the strong to devour the weak. And 'til but a few decades ago, thee and all thy kind were content with that sacred truth.' Lilidh watched the prisoners below, ruby lips curling. 'You . . . *people* . . . only believe our new world cruel because in it, for the very first time, *thou* art the prey.'

"The jester had won the bid and was taking possession of his stock now, while another group were being marched onto the steps. Lilidh turned to face Dior fully, engulfing her in the polished jet of her eyes.

"'What doth the Forever King desire of thee?'

"'I don't know, Mistress. I swear it.'

"'The bloodmage who slew Rykard on the Mère. Who was she?'

"'Her name is Celene. She's Gabriel's sister.'

"'Who was she to *thee*?'

"'Nobody. I only knew her a few weeks . . . Mistress.'

"'Esani.'

"The ancien hissed that word like venom, pinning the Grail in her bottomless stare. Dior held perfectly still, perfectly mute, cold wind filling the silence between them.

"'Know thee this name, sweet child?' Lilidh finally asked.

"Dior stared hard into those midnight eyes, and did what she did best.

"'No, Mistress,' she lied.

"Relief flooded us through at that—a single taste of Lilidh's ancien blood was not enough to have Dior betray us. But dread followed quick; the thought of what must come next. And the Heartless smiled, ocean winds rippling in her long, silken locks.

"'*Kneel*.'

"The Whip rang like a pistol shot in the night. And though we thought she might resist—that the gifts of the Dyvok might prove as useless as those of the Voss against her—the Grail immediately obeyed, sinking to her knees under that goddess's cold, dead gaze. Lilidh slipped her golden blade from inside her corset, and the wolf beside her growled then, ears pressed back to his skull.

"'Hush now, Prince.'

"The beast lowered his head, obedient, keeping Dior fixed in his one good eye as Lilidh smiled.

"'Forgive him. He is a jealous little brute.'

"And reaching down, she sliced the porcelain skin up the inside of her thigh, cutting deep through the tattoo and into the artery beyond.

"'*Drink*.'

"All our thoughts raged now—disgust, defiance, but most of all, fear. A second taste would leave Dior but one drop from servitude. Lilidh knew the name *Esani*. She was old enough to remember the Wars of the Blood, the Red Crusade, the fall of Illia's brood into near-catastrophe. And losing the Grail to this monster's clutches must surely push us closer to our final ruin. We prayed the Grail might resist, might refuse, might unveil some ploy she'd fashioned to escape this fate. But instead, Dior closed her eyes, and as if commanded by heaven itself, pressed her mouth to the smooth flesh of that devil's thigh.

"Its scent was autumn's rust and iron's end, that blood; heady and impossibly thick. Lilidh's hand snaked behind Dior's head, pulling her closer, tighter, deeper. Terror rushed over us as we watched, helpless, Dior groaning now, her hand slipping up and over the vampire's buttocks as she drank, clutching tighter. Lilidh smiled, but again, no hint of it reached those eyes, deep and lonely as a starless sky. Dior's mouth roamed the slice in that pale flesh, kissing higher now, licking up, up toward the dark shadow between Lilidh's thighs. But satisfied, the ancien pulled the Grail away, dragging her effortlessly to her feet.

"Dior's eyes were glazed, blood smeared thick and red on her lips, and she blinked like a drunkard, as if unsure of where she was. Lilidh leaned forward, serpentine, tongue outstretched to catch the long spool of ruby red dripping from Dior's chin. Drawing it into her own, Lilidh took the smooth swell of Dior's lower lip into her mouth and sucked it clean while we listened to the girl's heart thundering against her breast.

"'Kith dream not, did ye know that?' Lilidh whispered, sticky lips brushing gentle against Dior's. 'Our slumber is as death. But tonight, thou shalt dream of Lilidh, poppet, sure and true. And amorrow night, shall *Lilidh* have the truth of *thee*.'

"The monster glanced to one of the ladies beside her; the graceful older dame with the deep blade scar beneath the powder on her chin. Lilidh drew breath to speak, but at that moment, Worm returned from below, hands yet drenched with blood as she fell to her knees beside the ladies-in-waiting, gasping for breath.

"'I have returned, Mistress,' the lass wheezed.

"Lilidh smiled red. 'Timely arrival for once, Worm. Take our prize below.'

"The serving girl pressed her head to the stone. 'At once, Mistress.'

"Lilidh's gaze lingered on Dior a heartbeat longer, hungry, endless, cold as wintersdeep. And then she turned away, gazing out upon that auction of the doomed. Dior still looked dizzy, barely seeming to take note as she was whisked back to the dressing room. We followed, watching as she was stripped of her finery and wig by the dutiful Worm. And clad in simple servants' cloth, the Grail was escorted down to the dungeons once more. She seemed to be surfacing from the spell of Lilidh's blood now, looking about briefly for Aaron. But the capitaine's cell was empty as she passed it by.

"Worm locked Dior in her own cell, peering now through the slot.

"'A word of advice.'

"Dior blinked, looking up into those mismatched eyes.

"'If Count Nikita comes to you in the night, don't fight.' The maid sighed, blue and green deeping to grey. 'He hurts you worse if you fight.'

"And then she was gone.

"Dior hung her head in the dark, the maidservant's footsteps fading on the stairs. Fluttering in on tiny wings, we settled on the smooth skin of her left hand, wondering how soon it might bear the Contessa's mark. Above, we could hear that dreadful auction still going on, the wails of prisoners, the choir of a thousand crows.

"'God, I wish Gabe were here,' Dior whispered.

"We were saddened at that, fearful and sick. We beat our wings, gentle, just to remind her again that she was not alone in this hell. But she looked at us then, blue eyes shining a touch colder now, the scent of Lilidh's blood still thick on her breath as she whispered.

"'Celene . . . When we fought Kiara at Cairnhaem . . . when Gabe fell.' She licked her red-stained lips, swallowing thick. '*Did* he fall? Or did you—'

"*Tap Tap*.

"Our wings beat on her wrist. Furious. Defiant.

"*Tap Tap*.

"We spelled out the word for emphasis, tiny legs crawling on her skin.

"*No*."

"Tsk tsk tsk."

The Last Liathe glanced up as Jean-François clucked his tongue. Lifting a finger, the historian wagged it, as if in the face of a deceitful child.

"*When a man lies, he kills a part of this world, and a part of his soul besides.*"

"The Book of the Redeemer," Celene replied. "Thirteen, twenty-seven."

"Chapter and verse." Jean-François nodded. "Hardly becoming of a servant of the kingdom of heaven, is it, Mlle Castia? To lie to the last scion of the Redeemer's line?"

The monster lifted her chin, hissing behind the cage on her mouth.

"Everybody lies, sinner. But we did it only for the good."

"Ah, oui," the Marquis smiled. "The greatest wickedness is *always* done for the good, is it not? But what a relief it is, to learn that the Almighty's soldiers are just as hypocritical as the rest of us."

The monstress fixed Jean-François in her black stare, glittering with cold rage. The historian only tilted his head and raised his quill. And glowering, Celene continued.

"Dior chewed her lip as we gave her answer, watching us with those grifter's eyes, ever older than her years. We'd no knowing if she believed us, but still, she seemed to be slowly coming back to herself now; that crimson daze she'd fallen under fading away. And dragging one hand through her hair, she finally spat red off her tongue.

"'I have to get out of here,' she declared. 'I have to get out of here *tonight*.'

"We circled once upon her hand, batting our wings upon her skin.

"*Tap.*

"'Can you be my eyes? Find me a safe path through the dún? Over the walls?' The Grail shook her head, jaw clenched. 'I don't want to abandon these poor people. But I'm no use to *anyone* if that devil makes me her thrall.'

"The mote of me circled again, trying to convey confusion, agitation. We'd searched the château as she slept during the day, and while we'd found no sign of Mother Maryn, we *did* know a way by which she might make a run to us. Crawling over her hand, we spelled out five letters, painstakingly slow.

"'*Sewer,*' she whispered. 'Good. That's good.'

"It was a tiny flicker of hope, but while we ever sought to aid the Grail, in truth, we were unsure at all of this. God had brought Dior to this place for a reason, and to abandon the dún before we'd discovered Maryn's resting place seemed a kind of sin. Yet more pressing, while we might guide her to freedom, we could do little to actually *help* her escape; our mote was unable to steal a key or even lift a latch. Dior still looked a touch befuddled on the taste of that monster's blood. How was she to slip her cell in such a state?

"We walked over her hand again, spelling out a simple but all-important question.

"*LOCK?*

"'No fear on that score,' she whispered.

"The girl's lips twisted in the gloom, and reaching up to her growing mop of hair, she plucked a slender treasure from its pale tumble. It gleamed as she twirled it through her clever fingers, iron hard and dagger thin. The key to all our problems."

Jean-François lifted his gaze from his tome. And despite himself, the vampire smiled.

"A hairpin."

XI

UNANSWERED

"THERE IS AN art to picking locks, sinner," Celene said. "And a greater art to the lie of it.

"Tales speak of master thieves, who could but whisper to a keyhole and have it open, like a drunkard's purse at last call. But in truth, lockpicking is a trickier transaction than that. It took Dior twenty agonized minutes for her tryst, the threat of a visitation by Nikita Dyvok hanging over her head while the sweat burned her eyes.

"But at last, the most beautiful musical note a thief can hear kissed the air. "*CLICK.*

"Our mote took flight, up the dungeon stair. The jailor sat yet at his desk, and though his task must have bored him witless, the man was awake, alert, an ironwood cudgel close to his branded hand. This fellow had no doubt witnessed the cost of failure in Nikita's court, and had *no* desire to fill a foulblood's belly.

"We swooped out of the gloom like a dart and struck him full in the face, the jailor flinching and swatting at his cheek. Twisting aside, we wheeled about and hit him square in the eye. The man cursed, half rising from his stool and taking a more vicious swipe.

"'Fuggoff. Lil bastard.'

"We retreated, giving him a moment to settle before blurring out of the dark and slapping into his ear. The jailor rose, cuffing the air and setting his mug awobble.

"'Fuggin . . .'

"He reached for his cudgel, frowning as he realized it was not where he'd left it. And turning, he found himself face-to-face with an ashen-haired waif, cold fury burning in her ice-blue eyes.

"'WA—'

"His shout shattered along with his teeth, Dior catching his jaw with a northwind strike that would have made her former swordmaster proud. But spitting red, jaw hanging loose, the man grabbed Dior's throat and slammed her into the wall so hard she near blacked out. She squealed, he *squeezed*—possessed of all a thrall's awful speed and strength. And in the end, it was not a maneuver taught by the great Black Lion that saved Dior Lachance, but the first she'd learned on the hard streets of Lashaame.

"Knee met nethers with a damp crunch; the jailor's eyes bulged. And raising the man's cudgel in both hands, Dior brought it down hard onto the back of his head.

"She kept hitting him, blows falling like hammers onto his skull until he stopped moving. Dragging one sticky hand across her mouth, the Grail hauled the man behind his desk, tearing off his tunic to mop up the worst of his blood."

Jean-François raised an eyebrow, quill poised over his page.

"She killed him?"

"Not quite. But that was only his good luck. She certainly beat him viciously enough." Celene glanced across the river. "Such a portrait does not match the one Gabriel painted?"

"Hardly," Jean-François replied.

"Dear brother," Celene scoffed. "Ever you saw only what you wished to see."

The historian glanced in the direction of the tower high above them, twirling his quill through quick fingers. "Please continue, Mlle Castia."

"Dior wiped her cudgel clean, washing her hands in the jailor's mug, and taking his cloak from a peg. It was a dance then, the pair of us, our mote in front, she behind, slipping the candlelight gloom of the dún like thread through a needle's eye. But the higher we climbed, the more dangerous it became; night was day in a vampire's lair, and while that awful auction had finished, the keep was still a hive of servants, messengers, soldiers.

"In the end, Dior decided to hide in plain sight—she was dressed in servants' cloth, after all. Snatching a tray of mugs from a hallway table, she marched through the bustle as if meant to be there, hood pulled up over her hair, and our mote hid beneath.

"She slowed as she headed through the Hall of Crowns—a familiar figure barreled through the front doors and headed right toward her, flint eyes agleam. We tapped a frantic warning on her skin and Dior shrank back into the shadows beneath the banister. But Kane missed her entirely, storming up the great stairs six at a time and spitting bile to another fledgling beside him about 'that greedy bitch Kiara.'

"The Grail backed off farther, waiting for Kane to pass overhead. But heart agallop, eyes still on the Headsmun instead of where she walked, she bumped into another figure hidden in the shadows under the stair, dropping her tray with a crash.

"'Mothermaid, forgive me,' she said, stooping to retrieve the mugs. 'I didn't . . .'

"Dior's heart stilled as she looked up into the figure's eyes, her own gone wide.

"'Joaquin,' she whispered.

"All was undone, and I *cursed* myself a fool, knowing now she was caught. The houndboy of Aveléne stood before her, staring her right in the face, unmistakable. Dior's jaw clenched as she waited for his inevitable cry of alarm, the descent of the guards, the return to her cell. But the handsome lad only knelt and busied himself with the spilled mugs, helping stack them on Dior's tray before rising back to his feet.

"'God go with you, mademoiselle,' he whispered.

"The Grail blinked at that, glancing at Kiara's mark atop his hand. But the houndboy only cast a furtive glance about them, and with a nod, slipped off through the shadows.

"Sheened with sudden sweat, Dior could only follow as we took to the wing, leading her on through the bustling dún. She walked as if she belonged, past the copper-dark reek of the Hall of Plenty, the hustle and stink of the château kitchens, and finally out into the bitter, biting cold. And there, she stopped suddenly, breath stolen clean from her lungs.

"A pit lay before her, fifty foot at the square, the devil only knew how deep. And it was *filled* with human bones. Men and women and children, all tumbled together and blanketed nowhere near heavy enough with snow. Great piles of discarded clothing stood beside it; too vast, too high, too much to look at. The leavings of countless stolen lives; parents and offspring, lovers and friends, once alive with light and hope and now, *this*.

"'Oh, God,' Dior whispered. 'Oh, sweet Mothermaid . . .'

"We beat upon her cheek, frantic that she move. To be discovered here would cost everything, and there would be time enough for grief come the dawn. Dior made the sign of the wheel, whispering a soft prayer. Then she pawed at her eyes, clenched her jaw, turning her back on that pit, that abyss, that yawning mouth to hell.

"And onward, she marched.

"The ironworks stood nearby, and the night was aglow with the light of the Dyvok forges. A stone well stood in the shadow of the ramparts ahead, leading directly down to the sewers; easy access for servants tossing nightsoil from the dún. The well was covered by an iron grate, secured by a heavy lock, but we knew Dior could make short work of that. Crouching in the shadows, trying to ignore the fiendish stench drifting up from below, the sight of that mountain of discarded clothes, Dior pulled out her trusty hairpin.

"A scream rang in the night; the sound of some maid in the city beyond, suffering only God knew what fate. The Grail looked out through the gatehouse toward the shadows of Auldtunn, all those poor souls trapped between the highbloods in this dún and the foulbloods in Newtunn beyond. No hope of escape. No fate but that awful pit.

"'I'll be back,' she whispered. 'I'll come back for *all* of you, I promise.'

"We knew there was naught she could do for any of them—Isla, Aaron, little Mila—that to tarry here was to risk everything. And her alley-born pragmatism might have seen her through, had she not glanced at the last toward the ironworks. Because there, silhouetted in forgefire, she saw a man; broad of shoulder and mahogany of skin, his body glistening with sweat as he pounded at an anvil. A man who'd stood up for her when few in this world would. A man who'd risked his city to save her, and then lost it anyway.

"'Baptiste . . .'

"*TapTap. TapTap.*

"Dior glanced to the padlock, back to the blackthumb wreathed in flames. 'I could—'

"*TapTap. TapTap.*

"'He can't be thralled after only two nights. I *can't* just leave him like this, Celene.'

"*TapTapTapTapTapTapTapTap.*

"She brushed us away, heedless, and slipping down the château's flank, she carefully stole toward the smithy. The building was good stone, its roof tiled, the air around it blissfully warm. Hood pulled low, soundless, Dior stole through the rear door, into the shadows around the forge's light. The smithy was busy; men in its forecourt stacking armor and blades in long racks. But Baptiste was the only soul actually at work in the forge, his face lined with exhaustion, shadows carved under his eyes. He wore a leather apron and heavy gloves, no shirt, bright sweat gleaming on dark skin. Dior crept closer, swatting us aside as we battered her cheek, furious and helpless.

"'Baptiste,' she whispered.

"The blackthumb paid no mind, pounding hammer to anvil and thumbing the sweat from his brow. We realized he was forging sets of fresh manacles.

"'*Baptiste,*' Dior hissed, louder.

"The big man glanced up and saw her in the gloom, shock and wonder and fear all crossing his features in the space of a single heartbeat. He opened his mouth to speak, but she pressed finger to lips, eyes wild with warning. Baptiste glanced about him, shifting nearer and pretending to busy himself with the coals.

"'Sweet Mothermaid, child, what are you doing here?' he breathed.

"'Getting the *fuck* out. And you're coming with me.'

"He paused at that, handsome brow darkening. He threw a wary glance to the men stacking the weapons, the courtyard beyond, the dún looming into the dark.

"'What about—'

"'I don't know where Aaron is,' she said, eyes pleading. 'But Gabe's sister is nearby. She's hurt now, but when she's well, she'll be stronger than *all* these bastards. We can come back for Aaron. Come back for every one of them, I promise. But we have to go. Now.'

"He looked at her, tormented. 'But . . . how would we leave?'

"'There's a well by the château that opens into the sewers, and from there to the ocean. We can pick our way along the cliffs to the shore.'

"The blackthumb glanced back to the keep, torn to his very soul.

"'*Please,* Baptiste,' Dior begged. 'Aaron told me to get you out if I could. I can't save them all tonight, but if I can at least save *you* . . .'

"The man hung his head, a storm cloud now gathered at his brow. He dragged one gloved hand across his scalp, face twisted with anguish, and I could feel Dior's pulse hammering beneath her skin as she watched him fighting that war within; his blood versus his heart, his love versus his life. But finally, the smith of Aveléne won some bitter inner victory, heaving a sigh and looking to the girl in the shadows.

"'Let me get dressed. I'll meet you by the well, chérie.'

"She grinned bright, swiftly smothered by their peril. 'I'll get it unlocked. Be *quick*.'

"Soundless she turned, slipping into the night. We flew before her, spinning desperate spirals to bid her move quicker. Through the flickering gloom, she stole back down the château's flank, ducking into the shadows as two soldiers walked the battlements overhead. Crouching in the evil stench of nightsoil, glancing once more to that awful pit of bones, she drew out her hairpin and set to. Again, the lockwork was no magik trick, no quick twist and pop, but a dance of tumbler and iron and trembling fingers.

"*Tap Tap.*

"She fumbled with the pin, hands shaking, breath steaming.

"*Tap Tap Tap Tap.*

"'I'm hurrying!' Dior hissed. 'If you've nothing useful to do, say me a prayer.'

"*Tap Tap Tap Tap Tap Tap Tap Ta—*

"'Fine advice, little Mouse.'

"Dior whirled to look behind her, the blood draining from her face. There, silhouetted against the forgefire, loomed a half dozen figures, Kiara at their fore. The Wolfmother glowered, fists clenched, eyes agleam.

"'But best to pray for yerself, I wager.'

"The Grail scowled at the Wolfmother, the scorched gathered around her. Despite the odds, Dior slipped the jailor's cudgel free from her cloak and took up her northwind stance. But more thrallswords came through the servants' door now, others gathering on the battlements above, and the Grail's breath caught as their lanterns illuminated a figure behind Kiara. A man. A man who'd stood up for her when few in this world would. A man who'd risked his city to save her, and then lost it anyway.

"And now, lost himself besides.

"'Baptiste,' she breathed. 'Oh *no* . . .'

"'I'm sorry,' he said. 'I . . . Forgive me, chérie. I . . .'

"His voice was a burning whisper, tears shining as he covered his face with shaking hands. He'd removed the heavy smith's gloves he'd been wearing in the ironworks, and Dior's shoulders sagged as she saw Kiara's brand upon his skin.

"'But we've only been here two nights . . .' she whispered.

"'My blood touched his lips long before that,' Kiara smiled. 'I near killed him when I killed his man at Aveléne, see. He fell into a fury, to watch his Aaron fall. Almost took my head off with his bare hands. I had to feed him afterward to heal the thrashing I gave him, lest all this muscle be wasted. But we've put it to good use the last two nights, he and I. He doesn't miss his Aaron at all, anymore.' The Wolfmother ran her hand over Baptiste's head, drummed her fingers over his stubbled scalp. 'Is that not truth, pretty one?'

"'That is truth.' Baptiste hung his head, tears spilling down his cheeks. 'Mistress.'

"The cudgel slipped from Dior's grip, and the fight melted from her bones. Kiara's hand fell on her shoulder. Heavy as lead. Hard as iron. And the Grail sank to her knees, tears frozen on her cheeks as she looked to the empty skies above.

"'Oh, Gabe,' she whispered. 'Where *are* you?'"

XII

THE LESSON

"WE LEFT HER slumbering, back in the hole where they threw her. Jaw clenched tight. Cheeks wet with hateful tears. A wise woman once said there is no hell so cruel as powerlessness, sinner, but even rage must surrender to sleep eventually, and curled into a ball, silent and utterly spent, at last, the Grail's bloodshot eyes slipped closed.

"But there is no rest for the wicked, as they say. And as Dior drifted into the peaceful still of slumber, we crawled out from beneath her ashen hair, and took once more to the wing, flitting up through the dungeons, and into the dún above.

"My heart was heavy; guilt and fervor both. Though I'd have gladly seen the Grail freed, I couldn't help but see the hand of the Almighty again here, at work even in Dior's failure. We'd not been brought to the city where Mother Maryn slumbered, only to abandon it. We were *meant* to be here. And I was *meant* to find her."

The historian conspicuously cleared his throat, turning to a fresh page. The Last of the Liathe narrowed her eyes, glowering across the water.

"You have a question, sinner?"

"I have many," Jean-François sighed. "But I shall settle upon one, for now at least. Why was your Priori sleeping in Dún Maergenn?"

The monster shrugged. "Who can know? It was said she was born in the Ossway, centuries back. Perhaps she felt safest there. It is a dangerous thing, to enter the eventide; that sleep deeper than death. Master Wulfric told me that Maryn had slumbered for more than a century, and even thralls will die of old age in that time. It takes—"

"You misunderstand me, Mlle Castia. I do not ask why she chose Dún

Maergenn specifically. I ask why was your Mother of Monsters asleep in the first place?"

The Last Liathe sighed, lips pursed behind her silver cage.

"How much do you know of the Wars of the Blood, sinner? How much has your mistress told you about that righteous crusade?"

"Enough to know your so-called *righteous crusade* ended in complete failure."

"Not complete. Though lying historians would tell it so." Celene shook her head, dark eyes glittering. "The mortal church sought to eradicate the Redeemer's line, and Fabién and his Knights of the Blood to destroy we who safeguarded it. And they *did* achieve a kind of victory. When the Emperor's holy legions finally sacked the Aavsenct capital at Charbourg, when Illia herself was rendered unto dust, hope seemed utterly lost. Mortal histories purged all record of the Heresy, kith chroniclers spoke of the Esana in hateful whispers. But the Faithful endured. Only four of them. Four of God knows how many. But still, enough to carry the dream out of that cataclysm. A dream of saving this world."

"Rats *will* flee a sinking ship, I suppose. Even immortal ones."

"You mock," she sighed. "Again. But you have no conception of what was lost that night. Illia alone carried countless kith souls within her body. *All* of them damned to hell with her death. How many others were condemned to the abyss as Charbourg burned?"

"It depends how many your depraved cult had cannibalized, I suppose." The historian brushed a golden curl from his eyes. "In the end, we all get the hell we deserve."

"So it is said," the Liathe nodded. "And so it was thought. Too close to heaven had Illia's brood flown, and in their hubris, it seemed they had caused the extinction of the Redeemer's dynasty. But it was still whispered, hoped, *prayed,* that some remnant of Esan's bloodline might have endured. And so, those four Faithful who survived the Wars of the Blood made a pact. They would scatter to the corners of the realm, nevermore to gather in one place, lest they be caught, and Illia's dream extinguished forever. And alone, they would keep faithful vigil in the dark, looking for signs of the Redeemer's line, that hope still remained for this world, and that their dream was not truly dead."

The Last Liathe looked down at her hands, and the Marquis was surprised to see them trembling. Sighing, the monstress entwined her fingers to halt the shakes.

"But time is a *terrible* thing, sinner. And to carry the burden of hundreds of souls over hundreds of years is a weight that few can bear. The voices of the damned call to you in your sleep. Their memories bleed into your own, until you know not what is yours and what is theirs. The Four knew that madness would come for them all eventually. And so to ease their burden, it was decided only two would ever be awake at once—the others would slumber in the eventide, to be woken in turn after a century of watchfulness. And so it was. Wulfric in San Yves. Jènoah in Cairnhaem. Oleander in Augustin. And Maryn, eldest of the Four, 'neath Maergenn."

Celene shook her head in wonder.

"Four of them, to carry the weight of *ten thousand* damned souls. The fate of the world on their shoulders. But now, Jènoah was lost. Wulfric gone. Oleander might have been a million miles away. Yet I was still certain God had brought us to Maergenn for Maryn. And so, as Dior slumbered in her cell, we set out to search for our eldest once more.

"There was no hide nor hole in the city our wings could not reach, save those of the Holy Sepulcher, and we knew no fear at that—an ancient vampire could never sleep on hallowed ground. And so we started in the sewers; those dark tunnels twisting under Portunn and out to the sea. Empty-handed, we turned next to the cellars in Auldtunn, the oldest in the capital, most likely to house the Mother. The city's necropolis was next, a lone red moth flitting among the houses of the dead. And there, at last, we found a sliver of promise, carved upon the tomb of a mason long dead.

"The sigil of the Esana.

"My heart soared at the sight of those twin skulls, that chalice between. They were small, subtle, carved in old stone by the hand of one long gone to dust, but still, this was proof—the Mother lay *somewhere* in these ruins. All hope was not yet lost. But hateful dawn was coming now, and I too needed to sleep, to hunt, to heal. Answers still beyond our reach.

"In frustration we returned to the dún, soaring over her scarred battlements. The walls were peopled with scorched, gathered at flaming braziers and handing around a hipflask. It was a horrid-smelling brew they were sipping, conjured from potato peel and rotting weeds in the dún's distillery; a brand of Ossian rotgut known as *the Black*. Its stench is akin to cabbage mixed with cat urine, and we are told the taste is little better.

"We soared over those awful cages in the bailey, past the ironworks, poor Baptiste Sa-Ismael bent over his forge. We flitted through bustling corridors, past the Nineswords' statue, her legendary blade raised in her granite fist. But we slowed our flight, pressing wings to the rafters as four figures trudged up the grand stair below. The first was Kiara, looking dour, storm clouds over her brow. Behind her walked the two Ossian gallants who'd stood on guard outside Nikita's chambers, rescuing Dior from her treacherous heels. Their jaws were squared, hands on their swords, green eyes fixed on the figure between them.

"Aaron de Coste.

"He wore only leather britches, and a leather collar fixed about his throat. His handsome face was framed by golden hair, the scar gifted to him by my dark maker, Laure Voss herself, cutting hook-shaped down his brow and cheek. But on his back and arms, we saw new scars; dark lines tracing the path once graced by the aegis of San Michon.

"They'd carved out his ink, we realized, filling the wounds with ash so they'd no longer heal when he awoke each sunset; a relief from his endless pain. Whoever had done the work was an artiste—the Draigann, or his bride, Alix, perhaps—Aaron's tattoos had lost none of their splendor. But where once they'd shone silver, now they were black as night.

"Aaron's head was hung low, hands clasped before him.

"*Praying,* we realized.

"Again, we felt that kinship with this fallen son of Aveléne, to see he'd not abandoned his faith. Though we knew him not, still we feared for him. And so, though dawn was near, we found ourselves following as he was led along the landing to the boudoirs of the Count and Contessa Dyvok. Stepping into the foyer, they were greeted by the sight of young Isla in her beautiful gown, exiting Nikita's chambers. Her mouth was curled in a small smile, arms laden with bloody sheets. She glanced up as they entered, eyes on the former lord of her city, her lips smeared red.

"'Capitaine,' she whispered, smile fading. 'Oh *no,* not you too . . .'

"Aaron met her gaze, heartbreak plain on his face. One more soul he'd failed to safeguard. One more child brought to her knees before these monsters.

"'Courage, love,' he whispered. 'God has not forsaken you.'

"Kiara scowled at the girl, and Isla lowered her eyes, backing away with her bloody burden. Flitting past Lilidh's chamber, we saw the Contessa seated at a desk, reading some dusty tome by dimmest moonlight. She was still clad in those two strips of sheer black silk, dark lips pursed as she turned a page. Her great wolf, Prince, was asleep at her feet, and a pretty man was sprawled naked upon her sheets, throat punctured, chest rising and falling. We recalled her words to Dior, her questions about the Esana. Lilidh was ancient enough to remember the fall of Charbourg, the crusade against my kin. And though Nikita was the dread lord of this kingdom, we now knew here, in *her*, lay our truest threat.

"'Move,' one of the scorched growled, shoving Aaron's shoulder.

"Jaw set, Aaron obeyed. He was thirsting, we could tell—his pallor closer to death, shadows beneath his eyes. Yet though he was only a fledgling, we could see already how the Becoming had affected him. He may have been handsome in life, but now, he was awfully, *fearfully* beautiful—pale and fey and deathless. His skin was smooth, golden locks flowing down his bare back, thin beard trimmed razor sharp, eyes ablaze at the scent in the air. As Kiara drew back the doors to Nikita's boudoir, it washed over all of us in a flood, Aaron's long lashes fluttering on his cheeks, fangs bared in a snarl of perfect, animal hunger.

"*Blood.*

"The Count Dyvok awaited within. He was sat on a plush wooden chair of red velvet and dark ironwood, the tall window behind looking out on the Gulf of Wolves. The grand four-poster was dressed with fresh sheets, the bodies from his earlier feast cleared away by the dutiful Worm. But the perfume of murder still stained the room.

"An easel and canvas stood in one corner, more canvases scattered about— stripped from the walls and painted on their blank sides. They were portraits; nameless beauties, male and female, though several studies of Lilidh and Kiara and even young Isla could be seen among them. The Count Dyvok obviously considered himself an artiste in private, and though their flair was undeniable, there was something gauche and altogether brutish about the pieces; not only had the artwork of Maergenn been destroyed to serve as their bones, but each had been painted wholly and solely in blood.

"Nikita wore a black silk robe, tied loosely at his waist, little left to the imagination. Long, ink-black hair spilled over his broad shoulders, the marble plains and valleys of his bare chest, the hills of muscle running down his belly. His brow was crowned with iron thorns, his bottomless eyes fixed on Aaron, cold and dark as the waters in the bay.

"'Good eve, Golden One.'

"Aaron made no reply, fists clenched at his side. Nikita glanced to his daughter, the young scorched standing beside her, his head tilted. The gallants bowed low before their master, departing swift at his unspoken command. But Kiara lingered.

"'Daughter?' Nikita asked, one brow arched.

"'Priori,' she replied, her voice strangely gentle. 'I wonder . . . might we speak alone?'

"The Blackheart smiled soft. 'Anon, child. When I am done.'

"The Wolfmother bowed her head, lips thin. She was a slayer of the Ossian wilds. Murderer of countless men and women and children. The beast who had filled those cages in the courtyard to brimming. And yet, for a moment, she seemed a green maid.

"'Yer larder filled. Yer line strengthened. The Black Lion *slain*.' Kiara wrung her hands, meeting his eyes. 'Do my gifts not please ye?'

"'They do.' Nikita's gaze flickered to Aaron, his smile widening. 'They shall.'

"'Then can we not—'

"'Forget not thy place, Wolfmother.'

"There was iron in Nikita's voice now, and his daughter flinched when he spoke. As Kiara searched that dark, unblinking gaze, we saw no light nor warmth in it.

"'My right hand art thou,' Nikita said. 'Of all my court, stand ye the tallest. Be satisfied, my blood, with the blessings thou hast. For what is given can be taken away.'

"The Wolfmother lowered her eyes again at that, bowing deep.

"'My Laerd,' she whispered.

"And with a sidelong scowl at Aaron, Kiara departed, closing the doors behind.

"Silence fell over the boudoir, save for the song of the sea. Nikita's dark gaze fell once more upon Aaron, that dreadful smile lingering on his lips.

"'Solitude at last,' he said.

"Aaron made no reply. We knew that the ancien's blood was at work in the young capitaine—he had supped only once of Nikita's wrist, but even that is enough to forge a bond, same as we had seen budding between Dior and Lilidh. Nikita was *inside* of Aaron now, and as we watched from above, we could see how much effort it took for the lordling to ignore that pale incubus as he reached down slow, unbinding the ties of his robe.

"'Thirst, dost thou?' Nikita asked, voice low and deep.

"But still, the capitaine of Aveléne made no sound.

"'Astonishing, how swift the hunger rises,' Nikita mused. 'Glut thyself to brimming, and thou shalt know but one night's peace before torment begins anew. All too well I know the pain that grips thee, Golden One. All too well, I know thy need.'

"Nikita plucked a goblet of sparkling crystal from the table beside him. Eyes still locked on Aaron, the count lifted his wrist to his mouth, a soft hiss slipping his lips as he bit deep. Holding the goblet beneath his opened vein, he willed his ancien blood to spill into the cup, and though high in the ceiling above, still our wings trembled at the scent; that potency, that *power*, bathing the whole shivering world red.

"'Come.' Nikita proffered the goblet. 'Drink.'

"Aaron stood with fists clenched, defiant. 'Merci. But I am not thirsty.'

"The Blackheart only smiled. Setting aside the goblet, he met Aaron's eyes and shrugged his robe off his shoulders, leaving every graven inch of his perfect body unveiled.

"'Another kind of feast, thy desire? Thou art but young in the blood, after all. Still ye remember, the mortal man ye used to be. His hungers. His *needs*. In all of these, can Nikita well oblige thee.'

"Aaron stood in that boudoir, a pale droplet at the shores of a black ocean. His eyes roamed the peril of Nikita's body, his bloodless lips curling as he hissed.

"'You sicken me.'

"'Thy mouth protests. But I see the emptiness in thy soul.' Nikita reclined on the velvet, naked and perfect. 'And I shall see thee filled, Golden One. Nights of wonder await thee. Nights of bliss and blood, of pain and power and pleasure, all entwined. Nikita shall be thy mentor. Thy monarch. Thy master.'

"'Never,' Aaron replied. '*Never.*'

"'*Never* be a long time in the counting. Know ye, what I am? What I do?'

"'I know you are all I was raised to despise,' the lordling spat. 'I know you are a devil, wearing an angel's guise. But though you may bend my mind, for all your power, you cannot *touch* my heart. So hear me now, monster, then do as you will. All you shall have from me will be stolen. *Never* surrendered. I shall die before *ever* I call you master of my own will.'

"Nikita chuckled, low and long.

"'Thou art nobleborn, oui?' He waved his hand, as if to banish the question. 'Answer not, I smell its stench 'pon thee. I have met many who thought themselves born high in my years, Aaron de Coste. And in the end, I saw all of them on their knees.'

"The Blackheart toyed with the edge of his goblet, smile fading.

"'I myself was not. Nobleborn, that is. A shepherd's son was I birthed, on the dirt floor of a squalid hovel in Talhost. The hamlet where I lived does not even exist anymore. My father was a cruel man—men raised in cruel climes often are. But in his cruelty, there was a kind of wisdom, and *six hundred and forty-one* years later, still I remember the greatest lesson he taught me. Wouldst thou like to know, Golden One, what it was?'

"Aaron remained mute, glancing to the window, the fireplace, searching for some desperate escape. But Nikita spoke on, eyes fixed on his prey.

"'On a winter's eve in my eighth year, one of our ewes was torn apart by wolves. I found her body. There was so much blood, I could taste the iron in the air. A lamb had she, stood in the snow, bleating its fear, and my father told me to kill it—always could we use more meat for the pot. Yet though I told him done was the deed, instead, I hid the lamb in our barn. Fed her by hand. Slept with her at nights to keep her warm. She was the first thing in this world I truly loved.' Nikita smiled, midnight eyes twinkling. '*Treasure,* I named her.

"'One prièdi, Father summoned us for supper. And though we were oft hungry, that night, we had a feast laid out—a fine, hot stew of good, fresh meat. But after Father urged me to eat all I could, out to the barn he took me. And there he showed me the fresh-flayed hide, splayed 'pon the wall, and the empty loft where my Treasure had been hid, and I understood then who it was that filled my gurgling belly. And he beat me to within an inch of my life, my dear father. Beat me so hard that all that I had eaten came back up to greet me, the remnants of my first love spraying over the very hands I had raised her with.'

"'Is this tale meant to make me pity you?' Aaron growled, eyes flashing. 'You, who destroyed my city? Who slaughtered a *nation*?'

"''Tis meant to impart a lesson, as I said. The most important in life.' The ancien leaned forward, eyes fixing the lordling to the floor. 'What makes ye care, makes ye *weak*. The cruel will use the things ye cherish to strike at the very heart of thee.'

"Nikita leaned back, parting his legs slightly.

"'And the Blackheart is *nothing* if not cruel, Golden One.'

"'. . . Baptiste,' Aaron whispered, at last recognizing the threat.

"Nikita picked up the brimming goblet again, his voice soft and dark as smoke.

"'Die for him, wouldst thou?'

"'I love him.' The capitaine clenched his fists, trembling now. 'Of *course* I would.'

"The Count Dyvok smiled, and as those bottomless eyes bored into the lordling's, the ancien willed his blood down, down; his member stirring now on his thigh, swelling with the warmth and life he'd stolen from those poor souls murdered in his bed.

"'How benevolent a master, then, be great Nikita. For he commands not that ye die, Aaron de Coste.' The Blackheart slipped one hand down to his nethers, running one slow fingertip up his smooth and thudding length. 'Only that ye kneel.'

"Nikita held the goblet up to the light, studying his blood within, dark, warm, gleaming. With lips curled, he tilted the crystal, letting a few drops spill onto his bare chest, over one tight nipple; a splash of ruby onto polished marble. Aaron's jaw was clenched, but though he tried to look away, the fledgling found himself staring, lips parted. And with eyes still locked on the young capitaine, Nikita tilted the glass farther, blood scent kissing the air as he poured the entire goblet over himself, rivulets running down his smooth torso, the hard muscle of his belly, down, down to his member, now standing tall and taut between them. Here, he paid special attentions, upending the goblet entirely, painting his length and the smooth pouch beneath, letting the last of it *drip*, *drip* onto the tip of his swollen crown.

"'Tell me, beauty,' he breathed. 'Art thou still not thirsty?'

"Aaron gritted his teeth, wracked with despair. To fight, to bleed, to die, this he would gladly do. But to condemn his paramour to the fire? For pride's sake? Would he break before he bent, we wondered? Would he forsake his beloved, rather than his freedom?

"And we saw then, why Nikita Dyvok called himself *Blackheart*. Looking down into the hell below, we caught a glimpse of the abyss that yawned within his breast. A hint of the perfect evil that coiled beneath the skin of this pale prince of night.

"'. . . You will not hurt him?' the lordling whispered.

"'I vow it. So long as thou shalt give thyself utterly, *willingly*, unto me.'

"The Blackheart smiled, dark as all light's dying.

"'Kneel before me, Aaron de Coste.'

"Aaron stood frozen, hands curled into helpless fists. We could feel the thoughts ringing in his skull; nothing in him but rage and hate and the bleakest shade of despair. And head hung low, no choice left him, the lordling finally obeyed, stepping forward like a man toward the gallows, and slipping down to his knees before that black throne. Nikita dipped his thumb into the blood pooling at his navel, reaching out toward his prey. Aaron flinched, steeling his will, closing his eyes as that thumb was pressed to his lips, smearing them with red, slipping between his teeth, into his mouth.

"'What is my name, Golden One?' that dark prince breathed, withdrawing his hand.

"'Nikita,' Aaron whispered.

"'No.' Dark eyes flashed, bottomless and wroth. 'What is my *name?*'

"Aaron looked up then, his gaze matching the ancien's. Bloodshot blue staring into burning black, boiling with hatred absolute.

"'. . . Master,' he hissed.

"'Good,' that devil whispered. 'Very good.'

"One hand snaked out, marble fingers knotted in golden hair.

"'Now drink me.

"'Drink.

"'*Oh.*'"

XIII

WHEN RAVENS CALL

"DIOR'S EYES OPENED well after sunset, wide and blue in the deeping dark.

"She'd dreamed during the day; lips curling in a smile soft as winter's first snow. But we knew she had been dreaming of Lilidh—the ancien's blood at work inside her now, choking resolve and weakening will. And as she lifted her head from the hard stone, Dior's smile died, cold reality choking whatever sweetness she'd found beyond the wall of sleep.

"Her hands were manacled, an iron collar chaining her to a rusted ring on the wall. The Wolfmother had been ungentle returning her to her cage after her escape, and Dior's skin was splashed with bruises, shadows smudged under her eyes, the beauty spot at her cheek as dark as the blood crusted upon the floor. Her cell reeked of it, and she glanced to the gift they'd left her—the head of the jailor she'd not quite beaten to death, yet condemned to it all the same. The rest of the man had gone to the foulbloods, of course.

"Far be it from the Dyvok to waste a meal.

"Her throat was parched, stomach growling—they'd given her nothing to eat or drink all day. And now the fearful sun had fallen again, night's cloak gathered, and when those curtains fell, we all knew full well how the final act would play.

"'I'm so fucked,' she breathed.

"*Tap Tap Tap Tap.*

"We rested upon her cheek, near as afeared as she. For all we'd seen scouting the dún, we could see no way *out* now, and the thought of her bound to the Untamed was a terrifying one. Dior would be forced to tell all we'd revealed about the Faithful, and if the Dyvok unearthed our eldest's resting place . . . all that knowledge, all that power, all those shriven souls . . .

"'Are you still hurt?' Dior whispered, soft in the dark.

"*Tap.*

"'Too hurt to help me?'

"We could only flutter our wings then, frustrated and fearful. Our burns were healing, but not yet enough—we could not enter a lair like this alone and live.

"'It's aright.' Dior rolled onto her knees, brow to the stone. 'No sense throwing good coin after bad. I've been worse places than here, I'll think of *something . . .*'

"It was bravado, we knew it—but still, she dragged herself up, taking a familiar stance. And unarmed, hopeless, but trying to feel a little less helpless, she ran the sword-forms Gabriel taught her. *Belly, chest, throat, repeat.* She'd no chance of fighting her way free here; like her bluster, this practice was a bulwark against fear. But as footsteps rang on the stair and she flinched at the sound, we saw how desperately she needed it.

"'Working up a thirst, little Mouse?'

"The door was flung wide to reveal Kiara looming on the threshold.

"'The Heartless will see it sated,' she smiled, unlocking Dior's chain. 'Get her ready.'

"This last was aimed over her shoulder, and we saw Worm standing in the corridor outside, arms laden with silken finery. At the Wolfmother's command, the maidservant hurried into the cell, wordlessly peeling Dior out of her bloody clothes.

"The Grail stayed mute, allowing herself to be dressed, whatever trepidation she felt at being stripped in front of this monster outweighed by her hatred of it. Worm lacked the powders and paint she'd had the previous eve, but even ill-equipped, she did fine work, draping Dior in that same beautiful ballgown, adorning her fingers with jewels, and finally cinching her waist tight in the bonds of an ornate cream corset.

"When the maidservant was finished, the Wolfmother looked Dior over and sneered. And taking up the chain that had bound her to the wall, snapping it like a whip, Kiara led Dior up from the dungeon and into the dún, Worm on their heels.

"Walking through the stink of death and misery, Dior's gaze was downturned, cold sweat on her skin. But she glanced up as she was led through the Hall of Crowns, her face running bloodless at the sight of dead bodies being dragged in from outside. We recognized the corpses—the elderly and frail fed to the foulbloods in Newtunn yestereve. Their empty bodies were being carried toward the château kitchens now, hefted by scorched wearing bloody aprons, butcher knives at their belts.

"Worm bowed her head, making the sign of the wheel. Dior looked to the maidservant then, blue eyes gone wide as realization sank in.

"'That pit of bones outside . . .' she whispered. 'Those soldiers handing out meat to the people in Auldtunn when we arrived . . .'

"And she whispered then; Gabriel's words about the slaughterfarms at Triúrbaile.

"'*I can still smell the fucking stench when I close my eyes . . .*'

"Kiara glanced over her shoulder and shrugged.

"'Waste not, want not, little Mouse.'

"Dior's fists curled closed then, jaw clenched so tight her teeth creaked.

"'Why are you *like* this?' she hissed.

"Kiara stopped at that, turning to stare at the Grail. Dior looked frightened, furious, gesturing around at that symphony of misery. Worm took the younger girl's hand to calm her, but the Grail shook her off, stepping up to the Wolfmother and trembling with rage.

"'Why are you *all* like this?'

"'Ye think yerself better?' Kiara growled. 'Ye think yerself saintly? Yer kind hunted mine for *centuries,* girl, and not a tear they spilled for a one of us. I asked nae for this life, nor for my Laerd Nikita to take my old one from me. But take it he did, for the sake of the dún I owned, and I spent the next *five decades* in hiding, terrified of being burned in my bed or dragged screaming from it into the sun.'

"'Then why serve him?' Dior demanded. 'You were his victim, just like the rest!'

"'I was nae *victim.*' Kiara dragged off her gauntlet, lifting her hand before Dior's face. And there, branded upon her skin, was Nikita's mark. 'I was his *beloved.* Together we lived, as beau and bride. Fifty years hunted. Shunned as abominations. As monsters.'

"'But you *are* monsters!'

"The Wolfmother shook her head then, her eyes hard and cold.

"'If that be so, little Mouse, we are the monsters yer kind made us.'

"Dior grunted as Kiara tugged her chain, stumbling forth once more. Heart pounding, chewing her nails now, she and we both searched about desperately for some way out of this plight. God had brought her here for a reason, had he not? Surely it was not to suffer thralldom at the hands of the Heartless? But we could see no way through, and our prayers were still answerless as Dior was dragged into the Hall of Plenty, before Nikita's grisly court.

"They were gathered again, devils with the countenance of dead angels: the tattooed one called Draigann, his fearsome bride, Alix, in his lap, tipping a goblet of blood into his upturned mouth; the unholy sister, whispering with a smiling Kane; the grey jester, arguing with an old and apparently sightless man; Rémille with his coat stitched of the flayed hides of dead children. The rafters were strung with people, maids with knives and goblets waiting obediently below. And at the end of the hall awaited the king and queen of this Court of the Blood; Blackheart and Heartless, watching all atop their stolen thrones.

"Lilidh wore a daring gown of midnight silk and lace tonight, her long red hair circled by a crown of stag antlers. One gold-clad hand rested on Prince's head, the wolf as ever sat beside his mistress, his one good eye agleam. Her ladies stood about her, Worm taking up her place on her belly before Lilidh's throne. Nikita was resplendent in black and ocean blue, hair dark as midnight, his mighty greatsword at rest on the back of his throne. And in front of Nikita, down on his knees, was poor Aaron de Coste.

"He wore only leather britches again, muscle carved of pale stone, a leather collar cinched tight about his throat. As Dior was knelt beside him, the brave capitaine of Avaléne glanced her way, and we saw true pity on his face. But as Nikita stirred, Aaron's gaze was torn from Dior's, and thereafter, the lordling looked only at *him*. It seemed Aaron had been fed by his master already this eve, or perhaps he'd shared Nikita's bloody bed during the day, and feasted as the sun sank to rest. Whatever the case, we saw it in the fledgling's eyes now, his smile, his sigh; that hellish adoration he'd warned Dior of in his cell.

"*Love is mortal. Blood is eternal.*

"'Oh, Aaron . . .' she whispered.

"'Attend,' Nikita said.

"The hall stilled, all eyes now on that ebon king. Thorns on his brow agleam, Nikita rose to address his lords and ladies, a voice of iron reverberating on the walls.

"'My lords, my kin, my blood, these are the greatest nights the children of Dyvok have e'er known. After great Tolyev's murder at the hands of the thrice-cursed Lion, we fell to petty squabbling, bleeding each other as much as the cattle we were born to rule. But now, by the hand of mine own beloved daughter hath that murder been avenged.'

"Here, Nikita gestured to Kiara, black eyes agleam. The Wolfmother lifted her head, smiling as the monsters around the hall offered bloody toast.

"'The quarrels of the past hath been laid aside,' the Blackheart continued. 'United under Nikita, the Blood Dyvok hath brought all Ossway to its knees in two short years. And this whole *empire* shall follow.'

"He pointed to that vast map upon the wall, the realm of Elidaen taken in with a sweep of his hand. Sigils were marked upon it, outlining the points of kith conflict, the lines of their fronts. A flock of ravens was gathered along a river to the far east, poised above the Elidaeni capital, the whole Nordlund behind awash in their gold. Wolves were scattered about the south of the continent, dots of red indicating their strongholds of power. But in the west, a great multitude of bears were gathered, the whole country shaded blue.

"'The Chastain fumble in the Sūdhaem,' Nikita said. 'The Ilon cower in a few scattered cityports. The Voss still battle the Emperor in the east. And meanwhile, we rule Ossway as *kings*.' Nikita lifted his chin, meeting the stares of his monstrous court. 'Know we, my lords, that these lands are bled near dry. Know we, that thou hast hungered these past nights. But know we also, that all Elidaen can be ours if we have but the will to seize it!'

"A hungry murmur rippled among the kith, fangs bared, eyes narrowed.

"'Yet no dynasty may endure without new blood. One now kneels in homage before us, with desire to stand in service beside us. And we have found him *worthy*.'

"With a snap of Nikita's fingers, young Isla entered the hall, dressed in finery and bearing a golden bowl and iron rod. Wide green eyes fixed on Aaron, the lass proffered the rod to Nikita, one end glowing bright and smoldering. Dior's shoulders sagged at the sight of the brand, rippling with heat.

"Nikita turned to Aaron, still on his knees, iron ablaze between them.

"'Whom dost thou serve?' he asked.

"'Nikita,' Aaron breathed as if the name were God's.

"'Whom dost thou love?'

"'*Nikita.*'

"The Blackheart's lips curled, eyes deep and cold as the starless sky above.

"'I shall dear miss the sight of thee 'pon thy knees, Golden One.'

"Aaron looked up into Nikita's face, smiling just as dark as he.

"'Ask it of me, Master, and I shall gladly kneel again.'

"Kiara stood nearby, the smile that had curled her lips just moments ago now fled entire. We could feel a sob bubbling in Dior's throat, and she averted her eyes as the capitaine of Aveléne offered his hand to his lord. Lilidh caught her gaze then, smile heavy with dreadful promise. Dior turned away, Aaron's gasp cut the air, a sigh of something horribly close to passion slipping his fangs as the sound of sizzling flesh kissed the air.

"Nikita took Aaron's hand, rubbed the burn with ink and ashes from Isla's bowl. And with a triumphant smile, the ancien loosed the collar about the fledgling's neck.

"'Rise, Aaron de Coste, bloodsworn of Nikita, and—'

"The doors boomed open, and all eyes turned toward the southern end of the hall. Soraya stood there, framed in the light, her expression grim as death. The vampire strode through the gathering, shoulders and braids bejeweled with fresh snow, her mighty sword in one fist. She stopped a respectful distance from the thrones, sinking to one knee.

"'Daughter?' Nikita asked.

"'Forgive me, Priori. A message is come to the gates. From the Ironhearts.'

"The Dyvok ancien exchanged a glance, and we felt the mood in the hall grow heavier. Lilidh scowled, waving one lazy hand.

"'Tell the Voss begone. We are Dyvok, not Chastain. We speak not to dogs.'

"A mirthless chuckle rippled around the room. But Soraya looked only to Nikita.

"'They are . . . insistent, Father.'

"Nikita returned to his seat. 'They?'

"Soraya nodded, glancing to her sister, Kiara. 'The Terrors. Alba and Aléne Voss. They are come beneath banner of pax, and request Courtesy under the old forms.'

"The mood fell further, the vampires about the room whispering. For Fabién to have sent his eldest daughters to speak to the Blackheart in person . . .

"Lilidh turned to her brother. 'They shall offer nothing we want.'

"'Let them offer all the same.' Nikita's gaze fell on Dior, empty and dread. 'There be wisdom in listening when ravens call, sister.'

"Lilidh narrowed her eyes at that, but Nikita looked to Soraya.

"'Show the Princes in, good daughter.' He raised a warning finger. 'Politely.'

"Soraya bowed and marched from the hall. Dior was dragged upright by Kiara, propped beside the Contessa's ladies. Nikita bid his new soldier rise, and with a dark and knowing smile, Aaron bowed and backed away. Dior watched him sit beside beasts he'd spent half his life battling, tears welling to see him so twisted by so small a thing as three drops of blood. Her eyes drifted to Worm, on her belly before Lilidh's throne, and then to the monster on that throne itself. We could feel the Grail's heart thudding ever faster as those red, bow-shaped lips gently curled in a smile.

"*Soon*, it seemed to promise.

"'Alba and Aléne Voss,' came the call, Soraya's voice echoing in the hall. 'Firstborn of Fabién, ancient of the Ironhearts and Princes of Forever.'

"Sweating now, breath quickened, Dior lifted her eyes to watch the Terrors sweep into the hall. They stalked forward beneath the gaze of a hundred bristling Untamed, sparing none of them a glance. To step willingly into such a dragon's den may have seemed a fool's gamble to mortals, but Courtesy is a custom sacrosanct among ancient, and besides, the first daughters of the Forever King were likely more powerful than any in that keep.

"The twins walked in mirrored unison, heels clicking upon the stone. They were luminous in their finery, sweeping frockcoats and silken hose of black and white, eyes as dark as the siblings watching their approach. Behind them came a cadre of foulbloods, but not a rotten rabble as in the city below— these Dead walked with the voice of the Voss ringing in their minds, left foot, right foot, in grim parody of soldiers at parade.

"Alba and Aléne stopped some twenty yards from the thrones, sweeping off their snow-kissed tricorns, and curtseying like noble ladies at court. They spared Dior a glance, and we could feel them probing, failing, the air thrumming with fathomless power.

"'*Priori Nikita*,' they said. '*We offer greetings, and humble thanks for thy Courtesy.*'

"'Prince Alba. Prince Aléne. A singular pleasure, as always doubled.' Nikita's lips curled in a smile, sharp and wicked. 'How long hath it been since we danced? Eighty years since Ilhan's masquerade, methinks?'

"'*Ninety-two*,' they replied.

"'So many? Ah. The heart bleeds to have so long been denied such majesty.'

"'Majesty.' Lilidh sneered. 'Spake the night to the day.'

"Black eyes turned in unison to the Contessa. '*Lady Lilidh. We greet thee.*'

"'Ah, they deign attend at last, she who sits 'pon eldest's throne.'

"'*Forgive us, Lady.*' The Terrors bowed. '*A novelty, to stand in a hall where eldest and greatest sit side by side. Among the Ironhearts, they are one and the same.*'

"'We forgive thee, Princes, of course.' Lilidh scratched her pale wolf behind his ears, her tone mild as summer breeze. 'Counting to two is a difficult proposition, after all.'

"Nikita stroked his chin, still smiling. 'Thou hast journeyed far to exchange barbed pleasantries, cousins. Thy father's forces are to the east, we hear, his righteous crusade set to crush Montfort's walls to dust. How comes it thou art so far from his side?'

"'*Our dread father, Fabién, the Forever King, Priori of Voss, eldest of the kith and sovereign ruler of this empire, hath desire for return of his property.*'

"'Property?'

"The Terrors' eyes fell upon Dior. '*This child belongs to him.*'

"'Indeed?' Nikita raised one eyebrow. 'Yet, by time-honored pact twixt our great lines, there is naught west of the Mère and north of the Ūmdir that be not dominion of the Untamed. And whilst a king Fabién may *also* be, no emperor's laurel hath yet kissed his brow by our reckoning. Ye o'erstate, cousins. *And* o'erstep.'

"'By what right doth Fabién claim this prize?' Lilidh asked.

"The Terrors glanced to the Heartless. '*The child is his.*'

"'No. She is *ours.* By this very night's end, third time blooded and bound unto me.'

"A flush rose on Dior's cheeks at that promise, and fear gripped us as we saw her eyes roaming Lilidh's throat, licking absent-minded at the corner of her mouth.

"The Terrors' eyes slipped back to Nikita.

"'*Our father offers reward for return of his property, Priori. Two thousand head of mortal stock from his lands in the north. Delivered unto thee afore sweet winter's end.*'

"'Cattle have I in abundance aready,' Nikita said.

"'*Indeed?*' The Terrors tilted their heads. '*Thy lands appeared quite barren 'pon our journey here. We had e'en heard vicious rumor that to restock thy larder, thy captains were forced to raid east of the Mère, in violation of that time-honored pact made recent mention of.*'

"The ancien glanced to a bristling Kiara, then bowed in unison to Nikita.

"'*But of course, we were misinformed. No doubt Aveléne's fate was the work of lowly brigands, and wise Nikita hast some hidden cornucopia, that shall feed his bloodlords and foulbloods well after the summer thaw, when ice turns to rivers, and feast to famine.'*

"The Blackheart's eyes narrowed, and he leaned back in his throne, drumming sharp claws upon his leathers. 'Two thousand, ye say.'

"'So much cattle hath Fabién,' Lilidh mused, 'that he might spare them to feed us?'

"But the Terrors ignored the Heartless, eyes on Nikita.

"'*What say thee, Priori?*'"

In the belly of Sul Adair, Celene Castia fell silent, pausing now for thought. Dark eyes locked on the river between her and the historian, she leaned forward, legs crossed, steepled fingers hovering just shy of the silver cage over her teeth.

"There is no greater fondness in a vampire's heart than for a grudge, sinner. The Voss had galled the Dyvok since before most of those gathered in Dún Maergenn had fallen to darkness. Few knew how the animosity between their great houses began. Some whispered of ancient betrayal, or a war of the heart, or friendship soured to bitterest gall. But whatever the root, the hatred between these ancient lines had aged like finest brandy. Voss versus Dyvok. Ironheart versus Untamed. It is like—"

"Wine versus whiskey?" Jean-François murmured. "Blonde versus brunette?"

Celene blinked, scowling across the river. "I beg your pardon?"

"No matter." The historian smiled to himself, glancing upward. "Forgive me."

The Last Liathe frowned a moment longer before continuing.

"Despite the blow my brother had delivered at the Crimson Glade twelve years prior, the Dyvok had conquered all Ossway—an astonishing feat that made Nikita the first true king of the Dead in this new night. But in his haste to take his throne, the Blackheart had left his kingdom a wasteland. Summer was coming, and with it, the thaw. Rivers would flow once more, ending hope of further conquest 'til winter began anew. The mortal stock pledged by the Terrors would be a boon in the months of coming privation, that much was plain. But to truck with the Voss, for Nikita to admit he needed them . . .

"'I say thee *aye,*' he declared.

"Whispers rang among the Untamed, bared fangs and flint-hard eyes.

"'*Aye?*' the Terrors asked.

"'Aye.' Nikita raised his hand, the iron signet glinting on it. 'As soon as thou shalt drop to one knee afore my court, Princes, and gift kiss to this ring. And for thy affront to my sister and elder, ye may then drop to *both* knees, and press lips to mine other.'

"Grim approval rippled through the court, the Draigann's fangs glinting gold as he grinned, Soraya even going so far as to laugh. But if the Terrors were incensed, they gave no sign. Instead, with brows raised, they turned toward the foulbloods at their backs.

"'*Ah, sweet Nikita,*' came a voice, soft and lilting. '*E'er thou art ruled not by thy head, but the black heart thou hast named thyself for.*'

"The Count lifted his eyes, searching for the speaker. At some silent command, the foulbloods parted, and standing amid them, a boy was revealed, smiling and bloodless.

"He was foulblooded, that much was sure; eyes bleached white, dark traceries of rot's roots at his lips and fingernails. Ten or eleven when he died, hair shoulder-length and ashen blond, clothes bloodied. But he spoke flawlessly, his voice hard and cold, and across his pale eyes and down his brow, we saw a smear of fresh blood.

"A puppet, we realized. A marionette, being steered by another, darker will.

"Nikita rose to his feet, whispering a word.

"A curse.

"A name.

"'*Fabién.*'"

XIV

HOPE'S END

"DIOR'S FACE PALED, her skin crawling as that dead boy's gaze met hers. Though the corpse spoke with a child's voice, it was *he*, she knew it. The Forever King. All the miles, all the blood, all the murder—all because of *him*. A monster who had haunted her dreams, hunted her through the waking world, watching her now through the pallid eyes of some poor murdered child, lips curling in a ten-ton smile.

"The air seemed colder, as if winter had fallen within that grim hall, Dior's breath rolling in white plumes from her lips. We felt him then, this sire of our sire, hammering upon the battlements of the Grail's mind. The air fairly rippled with it, Dior shuddering as he tried to pierce the veil of her thoughts. And though for all his dreadful power, the Forever King's efforts were in vain, still he whispered through that dead child's mouth.

"'*We meet at last, little one . . .*'

"Dior shivered at those words, at the hunger in those eyes, and we could not help but wonder at all this. Daysdeath had been naught but a boon for monsters like Fabién Voss. And if Dior was the secret to *ending* this darkness, why under heaven did he want her alive rather than dead? What could Dior do we had not realized?

"What did *he* know about her that *we* did not?

"Fabién's puppet turned from Dior to Nikita, its smile growing wider.

"'*How fare, my old darling? An age hath it been.*'

"Lilidh glowered, gesturing to the dead marionette. 'Be this the measure of a Priori's worth in a Forever King's eyes? To come afore his throne clad in finery so rotten?'

"'*My dear Contessa.*' The dead boy bowed. '*E'er have I held thy brother in*

— 351 —

deepest esteem, well ye know this. But the miles betwixt us, like the years, sweet Lilidh, run treacherous and deep. And I have my own throne to sit.'

"'Pon no throne sit ye. Nearby must thou be, to ride Dead flesh to our halls.'

"Fabién's marionette chuckled, dragging pale hair from sharp teeth. '*Long years, as I said. E'en the changeless change in time. No idea, hast thou, what now I am capable of.'*

"Nikita bristled. 'We know *exact* what thou art capable of.'

"'*Ah, poor black heart. Still broken? Time mends all wounds, my old darling.'* Fabién's puppet tilted his head and smiled. '*E'en the ones I bestow.'*

"Nikita snarled, snatching up the mighty greatsword behind his throne and bringing it to bear. 'Get thee and thy rabble gone, Fabién. Afore I misplace my Courtesy.'

"'*Always hath ye been quick to passion, Nikita. But thou art in the end no fool. Thou hast made a charnel house of Ossway in thy haste to conquer it. Hungry months lie ahead of thee. And as we both of us know, e'er were ye possess'd of a . . . bottomless thirst.'*

"The smile on the dead thing's lips vanished, its stare boring into Nikita's eyes.

"'*With two thousand head to bolster thy larder, thou couldst spend a comfortable summer here, then press across the Gulf of Wolves come the freeze. Our dear cousin Margot is weak, Nikita. Her bloodlords scattered and squabbling. Thou hast strength enough to claim all the lands of Chastain, as well as Dyvok, as thine own.'*

"Pale eyes met Dior's, lashes gummed with blood.

"'*One girl be not so heavy a prize when weighed 'gainst two thrones.'*

"'Be she worth so little, why dost thou covet her?' Lilidh demanded.

"The puppet still stared at the Grail, eyes cold. '*Because she belongs to me.'*

"'Naught to do then, with the power of her blood?' the Contessa asked. 'The Lion who safeguarded her? The sanguimancer who accompanied her?'

"'*Sanguimancer?'* The puppet shook its head. '*The Faithless are extinguished, Lilidh. I saw to that, centuries past.'*

"The Heartless scoffed. 'Say we refuse thy generosity?'

"The puppet smiled. '*No desire have I for unpleasantness betwixt us, dear Contessa. And be assured; nor do thee. E'en with the new vintage thee and thine art drinking of late.'*

"The puppet's gaze drifted to the golden vial about Nikita's throat, then to Lilidh's eyes, the air fairly crackling between them. Prince growled beside her, the wolf's scarred face twisted as he rose, long fangs bared. And though she kept her expression as stone, Lilidh's eyes glittered with malice, one hand petting the beast's head to calm him.

"The marionette shifted its gaze back to Nikita.

"'*Consider my offer, beloved. My gifts are already en route to Dún Maergenn. I assure thee that the legions traveling with them are simply to safeguard them on the journey. My dearest daughters shall await their arrival and thy reply at the banks of the Órd. In the meantime . . .*'—the deadthing smiled—'*think of me.*'

"Fabién's puppet looked to Dior, the weight of hundreds of years in its gaze.

"'*Soon, child.*'

"The marionette shuddered, bloody lashes fluttering. The bitter chill in the hall receded. And then the Forever King was gone, only that hollow deadboy in his wake.

"'*Priori Dyvok. Lady Lilidh.*' The Terrors curtseyed, brisk and formal. '*Farewell.*'

"With one final glance to Dior, Alba and Aléne marched from the room, taking their cohort with them. Silence hung in their wake, a hundred highbloods now watching Nikita, propping his mighty blade upon one shoulder and meeting his sister's burning gaze.

"'No need hath we for them, brother,' she warned.

"'Need?' Nikita replied. 'No. But use? *That* we may glean.'

"'We can trust them not at all, Priori,' Kane warned.

"'Water-blooded bastards, all,' the Draigann spat. 'Cowards and sheep.'

"'They made short work of Nordlund,' the Wolfmother pointed out. 'And their armies are poised to sweep across the Ranger River and take all Elidaen.' Kiara's green eyes fell on Dior then, cold and hard. 'Two thousand cattle for one mouse seems a fine price to me.'

"'Perhaps we'd not need so many,' Alix muttered, glancing at Nikita, 'were we not so keen to paint the walls with the ones we have.'

"Nikita's eyes narrowed at that, and Alix looked away swift. The Draigann set his lover off his lap, rose to his feet, scowling at Kiara. 'You steal this pup from those dogs simply to hand her back when they bark? So swift to show your belly, cousin?'

"'I *stole* nothing,' Kiara growled, squaring up to her cousin. 'I *claimed* her on the field of battle, where afore me fell the Black Lion of Lorson and those same two Princes of Forever. And if ye've a hunger to know how, step ye forward and I'll gladly give demonstration.'

"Alix sneered. 'Try it, whelp. I'll tear your eyes out through your ars—'

"'*ENOUGH.*'

"Dior flinched, all eyes turning to Lilidh as she spoke. The Contessa sat with hand outstretched, studying her painted claws. 'Ye speak of bartering property thou hast no owning of. This prize belongs to Lilidh, and with Lilidh, it shall remain.'

"'All due respect, great Lady,' Kiara said, 'but Nikita, not Lilidh, is Priori here.'

"'And Lilidh is eldest,' the Draigann growled. 'Respect is owed for that, cousin.'

"'Respect, aye,' Soraya said. 'Yet obedience is paid not to the eldest, but the *greatest*. And Nikita is that. Who here in this court dares claim otherwise?'

"None spoke aloud, but many muttered, the length and breadth of that bloody hall. Lilidh glowered at her nieces, and looking around those whispering fiends, their dagger eyes and cutthroat smiles, Dior could only shudder at the sudden menace in the air.

"Nikita turned to his sister. 'Kept we this child because she hath value to the Voss. If that value be now measured in such a wealth of blood, should we not trade it?'

"Lilidh's face was stone, but in her gaze burned a terrible rage. 'Should we not *stop* first, brother, and consider why thy Fabién weighs her so heavy?'

"Nikita's eyes narrowed slightly. 'He be not *my* Fabién, Lilidh.'

"'Once, though. And wouldst thou not have it so again? Or art thou simply so accustomed to kneeling afore him, thou wouldst do so again to stand as equal beside him?'

"Every lady around Dior took one step back, trembling. And though he kept his voice steady, as Nikita turned to his court, we saw the fury in his eyes.

"'*OUT.*'

"The serving staff fled the hall, abandoning those poor fools still strung from the chandeliers. The vampires followed, those loyal to Nikita first, Aaron and Kiara among them. Others moved slower, the Draigann and Alix looking to Lilidh for approval before retiring. Yet the Contessa's mortal thralls remained—no small count of soldiers, her ladies trembling yet loyal, Worm on her belly before her throne, Prince on his haunches beside it.

"Dior stood still among it all, head bowed, heart pounding like a hammer.

"When they were alone but for Lilidh's servants, the Priori turned on his sister. His voice was graveled with anger, one marbled fist at rest upon his blade.

"'Ye o'erstep, Lilidh.'

"'Ye step blind, Nikita.'

"'I see *all*. Perhaps what ye do not. Thou art no warrior, and hath never been. E'en with our weapon, should Fabién strike at us, victory shall be purchased dear.'

"'No warrior, Lilidh, aye,' the Contessa nodded. 'But who was it that *gave* thee thy weapon, brother? Through Lilidh's design, thou hast conquered this wretched sty in but two years, where before, we languished *fifteen* in quagmire.'

"'Ye speak truth,' Nikita said. 'And ye *know* I am grateful. But why court conflict when Fabién offers advantage? We can *use* them, Lilidh.'

"'*Use* them?' she cried. 'He uses *thee*! Why think ye Voss offers us this feast?' Worm grunted as the Contessa stepped down off her throne, stabbing a claw at Dior. 'Because *she* is worth *more* than twenty hundred slit throats, Nikita!'

"'Then tell me *how*!'

"Dior flinched as the Blackheart rolled his massive blade off his shoulder and stabbed it into the floor, shattering the stone as he shouted.

"'What use this gormless slip to us? To dress as yet another doll? To primp thy hair and drape thy flesh and wait 'pon thee as fifth, where *four* will not suffice? Her blood may heal the ill, and so? One *mouthful* from either of us can mend the same!'

"'I know not *how*!' Lilidh snapped. 'But one more drop to her lips, and all her secrets are mine to plunder! The Esani bloodwitch who followed her did not do so out of charity! The Black Lion did not *die* defending her on a whim! I shall find her worth. *Patience*, brother!'

"'And if our bloodlords be not so? Already they quibble! *Ever* they scheme! Should Fabién bring his host to bear, how soon before our court weigh this brat's life worth less than their forevers? And who shall stand 'gainst the Terrors if they quail? *Thee*?' Nikita scoffed, cruel and cold. 'In seven centuries, thou hast spent not one *night* 'pon the field of battle. While use they doubtless have, neither thy tongue nor quim can assuage the Forever King.'

"Lilidh actually flinched at that, as if Nikita had struck her. With a snarl, she snatched up his sword from the splintered stone. It was almost half again her height, God knows how many times her weight. Yet Lilidh flung the weapon as if it were a twig. It flew across the room, and Dior gasped as it sheared through a bundle of those poor, dangling prisoners, bursting them like overfull waterskins. Gore sprayed, bright and thick, but Nikita's sword flew on, smashing one of the great pillars to splinters before crashing through the wall.

"'No warrior I be,' Lilidh hissed. 'But a *kingdom* have I yet brung thee with those gifts so swift dismissed. And though my swordarm be not so mighty, my heart hath twice the measure of thine own, Nikita. Three hundred years gone, and still, thou wouldst forgive all if Fabién did but *beckon* thee. Be ye so content on hand and knee? Wouldst thou borrow my ladies' dresses when next he asks thee to spread thy—'

"She got no further, her brother seizing her throat. As one, Lilidh's maids cried out as the Contessa was hauled into the air and smashed down into the floor so violently, the whole room shuddered. A deafening *boom* cracked the windows around the hall, and Prince rose to his feet, fangs bared, hackles up. But as the great wolf gathered himself for a spring, Nikita's voice Whipped the air, echoing on trembling walls.

"'*STOP.*'

"The beast stilled itself, ears pressed back, its pale blue eye glittering like sapphire. Through the settling dust, we saw Nikita looming over Lilidh now, hand on her neck.

"'Thou art my sister and mine elder,' he growled. 'But speak *ever* so to me again and thou shalt taste a reckoning undreamed.'

"Lilidh seized hold of his wrist as she glowered up at him.

"'Lay *hand* 'pon me again and thou shalt taste that reckoning doubled. Think ye thou shalt defend this city without the Draigann's fleet? Without Grey's or Alix's foulbloods? Without that prize dangling about thy throat? *All* this have I given thee.'

"Through the tumbling dust, the Heartless glowered up at her brother, squeezing the hand at her throat. She was *strong*, God, strong as the bones of the earth, and older than he besides. In nights before the death of days— nights where subterfuge and guile were worth a thousand times the weight of swords, she'd have been his match. No, his *queen*. But these were nights of war. Nights of chaos and conquest, where the blade cut sharper than the tongue, and deeds spoke louder than words."

Deep beneath the belly of Sul Adair, the Last Liathe sighed.

"What a thing, to pity such a monster. And yet I did."

"And Dior?" Jean-François asked. "Did she too look with pity upon her mistress?"

"She looked with dread," Celene replied. "She must have known there would be a price to pay for this humiliation. Nikita released his grip, and Lilidh's ladies rushed to help their mistress. But the Heartless snarled as they touched her, and the swans slunk back, anguished—aching to help the one they adored, yet terrified of her wrath.

"Nikita stabbed one claw at Dior. 'Find ye her worth, sister. And pray it be more than what we risk for her keeping. If it be not, Night help thee both.'

"And without another word, he stalked from the room.

"Lilidh rose from the rubble, gown dusted in powdered stone. Prince slunk forward, the wolf's eye fixed on the door Nikita had left by, licking Lilidh's hand and whining. The Contessa brushed stone splinters from her hair, dragging off her broken crown. A lesser vampire might have done *any-thing* in that moment—flown into a rage, painted the walls, torn everyone and everything in that room apart. But Lilidh Dyvok did not lose control.

"She *inflicted* it.

"'Come here, poppet.'

"She did not use the Whip, relying upon fear and the blood already at work in the girl's veins. But we knew she was strong, Dior Lachance, full of fire, and there was still some foolish part of us that expected her to fight. To spit. To defy as once she would have.

"Instead, there was but a second's hesitation.

"And then, Dior obeyed.

"Lilidh drew a now-familiar dagger from her bodice. And with her ladies watching like hawks, the Contessa slipped an arm about Dior's waist, lifted the knife between them, and ran her tongue up the blade, slicing it open.

"Lilidh licked her lips, slow, sumptuous, slicking them sticky red.

"'Drink,' she breathed.

"Again, no Whip, no command, save for the blood twice tied between them. And again, wings beating frantic on her skin, we burned with hope the girl might resist. The minds of countless mortals had been overthrown by that blood, but Dior Lachance was the Holy Grail of San Michon, heir to the Prince of Heaven.

"*Surely she'd not obey?*

"But slipping arms around Lilidh's shoulders, Dior pressed her lips to the vampire's, as if to a cup of finest wine. The Heartless opened her mouth, Dior sighed, tongues flickering like candleflames. Lilidh ran a hand up Dior's throat, clawed fingers slipping into her hair, and the Grail gasped as she was drawn closer, a drop of Lilidh's blood spilling down her knife to spatter on the floor; shattered like my heart to bear witness to that dreadful kiss.

"All was lost now. All hope was gone. The fate of every soul under heaven slaved to the eldest Dyvok outside of hell. All we had told her about Mother Maryn would be made known, any chance of unearthing her lost. And more, Dior would surely tell Lilidh about *us*—that we lurked outside the city, a Liathe of the hated Esani, wounded and frail. Should we flee now, we wondered? Abandon Dior as lost? Or should we throw ourselves onto this fire, simply so I might beg, '*At least I tried*,' when I faced my Maker on the Day of Judging?

"'Damn you, Celene Castia,' we hissed.

"'Damn you to hell.'

"Lilidh pulled back slow from Dior's embrace, the Grail moaning disappointment, lunging forward to suckle on the Contessa's tongue one last moment. Dior's eyes were glazed with passion as she gazed at her mistress, licking the blood from her lips.

"'. . . I *love* you,' she breathed.

"The Contessa smiled, triumphant.

"'Do not love me, mortal. Adore me.'

"The swans flocked to Dior's side, giddy, like bridesmaids at a wedding feast. The redheaded sisters embraced her, whispering felicitations, and with a bloodstained smile, Dior hugged them back, eyes shining to know such a perfect, awful love. Prince watched on, the wolf's ears pressed back to his skull, tail between his legs. Worm remained on her belly, silent, eyes glittering in the aftermath of that terrible communion.

"'You belong to Lilidh now, Dior Lachance,' the dame with the scarred chin declared.

"'Not Fabién,' the redheaded maid whispered.

"'Nor Alba or Aléne,' her sister smiled.

"'I am *yours*, Mistress,' Dior vowed.

"'Mine.' Lilidh looked the Grail over, lips pursed. 'But almost not. Ye flew thy cage yestereve, pretty poppet. Thy lock undone as if 'twere smoke.'

"Dior sank to her knees immediately, hands clasped before her. 'Forgive me, I—'

"Lilidh waved a hand, irritated. 'The fault lies not with thee.'

"As Dior bowed her head and whispered thanks, Lilidh withdrew a familiar sliver of metal from her bodice. It gleamed in her fingers, iron hard and dagger thin.

"Worm blanched as the Contessa tossed the hairpin onto the stone before her.

"'Again, ye fail me.'

"The serving girl breathed swift, mismatched eyes welling with an awful fear. 'Forgive me, Mistress, I was in haste after Laerd Nikita—'

"'*SPEAK NOT HIS NAME!*'

"Lilidh's scream was an awful thing, the walls shaking with her fury.

"'I'm sorry, Mistress,' Worm whispered, brow to the stone. '*Please* . . .'

"Lilidh stalked toward the prostrate girl, and Worm began to beg, voice rising with every step closer. 'Oh, please, no, please please*please* . . .'

"The Contessa seized a fistful of strawberry blond, and Worm shrieked, hauled to her knees. Lilidh gazed into the girl's eyes, emerald green and ocean blue. The pity I had felt for Lilidh was gone now, and where but a moment ago, she had been at her brother's mercy, now this poor girl was at hers. Such is the way of things, we suppose. Those hurt will hurt in kind. Cruelty is an infection, spread from one victim to the next; an avalanche rolling ever downhill and crashing worst upon those at the bottom of the pile.

"'Not again,' Worm sobbed. 'I *love* you. Please don't hurt me agai—'

"'Hushhhh,' Lilidh whispered.

"The vampire caressed the girl's cheek, soft as silk, brushing the tears away.

"'Hush, now, little faeling. I shall punish thee not.'

"'Thank you, oh, God, than—'

"'They shall.'

"Worm sucked in one trembling breath, looking now to Lilidh's ladies. The three women stood in a half circle, faces gone pale as their mistress spoke.

"'*Ye* shall,' she commanded them. 'And if *ever* the names of those Voss usurpers slip thy lips in my presence again, I shall gift thee twice the lesson, test me not.'

"The Contessa let Worm collapse to the floor.

"'Now punish her.'

"Without hesitation, without pity, the ladies obeyed. With gorgeous velvet heels and heavy bejeweled hands, those beautiful swans descended on the maidservant like vultures to a corpse, kicking, hitting, spitting. Worm could only curl into a ball, wailing, arms up to protect her head as they struck her, over and over again. Dior watched, her face death white, but mute as stone. And looking into her eyes, Lilidh spoke.

"'Thee also, Dior Lachance. *Punish* her.'

"This was the last of it. The final flame of hope inside us. It surged briefly—one moment where we thought we saw her tremble. But in a heartbeat, it was gone, Dior taking her place among the swans. And she kicked that poor maid. Again. And again. The sounds were wet, tearing, Worm's wails drowned beneath. And though to watch was all we could do, *I* could watch *this* no longer, taking wing and fleeing into the dark. Away from that sobbing maid, that girl I had failed so terribly. I thought I could protect her, I had meant all for the best, but now, I wondered if God were punishing me for what I had done.

"He had already chosen a guardian for his Grail, after all.

"And in my hubris and my hate, I had let him fall.

"Outside the dún in the bitter storm, hidden in a copse of trees long dead, something stirred. Scarecrow thin. Urchin ragged. She'd once been clad in a fine red greatcoat, a porcelain mask at her face. But she wore a dead man's clothes now, filched from a graveyard in a frozen hamlet, her face wrapped in scraps of dirty cloth. Her skin was cracked and dusty, like a river parched beneath the long-lost sun, and her voice was a croak, a whisper, thrown to the raging sky with no hope of answer at all.

"'Gabriel,' I whispered. 'Oh, God, where are you?'"

XV

OR ELSE BY NONE

"AH, VANITY. WHAT fools you make of your favorites."

The Marquis Jean-François of the Blood Chastain dipped his quill, chuckling to himself. He was finishing an illustration of Dior falling into the doom of Lilidh's arms, but he glanced up at the Last Liathe now, slender hands crossed at her lap, head hung low.

"You and your brother make quite the pair, Mlle Castia. I begin to see why you loathe him. For a creature who casts no reflection, you certainly do hate looking at yourself."

"I care as little for your critiques as for your flattery, sinner."

"Forgive me. But your conduct sometimes begs the former, nonetheless."

Celene sighed, looking up to the ceiling and blinking hard.

"It is only through falling that we teach ourselves to fly. Our measure be not in how many times we stumble, but how oft we rise. Failure is how we learn."

"Then you must have learned a great deal at Dún Maergenn, mademoiselle."

"Go to hell."

Jean-François laughed then. "I was under impression I was already there. Is that not what you Esani believe? That we all languish in purgatory, and that only you and your merry cult of cannibals could save us from ourselves?" The historian scoffed, lifting his crystal goblet and draining the last of the blood within. "God Almighty, I thought your brother's ego intolerable. At least he marries it with a sense of humor, puerile though it be."

"Perhaps you should keep him company for a time, then," the Liathe whispered. "We grow weary of your presence, Chastain. And your judgment."

"A pity, then, that decision is not yours to make. My Empress shall have her tale, and *you* shall have the pleasure of my presence *and* my judgment for so long as I wish it."

Jean-François glowered a moment before returning to his sketch. "Forget not who holds the leash here, whelp."

Celene lifted her gaze to Jean-François then, across the rushing river keeping her at bay. She would have been almost lost in shadow to a mortal's eyes, the dark staved off only by the globe on the historian's small table. That glow danced upon the river's surface, a million tiny points of light refracting on the water, his now-empty goblet of blood, the eyes of the thing watching him. She was leaning forward again, gazing at him through the veil of her lashes.

"Do you remember what it was like to die, Chastain?"

"Threats?" The historian tutted. "I thought we were past that, my dear."

"No threat. Curiosity." She tilted her head, a smile in her eyes. "Indulge us."

Jean-François matched those smiling eyes with his own. "I remember. Most vividly."

"Did you sigh when Margot killed you? Or did you scream?"

"Forgive me, Mlle Castia. But as I am constantly reminding your brother, we are not here to share my history. My mother is well aware of the details of my creation, after all."

"We think you died between the sheets." Celene stretched one hand out before her, weaving pale fingers in the air. "We think Margot was gentle with you."

"Indeed?" The historian arched a brow. "And what makes you say so?"

"You call her *Mother*. It's rather telling. And rather vile."

The monster's voice was cold, fingers stretching toward the goblet beside him. The historian heard it rattle, saw the congealed dregs trembling violently, as if the earth were quaking. He had time to draw breath before the glass shattered, glittering shards of crystal spraying the air. Droplets of blood spattered his coat, the illustration he had been finishing, and the shrapnel cracked the chymical globe on the table, plunging the room into darkness.

Jean-François was on his feet, claws unfurled, moving so swift he was almost a blur. He could see nothing; the cell pitch-black around him, the song of rushing water in his ears. But he heard a tiny sound beneath it, soft as a feather on the stone right beside him, mind suddenly filled with the image of that *thing* lunging out of the dark, no silver cage at her mouth, but teeth and hunger and hell awaiting.

"*Capitaine!*"

The door at his back *clunk*ed and swung open swift. Capitaine Delphine and his thrallswords flooded into the cell, their torches and blades raised, their eyes wide. It was only after their flickering light spilled across the stone at his feet that the historian realized the source of that feather-soft sound.

His quill, fallen from the pages of his bloodied tome.

"You are right to fear us, Marquis."

The Last Liathe's whisper echoed in the gloom, and Jean-François's dead heart flooded with relief as he realized her voice came yet from across the river.

"But you are a *fool* to mock us."

He saw her crouched on the far bank, watching like hawk to field mouse.

"Your histories named us *Faithless*," she hissed. "But we were far from that. And you are unworthy to judge us. Our cause was righteous. Our conviction so deep it shook the world of men to its foundations, and brought the world of the kith to its knees. Esan*a*, not Esan*i*. Faith*ful*, not Faith*less*. We were the reason elders cowered in their dens, frightened of shadows. We were the *reason* those monsters feared the dark."

"I warned you," the historian spat. "I *told* you what would happen if you tes—"

"And *we* warned *you*, sinner. All along. And still you do not *hear*."

The thrallswords were gathered at Jean-François's back, blazing torches held high. The Last Liathe glowered at those flames, dead eyes agleam as she spoke.

> "*From holy cup comes holy light;*
> "*The faithful hand sets world aright.*
> "*And in the Seven Martyrs' sight,*
> "*Mere man shall end this endless night.*"

The historian sneered. "I know the words to your so-called prophecy, madem—"

> "*Before the Five, come unto one,*
> "*With sainted blade, 'neath virgin sun,*
> "*By sacred blood, or else by none;*
> "*This blackened veil shall be undone.*"

Jean-François blinked, the silence a thousand years wide.

"...What did you say?" he whispered.

"Enough for now," Celene replied.

"You forget your place, mademoiselle," the historian snapped, jerking his lapels straight. "It is down here, in the dark, completely at my mercy. I say when you feed. I say when you suffer. And *I* say when it is *enough*."

Celene climbed to her feet, lithe and soundless, drifting toward the far-flung corner of her cell. She paused on the cusp of the torchlight to look at him over her shoulder; a silhouette against a deeper darkness. A shadow returned home.

"You should talk to my brother, Marquis," she said. "Though we have no doubts as to how keenly you will miss the joys of our company, we might both benefit from some time apart, oui? Absence does make the heart grow fonder, they say. And besides, the next piece of our tale will make little sense without his."

The historian glared at the monster's back, his tome heavy in his hand. His fright was gone now, replaced by cold fury, his need to see this thing suffer wrestling with his desire to get the hell out of this pit for a spell. In the end, the latter impulse won, the historian nodding brisk to Capitaine Delphine and his men. The thrallswords backed out of the room slow, eyes never leaving the thing across the river. But in a show of what he hoped would look like disdain, Jean-François turned his back on it, stalking from the room.

"Marquis?"

He stopped at her voice, but did not deign to turn. "Oui?"

The Last Liathe sighed, looking down at her empty hands.

"Give my love to Gabriel."

BOOK FOUR

THIS
BLIGHTED
BLOOD

I war with my sister, until,
We war with our kinfolk, until,
We war with the Highlands, until,
We war with the world.

—A SONG OF THE MOONSTHRONE

I

HELL DIVINE

A THOUSAND TONS rested in the palm of his tattooed hand.

At least, so it seemed to Gabriel. The bell was small, embossed with wolves and wrought of solid gold, though it weighed far more than its weighing. He'd been holding it for an hour now, staring at it for at least two more before he dared to pick it up. He'd paced the length of his cell a thousand times, pausing to stare out the window toward distant mountains and distant days, that golden bell muted in his palm and the certainty of what would happen if he let it sing weighing on his mind.

"Ring if you've an itch, de León. Someone will be along to scratch it."

The ache was in his bones now. Burning ice in his veins, cold fire under his skin. Unable to sit still. Unable to think clear. Sick and hurt and hollow. They'd let him smoke if he asked, but he knew he might not have the strength to settle for a mere pipe anymore. It had been too long, Mothermaid, *how* long . . . closing his eyes against the memory; the taste of her, the *feel* of her, slipping down his throat like molten flame and burning all of it away. That voice in his head, growing louder every year, every night, every mouthful, red, oh, God, *red*.

You pay the beast his due, or he takes his due from you.

"I can't," he whispered, sinking into his chair.

You must, it replied.

"I won't," he breathed.

Laughter, echoing on the walls and in his head.

You will. In the end, I always win, Gabriel.

The bell's song was bright, brief, but it was scarce moments before he heard the lock click in his door, heavy bolts sliding free. He looked up to find her watching him, tight lace choker and locks of blood-red hair framing the pale promise of her throat. Meline cast a careful glance around the room before entering, closing the door behind, hate etched in the pale blue of her eyes as she raised one brow.

"Your desire, Chevalier?"

"I'm thirsty," he whispered.

"As it please you." Stepping closer, the thrall bent to fetch his bottle and goblet, both dust-dry. "More Monét?"

His hand reached out to hers, stilling her with his lightest touch.

"I fear . . . I am not thirsty for wine, madame."

He watched her skin prickle at those words, at the caress he ran over the smooth thudding arc of her wrist. Meline met his eyes, lips parted, breath quickened. She shrank back as Gabriel rose to his feet, leathers creaking, his shadow swallowing her whole.

"A pipe, then?" She swallowed. "I could . . ."

Her voice faded as Gabriel shook his head, taking one step closer.

Meline did not step away. Meeting his eyes as she lifted her chin, wetting dry lips with her tongue. Though her hands shook as she loosed her choker of dark lace and jewels, she moved swiftly, as if she could not get it off her neck fast enough.

"If you must," she breathed. "Take what you will."

His heart raged at those words, every inch of him afire. This woman hated him, that was plain. Gabriel had hurt her beloved master, after all. But the Last Silversaint hated all that he needed too; that did nothing to lessen his *need* of it. And as he traced one sharp fingernail down the smooth line of her jugular, he saw how swift Meline's breast rose and fell above the bounds of her bodice, how her pupils widened so far her irises near vanished. Though she despised him, still he saw it carved in her every line and curve.

The same hateful Want he had of her.

"Say please, madame."

Meline met his eyes, biting her lip lest her tongue betray her. Her hand slipped down to his leathers, stroking the hardness she found there, toying with his belt buckle.

But she said not a word.

Gabriel laced one hand through her plaited hair, fingers closing to a fist, and Meline turned her head, baring her long, slender neck. He dipped his mouth toward her submission, lips brushing her skin as he growled, low and deep in his chest.

"Say . . ."

His tongue flickered against her vein, teeth brushing ever so light across her skin.

". . . *please*."

"Godssakes, Meline, give the dog his bone, will you?"

The pair snapped apart; Meline with a gasp, Gabriel with a snarl. Jean-François was sat in his leather armchair, a sly grin on his face, chocolat eyes sparkling in delight. Gabriel hadn't even heard the Marquis enter the room, but there he was, sketching in his damnable book. Meline bowed her head, stammering.

"Forgive m-me, Master, I—"

"Nono," the historian chuckled, giving a magnanimous wave. "By all means, continue. I love a good show after dinner."

Gabriel glowered, furious and ashamed. Dragging his knuckles across his lips, he willed his heart be still, his thirst and anger down, down into his boots, sparing Meline one starving glance before sinking into his chair with gritted fangs.

"No?" Jean-François glanced back and forth between the pair. "I don't mind, I assure you. I'd rather enjoy it, in fact. A dash of debauchery would make pleasant change from the hours of sanctimonious puritanism I've just had to endure, believe me."

Gabriel met Jean-François's eyes. "Celene."

"Last of the Liathe." The Marquis wiggled his brows. "She sends kisses, by the way."

"She actually spoke to you?"

"*Preached* at me would be a more accurate summation. But oui, we conversed."

Gabriel drew one steadying breath, trying to ignore the perfume of Meline's want. "You can't believe a word she says. That *thing* breathes lies like I breathe smoke."

"Speaking of, would you like some? If you're not willing to put yourself out of your misery in Meline, at least have a pipe, de León. The hour is late and we've much to discuss."

The Marquis snapped his fingers, and the door opened wide. Gabriel saw that same Nordish lad who'd bathed him earlier tonight, standing on the threshold with a golden platter; a bottle of Monét, a pipe of bone, and a burning lantern with a tall glass chimney. The lad stepped into the room, long black hair tumbling forward as he bowed low, casting one terrified glance toward Meline before his adoring eyes fell on his master.

"On the table, Mario, there's a love."

"Fuckssakes," Gabriel growled. "His name is *Dario*, vampire. Even I know that."

"Ah, oui, Dario." Jean-François kissed his fingertips, touched the lad's lips as he put down his tray. "Forgive me, beloved."

"Of course, Master," Dario breathed, dark gaze shining.

Meline had recovered her composure now, glowering at the other thrall as he set the lantern on the table. Jean-François fetched a phial of sanctus from his frockcoat, and, eyes narrowed against the lantern flame, he tossed it to Gabriel. The Silversaint snatched it in one hand, pipe already in the other. His thirst roared as he filled the bowl, screamed as he raised it to the lantern's chimney; that divine alchemy, that dark chymistrie melting blood to bliss. He could still smell Meline's desire above that thread of smoke, knowing how easy it would be to take what he wanted—God, what they *all* wanted—to hurl pretense aside and bury himself deep, soaring into a burning heaven and down to a flaming hell.

God, he missed it so badly he could *taste* it . . .

Instead, he breathed the sacrament in, warmth flooding into every tingling fingertip. He held it inside his lungs, eyes closed, smoke drifting from his nostrils as he finally exhaled, red and heady into the cold air. The thirst slunk back into the dark where it dwelled, but even the bliss he felt in that moment was soured by the knowledge it must return, intent to rule him. Ever patient. Ever watchful. That hole inside never quite filled.

To hate the thing that is completing you.

To love the thing that is destroying you.

What perfect suffering.

What hell divine.

"Better?"

Gabriel opened his eyes, blood-red, pin-bright, fixed on the monster opposite.

"Much," he snarled. "Merci."

"Are you certain you wish Meline and Dario to leave?" The historian waved his quill at the straining buttons on the Silversaint's britches. "That looks uncomfortable, de León. And honestly, it's rather distracting. I can wait outside and pretend not to listen if you're shy of an audience."

"Fuck off, vampire."

"Off you go, then, loves," Jean-François sighed. "We shall call if we've a need."

The historian brushed his quill along his maddening smirk.

"Or two."

Young Dario gathered lantern and pipe, set the new bottle of Monét on the table. Meline took up the empties, and with a deep curtsey, followed the lad from the room. As the woman turned to lock them in, her eyes met Gabriel's, dark and smoldering. Then the door shut, the lock clicked, hunter and prey alone once more.

"She's delicious, de León. And *quite* mad." Jean-François dipped his quill, turning to a fresh page. "You really should give her a roll, the occasional hate fuck is good for the soul."

"And what would you know about souls, Chastain?"

"Only that they appear to be an inconvenience at the best of times. And that many of us seem to get along perfectly well without them."

Gabriel chuckled at that, despite himself, filling his goblet with wine from the new bottle. Lifting his cup to the coldblood, he found the vampire smiling at him fondly.

"Santé, Silversaint."

"Morté, coldblood."

Gabriel could feel the vampire watching him as he tipped back his head and swallowed. Again Jean-François ran his quill over ruby lips, slow and soft.

"So," Gabriel sighed, refilling his cup. "What lies did my sister tell you?"

"I'm rather more interested in the lies *you* have in store."

"Did she talk about the Blackheart?" he demanded. "The faeling? Did she tell you of the colossal swamp of shite her idiocy landed Dior in, and what Dior had to—"

"It matters not," Jean-François sighed, raising a hand to stop the tirade. "Ignorance is a chasm, and knowledge is the bridge. You said after you fell in the battle of Cairnh—"

"After Celene *dropped* me."

"After you and gravity . . . had your little chat, that it was some time before you saw the Grail again. I would like to know what happened in the interim."

"What difference does it make? Margot wants Dior's story, not mine."

"There is no truth without context, de León. We have time. And meanwhile, your beloved sister is as uncomfortable as I can make her."

The historian met the silversaint's eyes, quill poised.

"So. You had fought to defend the Grail at Cairnhaem. But you ended up taking a rather long flight off a rather short bridge. What came next?"

Gabriel ran one hand along his jaw, leaned back in his chair with a creak.

"I fell." He shrugged. "A *long* fucking way. The wind was screaming, and so was I, thunder above as I tumbled below. I've no idea how far I plummeted. Farther than before or since, I know that. Eventually, I hit something that broke beneath me, crashing into fresh snow and rolling down in a bleeding, broken tumble. And then, darkness."

"Were you injured?"

"I *should've* died."

"Alone at the roof of the world. No horse. No sword. No supplies. I know palebloods perish with reluctance, but it sounds a divine miracle you survived at all, de León."

"Divine?"

Gabriel scoffed, taking a long gulp of wine.

"Believe me, coldblood. God had *nothing* to do with it."

A SONG OF SCARS

" 'BREATHE.'

"That was the first word I heard, somewhere dark and distant. Swimming up through bloodstained murk toward a point of light, a thousand fathoms above. All I felt was pain, no knowing where it ended and I began, barely enough in me to . . .

"'Breathe.'

"Red smoke. On my lips and in my lungs. It was harsh, burned halfway to bitter, and though I needed it more than words could say, I couldn't hold it in, gasping in agony as I rolled onto my belly and hacked blood into my hands.

"'*Breathe.*'

"'Stop f-fucking saying that,' I managed. 'It's n-not helping.'

"'Bollocks to ye an' all, then,' someone spat. 'Light yer own smoke, ye surly shite.'

"My pipe was tossed onto the stone before me. I coughed, opening one swollen eye, squinting at the blurry figure crouched over me. Freckled, tattooed skin. A collar of everknots bound about her throat. Flame-red curls tumbling over her scarred face, and, by the look of it, maybe forty yards of silk and tulle and Elidaeni lace covering her body.

"'What in God's n-name are you w-wearing?' I whispered.

"'The only other clothes in yer saddlebags,' Phoebe scowled. 'An' might I add, *very* sensible choice of attire, ye fuckin' cockwombler.'

"I looked around, saw we were in the depths of a mountain cave. Black stone and old ice, the stale musk of wolf. Outside, a fierce storm was raging, but a blessedly warm fire burned nearby, a pair of gore-soaked saddlebags beside it. My body was caked in clotted blood, broken in a dozen places. But

I was clad in my tunic, the greatcoat from Jènoah's lair; blood-red velvet, midnight-black trim. And Phoebe á Dúnnsair was wearing a dress.

"But not just a dress. A *ballgown;* shoulderless and wasp-waisted, mantled with fox fur. The fabric was a brilliant emerald to offset the flame of the duskdancer's hair, hugging her body to the hips, then spilling into a waterfall of skirts below. In the salons of Augustin, it'd not have turned heads so much as snapped necks, but in the frozen wilds of the Nightstone . . .

"'You l-look ridiculous,' I rasped.

"'Whose fault is that?' she demanded, hands on hips. 'It was in *yer* bag, ye twat!'

"'I didn't p-put it there, Kitcat. Dior p-packed it f—'

"My heart stilled. Kiara. The Terrors. The battle on the bridge . . .

"'*Dior.*'

"I pushed myself up, managing to reach my knees. Blood drooled from my lips, my left leg bent entirely in the wrong direction, but I clutched the wall and tried to rise.

"Phoebe pressed on my shoulders. 'Siddown, ye bloody fool.'

"'Get your damned hands off m-me.'

"'Take hold of yer ti—AAAAAAA!' The duskdancer jerked away, a whirl of emerald silk and burning curls. 'Watch the *silver,* ye bucktoothed gobshite!'

"I saw a bloody red welt in the shape of the sevenstar on her upper arm. Glancing to my palm, I realized I'd scorched her where we'd touched; the silver on me a burning brand to her. Coughing more blood, I slithered down the wall, struggling simply to breathe.

"'Apologies,' I wheezed. 'Y-you aright?'

"'Should've left ye in the damned snow, ye moonsstruck, cackwitted . . .' Phoebe stalked around the fire clutching her arm, mumbling a string of blasphemy so vile you could have dressed it in a red robe and called it a cardinal.

"'Why didn't you?' I asked.

"'Eh?'

"'Why didn't you leave m-me in the damned snow?'

"'Sweet Mothermoons, ye've got some talls on ye,' she spat. 'I think the words yer searchin' for are "Merci, m'lady, for savin' my sorry arse."'

"'What happened to Dior?'

"Phoebe sighed, curls tumbling over her face as she hung her head. 'Nae clue.'

"'Then I'll ask again,' I growled, temper rising. 'Why did you waste time saving me when you should be chasing *her*? Best-case scenario, my traitor sister has her in her claws. Worst case, she's in the hands of the fucking Dyvok!'

"'Ye think I dinnae ken that? I swore on my heartsblood to keep that girl safe!' The duskdancer stormed toward me, tossing her hair from her face. 'But in case ye weren't payin' attention, that leech put her boot so far up my cunny I can still taste the leather, so excuse me if I thought to bring help when I next step to!'

"'Phoebe,' I whispered, mouth agape. 'Seven Martyrs, your *eyes* . . .'

"She blinked, temper fading. 'What about them?'

"Looking to the scabbard at my belt, my heart sank as I remembered Ash-drinker was gone—smashed from Dior's hand by Kiara on the bridge. But reaching into my boot, I fished out my straight razor, unfolding the blade so Phoebe could see her reflection in the steel.

"'Oh, Mothermoons . . .' she whispered, hand rising to her face.

"The duskdancer's eyes were . . . changed. Where once they'd been emerald green, now they gleamed gold, the whites vanished entirely. No longer a woman's eyes, I realized, but those of a lioness. Like the talons at her fingertips. Like the shadow at her feet.

"'Shite,' Phoebe hissed, gazing at her reflection. 'Green suited me too.'

"I frowned, unsure at her expression. 'I was taught the more a duskdancer wears the shape of her beast, the deeper the beast marks her. Isn't this . . . a sort of normal for you?'

"Phoebe sighed, still staring at the blade. 'Before the death of days? It would've taken a *thousand* dances for me to be as changed as I am. But these nights?'

"The duskdancer handed back my razor, knelt by the fire in silence. With a wince, I sank down beside her, watching the flames dancing in that strange new gold.

"'What about these nights?' I urged.

"Phoebe looked at me sidelong, debating whether or not to reply. We'd both fought and bled beside each other to defend Dior, and battle makes the strangest bedfellows. But still, I was a silversaint; she, a duskdancer. We weren't exactly the closest of confidants.

"'We wealdlings are born of Moons and Mountains,' she finally sighed. 'Once, we were blessed by both. But since the death of days, our Mothermoons have been hid by the veil across the sky. Our Earth Father rots in the grip of the Blight, and his corruption infects our veins. The beast burns brighter inside us these nights. Every change twists us further, faster. And every time I dance the wealdshape, I know not what I'll become after.'

"'You mentioned this to Dior,' I murmured. '*The Time of Blighted Blood*.'

"She nodded. 'Now ye see why I journeyed with the Flower six months an' never danced once. *Now* ye see what the Godling means to my kind. An end to this endless dark. To restore the harmony among Earth and Sky, and our blighted blood between.'

"I sighed, unsure what to say at this revelation. But my temper had quelled at least, and I spared a moment to take stock of where we were. Last I remembered was tumbling off the Cairnhaem bridge—I'd no idea how I'd even got here. The pain in my body had dimmed thanks to the sacrament, but my boot was tattered and torn, the ankle beyond likesame.

"*Teeth marks,* I realized.

"I guessed the tale at last; Phoebe must've found me in her wealdshape, dragged me to safety in her jaws. Danced into human form come the dusk, then gone out into the snow wearing nothing but that bloody ballgown, gathering wood for a fire, the gear off my dead horse, clothes for my back. Paleblood or no, I'd have frozen to death without this woman. Her efforts were doubly courageous, given the price she paid to shift her shape.

"And here I was, chewing on her about it.

"'You know, you're right,' I murmured, dragging back a frost-caked lock of bloody hair. 'I *do* have some balls on me. Merci, Mlle Phoebe. For saving my sorry arse.'

"The duskdancer tossed a red curl from her face, breathing deep. 'S'aright.'

"'Your eyes . . .' I coughed, wincing. 'Gold suits you more than green.'

"'Stick yer chivalry where the sun don't shine.'

"'The sun doesn't shine anywhere anymore.'

"'Then stick it anywhere ye like.'

"We both chuckled, shadows retreating a little in that crackling firelight.

"'Sunshine aside, I *am* grateful,' I told her. 'Truly. I owe you my life.'

"'Nae bother.' Phoebe shrugged as if throwing off a cold, damp cloak. 'Moons only know why, but the Flower's fond of ye. She'd be vexed if I let ye perish.'

"'Not so sure of that anymore.'

"'Eh?'

"I scowled at my hand, remembering the awful sound of that slap. 'I acted . . . harsh to Dior before the battle. Did things I should've never done. Unforgivable things.'

"The duskdancer only stared. I shook my head, almost too ashamed to speak my sin.

"'I raised my hand to her. In anger. I *hit* her, Phoebe.'

"She shrugged. 'My ma gave me a whippin' or two when I was—'

"'You don't understand. My stepfather beat the shit out of me when I was a boy. Thrashed me so hard I couldn't walk some nights. I vowed I'd *never* do the same.'

"Phoebe watched across the fire with new, glittering eyes. 'Then why did ye?'

"'I don't *know*,' I hissed. 'I was . . . angry. Angrier than I've ever been in my life, but God, that's not *like* me. I *never* raised a hand to my Patience. Not once in eleven years.' I scowled at my hand again, fingers trembling. 'I'd rather cut the damn thing off.'

"'Well, buck the fuck up about it. Ye can lop off whatever body parts ye please later.'

"I glowered across the fire, Phoebe meeting my gaze.

"'A fool could see ye love that girl like kin, Silversaint,' she said. 'So save the self-flagellation for church on prièdi. Ye can atone to Dior once we get her back.'

"I chewed on that, and it tasted an awful lot like wisdom. Phoebe had a way of cutting sharp to the quick, but she was right. No sense moaning about what was done. All that mattered was what we'd *do*. Best pick my lip off the floor and get the hell on with it.

"And so, I closed my eyes, hand outstretched to the flames.

"'What're ye—'

"'Shhhh.'

"'Don't *shush* me, ye cocky fu—'

"'I gave Dior a phial of my blood,' I murmured. 'I can feel it if I try. But it's not easy.'

"I spoke truth; this was more akin to finding a piece of hay in a stack of needles than the other way about. But still, I reached across the freezing gulf, pawing through the storm, the night, the vast and lifeless spaces. I've no idea how long it took, groping about in that empty dark, but finally, I felt a tiny drop of red amid the black. Distant. Moving. Swift.

"'Seven Martyrs . . . I think the Dyvok have her.'

"Phoebe's eyes narrowed. 'Ye sure?'

"'No. But she's moving fast, and our ponies are dead. Either she stole a horse and started galloping toward Ossway without us, or she's being *carried* there on horseback. Either way, I doubt Celene is with her. She's not had time to thrall a beast to bear her.'

"'If those leeches have Dior . . .'

"'They won't kill her. The Wolfmother is many things, but a fool isn't one. She knows Dior has worth to the Voss now.' I climbed to my feet, gingerly testing the break in my leg. 'You *have* to r-run her down before she realizes how much.'

"'*I* do?' Phoebe blinked up at me. 'Ye got more pressin' plans? Washin' yer hair or—'

"'They're ahorse.' I gestured at my empty scabbard. 'And even if I could catch them, I'm unarmed. So amorrow dusk, you dance the wealdshape and give chase.'

"'An' leave you up here alone? Ye'll be frozen or starved within a week.'

"'That sounds an awful lot like Not Your Fucking Problem, Kitcat.'

"'Call me *Kitcat* one more time, Silverboy, and I'll bury ye up here myself. I know daft heroics are the ale and honey of yer kind—'

"'There you go again with that *my kind* shit, I swear—'

"'But were y'born stupid, or did ye just take one too many Dyvoks to the head?' Phoebe squared up to me, scowling. 'Did y'skip the chapter where that slag an' her boy kicked the shite out of me and chucked me off a *mountain*? And now ye want me to run them down alone, and what? Ask nice? Pretty please wi' my jugular on top?'

"'We can't just abandon Dior!'

"'Naebody's saying we should! But they won the battle, Silversaint! Take yer lumps and start thinking about winning the *war*! Moonssakes, I know yer fond of the girl—'

"'I'm not just fucking *fond of her*! She's . . .'

"I slumped back onto the stone, body still wounded and aching, yet nowhere near as bloodied as my heart. The thought of Dior in Dyvok hands, of what might be happening to her, the terror that the last time we spoke might be the last time we ever . . .

"'She's . . .'

"'She's all ye have left.'

"Phoebe sank down opposite me, golden eyes on mine. Her cheeks were flushed with rage, talons curled into fists. But in truth, neither of us was truly furious with the other.

"'I know what she means to ye. Past the auguries and destinies. What she *really* means.' Phoebe's voice was gentle, as if she knew she now stepped onto thinnest ice. 'Dior told me what happened to them. Yer woman. Yer little girl. I know what that feels li—'

"'*Don't*,' I growled. 'Don't you *fucking* dare . . .'

"My protest faded as the duskdancer lifted her hand between us. Her nails were claws, sharp and cruel enough to rip a heart from its chest. But around her ring finger, a scrolling design was inked in her skin, the same blood-red as the fae spirals adorning her body. A troth ring, I realized, not forged of silver, but carved in ink and blood.

"'Yer not the only one with scars, Silversaint,' she murmured.

"I glanced at the old wound etched down the duskdancer's cheek, the bite of her dead cousin's axe in her shoulder. Others were carved into her forearms, her neck. She was covered in them, I realized, just as I. A song of scars, singing the tale of her hurts.

"And it seemed Phoebe á Dúnnsair had been hurt a great deal.

"'I *understand*,' she said. 'Why ye're so afraid. And nae sin is that fear, save if ye let it rule yer wits. She's nae gone. Only lost. An' *we* can get her back.'

"I breathed a heavy sigh, dragging one hand down my bloodstained face. She was infuriating, this woman. Belligerent. Hard as stone. There were centuries of blood between her kind and mine—the very ink on my skin was a bane to her, and who knew what dark magiks flowed in her veins. But she was right, damn her. About the only thing Phoebe was better at than winding me up was talking me down afterward."

"She sounds *exhausting*," Jean-François yawned, turning a page.

"She was." Gabriel scoffed softly. "One of the things I appreciated most."

"Your masochistic streak when it comes to women is really *quite* telling, de León."

"It's naught to do with women," the silversaint scowled. "The folk I held dearest were always the ones I quarreled with hardest. Folk who weren't afraid to slap me out of my bullshit, or tell me I was being an arse. There's no friend under heaven like an honest one."

The Last Silversaint leaned forward, elbows to knees.

"That's the way to wisdom, vampire. The wise man learns more from his enemies than the fool from his friends, but even the fool can learn if his friends are willing to call him one. Surround yourself with folk who confront you. If you're not being challenged, you're not learning anything. If you're the smartest man in the room, you're in the *wrong fucking room*.

"Phoebe á Dúnnsair and I were nothing close to friends. From the day I entered San Michon, I'd been taught her kind were animals. Bloodthirsty heathens who drank the blood of the innocent and stole the skins of men. But though I'm not the wisest of fellows, I'm wise enough to heed wisdom when I hear it.

"'Aright,' I sighed. 'We work together.'

"Phoebe nodded, leaning back on her heels. 'So if they're headed to Ossway, where would they be bound? Dún Cuinn is closest. The Dyvok crushed that last year.'

"'Dún Sadhbh too. And Dún Ariss. Even Dún Maergenn has fallen if what Lachlan said is true.' I shook my head, bewildered. 'Fifteen *years* they've been in stalemate, and now the Dyvok have crushed all Ossway in a blinking? How the fuck did they get so *strong*?'

"'Nae ken. But tha's where they'd take her, aye? The Nineswords' capital.'

"I chewed the puzzle over, slowly nodding. 'Makes sense.'

"'Then ye need a horse if we're to catch them. Supplies if we're to chase them. And if I might be so bold . . .' She winced. '. . . a wash wouldn't kill ye either.'

"I opened my mouth for rebuttal, but looking the duskdancer up and down, I saw where I was splashed head to foot in bruises, ashes, and dried gore, she was absolutely spotless. I knew cats were fastidious, but this was just taking the piss . . .

"'A horse isn't the only thing I'll need.' I sighed. 'I lost Ashdrinker at Cairnhaem. After all we've been through, all we've seen together . . . She could be anywhere . . .'

"'Mmm.'

"I looked up at the odd note in Phoebe's voice. After a long moment of torture, she smiled, a touch of mischief twinkling in those strange, feral eyes. Standing swift, she pulled aside the bloodstained saddlebags, and there, wrapped in a blanket . . .

"'*Ash!*' I cried.

"I swept up my blade, eyes stinging as that beautiful silver voice rang once more in my head. She was talking to herself, I realized; a recipe for bloody spudloaf of all things. But her voice was wondrous, bright, warming my cold bones as no fire ever could.

"*One new p-potato, large and luvluvluverly . . .*

"'Ash?' I whispered.

"*Two cups goatsmilk, fresh and f-f-fine . . .*

"'Ash!' I said, louder.

"Her voice stilled then, that broken, silvered dame upon the hilt ever smiling.

"*Gabriel! Where did you g-g-go? I was w-worried wasworried!*

"'All's well,' I whispered. 'Fear not.'

"*Fear for them, not for us. Fear and the snikSNAK, aye. Not for p-peace was I hurled here, nor for parlay was I f-forged. But . . . w-w-where is Dior?*

"'South. Not far. We're going to go get her.'

"*Oh goodgood g-good. Was . . . was . . . was I talking to myself just n-now? What was I saysaysaying, I c-can't r-remember. I can never remember . . .*

"'You sleep now, amie,' I murmured. 'I'll call when I need you, eh?'

"*D-do ye?* she asked softly. *Still need me? Even if I'm . . . n-not what I was?*

"'Always,' I whispered, squeezing her tight. 'Shhhh. *Always.*'

"*G-good. Ohgoodgood. Sleep now. The quiet and thethethe still. The calm in the s-storm. Ye are a lucky man, my friend. K-k-kiss Astrid and P-Patience goodnight for me . . .*

"The blade's voice fell silent as I slipped her back into her sheath, caressed the beautiful dame on the hilt. I looked to the duskdancer, watching from across the fire.

"'That's twice I owe you, mademoiselle.'

"'Found her where she fell,' Phoebe muttered. 'She'd split the boulder she landed on in *half.* Should've heard the shite she was sayin'. Angels and devils an' all manner of madness. Messy as a pub floor at closin', that one.'

"'She wasn't always like this,' I protested. 'She has good nights and bad.'

"'What happened to her?'

"'No man of woman born can slay the Forever King, they say.' I sighed, old hatred burning in my chest. 'But still I tried. And Ash paid the cost, along with ma famille.'

"Phoebe's golden eyes roamed the silvered name on my fingers. 'Can ye nae fix her?'

"'Fix her?'

"'Reforge her or somesuch. Like in the auld tales. Daegann renewing the hammer o' the Tein'Abha. Or the damned Nineswords melting the blades of her foes to make her own.'

"'Doesn't work that way. You can't just melt a sword down and make another with it. If you liquefy the metal, you alter its chymistrie. Molten steel hardens into cast iron. Brittle. Weak. All those old stories about reforging shattered blades are just that, Mlle Phoebe. *Stories.*'

"I sighed, rubbing at bruised eyes.

"'A blade is like a heart. Once it breaks, it's broken.'

"Phoebe sighed, looking me over. 'Ye look like shite twice stepped in.'

"'Strange.' I peered out at the mountains beyond our cave. 'I feel on top of the world.'

"She chuckled, her scarred smile lopsided. 'We'll start remedying that amorrow. Where do we get ye horsed is the question.'

"I pouted, brow creased in thought as I considered options.

"'I know it's a dark road to get there,' I finally said. 'But if we sought help in the Moonsthrone, is there *any* version of that story where I don't end up slaughtered?'

"'Yer kind killed the Stormbringer, Silversaint. If ye go to the Highlands, ye die.'

"I nodded, sucking my lip. 'We could head down to Redwatch, I suppose.'

"'I thought ye told the Flower that place was dangerous?'

"'Dior and I fucked over some hedgemages from the Night Market last time we were in town. Murdered an inquisitor on holy ground to boot. If I get caught there, only question is whether they hang or quarter me. Maybe both.' I scowled, rubbing my stubble. 'But we've no time to waste. And I still have a few friends behind those walls.'

"Phoebe nodded, resolute. 'The City of Scarlet, then. Fast as we can trek. Get us mounted, then run Dior down and cut the Dyvok to pieces afore they reach Dún Maergenn.'

"'I don't mean to alarm you, but . . . did we just *agree* on something?'

"She scoffed. 'Sooner we get there, sooner we get to the Flower. Best sleep, eh?'

"I nodded, tired all the way to my bones. The bloodied saddlebags Phoebe had salvaged contained bedding at least, and I hauled some furs out onto the stone, curling down among them and wishing for nothing but a dreamless dark. I heard Phoebe drag another log onto the fire, fussing with the bags. And my whole body tensed head to toe as I felt her pull up the furs I'd wrapped myself in, and with a noisy rustle of emerald silk and tulle, join me underneath.

"'. . . What the fuck are you doing?'

"'Oh, quick round of ale and whores afore church. What d'ye think I'm doin'?'

"'I *think* you think you're sleeping with me, Kitcat.'

"'An' who ever said yer more pretty than perceptive?'

"'Is there only one blanket, or . . . ?'

"'There's three,' she said, pulling them all atop us both. 'Thing about blankets is they're warmer the more ye have. Same's true for bodies. Grow up.'

"I knew this was Phoebe's way; as heedless of personal space as any feline alive. I also knew it wisdom that we warm each other in this chill. But I'd never shared a bed with any woman who wasn't my wife. And so, I peeled off the blankets, made to crawl free.

"'Where the hell ye goin'?' Phoebe asked, lifting her head.

"'One of us should keep watch. The Terrors fell off that bridge too. You don't dance on a Voss grave unless you dig it yourself.'

"'Found their tracks this mornin'. Headed south. They're nowhere close.'

"'We shouldn't take that risk.'

"'Moonssakes, ye *do* have a high opinion of yerself.' Phoebe levered herself up on one elbow with a stare that could be safely described as withering. 'Take hold of yer bollocks, ye blouse. Yer virtue's safe with me. I don't bite.'

"I motioned to my bloodied leg, the teeth scars she'd left on my arm. 'That so?'

"'Well, not in my sleep,' she smiled. 'Trust me, I'm not hungry, man. Just cold.'

"I scowled a moment longer, but in the end, as if a prisoner on the way to the executioner's block, I crawled back between the furs. Phoebe sighed, snuggling up against my back without a care under heaven. She hissed as our hands briefly touched, silver burning her skin, but after mumbled apologies, I settled beside the flames, the duskdancer curled up against me.

"Phoebe was soon asleep, but I stayed awake, staring at the thing staring at me. She sat on the cusp between shadow and flame now, watching silently. She was clad only in firelight, heartbreak-shaped face framed by rivers of long black hair, tears of blood spilling down her cheeks. I couldn't move, couldn't speak, pleading with my eyes.

"'*I love you . . .*'

"Astrid hung her head, red tears falling like rain. She reached up slow, smearing the blood across her skin, and as I blinked, I realized her face was a mask, a bloody handprint painted upon it. Red circles were scribed around her eyes, midnight-blue hair whipping about her face as the lightning pulsed. And Celene looked down at me from the Cairnhaem bridge, ember rain swirling, mask twisting into a soulless smile as she let go of my hand.

"'*I* hate *you* . . .'

"I plunged into the dark, that lonely cold, that loss and longing. And as I fell, I heard screaming above; the girl I'd vowed to protect, yet failed like all the others.

"'*Gabriel, where are you?*'

"But the storm stole my reply."

III

THE WHITE RABBIT

" 'HOLD! STATE YOUR name and business!'

"The cry echoed in the freezing gloom, accompanied by the creak of a dozen bowstrings. The battlements above were wrought of redstone, forty feet high, dozens of firepots flickering along their length in the newborn night. The gates before us were made of ironbound oak, embossed with the key and shield of mighty San Cleyland. Breath steaming between us, Phoebe and I exchanged a weary glance.

"'Sweet Mothermaid, we're here,' I sighed.

"A fortnight we'd traveled, down from the Nightstone. Two weeks of howling storm, biting snow, and fungus-riddled deadwood. Phoebe had refused to shift as we traveled, and though I now understood her reluctance, Dior had only packed a fox-fur mantle and elbow-length gloves to accompany that impractical dress—not exactly winter attire. But even in human form, Phoebe seemed immune to the elements, walking trackless and barefoot atop the same snows I struggled through. It was only after dark the cold seemed to bother her, and strange as it was, despite our bloody history, a duskdancer and a silversaint slept beside each other for a few weeks that wintersdeep, beneath the hidden Elidaeni moons.

"Every night, I dreamed of Celene's face, the image creeping like a shadow into my quiet moments and unguarded thoughts. But all day long I fretted on Dior, reaching out every few hours to the blood she carried. Relieved to find her still moving.

"Still alive.

"We'd followed the Volta down from the mountains, through frozen valleys and wasted forests, all run to rot and ruin. The only signs of life were a few swift foxes and a single mousehawk, watching us with tawny eyes. We were exhausted by the time we spied it in the distance; a great crown of battlements encircling an island on the frozen river. A grand priory stood on its north side, looking over tangled streets below. A château rose in its heart, built of the red river stone the city was named for. Martyr's Cradle, some called it. Saintsholme. Birthplace of San Cleyland, the famed fourth Martyr.

"The grand cityfort of Redwatch.

"Dior and I had visited here before wintersdeep, but now, it seemed the gates had been closed to outsiders. A sea of tents and wagons had sprung up around the walls; a shantytown more akin to a city. Thousands of men, women, children, huddled in the cold, dirty and disheveled, wide-eyed and wounded. I saw different patterns on their clancloth; Cuinn and Sadhbh, Fas and Ariss, folk from all over the Nineswords' ravaged lands.

"A dozen burning arrows streaked from the battlements above, hissing as they sank into the snow about me. 'Not one step farther, by God!'

"'Hold, brothers, we come in peace!' I shouted.

"A grizzled fellow with an iron helm peered over the battlements, frosty beard quivering as he shouted. 'I'll not ask again! State your name and business, or begone!'

"I studied the soldiery above us; dozens of men at vigil on the towering walls. Burning fires and heavy mail and crossbows aimed square at us.

"'They're taking security a little more seriously these nights,' I murmured.

"'The closest château to here just got greased up, bent over, and arse-fucked by the Dyvok,' Phoebe whispered in reply. 'Are ye surprised they're nervous?'

"'What's surprising is you actually agreed to this. Now remember, we stumble here, I'm bound for the noose or worse.' I tugged the leather leash about her neck. 'So follow my lead, eh?'

"'Oh, *very* amusing.'

"I took off my glove, held up my hand to show my sevenstar. 'Fairdawning, Sergente! My name is Frère Philippe Montfort, brother of the holy order of San Michon!'

"'A silversaint?' The sergente squinted at my tattoo, his demeanor shifting a touch closer to warmish. 'What brings you to Martyr's Cradle, good Frère?'

"'The Hunt, sir! My abbot sent me to Beaufort to capture this unholy beast!' I feigned a kick to the back of Phoebe's legs, and she dutifully collapsed in the snow with a curse. 'I seek sanctuary for the night, afore the long march back to San Michon!'

"Refugees in the camp were looking at us now; flint-eyed men and hungry

children, elders shivering in their bloodied rags. The little sergente squinted at Phoebe on her knees in the snow, resplendent in her flawless emerald gown.

"'A beast, you say? She looks fair enough.'

"'And that's the evil of her, good Sergente! Let your eyes be not deceived; this sorceress is a duskdancer and skinthief, whose earthly temptations can enslave the pious with a word! A *glance*! No bishop, priest, nor God-fearing man is safe, and if she had her way, sir, *you* would be next to be flayed alive in her boudoir of blood!'

"'*Boudoir of blood?*' Phoebe hissed.

"'Easy, Kitcat,' I muttered through gritted teeth.

"'Who the *fuck* is gonna believe that shite?'

"'These men are press-ganged peasants,' I whispered. 'They stand on a damn wall for a living. So calm your tits before they perforate them.'

"'Why don't ye just tell them the truth?'

"'I want them terrified of you. That way, they won't waste time asking *me* idiotic questions, such as why you're only restrained with a few strips of saddlebag or wearing a bloody ballgown. I'm a wanted murderer in this city, Phoebe. If just one of these bastards recognizes me, they'll hang me twice over and burn the leavings at the stake.'

"I shrugged, lacing my collar tighter about my face.

"'Besides, this is more fun.'

"'*Fun?*'

"'Fun,' I nodded. 'Dior told me about it. I thought I'd try it for a while.'

"'Yer not the one on yer damn knees in the snow.'

"'Have no fear, mademoiselle. No doorman refuses entry to a member of the Ordo Argent. Those gates will be open quicker than you can say *fuck my face.*'

"'Fuck my—'

"Metal *clunk*ed, and with the groan of frozen hinges and a shower of broken ice, the gates began to grind apart. Phoebe glanced to me, scoffing as I winked.

"'Ye're cleverer than you look occasionally.'

"'Not difficult, according to some.'

"The Redwatch gates opened wide, revealing an arched tunnel leading through the gatehouse. Hundreds of refugees climbed to their feet as the portcullis rose, looking with hungry, frightened eyes at the city beyond. But a small army of soldiers barred their way, faces cold and hard. They carried spears and crossbows, and each was clad in the charcoal tabard of the San Cleyland gendarme. At their lead stood the little bearded sergente, iron helm on his head and hand on his sword. He cast a warning glance around the Ossians to ensure all were still, then turned fearful eyes to me and Phoebe.

"'You two, come forth,' he demanded. '*Only* you two. And if you move sudden, vile temptress, I swear you'll not move again.'

"I nodded to the gates. 'After you, vile temptress.'

"'Should've left ye on that damned mountain . . .'

"We marched forward under the eyes of the soldiery, Phoebe with wrists bound before her, me holding the leash about her neck. A dozen loaded crossbows were aimed at us as we stepped beneath the gatehouse arch, and I was on edge to be in close quarters—nowhere to run if the guards marked me for who I was. But on closer inspection, most looked barely more than boys—peasant lads raised in hamlets, where the greatest trade was rumor and superstition. A few kept watch on the ragged mob outside as the gates creaked closed behind us, just in case any should make a break for the shelter within.

"'I trust you know the custom, Silversaint,' the sergente said.

"He motioned to the stone font sitting to the right of the gates. It was crafted in the likeness of Sanael; the Angel of Blood's hands holding a large bowl, crusted with ice. I punched the surface to shatter it, dipping my hand into the freezing liquid beneath.

"'Whassat?' Phoebe asked softly.

"'Silence, villain!' I snapped.

"Turning, I flicked the liquid off my fingers, onto Phoebe's bare skin. And though holy water was no actual bane to duskdancers, she made a decent show of hissing in agony, teeth bared as she staggered backward and covered her face.

"'Sweet Muvvermaid,' someone whispered. 'Look at 'er eyes . . .'

"'You've stepped up the watch since last I was here, Sergente,' I said.

"The little man nodded. 'Gates are closed to all save citizens of Redwatch, or those on God's or the Emperor's business. By order of Lord Cédric Beaufort.'

"'Those folk outside are freezing, man. Lord Cédric has no charity for the poor?'

"'He's charity aplenty, Silversaint. Just no *room*. There's too many folk flooding over the border. The streets are awash with Ossian rabble, and food's aready scarce.'

"I sucked my lip, uneasy at the thought of those folk outside, but with no end of my own troubles to fret on. 'Well, I'll only be here the one night. But I'd best get this monstress into proper chains afore the witching hour.'

"The man nodded, frightened eyes on Phoebe. 'Where d'you plan to take it? I'll have to fetch the capitaine if you've wish to lock it 'neath the keep.'

"'Sanctified ground is the only place this beast can be safely caged. I'll take my rest in the priory this night, with the holy sisters of San Cleyland.'

"'As it please,' he nodded. 'I'll have my men escort y—'

"'No need, Sergente.' I slapped the man's shoulder, giving the lads around us a nod. 'You and your men stay your posts. The Dead are abroad, and all Saintsholme doubtless sleeps easier in the knowledge you brave fellows stand their walls.' I scowled at Phoebe. 'I know the way to the priory, and shall steer this heathen siren to God's house forthwith.'

"'Why's she wearing that dress?' someone asked.

"'Filthy whorespawn,' Phoebe spat, glowering at the man. 'I'll flay yer bairns to make my bedclothes, and fuck yer wife upon their sk—'

"'Silence, fiend!' I cried, flicking more holy water in her direction. 'Threaten not these faithful men of God! Come, give me your cloak, sir, and make a path, all of you. I'll have you goodly fellows hear no more poison from this acolyte of the abyss.'

"The young soldiers stepped aside, awed and fearful, a few flinching as Phoebe's golden gaze fell upon them. I took the sergente's cloak, threw it around her shoulders. Dragging the hood down over her eyes, I snapped the leash about her throat like a whip.

"'Follow, fleshwitch,' I growled. 'And speak no sinful word, lest you taste my blade.'

"The sergente returned my grim salute, and leading Phoebe on her leash, I marched into the torchlit street. Saintsholme's buildings were tight-packed, looming tall above us, its streets a tangled, overcrowded maze. I was awed at the flood of refugees; things must be going truly ill in the west for so many to have fled Ossway. But walking quick toward the priory, Phoebe and I were soon deep into the sprawl, and out of sight of the walls at least. Slipping into the lee of a cobbler's shop, I turned and unbound her hands.

"'That wasn't too disastrous, all things considered,' I muttered.

"'Nae the most fun I've had with knots,' she shrugged, rubbing her wrists. 'Nor the least. But we'd best get off the streets. Where are these friends of yers?'

"I nodded down the alley. 'Follow me, vile temptress.'

"'Pushin' yer luck now, Silverboy.'

"I drew my collar up over my smirk, Phoebe pulled her hood over her eyes, and I led us down a tangle of squeezeways and alleys, cutting toward the frozen Redwatch docks. We dodged two patrols, ducked into a doorway to avoid a third, the hangman's noose ever over my head. And at last, we came to a row of crooked buildings lining a cobbled thoroughfare, the street filled with touts and homeless Ossians begging for coin. On a grubby corner, stacked between a bawdyhouse and a smokeden, we found our destination.

"'*The White Rabbit*,' Phoebe murmured, looking over the taverne's sign.

"'The ragout's excellent. Whatever you do, do *not* order the Potato Surprise.'

"'Any particular reason?'

"'The surprise is dysentery.'

"A mountain of beef in a winter cloak stood in the doorway, sheltering from the wind. He looked me over, toe to crown, breathing into dishplate hands to warm them.

"'No beggars in 'ere,' he grunted.

"'Beggars?' I scoffed. 'Steady on, monsieur.'

"'I warned ye,' Phoebe muttered. 'That wash is *long* overdue.'

"Rolling my eyes, I jangled my purse in the man's direction, and he dutifully stepped aside. With one last glance around the street, Phoebe and I slipped through the door.

"The White Rabbit was a bustling affair, the commonroom filled with folk of all shapes and sizes, every shade of shady. The tables were packed, scullery maids slipping among the crush with laden trays. A trio of minstrels were hard at work in the corner, playing a brisk jumpstep on fiddle, lute, and drum. After so long wandering the frozen wilds, the taverne was a sudden rush of sensation—the heat of hearth and bodies, the perfume of woodsmoke and liquor, and beneath it all, sweet and hot and red, oh, *God* . . .

"'Ye aright?' Phoebe murmured.

"I shook my head, swallowing ashes. 'Need a drink.'

"We shoved through the throng, toward a booth in a smoky corner. Pushing a slumbering drunkard out of his chair, the two of us settled in, my back to the wall and eyes on the door. My stomach felt a knot of broken glass, drenched in cheap liquor and set aflame. Phoebe touched a passing scullery girl, hood pulled low to hide her eyes.

"'Drinks, if ye please, love. And food, eh? Ragout fer me. Potato Surprise fer him.'

"I opened my mouth to protest, but the maid had already bobbed her head, slipped off into the throng. Phoebe smirked in my direction, casting a glance around the room.

"'Fine place. Nae many horses in it?'

"'Food and sleep tonight. Amorrow we get ourselves saddled and gone.'

"'Ye don't want to spend a day resting up? Nae offense, but ye look—'

"'Every day we waste here is a day Dior draws closer to Dún Maergenn. Not to mention tempting the hangman.' I lowered my voice as the serving girl plonked two wooden mugs and a jug of rotgut on the table. 'The sooner we're gone, the better.'

"Phoebe nodded, hunkering down and waiting for the maid to depart before she spoke again. 'So this friend of yers. How d'ye know him?'

"'Met in the Ossian campaigns.' I poured myself a cup, another for Phoebe. 'I was part of the Ordo attachment under Niamh á Maergenn's command during the Dyvok war.'

"'What . . .' The duskdancer scoffed. 'Ye know the Nineswords?'

"'*Know* her?' I downed my spirits with a gulp. 'Niamh fucking *knighted* me.'

"'Knighted by a pretender's blade. Ye just get more impressive every day, don't ye?'

"'Niamh á Maergenn's no pretender,' I said, pouring another. 'She conquered the Ossway from the Splintered Isles to the Moonsthrone by the time she was twenty-five years old. Emperor Alexandre himself named her a duchess of the imperial court.'

"'Travel to the Highlands, see how many kneel for her,' Phoebe scowled. 'The Nineswords tried to invade the Moonsthrone, d'ye know that? After all those Lowlander dogs bent the knee, greedy bitch fixed her eyes northward and tried to take what was ours. There was seven different clanwars raging across the Highlands back then, and we still found the time to kick her arse so fuckin' hard her nose is yet bleedin'.'

"'Merci for the history lesson. But I *have* been known to read on occasion.'

"'. . . Ye can read?'

"The minstrels shifted tune; the crowd cheered as the fiddler jumped on a table. I winced, briefly entertaining the notion of jamming his instrument into an orifice with better acoustics. My head was splitting, stomach burning, this liquor doing next to nothing.

"I reached to my bandolier for a dose of sanctus, but instead of glass, my fingers brushed something heavy. Metal. Drawing it out with a frown, I recognized the golden vial that little Mila had given me after the battle on the Mère.

"You said a badword. But you're a goodman.

"'Wassat?' Phoebe asked, squinting.

"'The Wolfmother wore it,' I replied. 'Drank from it when we fought at Aveléne. And from another just like it before she smashed the Cairnhaem bridge to splinters.'

"'What's in it?'

"Unscrewing the cap, I inhaled. My mouth flooded with spit, belly tying itself into a burning tangle. Even sour, the perfume was so heady, so *rich,* I was sore tempted to upend it over my open mouth, to let those clotted dregs fall onto my tongue and bathe me in flame.

"Did they not warn you? Your preciousss Silver Order? What would happen if you indulged your desires night after night? Or were you sssimply too drunk with lust of the flesh to give a damn about your immortal soul?

"'Silverboy?' Phoebe asked. 'What's in it?'

"Red fire.

"Red thirst.

"'Blood,' I whispered, closing the cap. 'Just blood.'

"Phoebe's strange new eyes roamed my body; the clenched jaw and sweat-slick skin and white-knuckle fists. I filled my pipe, striking my flintbox with shaking hands.

"'Ye hunger fer it.'

"I looked up sharply at that. Pupils dilating as I dragged down a lungful of red. Phoebe looked from the vial to my eyes, her own glittering, feral and gold.

"'Why not just drink it?'

"'Because I'm not a fucking animal,' I growled.

"'Some of my favorite people are animals,' she said, lips quirking.

"I chuckled at that, despite my parched tongue, my dry and clawing throat, the pain in my belly easing as the sacrament flooded red and warm through my veins.

"'Palebloods who indulge their hungers can get lost in them,' I said, toying with my pipe. 'Falling to a madness we name the *red thirst*. It turns us into beasts. No better than the monsters who made us. That's why the Order smokes blood rather than drinks it.'

"'Trust monastery boys to find a way to drain all the fun out of life.' Phoebe watched me drag down another red lungful, her lips pursed. 'Is it true what's told in the auld tales? About the vampire's Kiss? They say it's a bliss unmeasured.'

"'I wouldn't know. I'm not a vampire.'

"'But ye used to drink. From yer woman, I mean. I heard ye and yer sister talking.'

"Anger flashed through me then, black and brittle. 'Perhaps once. But never again. And I'll thank you, Mlle Phoebe, not to speak about my—'

"A sheathed sword slammed on the table between us, embossed with sigils of the Mothermaid and Redeemer. Phoebe snarled, half rising as I scowled up at its owner.

"A woman, stout and tall, eyes of watery blue. She wore a jerkin and doublet, the sleeves split to show two shades of green, hatched with black and blue—the colors of Clan Maergenn. Her face was nicked with scars, crow's-feet at her eyes, plaited hair faded grey.

"'I heard tell ye were dead.'

"Her hand drifted behind her back, eyes glinting.

"'And by God, by the time we're done, ye'll wish ye were.'"

IV

EMERALD AND FLAME

" 'SEVEN BLOODY MARTYRS . . .' I breathed.

"I stood slow, hand slipping to my belt, brushing over my sword hilt. The old woman's eyes glittered as her hand closed behind her back. And simultaneously, we drew—her a bottle of dark Ossian homebrew, and me, my trusty hipflask.

"'Sweet Gabbie,' she laughed, opening her arms. 'Ye wee *rascal*!'

"I laughed also, catching the woman up and lifting her off the floor. Phoebe raised an eyebrow as I twirled the elderly dame about, my thirst and anger and the danger hanging over my head behind these walls all forgot. Patrons threw curious glances our way, the old woman yelling and thumping my shoulder.

"'Put me down, ye great lump!'

"I complied reluctantly, kissing both her cheeks. The dame smacked me on the backside like a disobedient brat. 'Away with ye! I'm too old to be manhandled such!'

"'Never was there a man alive who could handle you, Sister,' I grinned.

"'The cheek of him, talking so to a former woman of the cloth!'

"Phoebe watched us, eyebrow arched. 'This yer friend, I take it?'

"'Phoebe á Dúnnsair,' I declared, breathless with joy, 'this is Sœur Fionna, the White Rabbit. Hero of Báih Sìde and slayer of more coldbloods than I've had hot baths.'

"'*Three* vampires? Impressive.'

"I scoffed, but I was too happy to see Fionna again to quip back. The old dame thumped three fresh cups on the table, cracked the wax on her bottle, and poured us all a stiff dram of a dark, reeking liquid. Lifting her cup, she looked me in the eye.

"'*To those who fought*,' she declared. '*And those who fell.*'

"'*And those who lived through living hell*,' I replied.

"We smashed our cups together, and though Fionna must've been near-fifty, she matched my pace, slamming her empty down on the table when she was done.

"'Seven Martyrs,' I coughed. 'The taste of the Black hasn't improved with time.'

"'I brew it meself out back. A little taste of home. Takes me back to better times.' Fionna grinned, sitting down beside me. 'We've all seen finer days, Chevalier.'

"'Bollocks to that. You're as beautiful as the night we met.'

"'And ye're as full of shite as ever ye were,' she laughed. 'Time eats us all alive.'

"'The White Rabbit can never die,' I declared, topping up her glass with the reeking brew. 'You're going to live long enough to see your tits touch your hips, mon amie.'

"'Ha! Charm me out of this doublet, I can touch my *toes*.'

"Phoebe almost choked on her mouthful. 'Ye said yer a *nun?*'

"The old dame looked the duskdancer over, noting the golden gleam of her eyes. 'I *was* a swordsister, Highlander. In my foolish youth. Devoted to God and Mothermaid and Martyrs. But when I prayed . . .'—here, she touched her old blade—'. . . I prayed with *this*.'

"'Dame Fionna is one of the finest blades in the empire,' I said. 'She taught me a thing or three in the Ossian campaigns. Saved my life when I was still finding my feet.'

"'Ye got there in the end, sweet Gabbie,' she said, patting my knee.

"'Sweet *Gabbie?*' Phoebe scoffed.

"Fionna grinned. 'That's what I called him. Before they started this *Black Lion* palaver. Little Gabbie de León. Full of spunk and vinegar, he was. Scowling like someone kicked him in the bollocks every morn. And *shouting*! Mothermaid, *so* much shouting . . .'

"'This was when ye served the Nineswords?' Phoebe asked.

"'My first command,' I nodded. 'Emperor Alexandre commissioned a force to retake northern Ossway after Tolyev and his brood seized the coast. The good Sœur and I fought side by side for the next year.' I smiled, heart flooded with sweet nostalgia. 'Took back Báih Sìde. Pushed on to Dún Craeg. Saeth-tunn. All the way to Triúrbaile.'

"The minstrels picked up their pace, folk cheered, but Fionna's face had gone suddenly grim. A shadow fell over the pair of us despite the music, the dancing and laughter all about. The old dame's eyes grew clouded, no doubt walking the same streets as I in her mind; those awful cages, those wretched people. I topped up her goblet to the brim.

"'And that was the end of that,' she sighed.

"Phoebe looked back and forth between us. 'Were ye wounded or . . .'

"'Not in the flesh, Highlander,' Fionna replied, refilling my glass. 'But after the things I saw at Triúrbaile, the God in me just . . . evaporated. Young Gabbie and his Order chums marched on toward glory, and I quietly took my leave. Hung up my sword. Met myself a sweet Nordish man who preferred pouring drinks to cracking skulls, and shagging on a prièdi morn rather than going to mass. Never looked back. Good thing too.'

"Fionna lowered her eyes, her voice a murmur.

"'D'ye hear about Dún Maergenn?'

"'Only that it's fallen,' I replied.

"'The Dyvok took it months back. The Blackheart and his sister.'

"'*How?* Maergenn was the mightiest fortress west of Augustin.'

"'We hear only rumor.' Fi shrugged. 'Refugee tales. The Dyvok brought the walls down from afar, out of range of Niamh's cannon. Some say artillery; others, sorcery. They sank Lady Caitlyn's fleet in the Gulf of Wolves. Butchered Lady Una on the walls. Lady Reyne was killed defending the sepulcher. Three of the Nineswords' daughters, gone.'

"I sighed, remembering the girls I'd met at Niamh's court. Little Cat with her fierce smile and Una with her razor tongue. God, Reyne had been barely more than a babe . . .

"'And Niamh?' I asked softly.

"'She fought bravely, they say. Even after her girls fell. But when the city looked doomed, she sent parlay to the Dyvok, that her people might be spared. The Blackheart accepted her surrender, then threw her to his wretched. Drank her dry, the bastard, then fed the scraps to his dogs.'

"'Sweet Mothermaid,' I whispered.

"Fionna made the sign of the wheel. 'Take her in yer arms.'

"I was heartsick and afeared at this news. Niamh á Maergenn was a brilliant general, the veteran of a dozen campaigns against both the living and the Dead. For Nikita to have crushed her capital, for Kiara to have taken on the Terrors and lived—there was some new darkness afoot with the Untamed.

Some ill magik I'd no understanding of. And Dior was in the Wolfmother's clutches, headed right to the Blackheart's arms.

"'What brings ye here, Gabbie?' Fionna asked softly. 'What do ye need?'

"I dragged myself back to the now, finishing off my glass. 'Food. A bed. A horse.'

"'A wash,' Phoebe growled.

"'Oui,' I sighed. 'A bath wouldn't be unwelcome either, I suppose.'

"'Well, there we can oblige.' Fionna eyed me up and down. 'I'll have one of my girls scrub those clothes too. They look about ready to start walking on their own.'

"'We'll be gone amorrow, I swear. If we'd any choice, we'd not be here tonight. I know the Redwatch gendarme must be looking for me, I know y—'

"'Enough of that,' she scowled. 'It's a blessing to see ye again, love.'

"The music changed; shifting to an Ossian jig called 'The Riddle of the Fiddle.' It was a merry tune, as if the minstrels too wanted to banish my misgivings, to brighten my freezing night. The crowd cheered, Fionna clapped, several folk pushing back tables to open up the floor as people began to stomp in time. I was halfway to drunk now, but nowhere near close enough, pouring myself another and trying to hide the fact my hands were still shaking.

"'Dance w'me,' a voice demanded.

"I blinked at the outstretched fingers that had appeared before my eyes. Frowning, I followed the emerald glove upward, over a shoulder inked with blood-red fae spirals and at last, into a pair of shadowed, glittering eyes.

"'Eh?'

"'Ye can dance, can't ye?' Phoebe asked.

"'No,' I growled, knocking back my Black.

"'He can actually,' Fionna declared. 'He's excellent, I've seen him.'

"I scowled at the old sister as Phoebe wiggled her outstretched fingers. 'I love this song. So dance w'me. Or are ye plannin' to sit here mopin' all night?'

"'I'm not moping. I'm thinking.'

"'Drinking.'

"'Same thing.'

"'Dance w'me, damn ye.'

"'What's the magik word?'

"The duskdancer raised one brow, hand on hip. '*Now?*'

"'Tsk tsk.' Filling my cup to the brim, I took another long swallow. 'You'll find life a lot easier once you learn to say *please*, Kitcat.'

"Phoebe scoffed, shaking her head. 'The goddesses ruined a perfectly good arsehole when they put teeth in yer mouth, didn't they?'

"Tossing her curls over her face, the duskdancer spun out into that sea of bodies, stomping all in time. She moved like a blade, the fire of her hair burning like the flames in the hearth. Some around the room stared at her with envy, with awe, with desire, but she noticed not at all. I'd wondered if the change to her eyes might be troubling her, but I realized she kept them hidden only to avoid trouble, not because she was ashamed of what she was. Truth was, you could probably buy all the fucks Phoebe á Dúnnsair gave for the opinions of others with half a brass royale, and have change left over.

"I swallowed the rest of my cup.

"'The Gabriel de León *I* knew wouldn't have turned down a dance from a beautiful woman,' Fionna murmured. 'And that was *before* he got excommunicated.'

"I filled my cup with Black again, sighing. 'Heard about that, did you?'

"The old swordsister scoffed. 'I own a pub, I've heard the *songs*. There's not a maid alive who doesn't swoon a little at the opening bars of 'The Lion's Lover,' Gabe.'

"I scowled at the men in the corner, lips pressed thin. 'Fucking minstrels.'

"'Ye can't blame them. It's the stuff legends are made of. A boy and girl so in love they defied the will of heaven itself?'

"'Look how far it got them.'

"'How are they? The Lion's love? And his cub?'

"My eyes drifted up from my cup. My silence told the tale without me needing to speak a word. Fionna's face turned a lighter shade of pale, and for a moment, I could see my pain reflected in her gaze, raw and bleeding. Her voice shook as she whispered.

"'Oh, Gabbie . . .'

"'I did what a hero is supposed to do, Fi. I killed the monster. But the monster had a father who loved it.' I shook my head and growled. 'Fucking minstrels.'

"'This is no world for happy songs,' Fionna said. 'But that's exactly why we sing them. There's a joy to be found in something so simple as moving in time.'

"I glanced at her sidelong. 'Are *you* asking me to dance now?'

"She crowed aloud, head thrown back. 'With this hip? My dancing days are *long* past, old friend. But that's exactly my point.' She nodded to that flash of emerald and flame in the throng. 'Enjoy the music while ye can, Gabbie. The way we're headed, amorrow, the whole world might be silent as graves.'

"I sighed, meeting her eyes. 'We need to be back on the road, quick as we can. If you know someplace we can get horsed, I'd be in your debt.'

"'Anything for the Black Lion of Lorson,' Fionna smiled. 'Now, go on with ye.'

"I took up my cup, drained it to the dregs. Sharing an embrace that only those who'd fought through hell together can give, I kissed the old swordsister's cheek. And breathing deep, I walked through the whirling bodies and onto the floor.

"'May I?'

"Phoebe halted her swaying, turned to me with a scowl.

"'What's the magik word?'

"I bowed, hand to heart. 'May I please have the honor of this dance?'

"Her eyes were mostly hidden behind the curtain of her curls, but I thought perhaps I caught a twinkle of mirth in the gold. 'I s'pose.'

"With another bow, I took Phoebe's gloved hand, and together, we sailed into that ocean of rolling bodies. Her feet were still bare, and I'd no wish to tread on them, but I was surprised how quick we fell into step, moving as one through the smoke, the laughter and shouts of joy, all of us stamping the beat.

"Through the burning veil of her hair, I saw her lips curl as my other hand pressed to the small of her back, drawing her a little closer. It seemed then that the music grew louder, the laughter about us to dim, until even in the midst of that sea of people, the two of us were completely alone. The brutal history between our kinds faded a moment, the whispers of unholy magiks and tales of slaughter swallowed by that beautiful song.

"The tune shifted faster, and we pressed closer, holding tight. A part of me still felt this some kind of treason, the troth ring on my finger cold and heavy. But the woman in my arms was warm and fierce, laughing as she twirled out from my embrace. The crescendo built, the room about us fading further, and for a brief and blessed moment, I forgot all—who I was and where I'd been, what I'd done and must do, caught up entirely in the spell. Phoebe spun away from me, and I drew her back, lowering her into a breathless dip as the song reached its close. The crowd cheered, the minstrels bowed, and the duskdancer laughed in my arms, curls tumbling back from her face. It was a strange thing, but this close, I realized Phoebe's new eyes were not simply gold, but an alloy of precious metals—bright platinum and burning bronze and sharp silver, molten and wide and fixed on me. My gaze drifted from her feral smile, along her jaw, down the long, smooth plane of her throat.

"And there, I saw it, thudding, thumping beneath her tattooed skin.

"A vein.

"I felt my head snaking lower before I knew it, Phoebe's heart beating quicker as my breath tickled her throat. The thirst in me *smashed* itself against its bars, roaring, the blissful end of it all just one breath, one bite away. I wanted it, God, I *wanted* it more than anything before in my life, fangs grown long and hard, goosebumps prickling Phoebe's skin.

"Another song started. The spell between us broke. Phoebe and I straightened, stepped slowly apart, each watching the other. Her cheeks were flushed, eyes glittering like the heart of a forge. My heart was a wild thing, thrashing against my ribs.

"'The old dame was right,' she breathed. 'Ye *can* dance.'

"'Perhaps.' I swallowed, dust-dry. 'But I fear that was my last. I should abed.'

"Her gaze sharpened at that, eyes roaming the taverne around us.

"'Probably for the best. Long road ahead.' She curtseyed, smooth and graceful, curls tumbling forward as she dipped her head. 'Moon's blessings, Chevalier.'

"I tore my eyes from the thudding vein in her throat, my skin damp with sweat.

"'Godmorrow, mademoiselle.'

"And with the thirst inside me screaming, I near fled from the room."

V

SOME SLIVER OF JOY

"I WOKE WHEN dark ran deepest, and hope seemed farthest from the sky.

"Opening my eyes in the velvet black, I could still taste liquor on my tongue, a hint of woodsmoke, another scent strung beneath like an old promise. I wondered where I was, what had woken me. And I caught it again—the perfume that set my heart beating swift against my ribs and dragged me up through the tattered wall of sleep.

"Silverbell.

"*Astrid . . .*

"She drifted through the dark toward me, moonslight kissing her skin as if it adored her too. She was utterly bare, pale and perfect, my eyes drinking every inch of her; the mystery of her eyes and red promise of her lips, the dizzying curve of her breasts and the smooth arcs of her hips, and lower, to the dark heaven between her thighs. And though I knew in the heart of me this was only a dream, still I sighed at the simple sight of her.

"'*I miss you,*' she breathed.

"Standing at the foot of the bed, my bride lifted the covers, eyes sparkling to discover I was already naked and hard beneath. Slinking beneath the sheets, she prowled upward on hands and knees, long hair tickling my bare skin; a lioness of alabaster and shadow. She loomed above me now, wreathed in the perfume of silverbell, the sheet draped about her like a funeral shroud.

"'*I miss the way you kiss.*'

"Her face was framed by black rivers, red lips parted. She drifted closer, a serpent uncoiling, and I rose off the bed to meet her, dying to feel her mouth on mine. But Astrid allowed me only the faintest touch of her lips, placing one knife-sharp fingernail on my chest; the whole of me at her mercy with the press of her smallest finger.

"*I miss the way you feel.*'

"She knelt astride my thighs, razored fingernails skimming my chest, down the tattooed valley of my heaving belly until they reached the smooth heat of my cock. I groaned at her touch, her fingers flame, my breath quickening as her hand encircled me, slow and maddening. She leaned close, and again I lunged for her mouth, but once more, she allowed me only the briefest kiss before she pushed me back. And with a smile as dark as honeyed chocolat, she sank toward her prize.

"*I miss the way you taste.*'

"I groaned as I felt that first touch, warm and soft, licking me from root to aching crown. She teased me, fist tightening around me as her lips flickered over me, breath cool upon my burning skin. She toyed with me, stroking, kissing, kneading, pleading, and I sighed and thrust my hips upward, begging for more. She laughed, tongue tracing butterflies on me for one last, agonizing moment before she finally plunged me into her mouth.

"I was hers then. Wholly and solely. My head thrown back and my spine arched as time lost all meaning. All I knew was the rhythm of her lips, the deftness of her tongue, the tightness of her throat as she forced me deep, deep as she could take me. I gathered up a fistful of her hair to guide her, and she growled assent, but in truth, this tune was hers to play. And so she did—she, the maestro; me, now helpless in her song. Suckling harder, deeper, swifter now, that blissful tempo quickening with her moans as I closed my eyes and took hold of the headboard and held on for dear fucking life.

"'Don't stop,' I begged her. 'God, *please* don't stop.'

"The magik of her hands, her mouth, her lips dragged me ever higher into raging heavens, nothing left but the fall. I gasped as I felt my ending rushing up from the thundering heart of me, and as I tumbled, I cried aloud, eyes open wide and all my sky aflame, the oaken headboard shattering to splinters in my grip with a crack of thunder.

"She moaned as white fire flooded her tongue, drinking as if I were water in her desert, and when I had nothing left to give, still she tried, suckling and swallowing and whispering, '*More,*' until the pleasurepain was too much for me to bear. I wrapped my fingers in her tresses again, easing her away, and she let me slip from her mouth only reluctantly, gifting my still-aching cock a scattering of warm kisses, up and down its length, before her head sank to rest on my thigh.

"'Sweet Mothermoons, ye've been savin' that up for a while,' she purred.

"My heart lurched in my chest, and I shot bolt upright, snaking back toward the broken headboard. I could barely speak for my shock, mouth agape, eyes wide.

"'*Phoebe?*'

"The duskdancer raised herself up on one arm, curls tumbling over her pale skin. She was naked, dim moonlight spilling over tattoos and scars, sheet crumpled about her hips.

"'Anything to drink in here?' Her eyes roamed my body, and her smile turned sharp and wicked. 'Aside from the obvious, I mean.'

"'What the *fuck* are you doing in here?' I demanded.

"She blinked, looking at me like I was a simpleton.

"'You?'

"I was out of the bed, taking the blanket with me. We were in my bedchamber on the top floor of the White Rabbit, memory of the night before now settling in my addled head. I realized Phoebe must have stolen in here while I was dreaming, that I'd mistaken her for that same dream. I could still see the echo of my Astrid lingering in my mind's eye; long black hair and deep black eyes and a shadow that weighed a ton. My thoughts were a tempest; anger, shame, guilt, confusion, all further confounded by the beautiful naked woman now sitting up in my bed and gazing at me with utter bewilderment.

"'Ye aright?'

"'No, I'm not fucking aright!' I paced about, not knowing how to feel other than cold and naked. But as promised, one of Fionna's daughters had taken away my clothes for washing after I'd bathed, so I was forced to wrap the blanket about my waist instead. 'I never asked . . . Damn it, I'd no wish for you to do that, mademoiselle!'

"Phoebe's brow arched as she glanced to the headboard I'd just shattered with my bare hands. 'Apologies . . . but ye seemed quite enthused a moment ago?'

"'That was . . .' I flailed, utterly at a loss. 'I thought I was dreaming!'

"'I suppose a woman could take that as a compliment?'

"'I thought I was dreaming of my wife!'

"Phoebe fell still then, her playful smile fading. 'Oh.'

"She looked around the room, then slowly pulled the sheet up to cover herself.

"'*Oh*,' she said again.

"'Get out.' I leaned against the wall, sank to my haunches. The troth ring

on my finger felt made of lead right then. 'God *fucking* damn it, get the hell out of here.'

"'. . . I'm sorry.'

"I looked across the bedchamber and into those golden eyes, expecting the same sharpness I usually found there. But instead, Phoebe gazed at me with honest compassion.

"'The way ye danced wi' me, I thought ye wanted . . . and what ye said just now, ah, *shite,* I thought . . .' Phoebe hung her head, breathing deep. 'Yer right, I should go.'

"I watched her slipping on her chemise for the long, cold walk back to her room. And though my thoughts were still a flaming tumble of guilt and resentment and confusion, I saw Phoebe's cheeks burned with shame, and for a moment—perhaps the first in my sorry life—I tried to put myself in her shoes.

"She'd no knowing I dreamed of Astrid, nor the shape those dreams took. All Phoebe knew was that a man she'd shared a long and bloody road with had danced with her perilously near, and when she'd come to him in the dark, he'd pulled her closer rather than pushing her away. And now, even though the prick was casting her out of his bed, she still had heart enough to apologize to *him.*

"'It's not your fault,' I told her as she rose.

"Phoebe glanced at me, eyes hard, lips thin.

"'Please,' I said. 'You don't have to leave.'

"'Well, I cannae stay now. Ye've made me yer fool, Gabriel de León.'

"'You're not a fool.' I stood slow, matching her gaze. 'Forgive me. Stay.'

"'Sweet Mothermoons,' she sighed. '*Go. Stay. Kitcat. Mademoiselle.* Yer like summer and winter in one bloody day, man, I swear it. Yer problem is ye've nae ken *what* ye want.'

"I shrugged, not knowing what to tell her. I could still almost see my bride if I tried. Chest aching as the shadows lost her shape, as the scent I'd dreamed vanished in the dark.

"'I want her back, Phoebe.'

"She softened a little then, silvered pity shining on the hard gold of her eyes.

"'I know,' she sighed. 'I know ye do. And I lost one I loved too. I understand that want. That *bleed.* But I also understand this life is short, and this world is *cold,* and the warmth I feel atween us now might be the last time I feel anything a'tall.' The duskdancer shook her head, anger fighting sorrow.

'Moonssakes, Gabriel, she's *gone*. It's nae betrayal to find some sliver of joy without her. I'm not askin' ye to marry me.'

"'I know.'

"I sighed, dragging a trembling hand through my hair.

"'You know, most days I can keep a grip of it. Sometimes, I even remember them both and smile. But I still dream of her, Phoebe. Not as much as I once did, but . . . when she comes to me, she comes *so* sweetly, so fair and so fine . . . I should've known better than to mistake you for her.'

"Phoebe scowled then, tossed a flaming braid from her eyes.

"'Now *that*, nae woman could take as a compliment.'

"'No, that's not what I m—'

"She marched toward the door, and I was across the bedchamber in a heartbeat, reaching for her hand. But I was heedless in my haste, and as the silver on my palm again touched her skin, she snarled in agony and wrenched herself free with a curse.

"'Watch yer *DAMN*—'

"'I'm sorry,' I said, palms up as I backed away. 'Forgive me, Phoebe.'

"She glared at the welt my aegis had left on her flesh, sharp teeth bared. A reminder of the enmity between our kinds, the hatred; the simple touch of my hand a poison to her.

"'Ye know, yer wrong,' she snapped, eyes flashing. 'I *am* a damned fool. A fool who's forgot where she comes from. What she is, and what ye are. Ye spoke true in the mountains. I should've left ye in the damned snow and sought help wi' my kin. I've nae business bein' here, and I've sure as hell nae business bein' w'the likes of ye.'

"She spat on the floor, as if to rid herself of my taste.

"'See ye when I'm lookin' at ye. *Silversaint*.'

"'Phoebe—'

"The door slammed, and I winced at the thunderclap of her departure.

"I was left in the gloom then.

"Cold. Wretched.

"And once more, totally alone.

"'Outstanding job, de León,' I sighed. 'Just. *Fucking*. Brilliant.'"

VI

BEST SERVED COLD

HIGH IN A lonely tower of Sul Adair, Gabriel de León leaned forward slow, topping up his goblet of wine. Jean-François studied the Last Silversaint's features, the steel-grey eyes and sword-sharp jaw, the telltale scars wrought upon his tattooed skin.

"You certainly did have a way with women, de León."

"I think, rather, they had their way with me."

"Perhaps," the vampire chuckled. "Still, I fear your history with them is the sort I'd not wish upon my worst enemy."

Gabriel frowned, toying with his wine. "That saying always struck me as strange, you know. *I wouldn't wish it on my worst enemy*. It's supposed to describe a pain indescribable, oui? As if by refusing to wish it on the one you despise most, you place it in a tier above all others. But the worst pain I ever felt? Perhaps I'm a cunt, coldblood, but the thought of my enemies suffering it too makes the notion I had to live through it a little easier to bear."

The Last Silversaint downed his goblet with a single swallow.

"Seems to me if you're describing your pain as one you wouldn't inflict upon your worst foe, either you need a bigger vocabulary, or you need a better kind of enemy."

"And you had one now in Mlle Dúnnsair?" Jean-François licked his thumb slow, turned a new page. "Or did you kiss and make up once tempers had cooled?"

"Not exactly." Gabriel picked up the bottle with tattooed hands, refilling his goblet again. "When I knocked on her door the next morning, Phoebe was gone."

The vampire blinked. "She abandoned you?"

"Depends how you look at it." Gabriel shrugged. "I knew an old bookseller in Augustin, once. Kept a little shop off the Rue des Méchants. Mme Tatiana, her name. To keep her company in her dotage, Tatiana had two pets—a dog named M. Boots, and a cat named Spatula. She cared for them like her own children, and they loved her just as dear. But back in the fell winter of sixty-three, old dame Tatiana up and died.

"Took two weeks for anyone to realize. Breaking into her shop, her neighbors discovered Tatiana's body in the storeroom. M. Boots lay cold and still at his mistress's side, and beside him, warm and well, sat Spatula, cleaning his paws. The hound had starved to death. The cat had been chewing on his old mistress to keep himself alive. That's the difference between canines and felines, coldblood. The former will love you unconditionally. The latter will tolerate you until they don't."

Gabriel leaned back and took another long swallow of wine.

"I *had* made a fool of her. No woman I ever met took that with a smile.

"My clothes had been laid out for me at least, cleaned of the blood and filth of the road. A muddy dawn was blooming as I hurried down to the White Rabbit's commonroom, where Fi kissed me fairdawning and served me a swift breakfast. My old comrade handed me a heavy winter cloak and a few packs, bulging with supplies for my journey. Trying to buckle on her old swordbelt, she shot me a wry smile as she realized it no longer fit about her waist.

"'Time eats us all alive,' she sighed.

"I smiled, ruefully scratching my head. 'I . . . ah, might've broken your bed.'

"'That kind of evening, was it?' The old dame peered behind me, frowning as she realized Phoebe was nowhere to be seen. 'And where's yer fellow vandal?'

"'She was gone when I woke up.'

"'Ahhhh. *That* kind of evening. The way you two bicker, I should've known.'

"I frowned. 'Phoebe and I don't bicker.'

"'Seven Martyrs,' she scoffed. 'All the pair of ye need are some pet names and a dash of joyless shagging, and you'd be a married couple.'

"'Fuck off, Fi.'

"The old dame chuckled, shaking her head. Throwing on the cloak she'd given me, I looked upon the homely hearth of her little taverne one last time. Last night's revels had been welcome warmth on a long, cold road. But Dior was still in the clutches of the Dyvok, and only I could save her now.

Fi and I made our way through dawn streets crowded with the starving and dispossessed, over to a farrier's hold on the keepside of the city. I knew not by what magik she managed it—horses were worth a fortune those nights—but Fionna soon brought me around back and presented me with a fine gelding, already saddled. He was a tall warhorse with a braided mane and a distinctive pale pattern in the silver grey of his shaggy coat—white forelegs and a patch about his face that looked almost like a skull. He was that Ossian breed known as a tarreun, famed for their courage and endurance.

"'Is this your old Titan?' I whispered in wonder, stroking the beast's mane.

"Fionna shook her head. 'I put Titan to stud years back. This is the best of his sons. His name is Argent.' She smiled at me fondly, handed me the reins. 'Seemed appropriate.'

"I shook my head, lost for words. Here was another too-swift parting, just as with Lachlan—a friend resurfacing from past nights, vanishing in the flood I was drowning in today. World being what it was, I knew this might be the last time we met.

"'Godmorrow, Sister,' I said, eyes burning. 'And merci. For everything.'

"'Ye look after yerself,' Fionna warned. 'If ye're headed where I think ye're headed . . . Those bastards will never forgive what ye did to Tolyev, Gabbie.'

"I caught her up in my arms, squeezing tight. 'It was good to see you again, mon amie.'

"'Ye too. Remember what I said. About enjoying the music while ye can. And watch this surly arse out there, eh?' She squeezed me harder, then gave me a slap on the backside to part us. 'There's still a few of us who'd miss it if it were gone.'

"And then, I was. Riding through the crowded dockside gates, into a soup of cold mist dusted with thin snow. I rode through that shantytown around the walls; so many lives, so many futures perished to coldblood hungers. But still, my heart was warmed to be back on Dior's trail, and Argent was a sure-footed fellow, trotting across the frozen Volta without fear.

"'I feel it only fair to warn you,' I said as we reached the far bank. 'I don't have the best luck with horses lately. Or rather, they've not had best luck around me.'

"The tarreun nickered in response, looking unconcerned, and so, I nudged him into a trot. The woods were silent save for the howling wind, the thud of Argent's hooves across the frost. As my new steed seethed beneath me, rolling muscle and heaving breath, I kept my head down, tricorn pulled low, wondering if Phoebe had come this way. My mind was a storm when I thought of her—blood thrilling at the memory of her in my bed, tempered by the weight of the ring on my finger, the chill of that shadow that yet haunted my dreams. But the duskdancer never left tracks, and if she'd taken this path, I found no trace of her. The only signs of life in the deadwood were rabbit spoor and the occasional squirrel, and the shadow of wings passing swift overhead.

"Turning southward, I reached out once more toward Dior. I realized she was moving slower now, and I found my pulse quickening with the hope I might actually catch her up before the Dyvok reached their destination.

"I should've fucking known better."

Gabriel sighed, watching that pale moth flitting about the globe.

"They hit me on the third night.

"I knew they were coming by then. I'd marked those wings once too often, caught a glimpse of a mousehawk through the dead branches—the same one Phoebe and I had seen up in the Nightstone. They'd been tracking me awhile, it seemed, drawing closer as I rode southward, skirting the edge of dread Fa'daena, the Forest of Sorrows. But they were clever when they finally came, waiting 'til the small hours to strike. Brave Argent was slumbering beside a dead elm, the lonely figure of the tarreun's new master huddled among the tree's roots, my cloak pulled low, my boots protruding beneath the frayed hem.

"The crossbow bolt whistled out of the darkness, trailing a length of silver chain behind. It struck the cloak where my chest would've been, punching through the saddlebags beneath. The marksman cursed, my ruse spotted in a moment, but that moment was all I needed, striking from the shadows and burying Ash deep into the fellow's bowels.

"*Lovely red tasty red sniksnak snikSNAK!*

"The fellow grunted, I *twisted*, blood spraying in the night. The crossbow fell from his hands and I caught a glimpse of silver; a sevenstar embroidered on his greatcoat. But I'd no time to curse my ill-fortune, another figure barreling from the dark like a cannon shot, four feet thudding on frost. A hound, I realized; stout and pig-eyed, bright fangs bared. I stepped aside her charge, raising Ash, but shots rang out then, one two, *boom BOOM*, and I gasped as double slugs of silvershot blasted a couple of unasked-for holes in my favorite chest.

"*Oh, p-p-prettyone! W-w-w-w-we rememememember you . . .*

"I managed to keep a grip on Ash, turning as another shape flew at me from between the dead trees—black coat and silversteel greatsword, the gleam of another sevenstar. The 'saint's collar was laced over his face, tricorn dragged low, just a glimpse of hard green eyes as he flew right at me. I parried, desperate, blood spilling down my chest, spattering on my bare feet. Our blades met, the song of steel ringing bright in the halls of memory. He was dosed on sanctus, and I was dry, but still, we danced as once we'd done, matching blow for blow. If we dueled heads-up, I'd no clue who'd have proved the victor—he fought like the demon I'd trained him to be. But one-on-one wasn't the game we played.

"The hound flew at me again, seizing a mouthful of shin just as another crossbow bolt sang from the shadows. The sawtooth head punched through my shoulderblade, spring-loaded claw snapping open inside me. I was wrenched off my feet, roaring as I hit the snow, hound still tearing at my leg. She yelped as I kicked her, my hand clawing the frost as I rolled upright, coughing blood. But I gasped in agony as I felt something hard and sharp scrape across my spine, erupting out of my chest in a spray of red.

"'Yer back,' a voice hissed. 'My blade.'

"The first 'saint was on me then, holding his guts in with one hand as he tried to wrest Ash from my grip. Something crashed into my skull, sending me sprawling. I heard many feet then; a dozen pairs at least, charging from all around as a cry echoed in the night.

"'Do not kill him! But do *not* treat him well!'

"Boots rained into my ribs, the back of my head, the sound of tolling bells and cracking bone ringing in time with their kicks. I curled into a ball on the frost, forearms up to protect my face, night burning bright as the long-lost day.

"Gasping, bleeding, I was rolled onto my back. A familiar figure unlaced his collar as he looked down at me, square jaw dusted with stubble and silver roses.

"'L-Lachlan,' I whispered. 'Don't . . .'

"My old apprentice clenched his fangs, raised one tattooed hand.

"'Fucking *traitor*,' he spat.

"And like a sledgehammer, his fist fell."

VII
SOMETHING TO DIE FOR

"I WOKE ONLY slowly, blinking hard, blood in my mouth. It had been a while since I'd been tickled by another 'saint, and the bells in my tower were still ringing, the silvershot holes in my chest drooling red. My wrists and ankles were shackled with silversteel, my freezing feet bare. Squinting at the dirty grey sludge moving beneath me, I realized I was slung belly-down over Argent's saddle, raising my head to see how deep the shit I swam in truly was.

"Up to my fucking eyeballs, I realized.

"I was part of a convoy, two dozen footsoldiers trudging around me. They wore chainmail and heavy boots, eyes cold and knuckles scarred; a black-hearted pack of bastards if ever I'd seen one. Their tabards were crimson, embroidered with the flower and flail of Naél, Angel of Bliss. And my belly sank as I looked to the woman riding beside me.

"'Oh, shit . . .' I groaned.

"I recognized her immediately, of course; long dark hair and pointed fringe beneath her tricorn's veil, crimson tabard, and an iron gauntlet on her right hand. Last I'd seen her had been in the Redwatch Priory, fresh from a session of torturing Dior.

"Valya d'Naél, sister of the Holy Inquisition.

"'Fairdawning, heretic,' she said, lip curling.

"'Godmorrow, Sœur,' I sighed. 'Had a feeling we'd bump into each other again.'

"She smiled, bloodless. *No call unheeded that by faithful hearts is sung to heaven.*

"To have fallen into the clutches of the Inquisition would've been worrisome enough, but that wasn't half of my troubles. We were threading a thin path through rotten woodlands; weeping trees and grey ice and fungal snarls in the branches above. And right behind me, all in a row, rode three black-clad brothers of the Ordo Argent.

"The first I didn't recognize—too young to have been part of the Order when I served. He was Sūdhaemi born, dark hair cropped short, olive-skinned. He'd a sharp hazel stare, and his left ear was cut in half, left eyebrow scarred. His belly was still bandaged from where I'd stabbed him yestereve, and his expression was floating just north of hostile.

"The fellow in the middle of the trio was a mountain in his saddle, his greatcoat barely fitting over his barrel chest. He was Nordish, eyes dark blue, goatee running to grey. His right arm was missing at the elbow, and three scars cut across his face, brow to craggy chin. A mousehawk perched on his shoulder, watching me with tawny eyes, and the dog who'd attacked me yestereve walked beside his horse. She was dark grey, white on her paws and muzzle, possessed of the flat skull, piggy eyes, and steeltrap jaw of an Ossian staghound.

"'Xavier Pérez.' I coughed, tasting blood. 'Long time, Frère.'

"He gave me a grim nod, voice rough as sandstone. 'Chevalier.'

"'She's a beauty,' I said, glancing to the hound. 'What's her name?'

"'Saber,' the big man replied. Gesturing to the hawk at his shoulder, he added, 'This is Steel.'

"'Very pretty. Speaking of'—I nodded to the scabbard at his saddle—'it's generous of you to look after Ashdrinker for me. But could I have her back now, please?'

"'I fear not.' Xavier's scarred lips twisted in a mirthless smile. 'But if it's of comfort, she had some colorful opinions to share when I dared lay hands on her. My mother's virtue was mentioned. Repeatedly, in fact.'

"I chuckled, despite my predicament. 'Well. She's *my* sword, after all.'

"'The dead own nothing, traitor.'

"I looked up as the last 'saint spoke, my heart aching at the sight of him. My old apprentice took his tricorn off, brushing that whip of sandy-blond back from his brow. His green eyes were edged with kohl, a weave of silver roses and thorns scrolling down his cheek, fangs glinting at the edge of his snarl. I remembered the first time I saw those teeth; bared at me as we clashed upon the broken walls of Báih Sìde, steel to steel, butterflies rising in my belly as I realized what the boy was.

"What he could *become*.

"'Lachlan,' I sighed. 'Good to s-see you again, brother.'

"'Don't ye *dare* name me *brother*.'

"'I've not got any other names prepared, I'm afraid.' I spat red, prodding a loose tooth with my tongue. 'How about Buttercup? You look a Buttercup with that fucking haircut. Hit like one too.'

"'Ye jest?' He grasped the hilt of a beautiful greatsword, new-forged, scripture etched down the blade. 'Ye dare *jest* after what ye did, ye murderous fucking whoreson?'

"'Easy, á Craeg,' Xavier murmured. 'This traitor's for the noose, not the block.'

"'The noose?' I craned my neck to squint at the canopy above, searching for the strangled sun. 'We're headed east by my mark. They out of rope in San Michon?'

"'You are to be transported to Augustin, heretic.'

"I twisted to look at the sister riding beside me. Valya d'Naél didn't deign to glance at me as she spoke, eyes on the frozen woods ahead.

"'Empress Isabella herself has been informed of your malfeasance,' she said. 'You are to face judgment in the Tower of Tears under charge of heresy, and the murder of inquisitorial troops and members of the Ordo Argent upon sacred ground.'

"'It's not sacred ground if you're trying to butcher children on it,' I growled.

"'And butchering nuns upon it is better?'

"I looked to Lachlan as he spoke, his face dark with rage.

"'Lachie, you don't underst—'

"'I understand enough! Abbot Greyhand! Sœur Chloe and Fincher and the others! Ye murdered them all! Forgemaster Argyle *told* me it was ye!'

"'Did Argyle tell you why I did it? Did he tell you what th—'

"'Where are they, bastard?' Lachlan spat on the ground, lips twisted. 'Yer coldblood sister? Yer skinthief whore? And that ashen *witch* all three of ye are bound to serve?'

"'Seven Martyrs, Lachlan, Dior's no witch! And all I did at San Michon, I did to save her life! Chloe and Greyhand were set to cut her throat! To murder an innocent child on—'

"'Innocent? Is that a *jest?*' Lachlan shook his head, green eyes glittering like broken glass. 'I should've known. After yer fall into the arms of that lying jezebel, I should've known better than to trust ye. But I'd forgot just how *weak* ye were, Gabriel.'

"I breathed deep, ignoring the insult to Astrid, glancing to the 'saint beside Lachlan. 'We fought side by side in Qadir, Xavier. Again at Tuuve. You *know* me. You know I'd never—'

"'I know you bled for San Michon in your day,' the big man replied, voice hard as stone. 'I *also* know you shamed our holy Order, and broke your sacred vows, and returned from exile not to beg forgiveness, but to murder faithful servants in God's own house.' He shook his head. 'But no. I do not know you, de León. I wonder if I ever did.'

"I looked to the man beside me, my eyes pleading. 'Lachlan—'

"'Enough,' he hissed, raising his hand. 'Mothermaid, I can't bear the sight of ye.'

"Lachlan spurred his sosya on, hooves thudding in fresh snow as he broke away. I sought Xavier's eyes, but he laced up his collar and looked dead ahead, ignoring me completely. The youngblood was the only one to match my stare, hazel eyes cool and even. He was eighteen, maybe, dark hair shorn short, smooth jaw. From the size of the greatsword strapped to his saddle, I guessed he was Dyvok-born like Lachlan.

"'What's your name, brother?' I asked.

"'Arash Sa-Pashin. Though most call me Robin.'

"I smiled. 'Swift as a songbird, are you?'

"'My master said I sing like one. I had to take his word for it. Not many left these nights, after all.' He looked me up and down, lips pursed. 'You know, he used to tell me tales about you, hero. Back when I was an initiate. All the things you did when you were my age.'

"'And who was your master, swift Robin?'

"He made the sign of the wheel, gaze gone cold. 'Abbot Greyhand.'

"'Well.' I sighed. 'That's just fucking marvelous, isn't it?'

"We rode on through squalling snows, my body aching, hands shackled, bare feet freezing. I'd been shot with silver—the pain worsened by my constant, burning thirst, but after I complained, Valya simply ordered me gagged. And so I rode, days on end their prisoner, misery and pain compounded whenever I reached out toward Dior.

"I'd sworn I'd never leave her. But every time I pawed through the dark and cold toward that blood she carried, I found her farther and farther away.

"Every day. Every hour. Every minute.

"I was *losing* her.

"And that wasn't even the darkest of my troubles.

"I was sat on the snow as we stopped to camp the third night, my whole body numb with cold. The men lit a fire, Sœur Valya glowering at me across it—I swear that woman touched herself at night thinking about seeing me hanged. The 'saints were giving me only half a pipe per day, and to make matters worse, Valya was in her moonstime. I could smell her blood in every breath, and I'll put it down to' the thirst burning within me that it had taken three days to finally realize where we were.

"Young Robin was living up to his name as he did every eve, lifting a bloodwood harp from his saddlebags and singing a haunting tune. Bedding down a company thirty strong took a time, but after settling in, the hulking thug who oversaw my feeding and pissbreaks—an ugly trollson called Thibault—unbuckled my gag to give me a sip of brackish water.

"'What are we doing in here?' I croaked.

"'Shut your godless hole,' the thug replied.

"I ignored his command, looking Xavier in the eyes. 'Why are we going this w—'

"A fist crashed across my face, sprawling me into the snow with a crack of white light. I spat blood, glowered up at the prick who'd struck me. Thibault's bearded face was split in an ugly sneer, fist raised for another. 'I told you to shut your fuckin' hole.'

"'Easy there, brother.'

"It was Lachlan who'd spoken. He was sat against a tree with Saber, scratching the hound's ear as her leg joyfully thumped the snow. He'd slung off his brace of five wheellocks, and his gloves were off too, the letters G O D S W I L L etched silver below his knuckles. Atop his left hand was an old, awful burn; the skin healed mottled and red, never graced by the ink of his aegis. Firelight shone in his gaze as he matched Thibault's.

"'We don't go easy on heretics round 'ere, 'saint,' the big bastard growled.

"'This man slew Sada Ilon,' Lachlan said. 'Laure Voss. Danika and Aneké and dread Tolyev Dyvok in single combat. He doesn't deserve a dogpunch while he's clapped in irons.'

"'What he *deserves* awaits him in Augustin,' Sister Valya snapped. 'This man is an apostate. Slave to a thrice-damned minion of hell, hands dripping with the blood of the faithful.'

"'He's fallen far, Sœur,' Lachlan nodded. 'And I *will* smile as he hangs. But before he lost his way so completely, Gabriel de León taught me a lesson or three. About decency. About mercy. And I'll not sit silent while yer men beat a helpless prisoner.'

"Lachlan turned his gaze back to Thibault, his voice mild as a summer breeze.

"'Unless ye've the courage to remove his shackles?'

"The thug stared a moment longer, then muttered and turned away. I gave Lachlan a grateful nod, but he ignored me completely, returned to petting Saber. I knew it wasn't my defense he'd leapt to, simply the principle I'd instilled in him. He was a good man, my old 'prentice, despite the ire between us. Despite the pit of mud and blood he'd bloomed in.

"I knew I'd not long before they gagged me again, and so I turned to Xavier. Ashdrinker lay sheathed beside the old 'saint, my silvered dame dusted with snow. Xavier was oiling his own sword—remarkably well considering he only had the one arm now. Steel was perched on his shoulder, the mousehawk preening his feathers with a sharp black beak.

"'This route takes us through the Forest of Sorrows, Xavier.'

"He glanced at me, scarred face rent deep with shadow. 'And so?'

"'So, have any of you trekked through Fa'daena lately?' I looked to Lachlan, then to Robin. 'There's darkness afoot in the wild places of this empire, have you not seen it?'

"'I've heard tales,' Xavier replied. 'But Beaufort, where your ship awaits, is east.'

"'I tell you, it goes ill with this forest. We fought a stag in here that looked born in the pit of hell. And the shit I saw in the nor'weald would curl the hairs on your taddysack.'

"'Children's tales,' Valya scoffed, glowering across the flames. 'We are faithful servants of the Lord most high. We fear no darkness, heretic. It fears *us*.'

"I ignored the woman, fangs gritted, her very *scent* making me tremble like an autumn leaf. 'Trust me, Xavier. We walk a fool's path through Fa'daena.'

"'If I were you, hero,' Robin murmured, tuning his harp, 'I'd shut my mouth before someone shut it for me.'

"'But you're *not* me, boy,' I growled, temper and thirst getting the best of me. 'I'm the Black Lion of Lorson. Victor of the Battle of the Twins. Sword of the fucking Realm. How many babies have *you* had named after you?'

"'Gabriel,' Lachlan growled. 'Give it a rest.'

"'I taught you better than this, Lachie. I taught you to use your *head*.'

"'Ye also taught me to fight with honor,' he snapped. 'That it was better to die as a man than live as a monster. Well, it was no honorable man who butchered those innocents in that cathedral.' He shook his head, at last deigning to look at me. 'Great Redeemer, Gabriel, ye were the *best* of us. Bad enough ye broke yer vows at the beck of that harlot. But how in God's name could ye let it end like *this*?'

"'You speak ill of my wife again, Lachlan, I'll break your fuck—'

"'Look at yerself!' he cried. 'The *thirst* has you, Gabe! The *sangirè*! A blind man could see it! Ye can't even *look* at the sister for fear of her scent on the air! Is that how yer witch enslaved ye? Bending ye to her will with promise of her black blood?'

"'Dior's no witch, you stupid bastard!' I thrashed against my manacles, snarling. 'That girl is a miracle walking! She can end daysdeath, Lachlan! She has the blood of the—'

"'*Enough!*'

"Sœur Valya's cry echoed around the fire as she pointed one iron-clad finger.

"'I will have no heresy spread among this holy company! Silence him at once!'

"Her thugs descended, slapping the bit across my teeth and giving me a right kicking for my troubles. With a thoughtful frown at me, Xavier returned to oiling his sword. Lachlan sat scowling at the flames, refusing to meet my gaze. Robin stared daggers at my throat, then picked up his harp again, strumming soft hymns in the deeping dark. And I found myself staring heavenward, once more hoping that bastard up there knew what the hell he was doing.

"I wanted to speak to my brethren, to tell the truth about all I'd done and why. But Valya kept me silenced thereafter, gagged save for the few moments I was allowed to eat or smoke by that prick Thibault. And so we journeyed onward, two more days through Fa'daena, bedding down each dusk with that accursed bit in my mouth and my words seething behind my teeth as the thin red thread between Dior and me stretched ever thinner.

"Our first man went missing the next night.

"He was a Nordish lad named Leandro, sitting the night watch. We were in the heart of Fa'daena by then, the canopy so thick with fungus it smothered what little daylight we had. We were roused in the predawn black; Leandro's relief—a bruiser named Emilio—had woken to discover the lad missing. It was thought he might've gone to relieve himself, got turned about in the dark. But a search of the surrounds found no sign at all.

"'Seven Martyrs, look at this ...'

"It was Carlos, the duller of two brutish brothers, who'd spoken. He'd been searching Leandro's belongings as if the boy were hiding in his fucking rucksack or somesuch, holding aloft his discovery for his kinsman, Luis.

"It was a figure wrought of twigs, rough-formed in a man's shape. It wore a strip of red cloth like an inquisitor's tabard, a lock of dark hair knotted about its throat.

"Luis whispered, brow knotted. 'Is that ...'

"'Witchery,' Thibault spat, glancing to the woods around us.

"Carlos hurled the stickman into the fire, making the sign of the wheel. Valya ordered a search, but even with Xavier and Saber on the scent, they found no trace of Leandro, and after an hour, the inquisitor ordered we march on. The cohort shouldered their packs, leaving the lad's gear behind as if afeared to touch it. Gagged as I was, I could speak no warning save with my eyes, looking among the 'saints and shaking my head. But it would take more than an effigy of twigs to frighten men who'd fought denizens of the dark all their lives, and more than a warning from a murderous traitor to make them pay heed.

"The next men went missing two nights later.

"It happened during dinner, the fire blazing, young Arash Sa-Pashin singing as sweet as the songbird he was nicknamed for. It wasn't until the meal was served that the cook—a brawny slab of bucktoothed beef named Philippe—realized there were two bowls left over.

"'Where's Jean-Luc? And Luis?'

"Carlos rose to his feet, looking around the fire. 'Brother?'

"The other men stood, counting heads and searching their number. But as with Leandro before them, the fellows were vanished like wraiths.

"Torches were lit, a search conducted through the tight-packed trees. Robin and Sœur Valya stood watch over me, Xavier heading into the woods with Saber, Steel winging his way through the twisted branches above. I heard a shout, thudding footsteps, and Thibault and Carlos ran back to the inquisitor, breathless and pale.

"'Found piss-stains forty yards out, Sister,' Carlos gasped. 'And these.'

"Thibault held out two small effigies, both wrought of sticks. Again, they wore strips of torn red cloth like inquisitor's tabards, locks of hair tied about their necks.

"'What the *fuck* is goin' on here?' Philippe whispered, lifting his frypan.

"My heart lurched sideways as a scream sounded out in the woods. Faint. Terrified. Agonized.

"Lachlan squinted into the dark. 'Is that . . . Leandro?'

"'You're the one with five fuckin' pistols, mate,' Thibault growled. *'You* go find out.'

"'Calm yourselves, brothers,' Valya warned. 'Almighty God shall protect us.'

"The inquisitor's cohort circled the fire, steel and torches raised as the screams faded. I sat on the snow, still in chains, looking from Lachlan to Robin. We'd all seen hell, in one shape or another. But even Xav looked a little out of sorts as he returned empty-handed.

"I just shook my head, still gagged, speaking only with my eyes.

"*I warned you.*

"We broke camp next dawn, and despite protest from Carlos about his missing kinsman, it was decided to head south toward the wood's closest edge. It would take us longer to reach Beaufort that way, and worse, there was no path to follow; our compasses no longer worked, swinging like a pisshead in a pub brawl. But all save Carlos were now of accord it'd be best to get the fuck out of this forest as quick as feet could carry us.

"Steel was Fa'daena's next victim.

"The mousehawk slept on his master's shoulder, flying up every hour to check our course. But after midday, he was sent for a look-see and simply never returned. Xavier made no fuss at first, but as minutes stretched into hours, the men began to question, and the 'saint to fear. He and Valya spoke in hushed voices as the soldiers whispered. All looked frightened now, eyes bruised by sleepless nights. I met Lachlan's gaze, shaking my head again.

"*I fucking warned you.*

"We were lost now, tracking direction by what little we could see of the sun. Those on watch at night swore they saw shapes moving beyond the fire's edge. Eyes watching. Low growling. Men relieved themselves three or four at a time, not daring to leave the light. Each day was a slog through branch and bramble, trees with gnarled trunks that looked akin to human faces, blighted birds with feathers that wriggled like tiny tongues. The horses were skittish, the men sleepless, tempers frayed to threads.

"'*Why the hell did we come this way?*'

"'*Great Redeemer, did you* see *that?*'

"'*I dreamed of your death last night.*'

"'*The fuck you tellin' me that for?*'

"On the eighth day, when we broke camp, we found a row of small twig-men, encircling the dell where we'd slept. There'd been one made for each of us.

"On the ninth, we found more effigies in a small clearing. They were arranged in a circle, one on its back in the center, Leandro's sword thrust through its chest. Valya dashed them apart with a few savage kicks, roaring scripture to the empty woods. Her men muttered, dark stares aimed at the inquisitor's back, at those endless, silent trees.

"It was on the tenth night it finally went to hell.

"We were deep in the watch, four men posted to each shift now. I was dreaming of Celene again, smiling as she dropped me off the Cairnhaem bridge. But I was wrenched from shallow slumber by the most awful scream I'd ever heard in my life.

"I sat bolt upright, heart trying to burst from my chest. Saber was going berserk, men snatching up logs from the fire, faces bloodless, eyes wild. Valya lifted the wheel from about her throat, shouting Testaments quotes as that soulless screaming continued.

"'*Turn ye now, oh faithless kings of men! And look upon thy queen!*'

"'Martyrs, what the *hell* is that?'

"'SHUT THAT *BLOODY DOG UP!*'

"The screaming stopped, like someone had choked it. Silence thickened the freezing dark, Xavier hushing his hound with the powers of his blood. Lachie and Robin both loosed the buttons on their greatcoats, chests adorned with the bear of Dyvok. But there was no glow in their ink—whatever stalked us through these hungry trees was no coldblood.

"The screaming became singing, closer now; haunting and shapeless. And beneath that unearthly song, we heard a wail of agony, of terror, somewhere deep in the dark.

"'Fuck me,' Thibault groaned, squeezing his sword hilt. 'Oh, Mothermaid, fuck *ME*.'

"More screaming started, a different direction, faint and terrified.

"'Brother Luis?' Valya cried, wheel held aloft. 'Brother Luis, is that you?'

"'We have to go help him,' Carlos declared.

"'Fuck *that*,' Philippe spat.

"'That's my brother out there, you craven *dog*!'

"'Then *you* go bloody get him!'

"I wrenched at my shackles in vain, shouting behind the leather between my teeth. Saber was barking again, chaos breaking loose around the campsite, my eyes flickering from Lachlan's to Xavier's. The older 'saint scowled, unbuckling the bit from behind my head.

"'Give me my sword back, Xav,' I hissed.

"'What is this sorcery, de León?' Xavier demanded. 'Your witch come to claim you?'

"'I keep telling you Dior is no witch. Now give me my *fucking sword*!'

"'Shut him up!' Valya roared.

"'Brothers?' Robin murmured, eyes on his fellows. 'What do we do?'

"Lachlan snatched up a burning brand from the fire, held it aloft. His shout brought still to the men, calm in that breaking storm. 'Hear me, now! Those are men of God out there, and we shall not abandon the faithful to such a fate! Robin, Thibault, stay here and watch the traitor. Rest of you, march with me. Ten feet apart, torches all of you!'

"The soldiers obeyed, snapped from their fear by Lachlan's iron command. Xavier scowled at me, but followed Lachie into the dark. Robin drew the wheellock from his bandolier, his mighty greatsword held in his other hand. Thibault huddled close to the younger 'saint, blade shaking in his grip. My pulse was thudding, fear entwined with woodsmoke and rot as the deadwood echoed with calls for lost comrades.

"'Get me out of these shackles, Sa-Pashin,' I warned.

"'Shut the fuck up, hero.'

"I nodded to the keys on Thibault's belt. 'If the things out there are anything like I saw in the nor'weald, you're going to want a spare set of hands, man.'

"'He said *shut the fuck up*,' Thibault spat, kicking me.

"Silence fell, broken only by shouting soldiers, fainter screams. Thibault squinted into the dark, Robin scoured the shadows; pinpricks of light flickering among the trees like ghosts, a flash of fire on metal, quickly vanished. I thrashed against my manacles then, spitting. 'If I'm going to die, let me die on my feet, damn you!'

"'Damn *me*?' Robin scoffed. 'Damn *you*, de León.'

"The youngblood's voice was a low growl, eyes on that dreadful dark.

"'God, you should've heard the way Greyhand used to speak about you.

The stories he told.' He shook his head, sneering. 'Initiates used to go to sleep in the Barracks at night, whispering about the things you'd done. The Black Lion of Lorson. Butcher of the Crimson Glade. Knighted by the Empress's sword at sixteen. You were a legend to us. To *me*.'

"He chuckled, bitter, sparing me a hateful glance. On my knees in the dirty snow, wracked with the thirst, neck destined for the traitor's noose.

"'Never meet your heroes, I suppose.'

"'I never asked to be your fucking hero,' I snapped. 'And all you know about me is what you've been *sold*. The Emperor's armies were full of youngbloods like you, Robin. Boys who thought they'd grow up to be heroes like me. Fact is, most ended up in unmarked graves, or swelling the ranks of our enemies. That's a truth no minstrel song or fireside legend *ever* tells. But that's the fucking point of them.'

"'Your story gave us hope. It gave us courage to—'

"'It gave you a noose around your necks! Greyhand *despised* me! He didn't tell you those tales to give you courage; the bastard was giving you something to *die* for! And it wasn't because I deserved it that Isabella knighted me with her own sword. It was because that bitch knew it'd give a thousand *idiots* like you a reason to pick one up!'

"'Shut up,' he hissed.

"'You call me a traitor? You think me a monster?' I scoffed, shaking my head. 'I'm not half the fucking monster our cunt master was, boy. Nor half the *coward*.'

"'Shut. Your. *Mouth*.'

"'Truth is the sharpest knife, eh? You're right to loathe me, boy. I'm nothing close to the songs they sing about me. I'm nothing like the myth they made of me. I'm just a man. As flawed and frail and fucked up as the rest of you. But for all my failings, *all* my sins, never once did I think it right to spill the blood of an innocent child.' I met his eyes, smiling. 'I'm glad I put Greyhand down. He was a fucking *dog*, Sa-Pashin.'

"Robin snarled, sharp fangs gleaming, lifting his pistol and leveling it at my head. And as soon as the youngblood turned his back, the shape emerged from those twisted trees.

"'What in *God's* name . . .' Thibault breathed.

"It moved like water. Like lightning. Sharp teeth bared and wicked claws uncurled. I'd no idea the shape of the evil those men had imagined stalking us these past days. I knew the shape my *own* fears had taken until I'd glimpsed her in the shadows a few moments before. But it was not some fae horror or twisted blightling charging us through the trees now, nor some terror from a fireside tale. It was something entirely more welcome.

"Hair like flame.

"Eyes like gold.

"Beautiful as the long-lost dawn.

"'Bonsoir, Kitcat.'"

VIII

LIONESS

"WHEN DIOR HAD plucked that dress from Jènoah's wardrobe, I'm not sure what the hell she was thinking. Maybe she imagined we might find a moment's respite in some lordly château, or stumble across a quandary in which possession of a ballgown would prove essential to success. Maybe she thought Phoebe would look good wearing it, or perhaps she simply wondered what she'd look like climbing *out* of it. But whatever was going through the girl's mind when she chose that outfit, I'm reasonably sure she never imagined the duskdancer would find herself fighting for my life in it."

Gabriel took a long gulp of wine, shrugging to himself.

"But, here we were.

"She'd split the skirts to her hips, allowing her to move swifter, quieter. And move she did, silent as a wraith, right at Robin. The youngblood was no slouch—he'd been trained by the man who trained me, after all. But as he snapped off a hasty shot, I lashed out a kick at his knees, knocking him off-kilter, and then Phoebe was on him, splitting his guts with one swipe of her claws. Thibault screamed as Robin collapsed—his cry cut short as I reared up and wrapped my manacles around his throat. He stumbled, we fell, the big man grunting as I cracked his head over and over on the stones around the firepit.

"Shouts of alarm rang in the dark, Robin tried to raise his sword, one hand holding his ruptured innards. And Phoebe leapt astride him, knees pinning his shoulders, pressing sharp thumbs to his eyes.

"'Don't!' I shouted.

"The duskdancer glowered at me, hands dripping red. I'd already rolled Thibault onto his back, the big man groaning as I snatched the keys from his belt.

"'Don't kill him, Phoebe.'

"'Are ye mad? He tried t—'

"'Leave him be, grab the horses.'

"She snarled as a shout rang in the dark, footsteps approaching.

"'I know you enjoy it when my kind beg, mademoiselle,' I pleaded. 'But we've not the time to do it proper. Just trust me, eh? This boy doesn't deserve to die.'

"More shouts rang out in the woods, flickering torches heading back toward us. My wrists were unlocked now, and I was working on the shackles at my ankles as Phoebe tore away Robin's bandolier and hurled it into the gloom, rising swift to her feet.

"'Friend t-to duskdancers and c-coldbloods.' Robin coughed blood, guts steaming in the bitter chill. 'You're every bit the traitor they n-named you, de León.'

"'Were that true, youngblood,' I said, 'I'd be kissing you good-bye, not goodnight.'

"I swung my shackles into Robin's head, knocking him senseless. Giving the boy another for good measure, I dragged off his boots, snatched up my bandolier and supplies. Looking around the flames, I realized with sinking heart that Xavier had carried Ashdrinker off with him—there was no way to get her back without taking him on. But Phoebe was at the horses now, astride Valya's mare and hissing through bloody teeth.

"'Move yer arse!'

"I grabbed Robin's greatsword instead, hobbled across the clearing toward Argent. If I'd less heart and more brains, I'd have slaughtered the other horses to hamper their pursuit. But it takes a special sort of cunt to kill helpless beasts, Historian, and while I'm certainly a cunt, apparently I'm just not that special at it. Smacking their backsides, I shouted to scatter them instead. Climbing onto Argent's back, I looked the duskdancer over—dipped in emerald and drenched in red, eyes of molten gold.

"'*You* took your damn time.'

"She glowered at me, incredulous. 'I think the words yer lo—'

"'Merci, mademoiselle.' I tipped an imaginary hat. 'For saving my sorry arse. Again.'

"She scoffed, winding claws through her horse's mane. And then we were off, thundering into the deadwoods, my captors shouting behind. The night was black as pitch, chill as winter's heart, but paleblood and duskdancer eyes still saw true in that gloom, steering our galloping mounts through snag and bramble, faster than mere men could run.

"The inquisitor and her cohort wouldn't be able to pursue us afoot, but I knew better than most how far a silversaint would go to bring down his quarry, and we had three now at our backs. So, we traveled 'til next dusk, finally coming to a breathless halt beside a tall, twisted oak. Its belly had been split by lightning decades past, a hollow carved of its heart. I lit a small fire within, and the pair of us huddled inside as night fell soft and deep around us.

"Listening for pursuit, I heard only the moaning wind.

"'I don't mind confessing, that was some artful mind-fuckery, mademoiselle.' I chuckled, shaking my head. 'Even *I* was frightened to piss alone.'

"'We do the same up in the Moonsthrone.' Phoebe smiled. 'Seein' off strangers who stray too close to our lands. We made a game of it when we were little.'

"'A game?'

"'Aye,' she nodded, firelight dancing in wild eyes. 'We found a settlement at the foot of Bann Fìageal when I was eight. Missionaries trying to bring their One Faith to the pagans, aye? By the time we were done sportin' with them, they thought their goats milked blood, and a devil lived in their barn, whispering sins to their women at night.' Phoebe laughed, feral and sharp. 'They ran back to Dún Fas with naught but the clothes on their backs.'

"'And that was sport?' I scoffed. 'What kind of childhood did you have?'

"Her smile faded then, her voice gone low and soft.

"'There's a custom among my people. When a child turns twelve, they're given a seed by their eldest female relative. Oak or elm. Pine or birch.'

"Phoebe gestured to that tooled leather collar about her throat, and I noted a small brown pine seed, tight-bound among the everknots.

"'What's it for?' I asked. 'Good fortune?'

"'Ye wear it into battle. So something might grow from the soil where ye die. Ye ask what kind of childhood I had?' Phoebe shrugged, meeting my eyes. 'A short one, Silversaint.'

"I chewed on that a moment, studying the scar cutting down her cheek.

"'How'd you find me? And why . . .' I sighed. 'Why'd you come back?'

"'Five horses and two dozen men are easy to track. As for the second . . .'

"She tilted her head, looking into the fire, and I realized silence was the only answer I'd get. It mattered not, I supposed—the fact she'd returned at all was the important one. It was strange to think a woman I'd been raised to see as an enemy had rescued me from men I'd always thought of as friends. That this monster had become my savior.

"We settled into silence, wrestling quiet thoughts. The night was freezing, but our oaken shelter was warm, our fire burning near as bright as the memory of her in my bed.

"'About the other eve . . .' I began.

"'Don't tie yerself in knots,' she sighed. 'And spare me the fuckin' torture. I was a fool, you were an arse. Let's leave it at that, eh?'

"There was only a foot between us, but that foot felt a thousand miles. Yet I took off my glove, careful of the silver on my skin, placing my hand over hers.

"'You're not a fool, Phoebe á Dúnnsair. You're a lioness.'

"She looked at me sidelong, there in our tiny circle of two. But though her eyes were hard as iron, her lips curled in a smile. I nodded to the ink where her troth ring should be.

"'Who was your lion?'

"Phoebe blinked at that, as if it were the last question she ever expected me to ask. She held her breath for ten long beats of my heart before she finally replied.

"'His name was Connor.'

"'How'd you know him?'

"Again, it took some time for her to answer. I recognized the reluctance; saw it ever in myself. When someone you love is taken from you, their memory is all you have left, and sharing that memory can make it somehow feel less . . . *yours*. As if you're giving away a piece of it, and a piece of the person you lost besides.

"'I didn't know him at first,' she finally sighed. 'We met on our wedding night.'

"I raised a brow at that, but said nothing.

"'I know you Lowlanders spin tales that we steal the skins of men and beasts up in the Moonsthrone. I know ye think us sorcerers and fleshwitches. But the blessings of Fiáin—the gift to dance the dusk—it travels in the bloodline. Thing of it is, the gift never takes root in a child until the parent dies. Mothermoons and Father Earth keep the balance that way.

"'My ma had the gift. She was Rígan-Mor of the Dúnnsair. War-Maker, aye? Hard as a coffin nail, that woman. *Goddess*, she could fight. "*Burn bright*," she used to tell my sister and me. "*Burn brief. But* burn." She led our clan to victory through six wars.' The duskdancer sighed. 'But she lost the seventh. Slain at the battle of Loch Shior when I was nineteen. Angiss á Barenn, the Wolf who killed her, he still wears her skin as a trophy.'

"Phoebe shook her head, tracing the lines of her scars with one claw.

"'After Ma was killed, my baby sister, Torrii, and me were both blessed with the gift. But the Barenn were still pressing us hard. Dark things were rising in the weald. And the leeches had begun raiding the Highlands. The shitstorm ye caused when ye slew Tolyev Dyvok reached even so far as the Moons-throne, Silverboy. Impressive mess ye made.'

"'I'd have thought tangling with 'dancers would be the last thing on their minds.'

"Phoebe shrugged. 'The Untamed scattered after their defeat at Crimson Glade. Seeking shadows to lie low in. And their eldest daughter came home.'

"'. . . Lilidh?'

"Phoebe nodded. 'She was a child of the Moonsthrone. Centuries ago. Though no clan will claim her as their own now. The Heartless, the All Mothers named her. The Winterwife. She was a spook story parents would tell their bairns at night. *Do yer chores*, they'd say, *or the Heartless'll get ye.* But after ye slew Tolyev, she came back to lick her wounds. Chewing at edges of the weald, her and her children. Kane. The Draigann. Raiding us fer meat. One more problem my clan couldn't afford after Ma died.'

"Phoebe looked to the flames, her voice soft.

"'Saoirse's ma, my aunt Cinna, she's the Auld-Sìth of my family. The Peace-Bringer. She's a seer. A dreamwalker. The greatest healer in all the Highlands, ever seeking to mend what is broken. And to ensure our clan's future, she brokered a deal with others who'd warred with the Barenn. I was to marry the eldest blessed son of Clan Lachlainn. Torrii, a blessed son of the Treúnn. And with their strength, we Dúnnsair would survive.'

"I frowned, looking down at the hand I held, the ink on her finger.

"'You were forced into it?'

"'That's not our way. Women choose in the Moonsthrone. Men are chosen.'

"Phoebe shook her head, sighing.

"'*I war with my sister, until,*
"'*We war with our kinfolk, until,*
"'*We war with the Highlands, until,*
"'*We war with the world.*'

"I shook my head, not understanding.

"'It's an old song of ours. There's nothing that'll bring folk of the Moonsthrone together like a common foe. And while I loathed the thought of wedding a man I didn't even know, those blessed by Fiáin are rare. My sister and I had value, and that value could buy a future for our family. So, we swallowed our pride, and off to our bridal feasts we went.'

"Phoebe scoffed, her eyes clouded and distant.

"'I *hated* him at first. My Connor. He was older. Arrogant. He'd spent years traveling beyond the Moonsthrone. Even visited Augustin once. He knew poetry. Philosophy. Theology. Made me feel like some backwoods rustic. A moonsdamned know-it-all, that man.'

"'He traveled beyond the mountains? That's rare for your kin.'

"'Connor had greatness in his blood. A descendant of Ailidh Stormbringer, he was. The mightiest Rígan-Mor our kind has ever known. Connor had a dream of uniting the clans one night, just as she'd done. But he wanted to know the world before he tried to rule it.'

"I raised one brow. 'You were wed to royalty? Should I be calling you *Highness* or—'

"'There is nae royalty in the Moonsthrone. Not since yer lot slew the Stormbringer anyway. But his pedigree didn't help with his cockiness, let me tell ye.' Phoebe chuckled, eyes shining. 'He thought himself the goddesses' gift, that man. And though he was as tempting as all nine sins, I didn't let him touch me for almost a *year*.'

"She smiled, biting soft on her lip.

"'But it's true what they say; war makes the strangest bedfellows. And fighting side by side w' him, I came to see another side entire. He was brave. Noble. Merciful to foes and generous to friends. When Torrii was slain by the Untamed, it felt like my whole world came apart. My baby sister was only eighteen years old, and Lilidh and her children tore her and her husband to *pieces*. But Connor held me together. Kept me strong. And I found myself in love. Head over heels, like some green spring maid. Moons, I *adored* him.'

"'What became of him?' I murmured.

"Phoebe breathed deep, eyes shining now.

"'He died. Ambushed by the Wolves. The velfuil ... they skinned him alive, the bastards. Him and all his guard, flayed and hanged from the pines.' Her lips curled in a snarl, tears spilling down her scarred cheek. 'I should've been with him. But I was heavy with our daughter by then, and he bid me nae travel for fear of the danger.'

"'You've a daughter?' I whispered.

"'I . . .' Phoebe hung her head, pawing at her eyes. 'I . . . lost her. There wasn't room in me for her and all that grief. A woman can only carry so much.'

"I squeezed her hand, feeling an utter fool.

"'Not the only one with scars . . .'

"'That's why the Mothermoons make it snow so hard up the Highlands, they say. To cover all the blood. I came home to the Dúnnsair clanhold to grieve. To see if Aunt Cinna could heal my broken heart. And in the darkest of my hours, I had a dream. A star, fallen in the east. Voices, old and sweet, singing a song that burned in my mind like fire.

> "*Dead shall rise, and stars shall fall;*
> "*Weald shall rot to ruin of all.*
> "*Lions roar and angels weep;*
> "*Sinners' hands our secrets keep.*
> "*'Til Godling's heart brights hea'en's eye,*
> "*From reddest blood comes bluest sky.*'

"I sighed. 'Always a poem, isn't there?'

"'I thought I'd gone mad. But when I told Cousin Saoirse, she said she'd dreamed the *same dream*. The very same *night*. Long had my kin awaited the Godling's birth. It was prophesied she'd be born of the clans—but it never occurred to us she might be found among *Lowlanders*. I was still mourning. Still bleeding. But Saoirse was convinced the Godling would change *everything*. Aunt Cinna told me that in healing the world, I might just heal myself. And so, I agreed to travel with my cousin. Keep to the wealdshape, so I'd nae have to deal w' fuckin' people. It was good to be with someone who thought this place might be saved. Who could imagine those snows without blood.'

"Phoebe sighed, eyes lost in the flames.

"'And now Saoirse's gone. Bled the ground red, like my sister. Like my Connor.'

"I shook my head, mystified. 'How can you still be out here? If your goddesses put you both on this path and now your cousin's dead . . . how can you still believe?'

"Phoebe stared long into the fire, as if searching for truth in the flames.

"'I spent my time angry at heaven. When Torrii was killed. When the Wolves butchered my Connor. When my sweet Catir was denied her first breath. I know what it is to spit yer hate at skies above. But I also know there is *nothing* in that deed that does not make yer anger worse. There's nae joy to be found in embracing rage that isn't fleeing. In the end, it only deepens the darkness within. And so, it must—can *only*—be wrong.'

"She shrugged, meeting my eyes.

"'Hate is poison. Hope is salvation. And there's still some things in this world worth saving.'

"I frowned, looking down at the name tattooed across my fingers. I heard movement in the night beyond our firelight then. A little girl's laughter hanging faint upon the wind. The scent of silverbell kissing the air, and burning at the corners of my eyes.

"'Do you miss him?'

"Phoebe sighed. 'A little less each day.'

"My eyes were fixed on two pale shadows now, watching at the edge of the light.

"'That's what frightens me most, you know,' I murmured. 'The thought that grief is the only thing I have left of them. And once that fades, the last of them will too. The world feels half-full without them. I miss them like a piece of me is missing. But I honestly don't know what hurts more, Phoebe. Holding on to them, or letting them go.'

"'Ye've nae need to let them go. Ye just need something more to cling to.'

"I sighed, dragging my eyes from those wraiths who watched me, up to skies above. 'It matters not what you hold faith in, but you must hold faith in something.'

"Phoebe nodded. 'That sounds like wisdom to me.'

"'My friend Aaron told me that.' I shook my head. 'He's dead now.'

"She met my eyes, pity shining in that alloy of platinum and gold. I looked down to our hands, the silver on my skin gleaming in the firelight between us. But though her fingers were razors to me, and the ink on mine a poison to her, still she carefully entwined them together. Her touch was like spring rain; gentle and slow and perilously warm.

"I wondered if she were right. If I *did* need something more to live for.

Since the night I'd buried ma famille, I'd given no thought to the future. First, losing myself in the idea of revenge against Fabién, and then, of looking after Dior. Yet what might come if I somehow got all I wanted? The Forever King in ashes? The Grail redeeming the world?

"*What of the day after?*

"But beneath Phoebe's singing skin, I felt it then, silencing that foolish question in my head. Winding out in pale blue webs across her wrist, up her tattooed arm to the long, graceful line of her throat, thundering there like all heaven and hell awaiting.

"Pulsing. Pleading. *Needing.*

"I tore my eyes away. The scent of silverbell lingered on the wind, the sound of a little girl's voice calling me entwined now with the drumbeat of Phoebe's quickened pulse. But I turned aside from those phantoms of my past, that golden gaze, and I reached out into the freezing gulf for Dior; that slender thread of hope that was all I really had left to cling to.

"'Sweet fucking Mothermaid . . .'

"Phoebe looked up as I tore my hand from hers, snaking now to my feet.

"'Gabe? What is it?'

"'Dior,' I hissed.

"Fear filled her eyes. Despair flooding mine.

"'I can't feel her anymore.'"

IX

NO PROMISES, NO VOWS

"WE RODE LIKE a tempest, out of Fa'daena and into the rising winds. I'd lost ten fucking nights in the Forest of Sorrows—the thin red thread between Dior and me stretched so thin it had finally snapped. But still we gave desperate chase in the direction I'd last felt her, me upon brave Argent, and Phoebe on Valya's beast—a prickly chocolat mare she'd dubbed Thorn. Our days were spent in the saddle, hooves thundering, trying to make up our lost ground. Our nights were freezing and all too long, hope fading further with every dawn as I reached out toward the girl I'd sworn to give all protecting, feeling nothing at all.

"East Ossway had been wine country once, but now only hollowed farmsteads dotted the snow-struck valleys we galloped through. Dead vines clawed out of the earth like skeletal hands, barren as the plains of hell. The snow came blinding, a vast wall of dark cloud gathering to the north. Reaching a bleak rise on the sixth day, I searched behind us for signs of pursuit by Lachlan and the others. But Phoebe pointed through the howling snows, and the hammerblow fell—the first of two that would finally cost us *everything*.

"'Gabriel!' she called. 'Look!'

"I saw nothing at first, the weather too grim. But the wind shifted and swelled, and through a break in the flurries, I glimpsed them then; a column of dark figures, shuffling southward through a chill no mortal army would dare march in.

"Hope surged; the wild thought that we'd somehow managed to catch Dior, after all. But it died just as swift as the snows parted further, and I saw the extent of their number.

"There were *thousands* of Dead, marching like a cohort of mortal men, all in lockstep, left right, left right. A great wagon train came behind, filled with the doomed and the damned. And in the rhythmic tread of that grim procession, I knew at last what they were.

"What *led* them.

"'That's a wretched legion,' I breathed. 'Under command of highblooded Ironhearts.'

"Phoebe frowned. 'But they march like soldiers? The rottens are a mindless mob.'

"'The brains of the wretched decay with their bodies. But the Voss can still command what's left of their minds. There's a reason the Forever King has been so successful, Mlle Phoebe. A *reason* why his legions now threaten the capital of the empire itself.'

"'But they're marching *into* Ossway. Like ye said, the Forever King is in the east.'

"I lowered my spyglass, whispering through gritted fangs. 'Dior is south.'

"'Sweet Mothermoons. He's coming for her.'

"A terrifying thought, too awful to savor long. It would've been task enough to save Dior from the Blackheart, but now it seemed *two* armies might stand between us and her. Hope fading with every mile, still we rode on, wasting yet more time skirting round the Voss column, into the screaming winds. And the second blow fell then, the heartbreaker, stealing the very last of our hope. For while I'd vowed to fight my way out of the abyss to get back to Dior's side, it seemed that the abyss had heard me. And now, it gave bloody answer.

"A storm. Bearing down from the Moonsthrone, vast and black and boiling. It was a monster, set to devour all in its path, thundering across those mighty peaks as it came and falling upon us like the fury of God Himself. And though Phoebe and I fought through that tempest for long and frozen hours more, in the end . . .

"In the bitter end . . .

"'Gabriel, we cannae stay out here!' Phoebe roared, frozen braids whipping about her face. 'This storm will be the death of ye!'

"My hands were near frozen on Argent's reins, teeth chattering as I spat reply. 'I've taken b-baths c-colder than this! You just worry about yourself, mademoiselle!'

"'Damn ye, man, I know ye love the girl, but yer nae good to her *dead*!' Phoebe grabbed my arm, talons sinking through my sleeve. 'There's a château west of here named Ravenspire! It's just off the Lùdaebh River! We can make it if we ride hard now!'

"'If we stop, Lachlan and the others will be on us like scratch on a dockside doxy!'

"Phoebe shook her head, shouting over those hateful winds. 'They'll have to shelter from this shite too! We can bed down at the château, break as soon as the storm does!'

"I wanted to rage, to refuse, but I met those golden eyes, Phoebe's claws sinking just deep enough to pierce the fog of helpless fear and stubborn anger I'd shrouded myself in.

"'I swore to protect her too, Gabriel! We're *nae* leaving her!'

"I saw the lie just as clear as she did; we both knew what more delay must cost us. But with heavy tread and heavier hearts, still we turned westward, out of that storm's dreadful path. All was hungry thunder and bone-biting cold. The snows came sideways, clawing at our skin, our brave horses near dead afoot. But through the tempest, we finally made out a distant tower, etched in silhouette against the pulse of distant lightning.

"Ravenspire was a lonely keep atop a lonelier hill, guarding a lifeless stretch of river. The walls had been smashed like old clay, the gatehouse crushed to rubble by boulders the size of wagons. Blessedly, the keep itself was somewhat intact, and we found a safe enough space to hole up in against the weather; a small library upstairs, a long table, bedding stolen from the upper chambers. Wind hammered at the shutters, and all was deathly chill, but we lit a fire in the hearth with piles of old books, warm enough to banish death's cold hand.

"I set triplines at the stairs, strung with pots and pans. In the corridor leading to our room, I spread a dusting of glass shards; empty sanctus phials from my bandolier, crushed in one gloved fist. If attacked, we could fight in this bottleneck, retreat up another stair to the tower behind when pressed. But I hoped it'd not come to that.

"Three nights we sheltered in Ravenspire, that storm deepening every one. I kept vigil at the window, peering out through the rattling glass for any sign of my brethren, worrying about Ash, reaching into the dark for Dior over and over, hoping against hope.

"'Nothing,' I sighed.

"Phoebe glanced up from her seat by the hearth, brow raised as I slammed a fist into the wall. Cold rock sliced my knuckles, sweet pain momentarily swallowing my frustration and rage. The duskdancer only shook her head, firelight glittering in her eyes.

"'Nae sure how punching walls will help. It's nae the brick's fault, Gabriel.'

"'It's Lachlan's,' I hissed. 'We lost too much time fucking about in those damned woods. And now this *cursed* storm . . .'

"'It'll break soon. We'll be back after the Flower quick as silver.'

"But I shook my head then, cold dread in my belly as I spoke the fear that had been growing in me for nights now. 'I'm not sure we can catch her anymore, Phoebe.'

"'Well, we have to try. If they reach Dún Maergenn, we're *done*. The Anvil of the Wolf is the greatest fortress in Ossway. It'd take a fuckin' army to get inside it.'

"I sighed then, dragged one hand through my hair.

"'Then maybe we should start thinking about finding ourselves a fucking army.'

"Phoebe looked around the room with those hunter's eyes, finally hooking a talon into her décolletage and peering inside. 'None in here. Ye got one down yer britches or—'

"'Didn't you tell Dior all the Highlands are gathering for Wintermoot soon?'

"Phoebe sobered then, scowling. 'I did. But ye cannae be thinking of heading *there*. Only children of Fiáin and All Mothers might step into the Ma'dair Craeth and live.'

"Dior is bound for the Blackheart's clutches. And the Voss have sent a legion of the Dead on her tail. I'll take that risk, Phoebe.'

"'Then ye'll *die* fer it. Folk of the Moonsthrone nurse a grudge like a beggar his beer. The Ordo Argent killed the *Stormbringer*, Gabriel. Ye show up to a sacred moot w'naught but silver on yer skin and a grin on yer face, they'll wear ye like a fuckin' cloak.'

"'Well, you'd best do a damn fine job of vouching for me, in that case.'

"Phoebe scowled, golden eyes agleam as she looked me over.

"'You swore to give your last breath to keep that girl safe,' I told her. 'Don't ask me to risk less, not after what I've given already. I've not felt a trace of Dior for days. We've no chance to catch her before she reaches Dún Maergenn now, and she'll need an army to rescue her from it. So when this storm breaks, I go to raise her one. With or without you.'

"'Yer a bloody madman.' The duskdancer pouted, thoughtful, tossing another book onto the flames. 'I could make the trek up there alone, though, I s'pose. Plead our case.'

"'Bullshit. I'm supposed to just sit here and pray?'

"'I'm sure those silver brothers of yers will keep ye entertained.'

"'At the end of a rope, maybe.' I scowled, muttering through clenched teeth. 'Bloody *fools*. Ten days they cost us. Xavier, I understand. He was always thick as pigshit. Probably lost that arm of his trying to find his penis for a piss. But Lachlan should know better.'

"'The two of ye seemed thick as thieves when we first met at Aveléne. But now he seems intent on seeing ye hanged?'

"'Not sure if you've noticed, but I've a gift for getting on people's bad side, Kitcat.'

"She chuckled, sharp teeth gleaming. 'To *that* I can attest. But come now, who is he to ye? I know ye call all silversaints *brother*, but that one seemed special.'

"'He was,' I replied, loading my pipe. 'He is.'

"'Tell me a story, then, Chevalier.' Phoebe glanced around our little room, tucking one braid behind a pointed ear. 'Unless ye can think of a better way to pass the time.'

"I sighed, peering into the crackling flames.

"Embers rising in the halls of memory.

"Blood and silver and steel.

"'The first city we took in the Ossian campaigns was a port named Báih Side,' I said softly. 'It was really just a beachhead for Tolyev's main invasion; only a couple of highbloods and a hundred thrallswords left guarding his back as he advanced into Ossway.

"'By the Empress's decree, I led the attack. Nineteen years old, I was. Isabella's favored Black Lion. We hit them from the sea, striking at dawn. And though most of the Dyvok troops were the average sort of thrall, there was one among them who fought like a demon. Strong as a highblood, even with the black sun in the sky. I met him on the walls, all set to end him, but as we clashed, I realized from the brand on his hand and the fangs in his mouth what he truly was. A paleblood like me. Thralled into service to the Untamed.

"'I asked him who he was. He replied he was the child of Tolyev. Mortal son of the Priori Dyvok himself. And then he did his best to cut the head off my fucking shoulders.'

"'But the Black Lion was the greatest sword who ever lived,' Phoebe murmured.

"I shrugged. 'So the minstrels sing. All I'll say is I took his best, but gave a little better, and in the end, he lay on the bloody stone at the tip of my blade.

He was the enemy, I knew it. Son of the monster I'd been sent to Ossway to slay, but . . . he was just a *boy*. Fifteen at most. I'd never known my kind to serve the enemy. I felt pity for him. So I spared his life.'

"Phoebe gave a small nod of approval. 'Mercy is nobility.'

"'Lachlan didn't share the sentiment. He vowed he'd kill me when he got the chance. Tolyev had raised him among the Untamed, where only the savage survive. Compassion was for the weak. Mercy for the coward. Apparently, Nikita had started throwing Lachie into pits with starving wretched when he was only ten years old, just to see who'd come out on top. When I told him that was torture, Lachlan called me a fool. He informed me his big brother had been teaching him to be strong. That his noble father loved him true. That the Dyvok were born to rule the endless night, Tolyev its endless emperor.

"'But he was only a child. Raised in darkness and knowing no better. The father's sins are not the son's—I knew that better than most. And I refused to condemn him for them. Instead, I sat with him in his cage each night. Reading scripture. Showing kindness. Trying to prove we weren't the enemy he'd been raised to see. He'd have none of it, of course.'

"I shook my head, looking into the fire, and back through the red mist of time.

"'And then we liberated the slaughterfarms at Triúrbaile. Lachlan had no idea what his kin had been doing there. And when I *showed* him the atrocities unleashed by the famille he'd been forced to care for, the briefest sliver of horror and hatred cut through that dark counterfeit of love. It was Lachlan who told us where his father might be found. It was *he* who showed us the path to the Crimson Glade where Tolyev made camp. And though it was my blade that cut the Priori down that day, the victory was Lachie's as well as mine.

"'When Tolyev died, the bond of blood was truly broken, and Lachlan saw what his life had been. He marched toward the nearest bonfire, plunging his left hand into the blaze, intent to burn it off, his father's mark besides. But I dragged him away. Told him it wasn't his fault. Offered him a path from darkness into light.

"'Two years we fought side by side, through hellfire and blood. Lachie was more than a 'prentice. He was my little brother. The 'saint I loved and trusted most in all the world.'

"I hung my head, running a thumb over the name on my fingers.

"'And then he learned about Astrid and me.'

"'Oh, Moons.' Phoebe's eyes narrowed. 'He told yer brethren about the affair?'

"I shook my head. 'If he had, it'd be easier to hate him. But honor was more important to Lachie than life, and he breathed not a word to anyone. But I could see the disappointment in his eyes when he looked at me after that. To know I'd broken the vows I'd taught him to hold so dear. He blamed Astrid for most of it, I think. Still keen to keep me on the pedestal he'd built in his mind. But he warned me she would be my undoing, that God must punish us for our sin. I didn't listen. Such was my foolishness. My vanity.'

"I looked out at the thundering night, sighing from my heart.

"'I still wonder, you know. What might've come if I'd listened when Lachlan warned me. We'd not have been together, but at least Astrid would be alive.'

"'Ye cannae think that way,' Phoebe said, lifting her head. 'Blood spilled is blood lost. Take solace in the joy ye gave each other, and burn all else fer Father Earth.'

"I only scowled at that, staring out into the dark. With a sigh, Phoebe twisted to her feet, padding across the cold stone toward me. I could hear her heartbeat, smell the smoke in her hair and the fire in her veins. She sought my eyes, but I didn't meet her gaze.

"'Mothermoons, ye've such a shadow on ye, it might swallow the sun.'

"'Most would call it a shadow well-earned, mademoiselle.'

"Phoebe shook her head. 'I said it to the Flower, I'll say it again: There's a solace to be found in sadness. And I understand why ye'd think ye deserve that dark. Easier to find refuge in drink, in rage, to say hell with it all and push everyone away. Because ye think that cold is easier to live with than the pain that could come if ye let the warmth back in, only to be burned again. But that's the fire that lets us know we're *alive*, Gabriel.'

"I shook my head, two pale shadows now rising at my back.

"'You can't fix a broken blade, Phoebe.'

"'But don't ye see? We don't get broken. We're *made* broken. We are not whole alone. But if we're blessed, if we're brave, we might find those few whose edges fit against our own. Like pieces of the same puzzle, or shards of the same shattered blade. Those people who, in their own broken way, make our broken edge complete.'

"I could smell the perfume of silverbell on the air now, the shadows growing deeper at my back, the echo of my promise to the ground ringing in my mind as I hung my head. But Phoebe pressed clawed hands to my cheeks, forced me to look at her.

"'I am nae the one to unbreak ye, Gabriel de León. I am nae green maid, to swear troth to a man I barely know. I am the wild. I am the wind. I am thorn and bramble, blood and scars, and I do *not* love ye. But I ask ye fer nae promise, and make nae vow, save this: I am here. I am *warm*. And amorrow, the whole world might be swallowed by winter.'

"Phoebe leaned in, lips brushing mine, but heart thundering, I drew away.

"'Don't,' I whispered. 'Don't touch me.'

"She looked up into my eyes, firelight smoldering on molten gold.

"'Aright. I won't touch ye.'

"Stepping back, she reached behind her, loosed the stays on her gown. A part of me wanted to turn away, another to warn her, but most of me was helpless but to watch as, with a shrug, she shed that silken skin. Her dress tumbled in emerald waves onto the flagstones at her feet, leaving me undone at a single stroke. Phoebe slipped her hands behind her, wrists crossed at the small of her back, fixing me with golden eyes.

"'But ye can touch me. If ye want.'

"My eyes drank her in; the song of her curves, the smattering of freckles, the tattoos and scars. I felt my blood racing, my breath quicken. And though those shadows about me pressed down like gossamer and lead, still I found myself taking one halting step toward her.

"But she took one step back.

"'Do ye want?' she whispered.

"I stepped nearer, legs shaking like a newborn foal's, but again she stepped away.

"'*Say* it.'

"I'd no wish to be burned again. Yet, a part of me longed to feel that flame, if only for a moment. Fionna's warning about heeding the music, about holding on to what I could *while* I could rang now in my mind. And though the shadows pressed ever like tons upon my back, still I fancied amid the scent of silverbell and that soul-sick ache of loss, I heard my love whisper to me, as once she'd done in days fine and far from here.

"*Hearts only bruise. They never break.*

"I looked at Phoebe, bare and brave and beautiful, that song of scars upon her skin. My lips parted, ash-dry and hungry. And finally, I spoke a truth I never thought I'd say.

"'. . . I want.'

"And then, she was in my arms, crashing against me with all the fury and hunger of the tempest outside. Her kiss was fierce, burning, but true to her word, she kept her hands behind her back as if bound there, refusing to touch me. Leaving me to touch *her*.

"I was fumbling. Uncertain. The first woman I'd known in an age pressed up against me. Her body was an untamed realm, wild and beautiful, and I was aflame with the need to know every inch; to let my lips light fires among those hills and valleys, to brave the dangers of her darkest places. But I knew I must be careful of my silvered touch, and so I forced myself to trace her shape; a slow, torturous dance with just the very tips of my fingers, drawing long careful spirals on her prickling skin as our kiss ever deepened. I caressed the long, milk-pale path of her throat, that pulse calling my name, down over the arches of her collarbones to her breasts. Her heart thundered beneath my hands, her sighs stirring long-forgotten butterflies in my belly. Her breath catching as I stroked, gasping as I pinched, feeling her tremble as she groaned into my mouth.

"Phoebe stepped back again, and I followed; iron to starstone now. She bumped against the table, wrists still crossed behind her, lifting herself up and wrapping her legs tight around my waist. My britches were straining as we ground against each other, as my mouth slipped over the line of her jaw. Her scent was purest madness, flaming tresses spilling down her spine as her head drifted back. My hands caressed her arse, and my kisses roamed her neck, that forbidden hymn thrumming beneath her skin. My fangs had grown long and hard in my gums, and I dared not linger for fear of what I might do next, my mouth following her tattoos ever lower, taking one pebble-hard nipple into my mouth, licking, teasing. My fingers traced lines of fire up the inside of her thighs, and she hissed at the touch of the silver on my palm, shivering as she felt the brush of ivory needles on her skin.

"'God, I have to taste you,' I whispered.

"'I *want* ye to,' she breathed.

"She pressed me tighter to her breast, and I understood then what she spoke of. *The Kiss*. She wanted to feel it, I realized; to drown in the bliss it promised, to soar and burn among those dark red heavens. But though my thirst roared and bucked like a wild thing at the thought, I dared not

succumb, sinking lower instead. Phoebe relented with a sigh, legs parting wider as my kisses descended, blood-red spirals leading me ever closer, goosebumps rising as I sank to my knees and into the silken heaven awaiting.

"'Oh, Moons . . .'

"She melted as she felt my tongue flicker against her, sinking back on the table, spine arching and mouth wide. Her taste was fire and autumn's rust, honey and salt, my fingertips still roaming her skin as my tongue wrote poetry on her petals, fluttering on her swollen bud as she groaned and pleaded more, goddesses, *more*.

"I sang a song on her as old as time, wanting only to hear her sing in turn. Tension was writ in her every corded muscle, every tiny gasp, her legs rising up now, toes curling as her claws sank deep into the wood. She began to buck, to beg, undone by my touch, my tongue, and as she shattered, at last she broke her word, raking talons through my hair fierce enough to draw blood, a cry ripped up and out of her as she went taut as a bowstring, and her shapeless scream instead became my name.

"I smiled, reveling at that song. But I'd only a moment to savor her little earthquake before those claws sank into my shoulders and she hissed with all hell's hunger, 'Moons, get *up* here . . .' And as Phoebe dragged me up her body, lunging toward me now, our mouths collided with such force her lip split open on my fangs.

"*Blood.*

"I reared back. Gasping as it *crashed* upon me. A single drop of fire from her veins, mingled with the honey from her quim upon my tingling tongue.

"*BLOOD.*

"God, it was ecstasy. It was *agony*. Salvation and damnation entwined, racing in lines of white-hot fire straight down to my nethers. The thirst in me roared, and it was all I could do not to grab a fistful of her curls and wrench her head back as she tore my belt loose, dragging me free from my britches and sinking her talons into my hips.

"'Fuck me,' she demanded. '*Now*.'

"All was fire, all was want, Phoebe's legs cinched about me as she pressed my aching cock against her lips, heaven just one surrender, one thrust, one bite away. The want was deeper than any ocean, stronger than any vow, to dive, drink, devour. But above her ragged breath, the primal *scream* of that animal within me, I heard it; faint beneath the storm, but still, enough to plunge a dagger of ice right through my belly.

"I drew away from Phoebe's mouth, and she moaned and sought my kiss again, claws sinking deeper into my skin.

"'Moons, Gabriel, *fuck* me—'

"'Stop,' I gasped. '*Listen.*'

"And there it came again. Unmistakable. Unbelievable.

"The sound of crunching glass."

High in the reaches of a black tower in Sul Adair, Jean-François of the Blood Chastain, Historian of Her Grace, Margot Chastain, thumped his hands on the tome in his lap.

"Are you bloody *jesting*?"

The Last Silversaint sipped his goblet of wine, eyebrow raised. "Eh?"

"Right *then*?" the historian demanded. "You are not toying with me for your own sadistic amusement? Your enemies chose *that* exact moment to rear their idiot heads?"

"Their timing could've been better." Gabriel shrugged. "Could've been *far* worse."

"Great Redeemer!" the vampire cried, kicking back in his chair and searching the ceiling for patience. The monster finally found his calm, drummed fingers upon the page as he met the silversaint's eyes. "Tell me you made them suffer for the interruption at least?"

"No fear on that front, coldblood."

Gabriel shook his head, looking down at his tattooed hands.

"There'd be plenty of suffering to go around."

X

THE BEAST AWAKENED

"I BARELY HAD time to buckle my belt before he came through the door; Robin, abandoning stealth as he heard the glass crunch under his silvered heels. I shoved Phoebe aside, the duskdancer cursing as she tumbled naked off the table. And lifting his wheellock pistol, the young songbird set his sights on his hero.

"*BOOM!*" Gabriel roared, leaping in his chair and clapping his hands.

Jean-François paused his writing, raised an eyebrow.

"*Must* you, Silversaint?"

"Must I what?"

"Carry on like a drunken troubadour in a brothel pantomime."

Gabriel shrugged, refilling his goblet. "In life, always do what you love."

"I realize you're already three bottles into the evening's inebriation, but I know the sound a wheellock makes. There's really *no* need to shout about it."

"Your Empress demanded the whole of my tale, did she not?"

A sigh. "She did."

"And you're perfectly content to hear every lurid detail when I'm getting my kit off. I'm certain I could sing about swollen buds and aching crowns all night and I'd not hear a word of complaint."

The Last Silversaint arched one brow, but the vampire remained suspiciously mute.

"So, where were we?"

The historian rolled his eyes. "Boom?"

"*BOOM!*" Gabriel roared, leaping in his chair and clapping again.

"Night save me," the Marquis sighed.

"The shot grazed my throat," Gabriel continued, taking up his wine. "Just a half-inch shy of my jugular, and I knew then the game we played was Dead or Alive. I'd not smoked that pipe after dinner, too lost between Phoebe's thighs, and I cursed myself a fool for that now, diving across the floor toward my gear. Robin was charging toward me, Saber at his heels, big Xavier Pérez looming behind his staghound. I hit the deck, snatched up my wheellock, cracking off a shot. It was the wildest throw of the dice, meant only to buy me a moment, but sometimes Fortuna even smiles on me, vampire; the silvershot struck Robin in the shoulder, spinning the youngblood in a spray of red.

"Phoebe flew from the shadows, bare and beautiful, talons gleaming in the firelight. I rolled to my feet, drawing Robin's greatsword as the duskdancer carved four lines of fire across the youngblood's back. Saber lunged at me, her piggy eyes narrowed and jaws wide, and though it's ever a cruelty to hurt a beast, it's an easier one to bear if that beast is trying to rip your fucking bollocks off. Stepping aside, I planted a kick right into her ribs.

"The hound *flew* across the room, blasted through the shutters and into the howling dark as Xavier roared her name. Robin's blade cleaved the air just shy of Phoebe's head, the duskdancer and 'saint falling into a fearful ballet. Phoebe's talons could shred a man to the bone, but Robin was wielding Lachlan's new greatsword and the blade was purest silversteel, wrought by old Forgemaster Argyle's hand. One mistake from either . . .

"I'd no clue where the hell Lachie was, but Xavier was problem aplenty. Taking aim with his hand crossbow, he loosed a shot close enough to shave with, silvered chain streaming behind, punching into the bricks at my back— Xav at least seemed to want me breathing. And lifting Robin's stolen blade, I charged toward my old battlebrother."

Gabriel steepled tattooed fingers at his chin, eyes on the historian opposite.

"Now, here's the thing, coldblood. Greatswords aren't all that great when you're swinging them in a crowded room. And worse, Robin was born of the Blood Dyvok, possessed of a strength that would put most palebloods to shame. That blade was a fucking *beast*, half as long again as a greatsword had any business being, and broader and heavier than anything I'd wielded in my life. But I was *fighting* for that life now, for Phoebe's too, and you'd be surprised what a man can manage when he stares into the face of death.

"Xavier and I had fought side by side through the Sūdhaemi campaigns; we knew each other's styles to a stroke. But Xav had lost an arm since then, and even though he was dosed on sanctus, I still somehow fought him to a standstill, steel ringing on steel.

"'Heathen *bitch*!'

"I heard Robin's curse, risked a glance, saw a long slick of blood running down his chest now. To his credit, the youngster was fighting hard, but Phoebe was fierce as the storm, swift as the wind. A daughter of ancient mountains and warrior queens, her blood high and her heart athunder as she sliced Robin's swordarm bone-deep. The youngblood staggered, crying out as Phoebe slipped behind him, digging her claws into his throat.

"'Don't kill him!' I roared.

"She snarled, eyes flashing, but still she paid heed, smashing his head into the wall instead of opening his neck. Swinging him by one arm, she hurled Robin face-first through the broken shutters, roaring with triumph as the youngblood plummeted after poor Saber.

"'Call *me* bitch, ye fu—'

"The shot struck her in the shoulder, whipping her to one side, her blood boiling like fat on a breakfast skillet as it hit the wall. Glancing over my shoulder, I saw Lachlan at my back now, stomach sinking as I realized my folly; he'd climbed the tower wall with his dark strength, stolen down the stairwell to hit us from behind. I roared as I saw him raising a second wheellock, taking aim at Phoebe.

"'Lachie, *NO!*'

"The silvershot hit her square in the chest, opening her ribs up like a love letter. Phoebe's head was thrown back, mouth open in a soundless cry as she staggered, clutching the sizzling hole above her heart. I roared her name, and our eyes met; hers shining gold, mine burning with fury. A ribbon of blood spilled down her chin, lips parted as if she wished to say something. Say *anything*. But without a word, nor a whimper, Phoebe á Dúnnsair crumpled to the floor in bloody ruin as Lachlan hissed.

"'Die, skinwitch.'"

Jean-François sat aghast, one hand pressed to the place his heart might once have been. Chocolat eyes were fixed on the man opposite, ruby lips parted in shock.

"Almighty God. After you and she had just . . ."

"Oui," Gabriel nodded.

The vampire leaned forward, his voice a whisper.

"What did you *do*, de León?"

The Last Silversaint downed his wine in a gulp, wiping his chin on tattooed knuckles.

"There's a thing inside all men that even devils fear, coldblood. It's a monster most of us keep locked deep inside, knowing what will happen if we let it have its head. We feel a flicker of it when a stranger sets foot in our domain uninvited. We sense it stirring in the night at the sound of a creaking floorboard in our home. But we *truly* feel it waking when the ones we care for most are in danger; our lovers, our babies, and if we let it loose then, God help the fool who roused it. I'd felt it truly break free inside me only once before in my whole life—the night *he* came knocking on my door."

The silversaint poured himself another glass, leaned back in his chair.

"What did I do, coldblood?" The Last Silversaint shrugged. "I opened up the cage.

"My first blow caught Xavier across the shoulder, cutting to the bone. As Lachlan drew his third and fourth pistols from his bandolier, my pommel smashed into Xav's jaw, relieving him of most of his teeth. And as my old 'prentice lifted his guns at my back, I drove my sword up through Xavier's belly, the blade bursting out his back in a spray of gore.

"Lachlan fired, *BOOM BOOM*, but I pivoted Xavier about, stronger in my fury than I'd have thought possible. The shots struck Xav in the back, my old battlebrother gasped, my face painted thick with his blood. Kicking him hard, I sent him sailing across the room, right at my old 'prentice. Lachie stepped aside, drawing Ashdrinker from his belt, but then I was on him, roaring, smashing him into the wall so hard we punched clean through the crumbling stone, sailing out into the screaming night as I fucked his face with my fist.

"We fell three stories, crashed onto the flagstones, bones breaking, blood spraying.

"'Traitor,' he spat.

"'Bastard,' I hissed.

"'Coward!' he roared.

"'Fool!' I snarled.

"We were animals then, despite the years and ties between us—two dogs brawling, both lost in fury. I, the betrayer, the murderer, the heretic with hands drenched in faithful blood. And he, the man who'd woken that beast inside me for only the second time in all my years. Though he was born of Dyvok, I was somehow just as strong in my rage, each of us willing to smash himself to pieces if only he could cut his foe's heart out with the shards.

"Lachlan flipped me onto my back, punched me in my face. Climbing

astride me, he smashed my head into the flagstones, hard enough to crack my skull. My old 'prentice crushed his thumbs into my larynx, eyes flooded red as he choked me. I clawed his wrist with one hand, desperate now, the other fumbling at his bandolier. The world rushed red, thunder in my ears, black stars in my eyes. But at last, Lachlan froze, motionless save for the heaving in his chest as I pressed his final wheellock up under his chin.

"'Even the best m-marksman has the occasional bad day,' I hissed. 'But five pistols *is* a little m-much, Lachie.'

"My foe gritted his fangs, wheezing. 'Treacherous f-fucking dog . . .'

"'You say that l-like it's a b-bad thing. But I *did* warn you that I saved a few of m-my tricks.'

"'*Do* it,' he spat, bracing for the shot. 'I'll see you in hell, traitor.'

"My grip tightened on the pistol. Eyes locked on his. Picturing the look of surprise and pain on Phoebe's face as he gunned her down. The beast in me was roaring now, all the frustration and fear—for Dior, for Phoebe, for myself—rising up in my chest as I pushed the wheellock hard up under his chin. And I whispered, bloody lips and bloody hands.

"'If I were the traitor you think me, Lachie, I *would* k-kill you.'

"I threw the pistol away, silversteel skittering on stone.

"'But in your heart, little brother, you still know me better than that.'

"His hands were yet at my throat.

"Eyes hard as he glanced at the wheellock I'd cast away.

"'You k-killed them,' he whispered. 'Greyhand. Sister Chloe.'

"'I did. And I wish it otherwise. But I'd do it again, Lachlan. A *thousand* times over. Because not just the world, but the fate of every soul under heaven hung in the balance of it.' Looking him in the eye, I licked the blood from my split lips, and spat the truth I'd been longing to share since we met again. 'Dior Lachance is no witch, little brother. No sorceress or heretic. She's the Holy Grail of San Michon.'

"Lachlan's eyes narrowed then, wonder and suspicion in equal measure.

"'She was the treasure, the *weapon* that Chloe was sent to find,' I told him. '*She* was the reason Greyhand recalled all 'saints to the monastery. The Redeemer's blood flows in that girl's veins, Lachlan. That's why the coldbloods hunt her, why a duskdancer and a vampire and a silversaint stand together to defend her, why Chloe and Greyhand tried to *sacrifice* her. All I did in that cathedral, I did to save that girl's life. She's the only thing in this godforsaken world worth protecting anymore.' I gritted my teeth, heart aching in my chest. 'The only thing that matters since Fabién Voss took my wife and daughter from me.'

"His eyes widened at that, lips parted in shock. 'Oh, Gabe. Brother, I . . .'

"I reached up slow, easing his hands away from my throat.

"'I don't believe in much anymore, Lachlan. But I believe in Dior Lachance. And right now, she languishes in the hands of the Dyvok, and all the *world* stands in peril for it. I am sworn to protect that girl. So is that woman upstairs you just shot. So either kill me, or get the *fuck* off me. Because I happen to owe that heathen skinwitch my life.'

"I pushed Lachlan away, and he allowed me to rise, bewilderment and sorrow in his eyes. Clutching my broken ribs, drooling blood, I snatched Ashdrinker up and stood on shaking legs. Ash's voice was a silvered song in my head, full of fear, hurt, sorrow.

"*Oh Gabrielgabriel, the firehair . . .*

"My stomach was already twisting as I stumbled back into the shattered hearthroom, the floors soaked in blood. Xavier was crumpled by the broken wall, trying to push himself to his knees with his one good arm. But my eyes saw only . . .

"*Oh nonononono . . .*

"I ran to Phoebe's side, heart in my throat and belly in my boots. She was curled up in a pool of red, naked skin spattered with blood, an awful charred hole in her back. I rolled her over carefully, cradling her softly in my arms. But though she was wounded by deadly silver, two shots almost point-blank, still I was astounded to see . . .

"'Seven Martyrs,' I breathed. 'You're *alive* . . .'

"She whispered, almost inaudible under the howling storm.

"'W-who ever said . . . y-yer more pretty than . . . p-perceptive?'

"A bubble of blood burst on her lips, and she cried out as I lifted her over to the table to better inspect her wounds. The first shot had torn her shoulder up badly, but it was the second that had done the true damage; shattering her ribs just shy of her heart. To my horror, I saw the wound was burned black, the tracery of veins beneath her skin likesame. And with sinking belly, I realized there was no exit wound—that the shot was yet inside her.

"'Phoebe, can you hear me?' I whispered, shaking her. '*Phoebe?*'

"She groaned, and I grabbed my hipflask and poured vodka onto her wound. Phoebe yowled like a scalded cat then, spitting a rainbow of profanity through bloody lips.

"'Somethin's wrong . . . I c-can *feel* it . . .'

"'You've silvershot still inside you.'

"'Ohhhh, those *b-bastards*.' She laughed, spitting blood as she thumped her head back against the wood. 'They've fuckin' k-k-killed me, haven't they?'

"'Bull*shit*. You survived Danton Voss, you'll survive this.'

"'Won't heal.' She swallowed, lips wet and red. 'N-not silver . . .'

"'Just lie still,' I begged. 'Don't talk.'

"I'd an apothecary's kit in my saddlebags, stocked from the monastery stores. Xavier was still trying to rise, and stalking across the room, I laid him out with one jaw-shattering punch, fetching the kit and laying it on the table. The bleeding was bad, the light was shit, and I could see a dark stain slowly spreading through Phoebe's veins—the poison of the silver in her blood. Teeth gritted, I set to work, fingers shaking as I fished about inside the wound with a set of forceps. Burned blood oozed over my fingers, Phoebe moaned, finally screamed in agony, and I cursed a thousand times. But try as I might, wish as I must . . .

"'I can't feel it . . .'

"I pawed the hair from my eyes with one bloody hand.

"'God fucking *damn* you . . .'

"'S-stop,' Phoebe begged, taking hold of my wrist. 'P-please.'

"'Like hell I will.'

"'Moonssakes, I've n-nae wish fer the last thing I f-feel on this earth to be ye *butchering* me.'

"'Shut up, Kitcat. For once in your fucking life, just do what you're . . .'

"My voice faded as she pressed a red hand to my cheek, teeth slicked with blood. 'I told ye nae p-promises. N-nae vows. B-but swear . . . swear t'me y-ye'll save the Flower.'

"'I'm not swearing anything. And you're not going anywh—'

"'Dior n-needs ye, Gabe. Tell her farewell fer me. An' tell . . .' She snarled, head thrown back as her veins burned with silvered venom. 'Ohhh, I'm s-sorry, Aunt Cinna . . . I *tried* . . .'

"Phoebe curled up tight, whimpering as my eyes grew wide.

"'Aunt Cinna . . .' I whispered.

"*A seer. A dreamwalker. The greatest healer in the Highlands . . .*

"'Could she fix this? Your aunt?'

"The duskdancer only winced, wracked with the agony of the poison.

"'Phoebe?' I shouted. 'Could your aunt Cinna see this right?'

"'T-told ye, ye fool,' she groaned. 'If ye g-go to the Highlands, ye die.'

"That was all I needed to hear. As Phoebe moaned protest, I bound her wounds, dragging on her dress and wrapping her in our furs. Throwing all the gear I could over my shoulders, I lifted the wounded 'dancer in my arms. My blood was still afire, some desperate dark strength raging in my veins as I ran down to the keep's bailey six, seven steps at a time. Lachlan was on his knees in the broken courtyard now, a bleeding Robin helping him up from the flagstones, watching me as I dashed into the stables.

"I trotted out on Argent's back, Thorn behind us, Phoebe bloodied in my arms. My 'prentice's eyes were fixed on mine as I drew up short, breath steaming in the chill between us.

"'Don't come after me again, Lachie,' I warned. 'Or if you do, bring a silvered fucking army with you. Because *that's* what you'll need to stop me getting back to that girl's side.'

"With that, I wheeled Argent about, urged him on. Phoebe's eyes were shut, lashes gummed to bloody cheeks as we charged out into the dying storm, riding like all hell came behind us.

"'You hold on, Phoebe,' I told her, kissing her brow. 'Just breathe.'

"I knew this was a fool's gambit. That this story would likely end with me slaughtered and skinned like prey. But the woman in my arms had saved my life, perhaps in more ways than I was willing to admit, and the poison in her veins was on my account. So while it dragged me yet farther from Dior's side, while it likely led straight to my death, still I turned Argent's skull-painted face into the wind, and rode him hard as I dared upon our new road.

"Toward the blood-soaked spires of the Moonsthrone.

"Toward the shadows that danced in the dusk of the Daesweald.

"Toward the Highlands."

XI

NO DAY TO DIE

"SIX NIGHTS I rode, all of them ablur. Barely eating. Ever smoking. Curling down beside Phoebe to snatch a few minutes' sleep each night, terrified I might wake to find her cold and still beside me. The silver burned black in her veins, her breath thinned and her skin greyed. But I'd slowed her pulse with a tea of idleshade and neverhelm, gathered in the hollows of the thickening Daesweald. Never had I been more thankful for fungus in my fucking life.

"Yet as we rode higher toward the crags of mighty Bann Fìageal, my gratitude fled entirely. The trees loomed dark and twisted around me; laden with shadespine and asphyxia, contorted into nightmare shapes. The reek of decay stained every breath, strange shadows creeping through clawed branches. Dark birds sang with haunted tongues, webs too large for any spider under heaven strung between the branches. What little game I saw was blighted and fell; hides crawling with pale mold and lattices of dark rot. I could see why the Highland clans were so isolated; no sane or living man would brave these woods to reach them anymore. But if I didn't make it through soon, Phoebe would be buried in them.

"And so I rode, day and night blurring into one; an endless, freezing gloom.

> *"There once was a lad from Auld Lyles,*
> *"Who juggled five black ignis phials.*
> *"He blew his p-poor bollocks,*
> *"All over the hillocks,*
> *"And his j-jack all the way to the Isles.*

"'Awful.' I glanced to the sword in my hand. '*Bollocks* doesn't rhyme with *hillocks*.'

— 461 —

"*Nothing rhymes with b-b-bollocks, Gabriel. One of life's great disappointments.*

"I frowned at that, trying to think of a word to prove Ash wrong. My trepidation was such that I'd been riding with her in hand for three days now, and while her weight was a comfort in that blighted deadwood, her chatter was admittedly wearing a little thin.

"*I thought it m-might make ye smile. Ye never smilesmile anymore, Gabriel . . .*

"'I'll smile when Phoebe and Dior are safe.'

"*Ye c-c-care for her.*

"'Of course I do, Ash. That girl is the only reason—'

"*Notnotnot Dior. The f-firehair.*

"The beautiful dame on the blade's hilt stared at me; those silver eyes, sightless, yet seeing all. I stared back, the weight of her near as heavy as the troth ring I wore. Ashdrinker had been there the day Astrid slipped that band onto my finger. And even after I was cast from the Order, my blade had stayed true to me. Despite the grandeur of her beginnings, the glory she had earned over her centuries, she was content to remain a part of my life. Hung above the mantel in our little lighthouse as ma famille blossomed all around her. She'd been in my hand the night the Forever King came calling. She heard that promise I'd made to the ground afterward.

"*A shame, I n-n-name it.*

"I hung my head, cursing myself and my weakness as I glanced at Phoebe.

"'I know. I should've never let it get so far.'

"*Nonono. Ye grasp notnot my meaning. I n-name it no shame ye broke your vow, my friend. B-b-but a shame that ye swore it in the first place.*

"'What should I have done?' I growled. 'Bury her, and all memory of her besides?'

"*Ye do what all m-must do when Mahné's wings blot out their sun. Sing s-sweet songs for the beloved dead. But then pick up thy quill, and p-pen the next verse of thy life.*

"'I hate minstrels, Ash. And I can't sing worth a damn.'

"*What, then, thy plan? Remain a broody, m-moody celibate all thy days?*

"'I don't brood. And I'm not m—'

"*Shave thy head and g-grow thy beard and trade slayer's leathers for monk's sackcloth? Perhaps geld thyself also, aye? No good rhyme for b-b-bollocks, after all. Nor good use, neither, for forever's widowwidower.*

"'Ash—'

"*More use the bull for his teats than the eternal mourner for his manhood.*

K-k-keenest edge have I, to tackle thy troublesome t-tackle. So come, Chevalier, unsheathe thy blade and let me meet it, sniksnaksnikSNAK!

"I scowled, refusing to encourage Ash's little tirade with an answer. She carried on a while more, voice ringing in my head as I rode on through that gloom. And when she'd spent the last of her castration puns, I spoke with a voice sharp as her broken edge.

"'I loved her, Ash. I can't help it. I loved Astrid then, and I love her still.'

"Her voice softened then, musical and sweet in my mind.

"*I know it. Ye had something most men n-never possess. Yet I knew thy b-bride also, Gabriel. And never would Astrid have asked ye to mournmourn her eternal. To cut thyself off from all life and love. To suffocate on the past instead of b-breathing here and now.*

"I stared at that silvered dame, her words echoing in the halls of my battered heart.

"*Happiness, above all, would she w-wish for ye. And me beside her. My d-dearest friend.*

"A sting pricked my eyes at that, pawed away swift on my knuckles.

"*How is the firefirehair?*

"I looked down to the woman in my arms, sweat-lank curls plastered to her cheeks. I wore my gloves, of course, both to spare my hands the cold and Phoebe's skin the touch of more silver. But her breath was weak as a baby bird's, dark veins crawling under her skin.

"'Worse.' I scowled about us. 'And there seems no end to this cursed fucking wood.'

"*It is d-d-dark here. Frightening. I likelikelike it . . .*

"'Reminds me of the Crimson Glade.' I glanced among the shifting branches, the whispering leaves, the shadowshapes flitting through the dark. 'Do you remember that day?'

"*. . . No.*

"Her reply was a sigh, faint and heartsick.

"*S-s-s-some days . . . I can't rememember anything at all, Gabriel . . .*

"'Who?'

"The voice rang above me, talon-sharp over the moaning winds. Looking up into a pair of gleaming eyes, I raised Ashdrinker in my fist. But my pulse eased as I saw only an owl; tawny of feather and gold of stare, studying me with tilted head.

"'Whooo?' it demanded again, flapping its wings.

"'Gabriel de León, monsieur,' I muttered, lowering my blade. 'At your service.'

"I heard wings behind me, swift in the dark. Another owl joined the first, grey and thin, staring at me with eyes the color of flame. A cold wind blew at my back, a chill crawled my skin. Dusk was falling in the weald now; I should stop to rest soon. But though I knew not why, I nudged my horse instead, trotting faster. I was riding upon Thorn to give Argent a break, my tarreun clopping along behind us, and as we rode through the twisted trees, I heard the song of wings, noticed more figures on the branches above. A few. Then a dozen.

"Owls.

"They watched me pass, unblinking, eyes big as saucers or small as thimbles. Some were so tiny only a mouse might fear them, others big enough to carry off a toddler for supper. In the gloom after daysdeath, most of the birds in Elidaen had sputtered out and died. No fruit to eat. No flowers to drink. Owls were one of the few breeds to survive these nights, hunting prey small enough to have prospered in a world without sunlight. But to see so many in the one place, watching me of one accord . . .

"'Whooo?' one of them called.

"'*Whoooo?*' the rest replied, echoing in the trees.

"*What do they c-c-call a group of owls?* Ash wondered.

"'A worry,' I muttered, watching the branches around us.

"*Nono, that is not right. Is it . . . a f-f-f-flight?*

"I kicked Thorn, she and Argent now weaving quick among the nightmare trees. Phoebe stirred in my arms, and I held her tighter, kissing her cold brow. All around us, those winged shadows were gathering, bright eyes and sharp claws, calling, always calling.

"'Who?' they demanded. 'WHO!'

"*A murder?*

"'That's crows,' I hissed.

"'Whooo?'

"*A c-c-cauldron, then?*

"'Bats.'

"*A convocation? A swarm? A cloud a flock a gaggle a horde a run a brood a grist a—*

"'*WHOOOOO!*'

"I glanced behind, trees now ringing with their cries, eyes glittering in the freezing black. Shadows flapping around me, Thorn thundering beneath me, the lantern at my belt throwing flicker-mad patterns across the dark as we rode toward—

"*A bear!*

"'You don't call a group of owls a *b*—'

"*No, LOOK!*

"It lumbered out from the deeper darkness ahead, snow crunching under its massive paws, and my eyes grew wide as I saw it, just as Ash had said:

"A fucking *bear.*

"But not some honeythief or mountain grey, no, this was a monster spat from the mind of this nightmare wood, or else the black and curdled heart of hell. It reared up before us, a ten-foot tower, and its mouth opened in a blood-chilling *ROAR*. Its fur was midnight, its teeth swords, sharp enough to rend steel. Thorn shied sideways, and I cried aloud, throwing myself from her saddle as talons scythed just shy of my head. Twisting to protect Phoebe's body with my own, I felt something crack as we crashed into the snow, holding her to my chest as we rolled to rest. But I'd no time to bleed.

"No time to smoke either, sadly.

"Thorn panicked and galloped away, and I expected to hear the *crunch* of breaking horse behind me; for poor Argent to join the long list of unfortunate steeds I'd buried on this road. But I heard a fierce growling, glancing over my shoulder to find the tarreun standing on his hind legs before that massive beast; not rearing back in terror, but in defiance, the monster shying back as the warhorse stabbed the air with his front hooves.

"'Big balls for a gelding,' I muttered.

"I drew my wheellock and fired, the bear bellowing as the shot skimmed just shy of its skull, blowing off its ear instead. Cursing my miss, I snaked upright, Ash in hand as the monster charged me. I rolled across the tangled roots with another curse, drawing it away from Argent and Phoebe both. Thundering past, earth shaking, the bear pivoted to face me, swift as silver, Ash's voice lost under another thunderous *ROAR*. The beast lunged again, a blur of terrifying speed and strength, paws whistling toward my face, jaws snapping, forcing me back, back. I lunged around a twisted elm to buy me a moment to breathe, and slipping sideways around another flurry of blows, rolling low, I struck hard, eyes red, fangs bared, howling in triumph as I buried Ash deep into the monster's flank.

"It was a deathblow, I could've sworn it, but the bear only bellowed and swung about, wrenching my sword from my grip. I roared as it hit me, all the world burned white as I sailed backward, crashing through the branches of a rotten oak, owls screeching as they scattered. Hitting snow, I lifted my ringing head, stars in my eyes and blood in my mouth as that hellbear plowed into me, snatching me up in its jaws.

"The monster had me by the shoulder, shaking its head and flinging me about like a rag doll. I felt teeth puncture skin, bones breaking, and I screamed then, high and bright; a scream of agony, of fear, but above all, *rage*. I was Gabriel de León, after all. Savior of Nordlund, Sword of the Realm, the *Black fucking Lion*, and this was not the day I died. I punched the beast as hard as I could, face, snout, bleeding ear, and finally, with naught else to do, I bit that bastard right back, fangs sinking deep into its neck. The beast threw back its head and roared in agony then, releasing its hold, and I crashed onto the snow like a bag of broken sticks, blood gushing from my punctured chest and shoulder.

"The pain was . . . breathtaking. I was broken in a dozen places, flesh torn, chest bubbling, snow drenched red around me. But still, my world flooding crimson, boots filling with blood, I somehow dragged myself to my feet. The bear thundered toward me; two tons of muscle and fang and claw. Ash was still buried in the monster's back; I'd nothing to fight with save my bare hands. But bare hands have killed kings, coldblood. Bare hands have built empires. A man and his sword can carve a legend. A man and his army can conquer a nation. A man and his god can remake the world. But swords shatter. Armies falter. Gods betray.

"A man's hands are ever his own.

"The monster lumbered into me, knocking me onto my arse. But as its bloody maw opened wide to rip my throat apart, I seized hold; one hand locked around its chin, the other its snout. The beast pressed down with all its weight, tons of pressure on my chest, spit and blood drooling on my face as its tongue lolled from its open mouth. But though I knew not how, I kept those jaws held apart, fangs sinking into my palms, bare hands torn bloody. The monster surged, trying in vain to bite, but with fury and fear boiling inside my chest, I wrenched its mouth wider. The beast thrashed, claws ripping me open, the sounds of tendons popping and bone creaking rising over its agonized bellow as I flexed, and with a roar, tore its jaw so wide it simply snapped in my hands.

"Blood sprayed, the bear howled in pain and fury. I planted both feet on its chest, kicked hard, the monster sent flying despite its colossal weight. It struck a tree a few yards from where Phoebe lay, the oak tilting sideways in a shower of snow, earth shaking as the beast crashed into the frost and fell still, steam rising from its ruined mouth.

"I dragged myself upright, toppled and collapsed, crawling now across the blood-drenched grey. My tongue was tingling as I spat the bear's blood from it, all my senses ablaze, ablur, but I had only one thought, one fear, not for me, but for . . .

"'Phoebe . . .'

"She lay where she'd fallen, wrapped in furs, covered now in snow. Thorn had fled, but I managed a bloody smile as I saw Argent yet stood above Phoebe's body, like a loyal soldier at his post, his breath steaming as he whinnied at the sight of me. Crawling to his side on my knees, I pressed a bloody hand to his flank.

"'You j-just made a f-friend f-for life, boy.'

"The warhorse nickered softly, and I sank down beside Phoebe, coughing red. Peeling away the blankets, thirst burning bright as I listened for her breath. My heart twisted as I waited in silence, and I drew her arm out from the covers, feeling for a pulse. My gut filled slow with ice, but then; a faint thud beneath her skin, a small moan from her ashen lips.

"'Thank the Martyrs.'

"A whimper bubbled in the still, and I raised my head, realizing that monstrous bear was somehow still alive. It was trying to rise now, blood drooling from its broken jaws, eyes still fixed on me. Breathing deep, I hauled myself upright, staggered to its side, and dragged Ash from its bleeding flank. The sword's song rang in my head, near lost under the war drum of my pulse as I raised her high above that monster's body . . .

"*Stop, Gabriel, no STOPSTOP!*

". . . and froze still. Blinking, chest heaving, noting for the first time the collar of everknots around the beast's neck. The pattern of white spirals and moons daubed onto its fur.

"*A dancer see a dancer like firefirehair, d-d-don't hurt her, ye shitwit!*

"'Daen stiir,' came a voice.

"I glanced over my shoulder, saw a woman with a longbow of horn and ashwood, aimed right at my heart. Her leathers and furs were adorned with bramble and twig, painted in a slashed pattern of black and grey; she'd have been invisible among the shadows but for my paleblood eyes. Her face was covered by a hood and scarf, and she wore a mantle of feathers about her shoulders—a dozen different kinds. Owl feathers.

"'G-great Redeemer,' I wheezed, straightening. 'You—'

"'Daen stiir!' she bellowed. 'Ahlfunn drae'a ken!'

"I heard the creak of more bows, glancing to my flanks and rear, spotting new figures now; a half dozen women among the shadowed trees. They were dressed likesame as the huntress, bows raised and arrows aimed right at me.

"*Bright eyes looklook see true forest daughters so p-p-pretty.*

"Now, I was *fucked,* coldblood. My left arm was shredded, blood pouring into the snow. From the bubbling of my breath, one of my lungs was likely punctured, ribs crushed, shoulder wrenched, skull cracked. I'd no idea how I managed it, yet still I straightened, standing over Phoebe's body and raising Ash in one blood-soaked hand.

"'Aright then.' I sighed, spat blood. 'Which of you dames w-wants first dance?'

"'Maoic,' one of the painted women said. 'Dyasae'err skaenn'a?'

"The leader's gaze shifted from mine to the woman I guarded. Her eyes narrowed as she saw Phoebe's arm, pale skin run through with fine black veins and inked with fae spirals.

"'Fiáin dahtr,' she said, looking back to me with furious eyes.

"'This woman is under m-my protection,' I wheezed, swaying on my feet. 'You touch her, I'll m-murder every fucking one of you.'

"*Ye w-will N-NOT.*

"'Shut up, Ash,' I hissed, soft and furious. 'I'm trying to be intimidating.'

"*They are s-s-six ye are one they have bows ye've a blade they are hale ye are b-b-b-bleeding out of* several *new holes. How intititimidating do ye think ye look ye look?*

"I sighed. Listening to those bowstrings creak tighter. That these were clanswomen was in no doubt, yet whether they were friend or foe to Phoebe's kin, I'd still no clue. All the warnings I'd been given about the dangers of coming here rang now in my mind. But taking Ash's point, I scowled at the silver dame and thrust her into the snow at my feet.

"The huntress stared at me for an age, blood dripping from my empty hands. Finally, she lowered her bow, slipping from her hide and stalking toward me. As the woman approached, she drew back her hood, pulled her scarf low, and I saw beneath the greasepaint and muck, her brow was scored with a crescent and full circle, side by side, a pattern of everknots and moons trailing down the right side of her face—Naéth, the warrior tattoos of the Ossian Highlands. Her hair was pale blond, bound in a dozen slayerbraids and threaded with more feathers, tied with leather thongs.

"I sank to my knees beside Phoebe. Drawing back the blankets to show the black stain in the duskdancer's veins, I looked up to the maid with desperate eyes.

"'This is Phoebe, blessed daughter of Clan Dúnnsair.' I coughed, spitting blood. 'She's b-been shot with silver. And it's still inside her.'

"At mention of the word *silver*, the maid narrowed her eyes. Looking closer, she took note of the ink on my arms and fingers through my tattered coat and gloves.

"'*Se'yersan,*' she hissed, hand snaking to the blade at her belt.

"'Peace, mademoiselle.' I raised bloody hands. 'I'm with the Order no longer. I seek the Wintermoot and Cinna á Dúnnsair, in hope her niece's hurts might be healed.'

"Still wary, bristling, the huntress crouched beside Phoebe, pressing a palm to her brow. One of the others called out, the maid snapped reply, new fear in her voice. I coughed again, blood spattering into my gloved fist, breath frothing through pierced lungs. The snow around me was soaked now, my dusk swimming toward midnight—I should've dropped like a rock. But though I'd no ken how, I fought that darkness back. The huntress looked me over, her expression clouded. That I was somehow ally to Phoebe must be plain, but that I was an outsider, a Lowlander, a *silversaint,* was plainer still.

"'Will she live?'

"I turned at the deep, rasping voice. And there in the new-fallen dusk stood one of the biggest women I'd ever seen. She was broad and tall and muscular and, aside from her collar of everknots, unabashedly naked. Black waist-length hair bound in dozens of slayerbraids cascaded over blood-drenched skin, adorned with spirals and moons, daubed in white. From the bloody sword wound in her side and the shadow she threw on the snow, I knew her for who she was—that mountain of teeth and claw I'd just battled to a standstill.

"A duskdancer of the úrfuil.

"'Bear-kin,' I whispered.

"One of the huntresses tossed a cloak of clancloth, and the big woman bound it about her waist like a kilt. She limped closer, eyes locked on me, and I saw they were entirely brown, no whites showing at all. Ears trimmed with dark fur sat slightly too high upon her skull, one a ragged, bleeding stump. The hand she pressed to the wound in her ribs was more akin to a paw; clawed and covered with thick, dark fur that ran up her forearms to her elbows. Her nose and jaw were broken, mouth bloodied and bruised, but still she managed to speak, slurring, her brogue thick enough to butter bread with.

"'I'll have yer name, maebh'lair. An' one good r-reason nae to end ye n-now.'

"'I'll give you three, mademoiselle, since you asked so politely.' I raised one hand, counting on blood-soaked fingers. 'First, I'm not a vampire. Merely a vampire's son.'

"The úrfuil scoffed, touching the bite wounds I'd left in her throat.

"'Second,' I said, dragging myself to my feet, 'and please understand I cast no aspersions on your prowess here—but Phoebe á Dúnnsair would likely feed you your fucking heart when she found out you ended me.'

"The big 'dancer narrowed her eyes, folding massive arms. 'And third?'

"'Third . . .'—I scratched my stubble—'. . . and perhaps where I should've started in hindsight . . . the Godling is found.'

"I paused, listening to the whispers rippling around the group.

"'And *I* know where she is,' I added.

"Standing taller, I waited for their voices to still.

"'And as for my name, mademoiselle? I've been known by many. Savior of Nordlund. Sword of the Realm. The Black Lion of Lorson. But my first was the one my dear mama gave me, and the one I think you'll know best.'

"I shifted my gaze back to the duskdancer, looking her dead in the eye.

"'Gabriel de León is my name, mademoiselle. I am *quite* sure it precedes me.'"

Jean-François scoffed softly, scratching in his tome.

"You actually *said* that?"

Gabriel chuckled. "I actually said that."

"Well." The vampire shrugged. "Dramatic entrances *are* the best kind."

"Not always." Gabriel sipped his wine. "But when someone insists on measuring cocks and yours is the biggest, sometimes it's best to just whip it out and be done.

"'I know we've bloody history between our kin,' I said. 'But we're not enemies, mademoiselle. If we were, would one of mine be risking his life to save one of yours?'

"The úrfuil's eyes narrowed. The shadows whispered, new tension now strung thick in the air. The huntress still kneeling at Phoebe's side looked down as she moaned, pressing one hand to her brow. 'She's burnin', Brynne. We need to see her to. Or bury her here.'

"The big woman said nothing, staring knives at my throat.

"'Trust me, Mlle Brynne,' I said. 'The fate of the world hangs in the balance here.'

"Phoebe moaned again, sheened in sweat. The huntress looked to the big woman with wide, worried eyes. And the úrfuil finally sighed, squaring broad shoulders.

"'Ye set one foot wrong on this road, se'yersan, I'll make a cloak o' yer hide, ken?'

"'I fear human skin makes for terrible leather.' I managed a bloody smile. 'But I suppose it'd be warmer than what you're wearing right now.'

"The bear scowled, glancing among her sisters.

"'The smartarse comes wi' us.'"

XII

MOTHER'S CRADLE

"IT'S A STARE."

In the cold reaches of Sul Adair, Gabriel de León glanced up from the chymical globe, that pale moth beating in vain upon smooth glass. "What did you say?"

Jean-François smoothed back a lock of golden hair with his quill, dipped it swiftly into his pot of ink. "A flock of owls, de León. It's called a *stare*."

"Hmm." The Last Silversaint nodded. "You learn something every night."

"Several things," the vampire smiled. "If you spend your nights in the right company. You reached your destination alive, I take it? Bevy of scars aside, your hide is still intact, from what little you've been kind enough to show me."

Gabriel nodded, pouring the last of the Monét into his glass. "We made it to Wintermoot. But this is where it gets a little messy, coldblood. I might need another drink."

"I think three bottles is probably enough for now, oui?"

Gabriel scoffed, lifting his goblet. "You're no fun at all."

"We could call Meline and Mario back in? I can show you how much fun I can be?"

"His name is Dario, Chastain."

Gabriel sighed, leaned back in his chair, fingers steepled at his chin. He breathed deep, a dark frown between his brows, gathering his thoughts.

"It took us two nights to journey there, hurrying on secret paths with storm clouds whipping us on. The Daesweald was a dark stain all around, like mold creeping on old bread, but the Highlands were still *spectacular* country, coldblood; wild mountains and everskies, waterfalls of ice, frozen hundreds of feet high. I'd have appreciated the beauty more if I wasn't so afeared for Phoebe, but while there were no healers among the huntresses, the one named Maoic had some hedge magik about her; it was *her* that stare of owls belonged to, and she could speak to them in some wild tongue. Between the charms she strung about Phoebe's neck and the teas I brewed, we kept her breathing.

"They were guardians, I learned, these women. *Moonsmaidens,* they named themselves—warriors chosen from among the Highland clans, devoted to the watch of the sacred lands around the Wintermoot. They moved like wraiths, and spent most of their time in the shadows as we traveled; even with paleblood senses, I was stretched to keep track of them all. But Maoic led Thorn and Argent through the woods ahead of me, and the úrfuil woman stalked ever behind, dark eyes on my back, Phoebe on a stretcher between us. Her full name was Brynne á Killaech, and she hadn't returned to her weald-shape after our battle in the wood. She was clad in tooled leathers and a kilt of dark cloth now, strung with charms in the shape of crescent moons. The big woman wasn't much for talking, even after her jaw had healed, but it was clear she'd the deepest misgivings about my company.

"'Did Dahtr á Dúnnsair tell ye what Wintermoot is?' she asked one day. 'D'ye have *any* ken under the Mothermoons where ye were headed?'

"'Only that it'd be into danger,' I replied. 'Probably my death.'

"'And still ye came? Are ye that tired of livin', maebh'lair?'

"'Not a vampire,' I reminded her. 'And there are very few people in this world I consider friends, Mlle Brynne. But the Godling is one. Strange as it may seem to you, this woman between us is another.' I shrugged. 'And my friends are the hill I die on.'

"'Yer lucky ye aren't dead aready,' she growled. 'Yer heathen God smiled on ye, when last we fought. If we tangled again, I'd rip ye a new arse.'

"'I've no doubt. But given I'll be wearing the scars of your teeth for the rest of my days and that I'm rather fond of my arse as is, let's avoid further entanglements, shall we?'

"Brynne scowled, nodding to Phoebe between us.

"'Why's she wearin' a ballgown?'

"Despite my peril, my fears, still I chuckled then, thinking about that dauntless girl in the shadows of Cairnhaem, her smile brightening my dark.

"'Because there are always fucks to give for fashion.'

"We trekked on, owls fluttering through dead trees and thoughts of Dior flickering in my mind. I still felt nothing, each time I reached out for her now. Nothing but fear and regret.

"'Tis a festival,' Brynne finally said. 'Wintermoot. To celebrate the turning o' the frost, back t'ward spring. All Mothers and clanheads from across the Highlands gather under banner o' peace. Disputes are heard. Truces brokered. Weddings arranged.'

"'Alas. I fear I'm already spoken for, mademoiselle.'

"The úrfuil woman shook her head. 'Ye *are* tired of livin', aren't ye?'

"I winked. 'Perhaps I just like living dangerously.'

"We trudged up twisting mountain passes, toward the roof of the world. The cold was deadly, and every mile I could feel eyes upon me, hear whispers among the branches—how foolish I'd been to think I might make it through these woods unnoticed. Figures flitted among the trees, sharp eyes and swift shadows, Maoic's owls carrying word back and forth, hopefully warning them not to fill me with arrows. And at last, we arrived in a valley, nestled between two snowcapped spires, my eyes widening as I saw what awaited within.

"'Ma'dair Craeth,' Maoic murmured beside me, pressing two fingers to her brow, lips, heart. 'The Cradle of the Mothers. The heart of the Highlands.'

"'Twas here the Moons were suckled by the Night,' Brynne said. ''Twas here the first wealdlings were born, when the Mothers made love to the Mountains.'

"'Great Redeemer,' I whispered.

"It was a forest valley, frozen in winter's grip, but unlike the realm below, the trees here were hale and whole. There was no sign of rot, no fungus or decay, and I was at once reminded of the woods of my youth; hunting among green trees before the death of days.

"A great loch was frozen at the valley's heart, and two enormous statues of raw basalt rose up at its shoreline, forty feet high; a pair of regal, beautiful women, each holding aloft a crescent of stone. These were effigies of the moons, Lánis and Lánae, though I was struck with how akin to angels they looked; broad wings at their backs, long hair studded with stars. Between them, a bearded man with goat legs and a crown of antlers was carved, one hand outstretched to each—Malath, the Earth Father, guardian and groom to both.

"At the loch's edge stood a mighty hall with two tall towers, one to the west, the other, east. The architecture was awe-inspiring, ancient timbers and dark stone carved with everknots. Colossal trees stood beside the hall, great creepers crawled the walls, and my heart burned a little brighter at the sight—a *flower* this place seemed, a single bloom still growing, perhaps the last bastion of uncorrupted splendor in this empire entire.

"'It's *beautiful*,' I whispered.

"The path through the wood was lined with a row of figures; women all, dressed in long fur cloaks, dyed red as moonlight. Strange helms were sat atop their heads, covering their eyes, like crowns wrought of burning red candles. Silvered blades, curved like crescent moons, were planted in the snow before them, their hands at rest on the hilts. Every inch of their skin was covered in blood-red inkwork; fae spirals and snatches of ancient magiks.

"'Our sisters,' Brynne murmured. 'Priestesses of the Cradle. They keep this place unspoiled for the Mothers and Father, and ensure nae violence is done during the moot.'

"The first woman bowed and spoke with a deep, musical voice.

"'Mothers' blessings, dearest sisters. The Father smiles upon ye. But . . .'— here those masked eyes turned toward me—'. . . nae upon this one, we fear.'

"'I bring no quarrel, Sœur,' I began. 'I come only to help my—'

"'We know why ye are here, se'yersan,' the priestess said. 'We have word of yer coming on the winds, and the wealds have spake yer name to us these many nights. Ye shall cede yer weapons to us, and surrender yerself to our gentle keeping.'

"The thought sat ill with me; to be unarmed among a gathering who'd see me only as an enemy. But if I wished to enter here, it seemed I'd no choice but to obey. Brynne tensed at my back as I took off my pistol and powder, and unbuckling Ashdrinker's scabbard from my belt, I kissed the silvered maid on the hilt, handed her over to the priestess. Though her eyes were masked by that strange, burning candlecrown, the woman still took the blade unerringly.

"'Please take care of her, Sœur,' I murmured. 'We've been through hell together, she and I. And no finer company could I have asked for.'

"'The Drinker of Ash,' the woman breathed. 'The Soul of the Sky. The Heavensent.'

"Lifting the sword gently, she looked Ashdrinker over with wondering eyes.

"'Not so legendary as once they were, the hands that now wield her. But *her* legend remains undiminished.' The woman nodded. 'We shall treat her with all due reverence, se'yersan.'

"I wondered how it was this woman knew Ashdrinker's name, her past, but more sisters came forth before I could ask, lifting Phoebe's stretcher and carrying her swift down the forest path. I followed, Brynne looming behind as we walked past those unearthly maids to the valley below. Drawing closer, I saw beautiful lodges of wood and stone built around that mighty hall, a small town resting in this cradle's heart. And that town was peopled by the strangest folk I'd ever seen.

"I'd been raised on tales of duskdancers at the monastery, but in truth, I'd no idea what I'd find in Ma'dair Craeth. Hulking men and women with bodies covered in fur. Folk with tails and claws; half-human, half-animal. Some wore clancloth and armor, but others were so changed, they'd little use for either, simply walking in the shapes of their beasts. This was the only place in the empire I might see such sights, I realized—the regular mountain lions and bears and wolves had all gone extinct since the death of days.

"Fae spirals were painted on their hides, human intelligence glittered behind animal eyes. All stared at me in the gloom, a few with curiosity, most with hostility, and though I'd never spilled 'dancer blood in my life, I felt a tiny fish in an ocean of hungry sharks.

"Phoebe was taken with all haste into that grand hall, but I was marched to one of the towers at its flank. The priestess who'd taken my weapons led me up a winding stair, the candlelight from her crown flickering on the stones. Brynne thumped along behind, bristling with silent menace. I was led to a room at the tower's peak, thin windows overlooking those mighty basalt statues and the frozen loch beyond. I could see fires burning on the shoreline, shadows dancing around the flames, the song of bright pipes and the scent of feast hanging on the cold wind.

"'Ye shall remain here,' the priestess commanded. 'Young Brynne shall stand the watch below. If ye've need, call her name.'

"'How long must I wait?' I asked, fists clenched.

"'As long as the Mothers and Father will it.'

"'I've business to the south, madame. A dearest friend in deepest need. We come to ask the clans for aid, but if you'll give us none, we *must* seek those who will. And swift.'

"'We shall speak to the Fiáin dahtr.' She tilted her head, wax dripping upon the floor. 'All rests wi' her. If ye have the ear of yer heathen God, ye may wish to pray she lives.'

"'Or if she dinnae,' Brynne growled, 'that at least we kill ye quick, vampire.'

"I sighed, meeting the úrfuil's eyes. 'No marriage proposal, then?'

"The big woman muttered and turned to leave, but my voice brought her to a halt.

"'Merci, Mlle Brynne.'

"Scowling, she glanced over her shoulder.

"'For putting faith in me,' I said. 'It's no small thing, to be the one to take that first step. Folk who cannot trust each other are doomed to destroy each other. And Moons and Earth know, these nights are filled with enemies enough.'

"I offered my hand, clad in my tattered glove.

"'A debt is owed you. By me, and hopefully the world besides.'

"The warrior woman looked down at my hand. Grunting, she shook it, her paw, engulfing; her grip, bone-grinding. I winced, trying to match her strength as her eyes glittered with amusement. And with no farewells, the pair left my cell.

"It was no true prison—they'd no need for one in this sacred place, I supposed. I could've climbed out the window and tried my luck, but that'd serve me not at all. My future, Dior's, the world's, all was in the hands of fate now, and if I was the praying sort, I'd have been on my fucking knees. As it was, I waited, sucking on my pipe like a leech to a vein, burning with my ever-growing thirst, and wearing a rut in the stone from my pacing.

"It was late the next eve I heard footsteps on the stairs. Turning toward the door with fists and jaw clenched, I noted the song of sad pipes now gracing the mountain air, wondering if I were listening to a funeral song. But the door opened, and there she stood; a sight more welcome than I'd have ever believed when first we met.

"I could see she wasn't fully recovered, shadows drawn deep under her eyes. But she looked me over; my torn and muddied clothes, the stubble and dried blood on my face, one clawed hand resting on her hip as she smiled.

"'Seems another wash is in order, Silverboy.'

"'Phoebe,' I breathed. 'Thank the Mothermaid . . .'

"She laughed, and I caught her up in my arms, breathing in the scent of woodsmoke and fools' honey in her braided hair, crushing her so tight to my chest she gasped. I drew her back to look into those fierce golden eyes, knowing not whether to kiss or scold her. But she cleared her throat, nodded to the two figures behind.

"'Gabriel de León, this is my aunt Cinna, Auld-Sìth of the Dúnnsair, and my cousin Breandan, Saoirse's brother, an' Rígan-Mor of my clan.'

"The pair nodded, the woman warm, the youngblood cold as ice, and I released my grip on Phoebe, stepping aside so they might enter.

"Aunt Cinna was perhaps fifteen years older than I, emerald eyes scratched by crow's-feet, lines etched at the corners of her mouth. Her hair was strawberry-blond running grey, intricate braids draped to her waist, threaded with gold. The leathers she wore were tooled with exquisite patterns of ever-knots and long-dead flowers, the clancloth around her waist woven of fine lambswool. And down her face, around each finger on her hands, beautiful Naéth tattoos whispered of magiks, old and dark.

"Cousin Breandan was a brick wall of a man. His bearded jaw was square, his eyes the gold of a lion's, and his ears were pointed likesame—another duskdancer, I realized. His sandy hair was more akin to a mane, woven into slayerbraids and strung with gold and bone. Furred fingers ended in sharp black claws, and beneath his kilt of fine clancloth, I saw what could only be a *tail,* tipped with a tuft of dark fur. He wore a beautiful steel cuirass, dark leathers, and he moved like a warrior. A hunter. A killer.

"My room was hardly furnished—cot and table, furs on the floor. Cinna and Phoebe sat near the small hearth with sparse ceremony, Breandan re-maining by the window. Phoebe had at last rid herself of Dior's ballgown, clad instead like her kinfolk—tooled leathers and thick furs and a fine kilt in the black and three greens of her clan. Her hair was threaded with gold, tumbling in braids around her shoulders, and she looked every inch a warrior queen. But when she met my eyes, I could still see the woman I knew, shrug-ging that dress from her shoulders and leaving nothing and none between us.

"I tore my eyes away, looked to Cinna. She was watching me thoughtfully, her voice soft and hazy, as if she was new awakened from the deepest sort of sleep.

"'I dreamed of ye,' she said. 'A Black Lion in red snows. A white raven at its shoulder, a dead bear at its feet, a snake about its throat, and a star, falling from its bloody mouth.'

"The metal in Cinna's braids sang softly as she tilted her head.

"'Are ye a herald of weal or woe, Gabriel de León?'

"'I've never been one to put stock in dreams, Mme Cinna,' I replied.

"'Ye should. Truth dwells in them.' The woman glanced to the empty air over my shoulder, eyes glazed. 'I see they who haunt yers, and the halls of yer troubled heart besides. They forgive ye, Lion. Ye carry a burden they'd never ask ye to bear.'

"I glanced to Phoebe, bristling a little, eager to turn talk to task.

"'Your niece has told you about Dior Lachance, I take it? The danger she faces?'

"'My niece told me the Godling is found.' Cinna breathed deep, tattooed fingers entwined in her lap. 'And that my sweet Saoirse is lost.'

"Phoebe reached out and touched Cinna's hand, Breandan squeezing his mother's shoulder, heavy with sorrow. But Cinna stared at me, eyes shining with a grief and anger I knew all too well. There's no greater tragedy under heaven than for a parent to outlive their baby, coldblood. No crime that feels so . . . unjust."

The Last Silversaint peered into the globe's soft light, elbows to his knees. The historian wrote on, quill scratching on the page as Gabriel hung his head, ink-black locks spilling around his face. His voice was soft as pipe smoke.

"You know . . . Patience once asked me what happens when we die."

Jean-François ceased writing then, lifting chocolat eyes to the silversaint's.

"She had a pet bird," Gabriel continued. "A baby gull she found among the rocks. It was a sickly thing, but she had the softest heart, that girl. She kept him in a little box I made. Fed him by hand. Named him Star, since he'd fallen from the sky. But he was ever frail, and one morn, Patience came to Astrid and me with little Star in her hands, crying because he wouldn't wake up.

"It's a strange thing, to explain death to a child. The question they inevitably ask is *why,* and in truth, there's no good answer. We settle for telling them about the God who loves them. The good place we go afterward, where there's no hurt. No death. We raise our children to believe in that lie; that all will be wonderful once they die. But my Patience wasn't content with that. And she looked at me with eyes full of tears, and she demanded to know if God loved us so much, why did he put us in a place like this at all? Why didn't he *start* us in the good place, where there was no death to begin with?"

The historian smiled sadly. "She was a clever one."

"Like her mama."

"What did you tell her, Gabriel?"

"The truth. I told her I didn't know." The Last Silversaint turned his eyes heavenward, that storm-grey gone dark with rage. "But I know now, bastard."

Silence hung heavy in the room, the historian watching the man opposite him. The chymical globe cast long shadows across the floor, that ghost-pale moth beating its wings on the glass, forever in vain. And finally, Gabriel sighed, rubbing the stubble on his chin.

"Cinna brushed at her eyes, but her fingers came away dry. The woman's heart was heavy with grief, but she had a strength in her even a blind man could see.

"'I have talked to the Auld-Sìth of the other clans. Ye shall be granted leave to speak to the All Mothers amorrow, Lion, and put yer case afore the moot fer judging.'

"'Me?' I frowned. 'Silversaints have been hunting duskdancers for centuries. We murdered your greatest queen. I've no place in that hall. It should be Phoebe who—'

"'My niece shall tell the tale. But ye shall add voice to hers. For a se'yersan to risk his life to save a dahtr of Fiáin is a deed that will carry weight. The Time of Blighted Blood has been cruel, and long have we sought the one who might bring its end. But it was augured the Godling would be a child of the Highlands. Ye've need to convince the All Mothers our savior is born nae among the chosen of Fiáin, but is a daughter of Lowland heathens, and the ward of a man who served the Order that butchered Ailidh Stormbringer.'

"I sighed. 'Just that simple, eh?'

"'I fear nae.'

"I looked to Breandan as he spoke, furred arms folded over his chest. I could smell earth and a feral musk on his skin, see hard years and grim murder in those lion's eyes.

"'There is one other . . . complication, se'yersan.'

"I glanced to Phoebe, eyebrow raised. 'This wasn't difficult enough?'

"Phoebe's mood had darkened, a soft rage in her voice as she spoke. 'Troubles have bled the Highlands white since I was last here, Gabe. The ishaedh grows worse, the woods run to rot, the things festering within kill the game. All the Highlands are at war over the territory that remains unspoiled, and between those strifes and the battles against the blightlings . . .' She shook her head, seething. 'The clans could afford no further turmoils.'

"'. . . What are you saying?'

"'A truce was struck, Lion,' Cinna said. 'At Wintermoot two years ago. The Auld-Sìth of every clan tied their knot to it, our troth etched in stone.'

"'Truce?' I shook my head. 'I don't understand, truce with who?'

"'The Heartless,' Breandan said. 'The Winterwife.'

"I blinked at that, reeling. 'You struck a *truce* with Lilidh fucking *Dyvok?*'

"'To end another trouble we could ill afford to fight,' the 'dancer growled. 'The Dead were striking at us from the south, the clans were at each other's throats, the Blight turning all to ruin. We struck pax wi' the Heartless that we might solve our own troubles. She would leave our lands in peace, if we swore never to set foot in the lands beyond.'

"'That's fucking insane! You can't trust a vampire, they're murderous f—'

"'That *is* the truth of things, Gabriel de León,' Cinna snapped, cutting off my tantrum. 'In the two years since pax was struck, we have seen nae *one* maebh'lair north of Dún Fas. The Untamed have kept their word, and to break ours would mean war wi' the Dead when most of the folk in that hall below have spent the last two years burying daughters and sons and wives and husbands skinned at the hands o' their *neighbors*. So if ye want them to unite and fight a foe that they have *nae* quarrel with, ye'd best conjure a more compelling argument than *ye cannae trust a leech*. Because the Godling cannae remain in Untamed hands, and I'll nae have it that my only daughter died fer *nothing*.'

"Cinna spat that last word, furious, and as she blinked, a single tear ran down her tattooed cheek. Sniffing hard, she pawed it away and rose to her feet.

"'I take my leave. I must have quieter words to the other All Mothers. It might be within me to build support among the leófuil at least. But the Bears and Wolves . . .'

"She shook her head, looking me over with sharp, emerald eyes. The silvered letters on my fingers, the roses and skulls on my hands, the sevenstar on my palm.

"'D'ye pray to yer One God, se'yersan?'

"'Not anymore. He never listens, madame.'

"She met my eyes then, her voice hard and cold as stone.

"'If ye never pray to him, boy, what exactly is he supposed to listen to?'"

XIII

SNOWS RUNNING RED

"BY THE NEXT eve, I almost wished I'd taken Cinna's advice.

"The Wintermoot recommenced at dawn. As the frail sun blooded the horizon, I stood at one of the windows in my tower, watching as each clan was led into the great hall by a solemn procession of moonsmaidens. Phoebe told me the building was known as the Tael'Líed in the Ossian tongue; the Elderhold. She'd departed with her aunt the previous eve, still in need of rest after her ordeal, and—I suspect—under scrutiny from her kinfolk on the matter of keeping a paleblood's company alone. But she stood beside me now, perilously close, and I did my best to ignore the thrum of her pulse, the broken glass in my gut, the ash on my tongue.

"'The Whelans,' she murmured, nodding to a group entering the Hold. 'They were the most powerful clan among the úrfuil years ago. But Clan Slaene flayed their Rígan-Mor alive three winters back, along w' both her sisters and all three of her bairns.'

"'What the hell for?' I asked.

"'Naebody knows. The Slaene deny they were responsible a'tall. But old Deirdre á Slaene has hated the Whelans since her husband ran off w' one of them ten years ago.' Phoebe shrugged. 'Old feuds. Fresh woes. And always, snows runnin' red.'

"I watched a pack of velfuil entering next, decked in fine leathers and elegant steel. The leader was an elder, marked heavy by his beast—covered brow to boots in grey fur. Though still he walked upright like a man, his head was that of a wolf, and he wore a crown of brambles at his brow, a cloak of tawny fur at his shoulders. Three youngbloods I presumed were his children walked beside him, all clad as warriors, fierce and proud.

"'Clan Barenn,' Phoebe whispered. 'Angiss and his sons. They slew my ma.' She drew a long, shaking breath. 'And perhaps my Connor.'

"'Bastards,' I muttered, looking them over.

"'It was war. And war is complicated. But that's my mother's hide Angiss is wearing as his cloak.' She met my eyes as I looked at her in horror. 'So aye, they're bastards.'

"'Great Redeemer.' I nodded to a man among the gathering. 'Who the hell is *that?*'

"'Keylan á Meyrick. *De'Faene,* they call him. The *Red Wrath.* Impressive, aye?'

"'Impressive?' I shook my head, awestruck. 'Fucking terrifying, more like.'

"'Eh. He's my third cousin. We've known each other from bairns, he's a pussycat.'

"The so-called pussycat was the biggest man I'd ever seen. It was hard to tell with the hair, but I guessed he stood over seven feet tall. He was a brick shit-house of a fellow—I mean *huge*—muscle stacked upon muscle. But though he and Phoebe were near of age, it seemed the Time of Blighted Blood had left a heavier mark upon him than his cousin. His hands were paws, and the claws at his fingertips long as knives. He was covered in a coat of rust-red fur, and his head was not a man's, but a lion's; complete with whiskers, snout, and a thick mane, plaited into dozens of slayerbraids. He was shirtless despite the chill, wearing iron pauldrons and vambraces tooled with a beautiful pattern of everknots, a long kilt, and a thick iron belt hung with what looked to be human skulls.

"'Remind me not to piss him off,' I murmured.

"'But yer so gifted at it. Would be a shame to waste yer moonsgiven talents.'

"I appreciated the attempt at levity, but I couldn't find a smile. Looking out at the clanfolk—the friendly embraces or formal bows, sly smiles at greeting, spit on the ground at parting—I sensed a sea of alliances and enmities too intricate and old to see the bottom of. Though these walls weren't golden, this *was* a court, I realized, as perilous and twisted as the Emperor's halls of power in Augustin.

"'How the *hell* are you going to pull this off, Phoebe?'

"'Speak the truth. With ye beside me.'

"'I'm not sure my presence here is going to be anything but a burden, Kitcat.'

"'We fight for Dior now. Have some faith, Silverboy.'

"Phoebe squeezed my gloved hand. I met her eyes, butterflies loosed in my belly as I saw the memory of Ravenspire burning in that gold. But our hands slipped apart as the door opened behind us, and Brynne stepped into the room.

"The úrfuil was clad in leathers, a wolfskin cloak, the dark shadow of a bear cast on the stone behind her. Though she was ever dour and tight-lipped, I think the thanks I'd given had gone a tiny way toward thawing the frost between us. But Brynne was obviously enamored of Phoebe, speaking to her fellow 'dancer now while avoiding her eyes.

"'The moot awaits ye below, fair dahtr,' she murmured.

"'My thanks, dear dahtr,' Phoebe bowed. 'And thanks doubled, for the service ye and yer sisters gave in bringing me here. I'm told by Gabriel that I owe ye my life.'

"The big woman shook her head, gruff. 'My heart gladdens to see ye well.'

"'A debt is owed to ye, brave maid of Fiáin.' Phoebe stood on tiptoe to embrace the taller woman, kissing her cheeks. 'And it's a debt I'll nae forget.'

"The úrfuil grunted, stepping aside. As Phoebe descended the stairs, I stood with hands clasped, watching the heat rise in Brynne's cheeks.

"'Hell are ye lookin' at, maebh'lair?' she demanded.

"'Not a vampire,' I reminded her. 'And I'm just wondering if we might be treated to a marriage proposal, after all?'

"The big 'dancer scowled, clawed hands twitching, and I skipped after Phoebe before she could make use of them. At the bottom of the stairs, we were met by a procession of moonsmaidens, nodding silent greeting. And with swords held before them, candles burning in their crowns, they led Phoebe and me into the great Elderhold, and the moot therein.

"The Highlanders had obviously been warned of my attendance, but I still felt a shift in the current as I entered—if the daggers in the eyes of those who watched me were made of true steel, I'd have been flayed a thousand times. The Tael'Líed was as spectacular within as without; a vast circular room, with a broad firepit blazing at its heart, banishing all winter's chill. The ceiling was supported by three mighty pillars, each carved in the likeness of one of the duskdancer lines; a wolf, a lion, and a bear, facing each other around the flames, feet upon the earth, each doing their part to hold up the ceiling and sky above. The walls were etched with old magiks and fae spirals, the rafters carved with patterns of everknots. Incense was strung in the air, and long

wooden benches circled the firepit, cloaked with furs and filled to bursting with a throng of people.

"Again, I was awed at the strange folk there gathered, all of me on edge. Some seemed barely human, and others had abandoned humanity entirely. But there were ordinary folk among them also; elders mostly, and women almost all, grey hair braided to the floor. These were the All Mothers, the most venerable and wise of the clans. Women who'd survived long enough to remember the follies of the past, and hopefully had sight enough to avoid them in the future.

"We were escorted to a place beside Aunt Cinna, and though Phoebe still looked pale, she matched any gaze aimed her way, unblinking. Cousin Keylan, that massive so-called pussycat, met her eyes, returning her nod. The Barenn Clan watched her with subtle hostility, whispering among themselves. Their eldest, Angiss, still wore the cloak he'd made of her mother's hide, but I saw he wasn't alone in this practice—most of the 'dancers in the hall were clad in trophies of battle, bears wearing lions and lions wearing wolves. All around the room, I felt subtle whispers, the riptides of old grudges and bloody history.

"Three moonsmaidens stood around the fire, silver crescent blades in hand, those strange candlecrowns burning around their heads. They spoke in an ancient Ossian dialect, something between a song and prayer, and all in the room bowed their heads. The first of the three struck her sword upon the floor three times, voice high and clear.

"'Brothers and sisters of the clans, sans and dahtrs and All Mothers, we are gathered here amorn at the call of a daughter á Fiáin and Dúnnsair. Let her voice be heard clear, her wisdom judged true, and the will of the Highlands be known.'

"Phoebe stood slowly, all eyes in that hall—golden and slitted, blue and burning, green and kohled—fell upon her. And as she matched those stares, every one, I was struck with how regal her bearing, how fearless her voice. She was but one among many warriors here, the widow of a would-be king, but to me, she looked every inch a queen.

> "*Dead shall rise, and stars shall fall;*
> "'*Weald shall rot to ruin of all.*
> "*Lions roar and angels weep;*
> "'*Sinners' hands our secrets keep.*

""*'Til Godling's heart brights hea'en's eye,*
"*'From reddest blood comes bluest sky.'*

"Phoebe looked around that hall, firelight burning in her gaze.

"'So it was spoken years past by the augur of the úrfuil, the seers of the velfuil, the dreams of the leófuil. Long have the children of Moons and Earth prophesied this darkness would come. I see its mark upon yer skins as I look around this hall. I see it in the looking glass with my own new eyes. But now it is upon us, sisters and brothers, do we stand as one against this dark? Or do we quarrel twixt ourselves as we have fer generations, while the lands around us rot to ruin, and the world beyond our borders freezes to ice?'

"'What care we for the land beyond our borders, Phoebe á Dúnnsair?'

"It was a woman who'd spoken, an old warrior with a slash of Naéth across her eyes, a scar at her chin, and her grey hair still bound in slayerbraids.

"'What care we for the woes of Lowlanders? When my birthlands are stained red with the blood of my gran'children, flayed by those here gathered under the lie of peace?'

"Another woman spoke, her shoulders crowned with a mantle of wolf-hide. 'If ye'd talk of lies, Deirdre á Slaene, p'raps we might talk again of the deceits of yer kinsmen, who *every day* encroach farther into the lands of the Tiagh.'

"Grim murmurs circled the firelight, nodding heads and narrowed eyes.

"'What would ye have us do, Nia?' the older woman demanded. 'Blight-lings roam our domains, and our crops are dead in their beds. Would the Tiagh see us starve?'

"A grizzled fellow with a beard like a grey bush spoke then. 'Some might call that justice, Slaene. Longer than one winter have yer bloody-handed raiders harried the hunting grounds of Whelan and Tiagh, both.'

"'Aye!' spat the green-eyed woman, nodding. 'Murderers and skinthieves, all!'

"Cries of outrage and agreement filled the air until the moonsmaidens struck their swords three times upon the floor. Phoebe raised her voice in the aftermath.

"'I say nae that ye have unjust quarrel! But I say we are brought to quarrel by the hand of *one* doom!' She gazed around, meeting the eyes of those who'd shouted. ''Tis the Blight that rots the weald and corrupts the game we hunted to feed our families! 'Tis the *Blight* that eats our crops afore they come to fruit! And ever it runs worse!'

"'And so?'

"It was Angiss á Barenn who spoke, his voice a wet snarl. It was strange to see a wolf's mouth speak with a man's tongue, ears pressed back against his skull, long fangs flashing.

"'Ishaedh worsens. The Time of Blighted Blood is come. All sans an' dahtrs of Fiáin know this. All blessed feel the beast sing louder in their veins. Ye are gone from these lands two dozen moons, cub. Did ye return now only to chide us on the state of them?'

"More growls of agreement, Phoebe raising her voice to be heard.

"'I am returned to tell ye that the Godling is *found*!'

"Silence fell then, like fog on a winter's morn. Eyes glittering. Teeth bared.

"'Aye, found!' Phoebe cried. 'The one spoken of in the augury walks this earth, and *I* have seen her! Dior Lachance, her name. Blessed of the heavens! Daughter of the divine! Her blood a hallowed miracle, that can burn the maebh'lair to cinders with but a touch, and heal any mortal ill with but a *drop*! And it shall heal our lands and sky, also!'

"Keylan á Meyrick leaned forward, elbows to knees, massive paws entwined.

"'The Anabh'Dhai,' the Red Wrath said, his voice a rasping growl. 'A *Lowlander*?'

"'I swear it, Keylan. On the blood of my mother. In sight of Moons and Earth.'

"Scoffs of disbelief and furious whispers filled the Elderhold. An old woman was seated beside Keylan, stately and clad in fine leathers and gold. She glanced to Cinna, then up to Phoebe's eyes. 'What proof have ye of this, child?'

"Phoebe looked to me, then, and I breathed a heavy sigh. I wasn't sure anything I'd say here would make a difference, but still I stood slowly, looking around the hall. Slipping the glove off my left hand, I held my sevenstar aloft before the muttering crowd.

"'Some of you will know me by deed. More by name. I am Gabriel de León.'

"Angry hisses rippled among the throng, folk plucking hairs from their heads to curse me, and spitting twice upon the floor.

"'For years, I fought the Dead. In Nordlund, in Sūdhaem, in your own Ossway. In my time, I have seen miracles beyond reckoning, horrors beyond believing, but I tell you now, I have *never* seen a girl like Dior Lachance.

By the power of her blood, she brought men back from the dead before my eyes. Danton, the Beast of Vellene and child of Fabién Voss, was burned to *ashes* by her hand. The prophecies of your kin, of mine, of the Dead themselves have foretold her birth. She is born. She is *real*. On my life, on my name, I vow it.'

. "One of the Barenn rose, snarling. 'And what weight, the word of a se'yersan?'

"'Ye bring a heathen to swear afore the Moons?' another old dame spat at Phoebe. 'Get of the maebh'lair setting foot upon this hallowed Earth?'

"Angry words rang in the hall then, and Angiss á Barenn rose again, glaring at Phoebe. 'Have ye lost yer mind? Ye fled yer duty and yer family to chase madness among the heathens, and now ye bring a silver-painted *worm* to testify it sane?'

"The moonsmaidens slammed their swords upon the floor once more, demanding order be restored. As a fragile silence descended, Phoebe pointed at me.

"'This man saved my life, Angiss á Barenn. Brought me safe through blood and blight for nae reason save it was *right*. He risks his life to testify these truths to ye now. He is a slayer of ishaedh'ai and ancient maebh'lair. He is nae *worm*.'

"'Say then this is true.'

"All eyes turned to Keylan as he spoke. The mighty leófuil had golden eyes fixed on Phoebe, his growl echoing in my chest. I could see the power he wielded, fear and respect in equal measure. But I could also see how tangled this knot was; how deep the enmities and suspicions and misgivings among these people ran. There's no love so deep as that of family. But no hate so bitter either. Who can wound you deeper than your kin? And the hell of it was, I couldn't even blame them. My own sister had tried to end me, after all.

"'Say the Godling is born among the heathens despite the auguries,' Keylan said. 'And by the grace of the All Mothers, ye've found her. I might believe such a tale. Ye are Fiáin dahtr, Phoebe á Dúnnsair, and I've never known ye fer a liar.' Keylan shrugged, holding open his arms and gazing around the hall. 'So where be this miracle child?'

"Phoebe pressed her lips tight, glanced toward me. I could only nod.

"'She is held against her will,' Phoebe said. 'And there be none to aid her, save us. The Highlands must stand together, one and all, to see the Godling freed from her prison.'

"'And where be this prison?' the Mother beside Keylan asked.

"'She is on her way to Dún Maergenn.' Phoebe breathed deep. 'Toward the clutches of the Heartless and the Count Dyvok.'

"Tumult rose again, quickly silenced by the thumping of silvered swords.

"'I know I have little voice here,' I said. 'But if I can speak with authority on *one* subject, it is the Dead. And I tell you now, good people, the Dyvok are more a threat than any horror of the weald or enemy here among you. They were blooded after Tolyev died at my hands, but they were *not* beaten. They have come unto some new power—some dread sorcery that lends them a strength I've *never* seen. Dún Fas, Dún Ariss, Dún Cuinn, Dún Sahdbh, all smashed like glass. They took Dún Maergenn and the Nineswords' throne in a heartbeat, where four clans united could not *scratch* her walls.' I glowered around the hall, voice rising. 'I know you've struck pax with them. I *know* you have your own woes. But Dead tongues heeded are Dead tongues tasted, and once those leeches have drained the Lowlands dry, where do you think they'll turn next? They cannot be befriended! They cannot be trusted! Sweet Mothermaid, they're *vampires*!'

"'And ye're a vampire's *son*!' someone shouted.

"More agreement, more spitting, more plucked hairs and curses. I clenched my teeth, pressing my lips shut to hide my fangs. My frustration was boiling now, fear for Dior and worry for Phoebe, and God, I was *so fucking* thirsty . . .

"The old woman beside Keylan shook her head. 'Phoebe, we have had peace w' the Untamed for years. We vowed not to set foot below the Highlands, and the Dyvok have kept word not to set foot within. But though the Heartless may be our ally, she is nae our friend. If she has this prize in her keeping as ye say, what prize would ye offer her in trade fer it?'

"'Ye mistake me, wise Terin. The Heartless and her brother shall know Dior's worth. They'll nae hand her over freely. I dinnae propose we *trade* the Godling from the Dyvok.' Phoebe looked around the room, chin high. 'We will have to *take* her from them.'

"A hundred people rose at once to their feet.

"A hundred mouths drew breath to roar.

"And utter fucking bedlam broke loose in the hall."

XIV

RIVERS AND RAIN

"THE FROZEN VALE reached out below me, blessedly silent at last.

"The debate had raged for hours, the fire had burned down to embers, and by the shouting's end, I'd have killed every bastard in the Elderhold for a single cup of vodka. By Wintermoot law, no debate was permitted after dusk, and with resolution nowhere in sight, the clans broke for the eve. Phoebe assured me that *outside* the Tael'Lied was where the real politicking took place, and with her cousin and aunt in tow, she went out to argue for war against the Dead. I'd one-seventh of two-fifths of fuck-all to contribute in back-alley dealings among the All Mothers, and so, I nodded goodeve to Brynne at the base of the stairs and trudged back up to my room, intent on drowning thirst and sorrows both.

"I'd filched a bottle of what smelled like rotten spud boiled in old feet from the feast table, but it turned out to be some kind of Highland Black. Wincing at the taste, I stood by the window and watched shadows flit between lodges below; the whispers in the dark, the song of slow pipes. I reached out for Dior, knowing she was beyond my reach, yet trying to believe she was all right. That somehow, there was still hope.

"'We've nae fuckin' hope.'

"The snarl came from behind me, dragging me from dark thoughts. I frowned at the empty bottle in my hand—whatever this catspiss was made from, it had dulled me enough I'd not even heard Phoebe's feet on the stairs. But there she was, storming into the room and slamming the door so fierce the hinges near broke.

"I could see the tale on her face before she spoke. 'No joy, then.'

"'Nothin' close,' she replied. 'The Cleods and Barenns will nae be moved to war w' the Dead. The Hearns and Killaechs neither. Nae a single All Mother of the úrfuil or velfuil are swayed, and a few don't even believe the Godling is born among the Lowlanders. They just think me moonstouched, or p'haps held under sway of yer magiks.'

"I shook my head, astonished. '*Nobody* stands with us?'

"She shrugged. 'Keylan has pledged the Meyricks to the cause.'

"'That's good. Keylan holds sway among the leófuil, oui?'

"'Aye, but he'll nae march with us unless *all* do. To commit in strength against the Dyvok leaves their clanhold vulnerable, and Keylan has nae faith the Slaene or Killaechs or a dozen others won't stake claim on their lands while his back is turned.'

"'So they'll stay up here and fight for scraps of dying earth, rather than the entire world? The future of the realm is in the balance! Is there *nothing* that will sway them?'

"'A miracle, mebbe.' Phoebe shook her head. 'And then . . . only mebbe.'

"'Fuck my face,' I snarled.

"'Nae in the mood,' she sighed.

"I snatched up the empty bottle, hurling it at the wall.

"'Wintermoot, my arse!' I roared. 'See, *this* is why you need emperors, Phoebe! *This* is why you build thrones! Give every arsehole a voice, and you just end up drowning in their shite! And they'll *still* find a way to debate on the color of it as they sink!'

"'Aye, well, benefits of benevolent monarchy aside, what the hell do we do?'

"I turned to the window, searching that dark with paleblood eyes, looking to those statues of the moons below; crescents of granite and angel wings. To have wasted so much time and effort getting up here, to have failed Dior so completely, God, it felt like a sword in the gut. I could see no way out, no way through, but . . .

"'First thing's last. I have to get to Dior. She's bound to arrive at Maergenn soon.'

"'Aye, and what do we do once we *get* there?'

"I looked back to Phoebe as she spoke. Some small and foolish part of me still burned a little warmer, despite all that dark and cold outside. It's strange how a single word can change a world. Strange how so much power rests in the smallest of things.

"'We,' I repeated.

"'Aye.' She walked to my side, gazed up into my eyes. 'I care nae if a hundred armies of the Dead stand in our way. I swore blood oath to that child. So.'

"She put her hand on my chest, tossing back her hair, fierce and unafraid. "'*We.*'

"'I've no plan here, Phoebe. No prayer. We're likely headed straight to our deaths.'

"'We only die if we are forgotten, Gabriel de León. Burn bright. Burn brief. But *burn.*'

"I shook my head in wonder. Looking down into that alloy of gold and platinum, silver and steel. The liquor was warm in my veins, but despite the dark that lay ahead, or perhaps *because* of it, the sight of this woman warmed me more. Firelight danced on her eyes, the wind howled in the night outside, and I was reminded of her words in Ravenspire. About finding broken edges to fit against our own. About being brave enough to seek them out. And bleeding though I still was, vulnerable as it would make me, I reached out slow, brushing an errant braid from her cheek and listening to the song of her quickening pulse.

"'You're quite a woman, Phoebe á Dúnnsair.'

"'I am nae woman. I am the wild. I am the wind.'

"'Thorn and bramble,' I smiled.

"She nodded. 'Blood and scars.'

"I kissed her then, deep and soft and slow, slipping my hand to the small of her back and drawing her close. Phoebe sighed, throwing her arms around my neck with a hungry growl. She crushed lips and body against mine, and we stumbled and crashed against the table, almost falling. The dark was gathered all around us, no way through, no real hope for the morrow. Both of us desperate to fend off the cold if only for tonight.

"My fingers found the ties on her tunic, her hands slipped to my belt. Our tongues flickered against each other, her teeth nipping at my lip as she dragged me free of my leathers. I groaned as she stroked me, harder, longer, talons skimming along my burning skin. She sighed as I broke away from her mouth, hauling her tunic over her head, tearing her leathers down and kicking them free. And before I knew it, I was on my knees before that angel, lifting her effortlessly onto the table's edge and feeling her shiver as I blazed a slow trail of burning kisses up the inside of her thigh.

"'Oh, Moons,' she whispered.

"She leaned back, groaning, one hand behind my head to steer me true.

God, the want of her, the *need* of her washed over me like the sacrament itself. We were high in the tower where none would hear, but still Phoebe put a hand to her mouth, biting her finger to stifle her moans. She spread her legs wider, dragging me in, head thrown back and hips swaying as my tongue sang hymns upon her skin.

"I sighed at the taste of her, wanting to linger, to drown, but she was impatient, denied far too long, soon dragging me from my knees. I kissed my way back up her body, taut belly and soft curves, up to the heady peril of her throat. Her pulse whispered my name, my thirst *smashing* itself against the bars of its cage. It wanted to know her, own her, *devour* her, and as I kissed her neck, nipped her skin, I knew not where this would end. But Phoebe cupped her hands to my cheeks and pulled me higher, crushing lips to mine, hungry, hard, her honey mingling on our tongues as our bodies pressed close. She reached under my tunic, dragged it up over my head despite my murmur of protest. I gasped as she raked her talons down my belly, she hissed in pleasurepain as she leaned in to kiss me again, her pebble-hard nipples brushing the silver on my chest.

"'You'll hurt yours—'

"'I don't care,' she breathed around our tongues. '*Take* me, Gabriel.'

"My belly filled with butterflies at that command, all of me atremble. I'd no wish to burn her, nor be burned in kind, but if only for tonight, I wanted, *needed*, to make this woman mine. She gasped as I turned her about, bending her over the table before me. My eyes roamed the spirals inked down her back, the delicious dimples at the base of her spine, the perfect curves of her arse below. She groaned as I took her hands, crossed them at the small of her back, my fingers encircling her wrists to pin them, all of her now at my mercy.

"'Oh, Mothermoons . . .' she whispered, parting her legs.

"I ran myself over her quim, and Phoebe pushed back against me, pleading, sighing, so warm and soft it was all I could do to stop. She groaned as I slipped a little inside her, one slow, *agonizing* inch, all of me burning with the want of her. But I held myself still, willing myself to savor this moment, tracing featherlight fingertips over her tattoos and watching her shiver. A long sigh of protest slipped her lips as I withdrew, turning to a groan as I ran myself over and around her again, caressing her swollen bud with my aching crown.

"'Goddess, don't tease me,' she pleaded. '*Fuck* me.'

"'I remember a conversation in a pub about a certain magik word . . .'

"'*Now*,' she hissed, rising up and seeking my mouth.

"But I drew away from that kiss, prolonging our agony, drawing slow, hard circles on her petals and tightening my grip on her wrists as I growled.

"'That's not it, mademoiselle . . .'

"Phoebe moaned as I held myself poised, just a whisper, just a word away from what we both ached for. Her back was straight now, shoulderblades brushing my chest, silver hissing. Her cheeks were flushed, lips moving, her whisper too faint to hear over the thunder in her heaving breast.

"'What was that?' I breathed, sinking just a little back inside her.

"'Oh, you *bastard* . . .' she sighed as I withdrew once more.

"'That's not it either,' I smiled, lips drifting along her shoulder.

"Phoebe snarled, wrists still encircled by my hand, talons drawing blood on my belly. She turned her head again, lips parted, and I kissed her then, breathing her in, shaking with want. And as I let myself slip back into her again, one slow inch after another, she let her head drift back, flaming curls spilling down her spine as she sighed surrender.

"'Oh, *please* . . .'

"Her whisper, my command. I, her master and servant both. And she moaned as I sank inside her at last, slow and hard and deep, deep as I could go. Her whole body shivered, and she bent over again, curls tumbling about her face, grinding back against me. And so we danced, moving each in time, unleashed upon each other at last.

"'Ohhhh, Moons, that's—'

"My hand came down on her buttock, a sharp *crack* ringing in the air. Phoebe moaned, head thrown back as I slipped my hand between her legs, mindful of the silver on my skin. Her sighs were lost in mine as I caressed her, strumming long, slow circles as she shook like an autumn leaf. I was adrift in silken heat, still pinning her wrists, sinking to my hilt with each stroke and trying not to lose myself utterly.

"'Harder,' she begged.

"I obeyed, snarling, little more than a beast now, pulling her back onto me over and over again. The sound of our flesh slapping was near as loud as her cries, loud *crack*s echoing on the walls as I smacked her pinking cheeks in time. Phoebe was trembling head to foot, sweat gleaming in the valleys of her spine, the scent of her driving me mad. She began moaning louder, teeth gritted and toes curling, bending like a sapling in a raging storm.

"'Ohhh, please . . .'

"Releasing her wrists, I kissed my way up her arching spine, deeper, *harder,* rushing closer toward our ends. And Phoebe sighed, brushing the long, sweat-slick curls away from her neck; an invitation that made me shiver, the beast rising inside me now, hunger and madness and thirst.

"'Do it,' she breathed. 'Make me yours.'

"Her lashes fluttered on her cheeks, one hand knotted in my hair, the other braced against the table as we crashed against each other. She moaned as my kisses reached her throat, her pulse so loud it was all I could hear, and though I knew this was the path to damnation—*both* of us knew—that only made us burn the brighter for it.

"'I shouldn't,' I whispered. 'If I—'

"'Take me,' she begged. '*Taste* me.'

"I wrapped one fist in her curls, pulling her head farther back, a growl rumbling in my chest. My fangs brushed her skin, a feather-soft scrape that made her shiver and gasp, our bodies entwined and burning, the thirst boiling red and *screaming* inside me.

"*Just a mouthful . . .*

"'Please, Gabriel,' she whispered.

"*Just a drop . . .*

"'Please . . .'

"I groaned, shaking, my ending rushing up from the dark within. Her plea was a prayer, and my resolve was gone, that beast in me tearing it to ribbons. There was one last hesitation—that promise to the ground—already scorched by our kiss in the tower, now consumed in the flames between us. The thirst is eternal, coldblood. The hunger forever. And though I mourned for all things lost, after all is said and done, I am only a man. And so I reared back like a viper, like a monster, and God help me, I bit her. Heedless. Hard. My fangs sank into her skin, and my cock into her quim, and all my world was blood and fire.

"A flood; molten and thick with all her passion, *all* her want, soaking me through and filling me to my brim. I couldn't even cry out as I ended, so lost in the rush of her pulse, the storm of her heart, Phoebe screaming for us both, one hand behind my head, the other between her legs, utterly lost in the ecstasy of the Kiss.

"I drank her down, our bodies still moving in time, sinking to the root with every swallow. She was an ocean, and I the desert. I was the river, and she the rain. It had been more than a year since I'd succumbed so completely, and the thirst had swelled since then; wrapping me now in red arms and filling me the way no smoke or liquor or flesh ever could. Phoebe's eyes rolled back, whispering shapeless pleas as I swallowed all she gave me, and then, more besides. That fire never quenched. That hole never filled. That *need*, so hateful and sly, unsatisfied even as you sate it, never *ever* wanting it to end.

"'G-Gabe,' Phoebe whispered.

"*Just a little more, Gabriel . . .*

"'G-Gabriel, no more . . .'

"*Just one more mouthful, just one more drop, don't stop don't stop don't . . .*

"'*S-stop!*' she cried.

"And I came back to myself then; the fear in her voice a slap to my face, the man in me seizing that monster and choking it still. I was horrified, my mouth full of slippery warmth as with a growl, a gasp, I dragged my lips free of Phoebe's neck. I stumbled back, utterly aghast, blood spilling from my lips as Phoebe wilted onto the furs, gasping, holding her wounded throat. And that, right there, was the moment."

Gabriel leaned back in his chair, polishing off the last of his wine.

"That *exact fucking* moment, if you'll believe it."

Jean-François looked up from his tome, blinking.

". . . The exact fucking moment *what*, de León?"

Gabriel set aside his goblet, shaking his head.

"The exact fucking moment Brynne came bursting through the door."

XV

CRIMSON AND GOLD

THE LAST SILVERSAINT frowned, tattooed fingers steepled at his chin.

"Now, I'll be the first to admit this looked bad.

"Phoebe was collapsed on the furs, naked and bleeding, one hand to her throat. My chin was red and slick, her blood drooling from my fangs, and I knew my eyes must be flooded with it too. I was the son of a vampire to these folk, trusted by none and hated by most, and Phoebe's scream, while one of passion, might easily have been mistaken for otherwise. It's a slender line between pleasure and pain, coldblood."

The historian smiled, dark and wicked. "And with our kind, there's no line at all."

The Last Silversaint shrugged.

"All that by way of saying, I'm not surprised Brynne tried to kill me.

"A massive paw closed around my neck. Phoebe whispered faintly as the big úrfuil hauled me off the stone like I was a bag of cotton, her eyes burning in rage. Smoke rose from her skin as it began to burn from the silver at my throat, and with a blistering curse, she drew back one massive fist and sent it crashing into my face.

"I flew backward like a shot from a cannon, striking the tower wall. Phoebe cried my name, the bricks were blasted to rubble around me, white light in my skull. And naked, senseless, I flew out into the night, tumbling through the dark below.

"I fell twenty feet onto the roof of the Elderhold, broken stonework raining around me, tiles cracking beneath me. I'd time to roll onto my back, shake my ringing head before I saw Brynne flying out of the torn wall behind me with a blood-drenched roar. I rolled aside, gasping, but the 'dancer struck the roof so hard, she smashed clean through, shattering timber and tile to splinters and dust. And as the ancient ceiling gave way beneath me, I plunged another forty feet into the Elderhold below.

"Brynne hit the floor hard, fractures spiraling out across the flagstones. But as I plummeted after her, I found myself strong enough to seize one of the shattering rafters, slinging myself across the room as it collapsed. I landed in a crouch, still naked, tossing a whip of black hair from my face, blood spilling from the claw rents in my skin.

"'Peace, mademois—'

"The duskdancer roared, charging toward me, fangs bared and fists raised. I'd not smoked since early evening, but as Brynne bore down on me, I found my body flush with a new heat; a burning, feral rage rippling all the way to my fingertips, unlike *any* I'd known. The air sang as the 'dancer's claws scythed toward my head, but quick as silver, I seized her wrist and sent her sailing into the great carved lion holding up the roof.

"But not just sailing into it. Sailing *through* it; the force so immense Brynne blew the timber to splinters and tore the pillar from its moorings. I blinked at my bare hands, astonished; I'd thrown the woman like she was made of—

"'Gabe!'

"I looked up, saw Phoebe peering through the hole in the ceiling. She'd tossed on her cloak, pale and bloodied but moving, and I sighed in relief. 'Are you al—'

"The timber whistled as it sailed toward me—one of the massive, wooden benches encircling the fire. I rolled aside, crying out as another followed the first, Brynne hurling them like spears. Coming to my feet, I dashed toward her, Phoebe roaring for Brynne to hold as she tore up another. But with that same untamed fire in my veins, I slipped aside, rolled beneath, and bringing up both my fists, I slammed them into the big úrfuil's jaw.

"The 'dancer flew like a sack of chaff, crashing right through the wall. I flew out after her, heart pounding now, body bristling. My heart was a dragon within my chest, breathing fell fire into my veins. It had been a year since I'd drunk so much blood, but I'd not felt so alive since . . . well . . . since forever.

"Cries rang across the Cradle now; torches lit, clanfolk shouting as they saw a naked silversaint and an enraged 'dancer brawling like thunder and lightning. Moonsmaidens flew at me from all sides, silver blades gleaming. Again, I couldn't blame them—far as they knew, a halfbreed coldblood had just beat shite out of a daughter of Fiáin, desecrating their sacred site in the process. But still, I thought it a touch unfair when twenty came at me at once.

"'Peace, damn you! I meant no—'

"A silver blade arced toward my head, but in a blinking, I caught it—*SLAP*—right between my palms. With a twist, I snapped the blade like a twig, my backhand sending the moonsmaid fifty feet across the ice. More 'dancers were charging to the fray now—great bearthings and halfwolves and she-lions—but God, it seemed every mote of my blood was molten iron. With a shrug, I scattered a dozen slayers like straw; in a blink, I caught the clawed blow of a towering úrfuil at the wrist, punched him in the chest so hard his ribs shattered. I moved like a wave, seething and crashing, catching more swords and shattering them in my bare hands, breaking bones and cracking skulls with just the tips of my fingers.

"And then, Keylan charged me.

"Phoebe had described her third cousin as a big pussycat, but as all seven feet and five hundred pounds of the Red Wrath flew at me, he looked as far from a kitten as I from a saint. His talons skimmed my chest as my punch broke his jaw. My knuckles tore his face as his backhand clipped my head. The flames burning inside me were like *nothing* I'd known, my whole world washed red now, *red*, *RED*. But as I heard Phoebe screaming my name, as the realization I was taking on the entire Cradle and *winning* dawned upon me, another revelation crashed down, heavier and headier and far, *far* darker."

Jean-François leaned forward, chocolat eyes shining.

"And that was?"

"You tell me, coldblood."

"You had drunk your fill, true. Yet you are only paleblood, de León, and you'd just fought this entire moot of mongrels to a standstill. Unarmed, no less." The historian smiled, sly and wicked. "You were *stronger* than you should've been."

"*Far* stronger. But why?"

"Because you had drained Phoebe á Dúnnsair almost dry. Just as you had scratched her lip as you kissed in Ravenspire. Just as you bit young Brynne when you fought *her* in the woods. A few drops back then, to best three silversaints or an enraged úrfuil warrior unarmed. A *bellyful* now, to best an entire village of Highland slayers singlehanded." The historian smiled wider, twirling his quill through his fingers. "Because ever you are slave to passion, de León, and it seems the sin of Lust serves you as well as the sin of Pride."

"Well." Gabriel leaned back in his chair, smiling. "It *was* my favorite.

"'Phoebe!' I roared, looking up to the tower. 'Bring my bandol—'

"Keylan came on like hell unleashed, bounding across the ice on all fours, sailing toward me like a thunderbolt. But with a cry, I caught the Red Wrath midair, slung him into the effigy of Lánis; that great stone angel, holding her crescent toward the heavens.

"Keylan struck like a barrel of black ignis, smashing the stone to splinters. The figure of the moon goddess shuddered, cracking across her wings. Blood sprayed, bone shattered, and as Keylan collapsed in a heap beneath the statue, all hell broke loose.

"The impact had cracked the granite, the base splitting like clay. As someone screamed, the cracks spread farther, the great stone goddess tottering like a three-pint drunkard at last call. The statue began to fall with the awful hymn of sundered stone, folk about it scattering; moonsmaidens and 'dancers and All Mothers fleeing its descent. But beneath it, right in its path, lay poor Brynne, still bleary and bloodied, only just now dragging herself up from the snow where I'd punched her.

"I cried out, charging toward her. The shadow fell over my back, forty feet and God knew how many tons of stone headed right for us as I flew. With a deafening roar, the goddess fell, shattering the ground and the walls of the Elderhold, stone dust and snow, rubble and ruin. And as it settled, there I lay beside it upon the broken ground, gasping, covered in snow and blood, a bleeding Brynne groaning and concussed in my arms.

"Figures gathered around me, hundreds now, all set to rip me to ribbons. I rose to my feet, blood still aflame as Angiss á Barenn squared up and let loose an earthshaking roar.

"'HOLD!'

"It was Phoebe who bellowed, voice ringing clear in the night. She stood atop the fallen moon goddess, clad only in her cloak, blood spilling down her punctured throat. She'd seen it as clear as I while she watched me demolish her kin, the revelation giving her wings despite the fact I drank her near to dying. And in her hand, she clutched my bandolier, holding it aloft for the outraged gathering to see.

"'*Dead shall rise, and stars shall fall!*' she cried, pointing to the sky.

"'*Weald shall rot to ruin of all!*' she called, pointing to the dark woods around us.

"'*Lions roar and angels weep!*' she shouted, pointing to me, the broken statue.

"She reached into the bandolier.

"'*Sinners' hands our secrets keep!*'

"And then, she drew out the answer to the riddle: How the hell had the Dyvok crushed the Ossway in only two years, where before, they'd been foundering over a decade in quagmire?"

"A golden vial," Jean-François said. "That once a Wolfmother wore."

Gabriel nodded. "I'd known there was blood inside it; soured, true, but I'd smelled it in the White Rabbit. That same maddening scent now slicked upon my hands, upon my tongue, imbuing me with a strength far beyond anything I'd ever known."

Jean-François ran his tongue across his lips. "Duskdancer blood."

"It had deepened the potency of my own. I couldn't fathom it at first—if the blood of wealdlings was so special, how had it been kept undiscovered by San Michon, by hedgemages and chymists, by the Dead themselves? And then I realized; it had not always been so. Their blood had *changed* with the fall of daysdeath, Historian. Their Earth Father ascendant and corrupted, their Mothermoons veiled, the beast in them stronger than it should've been, and making those who drank from them stronger still."

"The Time of Blighted Blood," the historian murmured.

The Last Silversaint nodded, smiling.

"All eyes were on Phoebe now, standing atop that broken stone with that golden vial in hand. And as she met my eyes, I saw fire in her own—a righteous fury, a dark triumph. The clans of the Moonsthrone were hopelessly fractured, riven with rivalry, but the song she'd sung to me rang in my head now, the truth at the raging heart of these people.

> "*I war with my sister, until,*
> "*We war with our kinfolk, until,*
> "*We war with the Highlands, until,*
> "*We war with the world.*

"'Brothers and sisters of the Moonsthrone!' Phoebe cried. 'A truce struck with traitors is nae truce at all! An oath to a liar is worth less than nothing! And I tell ye now, by Moons above and Earth below, we are all of us betrayed!'

"'What in Malath's name do ye speak of, woman?' Keylan demanded.

"Phoebe threw the vial to the big 'dancer, tossing back her braids.

"'I speak of the Dead, cousin. I speak of Blackheart and Heartless. Of Dún Maergenn fallen and oaths broken and Godlings found.'

"She looked around the gathering, fire in her golden eyes.

"'I speak of *war*.'"

XVI

FIRE ON A DRAGON'S TONGUE

"HOW DID YOU know?"

In the highest tower of Sul Adair, the historian of Margot Chastain peered at the man seated opposite him. The silversaint was halfway toward drunk now, three bottles of wine emptied, his lips rouged a delicious dark red. Gabriel looked up from the globe, the moth circling it, dragging a lock of hair away from brooding, storm-grey eyes.

"You just said it yourself, Chastain. I drank Phoebe near to death, w—"

"Not the secret of 'dancer blood," the vampire said. "I mean, how did you know that all this effort was not in vain? All these miles, these trials. You could not even sense the blood you had given Lachance anymore. This is a world without pity, de León. It feasts upon the powerful and powerless alike. The Holy Grail of San Michon was set to be imprisoned at the seat of Dyvok power, in the cold grip of the Blackheart and the clutches of the Heartless. Even if you reached her, how could you know she'd be alive?"

The Last Silversaint smiled sadly, staring at that fluttering moth.

"You didn't know Dior Lachance like I did."

The vampire only scoffed. "That is no kind of proof, Chevalier. For all you knew, that girl would be filling a shallow grave by the time you reached the coast. And yet you were willing to march an entire nation to war on some vain hope—"

"Hope is for fools, Historian." Gabriel met the vampire's eyes. "Hope gets you killed. Hope walks into the fire. Faith leaps *over* it. I didn't hope Dior was alive. I *believed* it."

"And you were willing to risk your life for that belief?"

Gabriel shrugged. "What the hell else is worth dying for?"

"You mortals *fascinate* me," the vampire breathed, shaking his head. "Your lives burn like candles in a storm, one moment ablaze, the next . . ."

Jean-François blew a puff of breath, as if to extinguish a flame. "Had I but a handful of years ahead, I would guard each one like a dragon his gold. And yet, most of you fools act as if wed to your grave."

The Last Silversaint looked at the sevenstar on his palm, the name on his fingers.

"I'd rather die for something that matters than live for nothing at all. And because a man survived long enough to have a grey beard and wrinkles means not that he's actually *lived*. To live is to risk. To fear and to fail. A man must dance on the dragon's teeth to steal the fire from its tongue. Most are burned alive in the attempt. But better to dance and fall than to never have danced at all. Pity not the man who dies too soon, but the one who lingers too long. For those men who pass peaceful in their beds, who slip one night soft into sleep and wake nevermore . . . can they be said to have been awake at all?"

The vampire looked the silversaint over, toe to crown. His grey eyes were ablaze, pinpricks of light burning like long-lost stars.

"You turn into something of a poet when you're drunk, de León."

"Better a poet than a fucking minstrel."

Jean-François ran his quill across ruby lips, curling in the smallest of smiles. "I wonder what else you might turn into with enough encouragement."

Gabriel lifted his empty cup. "Get me another bottle and find out."

Smiling broader, the historian of Margot Chastain closed the tome in his lap with a heavy *thump*. Reaching into his frockcoat for a silken kerchief, Jean-François stoppered his ink bottle and began cleaning the nib of his quill with customary fastidiousness. Gabriel raised one brow, still toying with the stem of his goblet.

"Going somewhere?"

Jean-François sighed. "Back to hell."

Gabriel frowned. "I wasn't done yet, Chastain. We're almost at the best part."

"Be that as it may, de León, I fear you are near to overtaking your dear sister's recountings. And while the margin by which I prefer your company to hers be not measured in droplets but oceans, if we swim too much farther, I fear we might drown the drama." The vampire smiled. "And unless you were about to bend Phoebe á Dúnnsair over the nearest table and make her say *please* again, your definition of *the best part* differs from mine."

"You're a strange one, coldblood."

"Is it so strange?" the historian asked, chocolat eyes sparkling. "To live vicariously? To take joy in your joy and quicken as you quickened? To envy you?"

"... *Envy* me?"

The Last Silversaint burst into laughter. Raucous. Mirthless. Shaking so hard he lost his breath. He hung his head, shoulders heaving, laughter gone silent as he tried to bring it to heel. And at last, he leaned back, coughing, wiping tears from his eyes.

"My life is shit and misery, Historian. My country is in ruins. My wife is gone, my daughters beside her. And now I linger in this cell, dancing for your fucking amusement, at the mercy of the very monsters who have taken everyone I have *ever* loved away." He shook his head in wonder. "What in the name of Almighty God have you to envy?"

"That you may love at all, de León." Jean-François tilted his head, pouting in thought. "Perhaps *that* is why you mortals burn so fierce; because you know the flame must be so brief. For we immortals, there is *only* loss. All affection fades. Everything dies. Only the blood brings true peace. And you know that joy too; that perfect moment, as darkness is riven crimson and we feel truly alive." The historian looked the Last Silversaint over, smiling. "But you are also a man. You feel as a man, Gabriel. Live and love and lose as a man. One foot in two worlds, the suffering and bliss of both at your behest."

The historian finished cleaning his quill, slipped it away in the wooden case marked with the sigil of his house. Climbing to his feet, he walked to the silversaint's side. Reaching out with one pale hand, feather-soft and iron-hard, he caressed Gabriel's smooth cheek.

"You are *beautiful,* mon ami. How I wish we had met under different circumstances."

Gabriel said nothing, mute and still, though the historian fancied he heard the silversaint's pulse run swifter at his gentle touch. Jean-François sighed then, tossing golden curls back from his face as he lifted his chin.

"But. Duty calls. And hell awaits."

The vampire stalked toward the door, tome held under his arm.

"Jean-François."

The monster stopped, a small smile etched on pallid lips. He turned to the man still sat in his chair; hollow eyes and empty goblet, silver gleaming on tattooed fingers. The silversaint seemed to struggle with some silent enemy, dragging a shaking hand through his hair. And when he spoke, it was the voice of a man staring at the executioner's axe.

"I'm thirsty."

The monster's smile widened.

"I shall have Meline see to your needs, Silversaint."

Jean-François swept from the room, into the corridor where his major-domo awaited, clad in her black brocade. She stood with six thrallswords and their capitaine, the big man's hand at his sword, sharp eyes on the cell door as the Marquis closed it behind him. Straightening his lapel, Jean-François turned to his thrall.

"Bring our guest another bottle, Meline."

The woman lowered her gaze, skin prickling.

"You do not wish me to accompany you below, Master?"

"Alas, I must forgo the pleasure of your company for the sake of courtesy, beloved. Have no fear, good Capitaine Delphine shall see to my safety. And should I have other needs, I will make do with Dario and . . . Oh, God, what *is* her name? Yasmir?"

". . . Jasminne, Master."

"Ah, of course. Jasminne." The vampire took his majordomo's hand, kissed her knuckles, one at a time. "What would I *ever* do without you, my love?"

The woman blushed, dipping into a deep curtsey. Jean-François reached into his pocket, and placed a small black mouse upon the floor. With a glance to the capitaine, the Marquis spun on his heel and descended the stair, accompanied by the thralled cohort. Dario and Jasminne awaited him at the tower's base, falling into step behind, one carrying an unlit lantern, the other, a fresh bottle, filled to the brim with warm, lush red.

Down, down through the wending dark the company slipped, the Marquis running a red tongue over his lips. Dawn was approaching, the scent of Dario's skin and Jasminne's hair threaded the gloom around them, and the thought of a swift and sighing meal before bed had Jean-François's skin atingle. But desire was smothered at the thought of his mother waiting above, the monster lurking below. And at last, deep in the keep's bowels, below the reach of all light and laughter, he drew to a halt outside silver-clad doors. Taking the key his dame had entrusted him from his frockcoat, he handed it to young Dario.

"Do the honors, love."

The handsome lad bowed, wincing as his hands touched the silver lock and chains, slipping both free. The soldiers pushed the cell door wide, emitting the hymn of running water, the perfume of old blood, a sudden shiver of fear on the historian's marble skin.

"Come swift if I should call, Capitaine," Jean-François murmured.

Delphine bowed, and with a glance to Jasminne, Jean-François stepped into the cell. The lantern on the thrall's platter was the only illumination, a thousand stars refracting on dark, rushing waters. Jean-François took a seat in his leather armchair on the river's edge while the young woman placed the lantern atop the table, bottle and goblet beside it.

"Will there be anything else, Master?"

Jean-François's eyes were fixed across the water as he murmured reply.

"Merci, no. See to Meline, beloved. She may require assistance, depending how thirsty the good Chevalier decides he actually is."

Jasminne curtseyed, dark curls tumbling about her face. And never turning her back—always a clever thing, this one—she retreated, the door shut and locked behind her.

Jean-François's gaze never wavered, chocolat eyes unblinking. He could see her now; a shadow hovering on the cusp of lantern's light. A soft whisper of bare feet on stone beneath water's babble, the softer hiss of hunger as the Marquis cracked the wax seal on that new bottle, releasing a bloody fragrance into the frigid air.

"You are a brave man, Marquis," came a whisper.

Jean-François smiled, filling his goblet. "I am not a man, Mlle Castia. And if you believe it requires courage simply to sit in the same cell as you, you are as confused about the relationship betwixt jailed and jailor as you are about heaven and hell."

"You misunderstand. We do not speak of your presence in this cell with us."

Celene stepped into the trembling light, and Jean-François prickled at the sight—long midnight-blue hair, jet-black eyes, silver cage imprisoning those dreadful teeth.

"I speak of leaving my brother alone in *his* with one of yours."

"Your concern is touching. But entirely unnecessary. Dawn approaches on traitor's feet, and I would have the telling of this chapter done afore the sun rears its head."

"Why the hurry?" The monster took one step closer, head tilted. "You said your mistress had time abundant. Can immortals not take forever to sing our songs?"

"Forgive me, mademoiselle." He raised his goblet in grim toast, a cold smile at his lips. "But I do not find your company that pleasant."

"If we managed to cross this water, little Marquis, it might prove *very* pleasant." The monster took another step closer, black gaze on his. "For some of us at least."

Jean-François made a show of rolling his eyes as he sipped from his goblet, hand steadier than it felt. The blood was lush and warm, heavy on his tongue, banishing the chill he felt crawling up his spine as the abomination's eyes slipped to his throat.

"Your brother has been most accommodating, Mlle Castia. But I fear if we proceed much further, your paths shall stumble over one another." He set his goblet aside, opened his tome. "Will you continue your tale willingly? Or shall you prevaricate until I am forced to threaten you again?"

"There seems little sense keeping silent while Gabriel bleats like a docked lamb." The monster's eyes flickered to the table beside him. "But talking is thirsty work."

The historian inclined his head, tossing the bottle across the river. Thirty feet it sailed through that dark, green glass gleaming in the lanternlight, a pale hand snatching it from the air. The Last Liathe lifted his gift, upending it long enough to take a mouthful, then two. But she refrained from finishing the lot, tongue sizzling as she licked the bars of her silver muzzle clean. And placing the half-empty bottle beside her, she took a seat at the very river's edge, legs crossed, peering at him across the waters.

"So where were we," she whispered. "A houndboy and his Ever After. A capitaine and a blackthumb. A Grail and a worm. Strange the way the pieces fit. Stranger still the way they fall apart. To think the world's fate rested upon so few shoulders. So small. So young."

She looked toward the heavens, sighing soft.

"The Almighty moves in mysterious ways."

Jean-François drew his quill from within his coat, opened a fresh bottle of ink. "Let us begin, Mlle Castia."

She sat silent for the longest time, staring at the ceiling as if looking into the face of her wretched God. But finally, Celene turned black and hungry eyes to him.

"No, vampire," she whispered. "Let us end."

BOOK FIVE

CRUMBLING
NOW to ASH

And the hea'ens grew red as heartsblood, and the tempest cracked the skye, and the rain was like to the tears of all the winged host fallen. Those priests of gods false and covenants broken, numbering all the fingers 'pon hell's burning hand, did stand in bleak amazement. And the Redeemer raised his eyes to his Almighty Father's throne, and his heart did stain the bones of the earth, and with voice akin to thunder he cried:

"By this blood, shall they have life eternal."

—THE BOOK OF LAMENTS 7:12

I

LOVE AND WAR

"WE RETURNED TO Dún Maergenn a day later, flitting through the frozen dawn.

"We'd not the strength to bear witness as Lilidh Dyvok broke Dior's will, binding the girl with her blood and forcing her to beat that poor maidservant red. But nor did we have the strength to stay away for long. Our wounds were healing slowly, feeding as we were only on wandering wretched, but we *were* healing. And hopeless as Dior's fate seemed now, we could not simply abandon her. God would *never* forgive me that.

"We returned to the dún on small, red wings—just a mote of us, battling a storm raging in off the bay. But wending down into the keep's dungeons, we realized Dior was no longer there. And so, we spiraled upward, past the blood-drunk monsters slumbering in the Hall of Plenty, the scorched dragging corpses to the kitchens, and the maids washing gore off the floors, until at last we found Dior in the upper reaches, sprawled on a bed of red satin.

"Naked in the arms of Lilidh Dyvok.

"She was a picture, no mistake; ashen locks tumbled over the beauty spot on her cheek, bloodstains pinking her lips. Sighing in her sleep, the Grail slipped an arm around the monster beside her, nuzzling Lilidh's neck. But the vampire was awake, midnight eyes fixed on the ceiling as thunder crashed. She wore only her whalebone half-corset, black velvet trimmed red—in truth, she never seemed to take it off. And as the strangled sun dragged itself above the horizon, the Heartless pushed Dior's hand away and rose from the bed.

"'Where are you going?' came a murmur, muzzy with sleep.

"The Contessa Dyvok slipped on a black chemise, hair tumbling about her face like rivers of blood. Her every movement was preternaturally precise, nothing wasted, nothing spared. Alabaster poetry in motion, centuries in the writing.

"'The daystar rises. There be matters to attend afore I sleep.'

"'No,' the girl sighed.

"Dior rose from the bed, slipped gentle arms around the vampire's waist. Pressing close, Dior scattered Lilidh's cold throat with warm kisses, fingertips roaming the monster's marbled curves. And our hearts sank as we saw a fresh brand atop her left hand—an ornate crown set with twisted antlers, new-scorched in her flesh.

"'Stay with me.' Dior's lips curled as she whispered. 'Mistress.'

"Lilidh sighed, cold breath tickling Dior's throat. We knew there would be few pleasures that might move a creature so old, that a monster as ancient as the Heartless would have indulged her every darkest desire over her centuries. And yet despite the dust on her bones, we could see how Lilidh quickened at the girl's touch.

"'Mothermoons, that *scent*,' she breathed. 'Would that I could taste thee . . .'

"Dior shivered as those ruby lips brushed her neck, as those hands caressed her body. Letting her head drift back, sighing as ivory needles touched her prickling skin.

"'I want you to,' she breathed. 'But . . . I don't want to burn you.'

"She drew back, met the vampire's bottomless eyes.

"'I *love* you.'

"'Do not love me, mortal,' Lilidh smiled, dark and empty. 'Adore me.'

"'I *do*.' Dior kissed her mistress again, pleading. '*Stay* with me.'

"The ancien touched the Grail's cheek, one clawed fingertip tracing the bow of her bloodstained mouth. 'Alone Lilidh slumbers, poppet. And in the knowledge thou hast imparted, there be much to consider. Old enough am I, to recall the name *Esani* with all the poisonous hatred it is due. And I must ponder how best to turn revelation to advantage over the Ironhearts.' She smiled soft. 'Without sweet distraction of thy company.'

"Our heart quailed to hear those words, to know Dior must have confessed all to the Contessa—about the Faithful, about Mother Maryn in eventide somewhere in this city, even about *us*. Our wings froze still for fear of those dark eyes finding us on the ceiling above, the thought that our subterfuge was undone, that Lilidh would now *know* to look for us.

"*Great Redeemer, what was I to do?*

"Lilidh slipped her claws into Dior's hair, drawing her closer, lips but a

breath apart. 'We feast at sunset. Thou shalt kneel at thy mistress's right hand. Dress accordingly.'

"And with that, the ancien turned, opening the boudoir doors. Prince lifted his head from the threshold outside, the one-eyed wolf wagging his tail like a fresh pup at the sight of his beloved mistress. Lilidh caressed his spine as she stalked past, the beast turning to regard Dior with its one good eye. It was pale and cold, sapphire blue, glittering with feral cunning. But Lilidh called his name, and Prince turned, bounding down the hall after her.

"Dior closed the doors, sighing. The room seemed less chill now the monster had departed, and she stood naked in the dark for a long moment, fingertips pressed to bloodstained lips. Then she stalked to the cold hearth, and picked up the poker beside it.

"As we watched, she began practicing, running the sword-forms dear Gabriel had shown her, the poker her blade. *Belly, chest, throat, repeat.* Her body was toned from miles and trials, leaner and harder now, breath coming smoother; she was becoming quite adept with a blade. Yet we wondered why she practiced at all . . .

"Her bedchamber was one of many in the dún's reaches, plush and sumptuously appointed. Great windows looked out over the courtyard below, the bay beyond, the fixtures all mahogany and brass. The double doors were carved with the wolf and nine swords of Clan Maergenn, but as in many châteaux of the day, the bedchamber had doors beyond the obvious. And as Dior practiced, we saw the bookshelf behind her whisper open on silent hinges, a figure slipping into the room at the Grail's back.

"It was Worm.

"The maidservant was still bruised from her beating, black and blue splashed faint on her face. But she moved quiet and quick, mismatched eyes of emerald green and sapphire blue locked now on Dior's spine. And we felt a sliver of perfect fear pierce our long-dead heart as we spied a dagger in the serving girl's hand.

"She stole across the furs, jaw clenched, and though we knew it would place us only further in danger, we could not help but warn Dior; fluttering down from the rafters and battering her cheek. But the girl only brushed us away, speaking to the figure closing behind.

"'I was expecting a visit from you.'

"Worm froze, knife poised.

"Dior turned to face the older girl, motioning to the bed. 'Throw me that slip? I'd have dressed if I'd known you'd show up this early.'

"Worm looked Dior over, bruised eyes narrowed and split lips pursed.

"'Just what exactly is your game, girl?'

"Dior tilted her head, hard and bare and gleaming with sweat.

"'Do I look like I'm playing, chérie?'

"Worm pursed her lips, eyes never leaving Dior's as she tossed a pale silken slip at the girl's face. Dior stepped back, expecting some feint—gutter-smarts gleaming behind sharp blue eyes. But Worm made no advance, and scooping up the shift with her poker, Dior dragged it over her head, and her mop of ashen curls from her face.

"'You disobeyed Lilidh,' Worm murmured. 'When she ordered you to beat me. You put on a show, but you only *pretended* to kick me. You've drunk from her three times now; you're scorched by her hand. Her wish should be your command. But you disobeyed.'

"Worm drummed her fingers on her knife hilt.

"'You're not thralled to her.'

"'Neither are you,' Dior replied. 'Not anymore at least.'

"'. . . How could you know that?'

"'You were acting odd when you dressed me. Protected me from Nikita. Took time to give me counsel, even though it meant tempting Lilidh's temper. And you never call her *Mistress* when she's not in the room. But I didn't *know* until I ran into Joaquin.'

"Worm shook her head. 'That new houndboy?'

"'He spotted me escaping the dungeons a couple of nights back, but he never turned me in. Thing is, when I broke free on the way here, he was the first to track me down. He almost *died* for it. Stabbed three times in the chest trying to please his dear Wolfmother. So I got to wondering, why would he let me go now? What changed?'

"'. . . You healed him when he was dying,' Worm realized. 'As you healed me.'

"Dior nodded, speaking a handful of words that weighed as much as the world.

"'My blood breaks the bond between master and servant. It sets thralls free.'

"We could see a thrill in the maidservant's face at those words, the same we felt in our own Dead chest. We'd never *heard* of such a thing, nor imagined such a miracle ...

"'But why are *you* not thralled?' Worm demanded.

"Dior only shook her head. 'I've not the first damn clue. But the Voss can't read my mind. I only pretend to obey when Dyvok use their Whip. I s'pose it makes sense that vampire blood wouldn't slave me either, considering mine burns them to cinders.'

"'How is this possible?' Worm looked down at her hands, bewildered. 'My ties to Lilidh are broken, but the strength she gave me lingers. My bruises still heal quicker than they might have if I were only mortal. Are you a sorceress? Some servant of the pit or child of the Fallen?'

"'I'm ...' Dior shook her head, breathing deep before the dive. 'I'm a descendant of the Redeemer. I *know* it sounds blasphemy and madness, trust me. I still have trouble believing it myself some days. But the Almighty's son was a mortal man, and before he was put to the wheel, he had a child with Michon, his first disciple. A daughter named Esan.'

"'That name sounds ...' The maidservant frowned, quizzical. 'Old Talhostic?'

"The Grail's eyes narrowed at that, and we were awonder too; that a mere maidservant might recognize that ancient tongue.

"'It means *Faith*,' Dior said. 'Esan was the child of Michon and heaven, and her holy blood runs in my veins. It burns coldbloods to ashes. Heals any wound. And if what my friends have told me is true, it can end daysdeath, once and for all.'

"Worm lowered her blade, whispering, 'Great Redeemer.'

"Dior winced, apologetic. 'Just a distant relative, I'm afraid.'

"The maidservant stalked to the doors, checking they were locked. Her cheeks were flushed, pulse thrumming as she paced the room. Despite Dior's outlandish claim, it seemed this young woman was sensible enough to believe the proof of her own eyes.

"'Mothermaid, do you know what this *means*?' Worm hissed. 'We can take back this city! Free every conquered mind from their grip! Every soldier, every swordmaid! Break the shackles those monsters have locked us in, and burn the bastards in their beds!'

"Dior smiled, cold as a frozen river. 'Now you're catching on.'

"She looked to her shoulder as we alighted upon it, our whispering wings on her skin. We were ajoy at all this; to know our secrets were safe surely, but more, that Dior was safe also. We could not help but marvel at her courage, her guile—she even had *us* fooled with that kiss. To dance so close to this danger unflinching. To walk through this fire unburned. And in that moment, I knew the Almighty had chosen his Chosen well.

"'I told Lilidh nothing of worth,' she murmured to us. 'I talked about Sister Chloe and Père Rafa. I told her that the book with the ritual to end daysdeath was still hidden in the San Michon library. Give her a secret to believe, a task to turn her mind to. But I said *nothing* about the Esana. Or Mother Maryn. Or you.'

"'What is *that?*' Worm whispered, looking at my mote.

"'One of those friends I mentioned,' Dior replied. 'Celene can help us.'

"'A friend?' The maidservant shook her head. 'I have traveled the length and breadth of this empire, Dior Lachance. And I have never met a girl half so strange as you.'

"'I've not seen much of this empire at all. But I was running rips in Lashaame from the time I was eleven. And one of the first things I learned on the grift is how to spot other people on it too.' Dior studied the older girl, finally shaking her head. 'You're no maidservant. You're about as common as I am noble. Who the *hell* are you?'

"Worm breathed deep, mismatched eyes on Dior's own.

"'My name is Reyne. Fifthborn daughter of Niamh Nineswords, who was declared duchess and ruler of this nation by Emperor Alexandre III. I am a blooded child of the royal house of Maergenn, and after my sister Yvaine, rightful Laerd Lady of these lands.'

"Dior and we both studied the young woman, toe to crown. Despite the homespun cloth, the bruises and bloodstains, we could see a regal bearing unveiled now, a fierce pride in the girl's mismatched eyes. The Lady Reyne stood with chin high, strawberry-blond hair glinting in the dim dawn, and we could not help but think of the statue in the keep below; the mighty Nineswords herself. A woman who had conquered this nation by the age of twenty-five, and melted the swords of her defeated foes to forge her own.

"'Ossian princess,' Dior murmured. 'I told Gabe I wanted to meet one of your lot. You're not wearing a chastity belt under that homespun, are you?'

"'*What?*'

"'. . . Nothing.' Dior blinked, shook her head. 'We need to get to it.'

"'How does it work, your blood? Must it be touched to a mortal wound, or—'

"'I've no clue.' Dior scruffed her hand through her hair. 'If we have to stab everyone in the tits before we free them, this is going to get messy quick. But drinking blood is enough to thrall people. Maybe drinking is enough to free them too?'

"Reyne began pacing the boudoir again, hands clasped at her back. 'We should test the truth of it, then. My ladies often dine together, and I usually serve the fare. If you might spare me a dram, I will watch for chance to liberate them all at one stroke.'

"'*Your* ladies . . .' Dior blinked. 'Lilidh took your maidservants off you. Scorched them. Made them beat you.' The Grail sighed. 'Sadistic *cow*.'

"'They are not mere servants, Dior Lachance,' Reyne replied. 'Royal daughters of the Ossway are attended by swordmaids, not handmaids. Lady Arlynn and her sisters are warriors, born and bred.' She winced, prodding her bruises. 'More pity my ribs.'

"'Aright.' Dior snatched up a small vase, hand outstretched. 'Give me the shiv.'

"The Lady regarded the Grail in silence. She was obviously overwhelmed, and few could blame her, but in her faeling eyes, we saw the pragmatism of long roads and broad horizons. This was not a princess who'd spent her life in high towers and silken gowns. This was the daughter of a conqueror who'd carved her name into the pages of history.

"'Do I trust you enough to hand you a blade, is the question?' she murmured.

"'Truth told, I don't trust you either, Lady á Maergenn. I never had time to waste on the nobleborn. Never saw *Haves* do anything other than take from *Have-Nots*. But love and war make strange bedfellows, and in case it slipped your notice'—Dior looked around them and shrugged—'it's you and me against the fucking world right now.'

"Reyne stared a moment longer, then flipped the blade and handed it over, hilt first. Dior sat on the bed, pressing the knife into the soft arch of her foot.

"Reyne frowned. 'Why are you—'

"'My blood heals others, not myself.' Dior winced, carefully collecting the dripping crimson in the vase. 'If Lilidh sees the cut tonight, I'll say I stepped on glass. And if this works, bring a lantern next time. I'll burn the wound shut so she has less chance of smelling it.' The Grail handed over the small vase, brimming now with brilliant, holy red. 'Be careful with that. Be *quick*. The Dead can scent my blood, like hounds to prey.'

"'Fear not. I know the secret paths of this keep. And soon *they* shall be the hunted in it.' Reyne took the vase, her voice cold as winter dawn. 'These monsters slaughtered my sisters. Murdered my mother. Bled my country dry. And by my blood and breath, I vow they will *pay* for every drop of it.'

"Dior pressed on her wound to staunch the flow, extended one hand to Reyne.

"'Good fortune, Lady á Maergenn.'

"'Ossians put not our fates in the hands of Angel Fortuna, Mlle Lachance. My mother did not unite this nation by trusting to hope.' Lady Reyne gritted her teeth, fae eyes shining. 'We Maergenns light our own way, and make our own luck.'

"'. . . Mothermaid watch over you, then.'

"Reyne took Dior's hand, her callused grip making the Grail wince. 'And you.'

"Dior watched the Lady slip out the servants' door with blood in hand. And long after she'd left, the Grail sat staring, running soft fingertips over her lips as she sighed.

"'Ossian princess . . .'"

II

SOMETHING TO BELIEVE IN

"WINTER RULED THE halls of Dún Maergenn, and Dior's days seemed chill as night.

"Both had passed, handfuls of them, with not a word from Reyne. Days were spent in her boudoir, sleeping and practicing sword-forms while we fruitlessly searched the city for Mother Maryn's tomb. Nights were spent in that awful Hall of Plenty, caught up in the stink of brutality, and afterward, the cold embrace of Lilidh's arms. But she was ever a grifter, Dior Lachance, and though she played the dutiful thrall to perfection, we sensed her frustration was growing. And never content to sit idle for long, she soon decided to move.

"The stone was freezing, her skin prickling, breath hanging at her lips in clouds of white. But there was no chance to warm herself even for a moment—the only places fire burned in that damned keep were on the battlements or in those awful kitchens. And so, the Grail pulled her furs tighter, and stepped out from her boudoir.

"She was dressed in the finery her mistress had given her; the pearl-white gown of rich silk, a mantle of thick wolf fur. A choker of rubies encircled her throat, and we'd pressed our wings against those jewels, all the better to watch unseen. She was growing more adept on her dainty heels, barely wobbling as she walked now. Scorched were posted across the landing, those two redheaded gallants standing ever outside Nikita and Lilidh's chambers. But all took one look at the brand upon Dior's hand, and averted their gaze.

"There was merit to being handmaid to a horror, after all.

"Passing through the Hall of Crowns, she stepped out into the frozen courtyard. Though there now seemed a dim light in this darkness, the legions of the Voss were still on their way, and soon Nikita would be forced to choose—give Dior over to the Forever King, or do battle with the Iron-hearts for her keeping. In the end, the decision may not even be his—if Nikita's bloodlords decided Dior's life was not worth dying for, the Count might be forced to bend to Fabién's will to keep them appeased. Even supposing Dior broke every bond in this castle, the highbloods numbered near a hundred, the wretched in their *thousands*. And even if they took the city from the Untamed, there was still the Ironhearts to fear.

"What might one candle do against a flood?

"Battling winds across the bailey, she stumbled past the barracks, the stench of the distillery, the smithy's warm glow. We saw a silhouette within—her friend Baptiste, dark skin agleam with forgelight. Dior's breath caught at the sight of him, hand to her heart as she whispered his name. But we both knew he belonged to the Wolfmother now, and until Reyne got her word, she was unsure of the method by which his thralldom might be broken—to drink, or to bleed. So, the Grail passed him by, entering the stables instead.

"The pens were near empty—only a few dozen beasts left in a building that might've horsed an army in happier days. A dozen men were gathered around a cookfire; stablehands and grooms and muckrakers, drinking mugs of fresh-brewed Black from the distillery to stave off the chill. The scorched weren't forced to eat fare quite so horrifying as the Dyvok's cattle, sharing a stew of mushroom and sprout with their liquor instead. Dogshank sat among them—one of the brutes who'd brought Dior down from the Nightstone, blood beneath his fingernails and butcher knives at his belt. And beside the man, far too handsome for the company he kept, was the young houndboy of Aveléne. Joaquin Marenn.

"Elaina looked up as Dior entered, the hound's tail wagging.

"'Mlle Lachance,' Joaquin murmured. 'What are y—'

"'My beloved Mistress Lilidh bid me speak with you. Alone.'

"The stablefolk glanced to her brand, and without a word of dissent, all shuffled out into the storm. Joaquin held Dior's eyes as she sat beside him, his hound snuffling at her left boot. The lad seemed slightly the worse for drink—many of the Dyvok soldiers numbed themselves to the horrors of life in this keep with regular serves of homebrew. But his hand was steady as he scratched Elaina's ears, gifting the Grail one of his dark, crooked smiles as he sipped his mug of liquor.

"'Why haven't you run yet?' Dior whispered.

"He blinked, feigning confusion. 'Why would I run? My great mistress—'

"'You're not bound to Kiara, Joaquin,' she hissed. 'You haven't been since that day I healed you in the woods. That's why you didn't stop me the other night when I tried to escape.' She shook her head. 'But why the hell haven't *you?*'

"He drew breath to protest, Dior grabbing his wrist as he tried to rise.

"'I'm not bound to them either. My blood protects me from it. The same blood that broke your servitude, *and* saved your life.' She squeezed his hand, pleading. 'Trust me, Joaquin. I'm talking about the life of every poor soul in this city now. Those folks being fed to the wretched in Newtunn. Those people eating the flesh of the *dead* in Auldtunn. Every slave in this accursed fucking keep.'

"The boy remained silent, weighing Dior up. He looked to the new brand burned atop her hand, square jaw clenched tight. His fingers brushed at his chest, unscarred despite the mortal wounds he'd suffered. The death she'd saved him from.

"'Isla,' he finally whispered. 'I haven't run because of Isla.'

"'Your Ever After,' Dior realized. 'You won't abandon her.'

"'Of *course* I won't,' he hissed. 'I tried to get in to see her, but . . . she serves the Blackheart, and we're not allowed in the upper levels. I don't even know if she's . . .'

"'She's alive. She's well. I see her all the time in Nikita's chambers.'

"The boy swallowed, pale as death. 'Is she . . . Is *he* . . .'

"'She cleans for him. Nothing more. He dresses her well. Keeps her fed. She's faring better than most in that keep.' Dior's eyes fell, and she glanced toward the smithy. 'Nikita has been occupying himself with Aaron of late.'

"Joaquin kept his expression steady, but behind the liquor's haze, we saw a sliver of rage and hope break through his mask. We wondered at the strength of this boy—what it must have taken to keep his head amid these atrocities, to bend the knee in the vain hope he might somehow see his beloved again. And we knew him for what he was then."

Jean-François dipped his quill, muttering under his breath.

"An addle-witted fool?"

"A *believer*," the Last Liathe replied, staring across the river.

"Some would say they are one and the same, Mlle Castia."

"Some would say," she nodded. "But they do not know what *we* know.

"Dior looked deep into the houndboy's eyes, whispering. 'There's another in the keep who's been freed, Joaquin. And we've set our minds to freeing more. We may need your help out here, among the soldiers. Can we count on you?'

"The boy looked to the shadowed dún, to his beloved trapped within.

"'I've only known Isla eight months,' he murmured. 'She came to Aveléne after the Dyvok destroyed Dún Cuinn. She'd no famille left. No friends. She seemed *so* sad. But the dogs liked her. Elaina is a good judge of character.' He scruffed his hound's chin as she wagged her tail. 'Isla used to come with me when I walked the pups. She liked the quiet, she said. And one day, I told her she was pretty. Took a kiss without asking.' He shook his head, chagrined. 'You grow up looking the way I do, you become accustomed to girls not minding that sort of thing. But Isla kicked me for it. Straight in the taddysack.' The boy chuckled, rubbing his chin. 'I knew right then she was the girl I was going to marry.'

"Dior smiled, pale blue eyes shining. 'She *does* sound a keeper.'

"'I never thanked you,' he said, meeting her gaze. 'When you saved me. You'd no need to do that. But if you can save *her*, Mlle Lachance, you can count on me. To the death.'

"'We'll not let it come to that. I've no intention of anyone dying.'

"'Cheers, then.' The boy raised his reeking mug. 'To living forever.'

"Squeezing his knee, Dior rose swiftly. 'I'll get you word as soon as I can on how we plan to move. 'Til then, be careful, eh? I promise we'll make it through this. *All* of us.'

"He nodded. And in his eyes, we saw a light we'd come to know all too well among folk who met that girl. The awe of the believer, at last finding something to believe in.

"'God go with you, Mlle Lachance.'

"'With us both, M. Marenn.'

"She departed the stables, walking swift across the courtyard as if on her mistress's business. Passing those dreadful cages, forcing herself to breathe the stench, gazing at the folk within. Most of the prisoners looked down, away, each living in terror they'd be the next chosen to feed the wretched at suppertime. But one figure met the Grail's gaze as she passed by, staring out through the bars with bruised eyes.

"'Mila . . .' Dior whispered.

"The child who'd given Gabriel that golden vial at Aveléne. Grubby blond hair and tear-streaked cheeks. At the sight of her, Dior drew breath to speak, and we beat warning upon her skin—*TapTapTapTapTap*. She could say nothing to this waif, promise naught, or all might be undone. And so, she pressed a hand to her breast, tears in her eyes.

"'Mothermaid watch over you, chérie . . .'

"And then she turned, pawing at her frozen lashes as she strode past watchful scorched, back into the keep. Stopping at the base of the stairs in the Hall of Crowns, she gazed up at that mighty statue—Niamh Nineswords, armor-clad, her blade held in one raised fist. And in its shadow, wearing rough homespun and carrying only a lantern, stood the Nineswords' youngest daughter.

"Reyne á Maergenn threw Dior a pointed glance as she passed, disappearing through a servants' door. Slowly, Dior followed, only the thunder of her pulse and a new sheen of sweat to betray the storm within. Following the lanternlight down a hallway, past a maid with an armload of bloodstained cloth, she descended into a freezing stretch of dark stone.

"This part of the keep was mostly untended, the damage from the attack still evident; cracked mortar and broken glass. Ahead of Dior, Reyne motioned with her lantern, slipping through a door carved with the wolf and nine swords of her house. Dior joined the Princess inside; a simple reading room, lined with shelves and old, yellowed books.

"'Are you well?' Dior hissed. 'It's been bloody *days* since we spoke, I—'

"Reyne pressed a finger to her lips, twisted a candelabrum on the wall. Dior heard stone grinding stone, a soft breeze kissing her cheek as the bookshelf behind opened wide.

"The pair slipped into a narrow tunnel, Reyne sealing the entrance behind with the twist of another candelabrum. As the shelf *thump*ed closed, all was plunged into blackness, pierced only by the small lantern in Reyne's hand.

"'Well, this place isn't short of surprises,' the Grail murmured.

"'I told you, Dior Lachance,' Reyne whispered. 'I know my own mother's keep. Now move soft and keep your voice low. These cursed leeches have keenest ears.'

"Reyne lifted her lantern, illuminating a long stretch of cold stone tunnel ahead.

"'You've no fear of the dark, have you?'

"Dior shook her head. 'Just rats. You?'

"Reyne scoffed. 'I fear nothing.'

"The Princess marched down the corridor, Dior following slower, finally cursing and kicking off her dainty heels so she could keep pace. The pair wended secret paths, soft and silent, Dior's feet bare but for her silken hose now, her ridiculous shoes clutched in one hand. The tunnel was damaged from the Untamed attack, and as the demoiselles ducked beneath a spar of broken rock, we felt a strange sensation, building now with every step. Not painful as such, but uncomfortable; a sense of wrongness, of *unwelcome*, crushing our wings against the jewel we rested upon.

"'Listen, not that I don't trust you, Highness,' the Grail finally whispered, 'but you *did* almost stab me a few days back, and I've not heard a damned word from you since I gave you that blood. So might you be so kind as to tell me where the *fuck* we're going?'

"'My great-great-grandmother went to mass four times a day,' Reyne whispered. 'She had this passage built so she could travel back and forth untroubled by commonfolk.'

"'Commonfolk,' Dior scoffed, looking Reyne up and down. 'You might wear a maidservant's frock, but you surely speak like a bloody princess.'

"'If everyone was exceptional, mademoiselle, then no one would be.'

"'So you're saying we're going—'

"'To church, oui.' Reyne halted, pressed upon the wall, opening yet another hidden door. 'We're directly beneath Amath du Miagh'dair.'

"'The Sepulcher of the Mothermaid,' Dior whispered, glancing upward.

"Such explained why the world felt so wrong to us; we did not stand on holy ground so much as *underneath* it. But still, we felt an abiding unease, and as Dior stepped into the tunnel beyond, that weight only deepened, darkened. The corridor was short, ending at a grand door carved of ironwood, decorated with a beautiful engraving of the Mothermaid. She was carved in archaic fashion, more akin to an Ossian warriorwife than Heaven's Bride. She wore clancloth and a breastplate, her hair braided in the local style, and a snatch of scripture in auld Ossian runes encircled her head like a halo.

"Reyne pushed open the heavy door, stepping into the chamber beyond. But as Dior followed, we found ourself slapped backward, as if by the hand of God. We fluttered loose from her choker, dazed, spiraling to the floor outside. Dior saw us fall, stooping to retrieve us, but we shied back, wings shuddering. And looking around, the Grail at last understood.

"'Holy ground,' she whispered.

"We retreated, watching, and with a small nod for me, Dior followed

Reyne inside. The chamber was a crypt, vast and dark, lit only by a few flickering points of light. It had once been a grand affair by the look, ancient tombs of marble arranged in long rows. Statues of the ladies and laerds interred therein lay atop, attired as slayers in repose. But the destruction of the sepulcher above had wrought damage too below; the ceiling partway collapsed, tombs shattered by falling masonry, bones spilling forth onto the flagstones.

"Strange grooves were carved in the floor—some arcane geometry we'd no understanding of. Great mosaic portraits of the Seven Martyrs adorned the walls, but only one had survived the carnage almost intact; beautiful Michon, flaxen-haired and armor-clad, sword raised high as she led her army of the faithful in her holy war.

"Below that mosaic rested a mighty vault, large enough for half a dozen bodies. It was the finest marble, cracked and split in the attack, capped by a great sculpture in what we realized was pure silver, darkened with dust. A woman was wrought at rest upon a bed of skulls, long maiden's hair braided in a halo about her head. She was dressed in mail and plate, a longblade clasped at her breast. Cherubs at wing carried trumpets and garlands of flowers, great and fierce seraphim stood with silver swords drawn, guarding the empty coffin therein. For this was *Tà-laigh du Miagh'dair*, the Tomb of the Mothermaid, built in her honor after her body was taken to heaven, there seated at the Father's right hand.

"And before that monument to Dior's ancestor, four women waited.

"The first was Reyne, maidservants' cloth concealing the royal-blooded warrior beneath. But around her, three new players stood; those elegant swans who had waited on the Heartless hand and foot. They wore beautiful green gowns embroidered with the wolf of Clan Maergenn, decked in finery and jewels. But they carried themselves with a different bearing now, and we could not help but note the way they stood not with shoulders slumped and eyes downturned, but feet set apart for balance, hands poised as if they longed to hold swords. Looking into their eyes, Dior saw the truth as plain as we.

"'It worked,' she sighed.

"'Oui.' Reyne smiled as fierce as the wolf of her house. 'It took a time to do it safely, but I managed finally to mix your dram in with their mornmeal. All were freed by breakfast's end. It was like watching sleepers wake from a dark dream.'

"'Into a nightmare darker still,' one of the women murmured.

"She was the eldest of them; the swan with the scarred chin and hard

hands. A tall, lean switch of willow, late in her forties, long greying hair and fierce blue eyes.

"'Dior Lachance, this is Arlynn, first of my chamber, and Lady of Faenwatch.' Reyne nodded to the other two maids in the gathering, only a year or so older than she. 'This is Lady Gillian á Maergenn and her sister, Lady Morgana. Swordmaids all, cousins and friends and once more loyal blades of my household. And for that, you've our *deepest* thanks.'

"Each woman curtseyed, and as they straightened, all made the sign of the wheel. There was a touch of suspicion in the eyes of the eldest swordmaid, but the young redheaded sisters gazed at Dior with nothing short of wonder.

"'Our Lady Reyne told us who ye were when the black spell of Lilidh's blood was undone.' Young Morgana glanced to the mosaic above. 'A daughter of Saint Michon herself. The First Martyr reborn.'

"'I'm not a martyr,' Dior said. 'And I've *no* desire to be one. I just want to end this, to help those people up there, God . . .' She looked toward the bailey, thunder rolling overhead. 'There's already so few. And every night, less. We have to *do* something.'

"'No fear.' Reyne nodded. 'Now we know the workings of it, we can.'

"Gillian spoke then; a quick and fiery maid with a scar through her freckled brow. 'If one taste of yer holy blood might break the spell, we can serve it with evemeal tonight. Free every soul in the dún at one stroke.'

"'And how shall we get the blood into the meal, young Gillian?' It was Arlynn speaking now; hard blue eyes fixing the younger maid in place. 'It took days for Lady Reyne to find opportunity to liberate just three of us. Should we waltz into the kitchen with a bucket o' blood and hope Kailiegh and her hands dinnae notice?'

"'And how will she afford it?' Morgana asked, nodding to Dior. 'She's barely got any meat on her bones, ye think she's a spare bucket of claret inside her?'

"'I think they'd smell it anyway,' Dior muttered. 'The stink of those kitchens wafts through the whole keep, and my blood is like perfume to these bastards.'

"Gillian pouted, and Morgana rolled her eyes, muttering, 'Halfwit.'

"The maid elbowed her younger sister, hissing, 'Sod off, ye little tart.'

"Morgana punched her sister's arm. 'Dinnae call me a soddin' tart, ye soddin' tart.'

"'I'll call ye what I please an' knock yer block off while I'm—'

"'Ladies.' Reyne raised one brow at the sisters. 'Time and place, merci.'

"Arlynn paced, brow creased in thought. 'We have advantage here. Hidden as we are in the shadows, and yet unseen. We walk among them freely, trusted servants all. But if the Dead catch a *hint* of this conspiracy, we're undone with a word.'

"'We must walk slow,' Reyne nodded. 'Free those we trust most, first. Your husband, Brann, Lady Arlynn.' She glanced to Morgana and Gillian. 'Your beaus, Declan and Maeron, ladies. Start with a few, then spread like a plague. Six today, twelve amorrow.'

"'But what then, m'lady?'

"All eyes turned to Morgana, her stare bright and wide.

"'Say we free the keep entire, with nae a single woman nor man to lose their nerve.' The young maid glanced to the ceiling above, lowering her voice further. 'The highbloods took this keep with an *army* to defend it. How now shall our remnants take it back?'

"'I've been pondering that riddle,' Dior murmured, chewing her lip. 'And I don't think we need an army to end this. We just use the sword already hanging over Nikita's head.'

"Morgana only blinked. 'What sword, holy maid?'

"'I'd seen it before,' Dior breathed, eyes on the flickering lantern. 'Between Kiara and Kane on the journey here. In the Hall of Plenty when I first arrived. But it wasn't until I saw Nikita and Lilidh tearing at each other's throats I truly *understood*.'

"She looked up, gazing around those blank faces.

"'These things *hate* each other,' she whispered. 'Nikita doesn't rule through love, save the love he *inflicts*. He buys the loyalty of this court with blood. These bastards don't toil together through bonds of fellowship or nation or even famille. They just loathe each other a little less than the rest of the world, and are content for now to keep the company of monsters they despise to bring that world to its knees.'

"She smiled soft, speaking the truth my brother had given her.

"'The greatest suit of armor is only as strong as the buckle holding it in place.'

"Reyne and her ladies looked among each other, understanding between. Dior's smile faded, as if she were coming back to herself, the dark and cold around her. 'But we can't wait long to strike. I'm not going to sit by until those cages up there are empty.'

"'Oui. But small steps first.' The Princess á Maergenn drew a short blade from her bodice. 'Can you spare another few drams? Enough for my ladies' loved ones?'

"'You need to free Isla too,' Dior said, sitting on one of the tombs. 'The girl who cleans Nikita's chambers. She's Joaquin's sweetheart, he won't help us without her.'

"Reyne nodded. 'We sleep together in the maids' quarters. I'll find a way, no fear.'

"Dior sighed, dragging off her silken hose. Each of the swordmaids had brought a vessel—a stoppered phial or old perfume bottle or hipflask. And as they watched, Dior unwrapped the homespun about her foot and sliced it open again, wincing in pain. Young Morgana whispered a prayer, Arlynn signing the wheel as Dior filled a bottle to the brim.

"'Be careful with that,' she told Gillian. 'If they smell it on you, we're done.'

"The lass nodded, taking the bottle with the reverence due a holy relic. The swordmaids watched as Dior filled each vessel, blood dripping bright and thick. Even outside the crypt, our mote could smell it; all of us atremble at that heavenly perfume, at the fear of how close this girl now walked to disaster.

"'Give this only to those you trust,' Reyne warned. 'Only in secret. And risk *nothing* once the sun has gone down. We stand on knife's edge here, m'ladies. And should one of us fall, it will be to the ruin of us *all*.' She looked around the group, held the gaze of each until she was satisfied. Her voice was iron. 'Walk soft. And go with God.'

"Young Gillian hesitated a moment, then took Dior's hand and kissed it, curtseying low. 'Our thanks, holy maid. Mother bless and keep ye.'

"'Aye.' Morgana knelt and pressed lips to Dior's knuckles. 'Mother bless, m'lady.'

"The swordmaids nodded, old Arlynn touching Dior's cheek and murmuring a prayer. And one by one, the trio stole out into the shadows, the blood of God's Redeemer hidden in their dresses, and a spark of hope burning in their hearts for the first time any could recall.

"Reyne took her blade back from Dior, held it over the lantern's chimney.

"'This doesn't feel right,' Dior murmured. 'Doesn't feel like we're doing enough.'

"'We must move careful,' Reyne said. 'It helps no one if we're discovered.'

"'Tell that to the people who're going to get dragged from those cages tonight.'

"'It's an awful thing,' Reyne nodded. 'To consign folk to their deaths. Be they soldiers or innocents, with every loss, a part of you is lost too. But that's what it is to be a leader.'

"'I'm *not* a leader. I'm a whorechild. I slept in gutters. My fucking *fleas* had fleas.'

"Reyne gestured to the mosaic above. 'Michon was a huntress. As common as they came. And yet she led an army, and gave birth to the world's salvation. You are not where you were born, Mlle Lachance. Nor who you were born of.'

"'Easy for you to say. You were born of a legend.'

"Reyne scoffed. 'Hardly an honor to be envied, believe me.'

"Dior sucked a lock of pale hair, nodding. 'My mama didn't like me much either.'

"Reyne's mismatched eyes darkened at that. 'I never said my mother did not like me. Niamh á Maergenn was the greatest leader Ossway has *ever* known. My mother conquered nine warring clans to unite this nation. All I have, all I am, I owe to her. And I am *grateful*.'

"'It's just . . .' Dior shrugged, chewing her lip. 'The paintings. There's portraits of Niamh and her famille all around this keep. But . . . none of them include you.'

"Reyne bristled, jaw clenched. 'You've very keen eyes, Mlle Lachance.'

"Dior nodded, but kept her tongue still. Reyne's cheeks were pinked, her stare gone hard; this was obviously a sore spot for the Lady á Maergenn, and Dior chose not to press. Instead, she frowned down at herself, one hand rising to the choker at her throat.

"'I've just realized . . . if you were her youngest, these are probably *your* things I'm wearing. Your dresses. Your jewels. I'm sorry.'

"Reyne breathed deep, shrugging as if to throw some damp chill off her back.

"'You wear them well,' she murmured, smiling soft. 'Aside from the heels, perhaps.'

"'Honestly, why *anyone* would wear those things is beyond me.'

"'Such is the price of vanity, mademoiselle,' Reyne said. 'Beauty can be a kind of armor, as I've said. But I've other armor that would fit you better.

A suit of platemail and threefold chain, and a longblade of Ossian steel to match.'Their eyes met, emerald and sapphire watching old sky blue. 'I'll dress you suchlike one night soon, holy maid, I vow it.'

"Dior cleared her throat, blushing, and we were put in mind of that moment in the wardrobe; Reyne tying up her hosiery, hands slipping slow over her prickling skin.

"'I'm not a maid,' she murmured. 'I mean, technically maybe, but . . .'

"Reyne arched one brow, smirking. 'Either you are or you aren't.'

"'Well.' Dior dragged her hair over her eyes, her burning cheeks. 'I've not been with any men, is what I mean to say.'

"'. . . Ah.' The Princess's own cheeks pinked a shade darker. 'I see.'

"Dior coughed again, hardening her voice as she gestured to the blade. 'I should be about it. If Lilidh or one of these other bastards smells the bleed, we're fucked harder than a ha-royale dockson after last call.'

"Reyne smiled at Dior's commonborn tongue, glancing to her foot. 'Do you need me to . . . ?'

"'Merci. But I can handle myself.'

"'I have not failed to notice, Mlle Lachance.'

"'. . . You can call me Dior.'

"Reyne flipped the blade and passed it over, curtseying as if to a knight in old tales.

"'Mlle Dior.'

"The younger girl scoffed, took the hot knife from Reyne's hands, meeting her eyes as their fingertips touched. And gritting her teeth, Dior pressed the blade to the arch of her foot to cauterize the wound. The scent of scorched meat joined the dim reek of death, the spit and pop of burning blood accompanying her soft hiss of pain. But instead of wincing, Dior's eyes quickly widened, Reyne whispering in astonishment at the blood already spilled across the Grail's skin.

"'What in the name of . . .'

"Dior's blood was *moving*.

"Trembling, gathering in beads like quicksilver, it rolled *away* from the hot metal, as if reacting to the Grail's pain. Astonished, Dior withdrew the knife, and the blood stilled itself, dripping now onto the stone as if nothing were amiss. Thunder rolled overhead, and our mote was frozen still, bewilderment and disbelief washing us through.

"'Does your blood usually behave so?' Reyne whispered.

"'Not that I'm aware,' Dior breathed.

"'... What else can it do?'

"'I'd no idea it could do *that*!'

"We took the wing, whirling, spinning through the air on the tomb's threshold.

"'We should be gone from here,' Dior whispered, looking toward us. 'I've a need to talk to my friend.' Dragging on her shoe, she tested her weight gingerly, biting her lip. 'When your swordmaids have news, come find me.'

"Reyne nodded, helping the limping girl to her feet.

"'God go with you, Mlle Dior.'

"'And you, my Lady á Maergenn.'

"'... You may call me Reyne.'

"Dior flipped the blade and passed it back, curtseying as to a queen in old tales.

"'My Lady Reyne.'

"The older girl chuckled, the younger girl smiled, and like shadows, the pair slipped from that ancient tomb, into the gathering dark. But as their footsteps faded, we lingered on that grim threshold, our mote circling the cold air, all of us now awonder.

"We'd not seen it at first, perhaps not truly looking—*certain* there could be no trace of Mother Maryn on sanctified ground. But as Lady Reyne had scooped up her lantern, we'd spotted it, just as we'd seen it in the Maergenn necropolis; wrought in pearl-white shells in the mosaic on the wall. A sigil as familiar as my own name. The dream I'd sacrificed my soul for.

"The twin skulls of the Esana, etched in the clouds behind Michon's raised sword.

"And between, the sigil of the Grail."

III

THE VOW

"DIOR STOOD AT Lilidh's right hand, wreathed in the copper-dark stink of blood.

"The Hall of Plenty rang with roars and cheers, the hymn of metal upon metal. The Heartless and the Blackheart sat their thrones, still steadfastly ignoring each other after their altercation weeks past. Scorched stood guard around the hall, hapless prisoners strung from the chandeliers. Nikita's courtiers were gathered around the tables, cups filled to brimming, and the Wolfmother and the Draigann were trying to murder each other.

"Their weapons cut the air louder than the storm above, the vampires flinging themselves about the room in that style Dyvok name Anyja. The Tempest. The Draigann fought shirtless, sea monsters and maids inked on pale flesh, golden fangs glinting through a beard spattered with blood. He wielded a blade taller and wider than Dior, swinging it one-handed as he scythed through the air, skipping, leaping, whirling. The Wolfmother had stripped down to her leathers and tunic, Kiara's muddy braids whipping behind her as she rolled aside, the Draigann's sword shattering the flagstones where she'd stood.

"'Stand and fight, coward!' Alix roared.

"The Draigann's lover spat on the floor, dragging a hand over her cropped scalp. Beside her, Kane the Headsmun motioned to one of the serving maids, who dutifully brought over fresh goblets of blood for him and the grey jester. The courtiers cheered as Kiara broke the Draigann's arm with her mighty warmaul, Nikita raising a cup to his daughter as the dueling coldbloods fell back, circling each other. The scene was painted red, carnage and cruelty; a court of abominations ever baying for more blood.

"And at the head of it, Dior stood, her pulse quietly seething.

"It had been seething all week, truth told. She and we had spoken after her meeting with Reyne and her swordmaids—messages traced letter by painstaking letter upon her hand. We'd no explanation for the way her blood had reacted to that scalding blade, and that had been frustration enough. We'd told her about the Esana sigil in the Mothermaid's Sepulcher, but we still knew Maryn could not lie within that tomb—*no* vampire, ancient nor mediae nor fledgling, might slumber upon holy ground. But worst of all, we'd told her that though we were healing, we were still not ready to fight. Soon. But not *yet*. And that word burned in her eyes, boiled behind her teeth, fists clenched so tight her knuckles were white.

"*Soon.*

"It's a terrible thing to sit silent while others suffer. But those who run fastest stumble swiftest. To speak here was to die. To fight here was to fall. Sometimes the hardest thing of all to do is nothing, and we could see that though Dior was heartsick with it, she understood the rules of this awful game. And at least now she did not play it alone.

"Reyne's ladies were gathered behind Lilidh, the Princess herself prostrate before the Contessa's throne. And in the moments Dior's resolve quavered, she would look to the Lady Reyne á Maergenn—the daughter of a duchess, on her belly at Lilidh's feet to be used like a footstool. And the Grail's mask would slip into place, her will iron once more.

"Aaron stood beside Nikita, resplendent in dark silks and a greatcoat of blue velvet brocade. Long hair spilled over his shoulders like liquid gold, his beautiful face a mask as he watched his maker brawl with the Draigann. Aaron had been spending every day in Nikita's boudoir—we'd seen bodies being hauled from the room by poor Isla, crushed and torn and ripped. And though we still felt a kinship with this fledgling killer, we wondered what Aaron had been forced to do, and what he had chosen. Love is madness—or so the poets say—and a lover will do near anything to please their beloved. What darkness had been unleashed in the noble capitaine of Aveléne?

"Dior saw Aaron's suffering full well, but she knew just as we did that there was only one way he might be freed. He was kith, after all; he could not drink her holy blood. The Grail's one hope to rescue the fallen Lord of Aveléne was to destroy his master.

"But *how*? How could she overcome foes this fearsome?

"The Dyvok roared as Kiara bloodied the Draigann again, the Wolfmother sidestepping her cousin's strike and breaking half his ribs with her maul, using the weapon's weight to sail free of his fearsome counterstrike. Nikita chuckled as the pair circled each other once more, eyes flashing with shared hatred. Lilidh looked to her eldest son, limping now, hard eyes locked on his foe.

"'Stop toying with her, Draigann,' she called.

"The vampire glanced to his broodmother, spitting blood as he snarled. Crowd roaring, he stepped to his cousin like thunder, forcing Kiara back, too fierce to parry, little time to dodge. But Kiara was swifter, rolling back across the broken floor. With a furious cry, the Draigann pursued, the weight of his greatsword dragging him up, up into the air. But Kiara slipped aside his attack as he landed, slamming her mighty maul into her elder's chest in reply. The Draigann crashed into the flagstones so hard they were smashed to powder, the Wolfmother placing a boot upon his bloodied ribs.

"'So the Black Lion fell also,' she growled. 'Demonstration as promised, dear cousin.'

"'I y-yield,' the Draigann spat, blood gleaming on his golden fangs.

"'Untamed!' came the cry around the hall, cups lifted in toast. 'Santé!'

"Kiara raised her bloody maul in reply, throwing a triumphant glance toward her father. But her grin dimmed just a touch at the sight of Aaron, standing beside that dark throne and drinking from the cup a smiling Nikita had handed him.

"Lilidh lifted her own brimming goblet to her lips. The Heartless was clad in blood-red silk this eve, a crown of goat horns curling at her brow.

"'Thy daughter fights well despite her youth, brother.'

"Nikita sipped from his goblet in return. 'She is *my* daughter, after all. Thy Draigann perhaps underestimated the worth of skill, and overrated the value of age.'

"'A simple mistake to make.'

"'Fools often make the simplest.'

"Lilidh pouted in thought, tapping her lip as she studied her niece. 'She seems somewhat glum these nights, though, think ye not? Despite the new laurels her victory over the Lion hath brung? Perhaps she rankles, thy Kiara, to see her position usurped?'

"'Usurped?' Nikita scoffed. 'She stands as the right hand of my throne, as ever.'

"The Heartless glanced to Aaron, lips twisting as her bottomless gaze drifted below his belt. 'I speak not of her position in the throne room, brother.'

"Aaron gave no reply to his great-aunt, eyes fixed firmly ahead. Kiara's stare lingered on her father, the Blackheart glowering behind his cup. But if Nikita intended rebuttal, it was silenced as the doors were flung open, a *boom* echoing the hall's length. Soraya strode into the feast, dark skin gleaming, braids bejeweled with fresh snow.

"Nikita raised one brow. 'Daughter?'

"Soraya glanced to Kiara, standing in triumph upon the bloody stone. The sisters' eyes locked, the Wolfmother's brow creased at the look on her younger sibling's face.

"'Daughter,' the Blackheart growled. '*Speak.*'

"'Forgive me, Father.' Soraya bowed. 'A messenger is come to the gates.'

"Lilidh scratched Prince behind his ear, the great white wolf thumping his leg upon the stone like some overwrought pup. 'More Voss princes to beg for their pauper king?'

"Soraya shook her head, looking to Nikita, her desire to please her liege and father at war with the fear of being the bearer of ill news.

"'I . . . think it best if you come see for yourself, my Lord.'

"Nikita's fathomless eyes narrowed, pale fingers caressing the arm of the Nineswords' stolen throne. The weight of long years rested heavy upon the brow of this prince, and he was not one for guess a game. But he stood slow, straightening the line of his magnificent greatcoat before stepping down off the dais.

"'Best you bring Epitaph, Father,' Soraya whispered.

"Murmurs rippled the length of that bloody hall, Nikita's bloodlords glancing among each other. The Blackheart scowled, reaching for the weapon leaning upon his throne. The greatsword was terrifying; longer and broader than a man. A bear was fashioned upon the hilt, mouth open in a roar, its blade of darkest steel, etched with runes in Old Talhostic and notched by countless battles. Epitaph, Nikita had named it, and well was the moniker earned—God only knew how many its edge had written.

"With weapon at rest upon his shoulder, Nikita marched through the hall. As he passed, his bloodlords stood, suspicion in their eyes as they looked to Soraya. But the fledgling had already fallen into step at her sire's back, throwing another dark glance to Kiara beside her, others following now, until all the room was emptying, out into the snow.

"All save Lilidh.

"The Heartless remained, lips pursed, tracing one horn at her crown with a gold-dipped finger. Her swordmaids glanced to each other, to Reyne, the question of sudden opportunity so heady, the Princess almost missed Lilidh snaking to her feet with an exasperated sigh. Reyne grunted as Lilidh trod upon her back, down to the broken flagstones. Snapping her fingers, the vampire stalked off after her broodbrother, maids and wolf falling into step behind, Dior hurrying to keep up in her ridiculous heels.

"Out through the main doors, thunder singing over the bay. Past the curious thrallswords, Joaquin near the stable, Baptiste in the smithy, little Mila shivering in her cage. Nikita's procession stalked past the ruins of the Mothermaid's Sepulcher into Auldtunn, the mortal stock living there shrinking back in terror.

"A horn blast rang from the walls to Newtunn at their approach, the mighty gates cracking wide, opening into the shattered second city beyond. The thousands of wretched in the ruins turned at the sound, those with intellect enough left to vocalize whining or hissing their hunger. They slipped from broken homes, rancid drains and crumbled fiefs, fangs bared, ever hungry. But when they set eyes upon the Blackheart, they trembled like curs before a Lord of Wolves, slinking back, back into the shadows.

"Dior walked at Lilidh's side all the while, hands before her like a holy sister. But her eyes were a stormy blue, a faint line at her brow betraying her wonder at what might have drawn the Count Dyvok from his feast. As thunder rolled again, Nikita strode up the stairs to the highwalk along the crumbling outer walls. His bloodlords stepped aside as Lilidh took her place at his right hand, peering into the dark.

"They lined up along the broken battlements, hundreds of years and thousands of lives their tally. Kane and Alix, the Draigann and Grey the Jester, Soraya and Kiara and the rest. Dior heard the faint song of pipes in the dark, soft growls from among the kith. And though Lilidh kept her face a mask, a low hiss slipped her lips as thunder rolled again.

"The night was too deep for any mortal eye to pierce, and the Grail squinted into that black. But lightning cut the sky, a brilliant bolt illuminating the rubble before Dún Maergenn's walls, and Dior gasped as she saw the *legion* arrayed there. Hulking forms and glittering fangs, crescent blades and golden eyes, fur daubed with blood and ink-scarred skin. The world ran dark again, Dior blinking in the aftermath, faint pipes singing of death and war. But the lightning came again, a blade arcing across the heavens, echoing now with thunder and the memory of the vow he'd made her long ago.

"*I know not where this road will lead us, girl. But I'll walk it with you, to whatever fate awaits. And if God Himself should tear us asunder, if all the Endless Legion stood in my path, I would find my way back from the shores of the abyss to fight at your side.*

"Tears filled her eyes.

"*I'll not leave you, Dior.*

"Her whisper lost in the storm.

"*I will never leave you.*

"'Gabriel.'"

IV

BLACK NIGHT, RED DAWN

"I KNEW NOT what to feel at the sight of him.

"Joy and rage. Envy and pride. But the voices in my head sang mostly of dread. He stood at the head of the storm, that army of the Moonsthrone, cupped in the palms of cracking thunder, Ashdrinker naked in his hands. He strode forward, Phoebe á Dúnnsair beside him, the fleshwitch's flame-red locks bound into thick slayerbraids, threaded with gold. Gabriel's blood-red greatcoat and ink-black hair whipped about him in the winter winds, and his eyes were the grey of the clouds he roared over.

"'DYVOK!'

"Atop the broken walls of his city, the Priori of the Untamed stood. His jaw was set, dread Epitaph on his shoulder, bloodlords gathered about him like dark angels. Furious glares were thrown toward Kiara, the Wolfmother standing with head bowed, fists curled at the sight of the living legend she'd claimed to have killed, apparently living still. But Nikita spared not a glance for his child nor her shame, looking instead toward his foe.

"'The Black Lion! A guest most honored! Welcome, Nikita bids thee!'

"My brother shook his head as he called reply. 'Listen, I know none of your dogs have the balls to tell you this, but do you have any idea what a fucking *wanker* you sound, referring to yourself in third person?'

"Nikita laughed. 'I am delighted to learn rumor of thy death was unfounded, de León. To gods and devils did I pray that one night we might meet again!'

"'Apologies! I don't remember meeting you the first time! Were you at the Crimson Glade? I was too busy cleaning your father off my sword for proper introductions!'

"'Let us have them, then!' The Blackheart opened his arms to encompass the city his broodsire had never come close to taking. 'I am conqueror of Dún Fas! Destroyer of Dún Sadhbh! Despoiler of Dún Cuinn! Defiler of Dún Ariss! All Ossway kneels now at my feet, or lies buried by my hand! Welcome to the Kingdom Dyvok, de León! Nikita is its sovereign, and all in it pay him homage!'

"Gabriel's eyes roamed the shattered walls, the broken stone, the ruin Nikita had made of this realm in his quest to seize it. 'I *love* what you've done with the place.'

"Nikita laughed, fangs glinting as the lightning flashed.

"'A long journey thou hast made, by thy look. Desire for hospitality, hast thou?' The Count Dyvok motioned to the mighty gates. 'Enter and be welcome, de León. But pray ye, come alone? Well could we accommodate thee in settings more intimate.'

"Gabriel's fist tightened on his blade as he muttered. 'Soon, bastard.'

"'No?' Nikita smiled. 'Alas. We shall be forced to sate ourselves 'pon another of San Michon's pretty sons, then. But no fear, Lion. *Well* satisfied hath he kept us.'

"The Count Dyvok glanced over his shoulder, beckoning.

"'Be that not so, Golden One?'

"A figure moved through the flock of devils, taking his place at Nikita's side. And as Gabriel looked up into his face, I saw my brother's already-broken heart cleaved deeper.

"'That is so,' Aaron de Coste called. 'Master.'

"'Oh, God,' Gabriel whispered. 'Oh *no* . . .'

"Aaron and Gabriel stared at each other, across that falling snow and an ocean of time. Boys they'd been when they first met, hated foes, who had forged an unlikely friendship that burned bright as silver flame. A light in darkest times had their brotherhood been—if not for the Lord of Aveléne, Gabriel and the Grail would have fallen into the Beast of Vellene's clutches. But now, Aaron stood in the grip of one darker still.

"Gabriel's jaw was one clenched knot, eyes ablaze with hatred even as they filled with tears. One more loss. One more thing taken. And a part of me wondered then, how much my brother had left inside him to give.

"He looked to Dior; the Grail beside her mistress, tears frozen on her lashes. His eyes roamed the shattered battlements, that Court of the Blood, the get of great Tolyev. Untamed, one and all, strong as mountains and cold as winters, who had in two short years made a desolation of this country he had, in his youth, risked life and soul to defend.

"'I'm going to make ashes of each and every fucking one of you,' he hissed.

"'How comes it thou art here?'

"It was Lilidh who called now, blood-red hair flowing in the wind about her like a cloak, black eyes fixed on Phoebe.

"'A long trek be ye from thy clanhold, Fiáin dahtr,' she called. 'No foot hath Blood Dyvok set 'pon Highlands' hallowed soil since pax was fair struck. Yet now, ye stand arrayed for war upon our doorstep? In defiance of oath and troth, etched in word and stone?' The eldest Dyvok gazed among the legion behind Gabriel, raising her voice above the thunder. 'Be there no honor 'mongst the sons of Malath? The daughters of Lánis and Lánae? A shame upon thee, I name it, to break holy vow sworn on sacred ground!'

"Phoebe stepped forward, glowering up at the walls. Her eyes were smeared with a streak of moonsblood, sharp teeth bared in a snarl. She reached beneath the graven breastplate of steel she wore, snapping the leather thong at her throat and holding aloft a small vial for all to see. And with a curse, she hurled it toward those walls, the metal flashing the same gold as her eyes as an arc of perfect white light cut the skies.

"'There's yer fuckin' *honor*, Winterwife!'

"Nikita glowered at his sister, but Lilidh yet stared at the fleshwitch, lips thin.

"'Ye have stolen the strength o' Fiáin!' Phoebe cried. 'And by Mother-moons and Earth Father, by our blood and breath, we are here to reclaim it!' She pointed to the broken battlements, roaring to the legions behind. 'Death to traitors! Death to Dyvok!'

"'DEATH!' came the roar behind her. Hundreds upon hundreds of slayers, swords pounding shields, lightning flashing upon tooth and claw, wolves and bears and lions howling to their hidden mothers above. '*DEATH!*'

"A stone flew from the darkness, large as a horse, silent as smoke. Gabriel grabbed the fleshwitch and hauled her aside as it struck the snow where she'd stood, landing with the force of a thousand hammers. The frozen earth was blasted apart, splinters flying as the stone bounced toward the dusk-dancer legions. The figures scattered, the boulder crashing among them, snow spraying, thunder rolling. Another chunk of broken parapet followed the first, thrown by the Blackheart—the ancient flinging the massive stones like some vengeful god. Gabriel and Phoebe danced back again, the granite spar crashing to the earth and fracturing into a dozen smaller shards, spraying among the troops. Chaos reigned down their line, the 'dancer formation breaking apart as yet another massive chunk of battlement crashed among them, stone shattering as if it were glass.

"Nikita stood atop the walls of his city, another broken spar of masonry poised in one hand. It was huge, tons in the weighing, yet wielded as easily as a child with a stick. Fangs bared, he hurled it, godlike strength sending it sailing through the dark, farther than any trebuchet or catapult, crashing among the retreating 'dancers.

"'Aye, run!' he roared. 'RUN! Drag thy craven carcasses back to the mire that birthed ye, afore *bedding* I make of thy flea-bitten hides!'

"The Dyvok jeered, but none dared climb down from the walls to give the enemy chase. And though they spat at the retreating Highlanders, all knew their foes would return when the frail sun shone in the sky, vampires all the weaker for it. The claws and teeth of duskdancers could end kith swift as silver, and the number Gabriel and his fleshwitch had gathered must have been terrifying to anyone with desire to live forever.

"Let alone rule.

"Nikita descended the battlements, his court behind him, all of them amurmur. Reaching the flagstones, the Priori Dyvok turned to his bloodlords, dark eyes ablaze.

"'Thy scorched shall each ye set here 'pon outer wall. Let the cattle be the first to bleed. We highborn shall guard the walls to Auldtunn and Portunn, hold them there should they run the gauntlet of our foulbloods.' Turning to Kane, he spoke with a voice like iron. 'No food for the mongrels tonight. Let them be hungry when the 'dancers come. Soraya'—he turned to his youngest— 'take six riders to the Órd, there to seek the Ladies Voss. Inform the Terrors we shall have their father's prize trimmed and trussed when they arrive. But if they've a will to see this slip unharmed, hasten might they, to her def—'

"'What madness be this?'

"Nikita turned, glowering as Lilidh descended the shattered stone stair.

"'Preparations for battle, sister. No surprise be it, ye do not recognize them.'

"'Thou wouldst trade my property without my—'

"'MY property!' Nikita snarled, storming over to loom but inches from his broodmate's face. 'Nikita is Priori, and all thou hast, *he* allows! Content he was to indulge thee *this*'—he waved at Dior—'so long as it served to do so! Yet since thou hast failed—'

"'What failure, mine?' Lilidh demanded. 'Blood blighted for thy conquest, I hath given thee! Lords legion for thy army, I hath given thee! Truce with 'dancers, I hath—'

"'Ye dare bleat of *truce* with foes that mass outside, waiting only for dawn's light?'

"'I *crow* of it! By mine own hand was it carved in stone! And seek ye fumbling fingers to blame for its breaking, look not to thy sister, Nikita, but thy *daughter*!'

"The Heartless turned, scowling at Kiara.

"'M'lady, forgive me.' The Wolfmother frowned. 'But I've not s—'

"'Compound not failure with further deceit! We know full well thy vial was lost in pursuit of the Lion! Our secrets given unto the enemy and for what? Justice claimed, yet not delivered? De León looks spritely indeed for a *dead* man.'

"Kiara glared at Kane, standing in the snow beside the Draigann and Alix. And though butter will not melt in *any* vampire's mouth, Historian, the Headsmun made a fine show of looking cooler than most. All around the bailey, the Lords Dyvok whispered, Kiara's stolen laurels crumbling now to dust. Dior kept her face like stone, but glanced toward the swordmaids, her pulse running quicker as Arlynn met her eyes, as Gillian risked a tiny smile. The cracks were showing. Nikita's alliance beginning to crumble.

"How swift might it collapse, if they but pushed?

"'Ride ye for the Voss, daughter,' Nikita snapped, glowering at Soraya. 'Spare not the whip. Tell Alba and Aléne they shall have their father's prize if troops they bring to bear for her defense. If not'—he glowered at Dior—'they may have what is left by the crows.'

"Soraya bowed, and with a scowl toward Kane, a sad glance toward her broodsister, she marched for the stables. All about them, the highbloods were awhirl, giving orders for their mortal troops to man the outer walls. It was a brutal sort of plan, and we could see the Count Dyvok was a general to be respected; have the Highlanders wade through the mortal thrallswords first, spending their strength, then run the gauntlet of foulbloods in Newtunn before ever they reached the highbloods on Auldtunn's walls. The Draigann's fleet owned Portunn and the Gulf of Wolves, and besides, the Highlanders had no ships—a frontal assault would be their only choice. It would be a massacre, and the first to fall would be men and women who only stood the defense because the blood in their veins demanded they do so.

"Amid the clamor, Kiara walked up to her dark father, her once-lover, standing like stone in the falling snow. The alabaster of Nikita's brow was creased in thought, midnight eyes on the walls above. But as Kiara spoke, his gaze fell on her.

"'Forgive me.'

"''Tis true, then?' he asked. 'Ye lost me my truce in pursuit of the Lion?'

"'I sought only to please ye,' Kiara whispered, lifting her eyes to his. 'To slay the murderer of yer noble father. To have ye look upon me as once ye did. Nikita, I—'

"His hand flashed out, seizing the Wolfmother's throat. Kiara gurgled as she was hauled off the ground like she weighed nothing, flesh slowly pulping in Nikita's awful grip.

"'I gave thee this life, daughter. Just as simply might I take it.'

"'If s-such be my laerd's wish,' she whispered. '*Ever* will I b-bow to it.'

"Nikita looked his broodchild over, eyes dark and bottomless. There was no trace of old affection in him for her, we saw. Not one drop of love. Kiara had been Nikita's prey; a lamb unexpectedly become a wolf after its slaughter. A body to be used, then discarded.

"We wondered why she still knelt in his shadow—long years had obviously passed since she'd drunk from his wrist, and any false affection would have faded with the decades. Perhaps the devil you know is always better. Perhaps it was simply a matter of misery loving company, for surely, there are none more miserable than the children of the damned. But she spoke then; a simple truth we had *never* considered.

"'I love y-ye.'

"But Nikita only shook his head.

"'Ye bore me.'

"He tossed her backward, a flick of his wrist, sending her into the wall. She struck with the crash of thunder and breaking bone, flesh crushed by the ancien's strength. As the Wolfmother collapsed onto the flagstones, the other members of Nikita's court looked on without pity, Kane smirking to himself at his older cousin's fall from grace. Her father loomed over her, eyes black as heaven. And as all in the court watched, the Wolfmother crawled back up to her knees, and knelt bleeding in her father's shadow.

"'Deceiver,' the Draigann murmured, shaking his head.

"'Coward,' Alix sneered. 'The Untamed kneel for none.'

"Murmurs rippled among the bloody court, hissed curses, bloody spit striking stone. And the Blackheart looked down on his old love without pity, pale lips curled.

"'Get thy scorched to the walls. And thank thy God I do not stand thee among them.'

"Nikita turned, stalking back through the ruins, eyes of the wretched horde downturned as he passed them by. With a glance toward the battlements, Aaron followed on his master's heels. Lilidh walked behind, the Draigann flanking her, speaking swiftly to his broodmother. All about them, the court of the Dyvok made ready for battle.

"Lightning sliced the sky wide open, hungry thunder roaring.

"And in its wake, Kiara dragged herself up from her knees.

"Back at the keep, Nikita headed to the Hall of Plenty, there to take counsel with his bloodlords. Lilidh banished her handmaids to their chambers, ordered Dior locked in her boudoir, thrallswords on guard outside. While plans were hatched behind closed doors, the Grail was left standing at her window, staring out into the night. We felt her pulse flutter, her heart thrash quicker as she pressed one hand to the glass and sighed.

"'Bloody hell . . .'

"The bookshelf opened at her back, and Lady Reyne slipped into the room. The Princess á Maergenn strode to the Grail's side, squeezing Dior's shoulder, smiling fierce.

"'God and Mothermaid be praised.'

"'What the *hell* are we praising them for?' Dior muttered.

"'Salvation!' Reyne hissed, gesturing to the dark outside. 'The Black Lion of Lorson is come to your defense! A legion of Highlanders at his side! I remember meeting him when I was but a bairn, knighted in this very city by my mother's own hand. She always spoke tales of his prowess. His brilliance in battle. This is the miracle we prayed for!'

"'Miracle, my shapely arse. It's going to be a fucking *slaughter*.'

"'For the Dyvok, oui.' Reyne took Dior's hand, squeezed tight. 'Courage, now, Mlle Dior. We've not been idle. Lady Arlynn's husband is freed from his blood-bondage, as are Gillian's and Morgana's beaus, *both* of whom serve as guards of Lilidh's chambers. With a few more drams and the grace of God, we shall have force enough to strike—'

"'And what happens at dawn? When Gabe and his friends hit those walls?'

"'Don't you see, that is our *chance*! Lilidh is no warrior to stand upon the battlements with Nikita and his lords. She'll be alone. *Vulnerable.* And if we strike, blades anointed with your blood, all her household might be freed with one stroke! Hundreds of people, dozens of—'

"'I mean, what happens to *them?*'

"Dior pointed through the window to the bailey below. Preparations for battle were underway; anyone capable of swinging a blade was being handed one, and though mortal, the force there arrayed was no trifle. Behind their broken battlements and with the strength of their dark masters in their veins, the Dyvok scorched would paint those walls with Highlander blood before they fell.

"Black night above promised a red dawn amorrow.

"'Gabriel told me he'd fight through the legions of hell to get back to my side,' Dior said. 'He sure as shit won't think twice about cutting those poor bastards to pieces. But those people out there didn't choose to serve. They fight because they're *forced* to!'

"'This is war.' Reyne shook her head. 'I told you. It's no small thing to send folk to their deaths, but that's what it *is* to be a leader. If—'

"'I'm *not* a leader! I've no *fucking* idea what I'm doing!'

"'That is the best way to do something that's never been done.'

"Dior blinked at that, unsure if it tasted like wisdom or madness.

"'You've a golden heart, Dior Lachance.' Reyne shook her head, gaze soft. 'Perhaps that is why the Almighty chose you to be the bearer of his blood. But while we all of us pray nights like this never come, it's what we do on the *morrow* that will truly matter.'

"Dior scowled, dragged a shaking hand through her hair. 'We need to stop. *Think.*'

"'We've not that luxury.' Reyne's voice was filled with fire, eyes ablaze. 'The battle for this city begins at dawn, and I for one am willing to *die* for it.'

"Dior looked to the Princess then, her eyes taking the older girl in. She was taller, harder; every bit her mother's daughter. Her hair was summer flame, her eyes mismatched jewels, and though not a single portrait of her hung in this keep, it was easy to imagine her likeness gracing the walls of the Hall of Crowns below. Clad not in servants' cloth, but shining steel, a sword held aloft to heaven and God's fire in her eyes.

"'. . . I can't say I much fancy the thought of you dying,' Dior murmured.

"'Hold no fear for what is coming, Dior. It is coming anyway.'

"'I know, I just . . .'

"The Princess still held the Grail's hand, and as she spoke, Dior grazed one thumb, ever so soft across Reyne's skin. The Grail risked a glance, up, up into the older girl's eyes, searching those mismatched jewels for some hint of warmth. But Reyne's grip softened then, falling away from Dior's, her expression grown clouded and cold.

"The Grail sighed, scolding herself beneath her breath and turning toward the window. She searched the dark outside, lips pressed thin, jaw clenched.

"'I'm sorry,' she whispered. 'That was foolish. And fucking childish, this isn't the time—'

"Her voice faltered, skin prickling as she felt a touch on her hand, light as featherdown. She turned back, found the Princess looking at her, those faeling eyes aglow as lightning cut the sky outside. Her expression was not clouded now but pained; that they stood on the edge of some vast new shore, never to be wandered.

"'No time for sweeter things, Mlle Dior.' Reyne smiled sadly. 'No time at all.'

"The Grail chewed her lip, heart suddenly afire.

"'Then we need to buy some. I mean, not for . . .' Dior swallowed, nodded to the window, the troops mustering for a war they'd never see the end of. 'For them.'

"Reyne shook her head. 'Even if it were wise to do so, how could it be done? Dawn waits for no one, and the Black Lion comes with it.'

"Dior dragged a hand through her hair again, eyes on the storm outside. And though we knew with certainty what would come next, still our blood ran chill as she spoke.

"'Celene.'

"With heavy wings, our mote fluttered from the red jewels at her throat, alighting on her outstretched fingertip. She held us up to her face as if to study us; a droplet of blood given will and form, eyes of pale blue and gleaming red locked on one another.

"'I need you to talk to Gabriel.'

"*Tap Tap.*

"'I know he won't be pleased to see you.' She shook her head. 'I know you've business unfinished, that you had something to do with his fall at Cairnhaem, but th—'

"*Tap Tap.*

"'This is too important! This is thousands of lives, Highlander and scorched alike! You need to convince them to hold off their attack. Gabe always said there is *no one* more frightened of dying than things that live forever, and not a *one* of these bastards wants to be on that wall when hell hits it. If we end Nikita and Lilidh, this whole rotten house of cards comes tumbling down!'

"Our wings held still, save for the smallest trembling.

"'*Please*, Celene,' she whispered. 'I know there's a world of difference between us, and a part of me still trusts you not at all. But if you truly serve the Almighty as you claim, you'll not consign those innocents out there to death. Not if there's a chance to save them.'

"The daughter of the Nineswords watched on, but the Grail stared only into our eyes. This was foolish—to risk so much for one child's mercy. But we'd let fury and fear rule us once before when we let my brother fall, and all since had been fire and misery.

"The voices within me were a clamor, a storm, outrage and scorn and disbelief, threatening for just a moment to overwhelm me. I thought of Jènoah's tomb then, the words he had writ in his own blood upon it. *This wait, too long. This weight, too heavy.* I envied him the silence he must know now. But beyond their cries, the echoes of all those stolen souls who shared this immortal shell, there was a question only Celene Castia asked herself.

"*If I cannot trust my fate to the Almighty's hands, can I say I hold faith in him?*
"*And if I did not hold faith in him, why would he hold it in me?*

"And so, despite the roars of protest inside my skull, the echoes and tumult within me shrieking their dark discord, I gave myself to his keeping.

"Lifted up our wings.

"*Tap.*"

V

AMONG THE WOLVES

"DEATH WALKED SO close to us that night, we could feel her shadow in ours.

"We all knew how much I risked, how deep these waters ran. The legion of souls inside me was a choir of warning, overlapping, naught but a cacophony in my head. We walked with a dead man's clothes on our back, face bound with rags, a threadbare blanket for our cloak. Our skin was thin and cracking; too little paint and too much canvas, a hint of grey still lingering from the fire's dreadful kiss. We'd trod close to the shores of hell before, but I'd never known such fear—so much at stake here, and so much bad blood between us.

"*Brother.*

"Their fires burned low in the storm; hundreds of tiny pinpricks dotting a ridge above a forest of dead trees, well beyond the reach of the Blackheart's arm. We caught the scent of blood and meat, fur and leather, saw shadows of monsters crouched beside those flames. We heard snatches of pipesong under the moaning wind, thick Ossian brogue, and the crunch of light footfalls in the snow far to our left. Right. Behind.

"'I come in peace!' we hissed, a rag nowhere white fluttering in my hand.

"Bows creaked. Wind howled. Nobody spoke.

"'I seek parlay with Gabriel, the Black Lion of Lorson!'

"The footsteps fanned out around us then, and through the driving snows, we caught a glimpse of women clad in branch and bramble, bows of ashwood in their hands. Ahead, looming out of the dark, came another woman, near six and a half feet of her. She was an ugly brute; broad of shoulder and thick of arm, hair black as night bound in slayerbraids. Her skin was painted with spirals of blood from her moonstime, her face near an animal's—brown eyes with no whites, pointed furred ears, one half-missing, sitting too high on her skull. Her forearms were dark with fur, her fingers tipped with claws like curved daggers.

"'Give us yer name, maebh'lair,' the duskdancer demanded. 'And a single reason why we shouldn't make ashes of ye here and now.'

"'My name is Celene Castia, fleshwitch,' I replied. 'I am sister to Gabriel de León. And if that is not reason enough to let me pass . . .'—we sliced our palm, flicking our wrist to summon our bloody blade—'. . . I could slay you all where you stand and walk on anyway.'

"Bowstrings creaked tighter, our eyes locked on the leader, discord rising in my skull. It was a bluff, of course—had they tried to end us, we'd simply have fled on the wind before their arrows could fall. But we knew warriors such as these admired valor, not simpering, and quietly, I prayed Gabriel's name would carry us the rest of the way.

"The she-bear scowled, crooked teeth bared. But after a long staring match, she grunted, motioned we follow. One of the archers hissed softly, arrow aimed at our dead heart.

"'Ye put trust in a maebh'lair, Brynne? How do we know she is who she claims?'

"The slayer scoffed, looking me over.

"'Ego like that? She's *definitely* his bloody sister . . .'

"We were marched up the rise, incredulous guards assured by the one called Brynne that we were there to see the Lion. I'd only read of duskdancers in Master Wulfric's library, never seen one in the flesh aside from Phoebe á Dúnnsair, and though there were ordinary folk among their legion, I was aghast at how awfully their heathen magiks had twisted the rest of them. Hideous forms watched from around those fires; hulks of tooth and claw, half-human, half-beast. Animal eyes glittering in the firelight, pointed ears and tails and razored teeth, faces painted with spirals of moonsblood, imbuing the bearers with the strength of earth and pagan goddesses both.

"Stalking through that bestiary, we made the sign of the wheel.

"We were led to a tent in the heart of the camp, hung with banners of a dozen heathen clans. With a growl for us to '*stay*,' the one named Brynne stepped inside, leaving us surrounded. It seemed the entire Highland host was gathered at our back now, blades gleaming and fangs glittering and breath steaming in the chill.

"We heard a snarl, someone call my brother's name. And in blinking, there he was, ripping the tent's flap aside, his accursed blade naked in his hands.

His eyes were flushed crimson, fangs bared as he strode toward me, naught but murder on his mind.

"'Dior sent me, brother, *be calm!*' we cried.

"His fury lessened, but only a drop—testament to the depth of his rage. If not for our blood still at work within him, who knows what he might've done? It mattered not a drop to him that I'd *never* have gone into such danger without reason."

The Last Liathe shook her head and sighed.

"My brother was ever ruled by his heart, not his head."

"Not by one of them, at any rate," Jean-François smirked, sketching in his tome.

Celene turned her withering gaze on the historian, black as the waters between.

"Your desire for him is piteous, sinner. You know he would kill you in a *heartbeat* if given opportunity, do you not? How is it people look at my brother and see only what they wish? How is it he lives a life so charmed, when I was given *this?*"

"You speak as though you hate him," Jean-François mused, working on his illustration—a portrait of Celene standing in a sea of duskdancers. "And yet, at the heart of your rage lies a crime he cannot be faulted for. To lament ill-fortune is understandable, Mlle Castia, but to place the blame for the whim of heaven at a mortal's feet . . ."

The historian smiled, dark eyes twinkling.

"Well . . . it seems somewhat ungodly of you, mademoiselle."

"You do not see," she whispered. "You do not *know*. What he cost me."

"*Me*," the historian replied. "Not *us*. Your use of the plural seems to vary wildly. One moment you speak of yourself as many, another, you speak only of Celene. Forgive me, but it makes you seem somewhat . . . unbalanced. And worse, a rather unreliable narrator."

"Far more reliable than your other, sinner."

"Which is it, then? *Me* or *we?*"

"It is both. It is neither. It is *exactly* as we say."

The historian rolled his eyes, lifting his quill as Celene continued.

"We stood there in the snow, staring at each other, Gabriel's will against mine. Behind him, we saw the fleshwitch á Dúnnsair, further twisted by her dark magiks now; eyes that of the animal who wore her skin. But though she glowered at me, still she touched his wrist, whispered soft in his ear; *far* more familiar in touch and tone than once they'd been.

"We looked from her hand at rest on Gabriel's arm, up into his eyes.

"'You've spent *sleepless* nights in your efforts to return to Dior's side, we see. No time wasted at all.'

"The fleshwitch turned on me, cursed eyes flashing. 'Ye're but a few breaths away from slaughter here, leech. I'd spend them more wise if I were ye.'

"'You are not me. And will never be. Thank your heathen gods for that.'

"'What do you want, Celene?' Gabriel growled.

"'Dior bid me speak with you, brother.'

"'You've talked with her?' Phoebe demanded, eyes wide. 'How does she fare?'

"We glanced at the legion of shadows at our back, the folk within the tent behind my brother, their skins scribed with bloody spells and bodies twisted by blind idolatry.

"'Well enough, considering her plight. The Dyvok tried to slave her, but though she plays the part, her holy blood makes her immune to their mastery.' We met my brother's widening eyes. 'She can break the bonds of thralldom with it, Gabriel. Even now, she foments rebellion within the keep. She asks you delay your attack, that she may free more of those scorched by the Untamed.'

"'What difference does it make?' he demanded. 'If we burn every coldblood in Dún Maergenn to ashes, their thralls will be freed anyway.'

"'Nikita has ordered every mortal soldier to the outer battlements. You and your . . . new friends . . . will need to go *through* them before you can reach the Blackheart.'

"'And?' It was a wolfen man who spoke, his head that of his beast, voice like wet gravel. 'They serve the leeches. Let them die with their masters.'

"'. . . They don't choose that service willingly,' Gabriel said softly.

"We nodded. 'Dior asks you to give her time. The Heartless is the strap that binds the Untamed together, the Blackheart is the buckle. Without them . . .'

"'Nikita is ancien,' Gabriel hissed. 'Older than fucking empire. And Lilidh is the eldest Dyvok that walks this earth. Dior can't *possibly* think—'

"A shout rang across the encampment, all eyes turning behind. We saw figures marching through the snow; a dozen Highlanders, tooled leathers and faces daubed with blood. At their lead came the biggest man I'd ever seen; a giant more lion than man, a mane of slayerbraids arrayed about his twisted features, body covered in red fur. And upon one shoulder was slung a figure; torn, bloodied, struggling weakly against that monster's grip.

"He stopped dead when he saw us, sharp fangs bared.

"'Peace, Keylan,' Phoebe murmured. 'This is Gabe's sister.'

"'Who the hell is that?' my brother asked, nodding to the beast's shoulder.

"With a murderous glance to us, the fleshwitch dumped the body into the snow. We saw long black braids, dark skin run death grey, small circles of blood daubed on her cheeks. Her face was rent bone-deep by 'dancer talons, her arms ripped clean from their roots. Our eyes narrowed as the scent of her blood reached me on the air.

"'Soraya,' we whispered. 'Nikita's youngest daughter.'

"Murmurs rippled among the gather, swords and claws glittering the firelight. Soraya tried to rise, but the one named Keylan put a boot on her chest, crushing her into the snow. With no arms to fight him off, the vampire was left to writhe, hissing in pain and hatred.

"'My father will s-see you *flayed* f-for this!'

"'Caught it riding north with a half dozen others,' Keylan said. 'Jerrick ran her down.'

"'Rats,' the wolfen man growled. 'Fleeing the sinking ship.'

"'Nay,' the big lion replied. 'They were messengers, I think.'

"'For who?' my brother asked.

"Keylan shrugged. 'Nae ken. But we'd only the three of us, and there were six o' them. A few got past. Thralled horses, too swift to run down.'

"'Where were they going?' Gabriel demanded, eyes on Soraya.

"The highblood laughed, bloody face twisted. 'You will see. Have n-no fear, Lion.'

"'I don't.' He crouched at her side, face cold and hard. 'But I think *you* do.'

"We watched as my brother placed Ashdrinker at rest above the highblood's heart. And as the broken tip of that dread blade touched her breast, we saw indeed that Soraya quavered, her bleeding jaw clenched tight. She was decades old. Murderess of hundreds likely, thousands perhaps. But though she tried to hide it, as that starsteel sank half an inch through her leathers into the skin beyond, she was little more than a frightened child.

"'Tell me,' my brother murmured. 'And I'll let you go.'

"'You *lie*. You would n-never release me.'

"'You don't know me, madame. I'm no murderer.'

"'You slew Tolyev,' Soraya spat. 'You slew g-great Danika and Aneké. A score of my kin so g-great the snows are yet stained red. You *are* a murderer.'

"'That was battle. You're a prisoner. I'm not the sort to butcher a helpless woman.'

"We spoke then, voice soft on the wind. 'Gabriel—'

"'Shut the fuck up, Celene.'

"We knew the answer to the question he asked, of course. The hands Soraya was to deliver her father's message to. But the ice we trod upon was deathly thin here, and more, I think a part of us wanted to see what my brother was truly made of. Exactly how far he might go. The wolfen one rankled, growling as he glared at Soraya.

"'She's a leech, Lion. We cannae just let her go, she—'

"'She's got no fucking arms, Angiss. I think it's safe to assume she won't be swinging battle's tide.' Gabriel's eyes met Soraya's again, the vampire taut with fear. 'No, she wants to run, this one. She wants to *survive*. She'll live forever if no one kills her, can you imagine? No old age. No sickness. The only thing that will end her is the flame or the blade. Imagine what you'd give up to hold on to something that precious.'

"His grip shifted on Ashdrinker's hilt, starsteel glittering in the firelight.

"'Tell me what I want to know, coldblood. And I'll give you your chance at eternity.'

"Soraya met his eyes, her own flooded red. And though we wondered in truth if she actually believed him, in the end, a drowning woman will clutch even at straws.

"'The Terrors,' she hissed. 'They are come to Ossway with a legion of wretched at their command, and a m-missive from the Forever King on their lips. Voss has d-desire of the girl, Lachance. My father sends r-reply that he will give them the child if they come to his aid.'

"'And where is this so-called legion?'

"'They are encamped across the Òrd River. Awaiting word from my Priori.'

"'You're lying to me, coldblood.'

"'I do not lie!' She winced, torn flesh slicked with blood, eye filling with fearful tears. 'The Terrors come, but a few nights' d-distant. I swear it on my *soul*!'

"Gabriel nodded, rubbing at the stubble on his chin.

564   —   JAY KRISTOFF

"'You know, I still dream of the cages at Triúrbaile. Still smell the stink when I close my eyes.' He shook his head and sighed. 'I don't kill helpless women. But you're *nothing* close to that. And you can't swear by a soul you've no owning of, vampire.'

"'No!' Soraya spat. '*No,* d—'

"Pressing hard, Gabriel thrust Ashdrinker through the highblood's heart. Starsteel sundered her flesh, her mouth opening wide in a scream. And in a blinking, Gabriel drew the blade out and sliced Soraya's head from her body. Her corpse bucked, thrashing, the hands of time reaching out to reclaim all it had been denied. Grey flesh melted from the bones, blood curdled black, then hissed into dust, naught but a wasted skeleton left in the snow.

"Phoebe spat on the smoking carcass, snarling.

"'Enjoy eternity, leech.'

"All eyes now turned to us, storm-grey and glittering gold and emerald green. We stood wreathed in the smoke of Soraya's ruin, matching my brother's gaze.

"'You knew about this Voss legion, I take it? Were you planning to tell me?'

"'I tell you only what Dior asked me to. Brother.'

"Gabriel scoffed, wiping the blood off his smoking sword. 'Well, there's her answer, then. We saw a legion of Voss a few weeks back, marching south, thousands in their number. I fancied they were mustering to attack Maergenn, but if Nikita is now bargaining for their aid, we've no choice but to strike before they arrive.'

"'It will take time for the Terrors to march here, Gabriel. They are camped *days* away. Dior asks but *one* to strike her blow. To spare you and your fellows hours of slaughter, to spare the poor souls on that wall who only stand there because they are made to.'

"He shook his head, lips thin. 'We can't—'

"'She bid me remind you of the chessboard at Cairnhaem, brother.'

"He blinked at that, wind howling in the gulf between us.

"'She bid me ask you what you wanted victory to look like.'

"He glanced toward the dún, down to the figure on his sword, her arms spread along the crossguard. We wondered what that demon whispered to him with its silver tongue.

"'Have faith, Gabriel.' We looked into his eyes, pleading. '*Believe* in her, as I do.'

"My brother glanced to his fleshwitch, and in turn she looked to the slayers around them. We could see fury among the Highlanders; the righteous rage that their blood had been used to fuel Nikita's assault upon Ossway, leaving a carcass in his wake. There must be vengeance for that, we all of us knew. But still, we saw it in Gabriel's eyes—the same as when we faced down the Beast of Vellene on the Mère. For all his failures, all his frailties, I will say this one thing in my dear brother's favor: His faith in Dior never wavered."

The Last Liathe sighed.

"Not even at the end.

"'I saw Aaron at the Blackheart's side,' he said quietly. 'Is Baptiste in there too?'

"We nodded. 'Thralled to the Wolfmother. He will be in the vanguard for certain.'

"Gabriel dragged a hand down his face, sighing deep. We could see the fear in his eyes. The fear every parent feels, to let their child fly the nest alone. The fear for his friends within those broken walls; that hill he would die on.

"'We can give the Godling a day,' he declared.

"'Gabe . . .' the fleshwitch murmured.

"'One day,' he insisted, squeezing her hand. 'If it might spare those folk on the wall, we can give her tomorrow, Phoebe. We owe her that.'

"The fleshwitch looked among her kin, seeking consensus—Gabriel was a sort of leader here, but only one among many. None of the Highlanders seemed easy at the prospect; snarling teeth and narrowed eyes. But Dior was their Godling after all, Earthbooned and Moonsblessed, spoken of in ancient augury and entrails of the dead.

"Who were they to deny her a single dusk?

"'You've eyes within the keep?' Gabriel asked us. 'Some way to talk to Dior?'

"A droplet of our blood remains with her. A moth. What it sees, we see. What it knows, we know. It cannot speak, but it can pass messages nonetheless.'

"'Well, it can tell Dior she has 'til dawn on prièdi. The rest of you is staying here.'

"'We would rather—'

"'Count the fucks I give about what you would *rather* on no hands,' he growled. 'That's the deal. Dior wants a day, your treacherous arse stays *right* where I can see it.'

"We met his gaze, saw he would brook no dissent. And with a withering glance, we curtseyed, drawing up the hems of our ragged cloak like the finest dress at court.

"Phoebe spoke among her kin, asking that they pass the word. Thunder rolled above as the group broke up, staring a thousand daggers at our back. Gabriel's eyes brimmed with anger, misgiving, fear. But finally, holding the flap aside, he nodded into the tent.

"'Looks like we have all night, then. Perhaps we should talk. Sister.'

"Our gaze narrowed at that, boring into his. Our mother's eyes had been black as coal—Gabriel had his father's eyes, through and through. And standing there in all that dark and cold, I wondered what else he had inherited from that monster.

"Time to find out, I supposed.

"'As it please you. Brother.'

"And brushing the snow from our shoulders, we stepped inside."

VI

UNDERDARK

"DIOR STOOD BENEATH the earth of the Holy Sepulcher, staring at the mother of her mothers.

"A flock of conspirators were gathered now around her, arguing about the choices before them. There was the Lady Reyne, of course, royalty in homespun, eyes afire. The first of her household, noble Lady Arlynn, was debating with a pair of young men, red of hair and blue of eye, like enough to be brothers. These were beaus to the swordmaids Gillian and Morgana— that same pair of gallants that had saved Dior from her treacherous heels outside Nikita's chambers. An older man with a trimmed grey beard stood beside Arlynn—her husband, Laerd Brann. Last of all was young Isla á Cuinn, the maid of Nikita's boudoir, twin beauty spots on her cheek, and blood crusted under her fingernails.

"Our mote watched all from the threshold, still unable to enter the sepulcher's sacred ground. The figures snapped at each other, hushed voices echoing on the walls of the Mothermaid's empty tomb. And all the while, Dior stared at the mosaic of San Michon upon the wall, the sigil of the Esana wrought above the First Martyr in bright white stone.

"'Why nae free the kitchen staff?' one of the gallants demanded. 'Then we have access to the mornmeal of every thrall in the keep.'

"'Ye think it worth the risk, Declan?' Arlynn demanded. 'If we free those girls from their bondage, d'ye think any of them would have the stomach to keep carving up the *dead* for dinner? If but *one* of them breaks, we're all undone.'

"'The grey jester watches us eat anyway,' the other lad growled. 'Stands in the barracks and just *stares* at us. If ye say the Dead can scent the Lady Lachance's blood . . .'

"'They can,' Reyne nodded. 'It's like perfume to them.'

"'Then the jester may smell it.' Morgana squeezed Declan's hand, shaking her head. 'We cannae risk it, love. One misstep and we're buried.'

"His brother spoke again; a chiseled young warrior named Maeron, hands callused by bladework, and eyes far too old for his years. 'Well, we must do *something*. If not, when those heathens hit the walls, we die. Ye say we've bought a day until the Highlanders attack. That's nae time to free every soul in this keep one by one.'

"'Strike off the viper's head and the body dies, Maeron,' Reyne said. 'And this place is a *nest* of them. If we end Nikita and Lilidh, their alliance will crumble, I'm sure of it.'

"Isla spoke then, her voice soft. 'But . . . how would you *do* that?'

"'Aye, how?' Declan demanded, looking among the gather. 'They're monsters with the strength of *centuries* in them. The night they took the dún, the Blackheart was hurling boulders the size of *wagons* at the walls. I *saw* him. We cannae *hope* to hurt him.'

"'He *is* strong,' Arlynn nodded. 'But the tallest tree in the forest still burns.'

"'And even monsters need to sleep . . .'

"All eyes turned to Dior as she spoke, a hush falling on the tomb. Maeron and Laerd Brann bowed their heads, Gillian and Declan signed the wheel, as if it were a miracle every time the Grail opened her mouth. They looked at her, each and every one, and we could see the fire of faith absolute in their eyes. The girl who had freed them from slavery eternal, the clutches of a waking nightmare, the right hand of God Himself upon this earth.

"'My Lady Lachance—'

"'You can call me *Dior*, Laerd Brann,' she smiled. 'I've not earned a title.'

"'Ye've earned every accolade in this realm by my reckon, lass.' The older man smiled. He was a simple sort, grandfatherly and warm, but his sword-arm was hale, hands roughed by the blade. 'But neither the beast Lilidh nor Nikita slumber unguarded.'

"'No,' she agreed. 'But the Untamed have complete faith in the bond of their blood. They've never considered what could happen if it breaks. And half the people in this room are the ones who stand watch on Nikita's door while he sleeps. Isla cleans his chambers. Reyne knows a hidden path into his boudoir. Celene can keep watch for the moment his head hits the pillow. Then, we hit *him*.'

"'*Them*,' young Declan snarled. 'That blond one he's been bloodying his sheets with is a devil, through and through. He deserves the same hell as his master.'

"'No,' Dior said, sharpening. 'Nobody touches Aaron. None of this is his fault.'

"The young knight bowed low, hand to heart. 'My Lady Grail—'

"'Fuckssakes, call me *Dior*.'

"'. . . My Lady Grail Dior, ye've nae witnessed the things they do. I saw the state of the bodies Isla was cleaning up yestereve. Tell her, lass.'

"The maid swallowed as Declan looked her way, hands clasped tightly. 'The pair of them have been . . . busy together. But Master Nikita—'

"'*No*,' Dior said, harder. 'Aaron saved my life, he's not like that. Everything he's done, he's been *forced* to by the Blackheart. Aaron de Coste is off limits, understand?'

"Young Declan scowled, but still, he bowed low. 'Your will, my Lady Grail.'

"Dior massaged her temples, sighing.

"'What if they dinnae sleep amorrow?' Gillian said. 'There's an army of duskdancers on their doorstep, they may not have a will to hit the pillows.'

"'Then we ask Gabe to wait another day,' Dior said. 'They have to sleep *sometime*.'

"'And what of the beast Lilidh?' Arlynn asked, eyes shining with hate. 'Even without guards at her door, she is never alone. Always that accursed wolf skulks at her heels.'

"'Oui.' Dior sighed, eyes distant. 'But when she visits me in my boudoir, Prince waits outside. So long as we hit Lilidh and Nikita at the same time, a sharp knife and a few moments with her distracted is all I need.'

"'. . . And how will you distract her, my Lady Grail?' Brann asked.

"Dior raised one eyebrow, lips quirked. 'I'll tell you when you're older, m'laerd.'

"The old man grasped the hilt at last, blushing and staring at his boots. Reyne's faeling eyes twinkled, and she and Dior looked at each other and laughed, despite it all. Gillian and Morgana shared a glance, Lady Arlynn clearing her throat in the silence.

"'We risk much, striking like this. And though your coming is a miracle, Lady Grail, these monsters destroyed our *country*. Will your blood alone be enough to end them?'

"'I don't know,' Dior murmured. 'It burns them, I'm certain of that. But the only ancien I *killed* with it was stabbed through the heart with an enchanted blade, bathed in it.'

"'Don't suppose you've any enchanted blades in that dress?' Reyne asked.

"'This corset's barely got room for *me* in it.' Dior winced, adjusting her extravagant gown. 'Why the fuck you all wear these things is beyond me . . .'

"'Would a *silver* blade serve in their hearts?' Morgana wondered aloud.

"Dior chewed on that, sucking her lip in thought. 'Silver hurts them, sure and true. If I were the gambling kind . . . oui, I'd roll the dice on it.'

"'What difference does it make?' Gillian hissed. 'We've nae got a silver blade either.'

"Morgana scowled at her older sister, dragging a flame-red lock from her face and gesturing behind Dior. 'There's silver blades right there, ye dozy twat.'

"'Dinnae call me a dozy twat, ye doz—'

"'Ladies, *please*,' Arlynn snapped.

"Dior turned around, lips parted. 'Seven Martyrs, she's right.'

"Below the mosaic rested that mighty vault; Tà-laigh du Miagh'dair, the Tomb of the Mothermaid. Its marble was cracked and broken, but the vault was capped by that great sculpture of purest silver. The Mothermaid's likeness lay in mail upon her bed of skulls, longblade clasped at her breast. About her were gathered cherubs at wing and fierce seraphim at watch, silver swords held high to guard the empty resting place below.

"Reyne looked the sculpture over, faeling eyes glittering. 'Can we . . .'

"'Let's try,' Gillian breathed.

"Dior watched as Reyne and her comrades clambered over the Mothermaid's tomb, attempting to pry the blades free with the unholy strength of their masters, lingering yet in their veins. Standing beside the Grail, Isla made the sign of the wheel, whispering a prayer under her breath at the blasphemy of it all.

"Dior shook her head. 'We're a *long* way from the chapel at Aveléne, Mlle á Cuinn.'

"Isla nodded, her face grim. 'We are at that, Mlle Lachance.'

"Dior watched Reyne struggling with a sword, her gaze drifting over her ancestor as she murmured to the girl beside her. 'You know, I keep thinking about what you said that night we sheltered near the river. How it feels like it's been raining all our lives.'

"'I was wrong to despair,' the girl said, touching Dior's arm. 'And you were right to bid me hope. I feared I might never see the end of this road. But I truly believe God has delivered us to the place we're supposed to be. Here, with the ones we love.'

"'I saw Joaquin the other day.' Dior smiled at Isla sidelong. 'In the stable.'

"The girl hung her head, her voice soft. 'Is . . . is he aright?'

"'He's well. He asked about you. The coldness he showed you in the caravan was just a ruse, mon amie. He's not forgotten you.' Dior squeezed the girl's hand, looked into her eyes. 'Have no fear, Isla. You two will get your Ever After, I promise.'

"The others were still struggling at the sculpture, all to no avail. Maeron cursed beneath his breath, tugging at one of the blades in an angel's fist. Morgana's face had gone bright red with effort, Declan leaning all his weight into another blade, trying to pry it from that silvered grip. But even with the strength of the scorched . . .

"'I c-cannae do it . . .'

"'Bloody thing's stuck fast . . .'

"'Gilly, that's my *foot*, damn ye . . .'

"'It's no good.' Reyne cursed, pawing summer curls from sweating skin. 'This is all one sculpted piece of metal. It will bend before it breaks.'

"'We could cut it?' Morgana suggested.

"Her beau, Declan, rubbed his chin. 'With what?'

"'Saw from the smithy? They're bound to have one.'

"Her sister sucked her lip, gave a grudging nod. 'Nae a bad idea, Morgie.'

"Morgana smiled, genuinely pleased. 'Aye, thanks, Gilly.'

"'Did ye think of it all by yerself, or pull it out of yer c—'

"Morgana thumped her sister's arm, the pair cursing as they scuffled.

"'We don't have anyone in the smithy.' Red-faced and scowling, Reyne tugged at the longblade in the Mothermaid's hand, looking to Isla. 'Maybe your man Joaquin c—'

"The sword shifted in the Princess's grip, the sculpture shivered, dust drifting from the silver. Isla cried out, the others leaping clear as the whole tomb shuddered, chunks of marble façade falling away. The sound of stone grinding stone rang through the tomb, and as we watched from the threshold, that mighty vault of marble and metal rolled back, sliding by some ancient mechanism along those strange grooves in the floor. And beneath, we saw a hole in the stonework; a hidden stair, leading deeper into the earth.

"'Sweet Mothermaid,' Reyne whispered, signing the wheel.

"'What is this sorcery?' Arlynn whispered.

"Dior glanced to the mosaic above—the sigil of the Esana in the clouds over Michon's head. The Grail looked to us, spinning and whirring through the air, never more frustrated that we could not pass this threshold to see what lay beyond. We knew this could never be Maryn's resting place—not upon sanctified ground. And yet, scuffing the stone at her feet with the tip of her dainty heels, Dior pointed to a design carved into the rock.

"'Another sigil of the Esana,' she breathed.

"'The hell are the bloody Esana?' Gillian whispered.

"'Good God Almighty, it reeks,' Laerd Brann said, covering his face with his sleeve.

"His wife took his arm, Lady Arlynn's sharp blue gaze on Dior. Morgana stepped up to the brink, toeing a small pebble down the stairs. Her sister slipped up beside her, giving her a sharp nudge toward the hole, the younger sibling cursing and shoving her elder back. All around the gathering, eyes turned to Dior. But the Grail only shook her head.

"'I've no fucking idea what's down there.'

"Reyne stood at the edge of the stair, wincing at the evil smell. 'Should we . . .'

"'We should get back,' Isla said, wringing her hands. 'If their council in the Hall of Plenty ends and they find us missing . . .'

"Dior nodded to Reyne. 'Isla's right. I can go down alone.'

"'Like hell,' the Princess said. 'We go down together or not at all.'

"The Grail looked among the gathering, chewing her lip. Our wings battered the air, furious, praying Almighty God we might call out to her. But she looked to me, and we could still see her distrust, her trepidation—at what I was, at what all this meant. And lips pressed thin, she took up Reyne's lantern, nodding to the rest.

"'Aright, let's be quick.'

"We screamed silently, wracked with fear. Declan and Maeron insisted they go first, Morgana and Gillian next, the others following. They treaded down into that underdark, and we could do nothing, barred by that holy ground as if a wall of flame. Able only to watch.

"Pray.

"They were gone what seemed an age of the earth. My flesh sat with Gabriel in his tent, speaking of times past and blood spilled. But that tiny mote of me sat watching all the while, listening, straining for a sound, a clue. It was difficult for us to keep our thoughts grounded in two places at once; drifting back and forth between tent and tomb, torn between two worlds. We stared at the image of the Mothermaid carved into the ironwood door on the threshold. Her graven face was cold, hands entwined in prayer, a halo of ancient runes around her head. Time stretched out eternal, fear my only handmaiden, the voices in my head howling their fear, their rage. But after a dark forever, we heard soft footsteps, saw lanternlight brightening the stone, and at last, Dior emerged from that hole.

"Eyes wide. Lips thin. The look on her face not so much terror as *horror*. The Princess á Maergenn followed, her face so bloodless she looked a corpse. The others emerged, Isla silent and wide-eyed, Lady Arlynn leaning on her husband's shoulder, Morgana arm in arm with her sister, their beaus beside them. Their boots were wet with water that stank of a brackish sea, and all of that secret company looked changed; not in their features, but in their hearts. As if they'd caught a glimpse of something that could never be unseen.

"'I dinnae understand,' Gillian whispered.

"She looked to the ceiling above as if for answers, tears shining in her eyes.

"'I dinnae *understand . . .*'

"They stood in the dark, pale and frightened, the world somehow forever shifted beneath their feet. But the Grail lingered not, lantern in hand, stalking toward the entrance of the tomb. There was rage in her eyes along with horror now, damp skirts billowing about her as she stormed past the Mothermaid's graven door, back across the threshold.

"'My Lady Dior?' Reyne called. 'Where are you *going?*'

"We flew up toward her throat, but she battered us away, hissing.

"'To get a fucking saw.'"

VII

A FEW QUIET WORDS

" 'YOU WANT A drink?'

"Gabriel and we were sat in the command tent, winds howling in the dark outside. The walls were old hide, furs upon the floors, the air stifling warm. A fire burned in a stone pit at the tent's heart, and we sat as far from it as we could be, glancing up as Gabriel offered a wooden cup of what smelled like rotten fruit sprayed by drunken tomcats.

" 'You jest,' we hissed.

" 'I do, actually. You can die of fucking thirst for all I care.'

"Knocking back the cupful, he poured another. Lifting cup and bottle both, he sat on the furs by the fireside, Ashdrinker across his lap, fixing me with his father's eyes.

" 'I should kill you right now, Celene.'

" 'If you brought us in here to threaten me, save your breath. You survived the fall we gifted you at Cairnhaem well enough, so cease your—'

" 'Don't fuck with me, I'm not talking about the bridge! I mean the wine!'

"We blinked at that. A little impressed, I must admit.

" 'That Montfort bottle you just happened to *discover* in Jènoah's cellar?' he pressed. 'I've been *dreaming* of you, Celene. Every quiet thought, every unguarded moment, there you are. Your blood was mixed with that wine, oui? I'm two parts bound to you.'

"We said nothing, and Gabriel leaned forward, snarling.

" 'You told me Esani who steal the souls of other vampires steal their bloodgifts too. You've drunk the soul of an Ilon, haven't you?'

"We looked down at my hands, trembling as a scream rang faint within my head.

" 'My first communion. The first kith my teacher had me consume. She

— 574 —

was barely more than a fledgling. Her name was Victorine. I can still hear her voice in my h—'

"'On the Cairnhaem bridge,' my brother hissed. 'All those things you whispered while Dior and I argued. *You are ruled by Wrath. Your anger deepens.* You weren't calming me down, you were Pushing me with the power you stole. Trying to drive a wedge between Dior and me. I raised my fucking hand to that girl because of you.'

"'Do not blame me for—'

"'I blame us *both*,' he spat. 'I'm no coward, to deny my part in what I did. The fall was mine, oui. But you Pushed me right to the precipice, don't deny it.'

"'. . . We do not.' I lowered our eyes, lips twisting behind the rags. 'You said you were taking the Grail to the Highlands. I . . . *we* could not allow that, Gabriel.'

"He shook his head, incredulous. 'You poisonous fucking *bitch*.'

"'I *told* you!' I shouted, rising to our feet. 'I *told* you what was at stake! The salvation of this realm, and *all* the souls therein, including mine!' I tore the rags from my face, that he might look upon the horror of it. 'I am *DAMNED*, Gabriel, do you understand that? Trapped in this world, in this body, forever! A parasite, envying the dead yet terrified to die! Because when I do, unless the Grail fulfills her destiny, my soul will burn for all eternity! *That* is what I see when I close *my* eyes! The abyss awaiting me!'

"'And you blame me for that?' he snapped, rising also. 'Not your precious fucking God? Not that petty sadist up there who fashioned this hell for you and named it a life? Seven Martyrs, I was a *boy*, Celene! Laure Voss was orchestrating an invasion of the entire Nordlund when I burned her in Coste. But you put the blame for your suffering on *my* shoulders, instead of the creator of the fucking *universe*?'

"He shook his head, bewildered.

"'Great Redeemer, sister. What the *hell* happened to you?'

"'. . . That is a *long* story, brother.'

"'Well, we have until dawning after amorrow. And you're not leaving my sight.' He sat himself down, knocking back his cup of Black. 'But if you prefer, we can just sit here and glower at each other 'til the sun comes up. You've told Dior what I said, I take it?'

"'We are telling her now. She is . . . expressing displeasure with you.'

"'Doesn't sound like her.' His scoff faded, jaw clenched. 'Are you sure she has things in hand? Because I love Baptiste and Aaron, but if it's a choice between them or her . . .'

"'She is trying. It is thinnest ice she dances on. And Lilidh lurks beneath it.'

"'How did Lilidh do it?' he asked, brow furrowed. 'She and Nikita? We know they're using 'dancer blood, but not where they got it. I thought perhaps since Lilidh was born of the Moonsthrone . . . maybe there's something in *her* veins?'

"'We know not.' I sighed. 'We have been too busy searching for Maryn's tomb outside the dún to watch much within. But the Heartless is at the heart of this, we are certain.'

"Gabriel shook his head, and resigned to wait now, I sank back on our haunches. A lock of hair was glued to the flesh at our throat, and we dragged it loose, slick with dark red. Searching the floor around us, we found the rag I'd cast aside, made to bind it over our face.

"'You don't have to hide yourself from me, Celene.'

"I glanced up at that, into Gabriel's eyes.

"'You're my baby sister,' he said. 'No matter what you look like, or the hateful shit you do. You're the only famille I have left.'

"We lowered our gaze, rag curled in our cracking fist. Gabriel offered his cup again.

"'Sure you don't want a drink?'

"'It tastes like ashes.'

"'The Black's no strawberry liqueur, granted. But it's not *that* bad.'

"'Everything does.' We met his eyes again. 'Did you know that? Food. Wine. Water. It all tastes like ashes to me. Ever since that night. Ever since she . . .' I sighed, staring down at our fist. '*God*, I wanted to kill her. To look her in the eyes as she died. Every night in Wulfric's service I dreamed of taking back what Laure took from me. One more thing you robbed me of, brother. *Vengeance*.'

"'I didn't know, Celene. I didn't know what she'd done.'

"'You *still* do not know. What she cost me.' I hung our head, hair sticking to our torn flesh once more. 'Do you remember when Amélie died? When we were children?'

"Gabriel nodded, our sister's shadow falling across his eyes. 'Of course I do.'

"'I remember the day she disappeared. Gathering mushrooms . . . God, what a thing to die for.' We bit the tatters of our lip, sighing. 'I remember when she came back home. The way you fought her. The way they burned her. But most of all, I remember her funeral. After they scattered her ashes at the crossroads, we spoke, you and I. Do you remember?'

"He shook his head, and my face twisted into what passed for a smile.

"'Strange the memories we cherish, that others cast aside. We sat on the chapel stoop together, the stink of Amélie's ashes in our hair. I asked you if she was going to hell. You told me you didn't know, and I tried to be content with that. But in truth, I thought Ami dying was my fault. I had a secret, Gabriel. A sin. I thought God was punishing me for it.'

"'You were eleven years old, Hellion. What sin would warrant that?'

"I shook our head, avoiding his question.

"'You assured me all was well that day. *This is the work of the Fallen,* you said. *And you've nothing to fear from him while I live.* And you got down on your knees then, and you took my hands and said, *I am your brother, Celene. If ever you find yourself alone in the dark, but call my name, and I will be at your side. You are my only sister now. My blood. My kin. It is you and me against this world, Hellion. Ever outnumbered. Never outmatched.'*

"Gabriel smiled sadly, eyes shining as he whispered, 'Always Lions.'

"'Always Lions,' I nodded. 'God, I *adored* you. How could I not? Mama filled you with such fire that you filled the room, and I felt warmer just sitting near you. And then you were gone. Off on your grand adventure. Leaving me in the mud of Lorson.'

"'What was I to do, Celene?' he demanded. 'What could I have done?'

"'You could have answered my letters? Taken but one moment to pretend you cared? But no, you were busy, I understand. Except you had time to write Mama and ask about your father. You had time for things that mattered to *you.'*

"He hung his head then. We sighed, glancing toward that hateful fire.

"'Do you remember what Papa used to call me when I was a girl?'

"'Little Mountain.'

"'*Steel rusts. Ice melts. But stone stands. And that is what* we *do,* he'd tell me. *We endure the unendurable.* Quite a thing to be told as a child. Somewhat less inspiring than *One day as a lion is worth ten thousand as a lamb.* But still, I paid him heed. I did not begrudge my lot, nor bemoan my fate. No, I resolved to live a life of adventure, like my big brother, whom I so adored.

"'But as I grew older, Mama insisted I give up childish fancy. Even Papa hinted I must soon set aside the girl I was. *Grow up, Celene,* was the constant refrain around our dinner table. *Godssakes, grow up.* I knew what they had in mind for me. A little house. A little famille. A little life. Do you remember Philippe?'

"Gabriel nodded, taking out his pipe. 'The mason's boy.'

"'We used to pick mushrooms together—nobody went alone after what happened to Amélie. One day, he carved our names into a dying tree, circled with a heart, and I called him a dolt. And then he kissed me. Philippe wasn't the brightest flame in the bonfire, bless him. But he was a fine distraction, and we walked often in the woods after that, returning with fewer mushrooms than we might've, his lips bruised and leaves tangled in my hair.'

"My brother lit his pipe, red smoke kissing the air as I talked on.

"'León was my plan—a straight run to the coast. If I found no welcome in our grandfather's house, I fancied to take a ship to Dún Maergenn or Asheve. Those distant cities I'd dreamed of as a girl. The adventure I knew awaited me at the edge of the sky.

"'I knew Philippe would come if I asked. But truth was, I didn't want to. You had fled that nest, and so would I—shedding my skin and soaring far as I could, into the dark and toward who knew what end, save that it would be more than *this*.'

"I hung my head, Gabriel watching me, silent and still.

"'That day I lay in Philippe's arms, and I could feel his heart running quicker than usual. We were beneath our tree, and wintersdeep was coming, and I'd a mind to leave Lorson before it grew too cold to travel. I knew I'd miss him when I was gone, but that I'd go all the same. Arms open to embrace my future as Philippe murmured.

"'*Celene, I must ask you something* . . .

"'And he fumbled in his britches then, drawing out a strip of cloth, embroidered with flowers. A troth tie, I realized. To serve on my wrist until it was replaced with the ring. And I saw it then, as I'd *always* seen it, rushing toward me from Lorson's tiny horizon.

"'Grow up, Celene. Godssakes, *grow up.*

"'He started to ask, but I begged him to stop. He was a good boy, Philippe. He'd have made a fine husband, but all of it—the house, the famille, the life—it seemed a kind of hell to me then. Looking back now, I wonder if I'd have preferred it to the hell waiting.

"'The hell watching.

"'*Bonsoir, sweetlings,* she whispered.

"'We both started at her voice, sitting up in fright. And I saw her in the dark then, staring at me, and my skin prickled with her chill. She seemed a woman in a long crimson cloak, thick red hair spilling down her body. But as she stepped from gloom into light, beneath the shadows of her hood, I saw eyes, black and perilous as oceans.'

"'Laure Voss,' Gabriel murmured.

"'Philippe asked if she was lost, but she stared yet at me. I rose to my feet then, hand slipping to the knife Papa had given me on my saintsday, and I asked who she was.

"'*But a weary traveler, sweetling. Recent come from Coste, seeking dear friends in Lorson. Know thee, the famille de León?*

"'I opened my mouth to speak, and I felt it in my head then, like a whisper, like a kiss; that woman rummaging through my thoughts, my secrets, the images of my mama and the boy she'd loved so dear, the boy who'd not answered a single one of my letters, but promised to be at my side if ever I called, if *ever* I found myself alone in the dark . . .

"'I shouted at Philippe to run. But she was in our heads; shackles of her will, and though I wanted nothing but to fly from that place, she demanded we kneel, and we obeyed, sinking into dead leaves and new snow. And then, she showed us her face.

"'Oh, she was a *beauty*. Flaming hair and lips stained the color of wine. But her eyes were black and hard as stone, and her skin was marred—cracked and greyed from when you'd burned her, like leather too long in the sun. Her hand snaked out, lifting my chin, and I trembled then. Because I knew now those were not wine stains on her lips.

"'*His sister. Oh, this be poetry, sure and true.*

"'Philippe demanded she unhand me, and her eyes fell on the troth tie he'd offered me. She lifted it from the snow, and he roared that it did not belong to her.

"'*To whom, then, should I gift it? This lioness beside thee? Know thee not, her plan to flee the stinking mire she was birthed in, and the oafish hands of the mason's brat who thought that he might tame her? Celene Castia loves thee not, Philippe Ramos.*

"'I screamed at her to stop it, but she only stared at Philippe and smiled.

"'*Look into her eyes, and see, boy. Look upon the truth she denied thee. Let thy last sensation 'neath this wretched sun be that of thy breaking heart . . .*

"'I begged him not to listen. Not to look. But he did. Tears in his eyes as he whispered my name. And she crushed his throat. Just closed her hand and *squeezed*. His blood was all over me, and I was screaming, *screaming* his name. And she sank down before me, smearing his blood on my lips as she shushed me with her finger.

"'*Oh, angel. No tears now, love, but joy. Liberty be thy wish, no? To slip the smoth'ring cell of mud-flecked streets and seek bright nights in places far and flung?*

"'*Please* . . . I begged her, hand tightening on my knife. *Please* . . .

"'*Kiss me, then. Kiss me, and all thy desires shall I grant thee.*

"'And my stomach rolled as she pressed cold lips to mine. But I was a daughter of de León and Castia both. Little mountain. Stone lioness. And as our lips parted, I thrust my knife right into her neck. All my fear, all my hate was bent behind that blow, but the blade Papa made me only shattered on her skin. And as her hand closed around my throat, I screamed again. Not for my papa. Nor my God. No, I screamed for the boy who promised he'd save me.

"'I screamed for *you*, Gabriel.

"'She tore my throat out. Like a journal page unwanted. I felt bone rip like paper, heard the sound of tearing cloth, understanding it was my skin. And the Wraith sank to her feast then, and all would've been pain and fear but for the Kiss; that bleak rapture taking hold as her fangs sank home. Horror and euphoria. Terror and bliss.'

"I looked across the flames at the pipe in my brother's hand.

"'Awful, is it not? To love the thing that is destroying you? But she was hungry at least, Gabriel. Laure brought her appetite to Lorson that day. So in the end, it was quick.'

"My brother stared at me in the firelight, drawing on his pipe with shaking hands. I could see the glint of tears in his eyes, his voice thick and graveled as he whispered.

"'I'm sorry. I'm so sorry that happened to you. I didn't know, Celene. I didn't understand what they were like. Nor the lengths they'd go to for vengeance.'

"'But now you do.'

"He nodded, looking at the troth ring on his finger. 'Now I do.'

"He breathed red smoke, dragging one hand down his face. I could see he was tired, bruised, the heart of him torn open at all this; Baptiste and Aaron and Dior and me. But like a child staring at the eclipse that is blinding him, he could not look away.

"'But how did you find the Esani? How did you become . . .'

"'This?'

"He nodded, swallowing. 'That.'

"'The sin I spoke of.' I sighed, staring into those flames and back on far-flung years. 'The one I thought God was punishing me for. My deal with a devil.'

"'I don't understand. What devil, Celene?'

"'The first vampire I ever met.'

"Gabriel frowned. 'Amélie? Sh—'

"'No, not our sister, Gabriel,' I sighed. 'I was eleven years old when poor Ami was murdered. But I was ten the first time I met *him*.'

"My brother's brow darkened, suspicion creeping in on slippered feet. And though I think he knew the answer already, still he asked, staring yet at that eclipse.

"'Met who, Celene?'

"'Your father, of course.'"

VIII

TERRIBLY CLOSE TO
DANGEROUS PLACES

"DIOR LACHANCE WAS many things in life, sinner. Thief. Liar. Messiah. She wore many faces in the time we knew her; desperate urchin and fledgling savior and the Red Hand of God Himself. But beyond all that, it must be said, she was always something of a clotheshorse.

"She was not accustomed to wearing the guise of a mademoiselle, having spent most of her life hiding as a monsieur. Yet having noted the way the Lady á Maergenn's eyes followed her when Reyne thought Dior was not looking, we suspect the Grail was growing to appreciate the gown Lilidh had given her, despite initial misgivings.

"But as previously discussed, corsets are of little help when snatching some poor fool's purse, and additional layers of underthings help not at all when engaged in matters felonious. So, she'd abandoned the gown in her boudoir, dressed now in maids' homespun as she stole through the secret passage behind her bookshelf, slipping down a narrow stair, through a servants' entrance, and out into the storm-washed courtyard.

"The impending attack had all in disarray, and the bailey of Dún Maergenn was a scene of almost-chaos. Scorched were being sent to the outer walls in droves, runners and servants dashing to and fro, quartermasters bellowing for order. News had apparently spread among the prisoners in Auldtunn that an attack was imminent, and hundreds of hapless mortal prisoners were at the dún's gatehouse now, pressing to be let in. Squabbles were breaking out among the soldiers—the feuds of vampire masters spilling out among their scorched. And to finish all, the storm was raging harder, the snow so thick it was near to blinding.

"Through all this, stole the Holy Grail of San Michon, clad in plain servants' cloth. Though all was bedlam about her, she was a girl raised in shadow, thieving to eat and lying to live. Beneath the shouting and thunder, she made her way past the barracks, the distillery, finally to the smithy, there crouching in the forge-warm dark at the building's back. All was abustle within, Baptiste and other blackthumbs busy with anvil and flame, doing last-minute work before the assault. We could see an ironsaw hung upon the walls with other tools, sharp and saw-toothed. But even a girl born in shadow is not *made* of them, and there was no way she could filch it without discovery.

"She backed away, sucking her lip, batting us off again as we tried to settle on her skin. We knew not what she'd seen in that secret chamber beneath the Mothermaid's tomb, only that she appeared *furious* with us, pale blue eyes flashing as she swatted us away. And looking about her, the tumult and the rush, she spied young Joaquin Marenn by the stables, down on his knee and hugging his hound, Elaina.

"'Farewell, girl,' he murmured. 'You must take care of yourself now. I fear I'm—'

"'You don't have to say good-bye to her yet, M. Marenn.'

"The boy near flew out of his skin as Dior whispered, crouching now in the shadows at the stables' flanks. Sighing with relief as he saw her, Joaquin took a deep breath to steady himself. Elaina nosed up to Dior, tail wagging as she slobbered on the Grail's face. Her master was dragging his hipflask from his boot, taking a long swallow.

"Peering at him closer, we saw young Joaquin was armed for battle; an oversize chain shirt sat ill upon his shoulders under a threadbare padded tabard and a green cloak, a sword at his belt. The boy stood out among the soldiery like a wooden horse in a charge, and as he pressed the cork back into his flask, his hands were shaking.

"'They're sending you to the walls,' Dior breathed.

"'They're sending *everyone* to the bloody walls,' he spat. 'I've never swung a sword in my *life*, and there's an army of Highlanders out there, baying for blood.'

"Dior squeezed his hand. 'Fear not. They're my friends.'

"'Your *friends*?' he hissed, glancing about to make sure no one overheard them. 'Every able body is being sent to the Newtunn battlements, and when dawn comes, your bloody *friends* are coming right over the top of us!'

"'Breathe easy.' Dior crouched lower, her voice a whisper. 'We hit Nikita and Lilidh *today*. Cut off the head, and this serpent dies.'

"Joaquin swallowed thick, his face pale. 'Is Isla . . .'

"'She's well. She's with us.' Dior smiled. 'I promised her, and I'll promise you the same; you two are getting your Ever After if it bloody kills me. But I need an ironsaw, and the smithy is full. You think you can distract them? Half a moment is all I need.'

"The boy was breathing swift, clearly still afeared at the thought of the attack amorrow, and what might be happening to his beloved tonight. But he steeled himself, looked into the Grail's eyes, and in his own, we saw it again; that burning fire of total belief.

"'Oui. I can do that for you, Mlle Dior.'

"The Grail squeezed his hand, and he unstopped his hipflask again, swallowed another belt for courage. Apparently in need of the same, Dior snatched the flask, downed the remainder in a single gulp. Wincing, she dragged her knuckles across her lips.

"'Seven Martyrs, this shit tastes worse than it smells.'

"'Keeps us warm.' Joaquin gifted her a sad smirk. ''Til the killing starts at least.'

"She looked around the bailey—those men and women set to die at dawn. Most were terrified, barely half of them true soldiers, the rest press-ganged rabble like poor Joaquin here. They stood shivering in small knots, or staring toward that awful pit of bones, or marching out grim and silent toward the Newtunn walls. Dior ran a thumb over the hipflask in her hand, the initials of Joaquin and his beloved Isla engraved on the metal. She looked toward the distillery, then the forge, Baptiste's silhouette etched against the light.

"'Celene, go keep a watch for me in the smithy,' she commanded.

"Our wings fluttered at that, uncertain. We were perched on the stables above her head, a spot of crimson on snow grey. We pressed upon her thoughts to see her game, but as ever, they were a locked room. She looked up at us then, the reflection of whatever she'd seen in that chamber below the Mothermaid's Tomb carved upon her eyes as she spat.

"'*Now*, Celene.'

"We obeyed reluctantly, flitting across the courtyard, buffeted by howling winds. Through the snow-tossed air, into the forgelight, we settled upon the smithy wall, our wings shivering in the heat of those flames. We counted fourteen men in all, blackthumbs and dogsbodies, hammering, hauling, hefting.

But returning to Dior, we saw she'd already left her hide, stealing over to the rear of the ironworks. We heard a ruckus; Elaina barking, the crash of metal within the forge. And swift as the wind, Dior was slipping inside, into a babble of voices, Joaquin apologizing as the Grail stole out the back again, a conspicuous bulge under her skirts. We settled on her shoulder, and she seemed content to let us ride now, creeping back along the walls toward the dún, past that dreadful pit of frozen bones, back through the servants' entrance.

"She was stealing up the secret stair as Reyne caught her coming the other way. The older girl's gaze yet bore a trace of that shadow from beneath the tomb, but Dior's own eyes shone with excitement as she whispered, 'I have the saw. We need t—'

"'We need to get you upstairs, now,' Reyne hissed.

"Dior blinked, lowering her voice further. 'Why?'

"Reyne talked as she walked, dragging Dior back toward the bedchambers. 'Nikita is to make a speech in the Hall of Plenty before the dawn. All his capitaines and lords will be assembled. He's demanded your presence, properly attired.'

"'What the *hell* for?'

"Reyne reached the top of the stair, hauling Dior down the narrow passage. 'There's whisper of mutiny among the court. He means to hold you up as proof the Voss will come to their aid. Buoy the courage of his bloodlords before the Highlanders strike.'

"Dior looked down at her grubby servants' cloth. 'Shit, I'm n—'

"'I'll help you, fear not. But we must hurry.'

"The bookshelf creaked open, the pair stealing back into Dior's boudoir, closing the hidden door behind them. Dragging the ironsaw from beneath her skirts, Dior tossed it on the bed. 'I don't know if it'll cut silver, but it looked the sharpest they had.'

"Reyne nodded, hiding the blade beneath the covers. 'I'll get it to Gilly and Morgana after we're done. Come, let's be swift.'

"Dior kicked off her shoes, her hose, and I saw she was bleeding again; that gash in the arch of her foot reopened. Dragging off her homespun dress and casting it aside, she stood near naked—clad only in her silken shift, pale and thin and shivering.

"'This doesn't feel right.'

"'Nothing I've not seen before,' Reyne teased, slipping an under-tunic over her head.

"Dior looked at the older girl and scoffed, but her smile swiftly died.

"'That's not what I mean. I mean asking Gilly and Morgana to go into danger.'

"'You won't have to ask. They'll offer.' Reyne looked her in the eye. 'That's what love and loyalty are, and they hold both now for you, doubt it not.'

"'They don't even *know* me. How can they—'

"'They know you risk all for the sake of people you've never met. They know you freed them and the boys they love from service to a pair of the most twisted evils this world has ever known. They know you'd spill your last drop of blood for this if needs be.'

"Reyne sank to her knees, binding Dior's bleeding foot with a fresh strip of cloth.

"'They know you as well as I, Dior Lachance. They know you to be brave as martyrs and bright as heavens and fierce as wolves. That you are someone worth fighting for.'

"The Grail scowled, reaching up to drag her mop of ashen hair down over her face. But her cheeks were flushed with the Princess's flattery, heart quickening at the older girl's smile, her gentle touch as Reyne slipped a new brace of silken hose up her bare legs. Again, the Princess's hands were skirting terribly close to dangerous places, and perhaps to take her mind off how high those fingertips were drifting, Dior spoke.

"'Why don't you have an accent?'

"Reyne blinked at the strange question, tying a silken bow around Dior's thigh. 'I *do* have an accent.'

"'Not an Ossian one. Gilly and Morgana have accents heavy enough to anchor a ship in the harbor. But you sound . . . different.'

"Reyne breathed deep, finished tying Dior's stocking. Her fingertips slipped down the inside of Dior's thigh, and the girl's heart thundered like a warhorse at gallop. But standing, Reyne bid Dior raise her arms, lifting the gown of pale velvet over the Grail's head. The pair battled with the dress a moment, cursing, finally hauling it into place. Pawing her hair from her face, Dior saw the Princess was staring at her now, her mismatched gaze gone heavy.

"'You asked why I wasn't in any of the portraits around the keep.'

"'I never asked why,' Dior replied. 'It's none of my business why.'

"'My mother . . . that is to say, the . . .'

"Reyne fell silent, smooth brow furrowed. Dior reached toward her, uncertain, fingertips hovering just shy of the other girl's skin.

"'You don't have to tell me, Reyne. It's aright.'

"But the Lady shook her head, resolute. 'I told you my mother's husband died during the Clan Wars. She ruled Ossway from the Splintered Isles to the Moonsthrone by then. All she'd fought for had come to pass. But . . . she was lonely with her husband gone.'

"Reyne smoothed back an errant lock of hair, sighing.

"'She met a man on her campaigns. A wanderer. A young warrior from the north who knew poetry and philosophy, who charmed a battle-weary widow with his stories and smile. I think she loved him. But . . . only briefly. And then he was gone.'

"'He was your father,' Dior murmured.

"'I don't even know his name.' Reyne sighed. 'But I know when he left, he broke Mother's heart. And I think whenever she looked at me, she saw that man who'd made her such a fool. I think I shamed her. So, she sent me away. Raised in Elidaen by second cousins.'

"'That's pigshit,' Dior whispered. 'It wasn't your fault your papa was a dog.'

"'No.' Reyne sighed. 'Now close your eyes and turn around. I'll try to be gentle.'

"'. . . You what?'

"The Princess held up the dreaded corset between them. And groaning understanding, the Grail obeyed, holding her breath as Reyne began strapping her in.

"'Mother spared no expense in raising me at least,' she said, binding the stays. 'A matter of principle, I think. I was trained in swordcraft by the Chante-Lames at Montfort. Educated by the Holy Sisters of Evangeline at the Académie Grande in Augustin.'

"'Lucky for some.' Dior winced, insides adjusting as Reyne tightened her whalebone prison. 'My mama never even bothered to *feed* me most days toward the end.'

"'I wonder which is worse,' Reyne smiled, cold and mirthless. 'The mother who doesn't care, or the mother who only pretends to.'

"'I wager you dress and eat better with the latter, Highness.'

"Reyne chuckled at that. 'Touché.'

"Dior was sat down before the looking glass, closing her eyes as the older girl began powdering her face. 'What made you come back to Ossway, then?'

"'I returned when the wars with the Dyvok deepened. This was my home-land, and I wanted to help. But neither Mother nor her court nor my sisters welcomed me back. They treated me as the bastard. The halfblood. I stood silent in those war councils, I walked past those portraits every day, not a single painting of me anywhere, and I knew what they all thought of me. When the Blackheart attacked the city, Una was declared commander of Mother's legions. Cait was a captain in her fleet. I was charged with guarding the bloody foodstores.' Reyne scoffed, bitter and sharp. 'Thirteen years studying with the Bladesingers of Montfort for *that*. The soldiers who followed me only did so because they were ordered to. We never even got to fight.'

"Dior's eyes were closed as Reyne edged them with kohl, but she heard the girl sigh.

"'I was born a daughter of the greatest leader this country has ever known. And no one in my whole life expected a drop of greatness from me. Not even her.'

"'Then she was an idiot.'

"Dior opened dark-rimmed eyes, found Reyne scowling at her.

"'Do not talk about my mother so,' the Princess spat. 'Niamh á Maergenn united nine warring clans to sit her throne. She conquered all Ossway by the time she was—'

"'Twenty-five, I know, I *know*.' Dior rolled her eyes. 'She forged a blade out of her enemies' swords and shot fireballs from her arse and still had perfect tits and no stretch marks after squeezing out five puppies, I'm sure. Doesn't mean she wasn't a cunt.'

"'How *dare* you!' Reyne spat, stepping back. 'Who are you to talk so? Some common—'

"'I know what it is to grow up with a mother who doesn't care. I know a woman who has a statue of herself erected in her own bloody foyer probably had some demons, and growing up in that statue's shadow probably left you with some too.'

"Dior rose to her feet, eyes on the Princess.

"'But you told me yourself, Highness. We're not where we're born, or who we're born from. That's *doubly* true for you. The folk who follow you tonight don't do so because you were born Niamh's daughter. They do it because the fire in you warms all the folk around you. Because nothing feels quite as impossible when you're near.'

"Dior planted a soft kiss on the Princess's cheek.

"'You don't stand in the Nineswords' shadow, Reyne á Maergenn. You burn *far* too bright for that.' The Grail breathed deep and sighed. 'Now, I'd better get—'

"Dior fell silent as Reyne touched her cheek, running soft fingertips over her powdered skin. The Princess's hand was shaking, her pupils wide and dark as skies above. And drawing one deep breath, small spots of pink at her freckled cheeks, she stepped slowly forward as if in a daze, pressing soft lips to Dior's. The touch was tentative, gentle; a kiss and a question all at once. And drawing back for one endless moment to search her eyes, Dior answered, crushing her lips to Reyne's. They melted against each other then, all bright flame and soft sighs, Reyne enfolding Dior's waist in her embrace, Dior throwing her arms around the taller girl's neck. And there in the gloom, they kissed, as if for that moment all the world ceased to matter—not the rising cold nor the coming storm, not the battle looming nor the ending beckoning, but just those two, skin to skin, all of them ashiver.

"It lasted but a handful of heartbeats, that kiss, but it seemed to promise more, if only they were given the chance at it. And as they parted, Dior chased her quarry as she retreated, scattering the Princess's cheeks and lips with a handful of tiny kisses, each seeming a vow to return; not a good-bye, but a Godspeed, not an ending, but a beginning.

"'First time?' Dior breathed, lips brushing Reyne's.

"The Princess shivered. 'Not the last, I hope.'

"'Something to pray for.' Dior kissed her again, swift and burning. 'Now get my hair on, Highness, before they rip my pretty fucking head off.'

"That single word—that *they*—killed all the warmth left in the moment, inviting the bitterbleak cold back into the room. Working swift, Reyne fixed the tower of powdered curls atop Dior's head, applying a gloss of thin red paint to those bee-stung lips, a touch of darker ink to the beauty spot on Dior's cheek. But as the Grail stood, their fingers touched, just a breath, just a beat, and in that tiny fragment of stolen time, all the warmth returned, a fire burning now between them, the promise of something warmer still after the dawn, and one more reason to live to see it.

"Fingers parting, but no longer apart, the girls descended to the feast."

IX

FAMILLE IS FOREVER

"'MY FATHER.'

"Gabriel stared at us across the crackling flames, red smoke spilling from his nostrils as if he were about to breathe fire. This was difficult for me—paying attention to two places, two conversations at once. Most of my mind in the tent with my brother, but a sliver with Dior, watching as she followed Princess Reyne toward the Hall of Plenty.

"'Your father,' we replied.

"'You knew him.'

"'I *met* him. I do not know if anyone could say they truly knew him.'

"My brother shook his head, incredulous. 'Why the *fuck* didn't you tell me?'

"'I was a child, Gabriel. I was *frightened*.'

"'And afterward?' he demanded. 'All our time on this road together?'

"I fixed him with our dead eyes, the hate glittering in them my only answer.

"'Twenty-one. *Twenty-one years,* and you knew all along.' He glowered at me, storm grey deepening near to black. 'Tell me now. Who was he? How is it you met him?'

"We steepled fingertips together, pressing them to our bloody chin. Years and shadows so wide and deep that I was afraid to step back into them. The whispers of those souls I carried were crashing close to my surface now, roiling in the undertow of my thoughts. Some nights they grew so loud, they were all I could hear—never more so than when I looked back into years behind. I could understand why Master Jènoah had taken his own life—I could not forgive his weakness, Historian, but I could *understand* it. What must it have been like for those Faithful who lived for *centuries* with this weight?

— 591 —

How could a person not drown in the flood of those memories, those lives and thoughts not their own?

"What a price we paid, to be Faithful . . .

"'You fell very ill,' we told my brother. 'When you were twelve, do you remember?'

"'The flux?' Gabriel frowned, shaking his head. 'I remember a little . . .'

"'You were delirious for much of it. It laid you out so hard and swift, Père Louis gave you the last rites. The elderwives could fashion no cure. Mama could not sleep, sitting by your side—her only son, her favorite—whispering desperate prayers and watching you fade with each passing day. Until she could watch no more.

"'You scorned my papa for the way he treated you, Gabriel, but much as you two fought, he still ran seventy miles to Brinnleaf to fetch their apothecary. A Castia he was, through and through. Amélie went with him, but I refused to leave your side, instead sitting with Mama, praying and watching you fade. We were never close, she and I. Too much alike perhaps. But never closer than in our love for you.'

"I hung our head, staring down at the cracked skin on our hands.

"'I woke on the sixth night of your sickness. It took a breath to realize all was silence, and for an awful moment, I feared Mama's prayers had ceased because *you* had also. But peering down from the loft, I saw her not sitting with you, but standing by the hearth. In her palm, I saw a glint in the firelight—a ruby, I thought, big as a thumbnail. But as I watched, she tossed the gem into the flames, and I heard a *sizzle*, smelled a scent I'd no understanding of back then, but would come to know as well as my own name.'

"'Blood,' Gabriel whispered.

"'The next day, she acted no different. I thought I'd dreamed that strangeness. But three nights later, in the deep of the witching hour, I heard scratching at our front door.

"'Mama looked up to me, but I kept my eyes closed, watching through my lashes as she rose from your bedside. And lifting a log of burning rowanwood from the fire, she opened the door with shaking hands. A chill crawled down my spine as I saw no man nor woman waiting on our threshold, but a cat. Eyes red as blood. Fur black as midnight.

"'*Bonsoir, Grace,* Mama murmured. *Take me to your master.*

"'The door clicked as she departed, and I lay in the dark, wondering. I'd no clue what to make of this business, but it smelled of devilry to me. And so, checking you were well, and taking the knife Papa gave me for my saintsday, I slipped into the night. Mama was easy to follow, stealing through Lorson's muddy streets, into the woods beyond. I was very frightened and *very* cold, but if there was wickedness afoot, I'd see the bottom of it. I loved Mama in my own way, but I never truly *liked* her, and the notion she might be some sort of witch seemed not so far from possibility.'

"I met my brother's eyes, smiling with our ruined face.

"'God knows Papa had called her as much when he was in his cups.'

"Gabriel chuckled, hanging his head, and I continued with the tale.

"'Mama followed the cat, and I followed her, into the dark. The animal reached a clearing among the dead trees, and sat, cleaning its paws. Mama waited, burning torch aloft, pale and cold. I found a hide in the belly of a sundered oak nearby, peering out through dead scrub and wondering if I should have ever left my bed.

"'And then I saw him, Gabriel. Not so much stepping from the dark, but *shifting* into focus like a mirage. As if perhaps he had always been there, and only by some measure of his will had I been allowed to lay eyes upon him at all.

"'He was tall like you. Pale skin and long dark hair, rippling in the night wind like bolts of blackest silk. His eyes were grey like yours, and piercing, God, like *knives* fit to cut the heart from your breast. I was only a girl, but I knew what handsome was, and I understood this man surpassed the notion in ways that folk would die for. Kill for.

"'He was swathed all in black, like the night itself. A lord of it. A *prince* of it. When he moved, *it* seemed to move too. He knelt to stroke the cat, and she arched her back, adoring. And eyes on Mama, he rose and bowed deep then, like to a nobleborn lady at court. He spoke with a voice so warm and deep it made me shiver. And though he was more pleasing to the eye than any creature I'd seen, still that pale prince made me terrified.

"'*My darling,* he said as if speaking to an angel.

"'*My dearest,* she replied as if the word hurt to say.

"'*Ye look . . . different.*

"'*You look exactly the same.*

"'They both seemed saddened by that, and for a moment, he looked away. I crept closer, low, silent, the knife clutched in my fist. I knew not who this man was, but from the way he and Mama gazed at each other, I sensed something deeper between them; a secret, dark as wine and sweet as chocolat.

"'*Merci*, Mama said. *For coming when I called.*

"'*Would that I could have come sooner. But the road from San Yves is more treacherous than ever. Daysdeath hath all in disarray. The promise of blood hangs heavy in the air, Auriél. Blood, and the End of All Things.*

"'*I care not for all things*, Mama said. *I care for one.*

"He lowered his eyes then, black curtains hung about the portrait of his face.

"'*Ye were but a girl, Auriél. Ye gifted me something I thought forever lost, and I am changed forevermore by it. But never should I have taken what ye offered. It was wrong to claim it then. It would be doubly wrong to reclaim it now.*

"And she laughed then, cruel and cold. *You conceited fool. I speak not of you.*

"His mood grew fell at that. His pride stung. Mama steeled herself, hands in fists.

"'*Our son is dying.*

"'That word struck me like a hammerblow. Heart falling in my chest. But looking closer, at the cut of his jaw and the grey of his eyes, at last I understood why Papa beat you so hard when he loved Amélie and I so dear, brother. I knew, sure as my own name . . .

"'*The child's keeping was thy choice. He is* thy *son, Auriél. Not ours.*

"'She clenched her jaw, raised her chin. *My son, then, is dying.*

"'*Then send ye for a priest.*

"She held out a cup from our pantry. *You can cure his ills. As you once cured* mine.

"'I saw his face soften then; some tender memory between them. But the shadow returned, darkening those perilous eyes. As he folded his arms, I saw that black cat again, sitting nearby, watching Mama as the pale prince spoke with a voice heavy and cold.

"'*If it be the Almighty's will that he die, then he shall die.*

"'*You bastard*, Mama spat. *Do you know what I have lost for love of that boy? And you who lost* nothing *tell me I must sit meek and silent as I lose him too? I will not have it!* She lifted that burning torch, face twisted in rage. *You owe us! You owe* me!

"He stood taller then. All his dark sovereignty unveiled. The flame in Mama's hand sparked in his eyes as the shadows about him deepened. The birds in the dying trees whispered, the dark ran thicker about him, and his voice was iron and stone.

"'*Do not tell us what we owe. We have given more than thou shalt* ever *know.*

"*'If you'll not give it, then I will take it, damn you!* Mama snarled, and she lunged, torch swung like a club. But swift as sparrow wings, he knocked the flame aside, catching up her wrists. She might well have been wrestling with a statue, hair come loose from her braid as she thrashed and kicked in fury, that pale prince unmoving and unmoved.

"'*Stop,* he told her.

"'Mama fought him a moment longer, face flushed. And then she sagged, rage running to despair as she sank to her knees. She was a prideful woman, Mama. No man's serf. And yet, as she opened her mouth, I knew her next breath would be drawn only to beg.

"'*Give it to her,* I demanded.

"'They turned, the prince's eyes flashing with fury and Mama's with fear. I stood at the edge of the clearing, one hand clutching my knife, the other, the scruff of that pretty black cat. I knew not if the prince truly cared for the beast, but if he had the keeping of your salvation, brother, I was willing to risk his ire. Such was my love for you.

"'*I know not what aid you can give,* I said. *But give—*

"'I did not see him move. All I knew was one moment I stood with that cat at my mercy, and the next, I hung in his. Hauled against a dead tree, his face inches from mine, and that close, I could see his flesh was porcelain, his teeth sharp as a wolf's. I was *so* frightened. But it's not 'til we're thrown to the hellfire that we discover how bright we burn. *Little Mountain,* Papa called me, and that night, I learned just as he said, I was made of *stone.*

"'I stabbed the hand that held me, but his flesh was hard, and the blade did little but scratch him. Mama was screaming to let me go, but he heeded her not at all, glancing instead to the pearl of blood welling at the cut I'd gifted him. I saw hunger in him then; a beast so ageless and terrible I felt my bladder loose. And I whispered, frightened, oh, God, so *very* frightened. But somehow, yet more furious.

"'*Let m-me go, monster.*

"'And I saw that word strike him, sure as I had thrown a rock between those hungry eyes. It seemed he saw himself as we did, then—not a prince who wore the night, who mortal women would kill for, but a horror from some fireside tale. A devil, clutching a terrified, piss-soaked girl as her mother begged for her life.

"'*Almighty God . . .* he whispered.

"'He put me down, looking at his hands as if they were not his own.

Mama held me tight but my eyes were fixed on him, and my heart froze as I saw he was crying, save the tears in his lashes were made of blood.

"'*Forgive me, M*^{lle} *de León.*

"'*My name is Castia,* I spat.

"'He stared at me, his voice like a lost little boy's. *Ye bear thy father's name. But thou hast thy mother's heart. I had forgot how fierce that song.*

"'Stooping, he lifted Mama's cup from where it had fallen. Mama held me tight, sobbing as he bit into his wrist, filling the goblet to the brim. By the time he placed the cup back on the ground, that lost little boy I had seen was gone.

"'*Call upon me no more, Auriél. For thine own sake. And thy children's.*

"'Those storm-grey eyes fell on me, the beast lurking yet in their depths.

"'*It is said all cats have nine lives, little one. Lionesses too.* He inclined his head. *Have a care, how ye spend the eight that remain thee.*

"'The cat growled.

"'The shadows rippled.

"'And like a dream at dawn, he was gone.'

"We sat in the tent at the end of my tale, Gabriel and I, the song of the storm outside the only sound between us. He drew deep on his damnable pipe, eyes flushed red by the silversaint's accursed sacrament as they finally drifted up to meet mine.

"'Mama fed me his blood?'

"I nodded. 'And by dawn, you were hale and whole. I knew this was devilry, but Mama bid me tell no one. I asked her then if you were that thing's son, and I could see the grief in her eyes as she replied. *He is your brother. That is all that matters, Celene. Steel rusts. Ice melts. Even your papa's beloved stone becomes sand in time. But famille . . .*

"'She squeezed my hand then, so tight it hurt.

"'*Famille is forever.*

"Gabriel stared across those flames at me. Smoke drifting from his lips.

"'You saved my life.'

"I shrugged then, ragged face twisting in my almost smile. 'Always, Lions.'

"He hung his head, pawing at his eyes. And touching our own, I found them wet with blood. It is a strange thing sometimes, sinner, to be a sibling. So much rancor and love, hate and history, the storms of the present never quite enough to disturb the millpond of the past. It is quite a thing, to grow from children together, seed to sapling, side by side. It is a bond forged in iron, that tie, and it takes a great deal of work to sunder it entirely.

"'All my life, I wondered who he was,' Gabriel sighed. 'Why I never knew him. Sometimes I'd fancy the reason he never had anything to do with me was that he didn't know I existed. But he *did* know. He just didn't give a shit.'

"He nodded then, as if to himself.

"'Aright. I can live with that.'

"'He cared, I think. A part of him. But there were many parts to your father.'

"Gabriel glanced up at that. 'I thought you said you didn't know him?'

"'I did not. I cannot imagine anyone truly did. He was the bearer of countless souls, Gabriel. I do not think even your father knew where they ended and he began. He was cruel and cold most nights, but others, he was the brightest fire in the room. I would go to sleep, understanding why Mama had loved him, only to wake with him in a rage again. He was a thousand faces, a thousand moods, tearing himself in a thousand different directions. Faith was all that kept him anchored. His unfailing belief in Illia's teachings, the crusade of the Esana, the certainty that one day, the Grail would be found, the gates to the kingdom of heaven opened, and he and all the damned souls he carried inside him saved.'

"My brother's eyes bored into mine, and we saw understanding dawning at last in that storm grey. 'He told Mama where he came from that night. *San Yves.* And after Laure killed you . . . you went looking for him.'

"'And I found him. His name was Wulfric, Gabriel.'

"'My father . . .' he whispered.

"I nodded. 'Your father was my teacher.'"

X

EVER AFTER

"THE SUN DREW near to rising. The Blackheart's court was gathered. And Dior's heart was beating so hard it seemed set to burst out of her throat.

"The monsters watched her as she passed through the Hall of Plenty, clad in silk and velvet, white as olden snows, Reyne silent at her side. Nikita's lords were glutting themselves in one final feast before the coming battle, the iron and copper of fresh blood staining the air. The minstrels were playing a lively tune, and two scorched were battling for the court's amusement— starving prisoners stripped down to loincloths and hewing at each other with blunt knives. Other folk were strung up from the ceiling, throats opened like saintsday gifts and spilled into brimming goblets by the maids below.

"Kiara stood alone against one wall; the Wolfmother shunned by her fellows where once, they'd shown her raucous, bloody praise. Storm clouds were gathered at her brow as she glanced toward her father, but Nikita ignored her completely, intent upon Dior. Kane sat with the Draigann and Alix, Lilidh's children whispering among themselves, reveling in their cousin's humiliation. Lilidh herself reclined on her throne above it all, clad in her gown of blood-red silk, goat horns curling at her brow. Prince lay beside his mistress, the wolf's ice-blue eye fixed on the Princess and Grail as they approached.

"For her part, Dior never took her gaze off the Heartless, lips curling in a shy smile as she drew near. She played the part of the besotted lover with all her grifter's guile, but by the hammering of her pulse beneath our wings, we knew she thought only of the plan; the deathblow that, with fortune, would fall this very day. Gillian and Morgana need only saw the silvered swords from the Mothermaid's crypt below, and then, it was simply a matter of waiting for the time to strike. Gabriel had faith in her, Phoebe also, a whole army beside them. And blood-drunk as they were, these fiends *must* sleep sometime.

"Gilly and Morgana and Lady Arlynn stood at Lilidh's back as always, resplendent in gowns of green velvet brocade. Declan and Maeron waited among Nikita's scorched, gathered behind the Blackheart's throne. All studiously ignored her, playing their roles to perfection—to stumble here was to die, and all knew it. Aaron loomed at Nikita's right hand, swathed in black silk and pale majesty. As Dior glanced to him, we caught a glimmer of red in his lashes, as if he were close to tears. But the capitaine kept his expression hard as stone as Dior and Reyne reached those thrones and curtseyed.

"'Mistress,' they murmured, heads bowed. And turning to Nikita, 'Count Dyvok.'

"Lilidh glowered at Reyne. 'Tardy as ever, Worm.'

"'Apologies, Mistress,' Reyne said, dipping lower. 'I humbly beg your forgiveness.'

"'Beg as thou wilt. I've a mind to feed you to those savages outside.'

"'The fault was mine, Mistress.' Dior sank to her knees, gazing on Lilidh as a poet to her muse. 'I only wished to look my best for you. I want *only* to please you.'

"Lilidh's fury cooled then, ever so slight, black eyes roaming Dior's gown. A small cheer went up in the background as one scorched blooded the other with his shank, red spraying on black stone. The Heartless glanced to Reyne, picking at the carved armrest of her throne with one long claw.

"'Forgiveness I grant thee,' she growled. 'Thank thy God we have more pressing business this night than to break thee into pieces.'

"'Merci, my mistress.' Reyne swallowed hard, pulse thumping harder. 'Merci.'

"The Princess took her place in the shadows. Dior knelt at Lilidh's right hand, looking out over that sea of kith, the brawling thralls. Only an hour remained until the sun rose, and for all Nikita's bloodlords knew, the Black Lion and his Highlanders came with it. Despite the feast put on for them by their Priori, we could see tension writ on every face, disquiet in every stare. All save Nikita's, that is, his lip curling now as he glanced to his sibling.

"'Too forgiving of thy pet's ineptitudes, sister,' he murmured. 'Too attached thou art become, methinks. Whatever shall ye do, when forced to give her up?'

"'I shall obey the will of my Priori,' the Heartless replied, studiously avoiding her brother's gaze. 'And curse that same fool, who let this prize slip through his fingers.'

"Nikita chuckled then, sipping from his goblet of blood. 'Ye defy me, still.'

"'I defy thee not,' Lilidh murmured, voice low, features calm. 'I simply say we can win through this day without handing our treasures to the Voss.'

"'Thy years of military experience lead thee to this conclusion?'

"'Common *sense* leads me to this conclusion,' she hissed. 'At the very least, we control the Gulf of Wolves. Draigann's fleet awaits below.' She nodded to her broodson, still consorting with Alix and Kane. 'Be thou so afeared, brother, we could quit this f—'

"'Afeared?'

"A soft murmur rippled among the court as the Blackheart rose to his feet. "'*AFEARED?*'

"The minstrels fell silent, the battling thralls still, dreadful quiet settling over the hall as the echoes of Nikita's roar rang on the walls.

"'Tell me *I* fear?' he spat, glowering at his sibling. 'When ye propose we tuck tail and run from the city we *bled* to conquer? We are Dyvok! We balk not at the yapping of a handful of flea-struck Highland hounds!'

"'Thou art correct, of course, Priori,' Lilidh said, still not meeting his eyes. 'We should instead hand the Holy Grail of San Michon to Fabién Voss and his viper daughters, all three of whom shall sink fangs into thy throat the *second* they are given opportunity.'

"'Oh, ye see *so* far, Lilidh,' Nikita snarled, dropping into a mocking bow. 'So much farther than dull Nikita. How blessed are we, to have a sibling so learned, *so* wise.'

"And turning to his thrallswords, Nikita stabbed his finger at their line.

"'You. Come hither.'

"It was Maeron he pointed to. Young Gillian's beau. To his credit, the young knight didn't blink, didn't flinch, striding forward with adoring eyes fixed on his laerd, and smacking a fist against his black steel breastplate.

"'My master,' he said.

"'Unsheathe thy blade.'

"The lad obeyed, steel ringing crisp in the rafters. All in the hall now watched this drama unfolding, Dior's heart beating quicker as she risked a glance to Reyne. And turning to the swordmaids gathered behind Lilidh's throne, Nikita beckoned to Gillian.

"'Come hither, child,' he smiled.

"Now. Lady Gillian was bound to Lilidh, Historian, not her brother. And despite the danger of disobedience, the maid threw an inquiring glance to her mistress. Lilidh pinched the bridge of her nose, as if wearied by these antics, the threat of another tantrum.

"'What be thy game, Nikita?'

"'Aye, aye, a game, call it,' he smiled, gesturing to Dior. 'If Nikita shall pay so dear for this slip's parlor tricks, the very least she might do is entertain him with them.' He glowered at Gillian again, black eyes burning. '*COME HITHER.*'

"The Blackheart's Whip rang on the stone, and the young swordmaid obeyed, stepping down the dais to stand before Nikita and her betrothed. Morgana watched her older sister, paling beneath her freckles. Gillian's breath was coming swifter, pupils wide as she looked her beau in the eye. And as if ordering a snifter of port after supper, Nikita spoke a simple command.

"'Run her through.'

"An eternity, that moment. Dior's heart froze still, all in Lilidh's retinue held their breath. God only knows what went through that young man's mind. To look into the eyes of the girl he loved and know if he disobeyed, all would be lost—not just her, but the conspiracy entire, and his conspirators beside. But the Grail's blood had the power to heal the wounded, and Nikita *had* said this was only a game . . .

"Eyes pleading, Gillian nodded ever so slight, bidding her love to strike, Godsakes, *strike*. And with his face utterly bloodless, Maeron obeyed as would any thrall his master, driving his sword into his betrothed's body as her baby sister screamed.

"'Gilly!'

"'*BE SILENT,*' Lilidh snapped, scowling over her shoulder.

"Morgana watched her sister wilt, slithering to her knees. Her beau hadn't struck to kill—he'd not been commanded to, after all, instead driving his blade into Gillian's belly where the pain might be worse, but the danger less. Gasping in agony, Gillian pressed red hands to her stomach as her beau dragged his blade free.

"Dior was already stepping up to heal her when Nikita's eyes fell upon her.

"'I did not bid thee move, girl.'

"The Grail glanced to Gillian, pulse thrashing beneath her skin.

"'Forgive me, Laerd, I thought y—'

"'Fear not, fear not,' Nikita smiled, waving her away. 'In time, child. You,' he said, turning to his thrallswords and pointing now at Declan. 'Come hither.'

"The young knight strode forward to stand beside his trembling brother, thumping a fist against his breastplate. Maeron was pale as ghosts, eyes locked on the sweetheart he'd just stabbed, the pool of her blood slowly creeping toward his boots.

"The Blackheart looked from Declan to Maeron. 'This thy brother, aye?'

"'Aye, my master.'

"'Good, good,' Nikita smiled, waving between the pair. 'Run him through.'

"The boys looked at each other, eyes gone wide and cold, another moment as long as forever. Here was strife, Historian, sure and true, for all of Nikita's guard wore heavy breastplates and shirts of threefold mail. Even a thrall would struggle to drive a longblade through plated steel, and while young Declan might pierce his brother's mail under the arm or at the throat, that would spell a *far* quicker death than a blade to the belly.

"Declan looked to his laerd. 'His armor, Master—'

"'Here, here, let me help thee,' Nikita cooed, and glancing to Maeron, he smiled gently. 'On thy knees, boy.'

"'Aye, M-Master.'

"Eyes still on his brother's, Maeron sank now to the stone. All the Blackheart's court had fallen so still, I swear we could hear the song of distant pipes on the howling wind. Ignoring the frantic beating of our wings on her skin, Dior stepped forward, fingers curling to helpless fists. But Nikita's head snapped up, predatory, his voice Whipping the air.

"'*Stay*.'

"He raised a warning finger, as if daring she disobey.

"'Stay,' he repeated, softer now.

"It was Dior's intervention that spared poor Declan the agony of decision; his brother seizing hold of his blade, and pressing its point to the join of shoulder and neck. Their eyes locked, Maeron nodded, glancing to Dior in a silent plea. And then he gritted his teeth, dragging that blade into his own flesh, helping his brother drive the point home.

"Declan was gasping for breath, near to vomiting as he pulled his sword free. His brother's blood welled up in a flood, spurting rhythmically across Maeron's skin as the young gallant withered at Nikita's feet. Gillian groaned, reaching out to her beau with a bloody hand, pressing it to his gushing wound and looking first to Dior, then to Lilidh.

"'M-Mistress?'

"'What be this foolishness, Nikita?' Lilidh asked. 'Have we so many swords ye may squander them the very hour afore battle?'

"'Fear not, fear not,' he smiled. 'A game, as ye say. Soon played out.'

"He looked to Dior then, black eyes glittering, as if daring her to move. But the Grail remained motionless as if in the grip of his power, speaking only through clenched teeth.

"'My Laerd—'

"'*SILENCE*,' Nikita snapped, looking now to Morgana. 'You. Come hither.'

"There was no bond of blood between the swordmaid and the ancien; merely the fear that now dripped from the very walls. But glancing to Reyne, young Morgana obeyed, trembling as she stepped before the Laerd Dyvok and curtseyed. Dior was sheened in sweat now, her pulse unmoored. She looked to Aaron, but the capitaine avoided her eyes, jaw clenched tight, hair gleaming gold in that dying light.

"Nikita took Declan's sword from the boy's numb hands, handed it to his betrothed.

"'Run him through.'

"Morgana blanched, turning to Lilidh. 'Mistress—'

"'Look not at her!' Nikita roared. '*Look at me!*'

"Morgana obeyed, knuckles gone white on the hilt of that bloody blade. We saw a glimmer of mad possibility in her eyes then, the question *What if?* surfacing brief in the swordmaid's mind before sanity returned; fear for her princess, her sister, for all that would be undone if she struck this beast drenched in the blood of centuries and failed.

"'Brother,' Lilidh sighed, utterly exasperated. 'Be there reason in this madness?'

"'There be a *lesson*.'

"'In what, pray tell? Blooding the floors?'

"'Indulge me.' The Blackheart bowed low, hand to heart. 'Such gifts, such insight, *such* counsel hast thou given, sweet sister. What be one gift more to thy feeble brother, who doth owe thee oh *so* much?' He gestured to Morgana, fangs agleam at the corners of his smile. 'Pray, bid thy blooded servant obey me. A game, sister, all a game.'

"Lilidh pursed her lips, running one claw over her chin. Morgana stood paralyzed, terrified stare switching between her beloved and her princess and her mistress. Reyne's face was white as ghosts, agony welling in her faeling eyes. Dior hung like a broken mirror, every part of her atremble, our wings upon her skin likesame. We'd no idea what sport Nikita sought here, but to have plucked four members of the conspiracy by chance . . .

"'Do as he commands thee, child,' Lilidh said.

"Nikita smiled at Morgana, vulpine, gesturing to Declan.

"'Run him through.'

"Morgana obeyed, thrusting her sword at her beloved. Declan had turned himself sideways, exposing the gap in the fore and aft of his breastplate, and the blade sank through the chainmail and into his gut. Morgana's face twisted, Declan gasping as he sank to the stone beside his brother, red gushing over the flagstones, pooling in the cracks. Nikita placed one pale hand on Morgana's shoulder, took the bloody sword from her hand.

"'Good, child,' he cooed. 'Very good.'

"And with a snarl, he flung the girl across the room.

"Morgana struck the wall with a shriek, a wet *CRACK*, blood spattering on the stone. Reyne screamed her name, Lady Arlynn seizing her princess's hand, blue eyes locked on Nikita. In a blinking, the Blackheart had flashed up to Dior, his face now inches from hers, all midnight eyes and blood-red lips and pearl-white fangs.

"'Words to gift us, hast thou?'

"Dior clenched her jaw, swallowed hard. To speak, even to *move* would be to show Nikita's gifts had no power over her. But to stand here meek and silent . . .

"'No? Say ye nothing at all?'

"Dior met Nikita's eyes, teeth creaking as she clenched her jaw to still her tongue. We could see the darkness in his gaze, the murders untallied, the endless plains of unmarked graves. A monster who had destroyed a kingdom to sit now as its king. Nikita pressed the bloody sword into Dior's hands, leaning so close his lips brushed hers.

"'Then we shall keep playing, child.'

"He turned to the dais, patting his thigh and whistling.

"'Worm. Come hither.'

"Lilidh sighed. 'Nikita—'

"'Fear not, fear not. This sport is near its end.'

"Reyne's eyes were fixed on Dior's, muscle knotted at her jaw. She crossed the bloodied stone, all of Nikita's court watching, hungry eyes glittering like the embers of a dying fire. Gillian and Declan and Maeron lay in a widening puddle of red, the reek of blood and sundered bowel strung thick in the air. Morgana was crumpled in ruins where she'd been tossed, impossible to tell if the maid was dead or alive. Nikita hooked one claw beneath the Princess's chin now, peering into those cold faeling eyes.

"'Look at her.'

"Reyne obeyed, gaze falling on Dior, not a tear nor tremble in sight. The Princess á Maergenn did as she was bid—not to obey, mind you, but to protect those others who depended on this lie, no matter how slender the thread of hope now frayed. The Grail glanced again to Aaron, anguish welling in his eyes along with bloody tears. Her gaze pleaded with him, silent, begging, but ever so slight, the capitaine shook his head.

"'*LOOK AT ME, GIRL.*'

"Dior turned back to Nikita, lurking now over Reyne's shoulder. The Blackheart's cheek was pressed against the Princess's, eyes deep as the dark between the stars.

"'I made her mother scream before her end.' Nikita ran one sharp claw down Reyne's cheek, too gentle to even scratch the skin. 'But at least the mighty Nineswords died fighting. We found this one cowering in a grain silo like a worm. And so we named her.'

"Nikita exerted gentle but inexorable pressure on Reyne's shoulders, forcing her to her knees before the Grail. The vampire sank down with the girl, lifting the bloody blade in Dior's hand and resting the point against Reyne's breast. Dior still played the role, obeying as if under Nikita's power, not talking, not moving.

"'And now this worm dies on her knees.'

"Black eyes flickered up to the Grail's.

"'Unless thou hast some protest to speak?'

"Prince had risen to his feet, the wolf's hackles rising as the Contessa shouted, 'Nikita, enough! She cannot speak if thou hast Whipped her into silence!'

"The Blackheart raised one brow, still watching Dior. 'Nothing at all?'

"The Grail stood still as stone, blade poised in her hand.

"'*RUN HER THROUGH.*'

"Dior drew back the sword, blade steadied on her free palm for the strike, eyes fixed on Reyne's. Lilidh again shouted, '*Nikita!*' Prince snarled, fangs bared, but the Blackheart only glanced toward his sister and smiled.

"And in that moment, Dior struck.

"We knew now this *was* a game to him, and surely so did she—another torment dreamed up in the mind of a monster. The conspiracy was somehow undone. All hope had crumbled now to ash, all prayers unanswered, save perhaps this last, desperate one. And so, dragging her palm down that sword's razored edge, the Grail drenched the blade with her holy blood, and plunged it toward Nikita's twisted heart.

"Quick as flies, Nikita smashed the blade from her grip, Dior screaming in fury and pain as she clutched her wrist. The bloodied blade sang as it struck the floor, and Nikita rose like a serpent, seizing Dior's throat and hauling her off the stone. As the court clambered to their feet, roaring, Reyne lunged for the fallen sword, but effortless, Nikita kicked the Princess aside. Flying as if she were rags and stuffing, Reyne struck the dais, her skull smashed as she hit the stone. Dior screamed in hatred, flailing in the Blackheart's grip, Prince snarling his fury as Lilidh rose to her feet and roared.

"'Nikita, *hold*!'

"Dior grabbed the ancien's wrist with her bleeding hand, and with a howl of pain, Nikita dropped her, his own hand bursting into bright flames. The Grail struck the floor with a *crunch*, the Blackheart bellowing, and stooping low, Arlynn, Lady of Faenwatch, first of the Lady Reyne's household, snatched up the blade anointed with Dior's blood. Long had that old swordmaid suffered the indignity of surrender to these fiends, forced to humiliate the Princess she had sworn sacred oath to serve. And every drop of her fury rang in her cry as she plunged that sword toward Nikita's heart. But though the old maid's form would have put many a man to shame, alas, her foe was no simple man.

"Her wrist crunched like the bones of a baby bird as he seized it. Blood sizzled and flesh hissed as Nikita plunged his flaming hand through Arlynn's ribs, extinguishing the blaze on his skin inside her chest. Laerd Brann bellowed with terrible fury, the old soldier charging to his bride's defense, naked steel in his hand. But Aaron struck then, stepping between Brann and his beloved master, his greatsword slicing the old laerd clean in two. Blood sprayed as Nikita tore Arlynn's heart from its moorings, and the swordmaid near in half. And with black hand dripping red, the ancien turned on Dior.

"The Grail had crawled to Reyne's side, pressing bloody hands to the Princess's broken skull, smudging her holy blood over the girl's waxen skin. Eyes locked on hers, Nikita stomped on Declan's head, popping it like a waterskin, brains dashed on the flagstones. Dior screamed as he did the same to Maeron, to Gillian, her throat torn hoarse and bleeding as she called him *pig, animal, bastard, monster.* Boots dripping red, Nikita stalked toward her, burned hand curled into a claw as he reached for her throat.

"With a flash of white, a low snarl, Prince came to the Grail's defense, standing between the pair and snapping at Nikita's outstretched hand. The Blackheart drew back for one second, seethed forward in the next. Snatching the beast by the scruff, he hauled it skyward, claws poised before the wolf's snarling face.

"'Send thee to thy Mothermoons, little prince? Or merely take thy other eye?'

"'NIKITA, *STOP* IT!' Lilidh roared.

"The Count Dyvok turned eyes to his sister then, all in the room gone silent. He cast Prince aside, the wolf yelping as it crunched into the stone, skidding through the slick of gore. The Blackheart and the Heartless stared at each other, Nikita's sneer spattered red.

"'Name me fool, sister? Think me sightless? Speak to me as thou wouldst a *child*? Yet thou art so blind, ye cannot see the nest of vipers coiled at thy breast.'

"'What nest? Of what madness dost thou speak?'

"'Treachery,' he spat. 'Betrayal. All these here unbound, their red shackles broke by this brat's accursed blood.'

"Lilidh's black eyes narrowed, falling now on Dior.

"'She meant to murder thee, Lilidh,' Nikita said. 'And I beside thee. The pair of us burned in our beds. Gods, undone by *insects*.'

"'How d-did you know?' Dior looked at the vampire, hissing. 'How c-could you—'

"'Treasure?'

"Nikita's call rang in the rafters, lips curling ever so slight as he met Dior's eyes.

"'Hither come, beloved.'

"A figure stepped into the silent hall through a servants' door, clad in a long, beautiful gown. She strode through the monsters and the spreading pool of gore, blood crusted under her fingernails and splashing on her shoes, adoring gaze fixed on her laerd. And Dior's eyes flooded with tears as she whispered.

"'Isla . . .'

"The girl walked to Nikita's side, and the vampire caressed her skin, smiling as he cupped her cheek. A bundle of cloth was gathered in Isla's arms, Dior's heart hammering as we recognized the furs from her bed. And unwrapping them, the girl tossed the ironsaw onto the floor. The sound of metal striking stone split the air with a peal of thunder outside, the lass staring at Dior with eyes as cold and wild as the storm above.

"'But w-we *freed* you,' Dior whispered, horrified. 'I set you *free*.'

"'From what?' the girl asked, bewildered. 'Love?'

"Nikita smiled, standing at Isla's back and enfolding her in his dark embrace, the lass shivering as he scattered cold kisses down her neck. 'How think ye Aveléne was bought so cheaply, Mlle Lachance? Who think ye it was, who slew those guards, and opened those gates in dead of night? Ever faithful and true, my Treasure here. Ever loyal, since that night we met at Dún Cuinn's fall, and she begged to serve rather than die with the rest of them.'

"Dior looked into Isla's eyes. The prickling on the girl's skin as Nikita kissed her neck, the shiver in her breath as he deepened his embrace. And at last, we understood.

"*Some join willingly. Out of lust for power, or darkness of heart.*

"*Others are just fools who think they'll live forever.*

"'I am his,' Isla said. 'I have *always* been his.'

"'Your Ever After.' Dior shook her head, tears spilling down her cheeks. 'It's *him*.'

"The girl smiled, threading fingers up through the Blackheart's hair.

"'We'll be together. Forever. He'll reward me now, just as he did the capitaine.'

"'You *fool*,' Dior hissed. 'It doesn't *work* that way. He can't just—'

"Isla struck, heartless and swift, landing a brutal kick into Dior's face. She was lifting her bloody heel for another blow when Nikita laughed, gathering the lass back up in his arms, kissing her cheek as he murmured.

"'*Temper*, Treasure, temper. We must keep the Forever King's prize hale and—'

"A horn split the night, distant, feeble, near lost under the roar of the storm. But as Nikita tilted his head to listen, another joined it, louder, another now. The dún rang with the song of alarm, echoing on bloody and broken stone. The Dyvok court glanced among themselves, murmuring and muttering, all knowing what that song meant.

"The Black Lion was coming, his Highlanders with him, and all hell was about to rain down upon their heads. Drunk with blood though they were, golden vials glittering about their necks, still the fear hung thick in that great hall. Silver and fire and duskdancer claws—all manner of endings would soon be coming over those walls toward the kith of the Blackheart's court. And at the end of the night, forever is quite a prize to risk for loyalty.

"'Hear me now!'

"Nikita's bellow rang in the rafters, bringing stillness to the hall.

"'My children! My lords!' The Blackheart raised one bloody finger to the heavens. 'The Angel of Death hangs in the skies just a breath above our heads! And at Mahné's right hand, the Angel of Fear spreads her dark wings! Just as thee, I hear the beating of Phaedra's pinions upon the wind, and lo, I tell thee, I smile! For so *should* it be, that those dread siblings come to bear witness this day! Should the lamb not fear the teeth of the wolf? Should the cow not quaver before the butcher's knives? And what are they, who now gather in the mud outside our door, but *livestock*? *Cattle*? Pigs and mongrels, sheep and hounds, who dare to bark with mortal tongues at we who are eternal?'

"Growls of agreement drifted among the court, a few heads nodding.

"'This kingdom is ours!' Nikita roared. 'Carved in blood and conquest! We rule this land, this night, as we were born to! Balk not at the baying of those dogs outside, for we are the mighty! And those who dare come before our walls this day? They are the *weak*!'

"Nikita picked up Epitaph from behind his throne, raising it to the sky.

"'We are the hunters! And they are the prey!'

"A hungry murmur rippled among the kith, fangs bared, eyes narrowed.

"'We are the descendants of mighty Tolyev! Our triumphs be not measured in words but *deeds,* and I swear to thee, by the last drop of blood within these veins, thy deeds this day shall ring in the lamentations of the conquered for all eternity!'

"He snapped the golden vial away from his necklace of fangs, lifted it in toast.

"'Santé! Untamed!'

"'Santé!' came the roar, a hundred vials raised in answer. '*Dyvok!*'

"The shouts rang in the rafters, the clash of blades, the fury of forever unleashed. Nikita quaffed the contents of his vial in one swallow, dragged a red hand across his lips, looking once more to Prince. The wolf was hauling itself up from the bloody floor where he'd thrown it, blue eye flashing.

"'I shall kiss them goodnight for thee, little mongrel.'

"Nikita pressed cold lips to Isla's, the girl smiling up at her Ever After. Gesturing to the broken but still-breathing bodies of Dior and Reyne, he murmured, 'Take these two below and lock them tight. The Forever King shall have his prize, and the Princess may yet be of use. Kiara,' he called, turning to his daughter, 'My Golden One,' he smiled, glancing to Aaron. 'My lords and ladies!' he cried, turning now to his court. 'Draw thy steel, and steel thy hearts! We drink the lifesblood of the Moonsthrone this day!'

"He lifted Epitaph, shout ringing on the walls.

"'Deeds Not Words!'

"The vampires roared, and as one, the court stormed out toward the walls, the slaughter to come. Aaron bowed to his liege, Kiara scoffing and sparing Nikita a weary smile as he blew her a kiss. As all in the Hall of Plenty emptied out into the storm, Lilidh stood amid the carnage at the thrones, staring daggers at her brother's back as she hissed.

"'And what would the Count Dyvok have of his elder?'

"Nikita turned then, timeless, towering, slowly stalking up the dais to loom over his broodsister. Their eyes met, black and fathomless and ageless, more than a millennium between them. Who knew what they had seen and done together in all that time; the two oldest Dyvok that yet walked this dying earth. And as Prince watched on, snarling soft, Nikita lifted his hand to thumb a spatter of crimson from Lilidh's pale cheek.

"'Thy blessing for the battle to come?' he asked softly.

"Lilidh blinked at that, remaining mute. Nikita lifted his sister's hand, pressed ruby lips to her pale knuckles, a teasing smile curling the edge of his lips.

"'Thy forgiveness? For thy brash and boorish brother, who loves thee still?'

"She softened then; the first breath of summer on winter's frost.

"'Of course I f—'

"'And thy understanding,' he interrupted, his voice growing soft and deadly, 'why Nikita is Priori here, and why *ever* Lilidh shall dwell in his shadow.'

"Lilidh's eyes grew hard again, winter returning once more. Nikita smiled wider.

"'I go now to secure thy throne, sister. Keep mine warm for me while I am gone.'

"And dropping Lilidh's hand, the Blackheart marched out toward the slaughter."

The Last Liathe paused in her tale, head bowed, fingers entwined in her lap. In her head, beyond the voices that ever whispered there, she could hear the ringing of steel, the roar of crumbling stone, the terrified screams of the dying undying. The battle seemed so close now, the images bright in her head—so rare these nights, with so many memories and lives and pasts clamoring inside her. She could barely recall what it had been like to be alone with her thoughts. To have one moment's silence. To know one second's peace.

"Capitaine?"

Celene glanced up as the Marquis called, his voice ringing in the dark. Jean-François's eyes met hers for a moment, the air between them hung thick with the promise of the coming assault. She could still taste the blood on her mouth if she tried. See Dior's red hand and blue eyes raised high to heaven before all sank into hell.

"Calling for your dogs, sinner?" she asked. "Have I frightened you again?"

The historian gifted her a wan smile as the heavy door opened at his back, his thrallswords spilling into the room. The burning torches they bore were sunbright after an age in the dark, giving rise to more memories unpleasant. The silhouette of San Yves aflame. The taste of countless eternities washing over her tongue as her master screamed.

Celene averted her eyes.

"Marquis?" The capitaine looked around the room, hand to blade. "You called?"

"Be at ease, Delphine." Jean-François beckoned. "Come here, Dario."

The young thrall came forward, Nordish pale, handsome as a denful of devils. He kept his eyes downturned, sinking to his knees beside his master. Jean-François drew back the long locks of his hair, the thrall shivering as the vampire leaned close and whispered, bloodless lips tickling his earlobe. Dario glanced up to Celene, pupils wide, and he nodded, just once. Jean-François took his hand, scattering kisses across his knuckles, down to his wrist. The beau shivered then, lips parting, britches straining. And with a dark smile and a soft smack to his backside, the vampire sent him on his way.

Dario retreated, and with a nod of reassurance to the capitaine, the historian turned back to his tome. The thrallswords glanced around the room again, tight-wound and guarded, but with nothing amiss, they bowed to their master and departed. The door thumped shut, chains slipped back into place, the gloom in the cell growing deeper.

"Please continue, Mlle Castia," Jean-François said, waving his quill.

Celene narrowed her eyes. "Is everything well?"

Jean-François chuckled. "Are you honestly asking me that question?"

The historian dipped his quill, looked at her expectantly.

"Dawn approaches, mademoiselle. I would like to see my bed before the sun rises. The Grail's plan was undone, the Highlanders on their way, all stood poised on the edge of a knife. But what of you and your brother?"

"We stood there too, sinner."

Celene bowed her head, looking down into dark waters.

"We stood there too."

XI

NOT A PRAYER

" 'MY FATHER WAS your teacher.'

"I sat before my brother in the commander's tent, flames dancing and popping beside him, yet doing nothing to banish the cold between us. We could hear pipes drifting on the howling wind, the rumble of thunder above the dún. Gabriel was staring at me, our eyes narrowed against the light of the flames and the ink burning upon his hands.

"'Oui,' I murmured. 'Master Wulfric.'

"'You said your teacher was dead.'

"We nodded, swallowing with our ruined throat. 'He is.'

"We could see he was angered at this news, and that, we did not quite understand. Gabriel had never even known the monster who'd seeded him, and Wulfric had never cared a drop about my brother's life. Why should he care how his father's ended? But still he spoke, voice crackling like the hateful flames in that firepit beside him.

"'How?' he demanded. 'Why?'

"'That is an even longer tale, Gabriel. I do not think—'

"And our voice fell silent then, and we snaked up to our feet at once, the chill in the tent grown deeper still. Gabriel tried to speak, but we hushed him with one hand, turning the fullness of our gaze to that mote of blood in the Hall of Plenty, watching as Nikita Dyvok beckoned poor young Maeron to his side. We witnessed that red drama play out upon that awful stage, saw the Blackheart torture those children, spilling each other's blood rather than spill their secret, and end what little hope they had left.

"Gabriel looked at us, hand slipping to his accursed broken blade, and as our eyes met across the crackling flames, he knew at once what was wrong.

"'Dior,' he breathed.

"'She is discovered. All is undone, Gabriel, we mu—'

"But he was already gone, up and off, fleeing the tent with the speed of the terrified. He roared at the top of his lungs for his fleshwitch, for his heathen comrades, and we stood in the tent, watching that awful game in the Hall of Plenty play out. We watched Dior spit her defiance, sending her doomed strike toward Nikita's heart. We watched the traitor unveiled, cursing myself a fool; that I should have watched closer, that I might've *seen* had we not been searching so desperately for Maryn's tomb. And as the traitor Isla á Cuinn laid Dior out with that vicious kick to her skull, we heard it then, the sound on the wind, the peal of one bright horn, joined by another, the song of pipes stirring in the storm. The roar of the Moonsthrone rising, the call for vengeance, the bay for blood, the hue and cry for w—"

A heavy thumping sounded at the door, interrupting Celene's tale. The Last Liathe glanced up, brow darkening as the Marquis called, "Enter."

The sound of chains and lock being unshackled was again heard beneath the river's rush, the bite of stone upon stone. The door opened wide behind Jean-François, burning torches cutting the dark, heat swelling at his back. Capitaine Delphine and his men strode forward again, the young thrall Dario at their head, gaze downturned as he spoke.

"The prisoner, as you requested, Master."

Celene's eyes narrowed at that, a soft hiss slipping her lips as she spied the figure standing beside a bristling Meline. Long and bloody nights had passed since she'd last set eyes on him, and it surprised her, the effect the sight of him had. The gravity he exuded, the weight of his shadow, the way his very presence seemed to fill the room with fire.

God, how she *hated* fire.

"*Gabriel*," she whispered.

Under the watchful eye of the thrallsword capitaine, the Last Silversaint stepped forward to the water's edge, silvered heels scraping along the cold stone. She could see the stain of sleepless nights smudged under his eyes, weariness in the set of his shoulders, those twin teardrop scars wending down his cheek. But his clothes were spotless, his jaw clean-shaven, his eyes flushed red from the pipe. He seemed quite comfortable for a prisoner, given all the trouble he'd caused his jailors.

Gabriel looked at the rushing waters, smiling soft.

"Underground river. Very clever."

"I shall be certain to inform my Empress of your approval," Jean-François replied.

Storm-grey eyes fell on her like hammers, his hands curling into fists.

"Hello, traitor," he growled.

"Hello, coward," she spat.

"I see they're keeping you down below," he said, eyes roaming the cell. "A little closer to the place you're going to burn in the end."

Celene snaked to her feet, eyes alight. "We will see you there, bastard."

"Children, please." The Marquis rolled his eyes. "I did not bring the good chevalier down here so you might trade insults."

"Then why did you bring him?" Celene demanded.

Jean-François twirled his quill between his pale fingers. "As I told you, mademoiselle, I would like to see my bed before the sun rises this day. We approach the pointed end of this blade. And since you were both present at the Battle of Maergenn, I thought it prudent to have you both speak upon it. It will save me the trouble of having to determine afterward which of your contradictions are lies and which are truth."

"Truth?" the Last Silversaint scoffed. "From this snake?"

"I thought you said the Blood Chastain has no penchant for cruelty," Celene said. "His every word is tantamount to torture. Give me the rack and the flame—"

"*Enough,*" the Marquis said, looking between the pair. "This is not a request. And I grow weary of threatening you both. So let us simply say every minute the pair of you spend posturing now will cost you a night of starvation later, and be done with it."

The Marquis snapped his fingers and one of the thrallswords brought forth another leather armchair, placing it opposite the historian's. Dario set down a new bottle of Monét on the table, a fresh goblet embossed with golden wolves beside it. The chymical globe threw long shadows upon the stone, a ghost-pale moth emerging from the gloom and battering upon the glass. Jean-François glowered, eyes dark with wrath.

"Now *sit down,* the pair of you."

The siblings remained frozen, glaring at each other across that rushing river. The air between them rippled with hatred, Gabriel's fangs unveiled, Celene's eyes narrowed to knifecuts. But finally, as one, the pair relented, backing off a pace or two, Gabriel sinking into the chair set aside for him, Celene snaking back down to the bare stone, legs folded beneath her. And with a sigh, Jean-François adjusted his cravat and nodded to the capitaine.

"I think it best you and your men remain for this, Delphine."

The big man nodded. His eyes never left Gabriel. "I concur, Marquis."

The historian glanced to the soldiers. "Back in the shadows, there's some good chaps. I believe the scent of you might be exciting our guests."

Gabriel glanced to the big capitaine, blew him a kiss. Delphine scowled and nodded to his men, and the thrallswords retreated into the dark recesses of the cell. Dario backed off to stand with the soldiers, though Meline hovered at the historian's shoulder, eyes slipping every so often toward Gabriel. But the siblings stared only at one another, as if there were not another soul in that cell.

"So." Jean-François glanced to Gabriel. "Your sister and I had arrived at the point of no return, Chevalier. Lachance's plan to liberate Nikita and Lilidh's thralls had been foiled. An army of slaves faced you upon the walls of Maergenn. You had but three alternatives; retreat and consign the Grail to the keeping of the Forever King, wait and be crushed between the Dyvok anvil and the hammer of the Voss in a few days' time, or attack those walls that day. Your friend Baptiste stood upon those battlements, de León. Hundreds of innocents snatched at Aveléne, Cuinn, Sadhbh, Fas. Soldiers whose only crime was being captured rather than killed. If their masters were destroyed, they would be freed. But you could not *reach* their masters without carving through them. What path did you choose?"

"They stood between me and Dior," Gabriel said softly.

The historian opened a new page in his tome, smoothed down the parchment as he chuckled. "They never had a prayer, did they?"

Gabriel leaned forward, eyes clouded. His voice was soft as smoke.

"There's a saying among cavalrymen in Elidaen. *Everyone's a priest when the arrows start flying.* When all that stands between you and death is a few rings of chainmail, or a couple of feet of stone, it's hard not to give yourself over to God. *Everyone* in battle has a prayer, Chastain. Problem is, the one they pray to seldom listens."

"Everyone has a prayer except you, of course."

"No." Gabriel sighed heavy, looking skyward. "Not that day. We mustered there in the rising dawn, before those mighty walls. Phoebe stood beside me, her aunt Cinna before her, painting protection magiks on her skin in sacred blood. All down the line, the chanting rhythm was rising, like the pulse beneath my skin, the adrenaline in my veins. As the dim sun crested the horizon, I could feel the battle awaiting beneath that black sky. All I'd done, all I'd suffered, and it all came down to this—a headlong charge into a wall of teeth and swords, to rescue a girl with a blade already at her throat. We'd an ocean of slaughter ahead, but even if we survived it, Nikita *knew* all this was about Dior. If the battle went ill, martyrs only knew what he might do to her in retaliation. And there was nothing we could do to stop him. I knew it'd take a miracle for her to live through this."

The Last Silversaint shook his head.

"And so, I prayed for one."

"*You?*" the historian scoffed. "Pray?"

"We both did, sinner."

Jean-François and Gabriel looked to Celene as she spoke, eyes on the ceiling above.

"We stood among them, my dear brother and I, side by side. The army of the Moonsthrone was forming up before Maergenn's walls, baying to their heathen gods as the thunder rolled. The most bestial of them stood in their vanguard; towering figures more animal than human, wolves and bears and lions, fur and fang, kilt and claw. Wizened crones stalked up and down their lines, painting crimson blasphemies upon their skins to the tune of wild pipes and rhythmic chanting. They stomped their feet in time, snarling and heaving, a sea of roaring faces and flashing eyes. Gabriel's fleshwitch—"

"Don't call her that," the silversaint snapped.

"... Gabriel's *sorceress* stood at his other hand, her face daubed crimson. Bloodlust was building among the Highlanders, their spirits caught up in frenzy and idolatry and madness. And in the midst of it, I sank to our knees, and I turned our face to heaven, and closing our eyes, I prayed. The prayer on the lips of every Faithful soldier as they look upon the foe, and perhaps their death. The Benediction for Battle.

> "*The Lord is my shield, unbreakable.*
> "*He is the fire that burns away all darkness.*
> "*He is the tempest rising that shall lift me unto paradise.*'

"And I opened my eyes then, because there beside me, kneeling in the snow, was my own faithless brother, voice entwined with mine.

"'His light is my salvation, his love is my redemption.
"'His sword shall lay my enemies to rest.
"And should I face my ending, until the Day of Judging,
"'I give to him the keeping of my soul.'

"'Véris,' I whispered, signing the wheel.

"'Véris,' Gabriel replied, hands clasped before him.

"I looked at him then, the storm raging above us, the ocean raging between us. 'We thought you had vowed to ask nothing of heaven's sovereign, brother,' we said. 'Save the chance to spit in his face before he sends you below.' And he replied—"

"'I'm not praying for me,'" Gabriel said.

Celene nodded, staring across that black river with eyes dark as night.

"He was praying for *her*."

Jean-François, Marquis of the Blood Chastain, looked at Gabriel.

"I take it you should have fucking known better?"

The Last Silversaint sighed.

The Last Liathe hung her head.

"He should have fucking known better."

BOOK SIX

THE RED HAND
OF GOD

Judgment Comes.

—THE CREED OF BLOOD ESANA

STORMBRINGER

"WE ROSE UP from our knees," Celene said. "Dawn cresting the world's edge, black skies running to red. The tiny mote of us still with Dior was down in the dungeons of Dún Maergenn now, locked with her in her tiny cell. We beat frail wings upon her broken cheek, trying to rouse her, assure her that we were coming to save her. But she was still unconscious from Isla's brutal beating, her skin cold to the touch. And so the rest of me outside those walls sliced open our palms, bringing forth our blade, slender and sharp as broken bone, our flail, long and gleaming red. The scent of blood stained the air as I clenched our teeth and set our eyes upon the wretches we were set to slaughter."

Gabriel lifted the Monét, filling his goblet to the brim. Though it was his fifth bottle of the night, the silversaint seemed sharp, keen, eyes alight with memory.

"I'd fought in castle assaults before, coldblood," he said. "Dozens of them. I knew the hell that lay before us. Wading knee-deep through innocent blood, carving through a flood of wretched, under fire the whole time from Nikita's highbloods on the inner walls. Either way the scales tipped, this was going to be a massacre.

"I didn't know how to ask, didn't know if I even had a right to after I'd hurt her in the Cradle, knowing only that I'd need every edge that I could get in the battle to come. But as I turned to Phoebe, my mouth dry as ash, she'd already unbuckled the vambrace about her forearm, golden eyes locked on mine.

"'Phoebe, I wouldn't ask if . . .'

"'Nae need to ask. It's mine to give to whom I choose.' She touched my face then, and though she spoke of blood, I knew she meant more besides. 'I choose ye.'

"I took her hand, conscious of the eyes now upon us, the soft growls and muttered curses. Brynne loomed behind us, scowling as she watched on, big paws twitching. But though we stood in an ocean of tooth and claw, blade and blood, it seemed for a moment we were completely alone, as we'd been that night we danced in the White Rabbit. Eyes on Phoebe's, I lifted her wrist to my lips, and she smiled as I kissed her skin, feathersoft. But her smile faded, her lips parting as my own peeled back and I sank my fangs into her vein.

"Her blood washed over me, *through* me, that flood of heat and earth and flame I'd felt in the Mothers' Cradle, once more rushing out from my belly and into every part of me. Every muscle gone taut, every nerve afire, the strength of mountains and the rush of rivers and the might in the bones of this corrupted earth all within me. I swallowed deep, deeper, that thirst inside me roaring, needing, pleading, *Just one more mouthful, just one more drop*. But I pushed it back, not yet its thrall, roaring, *ENOUGH*. And shuddering crown to toe, I released my grip, drawing back from Phoebe's wrist and kissing the punctures in her skin.

"She was staring at me, her breath quickened, her hand shaking in mine. And she kissed me then, beneath those thundering skies, amid that song of pipes and the scent of slaughter to come. Her blood was still on my mouth, her talons snaking into my hair as she drew me closer, deeper, and I threw my arms around her and crushed her body to mine.

"She'd told me that we don't get broken, but that we're *made* so. And we were wounded, the pair of us, sure and true; both still bleeding from the wounds life had carved in us, the loved ones torn away from us. Honestly, I still feared my hurts would never be mended entire. But as I held that woman in my arms, I knew she'd spoken truth—that if we're blessed, we might find someone whose edges fit against our own, like pieces of the same puzzle, or shards of the same broken sword. Someone who, in their own broken way, makes our brokenness whole, and our shattered edge complete.

"I knew full well this might be the last time her lips touched mine. A kiss to remember and be remembered by. We'd had too little time, and now, we might be at the finish of it. And as we parted, all too soon, she spoke, ruby-red lips curling.

"'I don't love ye, Gabriel de León.'

"I kissed her knuckles, one at a time. 'I don't love you too.'

"She laughed then, eyes feral and bright with battlelust. 'See ye in the dún.'

"Turning, Phoebe stepped forward, raising her voice above the thunder.

"'Brothers and sisters of the Moonsthrone! We of the clans stand here united, one mind, one will, as has nae been seen since the nights of Ailidh the Stormbringer! Beyond those walls wait the thieves who have stolen our sacred blood, and pillaged our hallowed homeland! Curs and liars, oathbreakers and traitors!'

"'Death to Dyvok!' someone bellowed.

"'Death!' came the cry down the line. '*DEATH!*'

"'Nay!' Phoebe roared above the clamor. 'Nay, hear me now!'

"The tumult quieted then, bubbling just under a boil.

"'We are right to seek our vengeance!' Phoebe called. 'But beyond those walls lies the salvation of this world! The end to daysdeath! The Godling true! We fight today nae for the crimes of the past, but the hope of the future! So if we must fall, let it be for the sake of those bairns unborn, those days undawned, that the Godling shall bring soon to pass! And if ye must roar, let it be what we *fight for*! Let our foes tremble at the sound of her name!'

"Phoebe bared her teeth, pointing toward the broken walls.

"'Dior!'

"'DIOR!' came the cry down the line. '*DIOR!*'

"A thousand voices roaring as one, louder than the thunder above. Celene held her blade aloft, roaring the Grail's name, and I too found myself caught up in Phoebe's spell, dragging Ashdrinker from her scabbard and holding her up to the storm. The folk of the Moonsthrone had always spoken of the day Ailidh the Bold would be reborn, the queen who had united the Highland clans, and made all the heavens tremble. And looking at Phoebe as she screamed to the skies, golden eyes and flaming hair and talons sharp as blades, I wondered if there might be some truth in prophecy.

"*She is b–b–beautiful, Gabriel,* came a silver whisper in my head.

"'She is.'

"*What is her n–n–n–name?*

"'Stormbringer,' I smiled.

"Phoebe set her eyes on the walls, lips curled back from her teeth.

"'FOR THE GODLING!'

"The roar that echoed down the line was enough to shake the heavens above, and our charge began, trembling the earth below. Thousands of us, soldiers of the Highlands, moonsmaidens of the Cradle, úrfuil, leófuil, velfuil, pipes singing and blades flashing and claws curling as we hit that first fucking ditch."

Jean-François raised an eyebrow, glancing up.

"Ditch?"

The Last Silversaint nodded, swallowing a long mouthful of wine.

"Ditch," he repeated.

"You mean a moat around the walls, or—"

"I mean a ditch, coldblood. A simple hole in the ground. Dún Maergenn was the mightiest fortress west of Augustin, but it's not like its walls towered a hundred feet high, or that they were wrought from the bones of a dead god, or some other bollocks from a child's tale. Most fortresses aren't anything fancy. They're just a ditch surrounding a palisade. And the bigger the fortress, the more oft that pattern repeats. Ditch. Pre-wall. A deeper ditch. A bigger wall. This shit isn't fancy. But it *works*. Ditches break a charge's momentum, make the soldiers in it stumble. Ditches mean you can't bring siege weapons close enough to the walls without coming under fire while you set them up. I read somewhere that Dún Maergenn was only around three square miles in size, but it had over thirty miles of wall protecting it.

"The reason the Dyvok were so successful at siege warfare was that once they were wild on 'dancer blood, the bastards could hurl boulders at the defenders out of range of the defenses. That's why the walls of Newtunn were such a shambles—Nikita and his bloodlords had smashed up the pre-walls and hurled them at the battlements 'til the soldiers manning them were pulped. Then he repaired them best he could once he took the city.

"But we didn't have siege weapons, coldblood. We didn't have troop towers. We had brute strength and feral swiftness, magiks daubed in moonsblood, storm winds at our back and about five hundred yards of broken stone, ditches, and artillery fire before we reached the walls of Newtunn proper. And into that hell, we charged.

"The cannon fire came first—most of Niamh's heavy artillery had been destroyed when Nikita took the city, but a few of the bigger bitches still barked, booming and spitting fire along the wall. They'd been loaded with pepper shot, you know what that is?"

Jean-François opened his mouth to reply, but Gabriel rolled on as soon as he'd stolen another mouthful of wine.

"Anti-infantry. Designed to inflict carnage among ground troops. Phoebe had told me only silver or old age would slay a duskdancer, but I figured dismemberment or decapitation would serve just fine, and as the shots began hitting, I saw the damage they were doing. Arms torn from chests, legs from hips, bellies busted open and spattered across the snow. I kept running, ditch to wall to ditch, aflame with the fire of Phoebe's blood. Hunkering down beside a shattered battlement, I roared over the cannon's thunder.

"'Take cover on the fire, charge while they reload!'

"Phoebe was beside me, her cheek split and bleeding. I saw big Keylan crouching down ahead, Brynne just behind, the úrfuil gouging shrapnel from her shoulder with her talons. The cannon roared again, snow flying, earth shaking, the sound of metal splitting stone near deafening. But whoever was commanding the cannon was green; opening up with another volley while most of us had gone to ground. That's the problem with feeding enemy cap-itaines to your troops, vampire. If Nikita had kept a few more of Niamh's commanders alive, somebody up on those walls might've known what the fuck they were doing.

"The guns fell silent to reload, and we charged again, blinding snow and rising smoke. Phoebe ran hard beside me, but I'd lost sight of Celene, diving low as the cannon opened up again. We were off and moving swift right after, drawing ever closer to the battlements, the dark figures shouting atop them. But as soon as we got near enough, they unleashed their trebuchet, their ballista, stones and bolts raining down all around us, staggered enough that there was no safe window to charge anymore. I saw Keylan almost crushed— the big leófuil diving aside with only a second to spare as a ton of stone came crashing down on his cover. Angiss á Barenn had been hit by something vicious—the wolf was covered waist-down in blood. I could taste black ignis on the air, thunder shaking the ground as the trebuchet and cannon spewed death down our line.

"*Boom.*

"*BOOM.*

"We ran on. No choice. Hell and blood ahead, but worse backward than forward. Up and off, smoke and stench, thunder and snow, Phoebe's blood willing me on, lifting me up, bidding me run, on, *on* through that meat grinder toward the men I must kill. I was trying to spot Baptiste among those silhouettes atop the walls, hoping if I reached him first, I might some-how spare him the fate every other poor bastard up there would suffer once we reached the top. Because despite all they threw at us, we were coming."

Gabriel shook his head, quaffing his goblet.

"God help them, we were coming *fast*."

"May I speak now?"

The Last Silversaint glanced up, his face ice cold as he regarded his sister. Celene stared back at her sibling, sharp teeth locked behind that silver cage on her jaw.

"Must you?"

"We are certain you would prefer we sit in silent awe as the mighty Black Lion—"

"We," Gabriel scoffed, glancing to the historian. "Did she tell you what that actually means, Chastain? Did this fucking snake tell you who she's got—"

"But *I* was present also that day," Celene spat. "And I sit silent for none."

"Let her speak, Gabriel," Jean-François murmured. "Entertaining as it is, I did not bring you here to watch you spit venom."

"In every breath a lie." Gabriel refilled his cup, sighing. "But, as it please you."

Celene narrowed dark eyes, looking deep into the waters of memory.

"We moved swifter than my brother and his heathens, dashing ditch to wall to ditch again; dead man's clothes on our back, dead men ahead trying to kill us. We were close enough now that the crossbow fire began, burning bolts whispering past our cheeks. A stone crashed down but a few inches to our left, cannon fire peppered our body, but then, we were home—hitting the rubble at the base of the Newtunn wall and leaping upward, crack to crack, an arrow speeding toward heaven. Our flail snaked around the battlements above, our boots kicking hard, until we were running vertical up the wall. We heard cries of alarm, skipping aside blazing crossbow bolts, the men above screaming. But we saw it then, and if the heart in our dead chest still beat, it would have seized in terror as they dragged it up and made to tip it over—a trough, filled to brimming with burning coals.

"Fear froze me; the memory of those awful flames at Cairnhaem. I cried out, hand up to our face, trying to twist aside from that blistering shower. We felt the heat. Smelled the smoke. Imagined the agony. But then we heard a cry, meat striking stone. And the figures hefting those coals fell away, their trough tumbling back with them.

"We hit the battlements, flinging ourself over into a tumult of men, so close we could smell the reek of fresh liquor on their breath. But as we raised our blade, ready to split all around us asunder, we heard a voice we recognized, ragged with fear.

"'In Dior's name, no!'

"'. . . Joaquin,' we whispered.

"The houndboy stood with a dozen others, pale and frightened and splashed with blood. They'd attacked the men with the coals, holding them down, forcing them to drink from a flask of what we realized was Ossian Black. The liquor stank of rotten cabbage and tomcat spray, enough to make our eyes water if there'd been a drop of water inside us. But as we looked up and down the battlements, we saw the same refrain; scorched being brought down by their comrades, forced to drink, cursing and spitting.

"'What madness is this?' we whispered.

"Joaquin hefted his own hipflask, the stopper loosed. It was empty now, but our skin still tingled at the wondrous scent lingering inside.

"'Dior's blood,' we realized, remembering her bleeding foot. 'She filled that for you in the stable this morning. After she sent me away . . .'

"The boy nodded, pale and grim. 'I poured it all into the morning liquor ration before they sent me to the wall. Just like she told me to.'

"'The Black's reek covered the scent of her blood.'

"He nodded again, helping the man he'd knocked down back up to his feet. The cannon had fallen silent, the trebuchet gone still. All along the wall, those few who hadn't quieted their fears with a dram before battle were being forced to now—held down by their comrades and made to swallow, Dior's holy blood in the brew. And we thanked God then, for the frailty and courage of mortal men.

"The 'dancers hit the wall, Gabriel and his fleshwitch among them. But we climbed atop the battlements, screaming, 'Hold! *HOLD!*' praying God they would heed."

Gabriel nodded, eyes alight as he took up the tale once more.

"I was one of the first over, clawing my way up the wall with my bare hands. But as I hit the battlements, I heard Celene crying out, and as I raised Ashdrinker, she roared too, *Stop, ye shitwit, STOP!* All along the highwalk, I saw it now; free men and women breaking the last few bonds of servitude among the scorched. The Holy Blood of the Redeemer, secreted within a keg of homebrew Ossian piss by a girl who'd been on the grift in the gutter long before she'd taken on the mantle of Savior of the World."

Gabriel shook his head and smiled.

"Cunning little bitch."

"How did she know?" Jean-François asked, lifting his eyes. "How could she *possibly* know enough thralls would drink before they fought?"

The Last Silversaint chuckled then. "Spoken like someone who's never seen battle."

"But wouldn't fighting men want to be at their keenest when the battle is thickest?" Jean-François demanded. "When they have the most to lose?"

"That's precisely why they drink, vampire," Gabriel replied. "A soldier will take comfort in prayer. In thoughts of famille. In the love of his brothers . . ."

". . . But there's nothing like a dram of courage to hold you steady when the screaming starts." The vampire smiled, shaking his head. "Just as you told Dior at Aveléne."

The Last Silversaint raised his goblet.

"She was always a quick study, that girl."

"The heathens climbed over the battlements," Celene said, "ready to tear all to pieces. But Gabriel's voice joined my own, Phoebe now crying out too, and all along the broken walls of Newtunn, not a thrallsword raised a blade to fight. Keylan bellowed, '*Stay yer hands!*' and the word spread, the animals poised but a moment ago to wreak bloody carnage now confronted not by foes, but by welcomes, by blessings, by smiling faces and pleas for forgiveness. A legion of men and women dragged down into darkness, now awakened by the gift of one lone girl. A gift they had not even known to pray for.

"The gift of *freedom*."

Gabriel smiled, and they shared a glance then, these siblings who so loathed each other. And though her teeth were hidden, it seemed Celene smiled also, eyes shining in memory of that small victory upon those shattered walls.

"I heard a shout," the silversaint said. "Calling my name. Ash sang in my head then, *Blackthumb, oh sweet blackthumb!* and there he was, charging through the mob of scorched, the bewildered duskdancers, his smile bright as the sun had once been.

"'*Baptiste!*' I roared.

"'LITTLE LION!' he cried, crashing into my arms, and though I dared not hug him tight for fear of killing him, God, he near crushed the breath from my lungs, lifting me off my feet. Tears burned in my eyes as I wrapped my arms around my old friend, his big shoulders shaking with half sobs. I could only imagine the horrors he'd endured these past nights, but at least we'd been spared the horror of fighting each other. And as my old brother set me on the stone, I looked to heaven above and breathed quiet thanks to God for the first time in as long as I could remember.

"'I thought I'd never see you again, Gabe,' he whispered, pawing his eyes.

"'No such luck, I'm afraid,' I grinned.

"Baptiste looked to the battlements around us, Phoebe beside me, the legion of 'dancers arrayed upon the walls. 'All this for me? You shouldn't have, mon ami.'

"We laughed, but it was brief, our eyes turning now to Newtunn. Shapes were slinking from the ruins below, rotten and wasted, hungry and hissing—an army of Dead flesh, starved of blood, thousands of hollow eyes now fixed upon us.

"'Gabe,' Baptiste murmured. 'Aaron, he's . . .'

"'I know, brother.' I squeezed his shoulder. 'I'm going to get him back, I swear it.'

"'No.' Baptiste hefted a heavy maul in his hands, eyes on the sea of teeth below, the walls of Auldtunn beyond where his beloved waited. '*I'm* going to get him back.'

"I shook my head. 'Aaron belongs to Nikita now. The only way to save him—'

"'He was mine *long* before he was the Blackheart's.' The big man squared his shoulders, patting his maul on his palm. 'Love conquers all, Gabriel.'

"I clenched my jaw, wanting to steer him off, knowing he'd never listen. Baptiste and Aaron had given up everything to be together. I'd seen the love each bore for the other, standing side by side at the Battle of the Twins, the Forever King's Endless Legion not even enough to part them. I'd have been a fool to think Nikita's army would fare any better.

"'Aright,' I muttered. 'You just stick close to me, you hear?'

"'My old friend smiled, hefting his maul. 'You just try to keep up.'

"'Se'yersan!' came the roar.

"I looked down the wall, saw a bloodied Brynne amid a pack of moonsmaidens. The big úrfuil stood atop the broken stone, black slayerbraids whipping in the storm wind as she pointed to the shadows gathering on the battlements of Auldtunn.

"'What are we waitin' fer? A gilded invitation?'

"I glanced to the young fellow beside Celene, dark of hair and eye. His hands were unsteady as he drew his sword, and from his grip, I knew he was green as grass. Looking around the walls, among the hardened swords, I saw others just as fresh, just as frightened.

"'What's your name, monsieur?' I asked him.

"'Joaquin. Joaquin Marenn.'

"'Well, Joaquin Joaquin Marenn, this world owes you a debt. But I think you've done enough to square the ledger this day.' I looked to the wretched swarming below, the men and women newly-freed on the walls around us, calling above the thunder. 'You folk have walked through hell and darkness, but no command bids you fight here, nor any promise binds you to stay! There is no shame in living to fight another day!'

"But Joaquin shook his head then, calling to his fellows. 'I'll not stand aside while the girl who freed me is captive still! I will spill my blood for she who gave the same for me! Dior Lachance risked all to save us, and I say shame to *any* here who'll risk no less!'

"Shouts of agreement rang across the walls, Joaquin holding his sword high.

"'For the Grail Maiden! La demoiselle du Graal!'

"'The Grail!' came the roar, Highlanders and scorched both. 'The Grail!'

"*Fine s-s-speech,* Ash whispered.

"'Not bad,' I agreed.

"*Better than yoursthanyours . . .*

"'I don't speech,' I growled.

"Phoebe stood beside me, blood spilling from a cut in her cheek, eyes on the walls beyond. The vampires were gathered now, wretched and highblood, and there'd be no last-minute miracle here. Every inch of ground would be bought with blood. Every step a war.

"'How you feeling?' I asked softly.

"'Ready,' she replied.

"I turned to Brynne, gave her a nod.

"I held my broken blade to the sky.

"'FOR DIOR!'

"And as one, we charged down into hell."

II

SLAUGHTERSONG

"THREE PATHS LAY ahead of us," Gabriel sighed. "Three red roads."

"The first two ran east and west along the seawalls. The fortifications encircling Newtunn linked up to the battlements around Auldtunn—a man could walk from the dún gatehouse all the way to the city's entrance without his feet ever touching cobbles. Problem was, the battlements were narrow, and any force attacking along them would be caught in a bottleneck once they reached the inner walls; easy targets for the boulders the Dyvok would be tossing about like cheap liquor at an Ossian wedding.

"But the third path was no better—a straight shot up the guts of Newtunn, fighting house to house against Nikita's wretched and being used for target practice all the while."

"The proverbial rock and the hard place," the historian mused.

Gabriel frowned. "There was nothing proverbial about it, vampire. The highbloods were literally going to be throwing rocks at us."

Jean-François rolled his eyes. "So which path did you choose?"

The silversaint leaned back in his chair, legs crossed, drumming fingers to boot. "Well, none held particular appeal. But if I *were* to fall, I'd rather fall fighting than queued up like the sailors outside your mother's house when the fleet is in town."

"Ah, a jest about dear Mama's promiscuity." The historian yawned. "I was just thinking we were overdue. It had been a minute since the last one."

Gabriel snapped his fingers. "That's just what she s—"

"Great Redeemer, would you two *please* just kiss," Celene spat, "and put us all out of our bloody miseries?"

"We took the path up the middle," Gabriel said, scowling at his sibling.

"Heading into Newtunn. Better that than clog the seawalls, I thought. Keylan led a company of leófuil east, Angiss took a pack of velfuil west—"

"No," Celene said.

Gabriel blinked. "What do you mean—"

"No," the Liathe repeated. "Keylan went west, Gabriel. Angiss east."

"Bull*shit*. I saw them. I was *there*."

"As were we."

"Don't I know it," he snarled. "You're the fucking reason it ended the way it did."

"Children." Jean-François drew a slow, steadying breath. "Please."

The siblings stared at each other, knives in their eyes. The Marquis was certain if there were no river between them, they'd be at each other's throats, consequences be damned. He wondered at the rancor between them. The heart of their hate.

The girl, doubtless.

The cup was broken. The Grail is gone.

"Regardless," Gabriel finally sighed, cracking his neck. "The Wolves and Lions took to the walls. And the rest of us descended into Newtunn and dove in among the Dead.

"I'd visited Dún Maergenn in happier days; Lachie and I had traveled here after the victory at Crimson Glade. These streets had been flocked with cheering citizens on the day the Nineswords knighted me, and now, they were choked with the Dead. It was hard to know their number; driving snow and broken buildings and the bloody chaos of battle. Thousands, I'd guess. Old and young. Men and women and children. Empty eyes and black breath, naught in common save the cruel twist of fate that saw them rise from their graves.

"Street by street, house by house, we fought. Phoebe at my right hand, Baptiste my left. My silverbombs and shot were spent in the first few minutes. And though my aegis burned on my skin, I'd kept my greatcoat on for fear the glow would make me too much a target from the walls, relying on the fire of Phoebe's blood in my veins instead.

"God's truth, I'd *never* felt so strong. So alive. Thunder rang out around us—not the storm overhead, but a hail of broken granite, crushing wretched and 'dancer and soldier alike. The frost beneath us ran to red slush, the air so choked I couldn't tell ash from snow. Above the reek of burned flesh and torn bellies, I could smell the Gulf of Wolves beyond the walls, putting me in mind of our little lighthouse by the sea. I tried not to dwell on the fact these things had once been people, thinking only of my vow to Dior. And all the while, Ash sang in my head, not a nursery rhyme tonight, nor an aria, but a sailor's song of all things, echoing in my mind over the hymn of the distant waves, the cries of frightened gulls.

> *"I left you, love, in Maergenn town, to sail upon the sea,*
> *"And with a final kiss you vowed, that you would wait for me.*
> *"Across the Eldersea I sailed, to seek my fortune true,*
> *"And as the skies turn black above, my thoughts are all of you.*
> *"I still can see you now, my dear, so fair upon the quay,*
> *"And as the tempest closes in, I know you wait for me.*
> *"The waves they crash, the timbers break, and leave me now bereft,*
> *"Of all save love for you and fears, that I should ne'er have left.*
> *"And as I sink into my grave, my final breath, this plea,*
> *"My bride is now the ocean deep, love."*

Jean-François sighed as he finished.

> *"Do not wait for me."*

"We took the path along the battlements," Celene said, her voice quickening with memory of the battle. "I'd no stomach to cut down dead women and children, nor condemn already damned souls to hell. And we'd no time to drink a one of them."

"How generous," Gabriel scoffed. "Leave it to others to bloody their hands, instead."

"As if yours did not drip with it already," Celene hissed.

"*Chevalier*," the historian snapped, eyes flashing. "Do *not* interrupt."

Gabriel scowled, toying with his goblet as Celene continued.

"Instead, we ran *west* along the seawall, Keylan á Meyrick beside us, seven feet and five hundred pounds of furious duskdancer, dozens of heathen slayers howling in the Red Wrath's wake. The Dyvok hurled rocks the size of horses, obliterating the stone around us, smashing pagans to sludge— Nikita's courtiers had the stolen strength of the Moonsthrone in their veins, just as Gabriel did. And though my brother and his comrades were cutting a bloody swath through Newtunn, Nikita had saved his best for us.

"We saw him ahead, a whisper of midnight-black and ocean-blue silk, eyes as perilous as the sea. They were fixed on us, on the blade and flail of blood in our hand, and I knew he understood what I was. The Blackheart stood now, his two most loyal beside him; his former lover Kiara and his now-lover, de Coste. He raised Epitaph, that mighty blade singing as it cut the air. And without a word, all three *threw* themselves at us."

"I had never fought Dyvok before our brawl at Aveléne. Not ones this strong, at any rate. I did not quite understand what would be coming, else we'd have cried warning as Gabriel did, his voice ringing under the thunder, too faint, too late."

"Anyja," Jean-François murmured.

"The Dyvok Tempest," Celene nodded. "I know not how much Epitaph weighed. Half a ton perhaps? But when Nikita swung that mighty blade at us, it dragged him forward, like a typhoon of flesh and iron. And when he struck Keylan á Meyrick, the Red Wrath simply . . . *exploded*, bursting apart in a shower of limbs and entrails. Nikita flew on, cutting through the Highlanders like a scythe at reaping time, de Coste and the Wolfmother following. And as the trio skidded to a halt down the far end of the high-walk, where they'd passed, there was only corpses and heathens on their bellies, bewildered and drenched in blood."

"We'd stepped aside the Dyvok, our body splashing to the cobbles as we slipped past their blades; my trick of the eye, my spell of the Blood. But looking back, we saw Nikita raise his foot, and we roared to the folk still on their bellies amid that carnage."

"'Get up, GET—'

"His boot struck the highwalk like a hundred barrels of black ignis, the battlements before him shrieking and blasting apart. Almighty *God*, I had never seen such strength. The wall split to its very roots, ancient stonework torn apart as if it were straw and daub. And those who had managed to dodge his first strike were consumed in this second, screaming as the entire seawall collapsed with the sound of hellborn thunder."

"I'll never forget the sight," Gabriel sighed, gulping down his Monét. "A wall that had stood for centuries, hundreds of 'dancers and slayers and soldiers, obliterated with one stroke. The blood of the Moonsthrone, in the veins of an ancient of the Untamed."

"We stood at the walls of Auldtunn now," Celene said. "Picking ourselves off the stone, facing down the Dyvok highbloods alone as the dust settled behind us. On the eastern approach, the 'dancers battled tooth and claw, but they'd been bottlenecked just as Gabriel warned. My brother had done bloody work in Newtunn, and the streets ran red with it. But Nikita set eyes upon Gabriel now, bellowing above the slaughtersong.

"'De León! *Now* shalt thou remember Nikita's name!'

"The Blackheart launched himself upward, sailing through the storm. The flagstones splintered as he struck the thoroughfare behind my brother and his comrades, throwing up stone dust and snow into the churning air. And when that cloud was snatched away by the wind, there he stood upon the shattered cobbles—that black prince, carved of marble and washed in crimson, dark hair and greatcoat whipping in the moaning winds."

The Last Liathe looked to her brother then, expectant. Gabriel raised a brow.

"Oh, I get to tell my own story now? How kind of you."

"God, you are a child," she sighed.

Gabriel reached for the bottle, topping up his goblet.

"I'd turned at Nikita's shout," the silversaint said. "The shockwaves as he landed rocked the flagstones, smashing our moonsmaids asunder. And target though it might've made me, you'd best believe I tore off my greatcoat then. The ink on my skin burned like flame in that storm, the wretched around us melting away like smoke.

"Nikita stood, his most loyal behind him. The Wolfmother, eyes alight with hate, massive warmaul in her fist and slayerbraids seething in the howling wind. She'd thought me killed at Cairnhaem, and I had no doubt now she'd give anything to bury me in truth.

"My old friend Aaron stood beside her, clad in black and midnight blue, the whites of his eyes all washed with red. His sword had been broken when he died at Aveléne, and I saw he wielded another now—long as I was tall. He'd ever had a princely look, cold as winter, save when he smiled. But he was something else now, something more and less, and my heart broke at the sight of him. Baptiste stood beside me, maul spattered with gore, knuckles washed red. I heard his breath catch as he looked upon his beloved, whispering.

"'Oh, my beautiful man. What have they done to you?'

"Aaron met Baptiste's eyes and smiled. 'Nothing I did not want them to.'

"'I'm sorry, brother,' I called. 'I'm sorry I wasn't there to help you, as you helped me.'

"'Oh, Gabriel,' Aaron sighed. 'You fail *everyone* you love. Why would I be different?'

"I shook my head. 'I'll see your shackles broken this day, Aaron, I vow it.'

"'And what is that worth, exactly? The promise of a liar?'

"'Tell me something, de León.'

"It was Nikita who spoke now, brushing stone dust from his lapels. The chaos of battle raged around us, 'dancers killing highbloods upon the walls, scorched battling the Dead in the streets. But Phoebe's blood was burning in me now, the whole *world* pin-bright, every snowflake falling in slow motion, every scent cut crystal clear in the air—blood, smoke, ash, sweat, shit. And for a moment, it seemed in all the world, there was only we six; Phoebe glowering at Kiara, Baptiste watching Aaron, and my eyes now on the Blackheart.

"'They told me when ye slew my father at Crimson Glade, ye stabbed him in the back.' Nikita smiled, jet eyes narrowed against my burning light. 'That great Tolyev was aready wounded, the snow around him heaped with silvered dead. They told me ye stole up on him like a thief in the night. Like a coward. Like a cur.'

"'They told you I fucked your father from behind, in other words?'

"Kiara growled, lifting her maul. 'My Laerd, allow me to put this mongrel down.'

"Nikita shook his head. 'Ye had thy chance, daughter. And ye failed.'

"'Father, let me—'

"'*SILENCE*,' Nikita snapped, his voice Whipping through the ruins.

"He begged before he died, you know. Your mighty Tolyev.' I raised Ash between us, my rage at Aaron's fate boiling in my veins. 'You all beg, Nikita. That's what *they* don't tell you. When you see the end coming, past all the bluff and bluster, the *thees* and *thous,* in that final moment, you all beg like fucking children. And you die like fucking dogs.'

"I lifted one bloody hand, beckoning.

"'Come die, Blackheart.'

"Nikita bellowed, slinging his blade and himself, cutting toward me like a scythe. With a cry, I dove aside, bringing Baptiste with me as Epitaph split the air in two. The shockwave as Nikita passed was thunder, the broken houses around us crumbling. He skidded to a halt fifty feet down the thoroughfare, shredding the cobbles beneath him. With a curse, I rose to my feet, charging at his back, skin burning with the fury of my faith in the

girl beyond those walls; the girl I'd sworn to protect. Kiara raised her maul, Phoebe's talons glinting as the lightning flashed, and there in that slaughterhouse, our battle was joined.

"Kiara sought only to make right her failure in Nikita's eyes, rushing at my back headlong. But in a flash of flame-red and razored black, Phoebe cut through the snow and Kiara's flank besides, opening dead flesh to the bone. The duskdancer cared nothing about Kiara's sullied honor, nor her quarrel with me—Phoebe owed the Wolfmother for her beating at Cairnhaem, and there under that raging sky, she fancied to collect the due.

"Aaron raised his sword, also set to come to the defense of his master, to strike at his old brother's back. But as he strode forward, a figure stepped into his path, dark skin streaked with dust and blood, eyes filled with pain.

"Pain and boundless, *hopeless* love.

"'Don't do this, Aaron,' Baptiste whispered. 'Please.'

"'Step aside, Baptiste,' Aaron growled, hefting his greatsword. 'I warn you.'

"'I don't want to fight you, love. But I'll not let you hurt anyone else.'"

Gabriel took a moment then, a frown darkening his brow as he stared into his wine. He could hear the battle in his head now, smell the blood and metal, his heart athunder.

"So I was in the shit here, coldblood," he sighed. "My aim had been to steer Nikita away from Phoebe and Baptiste, but now I had his attentions, I'd not much clue what to do with them. The sun was up, and that was something. But for all my talk, Nikita Dyvok was no dog. Six hundred *years* he'd been a warrior, and worse, he was frenzied now on duskdancer blood. And while the doxyhouse minstrels might sing that I was the greatest swordsman alive, the Blackheart wasn't counted among the living.

"If not for my aegis, I'd be dead. But strong as Nikita was, you can't quite kill what you can't quite see. Fighting for Dior that day, the vow I'd made her, the light off my ink was *blinding*, and that was enough to keep me alive—back-footed surely—but skipping just shy of his blade as Nikita danced the Tempest, tearing all about us asunder.

"Baptiste and Aaron were wind and thunder, dancing among the ruins. The blackthumb kept his distance, and Aaron cursed as Baptiste backed away, parrying but never pressing, never fighting back. Yet as soon as Aaron would turn an eye to me, Baptiste would strike, hurling a rock or lunging at his man's flanks, keeping him off my back. Snarling, Aaron taunted Baptiste, using the gifts of Ilon that his immortal father had given him, trying to Push the blackthumb into the fray.

"'*Fight me!*' he'd roar.

"'No,' Baptiste would reply.

"'Kill me! *Hate me!*'

"'Never. I love you, Aaron. I *love* you.'

"And so they ebbed and crashed like the tides, a game of cat and mouse in the wreckage, the bodies and the blood. Poor Maergenn town fair dripped with it, I swear, 'dancers and slayers and highbloods and wretched, an abattoir washed so thick and deep I wondered if here too the cobbles might be forever stained. What would they call this place, when this day was done? The Drowned City? The Scarlet Grave?

"The Grail's Tomb?

"I was growing desperate now. I'd blooded Nikita twice, but he could afford to make mistakes, while I could risk none at all. If I closed in, I brought myself within Epitaph's deadly arc. But if I backed off, the Blackheart would stomp the cobbles and send a shockwave through the earth at me, or simply hurl his blade and himself along with it, slicing the air to ribbons. But if I could get my hand about Nikita's throat, I could boil the 'dancer blood in his veins dry, and his along with it. And so, I skirted closer to that terrible blade, slipping aside and rolling under his blows, watching for my chance.

"Phoebe had taken a hit from Kiara's maul, left arm hanging limp, but the Wolfmother had also been blooded—four jagged tears across her throat. Aaron stalked toward his old lover, face twisted with rage. But Baptiste fell ever back, ducking beneath the booming sweeps of Aaron's blade.

"'Stop running, coward!' Aaron roared.

"'I'll not fight you, love,' Baptiste said, stepping aside Aaron's blow.

"'Don't call me that! I *never* loved you.'

"The big man smiled. 'Now I *know* you're lying.'

"'...Am I?'

"Aaron slowed his assault then, staring at his old lover, his voice soft and sad.

"'None could fault you for believing so, I suppose. I thought what we had was love too.' Aaron looked to Nikita then, lips curling. 'Until *he* showed me otherwise.'

"'That's not true, Aaron. We were happy together!'

"'Happy?' The lordling laughed, cruel and cold. 'With *you*? Playing house in that wretched sty? Living on scraps and rutting in the crumbs? I'd no idea what happiness was.'

"'Aaron, that's his blood talking. He's twisted you.'

"'Ohhh, he's twisted me, aright.' Aaron ran one hand up his throat, biting his lip. 'Twisted me. Bent me. Tied me in knots. Left me wet and sore and *begging* for more.'

"'Don't,' Baptiste hissed, eyes flashing. 'I won't lis—'

"'*God,* the things he's done to me. Things you *never* did. Never *could.*'

"'Aaron, *stop* this.'

"'I never knew what love could be. Until I met him.'

"'STOP it, damn you!'

"It was a brief madness; a rage born of bitterness and fury, not for Aaron, but for the one who'd broken him. But still, Baptiste roared, maul raised, lunging at his beloved. And stepping aside the blow, at last within range, Aaron sprang his snare.

"'You always were a fool for love, Baptiste.'

"His grip closed around the big man's hand with the crunch of breaking bone.

"'And now, just a fool.'

"Aaron's other hand snaked around Baptiste's neck, the big man gasping, seizing his lover's wrist. Aaron dragged Baptiste off the flagstones, the blackthumb dangling in his dreadful grip, one twist from his ending. Clashing with Nikita, I yet heard Baptiste's choking cry, roaring, 'Godssakes, Aaron, *NO!*' Ashdrinker screaming with me as I hurled her through the air. The blade whistled as she came, a silver scythe cutting between the snow, striking Aaron in the chest. Baptiste tumbled from his grip, gasping and wheezing, Aaron flying backward, crashing to the bloody slush in an arc of gleaming red.

"But in saving Baptiste from Aaron's hand, I'd left myself open to Nikita's.

"To this day, I know not what hit me. All I know is I was struck from behind, flinging me like chaff and rags. I heard thunder raging around me, realizing it was the sound of my own body smashing through house after house after house, *boom, BOOM, BOOOOM,* stone shattering, roofs crumbling, white light and red pain and blackness.

"Phoebe's scream dragged me upward from the gloom, my mouth full of snow and blood, the ground shaking as Nikita crashed onto the cobbles beside me. As she saw me fall, Phoebe herself was caught off-guard, the Wolfmother gifting her a blow that sent her flying through the ruins of an old smoke shoppe. Nikita raised Epitaph above me, and as I looked up at him, blood in my eyes and mouth, I heard Astrid calling me in for supper, Patience laughing close by, warm and bright. And I smiled, because I knew I'd see them soon.

"The vampire smiled wider. 'Sleep well in hell, de León.'

"And it seemed then, behind his head, the sun came out from the clouds. Not the feeble star lingering behind the daysdeath pall, but the sun I'd known as a boy, kissing my skin as Celene and Amélie and I lay by the riverbank, in days so dim and distant I'd forgot their warmth. Its light was blinding, flame-red burning now to silver, and above the roar of too-close thunder, I heard a familiar hymn, soaring above the ringing in my ears.

"The song of a silver horn.

"Nikita cursed, silver caustic and black ignis bursting in the air, his skin and coat smoldering from the explosions blooming at his back. And he turned, scorched and snarling, looking at the figure now charging through the city gates. A man, green eyes edged in kohl, silver roses inked down his cheek, the bear on his chest ablaze as he cried.

"'GABRIEL!'

"I still remembered the day I'd found him; barely more than a bairn, his fangs bared in a hateful snarl, fighting for his life on the walls of Báih Sìde.

"God, to think where he'd started.

"What a man he'd become . . .

"'Lachlan.'"

III

CHAOS RISING

" 'LACHLAN . . .' Nikita hissed.

"The Blackheart loomed above me as my old 'prentice plunged toward us, glowing silver bright amid the storm of snow and ash. I lay on my back at Nikita's feet, stunned and bloody, Lachie letting loose with his fivebrace of pistols into the wretched around him, one after another after another. Nikita watched, Epitaph in hand, lips twisted in an empty smile.

"'Long years hath it been, little brother!' he called.

"Their eyes met, those two sons of Tolyev, mortal and immortal amid the carnage and chaos. Among the bodies that washed Maergenn red, those bairns in their nightshirts and the mothers swollen with babes forever unborn. The leavings of a thousand lives, of madness and hellish ambition that had left this city in ruins and this country in ashes.

"'Lachlan raised a pistol, eyes ablaze.

"'No brother of mine.'

"The blast caught Nikita in the face, smashing his cheek wide open, tearing out through the back of his skull. The vampire staggered, stumbled to his knees, hand raised to the gaping wound as he bellowed in fury. Lachlan lifted his horn in reply, blowing another peal upon it, that silvered hymn ringing across the battlefield again. And through that swirling pall of snow and ash, dazed, bleeding, still I saw them, charging through the gates at Lachlan's back—perhaps only fifty but worth a *legion*, angels and saints upon their skins glowing with the light of heaven's fury.

"'The Lord is my shield, unbreakable!' one cried.

"'For San Michon!' came the roar. 'FOR SAN MICHON!'

"'Silversaints,' I whispered.

"I saw Robin among their number, the youngblood's greatsword raised in defense of his fallen hero. Big Xavier Pérez and his faithful hound Saber ran at the songbird's heels, hurling silverbombs into the fray. But more, I saw faces I knew from my years of service to the Order; men I'd fought and bled beside at Crimson Glade, at Saethtunn and Tuuve and Qadir. Maxim Sa-Shaipr and Tomas Tailleur, Kurtis 'the Tower,' and even old Forgemaster Argyle, roaring scripture as he charged, a silversteel warhammer affixed in his iron hand. Behind them came sisters of the Silver Sorority, wheellock rifles pouring silvershot into the Dead, writing a twist to this script that the Blackheart was *not* prepared for.

"Lachlan dashed toward Nikita, drawing his greatsword as he roared. The ancien was yet on his knees, blood dribbling from the silvershot blast to his face. Lachie's eyes were ablaze with holy fervor as he charged the monster who'd helped raise him, all the might of Tolyev's bloodline now brought to bear as he swung his sword toward Nikita's skull.

"Metal rang upon metal as Kiara's maul turned Lachlan's blow aside, the Wolfmother smashing my old 'prentice back across the cobbles with the haft. She loomed tall in the blood and snow as Lachlan snaked back to his feet, the air around her ablaze with silverbombs and shot. She was torn by 'dancer claws, bloodied, outnumbered fifty to one, yet still prepared to defend her beloved fallen lord.

"'Here be a lesson ye should've learned, pup,' she growled. '*Loyalty.*'

"Lachlan smiled, pawing the blood from his chin. 'Teach it to *him*, leech.'

"Kiara turned at the scuff of boots at her back, her face falling. For rather than rising from the rubble to fight side by side with his daughter, Nikita instead raised Epitaph and slung himself into the sky. The vampire's coat was smoldering with silver caustic, a thin trail of smoke etched behind him as he flew through the air; back, back toward the dún, leaving his old lover abandoned in those bloody streets behind him."

The historian chuckled to himself, turning to a fresh page.

"There are none more afraid of dying . . ."

"Than those who live forever," Gabriel nodded, sipping his wine. "Aaron had crawled onto his knees, hands burned black as he dragged Ashdrinker from his chest, Baptiste gasping on the bloody cobbles beside him. A silverbomb burst upon Aaron's skin, setting his coat ablaze, my old brother tearing it off his shoulders lest he too go up in flames. Kiara was standing numb, watching her father flee, flinching as the bombs exploded, staggering as a burst of silvershot struck her in the shoulder, another peppered her chest. Aaron was on his feet now, hurling himself and his blade off through the smoke and storm after his master, and *that* seemed to galvanize Kiara at last, the Wolfmother scrambling behind him, up onto the broken stonework and raising her maul, flinging herself over the broken wall.

"The Untamed had fled the field.

"Newtunn was *ours*.

"I felt a hand grasp mine, and I groaned as Lachlan hauled me up from the bloody snow. My ribs were broken, lungs bleeding, and I could still barely drag in a single, bubbling breath. But all I felt was mad joy as I looked upon his face.

"'Good to see ye again, brother,' he smiled.

"I could only shake my head, wheezing, 'What the h-hell are you d-doing here?'

"'Ye told me to bring a silvered fucking army next time I came after ye.' Lachlan shrugged, green eyes glittering as he glanced at the miracle around us. 'So I did.'

"I looked to Baptiste, dragging himself upright, pale and bleeding, but yet moving. Phoebe emerged from the rubble, dusted in stone, dripping blood. She tensed at the sight of the man who'd shot her, but my old 'prentice raised a hand in peace.

"'Fairdawning, mademoiselle. God's truth, my heart gladdens to see ye well.'

"'It's aright, Phoebe,' I told her, meeting Lachie's eyes. 'He's famille.'

"My old 'prentice eyed me boots to bonce. 'Ye look like shite.'

"'Of course I do.' I dragged my hair back with one bloody hand. 'I'm *me*.'

"His eyes sparkled. My lip curled. Lachlan was the first to break, but I followed close behind, both of us falling into a hug so fierce it might have killed an ordinary man. I picked him up despite all my hurts, squeezing him tight, roaring at the top of my lungs.

"'Bring me those cherry lips, you beautiful little *bastard*!'"

The Last Silversaint leaned back in his chair, eyes shining at the memory. Jean-François's quill was scratching upon the page, his own lips curled in a smile. Celene picked up the half-empty bottle the historian had given her, pressing its lip to the cage across her mouth and splashing some of that clotting red across her tongue.

"Angel Fortuna was smiling on us at last, it seemed. We were fighting against the highbloods on the Auldtunn walls, but as the silversaints cut their way into Newtunn, we felt a tremor of fear run through the Dyvok line. And when Nikita broke, leaping back toward the Auldtunn walls, that tremor became a quaking, all through their number. 'BACK! BACK TO THE DÚN!' was the Blackheart's cry, the highbloods all breaking cover as he roared. The Dyvok rearguard were abandoned by their comrades, cut down by Angiss á Barenn and his wolves, Breandan á Dúnnsair and his lions. But the 'dancers didn't yet press, Gabriel's sorceress calling for her fellows to regroup on the Auldtunn battlements, the shout ringing up and down the line that San Michon had arrived, and salvation was come.

"Crouching low, belly to the stone, we stole alone along the western wall now, over the seagates to Portunn, ever closer to the dún. Amid the smoke and swirling snows, we peered over the battlements, eyes upon our foes. Nikita's court was cut deep, perhaps twenty of their number lost, their resolve hanging now by a thread. Retreated to the walls of his stolen keep, the Count Dyvok glowered at the figures swarming atop the Auldtunn walls, all he had worked for unraveling in the bright song of silver horns.

"His daughter stood beside him, eyes welling with rage.

"'Ye *left* me,' Kiara hissed, hand to her bleeding breast.

"'Survived thee, well enough,' Nikita muttered through his bloody jaw. 'Save thy bleating for the lambs, Kiara. This be a day for wolves.'

"'*All* those years. All I've done for ye—'

"'And what *exactly* hast thou done?' Nikita turned on his broodchild, bloody flecks at his lips. 'The Lion ye claimed to slay hath instead brought *two* armies to bear against us! Mustered by the very weapon ye let slip from thy fool's fingertips!'

"'I sought only to please ye! All I did, I did for love of y—'

"'*Love?*' he roared. 'Hast thou learned *nothing*? Love is frailty in iron's guise, Wolfmother! A lie the ram tells the ewe, that he might seed more *sheep* in her belly! That which is given may be taken away, and what makes ye care, makes ye *weak*! Now trouble me not with mortal trifles while our enemies gather in legion 'pon our doorstep!'

"Kiara bit her lip, eyes welling with bloody tears. Aaron stood at his master's side, skin scorched, chest bleeding—if not from his confrontation with his beloved Baptiste, then at least from the kiss of Ashdrinker's blade. Nikita's court flocked around him, streaked with the ashes of their fellows, flint-dark eyes on the Auldtunn walls. The 'dancers were unsealing the great gates into the inner city now, raising the mighty portcullis, those silvered figures flooding through. Aaron's jaw was clenched, the vampires around him grim and snarling.

"'What do we do, Master?' the capitaine asked.

"'Our fleet awaits in the gulf below,' Alix murmured, glancing to the waters at their backs. 'The oceans be yet ours, Priori. We could take to the boats, live to f—'

"Epitaph sang as it came, cleaving Alix's head clean off her shoulders; a blow so heavy and swift that it took a moment for the vampire's body to realize it was dead. As it tumbled off the wall, Alix's corpse crumbled to ashes, stolen years reclaimed by death's hungry hand, her skull turning to dust before it ever struck the cobbles. The Draigann roared as his lover was decapitated, eyes wide with outrage as they fell on Nikita. But the Priori Dyvok stood clad in smoking black, his bloody blade extended toward his nephew's throat, the empty midnight of his eyes still fixed on the foe as he spoke.

"'The next craven who proposes retreat shall suffer the same.'

"The Draigann trembled with fury. His golden fangs glinted as he snarled, tattooed skin smeared with the blood and char of battle, but still, he dared speak not a word of protest. There are few matters so deep as those of the heart, true. But no hearts beat inside the chests of the damned, Historian. And forever is a *long* time to give up for love.

"'What then,' he spat, 'would you have us do, Priori?'

"Nikita glanced at his defenses, pawing at the silvershot hole in his cheek. The battlements here were stronger, yet still cracked from his assault months back; plenty of footholds for a paleblood or duskdancer to take advantage of on the climb. There were no trebuchet or cannon here, only iron troughs to pour stones and boiling water down on ascending troops. But those troughs were empty now—the stone had been used to shore up the fortifications, and there was no scalding water in a dún where flames were all but forbidden. But looking at the basins, the Blackheart still smiled, turning now to Aaron.

"'Bring me the cattle.'

"Aaron glanced to those awful cages in the bailey behind; the feeble and frozen remnants of the bounty from Aveléne. 'Which ones, Master?'

"'All of them.'

"Aaron kissed his laerd's hand, the mark of his bloody lips painted on the Blackheart's skin. Nikita had turned back to the enemy; the silversaints spilling into Auldtunn, the Lion limping at their head, his fleshwitch and blackthumb and that accursed *traitor* beside him, all of them bleeding but unbroken. A legion of former Dyvok scorched came tumbling behind them, liberated by the craft of that damnable girl, the Blackheart's gaze flashing as young Joaquin raised his bloody sword and led the cries of those soldiers, ringing now on the winds.

"'La demoiselle du Graal!'

"He turned to Kiara, snarling.

"'Bring me that accursed girl.'

"The Wolfmother yet stared knives at her broodfather's throat, eyes drifting to the stain of Aaron's lips upon his hand. Her own lips were parted, her gaze—

"'*Now!*' Nikita snapped, his voice near cracking the stone.

"And with fingers curled into fists, the Wolfmother turned to obey."

"Why had you not already freed her?"

Celene glanced up at the historian's interruption. Jean-François was still writing in his tome, preternaturally swift, sparing her a brief glance as he dipped quill to ink.

"If you could take the form of your little winged legion at will, why not simply bypass the enemy entirely and slip into the Dyvok dungeons, there to set Lachance loose?"

Gabriel was pouring himself another wine, looking to Celene with eyebrow arched.

"Excellent question. Why *hadn't* you freed her, sister?"

"We knew we would do more good upon the walls," Celene replied. "Dior was locked in her cell, wounded, oui, but safe enough for now. Until the silversaints arrived, our assault upon the Untamed was failing, and every blade was needed in the fray."

"Awfully thoughtful." Gabriel inclined his head. "Or perhaps you fancied you might snatch yourself another cheeky feast in the chaos? Save another damned soul from perdition, as you'd done with Rykard at Aveléne? Maybe a mediae this time? Or a nice *juicy* ancien to wet your whistle? Do you earn more kudos from your beloved Maker the older your victims are? Or do you just steal more power for yourself?"

"You know nothing," she spat. "And *still* you whine like a kicked dog. Do you never tire of the sound of your own voice, brother?"

"You could've stopped it," Gabriel snarled. "What came next, you could've—"

"*Stop*," Jean-François snapped, slapping his page. "You were saying, Mlle Castia?"

"I was saying," she hissed, still glowering at Gabriel, "we fought upon the walls until the 'saints arrived. And soon thereafter, we were fighting for *all* our lives. So while my dear brother would love nothing so much as to place the blame for all that happened at my feet, I did the best I could." She sighed and hung her head. "Would that it could've been more."

Gabriel scoffed, but at a sharp glance from Jean-François, the silversaint held his tongue, sipping from his goblet instead. And with a final glower, his sister spoke on.

"Kiara stormed into the dún at Nikita's behest, her mood as wrath as the storm overhead. The rends Phoebe had torn in her skin, the silvershot holes blasted by Lachlan and his brothers, the bruises Nikita had left on her heart—who knew which pained her worse. We lost sight of her as she passed into the keep, but that mote of us with Dior deep in the dungeons was listening as Kiara approached the Grail's cell.

"Nikita's toy, the girl Isla, was on guard outside the Grail's cage at the command of her Ever After, a handful of thrallswords standing duty with her. Reyne á Maergenn watched from the barred slot in her cell door opposite. The Princess was bruised, but she'd been healed by the Grail's holy blood, glowering at the Wolfmother's approach.

"'Lady Kiara,' Isla curtseyed. 'How fares my laerd and love?'

"The Wolfmother ignored the girl, twisting the key in Dior's lock.

"'Lady Kiara?' Isla asked again. 'How fares the Laerd—'

"Reaching out slow, Kiara cupped Isla's pretty face, and with no word of warning, pushed it through the nearest wall. The girl's head burst like an overfull wineskin, her skull crushed to pulp. The thrallswords took a moment to react as the brains and blood splashed their boots, but by the time they reached for their steel, Kiara was among them, snapping necks like dry twigs, punching one fellow so brutally in the stomach, his innards escaped upward through his mouth. Floors washed red, hands painted likesame, Kiara wrenched open the Grail's door.

"'What are you doing?' Reyne demanded.

"Dior was laid on the floor, blooded at her ears and nose. The mote of us with her shivered, tiny and helpless, the rest of me on the outer walls seething now. Kiara rolled the girl onto her back, eyes brimming with red rage. And reaching to her boot, she drew out the short, sharp knife she'd used to flay de Coste on the long road to Maergenn town.

"'No, stop!' the Princess roared. 'Stop it, don't touch her!'

"The Wolfmother glanced at the girl, snarling, 'Shut yer fuckin' noise, whelp.'

"Reyne smashed her knuckles against the door. 'If you hurt her, I'll *kill* you!'

"'I'm nae hurtin' her,' Kiara spat, turning back to the comatose girl. 'I'm hurtin' *him*.'

"The Wolfmother stared at the brand atop her hand—that black heart circled by thorns, that mark of affection that should have faded long ago. And stabbing her blade into her marble skin, she sliced her scar of fealty away, pressing the bleeding wound to Dior's lips. The Grail moaned, crimson washing her tongue—the blood of a mediae, true, but enough to rouse her after that brutal kick to her skull. Slowly, the girl opened her gore-gummed eyes, widening as they saw the Wolfmother looming over her. Dior woke fully then, scrambling backward over the stone. She wiped her fingers across her bleeding nose, bloody fingers held out before her like daggers. But the Wolfmother only scoffed and rose to her feet.

"'Do ye still run swift, little Mouse?'

"Dior blinked. 'What?'

"'Get up. I'm taking ye out of here.'

"The Wolfmother turned, trudging across the corridor toward Reyne's cell, the bewildered girl watching as Kiara opened her door and nodded to Dior.

"'She'll need yer help. Highness.'

"The Princess held still a moment, uncertain, untrusting. Staring at the bleeding gouge atop Kiara's hand—the flayed mark of the one she was betraying.

"'What makes ye care,' the Wolfmother said, 'need not make ye weak.'

"Shouldering past the vampire, the Lady Reyne ran into the Grail's cell, slipping an arm around the groaning girl. Helping her to sit, Reyne pressed lips to Dior's brow, her cheeks, her bloody mouth, whispering fierce.

"'Are you well?'

"'Better now,' Dior whispered. 'Are y—'

"'Move yer arses, both o' ye,' Kiara snapped. 'Afore I change my mind.'

"Reyne took Dior's hands, helped the Grail to her feet. Kiara stood in the corridor, glowering at the pair before turning on her bloody heel and stalking back up the stairs. The girls followed slower, Dior limping beside Reyne, the Princess's arm around the Grail's waist. Dior frowned as she saw Isla and the scorched, splashed all over the walls.

"'What the hell is going on?' she whispered.

"The Wolfmother licked gore from her fingers as she climbed the dungeon stair, talking over her shoulder to the two girls following. 'Yer Gabriel is at the gates. But blood shall be spilled by the oceanful afore ever he reaches ye. Find ye somewhere to hide from the Blackheart 'til the battle is done.'"

Jean-François held up one hand, halting Celene's story. "Pray, let us not get too far ahead of ourselves, Mlle Castia." Dipping quill to ink, the historian glanced toward his other prisoner. "Where were you during all this delicious treachery, Silversaint?"

Gabriel drank from his goblet, dragged knuckles across his mouth.

"I'd no idea it was even happening. We were yet cleaning up packs of foulbloods, and mustering on the Auldtunn walls. We'd done well to press Nikita and his highbloods back to the dún, but I'd been fighting the Dead most of my life, Historian, and I knew you bastards are never more dangerous than when backed into a corner."

"Law the Fourth," Jean-François murmured.

"*The Dead feel as beasts, look as men, die as devils.*" Gabriel nodded. "But with the Silver Order on our side, I *knew* we could win now. Lachlan and the other 'saints had marshaled below, Joaquin and the scorched bolstering their number. Two contingents of 'dancers were set to hook east and west along the seawalls, closing around the dún while our silver sisters and moonsmaidens covered us with wheellock and bow. Phoebe stood beside me, and as we stared across the snows at the coldbloods on the dún's walls, she squeezed my hand. Raising Ashdrinker high, I drew breath to sound our charge.

"*G-G-G-Gabriel, Gabegabe, b-b . . .*

"I frowned at the silver stutter, looking at the dame upon my blade.

"'. . . Ash?'

"*B-b-b-b . . .*

"I pressed my bloodied fingers to her face. 'What is it, mon amie?'

"*B-B-B-BEHIND!*

"'Se'yersan!' Brynne roared. 'Ware ye!'

"I turned at the cry, my belly sinking. And there, slinking into the red rivers of the Newtunn streets at our backs, they came. The vanguard were foulbloods one and all, over a thousand by the look—beggars and lords, soldiers and peasants, parents and children. Their brains rotted to ruin, their bodies mere shells for the thirst within. Men marched behind, hundreds more their number. White ravens graced their shields and tabards, helms fashioned like skulls, their pauldrons, skeletal hands. Swordsmen in front, riflemen behind, wheellocks at their shoulders and death in their eyes.

"'It's the bloody Voss!' Brynne cried.

"'It *cannae* be,' Phoebe whispered. 'We caught those runners this morning. The Órd is *days* from here.'

"And I knew then, the simple truth. While the river *was* days distant, while Nikita's message would never have reached it in time, that only mattered if the Terrors had waited where they'd promised. If their master had kept his word to his old flame.

"'Fabién lied to Nikita.' I shook my head. 'He was planning to betray the Blackheart as soon as he had opportunity. And we just gave it to him. Let the Dyvok and us soften each other up, then mop up the remainder, and collect Dior on the way out the gates.'

"'Sweet Mothermoons,' Phoebe hissed."

The Last Silversaint licked at wine-stained lips, staring into his goblet.

"So there we were, Historian. Caught between hammer and anvil, balls-deep in hell, with a new hell greasing up our rears. Over a thousand more foulbloods, thrallswords behind them, fresh and unbloodied by battle. And squinting through the smoke and snow, I saw them, like a pair of good little emperors, *alllll* the way at the back of their lines. Two tiny figures, clad in white and black, hands all drenched in red.

"I could still see them in my mind's eye, gathered outside my home the night their dread father came knocking. They'd stood and watched while he did it. They'd *laughed* as my angels died. And I'd sworn I'd see them dead for it, every one.

"'What do we do, Gabe?' Phoebe whispered.

"I raised my blade, the ink on my skin ablaze.

"'Time to make good on a promise.'"

IV

COLDER STILL

" *'GABRIEL!'*

"The cry rose over the howling winds, the tromp of heavy boots at our backs. I looked down to the city streets below, Lachlan staring up at me as he pointed behind.

"'I see them!' I roared. 'Can you cover the Dyvok?'

"Lachlan glanced to the dún, then nodded, his face bloodied and grim.

"'Yer back! My blade!'

"'Angiss!' I shouted. 'Take your Wolves west over the Portunn gates, meet Lachie at the dún. Breandan!' I turned to Phoebe's cousin. 'Take your slayers east. Brynne, you and yours come with us! Silver sisters cover the 'saints, moonsmaidens at our backs!'

"I ducked for cover as a boulder the size of a small house demolished the walls alongside me. I saw Nikita tearing another chunk of battlement free in his hands.

"'All of you go! *GO!'*

"We charged toward our foes, half of us toward the Untamed ahead, the rest turning to deal with the Ironhearts behind. Phoebe and I leapt clear of the crumbling battlements, Baptiste landed beside us, flinching as the high-walk cracked overhead, stone dust and blood plastered to his skin. His arm was broken, a sling around his neck, a mallet of purest silversteel borrowed from Forgemaster Argyle clutched in his off hand.

"'Gabe, I have to go after Aaron!'

"'Damn it, Baptiste!' I snarled. 'The only way to free him is to kill the Blackheart! And I love you, mon ami, but you've not got that feat in you!'

"We winced again, more stone smashing overhead, Ironhearts closing in behind.

"'I can't just leave him! Would you abandon your bride among those monsters?'

"And I shook my head then, chest aching. I knew my old friend spoke truth—that I'd never leave my beloved behind, no matter the cost. I also knew that barring a miracle, Baptiste went now to his death. But God help me, I'd not the heart to stop him."

"The storybooks are full of fools who died for love," Jean-François murmured.

"That they are," the silversaint nodded, rubbing his stubble. "And though it might mark me a fool also, I'm glad for that fact, Historian. If you fight for nothing? That's exactly what you'll give to defend it. But if you fight for something worthwhile—I mean something that *truly* matters—there's no length you won't go to. Brotherhood. Famille. Loyalty. Love. All worth trying for. All worth *dying* for. In the end, that's what makes us different from you, vampire. And that which makes us different, makes us mighty."

Gabriel smiled.

"And so, I clasped my brother's hand, and spoke the words Aaron and I had said to each other at the Battle of the Twins, staring into the eyes of death side by side.

"'No fear. Only fury.'

"Baptiste kissed my bloody cheek and turned to join the silversaints, streaming now toward the dún. The Highlanders were rushing out to meet the Ironhearts, carving through the wretched vanguard. Brynne was a bloody powerhouse, fighting tooth and claw, painted to her elbows and surrounded by a sea of her howling kin. I saw a bear as big as a wagon plow through a half dozen wretched, tearing them asunder with claws and teeth. A shower of arrows sliced through the storm, cutting into the Voss thrallswords behind, wheellock fire crackling in the air. Parts of the city were ablaze, the Dead fleeing the flames, smoke biting the air black. Through the haze, I could see highbloods among the Voss troops, leading the thrallswords on, but my eyes were only on those two shadows, light and dark, lurking at their backs. Those dread generals, old when empire was young, hands entwined and drenched with the blood of ma famille.

"I heard a whisper of cloth, soft boots hitting snow, the scent of fresh blood on the air. Turning, I saw Celene beside me, bloody rags over her face, dead eyes on the Terrors.

"'You should go help Dior,' I told her. 'Steal inside the dún in the chaos and—'

"'Dior is sssafe for now. Kiara has her.'

"'*Kiara?* In what fucking nightmare is that safe?'

"'Mothers and sonsss. Fathers and daughtersss. Sisters and brothersss.' She shook her head. 'Quite a web we weave, we who call ourselves famille. But the Wolfmother has Dior safe under her wing. And you will need our help to defeat my aunts, brother.'

"'I didn't think you cared, sister.'

"She looked at me then, dead eyes rimmed with red, quiet in that storm.

"'I never ssstopped caring, Gabriel. That is why it hurt ssso badly when I thought you did.'

"She raised her blade and flail, glowering at the Terrors.

"'Now. Let usss go have blood for my niece.'"

The Last Silversaint leaned forward, empty goblet hanging limp in his fingers. His sister remained mute, watching across those dark waters, still as stone. Gabriel stared at her, breath hissing soft through his fangs, coming a little quicker now. Jean-François stopped writing, glancing toward Capitaine Delphine as the mood in the cell shifted a shade darker. Thrallswords tensed in the shadows, ready to move should the silversaint entertain the fury that burned bright and sudden in his eyes, but Gabriel only closed his fist, knuckles white, his golden goblet crumpling in his hand as he murmured.

"Do you know what a dejanic victory is, coldblood?"

The historian looked again to Delphine, motioned for the man to stand down.

"Oui." Jean-François nodded. "Named for King Dejan of Talhost, who fought Maximille the Martyr at the siege of Charinfel in the year 8 BE. He battled the Augustins to a standstill, but lost over ninety percent of his forces in the process. The phrase describes a triumph so costly it is akin to defeat."

Gabriel stared at Celene a heartbeat longer, the air heavy as lead. Dropping his crushed goblet, he picked up the bottle of wine, drinking straight from the neck.

"We ran along the broken westwall," he said, slurring soft. "Back toward the rear of the Voss line. Brynne and her fellows were slicing into the Ironheart vanguard, but the going was slow and bloody, and I meant to cut around their flank, strike at the Terrors from behind. I snatched up a dead soldier's cloak to cover my aegis as we ran, only three of us; Phoebe, Celene, and I, darting over the rubble and across the ruined highwalk. The smoke and snow were so thick, we were but shadows, the storm and battle so loud, we were but whispers, the stench of blood so heavy, they'd never smell us coming. And so we ran on, swift and sure over the rubble, the thundering storm, eyes locked on the pair of them.

"They stood on the crumbling arch atop the outer gatehouse, watching the battle unfold with dead black eyes. Patient, ancient, content to spend every drop of their troops' blood so long as they stole their prize in the end. Our warriors were torn and battle-worn, the Voss troops were fresh. The Dyvok wretched had attacked our forces mindlessly, but under the will of the Iron-hearts, the Voss foulbloods were feinting and maneuvering, pressing Brynne and our 'dancers where they were weakest, melting back to regroup. I saw that towering úrfuil go down under a mountain of foulbloods, moonsmaidens brought low by volleys of wheellock fire. Left to their own devices, Fabién's brood would win this day. But strike off the shepherd's head and the sheep will scatter, vampire, and between we three lions, I fancied we could take off a bonce or two.

"They felt us coming, eventually—even with my aegis concealed, there's lit-tle chance of stealing up on monsters that can feel minds. But still, we'd got close enough in the chaos, and as Alba and Aléne turned toward us, I saw them quaver, a ripple pass down their line of foulbloods below. Wheellock blasts rang out, thralls firing at us from the ruined streets, shots striking stone around us, but on we ran, Phoebe's claws glinting, Celene's blade dripping, Ashdrinker humming in my head to light a fire in my chest—that nursery rhyme I'd sing to Patience back when she was a little girl, woken by terrors in the night.

> *"Sleep now, my lovely, sleep now, my dear,*
> *"Dark dreams will fade now your papa is near.*
> *"Fear not the monsters, fear not the night,*
> *"Papa is here now and all shall be right.*
> *"Close your eyes, darling, and know this be true,*
> *"Morning will come, and your papa loves you.*

"Black eyes fell upon us, black wills following, battering upon my brow with the weight of bloody centuries. Minds so old and cold, they were simply unknowable. How many years, their counting? How many murders, their tally? But still, I felt a tremor as they looked to Celene, that blade of blood rippling in her hand, the fangs gleaming in her skull as she tore the rags away to reveal the ruin Laure had made of her face.

"I could hear it in their whisper.

"Their hate.

"Their *fear*.

"*Esani . . .*'"

Gabriel fell silent as Celene snaked to her feet. The Last Liathe seemed caught in the battle's spell now, just as the historian was, his quill moving swift across the page.

"We could see it also. Taste it on the very air. Alba and Aléne were daughters of Fabién, sisters to the beast who slew me, and to see even a sliver of disquiet in those Terrors bought a smile to our ragged lip. But as we fell to, there atop the gatehouse, Gabriel and his fleshwitch hewing at Alba, ourself at Aléne, all smugness ran to dust. As Aléne drew a blade from her riding crop and stepped aside our blow, we glanced back toward that mote of us within Dún Maergenn, a whisper slipping my lips.

"'*Kiara.*'

"The Wolfmother had reached the Hall of Crowns, the shadow of the Nineswords' statue, the Princess and the Grail limping behind her. But she froze still now, eyes widening as a cold voice spoke her name. Smoke hung on the wind with the hymn of silver horns and Highland pipes, the chant of doom come calling. Dior cursed, Reyne's jaw clenched. And turning, they saw three figures behind, eyes locked on the traitorous Wolfmother.

"The first was Kane, the Headsmun's terrible greatsword at rest on his shoulder. The second was Prince, snarling and scarred. And third, swathed in a beautiful gown of black and crimson, a crown of antlers upon her brow and a cuirass of steel at her breast . . .

"'Lilidh,' Dior hissed.

"'How now, sweet niece?' The Heartless smiled, petting her growling wolf atop his head. 'Wherefore dost thou travel with arms so laden?'

"'My dread Lady.' Kiara bowed, nodding toward the sound and fury outside. 'Saints of silver are come to the gates in aid of the Lion. The battle goes ill. Laerd Nikita demanded the girl be brought to the walls.' She glowered at Kane. 'Where *ye* should also be, cousin.'

"'The girl.' Lilidh's eyes flickered now to Reyne. 'Yet two such I count afore me?'

"The Contessa tilted her head, quizzical.

"'Or be it three?'

"'M'lady, I—'

"'Think me deaf as well as blind?' The Heartless glanced toward Kiara's bloody hand, her father's brand flayed off her skin. 'Think me fool, little niece?'

"The Wolfmother gritted her teeth, putting herself between Lilidh and the Grail. Dior was still looking limp and dazed, Reyne supporting her weight. But as the pair began slipping back toward a servants' door, Prince snarled, his eye flashing. Kane hefted his blade, glowering at his older cousin, but Kiara stared only at the Heartless, her mighty warmaul clenched in her fist. The ancien had never offered anything but cruelty to her niece, nor bestowed anything but scorn. We know not if Kiara thought herself Lilidh's better in battle. If she fancied the Contessa soft beneath that steel breastplate, a creature of whispers and silken sheets. Perhaps she was simply tired. Furious. Betrayed. Bleeding. We know not the Wolfmother's heart, Historian. We know only what she said.

"'I think ye a sadist,' Kiara spat. 'A viper and an oathbreaker. I think ye sister to a bastard,' she glanced to Kane, 'and a mother to cravens, and an architect of *ruin,* who sat upon a throne bought with blood ye were content to drink, but ne'er to risk.'

"The Wolfmother spat red upon the broken stone.

"'I think ye a *coward,* Lilidh.'

"And with that, Kiara drew back her arm and hurled her warmaul across the hall.

"She was only mediae, true, but she was dosed with duskdancer blood, and a warrior of the Untamed, hardened by decades of battle. Kiara's maul cut the air hard enough to shake the windows, and though Lilidh tried to move, the Dyvok are famed for their strength, not speed. The Heartless was struck, sailing backward in a gout of blood, colliding with the Nineswords' statue so hard it shattered into pieces. Granite cut the air like knives, Niamh's legendary blade singing as it crashed onto the flagstones. Lilidh flew onward, smashing into the wall beyond, the gables overhead creaking ominously as she collapsed to the stone.

"Kane roared at his broodmother's fall, lunging at Kiara with his greatsword. The Wolfmother wore two blows, the first taking her left arm off at the elbow, the second sinking deep into her chest. But spitting blood, cursing, Kiara smashed Kane aside with a vicious backhand. The armored suits about the hall trembled as the Headsmun struck the far wall, tumbling to the floor with a bubbling groan. And roaring in pain, Kane found himself pinned to the stone; his own greatsword torn from Kiara's breast and flung clear across the room, piercing his ribs and nailing him hilt-deep to the stone behind.

"Right hand curled in a bloody fist, the Wolfmother stalked toward her fallen aunt, murder in her eyes."

"Outside, things were running to shite now," Gabriel said. "Brynne and her kin were tearing the Voss apart, but being cut deeper in kind. Every death of theirs was bought with one of ours, Highlanders and foulbloods and thrallswords ripping each other to ribbons. Lachie and his silversaints had reached the dún, but there, the battle had run every shade of bloody. Silver ink burned in the dim dawn light, screams of the undying tearing the air. The 'saints hit the broken walls, leaping and climbing upward toward their foes on the battlements. But rather than stones raining down from above, Lachlan and his 'saints found another horror pouring onto their heads.

"It was Nikita's design. My gut still churns at the thought, even as my mind marvels at the genius. For in the time it took us to muster, those prisoners had been fetched from their cages, just as their laerd had ordered. The parishioners of Aveléne, the mothers, the children, all twisted open like ripe fruit and poured into the troughs along the battlements, then dumped in great steaming gouts over the silversaints leaping up from below."

"Blood," Jean-François realized. "Mixed with ash, snow, sticking to their skin . . ."

"It dulled the light of their aegis," Gabriel nodded. "Enough for the Dyvok to fight back at least. And as the silversaints reached the battlements, Aaron fell among them, fey and fell in that strangled silver light, Nikita beside him, dancing the Tempest with his dark lover; a dreadful duet tearing bloody furrows through the 'saints. Between them, they sent half a dozen brothers to their graves, young Robin beheaded with a single stroke, Tomas and Maxim, even old Argyle falling beneath their blades. From among the 'dancers charging along the seawall, Baptiste watched in horror, stricken to the heart at the sight of his beloved, *laughing* with Nikita as he slew those faithful sons of San Michon.

"At the gates, we clashed with the Terrors, the five of us a blur through the driving snow. Phoebe and I waltzed with Alba, but though we were two and our foe one, the Terror's skin was steel, and her mind pressed us constantly, whispering, half-heard echoes in the back of my head, shadows ever moving at the corners of my eyes.

"'*Papa?*'

"It was Patience's voice I heard, frightened and small. She was close, I could *feel* her, reaching out to me as she'd done when she was little, waking alone and afraid in the night.

"*'Papa?'*

"I heard Astrid's voice too, ringing in the dark halls of my heart. I saw her upon the battlements before us now, looking from Phoebe to me, heartbreak in her tear-stung gaze.

"*'You promised. How could you?'*

"*'Listen n-not, Gabriel,* Ash said. *Flowers fallen, pictures faded. She is g-g-gone.*

"*'Papa!'*

"*'You promised!'*

"*'They are g-gone.*

"*'Ye failed them, Lion.'*

"Alba smiled, head whipping aside as my blade crashed across her cheek, leaving naught but a scratch in her marble skin. Stepping aside Phoebe's strike, the vampire lashed out with the sword hidden in her riding crop, midnight eyes fixed on me.

"*'Ye failed them both.'*

"'Shut up!'

"'Dinnae listen, love,' Phoebe hissed. 'They're naught but lies.'

"*'Papa, where are you?'*

"'SHUT UP!'"

Gabriel halted in his tale, taking another long swig from the bottle. Dragging one hand down his face, he heaved a sigh that seemed to come from his boots. The Last Liathe stood at the river's edge, black eyes upon her brother, patient as spiders. But when it became obvious he would not speak, the Liathe continued instead.

"The Princess á Maergenn had turned to flee as the battle in the Hall of Crowns was joined. Reyne had no thought for the Wolfmother's safety, only the girl in her arms, dragging the still-dazed Dior around the grand staircase. But Prince flew out of the dark like an arrow then, the Princess and Grail both tumbling to the stone with a cry. Reyne screamed as the white wolf's fangs sank into her shoulder, blood spraying, bone cracking, the great beast possessed of a devil's strength. With a roar of fury, Dior lunged up from the flagstones, aiming a savage kick at the wolf's skull and striking true—her dainty pointed heel crashing right into Prince's open maw.

"'Good for something at least,' she gasped.

"Lilidh lay silent and still as Kiara reached out with her one good hand. But with a roar, the Headsmun struck at the Wolfmother's back. His skull was broken, his chest ruptured, but still he flew like a spear, crashing into her spine and bringing them both down to the ground. Kiara seethed, snarling and spitting blood, massive hand closing around Kane's throat. The Headsmun's thumb sank into her eye, bursting it like a grape, crunching through the socket behind. The pair struggled, cousin against cousin, the only blood between them thickened with hate. But Kiara was ever the elder, the stronger, and pressing down with all her might, she dug her fingers into Kane's neck.

"'I told ye to mind that tongue of yers, cousin.'

"With a snarl, the Wolfmother tore out a fistful of the Headsmun's throat, jaw and teeth and lolling tongue all coming with it. And with one final gasp, Kiara smashed her bloody fist back into Kane's skull, smearing it over the shattered flagstones behind.

"Prince hadn't taken kindly to the kick to his face, the wolf now turning on Dior. Beyond getting the beast away from Reyne, the Grail had no kind of plan, scrabbling back toward the statue's rubble. The wolf lunged, sinking his fangs into her shin and shaking, *shaking,* the Grail screaming over the beast's hollow growls. And behind him, Reyne á Maergenn lifted the sword she'd snatched up from the rubble; the sword of the mother who had never truly been a mother at all, who had never expected a moment of greatness from her. And with a fierce cry, she plunged the blade hilt-deep into Prince's back.

"The wolf wailed, bubbling and whimpering, sinking at last down to the stone. With a gasp, Reyne dragged the blade of the Nineswords free, grabbed Dior and hauled her upright, the girls bleeding and staggering away across the Hall of Crowns.

"Hand dripping with her cousin's leavings, Kiara limped toward her aunt. Lilidh still lay on the shattered timbers, breastplate crushed by the Wolfmother's maul, her ancien eyes yet closed. Kiara loomed above her fallen elder, shrouded in lightning's pulse and a shower of dust, lifting her bloody hammer in hand. And if this were a tale of redemption, of heroes, the Wolfmother might have slain the Heartless then and there. But as her niece raised her weapon high, a single drop of blood fell, spattering on Lilidh's ruby lips.

"And the Contessa opened her eyes.

"'*S-STOP.*'

"Seething, powerless before that Whip, Kiara stopped.

"'*KN-KNEEL.*'

"Helpless as a babe, Kiara sank to her knees as Lilidh rose up from the wreckage.

"'*DIE.*'

"And with the strength of seven centuries at her bloody fingertips, the Heartless tore the Wolfmother's head from her shoulders in a spray of bone and blood.

"And Kiara Dyvok died."

Silence fell in that dark cell below Sul Adair, Jean-François pursing his lips.

"Hmm. A shame. In the end, I rather liked her."

"She was a fucking fiend." Gabriel fixed bleary eyes on the Marquis, his voice thick with wine. "Butcher of thousands. Slayer of innocent women and children. A bloodthirsty murderess with nothing close to a conscience."

"As I say." Jean-François shrugged. "I rather liked her."

The silence was broken by a scribbling quill, the historian resuming his chronicle. The Last Silversaint shook his head, quaffing from his bottle.

"Outside the dún," he continued, "the 'saints were still clashing on the walls with the Dyvok. The toll the Untamed had taken was terrible, but the 'dancers had arrived now, Angiss and Breandan sweeping along the seawalls and crashing against the highblood flanks. Baptiste ran with the Wolves, broken arm and all; the bloody madman had doused his warhammer in pitch and set it alight with some 'saint's flintbox, swinging it like a burning silversteel club. The battle was spilling off the walls now, down into the dún's bailey, over into the streets of Auldtunn, Dyvok flinging themselves about in their Tempest, all order collapsing into the sweet arms of chaos.

"Nikita and Aaron had cut a bloody swath along the battlements, but the 'saints had rallied now, Lachlan fighting at their fore. He was the paleblooded son of mighty Tolyev, my old 'prentice, and he'd been raised among the Untamed before he was trained by me to kill them. Leaving one highblood legless, another in ashes on the stone at his feet, he lunged now at Aaron, meeting the lordling blade to blade.

"'They always told me ye were a bastard, de Coste,' he spat.

"'And do you know what they told me about you, boy?'

"Aaron hissed in reply, smashing Lachlan back across the stone.

"'Absolutely *nothing*.'

"Sparks flew as Lachlan's silversteel bit into Aaron's greatsword, fledgling and silversaint now clashing blade to blade. They were near equal in strength, perhaps in fury, both with all to lose. But in the end, Aaron had been only an initiate when he was cast from the Order, and Lachlan was a 'saint with seventeen years of war under his belt. With his foe still off-kilter in the dim light of his bloody aegis, Lachlan's sword found a way past Aaron's guard. Slicing the fledgling's shoulder bone-deep, Lachlan followed through, and with a twist, my old 'prentice disarmed my brother clean. Aaron's greatsword glittered as it sailed off the battlements, singing as it struck the stones of the bailey below. And fangs bared, Lachlan raised his silversteel for the deathblow.

"'I'll tell Gabe ye died well.'

"With a desperate cry, Baptiste threw himself through the melee, striking Aaron square in the chest. Tangled together, blackthumb and fledgling tumbled off the battlements, crashing into the bloody snow fifty feet below. Lachlan made to pursue the pair, but as Brother Xavier was cut to red mist but a few feet to his left, my old 'prentice found himself in far deeper water. It landed now on those shattered battlements before him with a crash, drenched head to foot in gore, eyes gleaming like voids.

"'Godmorrow, little brother,' Nikita smiled."

"Back at the gates," Celene said, "we still warred with the Terrors. Below us in Newtunn, thrallswords and foulbloods clashed with slayer and 'dancer, but atop the gatehouse, we fought alone. The fleshwitch had bloodied Alba, the iron of her throat torn by the duskdancer's talons. Gabriel pressed her back, bleeding from a slice across his cheek, another down his chest, burning red with the light of his aegis. And though it scorched the eyes of our foes, that cursed light blinded me too, making our own opponent ever more dangerous. Aléne's skin was dark grey marble, and though it shredded her finery, our blade left no wounds, only welts and tiny cracks on the flesh of her arm, her chest, her throat.

"She was in our head, I could feel her; preying on my fears, riddling me with doubt. Our swordarm was shaking, legs atremble, mind echoing with unbid memory. Their sister, my dread mother, tearing my throat and face asunder. The red hell of dying in Laure's embrace, awful pain and pleasure entwined, redoubled and reverberating in our skull.

"'*We know thee, traitor*,' the twins smiled. '*Acolyte of a line bereft of sight,* consigned to history's dust. We watched the best of thee burn aready, their ashes strung black and thick o'er Charbourg's ruins. We were there the night the belief of the Faithless faltered. Think ye, child, thou canst stand against us?'

"Silvered blades flashed, blood and snow and ash, dark eyes falling on Phoebe.

"'Stay out of my head!' the fleshwitch roared.

"'Poor kitten,' they whispered. 'To their deaths thou hast led thy kinfolk. No queen reborn, nor bringer of storms. Shadow of a glory long faded. Broken failure. Drunkard's whore. Widowed mother of a stillborn babe. How deep ye failed thy poor, dead husband. How shamed of thee, would thy Connor be.'

"'Shut your fucking mouth,' Gabriel snarled, reaching for the Terror's throat.

"'Silvered wretch. Cleaving to false hope as the beggar to his bottle. Think ye, if ye save her, thou shalt forget the music of their screams? Think ye Dior Lachance could ever fill the hole in the heart we watched our father break?'

"Gabriel roared, sending Alba skidding across the stone with a blow from Ashdrinker. His fury became awful then, terrifying; and we saw that rather than bruise his spirit, the Terrors had instead left the growing madness in him utterly unmoored. He crashed into Alba, heedless of her blade, the ancien stabbing his chest and throat as he brought her down onto the stone. Gabriel landed atop her, wounds gushing blood, his eyes wild, fangs bared as he pressed hands to her pale neck, the gift of his dark father finally unleashed. And as an awful scream tore the ashen air, Alba's blood began boiling in her veins.

"Aléne turned at her sister's cry, fear welling in those black eyes, and in that moment, we took our chance. The shell of me splashing red onto the stone at the Terror's feet, the rest of me rising up behind her, grabbing a fistful of her hair and wrenching back her head, forcing my fangs through the skin of her neck, knives puncturing that welted, cracking stone. Aléne's scream became a strangled cry, then a heartsick, trembling moan as our Kiss took hold, as we drank, I drank, the leaden weight of her blood, the awful strength of her years, the ever darkness in her soul crashing over our dust-dry tongue. It had been too long since I supped of someone that deep, all of us aflame, wrapping strong arms around the Ironheart as she tried to struggle, just as I had when her sister murdered me.

"Alba was yet flailing in Gabriel's grip, his thumbs now sinking into her melting eyes. She clawed his throat, spine arching, smoke seeping from the widening cracks in her skin. Phoebe looked on in horror at the pair of us; I, wrapping Aléne in my deadly embrace, Gabriel burying his fingers in the ash of Alba's skin. We could feel Aléne's terror, hear Alba's awful scream, rising frantic on the wind as Death reached out his cold hand.

"'*Gabriel?*'

"The voice was soft. Not in our head, but still cutting through the storm, the scream of battle, like a blade of broken glass. And looking up, my mouth full of glorious, leaden bliss, we saw him on the snow-clad battlements, pale eyes locked on my brother.

"'*Gabriel?*' he repeated.

"The foulblood boy who had spoken in the Blackheart's court. Traceries of rot at its mouth and fingertips, a streak of fresh blood smeared across its eyes and brow. It stood and stared as my brother glanced up, and though winter was in its fullness, the air about us grew colder still as that deadthing smiled. And Gabriel's lips peeled back in fury, eyes darkening as he recognized the monster that rode inside that rotten shell.

"'*Fabién.*'"

V

THE SIMPLEST TRUTH

JEAN-FRANÇOIS LOOKED TOWARD Gabriel, eyebrow raised. The silversaint was still as a statue, wine bottle in hand, scars cutting down his cheek like twin teardrops.

"It had been more than a year since I'd set eyes on him," he finally said. "But every time I closed them, I saw his face. Hundreds of nights had passed since we'd spoken a word, but in every one, I heard his voice. *Thou art a lion, playing at being a lamb. And* that *is why by God thou art abandoned, and why he hath unleashed me upon thee.*

"His eyes were fixed on mine, though he spared a glance for each of his daughters. Alba's veins were boiled all but dry, her flesh crumbling away under my fingers like the ashes of the life he'd unmade. Aléne had sunk to her knees, drained pale grey, Celene so glutted with her blood it spilled down her chin as she swallowed.

"'*F-Father* . . .' they whispered. '*D-d-don't let him take us* . . .'

"'*Release them,*' he commanded.

"And I laughed, then. Actually *laughed* amid that slaughter, that insanity, that churning, blood-mad thresher we name war. Thrallswords were running to the aid of their mistresses now, but Phoebe had met them on the stairs, cutting them to ribbons. All around us, folk were letting slip their final breaths; calling for their mamas, for their beloveds, for the God who didn't care a drop about any of it. And I stared into Fabién's eyes as I sank my fingers deeper into Alba's throat, feeling her flesh running to dust as she screamed again.

"'*Loss undreamed of shalt thou suffer, Gabriel, if thou shalt stay not thy hand.*' The Forever King bared his fangs, voice trembling with fury. '*Poor fool, ye know not what ye do.*'

"Those eyes bored into mine, that mind crashed upon me, all the weight of the time and rage and hatred behind it pressing me down into the stone. But I pictured my sweet Patience's face. Felt my Astrid's arms enfold me. And I was unbreakable.

"'I know I'm taking away something you care about,' I spat, eyes locked on his. 'How does it feel to lose something you love, bastard?'

"'*The same shall I ask thee, when Dior Lachance lies cold in her grave, and all hope of salvation is lost.*'

"Fabién glanced to Celene then, my sister's mouth still locked on Aléne's throat as she drank, desperate and groaning. I could see the ancien Ironheart's soul hung by but a thread now, terrible fear and awful bliss in her gaze as my sister swallowed her whole. I swore I saw tears shining in Fabién's eyes, boiling with the venom on his tongue.

"'Look *at* it,' he hissed. '*Abomination. Anathema. The Faithless were a plague, Gabriel, driven by madness and hubris and deceit. None upon this earth are more deserving of the hell we gifted them.*' He shook his head then, bleeding gaze falling back on me. '*With truest evil hast thou made thy bed, old friend.*'

"I shook my head then, almost speechless.

"'You . . . *dare* . . . speak to me of evil?'

"I looked back down to Alba, trembling in my grip. Black tears were welling from her molten eyes, that old familiar terror bubbling up in her voice as she tried to beg. To plead. And the thing of it was, I'd seen all this before. Countless monsters put to the grave. Ever the hero they raised me to be. Past all the bluff and bluster. All the *thees* and *thous*. In that final moment, you all beg like children, Historian."

Gabriel glared at his sister across the river then.

"And you die like dogs.

"'P-please,' it breathed. 'Father, s-save m—'

"And then it was gone. Obliterated. Annihilated. All the centuries crashing back into the void where it had lain beneath me, blasted now to char and ashes. I saw the Forever King flinch as Alba died, as if my hand had struck him. And rising from his daughter's ruins, I flew at him then, seizing his throat, fingers digging into rotten, freezing flesh. As I dragged it up off the battlements, I knew this wretched thing wasn't anything close to Fabién; only a puppet of meat he rode to torment me. But still, I prayed with all I had inside me that at least he felt the pain as I began boiling the blood from its veins.

"'You murdered my wife,' I spat. 'You butchered my baby. Everything I ever loved, you *took* from me. And I swear, by all I am and will *ever* be, you will burn in hell for what you've done.'

"I spat into his face, hate boiling on my tongue.

"'And I will see you there.'

"The Dead thing hissed, and it seemed that oui, he *did* feel pain; black blood boiling as it rolled down my arm, eyes filling with bloody tears as my aegis burned him blind. But still, Fabién remained in that body, enduring the agony so he might gift me one last barb.

"'*Thy famille I slew. Blood for blood the rule, we knew it both. And so might it be that one night thou shalt deliver me below. Verily, part of me still prays for it, old friend. But shall ye muster the same rancor for that* thing *behind thee, I wonder? Nurse the same malice? For the blood of thy famille stains also thy sister's hands, Gabriel.*'

"'You're a fucking liar. Dead tongues heeded—'

"'*Aye, aye.*' He smiled, eyes bubbling. '*But Celene Castia was born of my line, Silversaint. How comes it an Ironheart wields the power of the Faithless? She is only a fledgling in the tally of her years. How comes it the power of an ancien wells within her veins?*'

"I turned toward Celene, still latched onto Aléne's throat, swallowing the last dregs from her veins; her power, her soul, her *bloodgifts* with it. My sister's bloody eyes drifted now to mine, Fabién's voice fading in my mind.

"'*Poor Wulfric.*'

"The body in my hands shivered once, his whisper echoing in my head.

"'*Ask her how he died, de León.*'

"He collapsed into dust, blown apart on the wind.

"'*Then ask who it is ye should be serving.*'

"Aléne screamed, her body bucking, fingers curling into claws as the beast inside her struggled to cling on to something, to *anything*. And with a final choking wail, the Terror burst apart into a shower of ashes, snatched from Celene's arms and torn away on the storm. My sister knelt in the remainder, head thrown back, arms wide, black dust swirling all around her. And I saw it then, just as I'd seen at Aveléne; the awful wound at her throat and chin had lessened, muscles restitching onto bone, skin thickening on her ruined flesh.

"'By this blood,' she breathed, 'shall we have life eternal.'

"We, I realized.

"*We.*

"'You killed him,' I whispered.

"Phoebe shouted my name, raw with triumph. The foulbloods and Voss soldiers were breaking with their mistresses slain, the Highlanders rallying, Brynne roaring over the carnage. Celene's eyes flickered to me, and I saw their shade had deepened even closer to the brown they'd once been, the knowledge settling on my shoulders like dust.

"But she denied nothing. And I knew it true, then.

"'You drank my father.'"

There in the cell beneath Sul Adair, the Last Silversaint and the Last Liathe stared at each other, across those dark and treacherous waters. The 'saint's eyes were clouded, storm-grey, the whites stained deepest red. But the Liathe's were pure black, flooded to the edges, dark and bottomless as the river rushing between them. Jean-François glanced from one sibling to the other, the air between dripping with hatred. And in that uncomfortably heavy silence, the historian cleared his throat and spoke.

"What of the Grail? What was happening at the dún during all this?"

Brother and sister glowered at each other for an age before either spoke. It's a strange thing, to be a sibling. So much rancor and love. Hate and history. It's a bond forged in iron, that tie. It takes a great deal of work to sunder it entirely.

But it *can* be done.

"On the battlements," Gabriel growled, "we'd no eyes now. I only know what happened from those who survived it. Some Dyvok had broken as the 'dancers and 'saints tore them up, fleeing toward their fleet in the bay, living to fight another night. But around Nikita, all was storm and fury, the vampire clashing on the battlements with the mortal brother he'd nurtured, tortured, carved of stone. His duel with Lachlan was terrifying, I know that. A battle for poets to write about, minstrels to sing about; Blackheart against silversaint, brother against brother, all around them run to dust and ruin.

"But down in the wreckage of Auldtunn, Baptiste was on his last legs. He'd saved Aaron's life when he hurled them both off the battlements, but the impact to the flagstones below hadn't done him much good. His arm was already broken, his ribs now cracked too. Though Aaron had been disarmed by Lachlan, he'd fetched a greataxe from among the wreckage, big enough to take a man's head off his shoulders. And that seemed his intent as he pursued a limping Baptiste through the ruins of Niamh's city.

"Baptiste was calling to his beloved as he fled, still desperately trying to break the spell of Nikita's blood. In the midst of all that carnage and horror, he told stories of joy and sorrow and all things between; the little moments two people who shared a life knew as well as their own names. The time Baptiste made a bouquet of flowers out of scrap iron for Aaron's saintsday. The night they settled in Aveléne, and the terrible argument they'd had over who would carry who to the hearth. But it was when Baptiste spoke of their youth in San Michon there came a glimmer of hope.

"'You were training in the Gauntlet,' the blackthumb called. 'Running the Scythe, over and over. And I was setting up a new obstacle for the Scar, remember?'

"Aaron snarled with frustration, pursuing his quarry through a broken, roofless estate. Baptiste twisted backward from a blow, maul raised in defense, desperate now.

"'I suspected you might be watching me.' The big man somehow smiled, parrying the strike and stumbling backward. 'From the corner of your eye. So I took off my shirt to test the theory, and you got caught by one of the spars, remember?'

"Aaron stumbled at that, axe raised for a blow that never fell.

"'You almost broke your jaw.' Baptiste grinned, chest heaving. 'Remember?'

"The pair stood in the falling snow and ash now, twenty feet apart, across the rubble and ruin. A stillness had come upon them amid that chaos, the spell of Baptiste's words, and while Aaron's eyes still burned, they blazed not with rage now, but . . . memory.

"'You . . . laughed at me,' he whispered.

"'I did. And then I warned you to look after your face.'

"Aaron's lip curled, the tiniest fraction. 'I asked . . . what was wrong with my face.'

"Baptiste's voice softened, smile fading. And daring to hope, he took one small step closer to his love. 'I told you it was the most beautiful thing I'd ever seen.'

"Aaron was stood in the snow now, golden hair tossed in the roaring winds. The battle was deafening, but all was silence as his greataxe trembled, then slipped from his fingers, my friend looking down at his bloody hand as if it were not his own.

"'And then you kissed me,' he breathed.

"'I knew you were mine, then,' Baptiste said, stepping closer still. 'And I, yours. That nothing would *ever* part us. I remember like it was *yesterday*. Do you remember, love?'

"'I . . .'

"Aaron blinked hard, blood welling in his lashes.

"'I—'

"A black shape plummeted from the sky, landing between them with a crack of thunder. The flagstones split, Baptiste crying out as he was slammed backward, dropping his silversteel and crashing into the estate's wrought iron fence. And as the snow and stone powder cleared, there in the remnants crouched Nikita. His greatcoat was ripped and spattered, his left arm missing at the bicep. His chest and shoulder and belly were cleaved to the bones. But his blade was drenched in the blood of the brother he'd bested.

"Lachlan lay in the rubble beneath him, shattered, barely breathing, his aegis only a sputtering silver sheen through the ash and blood smeared upon his skin. Rising up from his brother's ruin, Nikita spat blood on the broken stones.

"'*Weak,*' he hissed.

"The Blackheart looked about him then, dead eyes falling first on Aaron, then on his beloved, still crumpled against a tangle of wrought iron. And with a cold smile curling his lips, Nikita reached down, and closed his hand around Baptiste's throat."

"They ran through the dún," Celene whispered. "Reyne and Dior. The Grail's shredded leg dripping blood, the Princess's shoulder bitten to the bone, her mother's blade hanging limp in one red hand. Dior begged Reyne, 'Stop, *stop!*' and breathless, she pressed her hand to the older girl's torn shoulder, the bite wounds stitching closed by the power of her holy blood. They could hear the song of ringing horns and soaring pipes outside, but hope yet seemed a thousand miles distant. And so they ran on, Reyne half dragging, half carrying Dior, both gasping for breath as they reached that little sitting room. The Lady á Maergenn twisted the candelabrum, whispering a prayer of thanks as the bookshelf slid open.

"They stumbled through, down the tumbled corridor toward sanctuary, turning now as a shadow swelled at their back. Whispering footsteps and winter's chill, Lilidh flashing down the tunnel toward them. She still wore her dented breastplate, the steel spattered with Kiara's ending, eyes as deep as midnight. She'd have taken them, I think, save for that sensation we also felt; that holy outrage bearing down from the sacred ground of the cathedral above, pressing on Lilidh's shoulders, stumbling her pace. As it was, the girls only barely made it to their sanctuary, slicked with sweat and blood, tumbling as they tripped over the threshold together, and into the tomb beneath the Holy Sepulcher.

"My mote had been left behind, torn from Dior's skin as she crossed onto holy ground. But as that red sliver of us fluttered to the flagstones, I was comforted to know that if *we* could not cross, Lilidh could not either; the Heartless brought to a hissing halt at that great ironwood door, the Mothermaid's graven likeness, fangs bared in a snarl.

"They were safe.

"Reyne dragged Dior backward, the floor slicked red beneath them, the Grail's leg torn and bleeding. Ripping her homespun hem, the Princess bound the Grail's wounds tight, staunching the blood as best she could as Dior hissed in pain.

"'Ye cannot run from me, Worm.'

"Reyne glanced up at that, face spattered red, mismatched eyes alight. Lilidh lurked on the threshold, glowering at the Princess she'd enslaved, beaten, humiliated.

"'I don't *need* to run,' Reyne spat, teeth bared in triumph. 'We'll just sit here on holy ground 'til the Black Lion arrives, and applaud once he's done with you.'

"'Cowering in the dark,' Lilidh sneered. 'Just as ye did when we took this city, when we butchered thy mighty dam and all her vaunted flock. Poor Worm. Ever the ill-favored. The unwanted.' Black eyes drifted to the bloody sword in Reyne's grip. 'Wretch's hands clutching a liar's blade. The bastard daughter of a legend failed.' That black gaze sharpened, pinning Reyne to the floor. 'But still I shall grant thee mercy, if ye give her unto me. I offer thee one chance. Serve me as ye once did, and I shall spare thee what is coming.'

"'And what is coming?' Reyne scoffed, dragging herself to her feet. 'An army of Highlanders? A legion of soldiers you tried to enslave? The hero who slew your father?'

"'Hell is coming, bitch,' Dior vowed, rising beside Reyne. 'For *you.*'

"Lilidh's eyes roamed the tomb's threshold, the ironwood door, the Mothermaid's etching, encircled by that halo of runes.

"'Educated in Elidaen, were ye not, bastard? By the Holy Sisters of Evangeline?' Midnight eyes fell on Dior. 'And thee, little whorespawn . . . can ye read at all?'

"'The fuck does that have to do with anything?' the Grail spat.

"'Don't listen.' Reyne squeezed Dior's hand. 'She's nothing but a liar, love.'

"'A liar, aye.' Lilidh nodded. 'But more besides. A murderess. A *monstress*. But a priestess too, knew ye that? My mother was a holy woman of the Moonsthrone. She read truetales from tablets of stone, augured in entrails of beasts, saw futures in stars above, oh, I remember *stars,* girls,' she whispered, looking upward. 'So many in skies of yestereve, to count them was to drive thyself mad. Intended was I, to follow in Mother's footsteps, afore mighty Tolyev took me for his own. But before my dark maker tore my heart out, my mother taught me to read, sweetlings. Those stones. Those entrails. And of course, the tongue of Ossway old.'

"Lilidh reached out to that ironwood door, caressing the runes about the Mothermaid's head. Speaking in a whisper; a snatch of scripture from the Book of Vows, the very same that had adorned the threshold at Cairnhaem.

"'*Enter and be welcome, those who seek forgiveness in the light of the Lord.*'

"'Oh, God,' Reyne whispered.

"Lilidh's midnight eyes fell on the Grail. 'An invitation, that reads to me.'

"'Oh, *shit,*' Dior breathed.

"I knew not how this would play, nor, I think, did the Heartless herself. No kith could set foot on hallowed earth, nor enter a home unasked. But to be invited onto sacred ground by the word of God Himself? How might that measure in the end?

"Lilidh closed her eyes, face upturned to the heavens as she whispered.

"'Forgive me, Father. For I must sin.'

"And fixing those girls in her endless gaze, Lilidh stepped into the tomb."

"'GABRIEL!'"

The Last Silversaint looked at his empty bottle, wiped his mouth across his sleeve.

"That was the scream I heard, rising on the winds. We were stood on the bloody gatehouse, Alba scorched to dying at my feet, Aléne drunk to ashes at Celene's. I looked at my sister, seeing the truth of the Forever King's words in her eyes. Now it made sense why she'd been released into the world with no true knowledge of what Dior needed to do. Now I understood why she knew so little about the cult she belonged to. She'd killed her teacher, stolen his power for her own, before he'd taught her all he could have.

"Her teacher.

"My father.

"And she'd never told me."

"And why would I?" the Liathe demanded, glowering now from across the river. "Why would I think you'd care a drop for the monster who cared not a drop for you?"

"I didn't," Gabriel replied. "I *don't*. But that's not the fucking point. It was one more lie, Celene. One more straw on the gelding's back. And it might've broken then and there, to know that all my little Hellion seemed to be made of now was deceit. But you looked toward the dún then, eyes filled with fear.

"'DIOR NEEDS US *NOW*.'

"And that was it. No breath to waste on rage. No time for accusation. For the last year, every night I lay down to sleep, I'd heard their voices. My beautiful wife. My baby girl. Walking yet upon this earth they rotted in, choking on the thought I'd failed them.

"If not for the girl in that keep, I knew I'd now be dead. My life spent in pointless struggle against the Forever King, or drowned at the bottom of a bottle. Dior had shown me there was something yet to believe in, and though we were flame and powder, fire and ice, I knew I could love her no more dear than if she were my own. Sometimes famille is more than blood, vampire. And when all is said and done, when the cheering stops and the music fades, when the stories they tell about you drift into silence, and the songs they sing are stolen by the lonely winter wind, a man is left with the simplest of truths."

"What truth, Gabriel?" Jean-François murmured.

"That there is nothing that grows as deep on this green earth, nothing that shines as bright in all the gables of heaven, *nothing* that burns as fierce in the blazing heart of hell, than a parent's love for their child."

The Last Silversaint shook his head, tears in his eyes.

"And so I looked across that burning city toward her, through the fire and blood, the death and screams, and I lifted my blade, and I charged."

Celene stared at her brother, eyes framed by locks of raven black. But he'd looked away now, gaze lost in those waters between them, dark and churning.

"They fled," she finally said. "Dior and Reyne. Scrambling back across the stone toward the Mothermaid's empty coffin, and down those secret stairs to the vault they'd found beneath. Lilidh followed, stalking slow across the stone, claws dripping red.

"My mote at least could bear witness, and as the rest of us prayed for forgiveness, that tiny droplet took to the wing, flitting through the air behind the Contessa. Ever suspicious, Lilidh stopped at the edge of that shadowed stair, toe brushing the sigil of the Esana etched into the stone. Glancing upward, she saw that same motif; the twin skulls and the Grail between, wrought in the mosaic above Michon's head. We could see uncertainty in her eyes now. Fear as she stood poised on that threshold, an eternity long. But the song of chaos and carnage rang deafening in the city outside, crescendo approaching, and with bloodied lips pressed thin, the Heartless finally descended into the dark.

"It was a crypt, we realized. A crypt more ancient and elaborate than the one above. The chamber ran *deep*, the light dim and distant, spilling only from the lantern Reyne á Maergenn had brought with her from the reading room above. It was sat far below now, at the bottom of a long winding stair, in the heart of a vast and frigid room. Of the Princess and Grail there was no sign, but our eyes picked out details as Lilidh slowly descended.

"The space put me in mind of Jènoah's chapel in Cairnhaem—the walls here too were circular, carved with a vast bas-relief of the Wars of the Blood. Hundreds of figures in antiquated armor were wrought there; vampire battling vampire, mortal slaying mortal. We saw the Forever King again, leading his Knights of the Blood against the Faithful, a raven on his shoulder and a sword in his hand. And we knew then what this place was.

"Who slumbered here.

"The room was shin-deep with dark seawater, leaked in over slow centuries, still and stagnant. From that fetid pool rose a field of tombstones, hundreds upon hundreds—filth-slicked marble arranged in concentric rings. Each stone was carved with a name, and each name was that of a slain vampire; Lyssa Chastain, Reynaldo Dyvok, Teshirr Ilon. In the very heart of them sat a stone box, heavy with the slime and grime of centuries. The capstone was carved in the likeness of an angel in repose, palms pressed together, mouth open as if in song. The flickering lantern was sat upon its chest, and above, a mighty marble statue of the Redeemer hung. God's son was nailed upon his wheel, mouth open like the angel below, as if caught in the moment he shouted his final words. His covenant to those who would build his church upon this earth after his death."

"*By this blood,*" Gabriel murmured, "*shall they have life eternal.*"

"But unlike other chapels in the empire," Celene continued, "here the Redeemer's statue was accompanied by five others, towering as tall as houses around that black pool. They were wrought in astonishing detail; priests and priestesses in antiquated garb, kneeling beneath the body of God's own son. They looked anguished, rending their robes and silently screaming. And in their open mouths, we saw their canines were long and sharp.

"As in Jènoah's chapel, a plinth stood before that coffin; an open book wrought of stained, grey marble. On the left page, that same prophetic verse Chloe Sauvage had given Gabriel was etched upon the ancient stone in Old Talhostic.

> *"From holy cup comes holy light;*
> *"The faithful hand sets world aright.*
> *"And in the Seven Martyrs' sight,*
> *"Mere man shall end this endless night.*

"But on the right-hand page, another verse was carved, black with time and grime, but wrought by that same ancient hand. And unlike its twin in Cairnhaem, the prophecy here was whole, our wings shivering as we read those ancient, sacred words.

> *"Before the Five, come unto one,*
> *"With sainted blade, 'neath virgin sun,*
> *"By sacred blood, or else by none . . ."*

The Last Silversaint spoke then, his voice hard and cold as his eyes.

> *"This blackened veil shall be undone."*

"'Have ye solved the riddle yet?' Lilidh called, her voice echoing in the dark. 'Know ye, whorechild, what thou art? What in the end this all means?'

"The Contessa stepped into the pool, drifting through the black like a shark. She wandered seemingly aimless, but all the while, she followed the honeyed scent of Dior's blood, hanging clear in the air. And stepping around the looming form of a screaming priestess, Lilidh lunged, ready to snatch the Grail up in her bloody claws.

"She found nothing but a slick of blood in the brine, her flawless brow darkening. Cloth whispered above, and she glanced up to the statue, too late, Reyne á Maergenn rising from the folds of that stone robe with her mother's sword in hand, and Dior's blood fresh upon the blade.

"'*STO*—'

"The blow fell true, hammer heavy; a princess this child, but trained by the great Chante-Lames at Montfort. The blade sliced the Contessa's face, shearing skin and muscle and bone, Lilidh cursing as she staggered away. Her flesh caught like tinder, the Grail's holy blood turning skin and bone to ash, her scream piercing the air.

"'That's for Lady Arlynn,' Reyne spat.

"The Princess leapt from the statue, splashing into the pool, Dior slithering down behind her. Pale blue eyes glittered like broken glass as Lilidh whirled and spun, tearing at her flaming skin, collapsing into the brine at her feet. Hissing, the Heartless slung back a curtain of sodden hair from her face, snaking to her feet. The blaze was quenched, but the damage was terrible; jaw dangling like a broken door, alabaster skin burned black. Reyne advanced, bloody blade cleaving the air. And though Lilidh raised her hand and spat a command, her face was so mangled that the Whip was garbled nonsense, blood-thick and gurgling.

"'No more orders,' Dior spat. 'Mistress.'

"Reyne lashed out at the Contessa's hand, and Lilidh shrieked as two of her fingers flew; blown to ashes before ever they struck the water. Her flesh blazed where Dior's blood kissed it, the ancien flashing backward with preternatural speed, blackening flesh dunked into the brine to smother that holy flame.

"'That's for Gilly and Morgana,' Reyne spat.

"The Princess came on, all the resentment and hate at her torment of the last few months now ablaze in her eyes. Her blade sliced the air, her form fearsome. And though Lilidh was drenched in the power of centuries, the Heartless in the end was no warrior, and unarmed besides. Lilidh backed away, unnerved by sight of the blood spitting and smoking upon that steel, her eyes narrowed in hatred. With the Grail at her back, Reyne á Maergenn raised her sword high, hissing through clenched teeth.

"'This is for me.'

"And with a bloody cry, the Princess lunged for her foe."

Gabriel leaned forward slowly, grey eyes alight.

"Baptiste dangled in the Blackheart's grip, the war on the battlements still raging above, Lachlan bloodied and motionless on the stone below. Nikita smiled, soulless, gazing up at the blackthumb as spider to fly. Aaron stood behind his master, looking between the pair; his old lover caught in the dreadful grip of his new one. His eyes were filled with bloody tears, but his face was serene. They'd shared a life together, he and Baptiste. Loved one another as fierce as any couple I've known. But love is mortal, Historian. Blood is eternal.

"'Master,' Aaron called.

"The Blackheart turned, brow raised, watching Aaron sink to one knee.

"'Please,' he said, glancing to Baptiste. 'Allow *me* to end him.'

"Nikita's red lips curled, midnight eyes shining. Turning back to Baptiste, he seemed to revel in the sight of all light dying in the blackthumb's eyes. The death of love. The murder of hope. God, what a fate. To be so empty, that joy might only be found in the sight of others just as bereft. What a hell. To think that which makes you care makes you weak.

"'I *do* enjoy the sight of thee on thy knees, Golden One,' Nikita said.

"And dropping Baptiste to the stone, he offered his sword to his servant.

"'Show me thy heart be mine.'"

"Reyne's blade cleaved the air," Celene said. "Whistling just shy of Lilidh's skin. The Heartless was back-footed, flesh scorched, jaw ruined. But she was ancien, after all, strong as mountains, never to be underestimated. And with her mother's blade anointed with the Grail's own blood, sadly, the Princess did just that. Her lips split in a smile as she paused to taunt her foe, twirling the sword in her hands.

"'I'm going to carve your chest open, devil. See how heartless you really are.'

"She lunged, blade cleaving the air, Dior shouting from behind to beware. Lilidh slipped back through the brine, swift and serpentine, and reaching out with the best of her hands, she tore one of the tombstones from the circles, rock splintering as if it were clay. Hurling the gravestone like a spear, she sent the Princess reeling sideways, the jagged marble spar whistling just shy of her head. Lilidh skipped backward, tearing another stone loose, hurling it like some vengeful goddess in the ancient tales. Reyne lunged aside again, gasping, another stone flying at her, another, faster, *another*, marble splitting, cracking, booming. Dior cried warning, limping forward with eyes bright. And as Reyne cursed, stumbling on a chunk of stone beneath the surface, a slab of marble the size of a wheelbarrow crashed into her chest.

"Bone shattered, the Princess cried out, blood and brine spraying as she fell. Dior roared her name, stumbling forward on her torn leg as Lilidh smiled, dead eyes alight. And with ashen hair plastered to sweat-slick skin, the Grail scooped up Reyne's fallen sword from the water. Wounded as she was, Dior had still been trained by the Black Lion, and dancing the northwind, she struck; *belly, chest, throat, repeat.* But the Nineswords' blade had fallen into the brine as Reyne did, Dior's blood washed from its edge. And as it bit into Lilidh's flesh, near harmless, the Heartless seized Dior's throat in one black claw.

"Lifting her high, Lilidh smashed Dior backward into one of the mighty statues; a screaming priest with a raven on a chain at his throat. Dior's palm had been sliced open to whet Reyne's blade, and she clawed toward Lilidh's ruined face. But the Contessa was the swifter, seizing her wrist, hissing as dead flesh smoked on Dior's bloodied skin. The Grail gasped as she was slammed back into the statue again; skull cracking, gorge rising. She managed one last stab of defiance, biting her tongue and spitting a mouthful of blood into Lilidh's face. The Contessa screamed, flesh burning, reaching into her bodice for that golden dagger. And raising it high, she slammed it through Dior's palm and into the stone behind.

"Dior wailed, Lilidh stumbled back, her face afire. She fell again into the brine, the flames extinguished with a blistering *hissssss.* Staggering to her feet, dripping and bloodied, the Contessa reached up to her mauled features, snarling as she fixed her jaw back in place. What was once the visage of a goddess was now a horror, flesh burned back to bone. But her lips were twisted in an awful smile as she whispered in that dark.

"'So too the spring c-cull to the lamb. Or the wolf's t-teeth to the doe . . .'

"Dior moaned in agony. Her left hand was pinned, the dagger driven so deep into the statue that the hilt had crushed her bones to pulp. The pain must have been breathtaking, but still she struggled to wrench herself free, holy blood flooding red and bright over her skin. And as she wailed, thrashed, she saw again as she had seen in the tomb above; that blood spilling down her arm, over her fingers . . . that blood was *moving.*

"She understood not what it meant, nor how it might be mastered, but still, she knew it was fire to her foe. And so, tears spilling down her cheeks, she stretched her red and dripping hand toward Lilidh and bid that blood obey.

"'*Move,*' she hissed.

"Move it did, her breath catching now, pale blue eyes gone wide as the droplets at her fingertips shivered. Lilidh stepped back, eyes narrowed, fearing some new spell. But though Dior's blood shivered at the tips of her outstretched fingers, trembling as if the walls were shaking and the world was ending . . . that was all it did.

"Nothing but tremble.

"'*Move!*' Dior wailed.

"Lilidh smiled, emboldened now, malice twisting her mutilated features. She stooped, snatching up the fallen princess like a sack of rags. Reyne screamed in pain, arm and shoulder snapped, broken bones grinding as she was hauled skyward, dangling now in Lilidh's cold claws. And reaching out with her smallest finger, Lilidh pressed soft upon Reyne's chest, splintering a dozen of her ribs.

"'NO!' Dior roared. 'Don't hurt her!'

"Reyne was struggling, breath hissing through her teeth, clutching the hand throttling the life from her with her one good arm. Lilidh squeezed gently upon Reyne's wrist, shattering it like glass as the Princess screamed.

"'STOP!' Dior roared.

"The Heartless turned to Dior, Reyne crying out as her spine creaked in that awful grip. The vampire's voice was gargling, glottal, her jaw burned wreckage. But still her hiss carried, knife sharp, echoing in that gloom beneath the Redeemer's cold gaze.

"'Beg me.'

"'Please!' Dior cried. 'Please, stop!'

"'Louder!'

"'*Please!* Don't hurt her, d—'

"'D-Dior,' Reyne whispered. 'D-don't.'

"And their eyes met then, across that dark water; those two girls with so little time given to them, now come to the end of it. The truth plain for both to see.

"'She's g-going to kill m-me anyw—'

"The Princess gasped as Lilidh squeezed tighter, cutting off her voice.

Dior screamed in horror, in rage, watching Reyne kicking and choking in Lilidh's grip. Lilidh's eyes were fixed on the Princess's, cold and black. The gaze of a shark closing in on a drowning swimmer, mouth slipping wide to reveal endless rows of jagged teeth.

"'We are the strong,' Lilidh gurgled.

"She drew Reyne closer, the girl gasping her last breath.

"'Thou art the w—'

"A shape flew from the darkness, a blur of hard white and gleaming red. It crashed onto Lilidh's back, sinking teeth into her neck. Lilidh screeched and dropped Reyne, lashing out with a backhand that sent the shape flying into the tombstones behind. It smashed through half a dozen graves with the dull crack of splintered stone, crashing into the water before twisting to its feet, blue eye narrowed as it snarled.

"'Prince . . . ?' Dior breathed."

"Phoebe cried my name as I charged toward the dún," Gabriel said, "but I paid no heed at all. And rather than leave me to fight alone, she charged with me, the Highlanders too, one and all, leaving the bloodied remnants of the Voss legions to flee the field, roaring as we flooded through the Newtunn streets, back toward Auldtunn.

"There, in the ruins of a nobleborn house, Nikita Dyvok stood wreathed in ash and snow. Aaron had climbed to his feet, eyes on Baptiste. The black-thumb was on his knees, mute and heartbroken as Aaron took up his master's sword. Nikita smiled at his dark lover, watching the last of Aaron's heart wither and die in his chest. And Aaron raised Epitaph high over his head, looking Baptiste in the eye as he whispered.

"'I remember.'

"Aaron swung Epitaph with all his might. And if this were a children's tale, Historian, he'd have turned on his heel and cleaved the Blackheart's head clean off his shoulders. He'd have proved that the poets write true, that the minstrels aren't bastards, that love ever conquers all. But though he'd not the strength to break the unholy spell of Nikita's blood, Aaron did have strength enough to hurl that blade *away*, sailing off into the ruins, glittering as it fell. And turning to Nikita, he spat.

"'You may have my heart. But not every part of it.'

"Nikita snarled, backhanding Aaron across the face with his one good arm. The blow was horrifying, sending the lordling flying through the iron fence, crashing through another wall. But in taking his eyes off Baptiste, the Blackheart had made his final mistake."

Gabriel smiled, his grey eyes shining.

"Because sometimes love *does* conquer all.

"The blow crashed into the back of Nikita's skull—a mallet of pure silversteel, wielded by a man who fought only and always from his heart. The ancien's skull splintered, he staggered, whirling with a snarl. The wound was a terrible one, yet not enough to fill a tomb, and Nikita lifted his dripping hand, intent on burying Baptiste instead. But another hand reached out then, seizing hold of his ankle and crushing the bone in a grip of iron.

"Lachlan lay in the rubble where the Blackheart had left him, bloodied and torn, but yet unbroken. He smiled, red and sharp, holding his brother in place as Baptiste's second blow smashed Nikita's jaw clean off his face. Ancien flesh tore like paper, Nikita stumbled, raising his good hand to ward Baptiste away. But the blackthumb was on him then, lost in roaring fury. The rage of a lover wronged, a husband betrayed, coupled with the strength of a thrall; falling atop the stumbling Nikita and smashing that hammer down, again, *again,* bone and brain pulping, blood and silversteel sizzling, the vampire shrieking, flailing, cursing.

"'He was mine before he was yours, bastard,' Baptiste spat.

"And bringing the hammer down, he smote the Blackheart's head to ruin.

"Nikita's spine arched, his arm flailed, a bubbling scream ripped up and out of his ravaged throat. All the pain, all the rage, all the terror of an immortal staring at the end of his forever. And then, he simply burst apart, Baptiste flinching, Lachlan hissing in triumph as Nikita was consumed, explosive, black and ashen, his remains whipped up into the hungry winds and scattered across the wreckage of the kingdom he'd tried so desperately to forge.

"Baptiste rose up from Nikita's remains, dark eyes aflame.

"'Some love is forever.'"

Gabriel fell silent, running his fingers across his smile. It seemed even the historian was touched, lips curling soft as he wrote swift in his tome. But the end was rushing on now, and caught in the spell of it, Celene spoke on.

"Prince lunged at Lilidh," she said. "Flying like an arrow at the Contessa's throat. For a moment, we wondered what had become of the lovesick puppy we'd seen following ever at her heels. But then we recalled—the wolf had bitten Dior, of course, *of course,* the ties that bound him broken by the Grail's holy blood. Lilidh clutched her ruined neck, stepping aside, lashing out as the beast passed and sending him into one of the great statues. And though the blow would have killed any ordinary wolf, Prince was back on his feet in a blinking, shaking off the water and leaping for the Contessa again.

"But though beast and monster now battled for her fate, Dior's eyes were fixed on . . .

"'Reyne!'

"The Princess had tumbled from the Contessa's grip as the wolf struck, falling into the water. Dior's hand was still pinned to the statue by Lilidh's dagger, the blade wedged deep into the stone, her palm crushed against the hilt. But Reyne wasn't moving, floating facedown in the reeking brine. And rather than hang helpless and watch her drown, Dior took hold of her own wrist, set her feet against the stone, and *pulled*.

"She screamed at the agony, steel slicing flesh, pulped bone ripping apart. Blood spilled thick and bright down Dior's arm, her face twisted, tears welling in her eyes as she braced her feet apart and heaved again. Her hand tore as if damp parchment. Tendons stretched and snapped like wet rope. And finally, with one last scream, Dior ripped herself free, leaving three fingers behind as she crashed into the water.

"Prince slipped aside from the gravestone Lilidh hurled, leapt once more at the vampire's throat. Her neck was already a ruin, jaw hanging loose again, the Heartless croaking a garbled command that the wolf ignored entirely. They crashed against the coffin in the tomb's heart, the Redeemer's statue crying silently above. Lilidh's hands closed about the beast's neck, her blood spilling over the angel at her back. Reyne's lantern splashed into the water, plunging the tomb into near darkness with a boiling hiss.

"All was carved in silhouette now, the light from the tomb above the only illumination. The wolf was insane with rage, but the Heartless was yet Dyvok, the blood of the Untamed in her veins, her hands closing around the beast's maw. The wolf gurgled and growled, claws ripping and finally tearing her breastplate loose. But with a roar, Lilidh wrenched the great wolf's head sideways, snapping his neck clean.

"She tossed his body aside, rising up from the beast's ruins. Her hands and arms were painted in blood, the coffin behind her drenched with the same; hers and the wolf's both. Lilidh's flesh was scorched, face mauled, body torn, but still, she stood unconquered. And with a snarl, she turned and stepped away from Prince's ruin.

"Straight onto three feet of bloody steel.

"Lilidh stared down at the sword, buried hilt-deep in her chest. Dior held the haft, gasping, blue eyes wide and locked on the Heartless. The Grail dragged her blade free, stumbling back toward Reyne, lying now against one of the broken statues. Dior's left hand was a mangled mess, fingers missing and dripping red; the same red smeared down the blade she'd just thrust through Lilidh's heart. The Contessa pressed one hand to her ruined breast, her flesh beginning to smolder as her gargling whisper broke the still.

"'N-not like this—'

"And then, she burst into flame.

"The scream torn from Lilidh's throat was an awful thing. A living thing. A black and twisted and wretched thing. She turned and spun as white and holy flame spewed from the wound, racing over her body like a brushfire on summer grass. Dior struck her again, the blade of the Nineswords biting into ancien flesh, the fire on Lilidh's skin now so bright it was blinding. And as her dress became cinders, as her body withered and flaked away, Lilidh's scream rose high until it was all Dior could hear, until she was forced to close her eyes and block her ears and scream herself, until the remains collapsed into the water and that voice was silenced forever.

"Dior fell into the brine, gathering Reyne now in her arms, tears spilling down her bloody cheeks. She daubed the Princess's wounds in her blood, but Reyne wasn't breathing, *she wasn't breathing*. Dior wailed her name, stroking her freckled cheek as she held that girl there in the darkness, sobs drowning out all the world around her.

"'Please don't leave me,' she begged.

"Tears like rain, pattering on the Princess's face.

"'*Everyone* leaves me . . .'

"She felt hands grab her then, a voice dim and distant beneath the thunder in her chest, the echoes of her sobs. And she screamed, lashing out, the jagged bones in the ruins of her hand cutting down his face, opening his cheek up to the bone.

"'It's me!' he roared. 'Dior, Godssakes, it's *me*!'

"She fell still, eyes grown wide as that cry rang on the walls, breath catching in her chest, not daring to hope as a figure in bloody black wrapped her in his arms.

"'. . . G-Gabriel?'

"'I'm here, love,' he breathed, squeezing her to his chest. 'I'm here.'

"And trembling, she threw her arms around his neck, sobbing like a newborn child. Gabriel too was weeping with that girl at last in his arms, and though he'd have crushed her had he hugged her as close as he wished, she squeezed him tight as she could, the pair on their knees in the bloody water. Dior was bleeding, shaking, and Gabriel looked torn to see how badly she was hurt, how much she had given, how much he had cost her.

"'Oh, Dior,' he whispered, taking her broken, bleeding hand. 'Oh, my poor girl.'

"'You c-came,' she whispered. 'I *knew* you would.'

"Phoebe barreled down the stairs now, I at her back, bloodblade raised as we looked for any sign of Lilidh, seeing only ashes. The fleshwitch ran to Dior's side, sinking into the red water and throwing arms around Gabriel and her both, kissing the Grail atop her head with bloody lips. Gabriel had torn his shirt, wrapping Dior's wounded hand, holding her and Phoebe both tight. Pressing his lips to the Grail's brow, he gazed at the Redeemer's statue above, the hate in him bleeding out into that dark water as all his prayers were answered.

"'Merci,' he breathed, voice shaking. 'Merci, my brother.'

"A cough rang out beside them, Dior shouting for joy as the Princess á Maergenn groaned and slowly opened her eyes. Reyne was drenched, blood and brine, but the Grail's holy gift had done its work. The girls fell into each other's arms, sobbing and holding on for dear life. Phoebe winced, peering at the wound Dior had torn in Gabriel's face; a long gash beneath his right eye, cutting downward and deep into his cheek. She kissed it with bloody lips, but he murmured that it would heal, that all would be well now, kneeling there in that crypt with his famille beside him.

"He looked at the surrounds, awestruck and bewildered; the broken gravestones, the bloodied angel, the marble tome, those five statues looming around the Redeemer's one. His eyes shone in the near-darkness, red with blood, looking now to me.

"'What is this place?' he whispered.

"But I gave no reply, all my body tensing as I heard something moving in the water, there in the shadows ahead. Gabriel heard it too, snaking up from the brine, his fleshwitch beside him and the Ashdrinker in his bloody hand.

"A shape limped from the shadows, breath coming heavy, pale fur dripping seawater and blood. His neck had been broken clean, we'd heard it true, but there he stood, one eye agleam in the darkness and fixed on the duskdancer.

"'Sweet Mothermoons . . .' Phoebe whispered.

"She took one step forward, bloodless and breathless and utterly bewildered.

"'*Connor?*'"

VI

ONE PERFECT MOMENT

"WE COULD SEE the heartbreak in his eyes as she said that name."

Celene watched her brother across the churning water, teeth trapped behind that silvered cage. Jean-François glanced at Gabriel sidelong; even Meline and young Dario looked at him with something close to pity. But the Last Silversaint stared only at the empty bottle in his hand, fingers drumming upon the glass.

"The duskdancer's voice was trembling as she staggered toward the beast," Celene continued. "And as if released from the grip of some horrid choker long cinched about his throat, the wolf bounded forward with something between a howl and a cry. They crashed together, embracing as best they could, the fleshwitch sinking to her knees and holding the wolf tight to her breast. Here was the riddle answered at last; the secret of where Lilidh had got the 'dancer blood that fueled her brother's conquest—a prince, stolen from his Highland home. Tears rolled down Phoebe's bloody cheeks, her prayers of thanks hoarse with joy and sorrow. He could not speak, but Connor's elation at their reunion glittered in the pale blue of his eye, the rumbling growl in his chest, and though he'd not be able to dance his wealdshape away until dim dusk fell, after *so* long apart, it would only be a matter of hours before Phoebe á Dúnnsair's husband could hold his bride in his arms once more.

"Her *husband*.

"We saw that thought darkening the grey of Gabriel's eyes, crawling up his throat as he desperately tried to swallow. Phoebe looked to him then, and we saw that same heartsick pain in her, shining in that gold flooding now with tears. That which was lost, found. That which was found, lost. It hung unsaid between them; a severing, cold as steel and sharp as a broken blade.

Gabriel looked away, jaw clenched, focusing instead on the girl in his arms; the tiny, beating, bleeding heart of his world. For he had moved heaven and earth, swum an ocean of blood, fought the legions of hell to return to her side.

"And in the end, if she was well, then *all* was well.

"'He h-helped us.' Reyne looked to the great bloodied wolf, her mismatched eyes locked on his singular blue. 'He saved us. I don't know why.'

"'Doesn't matter,' Gabriel murmured, kissing the Grail's brow. 'You're safe now.'

"'I hurt you.' Dior winced, touching his torn and bleeding cheek. 'I'm sorry.'

"'No, love, hush,' he whispered, smoothing her bloodied hair back from her face. 'You've nothing to be sorry for. *I* hurt *you*. And all the apologies in the world will never be enough for that, but still, I'll give them to you. I am *so* sorry, Dior.'

"She shook her head. 'You kept your promise. You didn't leave me.'

"'Never,' he vowed, eyes shining with tears. 'I am *so* proud of you.'

"'Merci,' she whispered, crying now. 'Papa.'

"They held each other tight then, each clinging to the other in the midst of all that dark and all that cold, warm and sweet and bright. For the Holy Grail was safe. The prophecy had been unearthed in full. Daysdeath could yet be ended. And it seemed for one moment, all was right in the world. The battle above had stilled. The storm held its breath. For that brief heartbeat, there was no pain, but joy. There was no death, but hope. There was no heaven, but here. One perfect moment, worth all the sacrifice under heaven to attain, if only here was where the story ended. But though they are as far apart as dawning and dusk, Historian, moments and lifetimes have one thing in common."

Jean-François raised an eyebrow in silent question.

"They never last," Gabriel murmured.

"Dior's hand was mangled and bloodied," Celene said, "the cloth Gabriel had bound it in already soaked red. She was pale, frail, Reyne holding on to her good hand now as the shock began to seep in. But still, Dior looked to me, a shadow across her eyes, sharpening as she gazed back up at my brother, at the statues around them, the Redeemer above.

"'Do you see?'

"That whisper hung in the air, heavy as forever. The sound of battle in the city above leeched back into the silence, wild pipes, rhythmic chanting, our blood-soaked victory ringing in the ruins of the Nineswords' dream. The storm's song seemed distant now, angry thunder echoing on the walls as Gabriel truly looked around the tomb we all stood in. Those five figures encircling the one, clad in archaic priests' garb, their fanged mouths open in anguish. My brother's face paled as he saw that each wore a different sigil around their necks—twin wolves, roses and snakes, a bear and broken shield, two skulls, and finally, a pale raven in flight. Looking up into the face of this last figure, he whispered a name into the dark.

"'*Fabién.*'

"It was him. An artist's rendition, but still, unmistakable. A youth, fierce and fey, beautiful even in his terror. And Gabriel spoke then, a quote from scripture every child in Elidaen knows. The Book of Laments.

"'*And the hea'ens grew red as heartsblood. And the tempest cracked the skye, and the rain was like to the tears of all the winged host fallen. Those priests of gods false and covenants broken, numbering all the fingers 'pon hell's burning hand, did stand in bleak amazement.*'

"'Five f-fingers.' Dior swallowed, looking from the bloody stains on her skin to those screaming figures beneath the Redeemer's wheel. 'Five priests.'

"'. . . Five bloodlines,' Gabriel realized.

"'Sweet Mothermoons . . .' Phoebe whispered, rising now to her feet.

"'*And the Redeemer r-raised his eyes to his Almighty Father's throne,*' Dior continued, turning now to me. '*And his heart d-did stain the bones of the earth, and with voice akin to thunder he cried . . .*'

"'By this blood,' Gabriel whispered, 'shall they have life eternal.'

"'Hell.' I looked to those kneeling figures, nodding. 'Eternal.'

"'At mass, they used to tell us that was the Redeemer's promise to the faithful.' Dior stood with Reyne's arm about her waist now, her voice shaking. 'His covenant to those who'd build his church after he died. But these are the priests who *murdered* him,' she said, waving to those five figures. 'His final words weren't for us. They were for *them*.'

"'He *cursed* them,' Phoebe whispered. 'With his dying breath. These priests . . .'

"'Dior nodded, cold eyes on ours. 'They were the first vampires to w-walk the earth.'

"My brother looked to those figures of pale stone, kneeling about the godchild they had murdered. And then, up to the Redeemer he had prayed to, that very dawn.

"'All of this,' he breathed. 'All the misery. All the blood. All these years we looked to you for salvation. But . . . you were the one who damned us.'

"My brother shook his head, tears on his bloody cheeks as he spoke to that statue.

"'You *made* them.'

"And then, he turned to me, fury boiling in his eyes.

"'And *you* knew.'"

Silence fell in the cell, save for the scratching of Jean-François's quill. The thralls glanced among each other, Meline and Dario and Delphine and his men, dumbfounded at this revelation. For his part, the historian simply continued writing, though whether he kept his composure through practice, or because he'd already known the truth, none could say. But the silence stretched long, and the quill fell still, and yet, Celene Castia did not speak.

She was glowering at her brother now, black eyes burning like tiny suns. He'd finally lifted his gaze from his empty bottle, cheeks flushed with fury and words slurred with drink.

"Well? What are you waiting for?"

"For you to finish it," she replied.

"Fuck you," he hissed.

"It was your fault, Gabriel."

"Fuck. *You.*"

"You and your idiot rage," she snarled, looking him up and down. "Your pigheaded, lack-witted pride. If you'd managed to keep hold of *either,* none of what came next—"

"You *knew*!" Gabriel roared, rising. "You'd known the whole *fucking* time! You'd deceived us for months! Lie after lie! Drinking souls! Risking Dior! Stabbing me in the back!"

"And *still* you bleat about it! You whining drunken *fool*—"

"ENOUGH!"

The historian's roar cracked the air, cowing the siblings into silence. Jean-François was on his feet too now, tome clutched in one hand, chocolat eyes ablaze with fury.

"I have listened to you bicker for the best part of a *night*! And though I have eternity ahead of me, I've not *one more moment* to waste on this child-ishness! The sun is rising, mademoiselle and monsieur, and I shall taste the pleasures of my bed before it is full in the sky, or by the *Almighty,* you will both pay the forfeit! Now sit your arses *down* and finish this!"

Stillness rang long and deep in that cell, the thralls not even daring to breathe.

"So help me *God*—"

"I flew at her," Gabriel snarled. "Right at her fucking throat. All the lies, all the rage, all the loss, her treachery at Cairnhaem, my father, this . . . it was too much for me to stomach in that moment. When we'd been children, we'd fought always side by side. Sticks in hand, back-to-back, facing down endless legions of imaginary foes.

"*Ever outnumbered,* we'd say. *Never outmatched. Always, Lions.*

"But all that was dust and past now. And no matter how much I ached for it, I knew the rift between us would never be made whole. I could still see the bloody bliss in her eyes as she drank Aléne to ashes. I could still hear her voice as she told me to trust in her hate. And so I did, spitting it, spewing it, flying at her through the dark like a knife and crashing against her in fury. Dior cried my name as Celene and I fell upon each other, Phoebe let go of Connor and roared at me to stop, *stop*. But I was blinded by it. The lies. The betrayal. But more, most, the thought that everything this world had suffered had been of *his* design.

"A part of me always knew it. When you *truly* think about it, alone in the deeping hour, when the music stops and the babble stills and you stare hard into that bloody mirror of your soul, it's impossible to reconcile the idea of a benevolent creator with a life that looks like this. To convince yourself the one above cares, when there's so much horror and hurt and hate in the world. Only the blind can look into hellfire and smile. Only the coward raises a fist to his child and calls it love. And I was reminded of that time I spoke to Patience, then. Her little dead bird cupped in her palms. Her questions about why he died. I told you it's hard to explain death to your child, vampire, but in truth, it's impossible to explain *any* of this to *anyone*. So we settle. For the myth of the grand plan. For the fable of the God who loves us. We teach ourselves to believe in the lie, that all of it will make sense once we die.

"But in truth, there's no truth to any of it. We suffer because he wants it. We hurt because he wills it. We die because he likes it. And if there *is* a plan, coldblood, then *this* is the extent of it." Gabriel waved at the walls; the dark stone around them and empty night beyond. "A world on its knees. Begging for just *one moment* of mercy. Bleeding its miserable last into the mouths of the monsters his own fucking *son* created.

"My hands closed around Celene's throat, and hers around mine. I could smell our blood boiling, the pair of us, Phoebe stepping in now to tear us apart. Dior screamed my name again, begging me to stop, Papa, *please*, eyes bright and blue and locked on mine.

"So she didn't see the shadow behind.

"She rose up from the water. A black and twisted ruin. Her hair had been burned away, her dress, her silks, barely more than a skeleton in a suit of charred skin. She'd no eyes left in her skull, but still she could smell that blood, thick and ripe on the air. And reaching out with both clawed hands, what was left of Lilidh . . . she . . ."

Gabriel's voice faltered, fading.

"She . . ."

Silence slunk back into the cell, swallowed by the rushing waters. The Last Silversaint's eyes were welling with tears now, hands shaking, long black hair draped about his face like a shroud as he sank down to his knees on that dark shore.

"I do not understand," Jean-François said. "Lachance had stabbed Lilidh through the chest. Her blood had been enough to bury an ancien son of Fabién Voss. A Dyvok would surely have ended after an anointed blade to the heart."

"She didn't have one."

The historian blinked, staring at the silversaint.

"She'd said so herself. Tolyev tore it out the night he killed her."

"We kith remain in the state we died in, Historian," Celene murmured. "Why think you she never removed that corset? Why think you they named her—"

"Heartless," Jean-François sighed.

"Connor was the first to move," Gabriel said, his voice gone hard and cold now. "Turning toward Lilidh as she reached out for Dior, but just not swift enough. Lilidh's hands closed around Dior's face, and Dior screamed, flailing, trying desperately to get away. But though her fingers were barely more than burned twigs, still that awful strength in Lilidh endured. Not a goddess, but a thing who slew them. And with a shapeless, hateful snarl, Lilidh twisted Dior's head so hard it almost came clean off her neck."

Gabriel hung his head.

Staring at his outstretched hands.

Trembling.

"We heard the awful sound," Celene whispered. "Even with our cursing and fighting, Phoebe shouting, still we heard it—wet crackling and Reyne screaming and all the light in the world running now to black. With a roar, raging, God, so much fury and hatred it shook the walls, Connor threw himself at the Heartless, fangs closing around her throat. His claws tore the ashes of her chest, his teeth sank into the blackened ruins of her neck. With one last hateful stab from the edge of the hell she fell into, Lilidh thrust her fist through the great wolf's ribs in a spray of red. And as brave Connor á Lachlainn, descendant of the Moonsthrone and Ailidh the Stormbringer, tore Lilidh's head from her shoulders, so too did she seize hold of his dauntless heart, and rip it clean from its cage.

"The pair of them fell, Lilidh bursting at last into a spray of charred ashes, Connor striking the water, black run to red. Phoebe flew to him, wailing, falling to her knees at her husband's side, pressing desperate hands to the hole in his chest. But all hope was lost. All life fled. The dark magiks in his veins at last gave way as death took hold of his hand, and his body took his true shape—bones twisting, fur receding, leaving only a man now, lifeless, broken, cradled in his weeping widow's arms. He was hard and beautiful, older than she; a prince of the Moonsthrone, torn by battles and scarred by trials, his one blue eye still open, his ashen hair sodden with water run through with blood. And Phoebe held him to her breast, and she threw back her head, and she screamed.

"Reyne was sobbing, cradling Dior's broken body and rocking her back and forth, back and forth. Gabriel and I still lay in the water, too shocked to speak, even to move, save to release the hateful, burning holds we had upon each other's throats. But the spell of stillness broke as my brother realized what had happened—what we had done and allowed to *be* done, scrambling through the bloody water now to Dior's side. He took hold of her, terror and disbelief piercing the heart of him, saying, 'No, no, baby, *don't, DON'T!*' and holding her tight to his heaving chest. He looked to me then, desperate, madness swelling and cracking at the edges of his eyes. But though the blood of ancien might snatch a soul back from the jaws of death, even a fool could see grim Mahné had already claimed his prize; the girl's head hanging limp upon her shattered spine, no pulse, no breath, no life.

"The Holy Grail of San Michon was dead.

"'Dior?' Gabriel whispered, shaking her.

"Bloody tears spilled down our cheeks.

"All the hope inside us died.

"'*DIOR!*'"

The Last Liathe shook her head, thick red spilling over her lashes.

"I have seen the abyss but a breath from my face, sinner. I have heard the pleas of countless immortals as they begged for their forevers. I have listened to the cries of a thousand orphaned babes, widowed grooms, childless mothers, of a realm run utterly to ruin, and I tell you, the scream my brother let out then was like no sound I have *ever* heard. It was not fury. It was not fear. It was . . . heartbreak. Perfect and awful and complete. It was the scream of a man who had dragged himself back from the very edge of despair, now plummeting into darkness. It was the scream of a man who had wagered *everything*—his heart, his soul, his sanity—on never failing someone who loved him again.

"It was the scream of the damned.

"I slithered to our knees, there in the dark, utterly lost. All I had done; every lie, every betrayal, every sin, had been done for this. For *her*. And now she was gone. I stared into the jaws of the abyss awaiting me, the souls I had stolen clambering up inside me, knowing there would be no escape for any of us now. Should I simply end it, I wondered? Now that all hope had fled? Should I go to meet my Maker, try to convince him my hand was not upon the knife? To beg, '*At least I tried*'?

"At least I tried.

"All was dark. All was tears, spilling down my face as Phoebe sobbed over her husband, as Reyne sobbed over her first, as Gabriel smoothed back the ashen hair from Dior's lifeless face and kissed her cooling brow, his song soft in the gloom.

"*Sleep now, my lovely, sleep now, my dear,*
"*Dark dreams will fade now your papa is near.*
"*Fear not the monsters, fear not the night,*
"*Papa is here now and all shall be right.*
"*Close your eyes, darling, and know this be true,*
"*Morning will come, and your papa loves you.*"

VII

DESOLATION

"HE DID NOT stay for her funeral," Celene sighed.

"They all of them gathered, there in the ruins of Niamh's city; all save for him. The Highlanders, poured out like red water on the ground and wondering what the hell it had all been for. Lachlan á Craeg and the ragged remnants of the Silver Sorority, mourning the Grail and their fallen brethren both; other than Gabriel's old 'prentice, not a *single* silversaint was found alive after the battle. The prisoners Dior had saved, crawling up from the basements of Auldtunn in disbelief. The thralls she had liberated, bruised and battered and never given a chance to thank her. A few children were discovered beneath the rags and frozen corpses in those awful cages in the bailey; a handful, spared by the slender mercy of Aaron de Coste during that dreadful final hour. Little Mila was found among them, standing in the snow with her moppet doll and her bloody dress and bewilderment in her too-old eyes. Reyne had found young Joaquin Marenn wandering the ruins with his hound, Elaina, calling for his dear Isla. Searching for his Ever After.

"To this day, we know not if the Princess told him the whole truth.

"She was laid in state in the ruins of Amath du Miagh'dair, the Sepulcher of the Mothermaid, where all came to pay her tribute. Reyne had dressed her as she'd vowed to that night they spoke in the crypt; garb that suited the Grail better than any silks stolen from an ancien's den, any finery from a princess's wardrobe. A suit of shining platemail and threefold chain, and a longblade of Ossian steel to match. Her long ashen hair had been washed and combed, arrayed in a pale halo around her head, her hands crossed at her breast. Her right was enclosed in a gauntlet, but her left was laid bare, so all could see the hurt she had suffered for their sakes; only a mangled forefinger and thumb remaining. *The Red Hand of God,* some named her. *La demoiselle*

du Graal. But more and most, the whisper that became a cry that became a hymn as they gathered there on the ruined steps of that mighty chapel, was a simple one, and true.

"San Dior, they called her.

"*San Dior.*

"The heavens rang in reply as they sang that name, dark and furious and heavy as lead. There was no joy in this parting, only loss, and in truth, none of us knew what now to do. Aaron de Coste stood watching the funeral rites from atop a distant wall, his beloved Baptiste beside him, and all the awful things he had done hanging between them like a shadow that wore the face of Nikita Dyvok. Phoebe á Dúnnsair spoke the eulogy, sang Dior's honors to her people and the howling sky. But her heart was torn so deep she was near a ghost, and the blighted blood ran still within her and all her kin, and back in her tent, wrapped in a bloody shroud, another beloved waited to be buried.

"And Gabriel was there for none of it.

"We know not when he left, nor if he told any farewell. We know only when we went to look for him, we could find no sign, and his brave Argent was missing from among the Highlanders' horses. We thought for the longest time about chasing after him."

The Last Liathe shook her head and scoffed.

"And then I thought the better of it.

"For my part, I could not bear to be there when they buried her. When Lachlan á Craeg dragged back the mighty silvered lid of the Mothermaid's empty coffin and laid her inside it, there to be forever guarded by those seraphim and their silvered swords. We sat below, far down in the vault of Maryn's tomb, waist-deep in bloody water, bloody tears spilling down our face. The hymns of the Silver Sorority sounded a dirge to me. All the prayers and names rang hollow. *Saint. Maiden of the Grail. Red Hand of God.* In the end, she had been a girl I cared for. A girl I had failed. A girl with a name that we whispered there in that awful dark, with heaven glowering above us and hell yawning below.

"'*Dior.*'"

"Cared for?"

The words were spat, not spoken. Gabriel rising up now from that dark shoreline, swaying on his feet. His eyes burned with drunken fury, his fists clenched tight.

"*Cared for?*"

Celene flinched as he hurled his empty bottle, the glass smashing to a hundred glittering shards on her silver mask, her marbled skin.

"You never gave a SHIT ABOUT *ANYONE BUT YOURSELF!*"

With a roar, at last, Gabriel threw himself across the river, long black hair streaming behind, mouth open in a hateful snarl. He cleared those dark waters before Jean-François had a chance to shout, crashing into his sister and bringing her down to the stone. Fists balled, bellowing with rage, he struck her across the face, once, twice, so vicious and fierce the metal cage on her lips dented, then snapped free with the scream of tortured metal. She was on him then, the pair smashing each other into the floor, up into the ceiling, twin shadows and twin flames, clawing and tearing each other in their hatred. Unable to follow the silversaint over the river, the Marquis could only bellow for Delphine, the capitaine and his thrallswords crying aloud, leaping out into the chest-deep flow and wading across while the siblings clashed.

The Last Liathe and the Last Silversaint were like children brawling, punching and kicking, gouging and spitting. But finally, Celene sank her teeth into Gabriel's throat, blood spraying, flowing, swallowing, lashes fluttering and breath whispering and lips curling until the swords arrived, stabbing at Celene with their burning brands so that she was forced off, shrieking her fear of the flames and flashing back, back into the darkest corner she could find. Jean-François could see little of her face behind the curtain of long black hair and blood, save her eyes, wide and bright with terror.

"Do not kill her!" he roared. "Bring the 'saint back *NOW!*"

The soldiers complied, helping a bleeding, drunken Gabriel to his feet, one hand pressed to his torn throat. But as he spied his sister cowering in the shadows, he snapped to, lunged for her again, only stopped by Delphine and five of his largest men.

"Lying BITCH!"

"Faithless COWARD!"

"I'll see you *dead*, I vow it!" he roared, bucking in their arms as they dragged him back. "You hear me, Celene? I swear to God above and hell below, I will tell them *everything* I know about you and yours just for the joy of watching you burn!"

"So steep your price?" she shouted, spitting his blood on the floor and looking to Jean-François. "Oh, be not fooled, little Marquis! My brother would sell you the keys to heaven itself for a bottle to drown in and a whore to drink!"

"*Die!*" Gabriel roared, reaching out toward her as they dragged him up the rocky shore. "Just step into this river, Celene, and wash yourself away! That's all you're good for! That's all you're *worth*! You're the fucking last of them all, so just end it and be done!"

"I will *never be done*! I am stone, do you hear me? I am the *MOUNTAIN*!"

"Get him out of here!" Jean-François bellowed. "Get him gone!"

Gabriel flailed, breaking one thrall's arm and another's jaw before they bludgeoned him into compliance. Bloodied, soaked through with wine, the Last Silversaint was hauled back out by Delphine and a half dozen of his swords, boots dragging on the flagstones. But through the sodden curtains of his hair, his eyes ever remained on his sister, twin scars cutting down his cheek like teardrops, fangs bared in hatred absolute.

Jean-François remained, standing on the shoreline in the ringing silence now, tome clutched in his hands. Meline stood at his side, her face drawn and bloodless. Brushing one golden curl from his flawless cheek, the historian stared across the water at that thing, that girl, that monster. She had retreated into the farthest, darkest corner of the cell, still trembling for fear of those flames. Her mouth was smeared with her brother's blood, dark hair splayed across her face like spiderwebs, black eyes fixed upon his.

His voice rang clear in the dark.

"Why do you not do as he suggested, mademoiselle?"

The Liathe tilted her head in silent question.

The historian gestured to the river.

"If the cup is broken, if the Grail is gone, then so too is any hope of your salvation." He shrugged. "Why delay the inevitable? Why not simply end it?"

"Steel rusts. Ice melts."

She smoothed the hair back from her face, unshackled from that silver cage, lips rimmed in red. And though the cell was dark, still he could see her mouth, her chin, her throat, unscarred and unspoiled. Flawless and whole below those ink-black eyes.

"Stone endures," she hissed.

The vampires watched each other across the water, fresh blood on her lips, on the stone, in the air. Jean-François's skin prickled, his eyes darkened, teeth sharp in his gums.

"There is far more to this tale than you are telling, Mlle Castia," he said quietly.

"There is always tomorrow, sinner," she murmured in reply.

Jean-François straightened his cravat, heavy tome tucked at his elbow, slender hands wrapping about it, possessive and protective. Meline hovered behind him, running her fingers feather-soft over his back as he stared Celene down.

"Do you require anything before I head to bed, mademoiselle?"

"Would you give it to us if we asked it?"

He smiled then, cold and cruel.

"No."

Smile vanishing, he gave her the smallest of nods.

"Au revoir, Mlle Castia."

"Give our regards to your Empress, little Marquis."

Footsteps receded across the stone, along with the globe in Meline's hand.

The heavy doors slammed shut, plunging all into darkness.

And in that dark, the Last Liathe whispered.

"Tell Margot we will see her soon."

DAWN

———————— I ————————

THE KILLER STOOD watch at the thin window, still waiting for the end to arrive.

The room was just as he'd left it when they'd dragged him down to hell. The flagstones scrubbed near-clean, old lambswool draped over the bloodstains. The hearth was bereft of flame, but not heat—they'd let a fire burn again while he was gone, banishing the chill. Two antique armchairs stood in the room's heart, a small round table between. A bottle of cool green glass sat upon it; empty, yet full of promise.

They'd hauled him up from that cell below, his sister's blood smudged upon his knuckles, his own blood running down his punctured throat. He'd been carried through the halls in the arms of the Marquis's thrallswords, past Margot's pale courtiers, the wondrous frescoes on the walls, counting every step in his head. And after it became clear that the rage was bled out of him, Gabriel had been allowed to walk, escorted back up the tower stairs, there to await the displeasure of the Marquis Jean-François Chastain.

He did not wait long.

As he stared out the window to the mountains beyond, he felt a tickling, as if a hand were brushing his hair back from his neck. Turning, he saw the coldblood twenty feet away, surrounded by his thralls; Meline and Jasminne and Dario, Delphine looming at his back.

"I trust you are feeling pleased with yourself, Chevalier?" the vampire asked.

"I'll be pleased when that fucking snake is in her grave."

"I did not give you permission to lay hands upon her."

"She deserved it. Every drop."

"Be that as it may, Celene Castia is my Empress's property, not yours." Jean-François glowered. "If you seek to do harm to her again, I will be forced to punish you again. And it has not been so long, methinks, that you have forgotten how unpleasant that can be."

The historian smoothed down his frockcoat, the smoldering rage in his eyes abating.

"But still. All in all, a fine night's work, mon ami." He gifted the silversaint a pretty smile, patted the tome under his arm. "Great Margot shall be well pleased. And though I am certain there be more to this story than either you or your beloved sister are telling, grim daylight has caught us for now. Sleep beckons, and my boudoir calls."

"Sweet dreams, vampire." The silversaint tilted his head, tapping his lip. "No, wait . . . you need a soul to dream, don't you?"

"Do you require anything before we retire?"

"No."

"Are you certain?"

The silversaint met the vampire's eyes then, amusement sparkling in that deep chocolat stare. Gabriel's gaze drifted to Meline, the choker cinched tight around the long pale line of her throat, the thin blue traceries of veins across her bosom. His eyes shifted next to Jasminne, wanton gaze and clever hands and dark, perfect skin, and now to Dario, long black hair framing his square jaw, the beat of his pulse thudding just below. Gabriel's cheeks were aflame at the memory of them in the bathhouse earlier this eve, the young-blood gifting soft kisses along his shoulder, the lass running slow fingertips up the inside of his thigh. The vampire's eyes drifted down to his crotch, lips curled in a knowing smile.

"Ask and ye shall receive, Silversaint."

"Merci," Gabriel growled, turning his back, sweat gleaming upon his brow as he clasped his hands tight behind him. "But I'm still not that kind of bastard."

"If the chevalier thirsts, Master . . . I could fetch him another bottle at least?"

It was Dario who'd spoken, smoky eyes drifting now to the historian's, the youngblood ever eager to please. Jean-François pursed his lips, covetous gaze roaming the youngster's body, his hands, his lips. But Meline ran a gentle touch down his spine, whispering in his ear, and the vampire seemed to draw conclusion that she and Jasminne could suffice for the day.

"What say you, Chevalier?" He glanced to Dario. "As I said, the vintage is *exquisite*."

The silversaint's jaw clenched. He could smell the heady perfume of Dario's sweat, hear the quickening drumbeat of the youngblood's pulse as he looked him over; the sharp planes of his jaw, the artery thudding just below, hypnotic. After the sanctus he'd smoked earlier in the eve, the thirst had slunk away into the dark where it dwelled. But as ever, it had returned now. That hole inside never quite filled. That need never quite sated.

To hate the thing that is completing you.

To love the thing that is destroying you.

"Perhaps . . . another bottle," he finally whispered, hoarse. "Oui."

Jean-François smiled, dark and vulpine, nodding to the thrallswords behind him. As Delphine and his men marched out of the room, he took Dario's hand, kissed his pale wrist, sending shivers along his skin, those dark Nordish eyes gone liquid and wide.

"See to all the chevalier's needs, love."

"As it please you, Master."

"Take your fucking eyes with you, Chastain," the silversaint growled, glancing back over his shoulder. "I'm not here to put on a damned show."

The vampire chuckled, reached out with his will across the room. A small black shape crawled from the shadows of the hearth, scampering swift across the floor toward him. Stooping, Jean-François gently lifted a small black mouse on the palm of his hand, gazing into the familiar's dark eyes.

"Come along, Armand," he murmured. "Our guest is a shy one."

Jasminne slipped out of the cell on slippered feet, Meline following, waiting patiently beyond the threshold with the swords, all prickling skin and bated breath. Jean-François stared yet at the silversaint's back, razorblades in his smile.

"In the end," he murmured, "you pay the beast his due."

Gabriel glanced back at him then, voice like ashes. "Or he takes his due from you."

The Marquis bowed.

"Santé, Chevalier."

"Morté, coldblood."

The vampire drifted from the room like smoke, the door barred and locked in his wake. Gabriel listened to their footfalls, fading down the cold stone stairs, the breath of the swords waiting just outside the cell. He could hear the quickened pulse of the youngster behind him, smell the perfume of his blood, mixed with his sister's across his knuckles, his own drying upon his throat, the memory of soft skin under his hands, warm and smooth and thudding against his tongue, rushing into his mouth and down his throat, all of him afire.

He turned from the window, storm-grey gaze falling on the prize the Marquis had left behind. Breath coming swifter. Hands curled in fists. He stared for an age, taking in the youngblood's beauty, dark brown eyes and snow-pale skin and ink-black hair. And when he was certain they were gone—the vampire retreated to the soft silk of his boudoir, there to drown that agony he knew all too well—the paleblood took one step toward his mark.

Another.

Another.

The youngblood raised his chin as the silversaint's shadow fell across him, swallowing thick, pupils dilated in the dawn's gloom. Gabriel's tread was as a man walking to his gallows, stopping close enough to feel the lad's warmth upon his skin. His heart was heavy as iron in his chest. His whisper, sharp as a knife in the dark.

> *"Before the Five, come unto one,*
> *"With sainted blade, 'neath virgin sun,*
> *"By sacred blood, or else by none . . ."*

The youngblood held the forefinger and thumb of his left hand over his heart.

> *"This blackened veil shall be undone."*

"You'd best be ready," Gabriel warned. "Joaquin Joaquin Marenn."

The youngster nodded, steel shining behind those dark Nordish eyes.

"For the Grail, Chevalier."

Gabriel nodded.

"For the Grail."

II

THE LAST LIATHE sat in the dark, alone but not alone.

Black rapids rushed in the river before her, swift as her brother's blood now beat in her veins. The hell they'd fashioned for her was lightless now, the Marquis gone to his bed and his serfs gone to his arms and his silversaint gone to his tower above. But below, amid the shards of shattered glass and the spatters of cooling red and the fragments of the broken silver cage that had bound her teeth once but no more, Celene could feel him.

A tiny pulse in the black.

"Come here, little one," she whispered. "We'll not hurt you."

She reached out with her gifts—stolen, oui, but still now *hers*—into the deepest corner of her cell. She felt his little mind, heard his little feet, scratching upon the rocks at her beckoning. Celene placed one pale hand on the stone, letting him scamper into her palm, and she lifted him up to her black eyes, Dead enough to see in that cold oubliette. A small black mouse, cleaning busy little whiskers with busy little paws, peering at her with eyes near as dark and hard as her own.

"What does your master call you, petit frère?"

He squeaked reply, small and sharp.

"Marcel," she repeated. "Pretty."

The Last Liathe smiled, sharp as a broken blade.

"Are you here to spy on us, Marcel?"

The little one squeaked affirmation, turning a circle on her palm. She nodded, sad.

"Your master truly does not know what he is dealing with, does he?"

Marcel squeaked protest, and she tilted her head, listening.

"No offense, petit frère. Nobody truly does. But let us give you a morsel, then, by way of apology heartfelt. One to fill your little belly to bursting. A grim and lonely day stretches now before us, and who knows how long shall pass until we speak again. We are cruel, Marcel, and we are cold, but not so much as to leave you so unsatisfied. So let us have an ending, little one. A finale worthy of the name."

She smoothed back the long midnight-blue hair from her face, licked the red on her lips, the same as her mother's had been; smooth and full and bow-shaped.

"We told your master of the Grail's funeral. Of the names they sang for her, and the heavens' black reply, and that we did not watch her buried. All of that was true. We waited below, in the crypt of Mother Maryn, surrounded by those silent effigies, that circle of broken tombstones, sitting in the water and staring at those words. Those truths.

"Knowing not their meaning.

"From holy cup comes holy light;
"The faithful hand sets world aright.
"And in the Seven Martyrs' sight,
"Mere man shall end this endless night.
"Before the Five, come unto one,
"With sainted blade, 'neath virgin sun,
"By sacred blood, or else by none;
"This blackened veil shall be undone."

Marcel squeaked, and Celene smiled, petting his brow with her fingertips.

"I know not how long we waited, petit frère. Long enough for the songs to fall silent at least. For the red thrill of victory in the city above to fade, and the shock of the price they'd all paid for it to begin to bleed through. The dark waters we lingered in were drenched red. Red like the tears I'd cried. Red like the life she'd spilled. Red like the stains on that marble coffin before us; the blood of ancien Dyvok mixed with a prince of the duskdancers and spilled upon that stone angel, dripping down its open mouth.

"Onto the mouth within.

"We could feel her quickening now. Fear stabbing our breast, settling like a dark and tattered shroud upon our shoulders. How would I explain it? What reason could I give, what excuse might I muster, what spell might I weave with these things so weak and frail as words to explain that I had found *all* we had searched for these long and lonely centuries, only to let it slip through my fingers at the last and shatter like glass upon the floor?

"'Mother, forgive me,' we whispered.

"And the angel stirred then; the slightest tremor in the marble, the colossal weight of that mighty capstone shivering as if the earth trembled. We rose to our feet, head bowed, the terror in me unbound as that angel was at last dragged aside, as that capstone fell free and crashed into the brine, and a dark shape rose up from the aching hollow within.

"A child she was.

"A girl. Barely more than a babe in stature.

"Skin pale as alabaster and teeth sharp as truth and eyes empty as forever.

"She crashed upon us with all the fury of heaven, all the hateful hunger of hell, starved by her century slumbering beneath that hallowed earth. We cried out as her little hands fell upon us, as her little teeth sank into us, as her colossal thirst was loosed upon us, desolate and dust-dry and my God so *deep*, we knew it must only destroy us. Strong as mountains, mighty as the very bones of this cradle, that little monster wrapped us up and held us close, ravenous, dragging all I was from within my veins, euphoria and terror entwined, the abyss yawning at our feet as still she drank, it *drank*, death but one more mouthful, one more swallow, one more bright red drop away.

"'Mother M-Maryn,' I whispered. '*Please . . .*'

"And then she stopped. Stilled. That gaping maw dripping red, little eyes deep as the abyss turning upward now, upward toward the tomb far above our heads.

"Inside the crypt they had buried her in, upon the slab they set her on, the Grail lay in repose. Still clad in her suit of plate and chain, ashen hair arrayed in a halo around her head. *The Red Hand of God*, they'd named her. *La demoiselle du Graal*. But more and most, the whisper that had become a cry that had become a hymn was a simple one, and true.

"'San Dior,' Maryn breathed.

"*San Dior.*

"She was a beauty, motionless in the dark after a life spent in struggle.

"Savior.

"Sinner.

"Saint.

"A girl I cared for.

"And there in the dark, that girl opened her eyes."

ACKNOWLEDGMENTS

Thanks and bloody kisses to the following:

Peter, Claire, Young, Lizz, Layla, Lena, Hector, Sara, Jonathan, Paul, Lisa, and all at St. Martin's Press; Natasha, Robyn, Vicky, Fleur, Chloe, Roisin, Sian, Emilie, Kim, Claire, Sarah, Alice, Fionnuala, and all at HarperVoyager UK; Michael, Thomas, and all at HarperCollins Australia; the amazing Marco, Sam, and all my foreign publishers; Bonbonatron, Jason, Kerby, Micaela, Virginia, Orrsome, Cat, LT, Tom, Fiona, Josh, Tracey, Anna, Samantha, Steven, Toves, Joseph, Emily, Vova, Tatiana, Alix, Ally, Tiffany, Clarissa, Andrea, Mara, Daphne, Avery, Taylor, Gonzalo, Bill, George, Anne, Stephen, Ray, Robin, China, William, Christopher, George, Pat, Anne, Nic, Cary, Neil, Amie, Anthony, Joe, Laini, Mark, Steve, Stewart, Tim, Chris, Stefan, Chris, Brad, Marc, Beej, Rafe, Weez, Paris, Jim, Ludovico, Mark, Randy, Vessel, Elliot, CJ, Will, Pete (RIP), Tom (RIP), Dan, Sam, Marcus, Chris, Winston, Matt, Robb, Oli, Noah, Philip, Robert, Maynard, Ronnie, Corey, Courtney, Chris (RIP), Anthony, Lochie, Ian, Briton, Trent, Phil, Sam (RIP), Logan, Tony, Kath, Kylie, Nicole, Kurt, Jack, Max, Poppy; my readers for the love, my enemies for the sales; the baristas of Melbourne, Sydney, Perth, Barcelona, Lille, Rennes, Bordeaux, Lyon, Montpellier, Toulouse, Frankfurt, Leipzig, Stuttgart, Strasbourg, Lucca, Roma, Milano, Venezia, London, Paris, and most importantly Praha.

Finally and especially, Amanda, for making my broken edge complete.

CÔSTE

TOLBROOK

CIIRFORT

ALMWUD

NORDLUND

KYEFALL

LORSON

SAN MICHON

LEON

CHÂTEAU
AVELÉNE

NIGHTSTONE
MOUNTAINS

CAIRNHAEM

REDWATCH

SAN
GUILLAUME

VENSPIRE

BEAUFORT

FA'DAÉNA

WINFAEL

DHAHAETH

Bay of Antoine

Gabriel and Dior's Journey